Satyrus nodded. 'So,' he said. He smiled. Looked from face to face. It was almost funny, the way they expected him to provide a magical spell of victory. 'So. Friends.' He hung his head, embarrassed by their trust in him. And then he raised his head. 'Listen. There is no trick to save us, now. I don't have a fancy plan. When we raise the paean to Athena, we go over the south wall and go for the monster.' He shrugged. 'First man there is King of Misrule.'

Anaxagoras sighed. 'That's it?' he asked.

Satyrus nodded. 'That's it,' he said. 'Kill everyone who gets in your way. It'll be dark. That can't hurt us.'

Abraham raised an eyebrow – for a moment, his old self. 'And when the sun rises?' he asked.

Satyrus locked eyes with Miriam. 'Die well,' he said.

Christian Cameron is a writer, re-enactor and military historian. He is a veteran of the United States Navy, where he served as both an aviator and an intelligence officer. He now lives in Toronto with his wife and daughter, where he writes full time.

By Christian Cameron

THE TYRANT SERIES
Tyrant
Tyrant: Storm of Arrows
Tyrant: Funeral Games
Tyrant: King of the Bosporus
Tyrant: Destroyer of Cities

THE KILLER OF MEN SERIES
Killer of Men
Marathon
Poseidon's Spear

OTHER NOVELS
Washington and Caesar
Alexander: God of War
The Ill-Made Knight

EBOOK EXCLUSIVES
Tom Swan and the Head of St George Parts One–Nine

TYRANT

DESTROYER
OF CITIES

CHRISTIAN CAMERON

An Orion paperback

First published in Great Britain in 2013
by Orion
This paperback edition published in 2013
by Orion Books,
an imprint of The Orion Publishing Group Ltd,
Orion House, 5 Upper St Martin's Lane
London WC2H 9EA

An Hachette UK company

1 3 5 7 9 10 8 6 4 2

A CIP catalogue record for this book
is available from the British Library.

ISBN 978-1-4091-2068-1

Typeset by Deltatype Ltd, Birkenhead, Merseyside

Printed and bound by CPI Group (UK) Ltd
Croydon CRO 4YY

The Orion Publishing Group's policy is to use papers that
are natural, renewable and recyclable products and made
from wood grown in sustainable forests. The logging and
manufacturing processes are expected to conform to the
environmental regulations of the country of origin.

www.orionbooks.co.uk

For my friends

GLOSSARY

Airyanãm (Avestan) Noble, heroic.

Aspis (Classical Greek) A large round shield, deeply dished, commonly carried by Greek (but not Macedonian) *hoplites*.

Baqca (Siberian) Shaman, mage, dream-shaper.

Chiton (Classical Greek) A garment like a tunic, made from a single piece of fabric folded in half and pinned down the side, then pinned again at the neck and shoulders and belted above the hips. A men's *chiton* might be worn long or short. Worn very short, or made of a small piece of cloth, it was sometimes called a 'chitoniskos'. Our guess is that most *chitons* were made from a piece of cloth roughly 60 x 90 inches, and then belted or roped to fit, long or short. Pins, pleating, and belting could be simple or elaborate. Most of these garments would, in Greece, have been made of wool. In the East, linen might have been preferred.

Chlamys (Classical Greek) A garment like a cloak, made from a single piece of fabric woven tightly and perhaps even boiled. The *chlamys* was usually pinned at the neck and worn as a cloak, but could also be thrown over the shoulder and pinned under the right or left arm and worn as a garment. Free men are sometimes shown naked with a *chlamys*, but rarely shown in a *chiton* without a *chlamys* – the *chlamys*, not the *chiton*, was the essential garment, or so it appears. Men and women both wear the *chlamys*, although differently. Again, a 60 x 90 piece of cloth seems to drape correctly and have the right lines and length.

Daimon (Classical Greek) Spirit.

Ephebe (Classical Greek) A new *hoplite*; a young man just training to join the forces of his city.

Epilektoi (Classical Greek) The chosen men of the city or of the *phalanx*; elite soldiers.

Eudaimia (Classical Greek) Well-being. Literally, 'well-spirited'. See *daimon*, above.

Gamelia (Classical Greek) A Greek holiday.

Gorytos (Classical Greek and possibly Scythian) The open-topped quiver carried by the Scythians, often highly decorated.

Himation (Classical Greek) A heavy garment consisting of a single piece of cloth at least 120 inches long by 60 inches wide, draped over the body and one shoulder, worn by both men and women.

Hipparch (Classical Greek) The commander of the cavalry.

Hippeis (Classical Greek) Militarily, the cavalry of a Greek army. Generally, the cavalry class, synonymous with 'knights'. Usually the richest men in a city.

Hoplite (Classical Greek) A Greek soldier, the heavy infantry who carry an *aspis* (the big round shield) and fight in the *phalanx*. They represent the middle class of free men in most cities, and while sometimes they seem like medieval knights in their outlook, they are also like town militia, and made up of craftsmen and small farmers. In the early Classical period, a man with as little as twelve acres under cultivation could be expected to own the *aspis* and serve as a *hoplite*.

Hoplomachos (Classical Greek) A man who taught fighting in armour.

Hyperetes (Classical Greek) The *Hipparch*'s trumpeter, servant, or supporter. Perhaps a sort of NCO.

Kithara (Classical Greek) A musical instrument like a lyre.

Kline (Classical Greek) A couch or bed on which Hellenic men and women took meals and perhaps slept, as well.

Kopis (Classical Greek) A bent bladed knife or sword, rather like a modern Ghurka kukri. They appear commonly in Greek art, and even some small eating knives were apparently made to this pattern.

Machaira (Classical Greek) The heavy Greek cavalry sword, longer and stronger than the short infantry sword. Meant to give a longer reach on horseback, and not useful in the *phalanx*. The word could also be used for any knife.

Parasang (Classical Greek from Persian) About thirty *stades*. See below.

Phalanx (Classical Greek) The infantry formation used by Greek *hoplites* in warfare, eight to ten deep and as wide as circumstance allowed. Greek commanders experimented with deeper and shallower formations, but the *phalanx* was solid and very difficult to break, presenting the enemy with a veritable wall of spear points and shields, whether the Macedonian style with pikes or the Greek style with spears. Also, *phalanx* can refer to the body of fighting men. A Macedonian *phalanx* was deeper, with longer spears called *sarissas* that we assume to be like the pikes used in more recent times. Members of a *phalanx*, especially a Macedonian *phalanx*, are sometimes called *Phalangites*.

Phylarch (Classical Greek) The commander of one file of *hoplites*. Could be as many as sixteen men.

Porne (Classical Greek) A prostitute.

Pous (Classical Greek) About one foot.

Prodromoi (Classical Greek) Scouts; those who run before or run first.

Psiloi (Classical Greek) Light infantry skirmishers, usually men with bows and slings, or perhaps javelins, or even thrown rocks. In Greek city-state warfare, the *psiloi* were supplied by the poorest free men, those who could not afford the financial burden of *hoplite* armour and daily training in the gymnasium.

Sastar (Avestan) Tyrannical. A tyrant.

Spola (Classical Greek) Body armour of leather. Herakles in heroic depiction has a spola in the form of a lion's skin, but soldiers might wear anything from a light leather tunic to stiffened abdomenal protection and call it a spola.

Stade (Classical Greek) About 1/8 of a mile. The distance run in a 'stadium'. 178 meters. Sometimes written as *Stadia* or *Stades* by me. Thirty *Stadia* make a *Parasang*.

Taxies (Classical Greek) The sections of a Macedonian *phalanx*. Can refer to any group, but often used as a 'company' or a 'battalion'. My *taxeis* has between 500 and 2,000 men, depending on losses and detachments. Roughly synonymous with *phalanx* above, although a *phalanx* may be composed of a dozen *taxeis* in a great battle.

Thorax/Thorakes (Classical Greek) Body armour – literally, that which covered the abdomen. Could be bronze, quilted wool or linen or a mixture of textile and metal armour; could also refer to a leather armour like a spola. The so-called 'muscle cuirass' forged by the armourer to look like the male abdomen was one form, and probably the most expensive.

Xiphos (Classical Greek) A straight-bladed infantry sword, usually carried by *hoplites* or *psiloi*. Classical Greek art, especially red-figure ware, shows many *hoplites* wearing them, but only a handful have been recovered and there's much debate about the shape and use. They seem very like a Roman gladius.

PROLOGUE

Stratokles the Athenian sat on an iron stool in his mistress's receiving chamber, and crossed his legs comfortably.

'Interesting times, Despoina,' he said.

She was reading through her correspondence – he'd already read it, of course – and making notes. 'Demetrios has taken Athens!' she said. She snapped her fingers at a maid for more milk, and tapped her fingers impatiently until the maid had warmed the milk in a silver cup, mixed in honey and transferred the contents to a second cup, before presenting it with averted eyes.

Quietly, firmly, she spoke to her slave. 'Listen, girl. I expect you to have this ready-mixed. Understand? Don't wait for me to demand it. How long have you been with me?' Amastris of Heraklea snapped her index finger against the maid's forehead and the girl cried out. Then Amastris turned back to her Athenian. 'Does this change your views on Antigonus One-Eye?'

Stratokles shrugged, wondering idly if, by comforting the slave-girl after his interview with her mistress, he might put himself between her legs. He allowed himself to catch her eyes, and she hesitated before looking away. Interesting. Slaves were always so *lonely*.

'Are you attending to me, sir?' Amastris asked sharply.

Stratokles was unflappable – at least, by his mistress. 'It relieves me of any responsibilities towards Demetrius of Phaleron or Cassander,' he said carefully. 'I remain loyal to the city of Athens. Demetrios the Golden will pretend to be a democrat – everyone always does when they come to power in Athens. We shall see, after the first few months. But, for once, the news from Athens is not the most important. There's more news – more immediate, if not more important. Look at the dispatch from Byzantium.'

I

Amastris shook her head, the blond ringlets staying crisp and perfect as her head went from side to side. She drank her honeyed milk absently. 'When I finish this.'

Stratokles got up and poured himself a cup of wine.

'Satyrus is coming here!' Amastris said, eyes on the scroll, and her hand went to her hair as if she needed to preen a little.

'Yes, Despoina,' Stratokles laughed. He wished that he might affect her – or any woman – the way Satyrus of Tanais affected her. He shot a glance at the maid, who met it – and then dropped her eyes. *Played this game before, have, you?* he thought with satisfaction. 'He's coming with his fleet and his merchants, moving the grain south to Alexandria.'

'As usual, not coming just to *see me*.' She sat up. 'Why does my uncle continue to forbid the match? I want to be wed.' She read further. 'He's too devoted to that slut of a sister. He'd be well rid of her.'

'Your father is about to crown himself *king*,' Stratokles said with unfeigned distaste – distaste for kings, and distaste for his mistress's obvious jealousy.

'Melitta is Queen of the Assagetae in her own right,' he said. 'Your princely Satyrus needs her.'

Amastris snapped her fingers and another maid brought her a wrap, a costly piece of work imported from India. 'I need him to need me,' she said with a sweet smile. 'And if my uncle wants to be a king, why must you sound so sour about it?'

Stratokles, whatever his faults, and he admitted that he had a phalanx of them, nonetheless saw himself as a true democrat in a world of aristocratic despots. 'As *King* of Heraklea, he expects to marry you a little better than the *King* of Hyperborea.'

'Satyrus is the King of the Bosporus,' Amastis said with asperity. 'He is as much a king as my father. And Stratokles – why is it that when you say the word "king" you render it like an insult?'

'Despoina, if you don't know by now, it is too late for me to teach you. I loathe tyrants.' He shrugged.

'And yet you serve me,' she said.

'You need me, Despoina. And Athens needs this city and her grain, and my eyes on the north. I have never pretended to love your uncle's tyranny, nor your lover's kingship.' He rolled his shoulders, flexing his fighting muscles and wondering, in the way of middle-aged men, if he didn't need to spend more time in the gymnasium.

'You might give pretence some consideration, or Nestor will have your head.' Nestor was the captain of the Tyrant's bodyguard, and no friend of the Athenian's.

Stratokles chose to ignore her. 'Satyrus won't just be an ally if he weds you,' Stratokles said. *I'll be out of a job*, he thought. 'He'll be master here. He has a fleet, an army and a core of professionals that we can't really match. With Pantecapaeaum and Olbia behind him, surely you can see that we're next.'

'Hmm. I look forward to his being my *master*,' Amastris said, and licked her lips. She laughed at his discomfiture. 'Don't be a prude. Satyrus isn't half as bright as I am. Who'll run whom, do you think? Heraklea won't be the loser. Melitta might be, though,' she said with a smile.

'Your uncle is not interested in ruling through your womb,' Stratokles said. 'And you will need Melitta's good will as much as Satyrus does, if you come to be his wife.'

'Now that's the sort of thing I employ you to say,' Amastris nodded. 'He's old, though – my uncle, I mean.'

'Don't be rushing him to his grave, Despoina. Please read the dispatch from Byzantium.' Stratokles wasn't always perfectly pleased with his charge. She was past the first innocence of youth and she was becoming headstrong, just when he felt she most needed a rein. And with Demetrios in Athens … The world was changing. Stratokles was beginning to wonder if he had lingered too long in Heraklea. Although he had other ideas—

She flipped through the scroll tubes. 'Demostrate is dead?' she asked.

'Got it in one!' Stratokles pounced like a cat taking a rat off a post.

'By Aphrodite, lady of ladies!' Amastris said, and shook her head. 'The old pirate is *dead*? Who killed him?'

'Who cares? The point is that a new man has Demostrate's fleet – if he can hold it. They are pirates. And now Antigonus One-Eye will have a clear run at allying with them – the pirates – a fair shot at buying all of them.' Stratokles swirled the wine in his cup.

'But we're no allies of old One-Eye. My uncle broke that chain.' She drank off the last of her milk.

Stratokles swirled his wine again. 'There are never just two sides in politics, my dear. Antigonus would like to be master here. So would Lysimachos and so would your Satyrus. By naming himself "king", your uncle puts himself on the same level as all of them. He can only maintain that level by ceaseless vigilance and a willingness to play one against the other.'

'And my beloved has just lost his guarantee of passing the straits unmolested,' Amastris said. 'Perhaps he'll come here and stay awhile.' She smiled.

'He's lost more than that, dear,' Stratokles said. 'He's lost his immunity, and some of his status with the great powers. Now he'll have to buy the pirates like the rest of us. And if Antigonus has Athens' fleet, and the pirates,' Stratokles shrugged, 'well then, so much for Ptolemy.' He leaned back and recrossed his legs. 'Times are changing, dear.'

She looked at him from under her eyelashes. 'You don't love my Satyrus,' she said.

'I helped him achieve his kingdom,' Stratokles said. 'But no – he's no friend of mine.' He didn't mention that in another dispatch – one he didn't need to pass to her – he'd had news of Lysimachos. Lysimachos, the fourth contender for Alexander's power. Lysimachos, whose Thracian wife had just died.

The perfect husband for his little princess. With Lysimachos and Amastris, Stratokles could guarantee Athens' grain trade for fifty years, and to Hades with Satyrus of Tanais.

And why dream small? With the two of them, Stratokles could aim higher.

Whereas her marriage to Satyrus would mean that he would have to start all over again.

BOOK ONE

EUXINE

1

Late winter, or perhaps early spring on the shores of the Euxine. The first crocus buds were peeping out of the earth, and the lambs were coming, and the horses were foaling, and in just a few weeks there would be fresh green on the Sea of Grass.

Two archers stood on the city's Field of Ares, shooting arrows into a distant target made of linen canvas stuffed tight with rags and straw. Shooting with a precision that bored the onlookers, who mostly sat on the dead winter grass enjoying the first day of sunshine. Until both archers started shouting.

Melitta touched the corner of her mouth with the fletchings at the peak of her draw, and loosed her arrow at the target.

It struck home with a satisfying *thwack* as the barbed head cut the taut canvas. 'When is she going to marry you, if she loves you so much?' she asked her brother.

Satyrus pulled an arrow from the *gorytos* at his waist and nocked the arrow. He drew a breath, raised the bow and shot – a continuous motion that sent the arrow into the target with the same flat *thwack*. 'When her uncle is done traipsing about pretending to be one of Alexander's men,' Satyrus said. He didn't hide the disappointment in his voice. Every spring brought a new delay in his wedding plans. He was twenty-four, and Amastris was older.

Melitta nocked, drew and shot. *Thwack.* 'You have a slave in your bed,' she said, accusingly.

Satyrus nocked, drew and loosed. His arrow flew over the top of the target. 'By the Lord of the Silver Bow, sister, is that any of your business?' he asked pettishly.

'We swore to *Mater* that we would not lie with slaves,' she said. 'You missed, by the way. The horse is mine.'

Satyrus struggled with his temper for as long as it took his heart to beat three times. 'Yes,' he said after the third heartbeat.

'Yes, you are sleeping with a slave? Or yes, the horse is mine?' Melitta asked. Just for emphasis, she drew, nocked and shot again – and her arrow struck dead in the centre of the mark.

'Yes, I think it's time you got moving on your spring progress,' Satyrus said. He didn't do a very good job of keeping the anger out of his voice.

'Splendid!' Melitta said. 'What a very good job you are making of living up to *Mater*'s desires. And Philokles'! And Leon's! We said we would *not* have slaves. How are you doing with that, *brother*? I seem to see more agricultural slaves arrive every day.'

'Some of them on Leon's ships!' he shot back. 'This is the real world, sister! You go and ride the plains and pretend to be a nomad princess. I have a kingdom to manage. We need agricultural labour.''

'In our beds? Get me one, brother. A nice one with a big cock.' She rolled her hips. 'How's that!'

'Ares! You are the limit! It is not your business who's in my bed!' The King of the Bosporus realised that he had shouted the last, and that even on the Field of Ares outside the city people were watching them.

Melitta shrugged. 'Handsome boy like you ought to be doing better than agricultural labour,' she said.

'Perhaps I could sleep with the captain of my bodyguard?' Satyrus asked his sister.

'Shut your mouth!' she hissed.

'Of course, he's twice my age – but surely Coenus is still a good-looking man,' Satyrus finished, satisfied that he'd punched through his sister's air of superiority. He had long suspected that she slept with her guard captain, Scopasis, a former outlaw.

They stood and glared at each other for ten heartbeats.

'At least he's not a slave,' she said – and she meant to hurt.

'That's all right,' he shot back. 'Go out on the plains and leave your son with me to raise.'

In fact, she wasn't the most devoted mother, and that shot hit its target squarely so that she turned bright crimson from the roots of her black hair to the tops of her breasts, just visible under her slightly open Persian coat.

'You owe me a horse,' she said, and walked away. She walked ten steps and turned, unable to stop herself. 'You need to stop pretending that Amastris will marry you. Find yourself a girl. Fuck her and make some children, and then you can talk to me—' She was choking up, getting angry, threatened with tears and hating herself for it. 'Then you can talk to me about children.' She walked to her horse, leaped into the saddle and dashed away.

'That is the king?' asked a foreign voice. The man sounded puzzled.

'The king's not available just now.' Satyrus turned his head, anger still pounding away in his bloodstream and saw his hypaspist, Helios, standing with a powerfully built man – Satyrus had seen him arrive – Antigonus' ambassador Niocles, son of Laertes of Macedon. Or so his morning report had said.

Helios hurried to his side, and Satyrus handed him his bow and *gorytos* to carry. 'What's next?' he asked, walking to his horse.

'The new plough, lord,' Helios said.

'I'll skip that,' Satyrus said. Anger was still heavy inside him, so big that it seemed to fill his breast and choke him. *How dare she tax him with his slave-girl.* He took a deep breath. *How disgusting it was of him to hit back at her motherhood.*

The problem of being twins was that you were born able to hurt the person you loved the most.

'Lord, you said you had to see the plough today or it would be too late—' Helios sounded contrite, but he knew his master and he knew his duty.

'Then I shall.' Satyrus cut short a lecture on duty by jumping onto his charger's back and putting his heels to the animal's sides, and he was gone as fast as his sister.

Satyrus owned a number of farms around the perimeter of Tanais, the city that he made his capital. It was the city founded by his father – posthumously, it is true. The bronze statue of his father still loomed over the agora, although other statues were joining it.

Thinking about his father – heroised, and almost deified – didn't help him dismiss his bad behaviour. Nor, as he rode along the escarpment and looked down into the valley of the Tanais River, did thoughts of Philokles, his tutor, with whom he had often galloped these same stades.

He rode down the near cliff at a reckless pace and his horse carried him in great bounds, his four feet seeming to skim the earth. Satyrus kept his seat at the base of the ridge only by leaning well back and clamping his knees like the vice in a bootmaker's shop. And when he felt his charger's pace ease, he righted himself, leaned low over the stallion's neck and galloped along the road – the road where he'd killed his first man.

And his first woman.

Right here, he'd shot her. She'd been lying wounded, and he'd leaned over and put an arrow in her and watched her die. Just his age, at the time; thirteen or fourteen. He still saw the look on her face. He still wondered where she went when she left her body – and what awaited him.

He flew along the road, past the stream where the salmon went to breed and up the next hill to where he kept his own farm. It was a wealthy farm, with stone barns and a good house, and he rode into the yard, his stallion throwing clods of earth from the wet road.

He'd left his attendants far behind, except for Helios who was hard on his heels. His farm manager, Lekthes, was waiting by the ox shed.

'You came, lord!' he laughed.

'Am I so unreliable?' Satyrus asked.

'Reckon there ain't many kings in the circle of the world who till their own fields,' Lekthes said. He spat. 'Plough's hitched. How do your courtiers say it? He *awaits your pleasure.*' Lekthes was a freedman, a former slave who'd been purchased by Leon to run farms and train new farmers. He didn't have the habits of a slave, though. In some ways, he was the most arrogant man Satyrus had ever met. He had the arrogance of a craftsman.

'I'll get started,' Satyrus said. 'All my people are close behind, and I can't avoid the Macedonian ambassador for ever.'

Helios allowed a grim chuckle to escape his lips.

Satyrus stripped his chiton over his head so that he was almost naked, tossed the garment to Helios and clucked to the oxen.

They were well trained, and very strong. As soon as he made the noise, they started forward, and the blade – the *hynis* of the new plough – bit immediately, penetrating the winter sod and cutting deep, more than a handspan deep. After a single furrow, less than a stade, Satyrus could feel the strain in his wrists and lower back. He clucked again and the beasts snorted and rumbled to a stop, and he leaned over the handles of the plough to examine his furrow. Straight enough. And deep. The black soil was turned in neat mounds on either side of the furrow. The sexual imagery of ploughing was obvious; even the smell—

The king shook himself. Sex was very much on his mind, and he forced himself back to the matter at hand. He clucked again, and his two beasts pushed forward against their yokes – the *zygotes* that gave the hoplite class their name.

Up and down, and up and down. After three full furrows, Satyrus understood all over again why farming was the best training for war. He motioned to Helios, had a drink of wine from his flask and ignored the arrival of the Macedonian delegation and got back to work.

He lost himself in it for a while. Ploughing – which he had only begun to practise the autumn before – required his full concentration, body and mind. The management of the oxen, the depth of the plough blade, the shifting of the machine under his hands and the pain in the small of his back—

The oxen shambled to a stop, the offside beast shying at a fly. Satyrus considered that there was something poetic, even oracular about a beast the weight of three horses shying from the furrow because of a fly the weight of a grain of wheat. While he indulged in this bit of petty philosophy, he had to use the full breadth of his shoulders to keep the plough on course.

The erring ox stopped, flicked its tail and lowered its head.

Satyrus let the handles of the plough down, easing the weight of the machine onto the turned soil. Then he rolled his shoulders, stretched his back and stood straight for the first time in five long furrows.

Satyrus the Second, King of the Bosporus, was naked like a slave – or a farmer – toiling in the hot spring sun of the Euxine. He stood a full six feet, with shoulders that seemed as wide as he was tall. Men likened him to Herakles, which made him laugh. He was twenty-four years old, and he had been king for three years, and those three years seemed to him to have aged him more than all the years before, as if time were not a constant, whatever Aristotle and Heraklitus might have to say on the subject.

Helios came running from the trees with a chlamys, a strigil and a linen towel – and the canteen of wine. Satyrus took the wine first, drinking a long draught of thrice-watered red before he used the strigil, wiped himself down with the towel and pulled the purple-edged white chlamys over his head. Satyrus gave the younger man a smile and walked across the field towards the foreigners.

'You don't have to see them until tonight,' Helios muttered.

'I'm all right now,' Satyrus said.

Many of the Macedonians were mounted, and there wasn't much to tell them apart. They had the same dun-coloured cloaks and the same look of arrogance. Satyrus laughed because the thought came, unbidden, that Lekthes might have been the Macedonian ambassador's brother.

Satyrus walked across the furrows to greet the ambassadors of the world's most powerful man, Antigonus One-Eye, naked except for his short cloak. He paused, just short of the range at which men begin social interaction, to note the workmanlike nature of his furrows with pleasure.

'Crax?' he called.

'My lord?' Crax responded, pushing through the crowd of sycophants and courtiers. Crax was Satyrus' Master of the Household. He was tall and red-bearded, and his voice still had a hint of the Bastarnae brogue that he had been born to – before slavery, freedom and war made him a powerful officer in the Kingdom of the Bosporus.

'The new plough is a fine machine. Order ten for our farms, and suggest to Gardan that a meeting of the farmers be held on one of our farms so that they can see the benefits.' As he spoke, he noted Coenus – one of his father's most trusted men – standing at his ease, surrounded by soldiers of the bodyguard. He winked, and Coenus responded with a wry smile. Satyrus turned to Helios. 'Make a note for me. Meet with Gardan. He's been requesting it.'

Helios wrote some notes on a wax tablet. Crax wrote something as well, on his own tablet. The sight of a tattooed Bastarnae writing on a wax tablet might well have been mocked, in other company.

'And these gentlemen?' Satyrus asked with elaborate unconcern. As if the last day hadn't been spent preparing to receive them.

'An ambassador, my lord,' Crax said. 'Niocles son of Laertes of Macedon from Antigonus, Regent of Macedon,' Crax said, indicating a middle-aged man – strong, of middling height, who looked more used to wearing armour than the long robes of officialdom.

The man so named came forward, his white chiton held carefully out of the newly turned furrows by a pair of slaves. 'My lord,' he said. His voice was gruff, and his face said that he was none too pleased with the morning's proceedings.

'A pleasure to receive you,' Satyrus said. He clasped hands with the older Macedonian, and if he was discomfited to be greeted by a nearly naked Herakles, he didn't show it.

'A pleasure to meet such a famous soldier,' the Macedonian said.

'Welcome to the Kingdom of the Bosporus,' Satyrus said. 'I expect that you have come wanting something?'

Niocles might have made a face, but he was made of sterner stuff. 'Aye, lord. It pleases you to receive us in a muddy field – and to go straight to the point.'

'I'm busy,' Satyrus said. 'It's ploughing season.'

'As if a king needs to plough his own land,' commented a man in the delegation. The sneer was almost audible.

'I'm sure you came here with business to transact,' Satyrus said.

'I have come on behalf of Lord Antigonus, who men call "One-Eye", Niocles said. 'To demand reparations.'

'Are you sure this isn't your speech for Ptolemy of Aegypt?' Satyrus asked, and many of his men laughed. The Macedonian flushed and there might have been violence, except that Coenus' men of the bodyguard appeared as if from the grass and stood in neat array between their king and the ambassador's men – every bodyguard in the somewhat archaic uniform of bronze breastplates, greaves, attic helmets and long, indigo-blue cloaks. They carried the heavy round aspis of old Greece and short, heavy-bladed spears.

Niocles waited, calming himself. Satyrus wished him luck.

'We understand that you are not so close with Lord Ptolemy as might formerly have been the case?' he asked.

Satyrus smiled. 'Am I not?' he asked. 'How may I help you, and your lord?'

Niocles shrugged. 'Why, with a treaty making us allies in war and peace, of course, lord. But for the moment, I am here to resent the behaviour of your merchants at my master's port of Smyrna.'

Here it comes, Satyrus thought. 'Yes?' he asked, all innocence.

'My lord must know that two of your ships attacked my master's ships in the port of Smyrna. Men were killed. We demand the captains.' Niocles smiled, and now his tone hardened as well. 'This is not negotiable. It might have been better for you if you had given them of your own free will.'

'Better how?' Satyrus asked. He stepped forward, so that he was quite close to the Macedonian. 'Let me see ... I have heard of this incident, of course. Two of my ships are riding at anchor in Smyrna, your master's port. Hmm? And they are attacked. Yes?'

'Men were sent to demand the taxes,' Niocles said. He shrugged. 'Violence only ensued when they were refused.'

'Taxes that included the seizure of the ships?' Satyrus asked.

'My master may make any law he pleases within his own dominion,' Niocles said. Now he all but purred with pleasure. 'And unlike some lords,' he said with a glance at Satyrus' guards, 'my master has the power to enforce his demands.'

'Let me get this straight,' Satyrus said. His hypaspist handed him a golden cup of wine, which he drank without offering any to the Macedonian beside him. 'Your master set a ridiculous "tax" in the port of Smyrna as a pretext to allow a band of pirates to attack my ships. They were roundly defeated. Now I am to hand over my captains, and what? Pay an indemnity? For my presumption in resisting the tax?'

Niocles nodded. 'Exactly.'

'And our crime in this matter is ...?' Satyrus asked, and took a sip of wine.

'Trading with Ptolemy,' Niocles said. 'Your ships had traded with Ptolemy.'

Satyrus laughed. 'That's a crime?' he asked.

'In Smyrna,' Niocles said.

Satyrus nodded. 'So,' he said. 'A lord has the right to make any law he pleases, if only he can enforce it?'

'That's right,' Niocles said.

Satyrus handed his wine cup back to Helios. 'Ploughing is excellent exercise for war,' he said, 'as my ancestors, who defeated the Persians when Macedon was an ally of Persia, could attest. The pretence' – and here Satyrus' voice took on a tone he had not possessed just a few years before, the sharp tone of a king dealing with a fool – 'the pretence that your master has the power to inflict his will on me, here, on the shores of the Euxine, is sheer folly.' Satyrus smiled. 'But as you have yourself noted the precedent, I'll be happy to free all the slaves that you so obviously have in your tail, there.' At this, Satyrus began to walk across the furrows towards the Macedonian embassage.

'What – what?' asked Niocles.

'You – are you a slave? All of you who are slaves, step away from the others. Good. Yes. Coenus? See to it.' Satyrus rounded on Niocles, who had followed him across the ploughed ground and up onto the grass. 'Slavery is a carefully controlled institution in my kingdom,' he said. 'Such is my whim, and the whim of my sister. And since I have the power to enforce my will,' he said, 'you can go home to your master and tell him that the next time he attacks a couple of my ships, I'll have my fleet begin to burn cities on his seaboard. I hope that's clear enough.' Satyrus waved. 'Get you gone. And leave your slaves. I suspect they'll be happier here, anyway.'

Niocles stood his ground. 'You are declaring war?' he asked.

Satyrus shook his head. 'No,' he said. 'I'm just playing this foolish game the way you people play it.'

'What game, lord?' Niocles asked.

'The game of diplomacy,' Satyrus answered. 'Where you pretend to be powerful and I pretend to be powerful and we posture like boys around the Palaestra. I don't want war. Understand? My little realm has had too much war. But neither will I play. At all. Your master has neither the time nor the inclination to come into the Euxine, any more than Ptolemy does. Come back when you want to speak my language.'

Niocles made a face and then shook his head. 'You're more a Macedonian than most Greeks,' he said.

Satyrus shrugged. 'I assume you meant that as flattery,' he said. 'But your flattery won't get you your slaves back.'

'When Antigonus is Great King – King over Kings – you will be sorry you indulged in this petty insubordination.' Niocles stepped closer to Satyrus, and men among the bodyguard shifted. Hands went to spears.

Satyrus shrugged. 'You may judge my views on the subject,' he said, 'by my willingness to behave as I do.'

*

Tanais was a new city, so new that the smell of linseed oil and fresh-cut pine seemed to fill every room in every house, rivalled only by the dusty-dry smell of fresh-cut marble and limestone. It was less than fifteen years since the city had been burned flat by Eumeles of Pantecapaeaum, and less than three years since serious rebuilding began.

Once again, there was a bronze equestrian statue of Kineas, Hipparch of Olbia, in the agora. Once again there was a golden statue of Nike in a temple to Nike at the east end of the agora, and this time the temple was built of Parian marble, shipped block by block from far-off Sounion on the coast of Attica. The 'palace', a small citadel with six tall towers, was small but built entirely of stone, and its central hall was great enough to entertain the whole of the city's thousand citizens, crammed tight as sardines in a barrel, on feast days when it rained.

The loot of four campaigns and the tribute of the northern Euxine cities had rebuilt Tanais with dramatic speed. But it still had the air more of a rich colony than a real city. Many of the citizens were farmers who tilled the land themselves, and hundreds of the local Maeotae had been admitted to citizenship to balance the mercenaries who received land grants in lieu of payment for services.

Besides Greeks and Maeotae, the Valley of the Tanais had a third group of citizens, if they might be so styled. Melitta, Satyrus' sister, was Queen of all the Assagetae – in truth, the leader of the horse nomads from the edge of distant Hyrkania in the east to the far western lands of Thrace and the Getae. She too ruled from Tanais, when she wasn't out on the steppes, ruling from the saddle. As it was spring and the grass was fresh, she was getting ready to escape the confinement of the city and ride free, away to the north, for the yearly gathering in of all the Assagetae when the census, such as it was, was taken. But the Assagetae were as much a part of the kingdom as the Greeks or the Maeotae.

Satyrus left his horse in the 'royal' stable just inside the main gate of the city. The building of stone walls – not just stone in the socle, or foundation courses, but stone all the way to the rampart's top, like the richest cities of the world – had been the twins' first priority. The main gate was flanked by two recessed towers, each three storeys tall and holding three levels of heavy artillery – big torsion engines capable of firing a bolt of iron two yards long. A permanent garrison manned the engines in every tower, and the city had twenty-six towers. Standing as it did on a low bluff over the mouth of the Tanais as it flowed out into the shallow Bay of Salmon, Tanais was as impregnable as the hand of man and the expenditure of gold could make it.

The towers alone had cost the equivalent of a year's revenue from the whole kingdom. That's how Satyrus had begun to see everything in his kingdom – as a price tag. The street from the main gate ran past the royal stables (seventy minas of silver, needed a tile roof) along the wide Street of Heroes with statues of Satyrus' ancestors and some of Kineas' friends (Philokles' statue was due any day from Athens, bronze with silver and gilt, four talents of silver, delivered and already waiting in a pile of wood shavings, along with a statue of his most famous heroised ancestor, Arimnestos of Plataea in bronze, silver and gold), past the gates of the citadel, whose defensive artillery covered the road and gate (four hundred and seventy talents of silver, complete) to the sea gate (five hundred and ninety talents) beyond which stood the masts and standing rigging of Satyrus' fleet, the strongest in the Euxine. Without straining himself, the young king of the Bosporus could count twenty-two trieres, or triremes, whose hulls, repair, sails, rigging, sailors' wages, rowers and marines cost him eighteen talents of silver a year in wages. Each. With his six hemiolas, or sailing triremes (twenty-four talents a year) and his four penteres or 'fivers' at a little more than thirty talents a year, his docks and ship sheds to protect the hulls from Euxine winters, and the fortified mole which protected his fleet and its maintenance, his naval expenditure topped seven hundred talents a year – a noticeable amount even in the revenues of the leading grain producer in the world.

And that was without his magnificent new ship, the *Arete*. New built from stem to stern, and all to his specification. He could see the towering mainyard above the sea gate. She was cubits taller than any other ship in the harbour, and broader in the beam, with room for two men sitting on every bench – a hexeres, or 'sixer'. He longed for his wide deck the way he longed for a girl – any girl – in his bed. The way he longed for Amastris, except that he didn't always think of her when he wanted a woman. Amastris, whose birthday gift, a golden dolphin, had cost two talents of pure gold.

Satyrus sighed, tried to forget the price of everything and walked towards the agora, trailing Helios and Crax and Coenus and two dozen guards. No one bowed. Men did run to him, demanding his attention concerning their lawsuits, or seeking his approval for their wares, or for merchant ventures.

It took him the better part of the afternoon to cross the agora.

Finally he freed himself from the last anxious citizen – a farmer complaining about the moving of his boundary stones – and walked under the gate to the citadel where he was, at last, on his own ground. And this was Tanais – next to Olbia the easiest of his cities to administrate. In Pantecapaeaum, it might have taken him all day to get across the agora and he'd have needed the soldiers at his back. There were still many men who hated him in Pantecapaeaum.

'My lord?' purred Idomenes. Idomenes was the Steward of the Household – the man who made sure that the king was fed and clothed and had a place to sit. He was also the Royal Secretary. He'd held both of these jobs for the former occupant of the throne, and Satyrus suspected he'd do the same for the next.

'Dinner – just friends.' Satyrus dropped his chlamys on the tiled floor of his own apartments. A dozen servants came forward to lay out his clothes for dinner.

'Bath?' Karlus asked, a giant German who served as Satyrus' personal guard and often worked as his manservant, as well. The big German was getting white in his hair, and his body was criss-crossed with scars earned in thirty years of near-constant fighting.

'Yes, Karlus. Thanks,' Satyrus said. The living areas of the palace had hypocausts – heated floors – and a central furnace that kept water hot all day. Satyrus slipped into the water, swam around his little pool for a few minutes and climbed out to be greeted by a pair of attendants with towels.

Massaged, oiled and clean, Satyrus lay down on his couch for dinner as the sun set in red splendour over the valley of the Tanais River. Satyrus rose only to say the prayer to Artemis and pour the libation of the day, and then he led the singing of a hymn to Herakles, his ancestor, before he reclined alone.

On the next couch, Coenus raised a wine cup. 'You did well, lad,' he said.

Satyrus made a face. 'Posturing. Philokles would laugh. I had a spat with Melitta, and took my aggression out on the Macedonians.'

Coenus shook his head. 'Philokles would say that it was well done.

He was the very master of deceit when he needed to be, lord. You should have seen him fool the Tyrant of Olbia with spies—'

Satyrus nodded and cut off the impending story. 'I did see him fool Sophokles, the assassin of Athens,' he said.

Coenus laughed. 'I'm getting old, lord. You did, right enough.'

Satyrus shook his head. 'Never say old.'

Crax scratched his head. 'I'm just a dumb barbarian,' he said. 'Why exactly do we have to do this dance?'

Satyrus exchanged a long glance with Coenus. 'To keep Antigonus off balance until our grain fleets are safely in Rhodes and Athens,' Satyrus said. 'We're at sea in what, two weeks? Antigonus has more than two hundred hulls in the water, and he could pick our merchants off like a hawk takes doves.'

'So we offended his ambassador?' asked Hama. Hama was another barbarian – a Keltoi from the far north, who had served Satyrus' family for twenty years as a bodyguard and war captain. 'How does that help?'

Coenus gave a half-grin. 'Listen,' he said. 'It's not simple. We offended the ambassador to make him believe what he saw and heard here. If we'd been nice to him, he'd have wondered what was up – after all, we've never exactly been friends. The truce between Antigonus and Ptolemy is a dead letter, now. It's war, across the Ionian Sea, and our people have to sail through the middle of it.'

Hama sat up on his couch. 'I see it!' he said. 'By appearing to offend One-Eye, it seems possible that Satyrus is ... available.'

'Or mad,' Coenus said. 'Niocles can report it either way, and Antigonus might choose to keep his distance from our merchantmen this summer.'

'Ares,' Crax spat. 'What do we do *next* summer?'

Satyrus raised his cup and slopped a libation. 'Next summer is in the hands of a different *Moira*,' he said. 'Let us remember the Fates and Fortunes, gentlemen. This summer will be tough enough.'

'You are determined to accompany the fleet?' Coenus asked, for the fifth time.

Satyrus shrugged.

It was morning – a glorious spring morning. From the height of the palace towers, he could see men ploughing in their fields beyond the walls, and far off to the east, an Assagetae horse-trader riding briskly west towards the city with a string of stout ponies raising the dust behind him. Closer to hand, a gaggle of girls went to the public fountain in the middle of the agora (sixty talents for the fountain of marble and bronze, a hundred and seventy for the well, the piping and the engineer and the workmen to dig down into the rock and make a channel so that the waterworks would provide water all year round).

Satyrus watched them draw water; watched the shape of them as they leaned out over the water to draw it, watched as one young woman drank from the pool provided for the purpose and then washed her legs.

Why can't I just summon her? What a fool I am – as if my sister actually cares. And who am I harming? Hyacinth takes no harm from me.

Because I know perfectly well it's wrong, of course. I'm not avoiding my slave-mistress to please my sister. I'm doing it because it is right.

I think.

'I don't think I have your attention,' Coenus said from a very great distance.

'You do, of course,' Satyrus said. He forced his eyes back over the parapet and onto his father's friend. 'But I do request you say that last bit again.'

'I thought that you were going to take an embassage to Heraklea this spring,' Coenus said.

'And so I shall,' said the king.

'You mean, you'll cut a more dashing figure with a war fleet than with some ambassadors,' Coenus said. 'Your prospective father-in-law – now, I'll note, the "king" of Heraklea – may not see it that way.'

Satyrus disliked having his mind read. He disliked it all the more when he felt that he was being mocked – as all of his father's friends tended to do, all the time. His sister Melitta called it the 'conspiracy of the old'. In fact, Coenus was exactly right. Satyrus wanted to see Amastris with twenty ships at his back and resplendent in armour – perhaps fresh from a victory or two.

'Coenus, with what we spend on the fleet, we might as well get some use from it,' Satyrus said.

Coenus grunted. 'You've got me there, lord.'

'And I'm the best navarch, if it comes to a fight,' Satyrus said. 'You've said so yourself.'

'If you get into a fight with Antigonus One-Eye's fleet, all the skill in the world won't be worth a fuck,' Coenus said. Then he shrugged. 'I'm sorry, lad. I'm not myself. You are the fittest navarch. I dislike the both of you gone at the same time – you at sea and your sister out on the Sea of Grass. And neither of you with an heir old enough to rule.'

'If we both die,' Satyrus said, 'feel free to run the place yourself.' He grinned. 'You already do!'

Coenus grunted. 'This is not the retirement I had planned,' he said.

Three days, and Satyrus did not summon his concubine – bought in secret and enjoyed with considerable guilt even before Melitta discovered her. He and Melitta were correct with each other, and no more, and neither offered any form of apology.

But on the fourth day, Satyrus sent the horse. It had started over the horse, a descendant of his father's wonderful warhorse and a fine prospect for a three-year-old, with heavy haunches and a lively spirit – the same slate-grey, silvery hide, the same black mane and tail. A fine horse, and perhaps more ... Thanatos had been a great horse.

Both of them wanted this new horse, and they had wagered him on an archery contest – itself foolish, because Satyrus knew that he was never his sister's match with a bow.

But he conceded defeat and sent her the horse, and then watched from his balcony as a groom took the horse to her in the courtyard, where her people were loading her wagons for her expedition to the Sea of Grass.

He wasn't going to let her leave until they were friends again.

She looked up from a tally-stick, eyed the young stallion greedily and ran a hand over his flanks. Then she shook her head and went back to her packing.

'Look up!' Satyrus said quietly.

But she didn't.

That night, he invited her to share dinner, as it was her last night before leaving.

She declined.

Satyrus went downstairs to the nursery, where his three-year-old nephew was playing with his nurses.

'Hello,' said Kineas. He had bright blue eyes.

'Bow to the king, lad,' said the older nurse. She was Sauromatae, tall and probably as dangerous as most of the bodyguards. She flashed Satyrus a grin.

Kineas bowed. 'Will I be king someday?' he asked.

Satyrus shrugged. 'If I don't get a move on.'

'What does that mean?' Kineas asked.

Satyrus shook his head. He often made the mistake of answering his sister's son as if he were an adult – or as if he were too young to understand the complexities of his position. Kineas was three, and already wise.

'Would you like to go riding tomorrow?' Satyrus asked.

'Only after I watch my mother ride ... away.' The fractional pause told Satyrus too much – and made him angry.

He played with the boy until the sun began to set, romping on the carpets and helping him shoot his toy war engine, a tiny ballista that the sailors had made for the boy. It was really quite dangerous, as Satyrus discovered when one of his shots stuck a finger's-span deep in a shield on the wall.

'Oh!' he said. He'd given the boy the ballista himself. 'Kineas, I have to take this away.'

The boy looked at him a moment and his jaw worked silently.

He was trying not to cry. 'I didn't— I *am* careful!' he said. He grabbed his uncle's knee and raised his small face. His eyes were already looking red around the edges. 'Please? I *am* careful.'

Satyrus took a deep breath. Someone had to take care— 'No,' he said. 'That is, yes— Oh, don't cry! Listen, lad. This is a little too powerful for a boy your age. I didn't know. We can play with it together, but I can't let you play with it by yourself.'

The sun had fully set before Kineas was content. He wasn't a spoiled boy, or a bad one – he was merely a bright lad who spent most of his day with a pair of nurses. He deserved better.

Satyrus got a big hug before he left, and found that his anger was fresh and new. He stood at the entrance to the wing that led to his sister's quarters for as long as it took his heart to beat twenty times, and then, common sense winning out over rage, he walked away.

He went into his own wing, closed the door to his apartments and picked up a cup of wine.

'Lord?' asked Helios.

'Send for Hyacinth,' Satyrus said.

And instantly regretted it. Anger at his sister did not justify excess.

But in Hyacinth's embrace, he lost his anger. It was replaced by sadness. Satyrus had made love often enough to know the difference. He made little effort to please Hyacinth. She, on the other hand, made a dedicated effort to please him.

She was, after all, a slave.

2

Melitta's column rode out through the landward gates of Tanais the next morning, and Satyrus stood with his three-year-old nephew's hand clutched in his own and watched the procession.

She stopped her horse when she came up to them and dismounted with an easy grace. She leaned down and kissed her son. 'I'll be back soon,' she said. 'I love you.'

'I love you!' Kineas said, and threw his arms around her neck and clutched her as if he was drowning.

'Kineas,' she said, after a pause. '*Kineas.*'

The boy relinquished his hold and put his arms by his sides. 'Sorry.'

'Thank you.' Melitta looked at her brother. 'Take good care of him,' she said.

'I always do,' he answered, and wished the words unsaid as soon as they had crossed his lips.

She was mounted and gone before he could think of anything more to say.

Satyrus waited for his ships to sail with the eagerness of a child anticipating a feast, or a holiday from school. But unlike a child, he had plenty to fill his days. He sat with Theron, Coenus and Idomenes for hours, going over long lists of items – of luxury and necessity – that they needed from Alexandria and Rhodes.

'We need more smiths,' Theron insisted.

'Temerix is probably the finest smith in the wheel of the world!' Satyrus said.

'That may be, but men now wait years for him to make a blade.' Coenus shook his head. 'His very excellence has blinded us all to the scarcity of other smiths.'

'He has apprentices,' Satyrus put in.

'He has twenty apprentices. We need twenty smiths – just in the

Tanais countryside. And bronzesmiths, and more goldsmiths.' Theron shook his head. 'We need to have the ability to manufacture our own armour.'

'We need tanners,' Idomenes said quietly.

'Tanners?' Satyrus asked.

'Tanais is growing as a place where animals are slaughtered and hides are gathered,' Idomenes said. He held up a bundle of tally-sticks. 'Last month alone, from the Feast of Demeter to the Feast of Apollo, we gathered in six hundred and forty hides of bulls and big cows. If we had a tanner, we'd make ten times the profit on them.'

'Tanner means a tannery and a lot of stink,' Coenus said. He rubbed his beard and his eye met Satyrus', and both of them smiled.

'Beats the hell out of being an exile in Alexandria, doesn't it?' Coenus asked him, and Satyrus chuckled.

'It does, at that. But somehow I never thought that being a king would involve quite so much *maths*.' He laughed. 'Very well, Idomenes. Your point is excellent. We need a master tanner, some slave tanners and some silver to build a tannery.'

'Slaves?' Idomenes asked.

'I'll buy 'em as slaves and free them here,' Satyrus said. 'Good way to start.' He looked around, grinned and said, 'Basically, you want me to buy everything on the skilled-labour market.'

Theron nodded. 'Where would we put the tannery?' he asked.

'Up the coast. There's that black stream up by Askam – flows all year round. Stinks already.' Idomenes was making a catalogue of all the terrain in the kingdom, and he knew every landmark within five days' ride. He raised his eyes, found no disagreement and wrote a note on his wax tablet.

'If we all die, let's leave the kingdom to Idomenes,' Satyrus said.

Idomenes' head came up. The other men were all smiling. He flinched.

'Hey!' Satyrus said. 'I'm not Eumeles!' He leaned back and held out his cup for cider, which a servant poured for him.

'Lord, such a comment . . . scares me.' Idomenes had served the old tyrant, a ruthless man who taxed and killed without meaning or warning, bent on making himself a major player in the game of succession to Alexander.

'I merely meant that you seem to do this better than the rest of us,' Satyrus said.

'I'll just write my notes up and make a smooth tablet, shall I, my lord?' Idomenes clutched his tablets to him as if to protect him from wrath, and slipped out.

Theron shook his head. 'He's not even slimy. He's a good man. Why does he *act* like a snake?'

Satyrus shrugged.

Coenus pursed his lips, rubbed his beard and took a drink. 'He lived too long with snakes, I think. Never mind – he'll get used to us.' He took a stylus from behind his ear and made a note in his own tablet. 'Where do you think Diodorus is, anyway?'

Theron shrugged. 'Idomenes has the latest letter – but you've seen it.'

'I haven't,' said Satyrus. He turned to his hypaspist, who stood by the wall. 'Helios, fetch Idomenes back and ask him to bring the latest letter from Diodorus.'

Helios bowed and vanished through the door.

'You're spending a fortune on your fleet,' Coenus remarked, looking at a list.

'Yes,' Satyrus said. He was tempted to add *it's mine to spend*, but he bit it back. The 'conspiracy of the old' made him react like a callow youth, but he wasn't so callow any more.

Coenus shrugged. 'Well – it's yours to spend.' He looked up when Satyrus made a choking sound. 'Artillery?'

'We were already getting weapons for the towers,' Satyrus said.

'Draco and Amyntas are installing the new pieces today,' Theron put in. 'I saw Draco on the wharf, covered in shavings.'

Satyrus glanced around. 'I want to see that!' Then he sat back and fiddled with his belt of gold links. 'When we've finished here, of course.'

The two older men laughed. They were still laughing when Idomenes came back with a sheepskin bladder of scrolls. 'Letters from Babylon?' he asked.

'Latest from Diodorus?' Satyrus asked.

'Came yesterday. My apologies, lord – I read it out for Theron while you were playing with the ambassadors.'

To Satyrus, King of the Bosporus, and Melitta, the Lady of the Assagetae, and the rest of you: greetings.

We appear to be in for another summer without fighting – a mercenary's dream. Demetrios seems to be in Greece, facing Cassander and 'liberating' Athens. It occurs to me that if Demetrios really does take Athens, Stratokles will suddenly be tempted too – and Heraklea could be a dangerous ally. But I'm an old and very suspicious man.

'Lord, it would appear that Demetrios has entered Athens.' Idomenes raised his eyes from the scroll. 'We have that news from several sources.'

Coenus nodded. 'All the more reason for you to hurry down to Heraklea.'

Antigonus is rumoured to be building up his fleet and preparing to have a go at Aegypt. If so, Ptolemy is more than ready for him – he declined a contract with us, saying that we cost too much! So he must be confident, the old skinflint. But Antigonus is serious, and he's busy buying the alliance of all the pirates in Cilicia and Ionia. Rumour in Alexandria before I left suggested that your old friend Demostrate declined his offer.

Demostrate was the king of the pirates of the Chersonese, and had long been an ally. His ships had been instrumental in taking Tanais from its former tyrant. 'Thanks the gods for that,' Coenus said. 'Demostrate going over to Antigonus would be the end of our shipping.'

Satyrus shuddered at the thought of the golden horn being closed to his merchant ships.

I'm going to accompany an embassy to the Parni, as our squadrons have more Sakje speakers than anyone else in Babylon. I will be out of contact for several months, but I'll see more of the world. Darius sends his greetings, as do Sitalkes and a dozen others. Keep well – I plan to retire there, lad!

Of all of them, only Diodorus – the commander of his father's former mercenary company, the 'Exiles' – and Coenus and his father's other friends still called him 'lad'. He laughed. The letter was like having Diodorus present in the room, if only for a few lines.

'Who are the Parni?' Satyrus asked.

'No idea,' Theron answered, and even Idomenes shook his head.

Two hours on the grain tax, and more on warehouse space in Olbia – he really needed to visit Olbia, and soon. Eumenes the archon was an old family friend, but he was a gentleman farmer, not a merchant, and the town merchants were none too happy. The warehouse space for the grain tax was so damp and rat-infested that they were losing money.

A farewell meal was given for Antigonus' ambassador. Satyrus was pleasant, and Theron was the picture of a gentleman and former Olympic athlete. Niocles was charmed and annoyed by turns.

'You intend to send your grain to Rhodes this year, my lord?' he asked, as the roast duck was served and the tuna steaks were removed.

Satyrus had hoped to avoid serious talk, and he saw his precious artillery slipping away. All the frames would be installed before he even got to the wharf.

Satyrus shrugged with well-feigned nonchalance. 'Wherever we get the best price,' he replied. 'A matter for merchants,' he said, hoping to chill the topic.

'My lord would prefer if your grain bypassed Rhodes. And Alexandria.' Niocles drank some wine. 'Your cook is to be praised. The tuna was better than anything I had in Athens.'

'You were in Athens, with Demetrios?' Satyrus asked. Theron grinned and turned his head.

Niocles looked around. 'Yes – yes, I was. It is not widely known yet that my lord has taken Athens.'

'Perhaps not known by those who lack the proper conduits of information,' Satyrus said with a smile. 'So: you have Athens. And Athens needs grain.' He nodded. 'Take it up with my merchants,' he said firmly.

'Athens needs grain. As do many other cities.' Niocles nodded. 'I'm sure that your merchants would find it worth their while to turn west when they pass the Dardanelles.'

Satyrus shook his head. 'My ships go where they will,' he said. 'Most of our cargoes go on foreign hulls anyway. Athens, for instance, buys most of Olbia's grain.' His voice carried the clear message – *this subject is closed*.

'But you have grain of your own, lord. You are dissembling, but there are fifteen ships in the mole, all loading grain from *your* warehouses.' Niocles leaned back, sure he'd scored a point.

'You sound more like a spy than an ambassador,' Satyrus said. He was bored, annoyed that he was missing the installation of his artillery and even more annoyed that Antigonus' ambassador continued to make all these demands. 'I declare your embassage over. This instant. Begone.' Satyrus rolled off his couch. Helios stepped to his side and handed him his sword, and he put it on over his head, donned his chlamys of royal purple and turned back. 'If he's not on his ship in an hour, kill him,' Satyrus said to Hama. Hama nodded.

'You're insane!' Niocles said. 'Lord, I meant no – that is – ambassadors!'

Whatever he was going to say was lost as Satyrus walked in through the doors of his private apartments.

He changed into a plain natural wool chiton and a fine dark red chlamys with plain silver pins and a hat to hide his face. He put on boots.

Theron came in as he got the left boot laced.

'That was a little precipitate,' Theron said.

'Was it really?' Satyrus asked. 'He's a fool. And he doesn't seem to care whether he offends me or not.'

Theron nodded. 'Well, you have a point. And I suppose it can't hurt. After yesterday. As you said this morning, either you are mad, or very strong, and either way it should give his master some hesitation.' Theron had been Satyrus' athletic coach and tutor. He had special rights in terms of criticism. 'Besides,' he said, 'now you have a free hour to look at your ships.'

Satyrus laughed. 'Am I so transparent?' he asked.

The sun pounded down on the wharf, and on the naked backs of the work party that was installing the artillery aboard Satyrus' new-built flagship. *Arete* was going to be the most powerful ship in the Euxine – a Rhodian-built penteres with a hemiolas deck.

Satyrus walked down the wharf with Helios at his back, doing his best to be a private gentleman and not the king, but sailors and oarsmen stopped whatever they were doing to smile, wave, bow, or simply stare.

'She's huge!' Helios said.

Satyrus knew there were bigger ships on the seas, but *Arete* towered over the rest of his small fleet – taller and broader than his triremes and slightly longer as well, like a warhorse in a stable of racehorses.

'Permission to come aboard?' Satyrus called up the companionway.

The marine on duty nodded.

Neiron, his helmsman – technically the trierarch of the *Arete* – met him on the central command deck. Unlike a small trireme, the mighty penteres had a deck that went from gunwale to gunwale the whole length of the deck – armouring the rowers against archery but condemning them to airless sweat wherever they rowed. However, with the after half-deck for the sailors to work the permanent mainmast, the ship had the deck space to carry a huge marine complement – thirty or forty men, if he wished it. More important, the deck had room to support outboard sponsons – small decks – with the new artillery pieces. *Arete* was built to hold six ballistae – three to each side – and a seventh over the ram.

It was the weapon over the ram that Draco was installing as Satyrus came up the companionway, and he seemed to ignore the king, lying full length and squinting at the deck. The frame of the ballista lay across the bow, and there was a hole bored through the deck and into the main timber that supported the top of the ram – a timber of Euxine oak as big around as Satyrus' leg. Two shipwrights stood by, one with a brace and bit, and the other with a saw.

Satyrus crouched by the Macedonian. 'You've done this before,' he said.

'Nope,' Draco said. 'Diokles! You asleep?'

'Didn't go through the beam,' came a voice from below.

Draco shook his head. 'Needs some kind of collar, I think. Look – we put a pin in the base of the main frame, so the piece can rotate.'

'Excellent!' Satyrus said, celebrating his freedom from the finances of his polis.

The ballista over the bow was the heaviest piece on the ship – in fact, in the whole fleet. It could shoot an iron bar out over two stades. Allowing the piece to rotate would more than double its effectiveness.

'The pin goes deep into the oak of the frame – and deep into the beam below.' Draco shook his head. 'But the thing weighs fifty talents. When it looses it could kick like a mule. Shear the pin – crack the beam – break the frame.' He shrugged.

'We won't know until we try,' Satyrus said.

'I'd prefer bronze. A nice bronze base – cast. And a matching piece on the frame, to hold the pin.' Neiron shrugged.

'What's to *stop* it from rotating?' Satyrus asked suddenly.

'What?' asked Draco. His tone indicated that he was taking the criticism personally.

'When there's a sea running, won't it just swing around like a mad thing, useless as tits on a boar?' Neiron asked, his eyes on Satyrus. He shrugged. 'I'm just an old man. I don't like all this innovation. What next – we'll all forget how to ram, and just sit back and pound our opponents to flinders with these things? Not exactly glorious, if you ask me.'

Satyrus slapped his helmsman on the back. 'I'll remind you of that sometime. But Draco – he's got a point, eh?'

'More reason for a bronze base plate. With stops, or catches, or releases. I'm not a sodding engineer, am I? Just a Macedonian who's actually loosed one of these.' Draco knelt back down by the hole bored in the deck, still mumbling to himself.

Satyrus expected someone to step forward, but they were all deferring to him. 'Well?' he asked.

Neiron raised an eyebrow.

'Do we have a bronzesmith who can cast a base plate?' Satyrus asked. But he knew the answer, and he was suddenly back in the realms of finance.

'Not really,' Neiron admitted. 'We need one!'

'Take a note,' Satyrus said to Helios, who took a tablet from his leather sack and scribbled. Then he turned back to Draco. 'Well? Rig the tackle and put it in. Let's shoot it and see.'

Draco smiled. 'Yes, lord.'

In a matter of moments, a dozen sailors swarmed up the mainmast, rerigged the yard to run fore and aft, belayed the aft end with a heavy rope and put a sling over the bow end with a system of hitches. Then they attached the frame of the forward ballista and used the contraption to raise the frame off the deck and lower it – swaying slightly in the very gentle motion of the Bay of Salmon – until the pin slid home into the deck and the beam below.

'Needs a cross brace,' Neiron said, getting into the spirit of the thing. 'Look here – something that comes out of the base and pins into the deck.'

In fact, the whole weapon rotated slowly back and forth on its pin – a two-fingers-thick rod of iron – swaying with the motion of the waves.

'Never thought of the waves,' Draco said.

Neiron made a sound of derision.

Satyrus moved the weapon back and forth with his hand. It was heavy, but well balanced. Then he got down on his hands and knees and looked at the place where the pin entered the deck.

'Wearing against the deck boards already,' he said. 'Draco's right. It has to have a bronze mounting plate. But let's shoot it anyway.'

He walked over and looked at the port-side forward weapon, which was fixed in place. It could only be moved if a dozen men lifted the entire frame. Out beyond the mole, he could see a ship putting to sea – the Macedonian ambassador.

He walked back to see Diokles, his former helmsman and now captain of *Oinoe*, a heavy teteres, or 'fourer', emerge from below decks with a heavy iron spear.

'Shooting away a couple of drachma every round,' he said as he came up. 'Like throwing money at the enemy.'

'I'll just have the new weapons stripped off *Oinoe*, then,' Satyrus responded.

'Not my money!' Diokles laughed. 'It's yours!' He gave Draco the spear.

Between them Draco and Neiron spun the winding handles on the weapon's torsion mechanism. The gears made a curious noise, almost musical, as the handles turned. Satyrus and Helios took a turn.

'Not exactly *fast*,' Satyrus said.

'That's tight enough. Never overwind – that's how you break a rope, and then you're done for.' He put a hand carefully on the string of the giant bow. Satyrus did the same.

The bowstring was as thick as rope, woven of horsehair. It was as hard as a tree branch under his hand.

'Load!' Draco called, and Neiron and Helios swung the iron spear up and onto the weapon's loading trough. The nock slid effortlessly onto the string. 'Ready!'

'You want to do it, lord?' Draco asked.

Satyrus didn't pretend. 'Yes!' he said, and placed himself behind the frame, his hand on the releasing handle.

'Stand a little clear, like this. Sometimes a string breaks, or the winches give way. Either way, you don't want to be right behind her, the bitch.' Draco nodded.

Satyrus ignored him, to line up his shot. 'Ready to shoot,' he said.

Draco stood back.

Satyrus pulled the handle and the spear flashed away, so fast that none of them could trace its flight. The frame shook and twisted on its pin, and the deck groaned, and the arms of the heavy bow made a curious *thwack* as they hit the limit of their travel.

The spear vanished. It went far enough that none of them saw the fall of the shot, and they all stood around, disappointed.

Neiron shook his head. 'Look at that,' he said. He pushed against the weapon's frame, and it tilted.

One shot had bent the pin on which it rotated.

'Thetis' glittering breasts!' Draco said.

'Best put it on a fixed frame until we can get ourselves a bronze-smith,' Satyrus said. He was watching the ambassador's ship. 'How many men do we have who can use these things accurately?'

Neiron snorted.

'Looks to me as if we need to have trained crews,' Satyrus said. 'And targets on the shore. And contests and prizes. We go to sea in two weeks. I'd like us to be able to hit something.'

Neiron nodded. 'And what will one of these here spears do to a ship?' he asked. 'Anything?'

Draco nodded. 'Marines?'

Satyrus and Neiron nodded. Diokles shook his head. 'Better train some sailors, too.'

Satyrus left them debating where they should hold the drills. He was in a much better mood, although as usual, these days, part of his mind was calculating the cost of exercising the new weapons, with the spears at two and a half drachma each (a day's wage for an oarsman).

He consoled himself that the price was far lower than the value of the loss of a merchant ship. And then he went back to worrying about warehouse space and which towns needed better water supplies.

Two weeks and I'll be at sea, and will leave all this behind me, he thought.

3

Melitta sat on a stool covered in furs, wearing her best silvered-bronze scale and her favourite white caribou-hide boots and her mother's caribou coat over her armour. Despite the stool, she sat with her back straight. Her right hand was supported by her mother's sword, which, according to Assagetae tradition, had been taken as spoils from Cyrus the Great after a battle in the distant past.

Behind her stood – or sat – her bodyguard, twenty young knights of her own household led by her lover, Scopasis, who stood at her side like a heavily muscled statue.

Arrayed in front of her were ten days of heavy work – the men and women of the Assagetae who had brought their cases to her to plead. It was the spring gathering of the Assagetae in their 'city' of dykes and temporary walls, hidden in the upper reaches of the Borysthenes River where most Greeks had never travelled.

Merchants had been arriving for days. Hundreds of them: sword-smiths and goldsmiths and fine potters and leatherworkers from as far away as Athens and Alexandria, lured by the promise of rich profits and a sense of adventure. The Tanja of the Assagetae was like a combination of law court, agora and religious festival, with a trade fair thrown in for entertainment. There were twenty thousand tribesmen and women in the dykes, their great herds penned, tribe by tribe, with two hundred thousand horses and twice as many sheep spread over hundreds of stades. Cattle wandered from encampment to encampment, lowing loudly, eating whatever grass was already available, watched by children whose attention was more on the wonder of the Aegyptian priest and his wagon than on their charges. Horses trumpeted to each other – uncut stallions roared with irritation at the smell of so many other strange stallions, and mares rolled their lips back in scent-inspired appreciation of all the possibilities. Adolescent warriors of both sexes did approximately the same as their horses.

Melitta could remember coming to the Tanja with her mother: the adulation of the adults, the praise for her six-year-old accomplishments, the wonder of the trade fair, the fine horses and the beautiful clothes. But mostly she could remember her mother's disgust that her people could behave so often like fools, and her annoyance at dealing with their failings in the giving of law. Adultery, drunkenness, child abandonment, horse-thieving, witchcraft, murder – she heard them all.

Are you children? her mother would often ask of the men and women brought before her.

Her attention snapped down to a pair of her own tribesmen – Cruel Hands – veterans of her summer campaigns of three years before, and men who had ridden to raid the Sauromatae these last two years. Impatient with a grain trader, they had killed him and taken his mules and his goods.

'He was trying to cheat us!' the shorter one said, as if this made it all right.

'You murdered a foreign merchant in cold blood,' answered Kairax. He was their immediate lord and was acting for the merchants.

'Wasn't cold blood!' shouted the bigger of the two. 'I was mad as fuck!'

'Are you two children?' Melitta snapped. For a moment she paused because she heard her mother's voice emerge from her own lips. 'He made you angry, so you killed him?'

'He was cheating us,' the smaller man said again.

Melitta took a deep breath. She looked at Kairax. 'What do the merchants want?'

'Restitution,' Kairax said. 'Fifty horses for the life of the man, twenty more for his goods.'

'By the Heavenly Archer!' the smaller man said.

'That fuck wasn't worth no fifty horses,' said the bigger man.

Melitta's eyes strayed around the enclosure. Carpets – fine carpets – hung on three sides of her, blocking the chill spring wind, separating her deliberations from the riot of the market on the far side of the barrier, although all Sakje were welcome and several hundred of them crowded around, more than a few on horseback.

Her wandering eyes crossed with Scopasis', and she smiled at him – an automatic smile, as she was beginning to doubt the wisdom of taking him as a lover. He was brave – loyal – and deeply in love with her.

She sighed inwardly, and thought about how easy it would be to be a bad queen; to ignore these petty cases, give quick judgements and be free to roam the booths, spending her riches on golden cones to hang tinkling at the edge of her caribou coat, or fine saddles—

Drakas. That was the short one's name. He'd been with her in the last charge at Tanais River when all the tribes became intermixed. But she could remember his ugly nose under his helmet, and his grin.

'Drakas,' she said.

He stiffened. 'Lady?'

'Drakas, how many horses do you own?' She leaned forward and pointed her mother's sword at him. 'How many?'

'More than a hundred,' he admitted.

'And this lout?' she asked. She didn't really know his companion.

The big man shrugged. 'A dozen,' he admitted.

She shook her head. Drakas had enough horses to be treated as a nobleman, but his friend did not. She suspected that this apparent inequality had something to do with the killing – and she further suspected that Drakas' success as a hunter and raider had something to do with the fact that Kairax was willing to see him punished. Rivalry? Jealousy?

You're like children.

'Who struck the killing blow?' she asked.

Drakas shrugged. 'I did,' he admitted, pursing his lips. He spat. Among Sakje, that wasn't a gesture of disrespect – she needed to remember that. Among Sakje, he was being contemplative and polite.

'What was the actual value of the man's goods?' she asked Kairax.

Kairax shrugged. 'They say twenty horses,' he said, and shook his head. He and Drakas exchanged a glance that suggested their relationship was even more complicated than she had guessed.

'Bring me a merchant who knew this man,' she said. She raised her head to Scopasis. 'Who's next?'

He raised an eyebrow – an expression she loved. 'Astis daughter of Laxan of the eastern Dirt People.' He made a face. 'Her father and brothers were murdered.'

'Sauromatae?' Melitta asked, suddenly interested.

'Perhaps,' Scopasis said. 'A matter for your attention, anyway. I have heard her story and believe it.'

'Have her brought,' Melitta said.

An eddy in the crowd announced the arrival of a pair of long-robed merchants – Syrians. They bowed to her.

'They ask if we will use their interpreter,' Kairax asked. He grinned.

'Tell them I would be happy to use their interpreter,' Melitta said. She grinned too.

Their interpreter stepped forward. He looked sheepish, and they spoke among themselves for a moment.

'How big was the dead man's family?' Melitta asked in Sakje, and the translator put the question to the two merchants in Greek.

'No doubt she'll use the size of his family to assess the total value of the judgement,' muttered one merchant. Greek was not his first language, either.

'So make it big. Eight children,' said the other merchant.

'Lady, the merchant says eight children,' the interpreter said. 'That's what he told me to say, lady,' the man added.

'Ask him if he knows the family well,' Melitta said.

'Now what do I say?' asked the second merchant. His Greek was better. 'If I say I don't know them—'

Melitta leaned forward and pointed her sword at the second merchant. 'You could just tell the truth,' she said in Greek.

Gaweint, one of her knights, and the one whose Greek was best, translated this sally for the audience, who roared with appreciative laughter.

The merchants glared around.

'Come forward. Talk to me,' Melitta said. 'How many children did the man have?'

'I don't know,' admitted the merchant. 'He only worked for me this one trip.'

'And if I give you horses, will any of them go to his wife and children? Where was he from?'

'Far, my lady, by the great salt—'

'Spare me, Syrian. I grew up in Alexandria and I've ridden a black-hulled ship into every port on the Syrian coast.' She laughed at their discomfiture. 'You people need to do more research before you come to the Sea of Grass. Now, no horse shit – do you even know where he's from?'

'No,' admitted the Aramaic merchant. He shrugged expressively. 'No. But that shouldn't mean your man gets off free.'

'How much merchandise did the man lose? Really lose?' Melitta asked.

'About ten good horses' worth,' the merchants admitted, after a whispered discussion.

Melitta nodded. 'Kairax, step forward. Here is my judgement. Each of these two,' she pointed at the two Cruel Hands tribesmen, 'will give five good horses to these merchants. Yes?'

Both men nodded, although the bigger man – the poorer – grew pale.

'Drakas will pay ten horses each to me and to Kairax for his breach of the lady's peace.' She looked at Drakas.

He jumped forward. 'Where is the fairness in that, lady? Alkaix here did the same as me—'

'You struck the killing blow and you, the nobleman, led him into this crime. Did you not?' she asked.

Drakas mumbled something.

'Twenty horses will not break you, Drakas. But it ought to remind you to keep your temper in check.' She motioned him forward. He came to her side, and she gestured for him to kneel so that she could speak into his ear.

'You desire to be treated as a nobleman, do you not?' she asked.

Drakas nodded. 'I have—'

'Spare me. What do you have for armour?'

Drakas shrugged. 'A good helmet.'

'Noble status cuts both ways. Arm five men as knights, mount them yourself and bring them to me, and I will see to it that Kairax grants you your due. See to it that one of them is your friend here. Otherwise shut up and obey your betters.'

'Yes, lady!' he said.

'Anything further?' she asked of the assembly when Drakas had backed away.

Silence reigned.

'I have spoken my will. Will you see it carried out?' she asked the assembly.

Men – and women – nodded. Many voices were raised in assent. Kairax gave her a nod. Scopasis gazed at her with adoration.

She felt a certain satisfaction. Giving justice well was a good job. 'Next,' she said.

Scopasis stepped up. 'Astis daughter of Laxan the farmer requests that the lady and Lord Thyrsis help her achieve revenge.'

Astis was a strong-looking woman with a square face and blond-brown hair. Her nose had been recently broken and her eyes had the look that hunted animals and damaged people hold. But she stood erect in front of the assembly of the people in a good Parsi coat of blue wool and deerskin trousers.

'Who speaks with her?' Scopasis asked.

Thyrsis stepped forward. Melitta thought of Thyrsis as the Achilles of the Assagetae. His father, Ataelus, had been her father's right hand on the plains, his chief scout and a hero of every battle he'd ever fought. After her father's death, Ataelus had served her mother. When she was murdered, he'd held the high plains to the east against the Sauromatae in a six-year campaign of raid and counter-raid. In the process he'd built a mighty clan out of broken men and outlaws from both sides of the Assagetae-Sauromatae divide. Thyrsis was already a famous warrior – handsome, tall and utterly honest; loyal, strong in battle, clever in council. Too good to be true, really.

Both of his parents had died preserving her kingdom; his mother in the battle, his father shortly after, and he had a special call on her attention. Many Assagetae felt that she should marry him.

He and Scopasis hated each other, but both adored her.

They glared at each other for a long moment.

Melitta laughed. 'Hey, stallions!' Melitta called. 'The mare is waiting.'

That got a roar of approval from the crowd.

Thyrsis stepped forward. 'Lady, this woman is the daughter of Laxan, who served with the archers at the Battle of the Tanais. I have this word from the smith, Temerix, on her behalf. Her people settled the upper Tanais high ground, east of the Temple of the Hunting Goddess, and her father's father held land by Crax's fort.'

Melitta nodded to the woman. 'You are welcome, and doubly welcome for the service of your father.'

'Thank you, lady. Temerix and Thyrsis both say you are the Lady of the Dirt People as well as the Sky People, and I pray this is true.' Her eyes were slightly mad, and there was something flawed in her voice, as if she was afraid to talk and afraid to be silent.

'I am here,' Temerix said. He was a giant of a man, his shoulders as broad as the full length of a child, his arms heavy with muscle like the roots of a strong oak. He was a master smith, and his best work could rival that of the Aegyptian smith-priests or the best ironsmiths of Chaldike or Heraklea. He was another fixture of Melitta's childhood, having served her father.

This no-account Dirt People woman had two powerful advocates. That was interesting.

'Speak, daughter of Laxan.' Melitta smiled at her, trying to disarm the tension in her shoulders and the fear in her face.

'Lady, raiders came to our farm and killed my family.' She laughed – a terrible sound. 'They took me and my sisters. I lived with them – almost a year.' She took a deep breath. 'Last autumn I took a horse and rode away. I would not be one of them. I ask that you ... ride against them.'

The broken nose and the odd motions of her face told that this was a woman who had been beaten – many times. 'Who are they?' Melitta asked.

'Sauromatae?' asked Scopasis. The Sauromatae had become the enemies of the Assagetae, but it had been three years since their defeat and now many of the beaten tribesmen had simply moved into the tribes of the victorious – as was always the way on the plains. Many of the men and women gathered around the assembly were Sauromatae, but they were no longer the 'people of Upazan', the leader who had ridden to defeat and death. Now they were her own people. Scopasis' failure to understand these things was one of the reasons he could never be her consort.

'They were not Sauromatae,' Astis said. She gave her curious laugh again. 'In the year of the War, Sauromatae came and burned our farm and my father took us and led us into the woods. I killed a Sauromatae. I know what a Sauromatae looks like. I know a Sauromatae horse from an Assagetae horse, although I am a farmer.'

That provoked a growl from the assembly.

'What clan would dare to breach the peace and kill your father?' Melitta asked. *This is bad*, she thought, and inwardly she cursed Scopasis for not bringing her this in private – and Thyrsis for not bringing the matter to her attention *before* the assembly. If one of the clans had done this ... so much for her pleasant spring progress.

'No clan of Assagetae,' Astis said.

Now she had silence. Every ear was turned to her. Melitta found herself leaning forward.

'They call themselves *Parni*,' she said. 'Big men with yellow hair from the east. What they speak is like Sakje, but not Sakje. I heard them say that after they take Hyrkania, they will come here.' She looked around. 'I went with them, east of the Kaspian Sea. Twenty days east of the salt water.' She raised her mad eyes and Melitta looked into them – into a year of horror, slavery, beatings and rapes, degradation. 'I ask for revenge – for my father and brothers, for my sisters who died under them.'

Melitta rose. 'Astis, you have suffered, and we will discuss your revenge, but this is not a matter for the assembly. I cannot offer a single judgement on this, the way I might on the murder of one man by another. If we are to punish these Parni, it would require the agreement of a dozen clan leaders. But when we meet, I will ask you to speak.'

A hundred heartbeats later, in the relative privacy of her own tent, she turned on Scopasis.

'Why was I not warned?' she asked. 'This is a matter for all the Assagetae!'

Scopasis shrugged. 'A woman was taken in a raid,' he said. 'These things happen.'

'Artemis! Gentle lady, deadly archer – Scopasis, are you a fool? This is not a simple abduction. That woman has been used – brutally. And not by some tribal youngling with a delusion of power – this is some clan about which we know nothing, attacking our high-plains farmers!'

Thyrsis pushed into the tent behind Scopasis. Melitta's main tent space was big enough for four men on horseback. She waved her hand automatically, inviting him to sit. 'Wine for my guests,' she said to her servants. She and her brother had outlawed slavery in the city of Tanais – but the Assagetae had paid no attention at all. They had slaves, especially after a successful war.

'Pardon me, lady,' Thyrsis said.

'And you!' she turned on him. 'If he's a fool, you're two fools – once for not warning me in advance, and again for not sending her to Tanais.'

Scopasis was angry, she could see that. No man enjoys being called a fool in front of a rival. But Thyrsis bore her anger easily.

'Lady, this woman presented herself to me just yesterday, when I came into the camp. She travelled far to the north, and came among us with the Standing Horses, even though she is one of ours. And she is from far to the east, lady – I'm not even sure that she can claim to be one of our people, except that her father served with Temerix – and I did not even know that until she brought the smith to me this morning. Then this one,' Thyrsis pointed at Scopasis, 'told me that it was a matter of little moment, and that you would deal with it in due time.'

Melitta turned on Scopasis. He shrugged. 'I was wrong, it appears. I cannot always be correct.'

Melitta drew breath to speak her mind – and all but bit her tongue. The Lady of the Assagetae was not the same person as Melitta, lover of Scopasis, nor yet again the same person as the warrior Smells Like Death. In Assagetae terms, these were different people who shared her body – a belief that would have angered Aristotle, she thought. Regardless, if she unleashed her rage on Scopasis—

'We will talk of this later,' she said. 'In the meantime, you can best serve me by summoning the clan leaders.'

The *Tanja* was the largest in years – so most of her clan leaders were readily available. Parshevaelt of the Cruel Hands, with Kairax, were close by, and came to her tent before the wine was poured. Urvara's daughter Listra Red-Hand was just sixteen – but Urvara had inherited the Grass Cats from her father at a young age, and Listra had already killed men in battle, led the great hunts for which her people were famous and was undisputed lady of the clan.

The lords of the Silent Wolves and the Hungry Crows were harder to find, and were less her men. Their clans had come late to the great fight at Tanais River – perhaps due to some treachery, and perhaps not. Her decision to give them only small shares of the spoils had been popular with her other clans – but not with them.

And in truth, clans came and went from the great tribes such as the Assagetae in the same way that warriors came and went from clans. The People of Ataelus now numbered more Sauromatae than Assagetae – while the Grass Cats had absorbed many of the former Standing

Horses, and the current Standing Horse clan was a pale shadow of its former numbers although its new lord, Sindispharnax, was rebuilding. He had so few warriors that he might not have warranted a place in her council but he was a member of her household, one of her own knights, and he was already present. Besides, she wanted him to succeed in rebuilding what had once been the greatest of clans, after the Cruel Hands.

To foreigners, the Horse People – the Sky People, as they called themselves – were a mass of faceless nomads with an alien, impenetrable, unchanging society. The Greek called them the Royal Scythians. But Melitta knew that they were as changeable as the sea, as different, tribe by tribe, as Athenians and Spartans.

Tuarn of the Hungry Crows was next – small, dark-haired and bearing an uncanny resemblance to his totem animal, from his stooped shoulders to his beak of a nose. He took his wine with a good grace and his eyes twinkled.

'I gather we have a border problem,' he said.

Scopasis stood stiffly by his side. 'I explained,' he said, like a man who fears that anything he does will prove to be wrong.

Kontarus was last, lord of the Silent Wolves. He was old and bent, and his tanist, a tall, thin woman with remarkably red hair, stood at his arm, supporting him. He glanced around, refused the wine and grunted. 'Saida,' he said, pointing at the red-haired woman. His tone suggested that he was not pleased to be summoned.

Melitta couldn't decide whether Saida was haughty or merely nervous. She'd never been introduced. Melitta crossed the carpet to her and offered her hand to clasp. 'Saida, I'm Melitta,' she said with deliberate informality.

'Yes,' Saida said. 'I know.' She took the hand clasp as lightly as possible, as though Melitta's touch held some disease.

Melitta refused to act like a boy. 'You are the daughter of Kontarus?' she asked.

'No relation at all,' the woman replied with cold finality. 'Not really your business.'

Melitta wanted to roll her eyes. Rudeness like this was not acceptable. It had political overtones. 'My dear,' she said, switching to a Greek approach, 'if you are not a relation of the lord of the Silent Wolves, then you can't expect us to play twenty questions until we discover how he came to name you his heir. And it is, in fact, my business, as I am your lady – the lady of your clan and all the clans.'

Saida didn't quite meet her eyes. 'As you say,' she pronounced. 'My relations are my business. I'm his heir. No one need know any more than that – *lady*.'

Melitta shrugged and marked the woman for a later conversation. This sort of thing she knew how to handle. Uppity girls – no problem.

'Lords of the horses, we have a problem,' Melitta began. As quickly as possible, she outlined the story as told by the woman Astis, and then she sent for the woman to tell her own story.

When she had told her story and gone again, leaning on the strong arm of Temerix the smith, Melitta looked around.

'I would value your thoughts,' she said, and was greeted by silence.

Oh, how I miss Ataelus and Urvara, she thought. The two older leaders had supported her – and taught her a great deal. Even Geraint – the former lord of the Standing Horses, dead at Tanais River like his former rivals – had taught her, sometimes merely by the way he opposed her. Her new horse lords were as young as she was and, in some ways, even less trained.

It was the Hungry Crow, Tuarn, who broke the silence. 'We can't fail to act,' he said. When no one commented, he shrugged. 'This is how the fighting with the Sauromatae started, back when Marthax was king. The rest of you are probably too young to remember, and the lady wasn't among us. The Sauromatae were once strong allies, eh? But Upazan came to be their lord, and his young men pounded away at our eastern valleys. And we did too little.'

'That is not the way my people tell the tale,' Thyrsis said. 'Among Ataelus' people, we say that we fought, and no one came to our aid.'

Tuarn refused to be offended. 'Young man, is that any different from what I just said? I did not mean that some of the Assagetae didn't fight. I mean we didn't act together. And later, we paid.'

'Of course, some of us paid more dearly than others,' Listra said. She was standing with Parshevaelt and Sindispharnax – all three veterans of campaigns with Melitta. The positions in which they were standing – closer to Scopasis, her bodyguard – said a great deal.

'And some of you *profited* a great deal more than some of us,' old Kontarus added.

'Those who fought were rewarded.' Melitta was tired of this

foolishness. 'Those who did not fight were not so rewarded. That is the way of the people.'

Saida shrugged. 'Perhaps it is time we found our own way,' she said.

'That is a discussion for another time,' Melitta said. She schooled her face carefully. 'Or not. If you decided to ride the Sea of Grass, none of us could stop you, or would. It is the right of any of the people – to ride away. In the meantime, let us keep to the issue at hand.'

Scopasis nodded. 'I agree with the lord of the Hungry Crows,' he said.

Melitta glared at him. He was a former outlaw and the captain of her knights, not one of her lords. But among Sakje, a warrior included in a council always felt he had the right to speak, and she was in danger of thinking like a Greek.

Thyrsis laughed. 'At last we find something on which to agree, outlaw!' he said.

'Arrows on the wind,' agreed Scopasis. The Sakje had a saying: if you shot a hundred arrows into the wind, at least two would fly together.

Listra looked around. 'We have had too much war,' she said.

Every one of the clan leaders nodded at that. The population of the Sakje – even with the addition of new people from the east – was down. In three generations they had fought four great campaigns, and the results were obvious in every camp.

'We don't even know who these people are,' Melitta said. 'I have a mind to go myself. To see them.'

That shocked them, but Melitta saw something on Saida's face that she didn't like. She glanced at the red-haired woman, but her face had closed again, and Melitta went on:

'My thought is to ask every clan for fifty warriors – your best, with five horses each. Together, we would ride east, as quickly as the wind blows in the grass, and find these Parni. To talk – or to kill.'

'No.' Saida shook her head. 'No. The Silent Wolves will send no warriors.'

'No,' Thyrsis said, mocking her voice. 'The Silent Wolves are a clan of children, and have no warriors to send. We never do—'

'Thyrsis!' Melitta said, though in truth she appreciated his comment.

Saida stared at the other horse lords. 'Pah. War and more war – that's all this one wants. We will be out on the grass.' She turned to leave, but Scopasis had caught Melitta's glance and he blocked the entrance of the tent.

'You have not been dismissed,' Melitta said. 'Saida, you seem to crave my ill will. Listen, then. We have not yet chosen a path. Every leader – aye, and every tanist – can speak her mind in council. But if we choose to send riders, and you refuse – then you may indeed go to the Sea of Grass. And don't come back. Please understand: that will mean you will have no share of the grain and gold that the Dirt People earn for us, and you will hold no land from the Assagetae. You can go north, or east, and fight for grazing as our people did in the old times. Is that plain?'

Saida looked at Kontarus, and he shook his head. 'As if you would – or could – push us off our lands.'

Melitta was suddenly tired; tired of their childishness. This was an old and insular man who was speaking from ignorance because he had *not* ridden to the fight at Tanais River: he had no idea of how much power she and her brother had.

Scopasis spoke from behind him. 'The lady has the power of all the clans, and her brother has fifty ships and five thousand soldiers. And you two represent one small clan that behaves as if you were all the people.'

'You may go,' Melitta said. 'I mean what I have said. If you refuse to serve – begone. If you try to choose a middle path, I will eliminate you. And frankly,' she said, her temper getting the better of her, 'I'm tempted to be rid of the pair of you now, as your actions suggest that neither of you is fit to lead one of my clans.'

Scopasis drew his akinake. 'Say the word, lady,' he said.

Kontarus glared around. 'Kill an old man and a woman – murder in council! Bah. Empty threats. We are the greatest of the Assagetae clans – why will you not treat us with the respect we deserve? We have more wagons, more lodges, more horses—'

'—and no warriors,' Listra said. 'The lady is right. Go – or stay. Your own warriors mutter against you because you shirked the fight at Tanais. Try to face us, and see what you get.'

Saida looked around again, still blank-faced. 'Very well,' she said. She looked up at Scopasis. 'Out of my way,' she ordered.

Scopasis looked at Melitta. 'I have said they may go,' Melitta agreed with a nod. When they were gone, she turned to the rest of her lords.

'Those two have to go,' she said. 'I hadn't realised how bad they were.'

'It is just ignorance,' Tuarn pleaded. 'I, too was late for the Tanais battle. But I saw the forces on that field. Kontarus has no idea – he lives in the days of your grandfather's father, lady. The Silent Wolves have not ridden to battle in many years. Not under their lords.'

Melitta shrugged. 'Let us deal with these issues one at a time. Are we all agreed in sending a force east?'

All of the clan leaders agreed, although none of them was happy about it.

'Can the Standing Horses send me twenty-five warriors?' she asked Sindispharnax.

He took a deep breath. 'Yes,' he said. 'I can send fifty.'

She smiled at him. 'I do not want fifty. I'll ask you to provide me with twenty-five young scouts. I'll ask Thyrsis to provide the same – people who know the country. The rest of you I ask to provide fifty knights and a leader who can speak for your people, if I find that I need to negotiate.'

Thyrsis grinned. 'May we come ourselves?' he asked.

She nodded. 'I hope that some of you will, and that others will stay. I will name a tanist of my own, to watch the people while I ride east.' She forced a smile. 'This will come between me and my son,' she said. 'But Tuarn speaks correctly. The last time we were threatened, we were slow to react.'

They were not Greeks, who argued everything endlessly and then voted in slow-moving assemblies. The next day, she told the whole of the people who were assembled about the Parni, and that there would be an expedition to the east.

They roared their approval. Three days later, Melitta discovered that Kontarus had ordered his people to pack and leave the Tanja, and he departed – but fewer than four hundred of them accompanied him.

This was the way that politics happened on the plains. People didn't meet in assemblies to vote – usually. Most of the time, they 'voted' by moving their tents and wagons to another clan. Suddenly, the Standing Horse clan was larger than it had been in five years. The

Cruel Hands had to turn new adherents away – they had no more grazing land to share.

'I didn't like the look of Saida,' Melitta commented to her captain of the guard. They were both mounted, having ridden out to review the warriors that each clan were contributing to the force for the east.

'She means to trouble you,' he agreed. 'Shall I follow her and kill her?' he asked.

'No,' Melitta said, but only after a pause. 'No, Scopasis. I don't want to rule in that way.'

Scopasis hadn't been in her bed for five nights. He turned and looked at her for a long time. 'You are angry at me because I am who I am,' he said. 'What I have to say will not make you love me better.'

'You might be surprised,' she said.

'You cannot be the Lady of the Assagetae and let this woman defy you,' he said.

She shook her head. 'I can. And I will. Do not – I repeat, do not – take action against her.'

Scopasis turned his head to watch the sun setting on the plains. The grass rolled away in waves like the sea, a carpet of fresh green that went north as far as the eye could see, and west into the setting sun, which turned the seed heads of the new grass a ruddy gold. He watched the sunset for a while.

'Would you like me to ride away?' he asked, after a while. 'I would be gone, and never trouble you again.'

Yes and *no* both crossed in her head. 'You must do what is best for you,' she said carefully, hating the foolish sound of the words, and the pomposity with which she said them. In a moment, she saw what Xeno's death had spared her. 'Can you be my guard captain without being my lover?' she asked – and was proud that she'd said it.

Scopasis groaned. When she turned to look at him, he was weeping.

'Are you a child?' she asked, suddenly angry. 'Grow up!'

So much for mature reflection. She was glad she was riding to war in the east. She felt as if killing someone might make her feel better. She wished that Scopasis was less of a foolish man, so that she could have his long, hard body next to hers and not be lonely at night. The truth was that picking a lover was a hard task for the Lady of the Assagetae –and it would be easier to keep the one she had.

She feared he would do something stupid and dramatic.

'I want a gallop,' she announced to the air, and turned her horse's head and started away across the grass.

She saw him look at her, as if tempted to follow.

But he didn't.

Two days later, she cut her time at the spring Tanja short, gathered her warriors and headed east. She had more than three hundred riders – she even had twenty-five of Temerix's people on ponies, big bows on their shoulders and jars of grain in their wagons. They had fifty wagons. The grass was green and fresh, and the game was plentiful as soon as they rode clear of the circle of the Tanja where everyone had hunted everything.

Listra came along with her young cousin, Philokles of Olbia, and a dozen of his friends – Olbian gentlemen, members of the new aristocracy, part Sakje and part Greek that was the legacy of constant intermarriage. They had been at the Tanja and now they rode east, as if it was the most natural thing in the world. She was glad to have them – they were well-armoured, capable men who, despite their youth, had already made a campaign or two.

Tuarn of the Hungry Crows came in person as well, riding a black stallion of magnificent size.

She admired the horse and called out to praise him, and he rode out of his part of the column. 'When you are lord of the Hungry Crows,' he joked, 'you had best ride a good black horse.'

'Why have we not been friends before?' she asked him.

He made a face. 'You always speak your mind like this, lady? I thought that childhood among the Greeks would have made you ... subtle.'

'Much the opposite,' she said. Her eyes happened to stray across her guard – and there was Scopasis, in his place, wearing his armour – and she found that her heart gave a little leap.

'I was Marthax's man,' he said. 'Sometimes I represented him to Eumeles. I didn't expect you to forgive me.'

She digested this.

'You didn't know,' he said.

'No,' she allowed.

'Shall I ride away?' he asked.

She shook her head. 'No. No, let's share this little war, and be friends.'

He nodded. 'This bluntness has its benefits, I see.'

And, of course, she had Thyrsis. He chose his warriors carefully, and offered to bring three times as many, but she shook her head. 'Bring what I ask,' she said. 'I need to know that there are many warriors here, if we're all killed. So that my son will come to avenge us, in time.' She thought of young Kineas, left behind again. She'd left him back in Tanais with her brother – in the care of Temerix's exotic wife, who had been her nurse once, and a circle of Sauromatae matrons. Her brother, who openly accused her of being a poor mother.

I should not have left Satyrus without making peace, she thought. *I should not be riding away from my son.*

She rode easily, breathing deeply of the new grass and the smells of spring – the flowers on every stream bank, the smells of the horses, the woodsmoke at their first campfire. It was hard to concentrate on her winter life as a semi-Greek woman when she was here, doing what she loved, riding the plains.

It was glorious to be young, and to be Queen, leading an army to the east. Or rather, it should have been glorious, but even while she drank from the spring, she wondered if she had made the right decision. On the word of one mistreated farm girl she was leading the flower of her people east on a war of vengeance. Was she being decisive, or merely reacting from boredom?

Scopasis rode up behind her. 'Is the camp satisfactory?' he asked.

She nodded. 'Beautiful,' she said.

That made him smile.

'Scopasis, am I doing the right thing?' she asked, suddenly.

He sat behind her and his gelding snorted, sniffing her mare with a sort of vague interest. Her mare sidled away.

'You ask me these things,' he said, when they had both reined in their mounts. 'But the truth is, I'm no king. I can't answer. And I only sound like a fool when I try. You must ask Thyrsis or Listra. They are lords. I was an outlaw, and now I command your guard. I can make a good rabbit stew, and I will match any other man arrow for arrow, but in truth,' and he managed a smile, 'in truth, I'm not able to advise you.'

'You lay out a good camp, too,' she said.

'I have much experience,' he allowed.

'You could learn to be a clan leader,' she said. 'As good as Sindispharnax, or better.'

He shrugged. 'Perhaps. Yes – if I rode hard this campaign, and started speaking to the young men and the old outlaws of my youth who still live in the high ground.' He shrugged. 'I could be that man, I suppose. But—' He looked around, struggling for words. 'But that man might not be me. I don't know.' He looked at her. 'If I became a clan leader, would I then be worthy of you?'

She shook her head. 'No – or no more than you already are. I'm sorry, Scopasis. Have I treated you badly? I think I have.'

He grunted. 'I find it hard to know what you want.'

She nodded. 'Dinner,' she said. And rode away, before she threw her arms around him and started all over again.

4

Ten days until he sailed, and Satyrus was meeting with the farmers of his southern shore about taxes.

They were a special case in a kingdom burdened with more special cases than uniform taxes and laws. All of the other citizens of the Kingdom of the Bosporus (as it said on the coins, of which he was very proud) were really citizens of Greek city states whose loose alliance he headed – Pantecapaeum, Olbia, Tanais – while to the far west, near the border with Lysimachos' Kingdom of Thrace, and to the far east, near the wild lands of Hyrkania, his 'kingdom' possessed 'citizens' who had no intermediary. They had no city to which to report or to pay taxes, no easy place for refuge or law courts.

The westerners were a special case within a special case, as most of them were controlled – ruled – by Sakje overlords who owed their allegiance to his sister, Melitta. And the fact that the King of the Bosporus and the Queen of the Sea of Grass were brother and sister – twins, in fact – was convenient, but it did not represent a union of the crowns in any way, except in special cases.

But in the east, his Maeotae and Sindi farmers along the Hypanis River had no horse-nomad overlords, no archons, no tyrants. And they were wealthy men – or wealthy enough, with good stone houses, barns heavy with grain, slaves, horses and cattle – men of property who deserved his consideration. More than his consideration.

He looked at Gardan, who had fought for his father at the Ford of the River God and had raised a *tagma* of archers for the campaign that ended at the Battle of the Tanais River. Gardan was, in his quiet way, an important man in his kingdom. A man who had saved him, and his sister, when they were penniless, hunted exiles.

'A fortification on the Hypanis River would appear to Sinope to be a provocation,' Satyrus said to the group. They were not well dressed, by Greek standards – large, dark men with furry wool cloaks and homespun chitons. Many of them wore trousers, like the Sakje. 'And your farms are under no threat.'

'Three summers ago, Sauromatae raiders burned my house,' Gardan said. 'Lord, you can't tell us it couldn't happen again.'

'The western Sauromatae are settling our lands,' Satyrus said. 'In a generation they will be neighbours.'

'Raiders attacked out east. I heard it from a trader when the river opened.' Scarlad Longshanks was another veteran of their campaigns. He shook his head. 'Lord, we don't have a city. Give us a fort.'

'Does this fortification need soldiers?' Satyrus asked.

'Wouldn't be much use without them,' Gardan said. 'Lord – we pay taxes, and we fought for you.'

Satyrus heard them out, because one of the tricks of ruling that he'd already learned was that listening cost him nothing and often went a long way to satisfying dissent. He listened, he talked of the new plough and showed it to them, and then he met with Coenus and Nikephorus, formerly an enemy and now the commander of his infantry.

Coenus just shook his head. 'It'd be the last straw for Heraklea and Sinope,' he said. 'They already think we're out to take them.'

Nikephorus shrugged. 'That's as may be. It'd be nice to have a couple of garrisons where we were welcome, and where the lads could have their own places. Billets on the populace make trouble in the end – always.'

Satyrus sat with his chin in his hand, picking at his beard. 'I hadn't expected to keep you all sitting around so long,' he admitted. In the aftermath of his victory at Tanais River, he'd had two thousand of his own mercenary foot, mostly Macedonian veterans, and he'd captured Nikephorus and his equally good Greek mercenary foot – another two thousand. He'd expected further campaigns – at least in the east – but the complete collapse of the Sauromatae Confederacy with the death of Upazan left him with no external enemies unless he chose to invade his neighbours. No external enemies, and five thousand veteran soldiers (12,500 drachma per day, plus officers and bonus payments, food and equipage). He used them as marines, and he loaned a thousand of them to Heraklea during a slave revolt, but day to day they were the second largest expense in the kingdom, after the fleet.

Coenus raised an eyebrow. 'But?'

Satyrus sat up straight and spread his hands. 'It seems foolish, but the whole world is at war and the cost of the fleet and the army seems to me to be an insurance. We're strong enough to discourage any attempt that any of the main players could make. With the city militias and the Assagetae, we could defeat anything they could roll at us.'

Coenus smiled, and his eyes narrowed. 'In fact, we have.'

Satyrus nodded. 'So I'm no better than the farmers. I want to keep the army and the fleet together *just in case*. And we can afford it. Stability is the key to the future. Good walls and a strong army.'

Nikephorus grinned. 'Glad you gentlemen intend to continue our employment. That being the case, how about farms for the veterans? You have the land – the top of the eastern valleys has some good land, or so I'm assured, and much of it is still empty.'

Satyrus looked at Coenus. Coenus shook his head. 'The Macedonian farm boys will make farmers, but will the Tyrian guttersnipes? They won't know how to hold a plough.'

Nikephorus shook his head. 'Then they can buy a factor or a couple of slaves to work the ground.'

'I didn't like that report of a raid in the Tanais high ground,' Coenus said.

Satyrus took a sip of wine. 'Nor I.'

Coenus nodded. 'If I take a patrol – Tamais Hippeis and some of your men on ponies – we could take a look at the ground for settlement. I want to go back and see to the restoration of the Temple of Artemis, anyway – I've arranged for a priestess from Samos to come and train some of our girls, and I was rather hoping that you would fund it.'

Satyrus was not in the position to refuse his principal councillor and the architect of his kingship the cost of restoring a small temple on the Tanais River. 'Of course,' he said.

Coenus smiled. 'I think I'm as anxious to get out of town as you are.'

'You said you'd come to Pantecapaeaum with me,' Satyrus pointed out.

Coenus shook his head. 'Lord, you are on your own. Take Theron. He likes cities.'

*

Nike of Salamis swept into Tanais' harbour, her oars perfectly controlled, her helmsman kissing the long pier by the mole with the practised
efficiency of the Middle Sea's fastest courier ship. Her navarch, Sarpax
of Alexandria, was across the prow before the oarsmen had moved
off their cushions. He moved quickly across the wharf, and Satyrus
watched him with some alarm from his own window in the citadel.

'That's Sarpax,' Satyrus said to Theron. 'In a hurry,' he added.
Helios was pinning him into a new chiton – a huge piece of superfine
wool meant to be worn under armour.

Theron was munching his way through an apple. He stood in the
window for several minutes. 'Can't be good news,' he said. 'No one
hurries like that to tell you anything good.'

Helios stepped back. 'Done,' he said.

Satyrus shrugged his shoulders and motioned with his arms as if
he was making overarm cuts with a sword. 'Feels good. Wonderful
cloth.'

'Sarpax of Alexandria to see you, lord,' Nearchus said from the
doorway.

'Lord – your uncle Leon sends his regards, and would you please
get to sea immediately?' Sarpax accepted a cup of wine, but his face
was red with exertion and he carried with him an aura of urgency.
'Demostrate has been dead almost three weeks. The word at Rhodes
is that he was murdered by Dekas – Manes' former catamite, as you'll
remember.'

Theron rubbed his beard. 'Will Dekas take command of the
pirates?'

'The word is that he has already done so, and that he's taking them
over to Antigonus – as a fleet.' Sarpax took a deep breath. 'I'm to get
you to arm and put to sea, and to accompany you south. Leon will
have his squadron at Rhodes.'

Satyrus knew that the defection of the Euxine pirates would have a
profound effect on the naval balance of power. They had been allies
– unreliable, morally dangerous allies. Now they would be enemies,
and they would prey on his shipping.

'I guess this is why we keep a fleet,' Satyrus said. 'What did you see
as you came through the straits?'

Sarpax drank off his wine. 'Twenty sail at Timaea. Byzantium
was empty. At Rhodes, they say Dekas has defeated a force sent by

Lysimachos, and the King of Thrace has already lost part of his spring grain fleet. The Tyrant of Heraklea is holding all his ships in port.'

'Stratokles knew what was coming, then,' Satyrus said. 'Tell Leon that I was going to sea in five days as it was. With a little effort, I can sail tomorrow. Theron, you will have to go and be my vicar in Pantecapaeaum.'

Theron made a face. 'While you play navarch? The unfairness of the world.'

'You don't like the sea,' Satyrus said. 'Twenty hulls in Timaea? That's a third of Demostrate's fleet.' He turned to Helios. 'Run down to the docks and get Diokles to sound All Captains. Tell them I intend to go to sea tomorrow morning. Tell them why.'

Sarpax handed a servant his wine cup. 'I'll be gone, then.'

Satyrus allowed his surprise to show. 'Stay the night – rest your rowers.'

'Leon thinks that Antigonus is going to have a go for either Rhodes or Aegypt,' Sarpax reported. 'Every day counts. Rhodes is recalling their cruisers. Ptolemy has half his army on Cyprus.'

Satyrus narrowed his eyes. 'That makes him vulnerable. Where is the fleet? The Aegyptian fleet?

'Alexandria, or it was three weeks ago. It's probably off Cyprus by now.' Sarpax paused in the doorway. 'Demetrios is on Cyprus, fighting Ptolemy.'

Satyrus exchanged a look with Theron. 'Tell Leon that we'll be at Rhodes in ten days.'

Neiron had the helm, and Tanais was a smudge on the northern horizon.

The whole of Satyrus' fleet formed a long, trailing arrowhead that covered forty merchants, ranging in size from the enormous high-sided, Athenian-built grain ships, each capable of hauling several hundred tons of wheat, to the smaller ships – local merchantmen, oversized fishing smacks and former warships, as well as a dozen small vessels under sail. Altogether they represented sixteen thousand tons of grain, or a little more than a third of his kingdom's entire autumn harvest.

'What if fucking Ganymede commits his whole fleet to taking us on? Sixty ships?' Neiron asked.

Satyrus shrugged. He couldn't help it – a grin covered his face from ear to ear. 'So what?' he asked.

Neiron shrugged. 'I'm just saying. We could have sent to Athens for ships – we could still stop at Heraklea.'

Satyrus nodded. 'I expect that the straightforward approach would be to stop at Sinope and Heraklea, gather their warships and their merchants and take this great armada of grain slowly through the horn and across the Ionian to Rhodes.'

Neiron sounded resigned. 'But we're not going to do that,' he said.

'No,' Satyrus laughed. 'No, we're not.' The grin that split his face made him look years younger. He *felt* years younger. He was going to risk his grain fleet and perhaps his life, but that was fine. He was at sea. And the sea was clean, neat, wild and much, much simpler than the land.

5

Fifteen days' travel over the steppes, and her war party emerged from the Sea of Grass into the high ground north of Tanais, with its stands of trees, high hills and beautiful, fertile valleys. It was more her brother's ground than hers, but they had yet to quarrel about such things. They ruled together, two lords of the different peoples who occupied the same land.

Thyrsis rode up, his golden bow case throwing brilliant ripples of reflected light in the early-morning sunlight. 'Riders,' he said. 'Scouts say more than fifty men with a hundred horses, moving slowly on the river road.'

Melitta was troubled. 'They shouldn't be my brother's men,' she said. 'I've only been gone three weeks, and there was no—' she trailed off. 'Look them over and make contact,' she said, pointing downriver with her riding whip.

Scopasis pressed his horse closer to hers. 'Now what?' he asked.

She shrugged. 'If I've heard about raids in the east, Satyrus probably has as well. Let's ride.'

She was delighted to find Coenus, although less enthusiastic to find Nikephorus, a man whose talent she admired and of whose motivations she remained suspicious. But the two of them were riding together. They had a strong troop of farmers' sons on ponies and two dozen of Nikephorus' men, armed as cavalry and mounted on steppe horses.

'Well met, Coenus son of Xenophon!' she called, as she got her best charger up the far bank of the Tanais. It was still chilly enough that swimming the river, even this far north, was a damp and uncomfortable business.

Coenus came forward to embrace her. His men had already set their camp, and had fires started, and he led her to one of them while

Scopasis dealt with settling the rest of her little army. But the Sakje knew every pasture and every natural meadow in the Tanais high ground – Melitta had fought a war here, and Coenus had lived here for ten years.

'You look happy,' he said.

'How's my son?' she asked. 'Your grandson,' she put in.

'Happy and healthy when I saw him, less than a week ago,' he replied. 'The image of his mother – and his father.' Coenus didn't flinch to say it, although the boy's father was his son Xeno, dead at Gaza. Her first lover. She flinched more at the memory than Coenus did. He looked at her. 'Shouldn't you be dispensing law to the clans, away west?'

She shrugged. 'It was a slow winter for crime, Coenus,' she said. 'I have reports of raiding in the east. I felt that I should look into them. And I have some restless clan leaders, and I thought I should take them for a ride.'

'That's my girl,' Coenus allowed. He scooped up a horn cup full of warm wine and passed it to her, and she inhaled the fragrance deeply before drinking it off. 'We're looking at land for settling our veterans,' he said. 'But I've five reports of these raiders – all from last autumn.'

'I have a survivor in my train,' Melitta said. 'Taken two autumns ago. So the first raids were a year after the battle.'

Coenus nodded. 'I think I – that is, we,' he looked at Nikephorus, 'would like to interview her.'

'What do your reports say?' Melitta asked.

'Not Sauromatae and not Assagetae,' Coenus said.

'My victim says they are a people called *Parni*.' Melitta shrugged. 'It's a Sakje-sounding name, but I've never heard it.'

Coenus made a face. 'Sounds damned familiar,' he said. 'Why do I know that name?' He shook his head. 'No matter – that's quite a little army you have there. You planning on a raid?'

Melitta was happy to have Coenus around. He was level-headed and good at giving her advice. When she was a girl, she'd called him 'uncle'. Now, as he was the father of the father of her child, he had status among the Assagetae as a sort of stepfather for her.

'Perhaps,' she said. 'I'm going east, to Hyrkania. That's where my survivor says the Parni wintered. I may find them and talk. I may raid their wagons. It depends on what they have to say for themselves' She looked pensive. 'Most of my clan leaders felt that we needed to be strong and act decisively to prevent ... another Upazan.'

Coenus nodded and drank some of the warm wine. The last of the Sakje wagons had crossed the river down at the ford, and they were being drawn up in a loose circle, the horses picketed, the sentries set.

Coenus had trained Scopasis, and he watched the former outlaw with something like parental pride. 'Still sleeping with him?' Coenus asked. There was some judgement in his tone, and it made her angry, even as she realised that he was probably judging her just as she judged herself.

'No,' she said.

He nodded. 'Sorry, honeybee. You're not fifteen any more.' He stretched. 'And I'm not forty any more. Zeus Sator, do you know Antigonus is nearly *eighty*? I don't want to be riding and killing when I'm eighty. I'm feeling tired and old *now*.'

She shook her head. 'You're not old!' she said.

Coenus grinned. 'The blessing of Artemis upon you, lass.'

'Will you come east with me, Coenus?' she asked.

'I was afraid you'd ask that,' Coenus said. He motioned to Nikephorus, who was lying with his head propped on an aspis, looking up at the sky, allowing them their privacy with the ease of a man who'd spent his entire adult life in the field.

The mercenary officer rose, pulled his chlamys tight around himself and came over. 'Lady,' he said with a nod to Melitta. She'd bested him in a skirmish, and she wasn't sure he'd forgiven her for it. But Coenus obviously liked him. She was prepared to deal with him to make Coenus happy.

'Lady is going east, looking for our raiders,' Coenus said. 'She has reason to believe they're from east of the Hyrkanian Sea. I'd like to go with her. How do you feel about it?'

Nikephorus looked at her, and then glanced up the hill at the wagon fort. 'With our boys?' he asked.

Melitta nodded.

'Lady, will you let my men settle these valleys?' Nikephorus asked.

Melitta shook her head. 'I'm not going to hand you blanket control of the Tanais high ground,' she said. 'On the one hand, it's all under the hooves of Thyrsis, Lord of Ataelus' people. On the other hand, it is very much part of my brother's kingdom.' She raised her hand. 'But

I could see us negotiating one parcel of land at a time, as required. This, right here—'

Coenus shook his head. 'They'd like the ground north and west of the Temple of Artemis.'

That was fifty stades downstream. 'That's good land,' she said. 'What does Gardan say?'

'Haven't asked him yet, or Satyrus, either,' Nikephorus said. 'I understand that it's complicated. Some of those farms were recently burned. There may be survivors. But it's good land, and my men could help hold it. For everyone.'

'We're talking about a fort above the temple,' Coenus said.

'We should include Thyrsis in this,' Melitta said. 'But it doesn't sound too outlandish to me.'

Nikephorus flashed her a smile. 'Thanks, lady,' he said. To Coenus, he raised an eyebrow. 'So?'

'I hate leaving Theron with everything.' Coenus looked at Melitta. 'A lot of things went to shit after you left. Demostrate's dead.'

Melitta understood immediately. 'The grain fleet!' she said.

Coenus nodded. 'Your brother has gone to sea with the fleet. He's going to try something fairly risky. I don't think any of us imagined that both of you would be at risk this summer.'

Melitta nodded. 'I understand – but I have to do this. How big is the threat to the grain fleet?' All she could think of was that the grain income – the gold generated by what was, in effect, her direct tax on merchants buying the grain of her Dirt People – was ultimately what gave her power over the clans. There was sentiment and loyalty, but the money mattered. Loss of that income would limit her ability to deal with the likes of Kontarus and Saida.

It was all so complicated.

It was all as simple as breathing, if only people would behave like horses.

She laughed aloud, and realised that Scopasis was sharing wine with Coenus, like friends. On the other hand, Nikephorus was watching her as if she were a dangerous animal. 'I don't bite,' she said.

Nikephorus raised both hands in mock surrender. 'I think you just say that,' he replied.

Coenus laughed at something Scopasis had said, and slapped the younger man on the back. 'Well, we should have plenty of time to work it out,' he said.

Melitta smiled. 'So you'll come?'

Coenus nodded. 'One more campaign,' he said. 'Who knows – perhaps just a good ride over the spring grass and a nice negotiation at the end.'

Melitta nodded. 'I'd rather it was like that.'

Nikephorus pulled his cloak tighter. 'We'll need wagons and grain and some more ponies,' he said. 'You folks will move fast, no doubt.'

'Two to three hundred stades a day,' Coenus said, his eyes on the high ground rising away to the west. 'I haven't been this way in ... twenty-five years. Niceas died out here. Kineas, too, for that matter.' Coenus pointed west. 'Thousands of stades west. But it wakes memories. Last time I lay in this camp, it was with Niceas – he'd been wounded – and some Sauromatae girls.' Coenus shook his head. 'And I swore I'd build a temple to Artemis if Niceas lived.' He smiled into the distance. 'I lived here when my wife was still alive. Xeno was born here.'

They were all silent. Out in the darkness, a thousand horses cropped the new grass, farted and whickered to each other. Closer in, one of the mercenaries played an aulos flute, and a couple of other soldiers danced and a dozen Sakje watched them, smiling.

Melitta felt tears come to her eyes, as they often did when her father was mentioned.

'Who was Niceas?' Scopasis asked.

Coenus spread his cloak on the ground and patted it for the Queen of the Assagetae to join him. 'Settle down,' he said, 'and I'll tell you a story. You all know that the Queen's father was Kineas? He was a Greek mercenary ...'

6

Heraklea. One of the strongest cities on the Euxine Sea, with high walls and a servile populace of peasants conquered by Greeks and made into serfs, like the Spartan helots. Dionysus of Heraklea was tyrant.

Satyrus' grain fleet anchored without asking permission – twenty warships and more than forty grain ships that rose and fell on the late spring swell.

'And we're buggered if a storm comes up.' Diokles shook his head. 'Why not take the ships inside the mole?'

'First, because Dionysus will be worried enough already,' Satyrus said. 'Second, because everyone is a spy, and I don't want any of our sailors talking.'

The arrival of the grain fleet was hardly a surprise to Stratokles, who had advised both Amastris and her uncle to keep their own merchants and warships home until it came. 'Satyrus will come like the wind when he hears Demostrate is dead,' Stratokles had predicted, and here was the fleet, making him look like exactly what he was – a first-rate intelligencer. It had sat off the entrance to the harbour for a full day.

Their appearance outside the mole – and their inaction – had been cause enough for Stratokles to be summoned to the tyrant's presence. The enormously fat man lay, as he usually did, on a stout couch with heavy rawhide cording under the mattress to support his bulk. His niece, Amastris, sat on the edge of the *kline*, as if her beauty could somehow help the tyrant's ugliness. Stratokles had joked to his captain, Lucius, that he liked to work for the tyrant because the fat man made Stratokles seem handsome. Stratokles had never been graced with the looks that made men heroes – and a sword cut to his face a few years back had made it worse.

Satyrus' mother, that had been. Stratokles sighed. *What an error her murder had been.* Not his idea, of course.

'So.' Dionysus had a carefully trained voice, like an actor's. Not what you expected from such a fat carcass, but then, Dionysus of Heraklea was never what anyone expected. 'So, Stratokles of Athens. You predicted this. Now what happens?'

Stratokles smiled at his mistress. She was without doubt the most beautiful woman he'd ever known – or at least, known well. And her beauty seemed new – or at least, subtly different – every time he saw her. She had considerable intellect, and she used a good deal of it on her looks.

'My lord,' Stratokles said, 'Satyrus needs your fleet to support his own fleet. Together they will be strong enough to try to move our combined grain fleets across the Ionian to Athens.'

'Satyrus generally sells his grain at Rhodes,' Dionysus said.

'I understand, my lord.' *I am, after all, somewhat famed as a spy.* 'But this year, my lord can call the tune. Satyrus cannot sail without your ships and your marines. You do *not* want to sell your grain at Rhodes, I take it?'

Stratokles was playing a dangerous game. Of course it was his duty, as an Athenian, to get as much of the Euxine grain trans-shipped to Athens as was possible. A glut was fine. A glut would mean low prices and exports. But he couldn't force events. He could only manipulate them.

Dionysus shrugged, and his chins wobbled. 'You know perfectly well that we sell our grain to Athens,' he said. 'You argued for the policy, and you pushed me to support Antigonus. Now he has all the warships. Surely my grain fleet can proceed as it would?'

Stratokles shook his head. 'If only it were so simple,' he began.

'Don't patronise me, Athenian!' Dionysus shot back. 'Dekas can't really control the pirates, is what you mean. Or he may not *want* to control them. So we need young Achilles out there to help us punch through the straits.'

Stratokles nodded. 'My lord, that is *exactly* what I mean.'

Dionysus nodded, and the nod spread over the fat of his body like ripples spreading in a pool from a thrown rock. 'So – if that's the situation, where is young Satyrus?'

At this question, Amastris looked up. 'Exactly. Where is he?'

Dionysus pointed out over the mole. 'His ships have been there all night, but the boy has yet to come ashore. And Nestor says that some of the ships have slipped away.'

Stratokles felt a touch of ice in his spine. 'Slipped away?' he asked. He walked to the edge of the balcony and looked out over the bay.

His self-control was excellent, but it didn't prevent a single, sharp curse.

'Well?' Dionysus asked.

Stratokles didn't need to count the ships riding at anchor in the strong spring sun. He had been guilty of seeing what he expected to see. He shook his head. 'My lord, Satyrus has taken his warships and gone.'

'Gone *where*?' Amastris asked. The whine in her voice boded ill for her maids – and for her intelligencer.

Stratokles shook his head. 'He didn't ask for your fleet?' he asked the tyrant.

'Satyrus of Tanais hasn't even been ashore,' Nestor said from the door.

Nine hundred stades to the south and west, Satyrus' entire war fleet, minus just two triremes away at Olbia, rode under oars in the last light of the sun, their masts struck down on deck. Behind them were all six of the gargantuan Athenian-built grain ships.

'Well,' Diokles said, watching the sky, 'the weather's with us. Any last thoughts?'

Satyrus looked around the deck of *Arête* at all of his other captains – Neiron himself, Sandakes and Akes and Gelon of Sicily. 'Let's sacrifice,' Satyrus said. He went into the stern – still feeling as if he was walking across the agora, his flagship was so big – to where the altar of Poseidon was set into the rise of the stern boards that covered the head and back of the helmsman. Satyrus took the lead of a young kid, a black one, and looked into its eyes. The animal had perfect horns and bright eyes, and it looked at him—

He drew and slashed its throat in one trained movement, then stepped slightly to the side to let the blood flow past him, and the priest of Poseidon, Leosthenes, caught the blood in a bowl. Then the priest used his own knife to open the animal.

He looked at the entrails carefully, rubbing the liver back and forth between his hands. He put his nose down and smelled it – not something that Satyrus had seen before from a priest. Then he nodded.

'Victory,' he said. 'Complete, entire and yours, lord.'

Satyrus was not used to hearing such emphatic pronouncements. 'May you be correct,' Satyrus said.

The priest cut the liver free from the animal and raised it, still dripping blood. He turned to the sailors, oarsmen and marines who waited a respectful distance down the deck. On an older ship, they couldn't have approached even this close as there'd have been no deck to stand on, only a gangway over the rowers' benches.

'Victory!' the priest shouted.

The men roared, and on twenty other ships, they took up the cry.

Night, and full darkness. Satyrus' *Arête* led the way, with the tide running hard out of the Euxine and the current moving them briskly south and west towards Byzantium, which was stades away on the far bank.

Satyrus and Diokles had fought an entire season in these waters. They knew the tides, which were shallow, and the Dardanelles, which were as treacherous as the pirates who infested them.

'Regrets?' Neiron asked Satyrus.

'Pah,' Satyrus answered. He wasn't sure what he thought of the new priest and his confident assertion of victory. It seemed like hubris.

An hour later, and the lookouts told him that Timaea was in sight. He climbed the foremast and peered into the gloom and saw lights, but they might have been any of the fishing villages, Thracian and Greek, or pirate havens that flourished along this coast.

Was it really possible that Dekas had left twenty ships in Timaea and that they wouldn't even keep a watch? Or was it a trap? It would have to have been a very elaborate trap, counting on his headstrong ways.

Satyrus began to drum on the weather rail as he contemplated all the ways his risk – his rather colossal risk – might fail.

'They'll hear you in Timaea,' Neiron called. 'Relax, lord.'

Another hour, and they were under oars, ghosting along a stade from the muddy banks of the strait, and it was obvious to every man aboard that the harbour of Timaea was crowded with ships. More than twenty ships, and at least fifteen more pulled up on the beach. There were merchant ships anchored out at the wharves, and beached so that they tipped to lie on their high, round sides.

Satyrus blew on his cold hands and leaned over the fighting platform that sat above the huge ram of his *Arête*.

'I count forty-four warships,' said the lookout as quietly as he could manage.

Neiron made a sound with his tongue behind Satyrus, who gave a low whistle.

Satyrus was silent for fifty agonising heartbeats, during which he lived, and died, a dozen different ways. He made a decision, then another, and then another. Then he took a deep breath.

Satyrus caught the glint of Neiron's eye in the dark. 'Do it,' he said.

Neiron's eyes said that he agreed. He turned to Helios. 'Light the rest of the lanterns,' he said. 'On my command – battle speed.'

There was a growl from the oar deck. Satyrus rose from his position in the bow and stretched to counter the sudden pain in his legs – too long in one position, and insufficient exercise the last three days. A private smile came to his face. Plenty of exercise in the next hour, either way.

He went aft to the base of the mainmast and dropped through the deck to the cramped oar deck below. He had to stoop to move, and the cross braces that supported the main deck made him crouch to pass under them. Even on a cool spring evening, the top oar deck was stuffy and warm. In high summer, in action, it would be unbearable. And it was the coolest and draughtiest of the three oar decks. The top deck was just leaning into the stroke, and men grunted or swore or chatted – a fair amount of noise, but nothing that would keep them from hearing the oar master or the rattle of the oar pace.

'Evening, friends,' Satyrus said. He walked down the central catwalk that passed between the benches. A sixer like *Arête* had three decks of rowers, with two men on every one of one hundred and seventy oars. The oarsmen in the top deck had a boxlike outrigger to give them more leverage and stability for their stroke, and to make more room for the lower-deck oarsmen, the *zygites* and the bottom-deck *thalamites*. Only the upper oar deck had room for a catwalk.

The lower-deck rowers completed their pulls and their arms moved, hundreds of men rolling forward, sliding on their oiled leather cushions to get the most out of their muscles. These were highly trained oarsmen, just getting into top condition from a row down the Euxine. The top-deck oarsmen rested, their oars crossed in front of them so that Satyrus could barely see the end of the deck in the near darkness.

He was answered with a murmur – almost a growl.

'Dark out there,' Satyrus said, enunciating like a trained orator. *That's why they train you*, he thought. *So that your voice carries in the assembly – or the oar decks.* 'We're going after the pirate fleet in the dark,' he said, slowly and carefully. 'We'll be landing our marines to take the town. If we win, every man here will share in the loot. Understand?'

This time, the answering growl was loud, like that of an animal ready to leap. Some men said, 'Do the thing!' and others merely grunted, 'That's right.'

An older *thranite* at Satyrus' left hand barked a laugh. 'We heard the omen,' he said. 'Silver in our hands!'

Satyrus slapped him on the back and climbed the short ladder to the main deck. It was brighter towards the stern – a triangle of oil lamps had been lit – fifteen lamps, carefully primed and maintained half the night for this moment. In less than a hundred heartbeats, similar lamps were kindled on all the rest of the ships, so that Satyrus' small fleet seemed to glow.

'Battle pace,' Neiron said to the drummer who kept the oar beat. On a ship as big as the *Arête*, the oar master couldn't keep the stroke by voice alone. Before he finished speaking, the ship seemed to cough – a short, sharp scrape as sixty-two upper-deck oars were run out of their oar ports together.

The drum had been silent as they crept down the channel, but now, on all the ships, drums rolled.

The oars slid out and bent as the full crew pulled on them.

Even the *Arête*, easily the biggest ship in the squadron, leaped ahead.

Satyrus went forward and leaned out over the ram, watching the water flow by, feeling the speed and power of his ship. His eyes flicked over the big ballistae, unmanned and encased in painted canvas. Too dark for shooting; but he longed to use them.

Neiron was at the steering oars, and he took the big ship in first. The original intention had been to clear any opposition, but there wasn't a single enemy ship manned, and now the *Arête* swept forward, the deepest hull and the most likely to run aground. They steered for the beach, passing just inshore of the moored warships, tied in long rows with heavy canvas thrown loosely over their rowing benches.

'Pirates,' Satyrus said, with contempt. 'Bastards can't even be bothered to maintain the ships they use to prey on others.' But in his mind he saw men hiding under that loosely flung canvas.

Helios choked something in the dark. The young man had been taken by pirates as a boy. Left to himself, he'd have killed every pirate on the sea. He, at least, was entirely in favour of his master's choice of campaign.

A stade from the shore, and there was shouting in the town. Men were running onto the beach, calling out in fear.

'Rowed of all!' called the oar master from amidships. Satyrus wasn't commanding anything this night – or rather, he was commanding everything. He had his armour on, and a cloak, and once they were ashore he'd take command. But he was letting his beautiful ship have her first fight in the hands of other men, and he wanted to leap in and shout orders, ram an empty ship for the sheer joy of it—

'Brace!' Neiron called from the steering oars, and all the marines and deck crewmen caught hold of something.

The ram clipped one of the beached warships, bow to bow, except that *Arête*'s ram towered over the smaller ship the way an elephant towers over a horse, and the beached pirate ship had her bow crushed as if she were made of paper. Then the bigger ship ground to a halt, cushioned by the shattering of the smaller ship's frames and sewn planks.

Satyrus rose from his brace, put his helmet on his head and toggled the cheekpieces under his chin.

'Marines!' he called, and Draco roared behind him, and then they were pouring over the bow into the stricken vessel and racing down her central catwalk, using the pirate vessel as a bridge between the gargantuan *Arête* and the land.

Labours of Herakles, the penteres, did the same, coming to lie alongside a beached trireme and using her as a wharf, but the rest of his fleet beached themselves, except five triremes that stayed out in the dark, putting marines aboard the moored ships.

'The wharves!' Satyrus shouted as soon as his feet hit the beach.

'Take the wharves!' The marines had been told to offer no quarter, and they weren't being too choosy about who they killed. It was ugly work, but the first resistance was quickly crushed and the wharves had to be seized at all costs. They were central to Satyrus' plan.

The King of the Bosporus was himself in the front lines, for no better reason than that he needed the wharf area taken fast, and there was no one better suited to the task than he. Or that's what Satyrus told himself. He was one of the first men onto the wharves, and he could hear junior officers shouting to get the marines – most of whom were unused to working in groups larger than ten or fifteen men – to form a line across the cobbled square.

But the pirates were not slow to react. The alleys west of the wharves were suddenly full of men and javelins, darts and arrows coming out of the darkness. Helios was hit on the helmet by a heavy tile thrown from the roof of one of the nearest warehouses.

Then, before Satyrus and Draco and Apollodorus had the marines steady, the first counter-attack came. There were more than a hundred men, most with spears, some with axes, and they came at the marines like Thracians, yelling defiance.

The marines were veterans, and most of them carried the small Macedonian aspis and a long spear. All of them had good armour. Armour that, even in the dark, made them confident. They locked their shields, the second and third ranks pressed forward on the front, and the pirates met with a volley of javelins at point-blank range. Their charge never reached the aspis wall. With little armour and few shields, the javelins knocked a fifth of the attackers flat and the rest ran.

Satyrus led his own marines into the maze of alleys west of the wharves, following the broken men from the first counter-attack. Some men stopped to execute the wounded, and Satyrus did nothing to stop it.

A javelin flew from the dark, and the shaft hit his helmet with a heavy *clang* and he had to drop to one knee, the pain was so intense.

'On the roof!' called Apollodorus, behind him. 'Archers! On me!'

The rush into the alleys had slowed when they reached the narrowest passages and the long back walls of the second street of warehouses, shops and residences. The air here smelled of smoke and blood.

Helios pushed forward and held his aspis over Satyrus' head. 'Lord?'

'Give me a moment,' Satyrus grunted. He unfastened his

cheek-plates and raised his helmet over his head, pulled off his arming cap and felt the spot on his skull. Blood – his hair was full of it. Then he put it all back on again. 'Ouch,' he said.

Men around him laughed.

More javelins were coming off the roofs around them, and no archers were to be seen.

'We either have to back off and give them this street, or take it to them,' Satyrus said.

Apollodorus winced and Draco grunted.

Satyrus looked around. The alley, and the cross alley behind him, had about forty marines in it.

'Let's take it to them,' he said. 'Right onto the roofs. No quarter. Try not to kill captives and slaves, but if in doubt, put your man down.'

Draco's golden Thracian helmet shone in the firelight of the buildings already aflame to the south. 'Listen to the king!' he said. 'More men go down in a house-to-house fight than in a field battle. Stay with your file, and don't let up the pressure once you start.'

Satyrus looked around, down the alley and into the smoke. 'We used to have a warehouse at the end of this street,' Satyrus said. 'On the other hand is a big cross street. No advance beyond that.'

'Yes, sir.' Draco looked around. 'Everyone got that?'

Apollodorus laughed. 'I get it that the taxiarch and the navarch are about to lead a reckless charge in the dark,' he said. 'Perhaps the king should sit this one out, eh?'

Draco laughed. 'Good times, lord. My sword has touched nothing but wood in three summers.'

'By Ares and Herakles,' Satyrus said. 'I'm here.' He was afraid and exalted at the same time.

The marines pressed in around him, shields raised against a rain of missiles, huddled up together at the corners of two buildings and waiting for the next shower of javelins, which obligingly came down at them from just ahead.

'Go! Go! Go!' the officers shouted. As soon as the missiles rang against the roof of shields, the men were up and running, one file of six men for each of the first half-dozen houses and warehouses on the narrow alley. It wasn't well planned or neat, and men fell, or tangled in their armour, but they made quite a lot of noise.

Satyrus was in front, Draco running hard beside him, and their files were aiming farther up the street, well beyond where the javelins had come from.

A woman screamed and a large tile shattered next to Satyrus' foot. He almost fell from the pain, but he managed to keep his footing and he and Draco hit the gate of their chosen building together, and it burst inward. The yard was full of people. Satyrus narrowly avoided cutting a young woman in half. She saw him and screamed, and then the whole courtyard started screaming.

Slaver's yard, he thought.

'On the ground and you won't be killed!' he roared. He pushed through the crowd and they fell to the ground as if dead. Then he was at the steps to the main house, while Draco took his file into the warehouse. There were shouts. Screams. All the sounds of despair and death.

It occurred to Satyrus that his men were too thin on the ground already, the forward edge of the bloody bubble that might pop at any second. That's why he needed the wharves clear – and without them, his men were going to start dying.

There was a man in the stairwell with an axe. He took a cut at Satyrus, and Satyrus took the blow on his shield and felt it on the old break but shield and arm both held. Then Satyrus punched out with the rim of his shield, caught the axe head, pushed against it and stabbed under his shield until the man was down and dead.

An arrow hit his shield.

'Need some help, here!' he called.

There was no answer. Another arrow hit his shield, and this one punched through the bronze facing to gleam three fingers clear of the inner face of his aspis.

'Herakles, Son of Zeus,' he roared. Then he slammed his shield face into the wall next to him to break the arrows and ran at the stairs, holding his shield in front of him.

Another arrow hit the shield when he was halfway up the stairs, and then he reached the top.

There were three of them.

One shot him, point blank. The man was partly behind him, and the shot should have been deadly, but in his excitement the man hurried, or simply missed, and the arrow vanished into the night.

I have as long as it takes him to reload, Satyrus thought.

Satyrus leaped forward, slammed his shield into the larger man and sliced hard to the right with his sword at the same time, at the other opponent. His blade touched home – high, somewhere on the man's face or head – and then Satyrus was rolling to the left, keeping his shield pressed against his opponent.

The man cut under his shield and Satyrus couldn't do much about that, as his aspis was entangled and his sword elsewhere. His greaves took most of the blow, and his right shin suddenly exploded in agony and he stumbled back, placed his good foot and sank to one knee with his shield facing the archer.

'Let me shoot!' the man was screaming, but Satyrus' first attacker had blocked the other man who was also screaming, and the three of them were uncoordinated. Satyrus backed up a step, and the closest man came at him – blocking the archer.

Satyrus let him come, and then slammed his shield forward, his shoulder in the blow, stepped up close and cut at him overarm, and their swords rang together. The other man backed up a step and Satyrus cut at him again, another heavy overarm blow and the man flinched and parried, but his much lighter – and cheaper – sword had had enough, and the blade snapped and he lost fingers. He cried out and fell back, trying to get his shield up, back-pedalling across the roof and into the archer.

Satyrus didn't give them a moment to untangle, but cut at everything he could reach, blows too fast to count in the dark – and then he whirled, wondering where the third man had gone.

He was kneeling with his head in his hands. 'I'm *blind*!' he screamed with the raw intensity of a woman in childbirth. Satyrus' blade had cut through his ocular region and his nose. There was blood everywhere, shiny black on matt black in the fire-stabbed darkness.

Satyrus decapitated him.

The roof was still. Women were screaming in the courtyard, but the roof was clear, and against the fires back by the wharves, he could see the great grain ships landing.

They weren't full of grain.

They were full of two thousand Macedonian veterans, who poured out onto the newly secured wharves, formed up in a rough approximation of their usual formation and proceeded to storm the town.

They were ruthless, they were thorough, and the pirates had nothing with which to match them.

There was more fighting, but Satyrus was out of it – his ankle burned, he had a nasty cut down his leg and his damaged greave needed to be pulled clear of the wound.

He stumbled back off the roof, his right sandal squelching blood at every step. In the courtyard, the slaves lay prone amid so much blood that it appeared they might all have been butchered.

A thin trickle of blood flowed out of the courtyard and into the street's central gutter.

His Macedonians were pouring up the street, bellowing, scenting victory and a town to rape. Satyrus had to flatten himself against the wall to avoid be trampled – or worse – as a *taxeis* fought its way through the skein of alleys towards the town's agora and public buildings. Satyrus saw Draco emerge from the warehouse behind him. The Macedonian officer gave him a sketchy salute and plunged into the river of phalangites screaming orders, and vanished, leaving the King of the Bosporus to bleed in relative peace.

Satyrus swayed, caught himself on a warehouse wall and limped back down the cobbled street towards the wharves. He was losing blood, but he could see where men had fallen – a marine with his face a red ruin from a paving stone, another with a javelin in the back. At the corner where they'd started their charge, Helios was lying on his aspis. There was a deep dent in his helmet.

Satyrus bent and picked the boy up. Even in armour, he didn't weigh much. Helios coughed and spat and cursed. Several steps later he gave something like a choked scream.

Satyrus carried him down to the wharves where the *iatroi*, the healers, were gathering the wounded. They were a recent innovation – every ship had one – and Satyrus didn't really know any one of them from the others. He stumbled over a bale of cloth and fell with his hypaspist on top of him. They both cried out.

'My lord!' called a man, and suddenly he was surrounded by men with torches.

'You take the king, I'll get the man he carried,' said a voice, and then Satyrus was gone.

He came back to life stretched across a pair of upturned barrels. After a long – and painful – moment of disorientation, he realised that he was in the courtyard of what had once been Abraham Ben Zion's warehouse, having his shin bandaged tight in a whole length of superfine linen while around him, men screamed under the knife or murmured thanks to the men who tended them. The courtyard was bright with new sunlight and the air reeked of dirty smoke – burning buildings, charred meat.

Diokles found him about an hour later, when the pain had started to build in his leg and in his shoulder. He didn't even know why his shoulder hurt, and he'd had to decline the poppy juice that kept most of the other wounded men quiet.

Helios was lying on the cobblestones on top of his cloak, deeply unconscious and with a line of sewing up his sword arm and a bruise on his head so deep that the *iatros* feared that his skull was broken. Satyrus was looking at him and contemplating his bold, rash, brilliant attack in the light of the cost.

'I think we won,' Diokles said.

Satyrus was light-headed from blood loss and some related drunkenness. 'Oh yes. Very glorious. Any idea of losses?' He took a pull on the wineskin in his hand and shook his head. 'Losses beyond those I can see here?'

Draco stepped up out of the street and seized the wineskin. 'Lost a dozen in the first fights, before we had the numbers,' he said. He had blood dripping from under his helmet and his right arm was brown-red to the elbow. He took a long drink. 'I haven't taken a town in a long time. Makes the boys happy, it does.' He grinned. 'Once the rest of the boys were ashore, there wasn't much fighting.'

'Not that we took a lot of prisoners,' Diokles said.

Satyrus shrugged. Pirates were vermin. That some of them had once been his allies was – *Moira*. He fought with that thought to establish it in his head as what he *really* felt. *Because otherwise he would vomit, and be unfit to command men.* Or be a king.

He sat up, forced himself to look away from Helios and nodded. 'Light casualties and, I assume, some worthwhile loot.'

Draco nodded. 'A good start. We've been lax – and the boys have had three easy summers. This will get their blood up.'

Satyrus considered a number of replies – their blood was all over the courtyard – but finally shook his head. 'I want to be away before nightfall,' he said.

Diokles saluted with his fist and Draco grunted. 'Easier to pull a drunk out of a brothel than a soldier out of a taken city,' he said. 'Brothel costs money.'

Satyrus tried putting weight on his shin. That made it hurt more, which seemed to clear his head. 'Nightfall,' he said.

Satyrus sacrificed to Apollo at the setting of the sun, and before the calf was split for butchering and burning Draco declared the town secure. The captured ships – those worth saving – were towed. The rest were burned. The town, save only the wharves and warehouses, was burned. The survivors were either herded aboard ships to be sold as slaves, or, if too old or useless, were pushed into the *chora*, the farms around the city, to make their own way. Many would be taken by Thracians and sold as slaves anyway. Others would starve, or succumb to disease, or simply be killed as useless mouths.

Satyrus hardened his heart and reminded himself that these were *pirates*. Their fate was justice.

Of course, he knew perfectly well that most of them were the pirates' baggage – wives, whores, slaves, servants and the small craftsmen who were attracted to any community. They had chosen to come here to live. Most of them were innocent of any crime save poverty.

Four days of no news – of an ever more restless grain fleet anchored off Heraklea. And then the warships returned.

Stratokles watched Satyrus of Tanais sail up the coast. He had good eyes, and he could see at quite a distance that Satyrus' warships had either bred like rabbits or met with friends.

Or taken enemies. Stratokles shook his head. The boy was good. Stratokles hurried to his mistress.

'He's taken Timaea?' Dionysus asked. He was quite calm, for a man who had just heard that a potential rival now owned the closest sea base.

'That's my guess, lord,' Stratokles said. 'I'm sure he'll be here soon enough, ripe with his triumph, to explain.'

Amastris was not amused. 'He might have told us!' she said.

Dionysus watched the fleet now at anchor. 'He might,' Dionysus said slowly. 'But he did not, nor did he allow his sailors to land. He didn't trust us. This is the man you wish to marry, my dear?' he asked Amastris.

Amastris shrugged. 'Yes. Although I am not happy with this turn of events. It's your fault, Uncle! You've kept him dangling for so long – he will find another wife and come here—'

'Silence,' Dionysus said. He sat up on the *kline*, and it protested. 'Let me think. Dekas has lost his base and a third of his fleet. And probably his treasure.'

'Now he has no choice but to serve Antigonus,' Stratokles put in.

'And Satyrus of Tanais holds the entrance to the Dardanelles,' Dionysus said. 'He can control *our* grain.'

'We won't know until we hear what he has to say,' Amastris said. 'I will speak to him.'

'He may just come and take you,' Dionysus said. 'I hadn't considered the possibility that Demostrate was a better neighbour than Satyrus.' He laughed without mirth. 'And to think that I gave that boy his start.'

Stratokles nodded, because he hadn't considered the *weakness* of the pirate position at all, only its strength. *I'm getting old*, he thought.

'Satyrus, King of the Bosporus, and attendants,' intoned Nestor.

'You might have told me!' Amastris said as soon as they were alone. Alone meaning together with a dozen attendants, slaves and Nestor.

Satyrus was not wearing armour. He had imagined, in the winter, coming ashore to her wearing his splendid scale *thorax* and his magnificent silver helmet, itself a trophy. He'd imagined coming fresh from a sea fight.

The taking of Timaea wasn't something he cared to brag about, nor was he interested in wearing armour. He wore an old sky-blue chiton that had been washed so often it felt like an old friend on his shoulders. He wore Boeotian boots because he always wore them at sea. He did not look like a warrior king, and he could see the plainness of his appearance reflected in her glance.

'I needed to move swiftly,' he said. He was surprised to hear how *normal* his voice sounded.

'You *needed* to reassure your allies, who include my uncle and me. My uncle thinks, even now, that you might pounce on us, seize Heraklea and put it under your crown as "king".' Amastris didn't sound angry – just detached. A good stateswoman, he realised. Probably far better with ambassadors than he would be. Her beauty – more than

77

beauty – made his loins ache. Her breasts showed – just the very tops of the rich fruit of them, pale – he could remember the feel of them—

'I'm sorry,' Satyrus said. He changed the tone of his voice; no more the detached statesman. 'Amastris, if I had come ashore, when would I have ever left?' He reached out and took her hand, but she pulled it away before he touched her and turned her shoulder.

'You paw me. It makes people talk.' She stood suddenly. 'I think that you have to make me a better apology than that empty flattery, based solely on lust.' She only came to his chest, but her eyes burned into his. She was angry – so angry that her shoulders trembled. 'You didn't trust me!'

'How could I?' he said, before he thought too much about it. 'You employ the man who murdered my mother.'

'You know that is not true,' Amastris said. 'I defy you to prove it. Anyway, even if he *was* involved, it was just politics. Nothing personal.'

Satyrus shook his head. 'That's exactly what he said, or so my sister tells it.'

'So what?' Amastris said. 'You don't want me to have a councillor as good – as thorough – and as deep as Stratokles. Better I be a nice ignorant virgin, ripe for the wedding market. You can tell me whatever you see fit, and I'll at least pretend to be happy to have such jewels of your manly wisdom shared with me. *You are no better than my uncle*, except that you are better to look at.'

Satyrus had never seen her like this. He wasn't sure that he didn't like this Amastris – enraged, uncaring and strong – *better* than the complacent temptress of Ptolemy's palace. 'Very well,' he said. 'Let's talk like rulers, shall we?'

'Don't patronise me,' she spat.

'I'm not patronising you, Amastris. I'll tell you the unvarnished, unflattering, unstatesmanlike truth.' He sat carefully on a couch. 'My attack depended on speed and surprise. Speed to catch Dekas' warships still in their berths. Surprise because it saves casualties and, as it turned out, I was hideously outnumbered. I—' He fingered his cup, 'I miscalculated pretty badly, and only the favour of divine Herakles—'

'You are such a depressingly pious man,' Amastris said, shaking her head. 'The favour of divine Herakles. Did you grow up in a mighty city? Or are you secretly a shepherd from Attica?'

Satyrus began to smile – much the same sort of smile that came to his face in a fight, although he didn't know it. 'Perhaps I *am* a shepherd boy, at that,' he said. 'Nonetheless, I needed surprise to take Timaea. I don't trust Stratokles. I'm sorry that you like him – sorrier that you trust him.' He paused to take a sip of wine.

'He helped you win your throne,' she said carefully.

'I suspect you pushed him to it, and I further suspect that it co-incided with the interests of Athens.' Satyrus shrugged. 'It's not about Stratokles, my dear. We always argue about him – and for nothing, this time. Even if he was not at your side, I would not have come ashore. Most of my oarsmen and marines already know too much. If I had landed here, rumour would have gone on falcon wings over the isthmus to Timaea.'

She shrugged. 'So? Perhaps some things should be more important to you than the lives of a few mercenaries.' She smiled at him, her dimples appearing as if summoned.

'I thought we were speaking as statesmen?' he asked her. He wasn't sure what he felt. He had come – why had he come? Leon was wait-ing, and he was wasting a day.

Suddenly, in the space between heartbeats, he felt the change, like the moment when the rim of the sun appeared above the world.

'My lady, I need to be in Rhodes,' he said.

She appeared confused for a moment. Satyrus had never seen her confused.

'I am sorry if my tactics confused you, or your uncle. I meant no harm to you or yours. The straits are open to your ships. I must be gone.' He leaned forward to kiss her cheek, but she bolted from her chair and put it between them.

'You are *leaving*? Do you have any *idea* what you are doing? We have plans to make—'

Satyrus shook his head. 'Plans we can make another time. The wind is fair for me, and my uncle is waiting for me at Rhodes. I'll be back in a few weeks and we can make arrangements then.'

'Aphrodite, stand with me. Are you leaving me, Satyrus? Are we not lovers? What service is this?' She was angry again – or perhaps had been angry all along.

Satyrus was angry too, although he was only just discovering it. 'Perhaps if we were married, I'd take these protestations more seriously,' he said. 'As it is, we are a pair of rulers duelling for power. I can do that elsewhere, and I am needed elsewhere. I long to marry you, Amastris – but until your uncle agrees, what's the point in these meetings? Anger, recrimination—'

'Then go,' Amastris said. 'You're quite right. There is no point. Please leave, immediately.'

Satyrus picked his chlamys off a stool. He'd said too much – said the unsayable. And now he regretted it.

But there was nothing he could add without surrendering, and he'd never been much for surrender.

So he looked at her, hoping to communicate with his eyes, but she swept from the room. He heard the sound of metal impacting plaster.

Satyrus sighed and left the room. He collected the silent Helios from the kitchens, and found his guard of marines waiting under the eaves of the palace. Nestor was there, talking to Apollodorus.

'Evening, Nestor,' Satyrus said as he came up.

'Lord,' Nestor said, inclining his head. 'A famous victory.'

'A lot of dead women and children,' Satyrus said with some bitterness.

'Nest of vipers, if you ask me,' Apollodorus said.

'I didn't ask you,' Satyrus said.

'Not a good day with my mistress, then?' Nestor said with half a smile.

Satyrus shook his head. 'I think it's over,' he said. He felt like weeping – felt that saying it aloud might make it so.

Nestor shook his head. 'Not unless you no longer want her,' he said. 'It is just the poison of that Athenian hyena.' He shrugged. 'Perhaps one day I will kill him for my king – and for you.'

Satyrus shook his head. 'Heraklea has never been lucky for me,' he said. He caught the eyes of his escort. 'We're needed in Rhodes. We should be gone.'

7

Days under sail and oar – nights under canvas on beaches from the neck of the Bosporus to the coast of Asia. The second night they camped below the ruins of Troy, and Satyrus went and sacrificed to the shades of Achilles and Patroclus and Hektor. The fourth night they camped under the walls of Mythymna, on Lesvos, and Satyrus drank wine with the garrison commander, Phillip Xiphos, an old friend of Draco's.

'Catamite bastard is waiting for you off Chios,' Phillip said with no preamble.

Satyrus nodded. 'Thanks for that,' he said.

Phillip laughed. 'Draco says you're a good man, for all you're an effeminate Greek and a barbarian, too,' he said. Phillip had lost an eye, like his namesake, and had a pair of scars that looked like fingers reaching across his face. His couch-mate at dinner was a beautiful boy with the body of an Olympic athlete, one of Sappho's descendants.

'I'm descended from Sappho *and* Alcaeus,' he proclaimed proudly.

After he had sung some of his ancestor's poetry, and played very well on the lyre, the boy came and joined Satyrus on his couch. 'Would you take me to be a marine?' he asked. 'I want to go to war. All I do here is train.'

'What's your name?' Satyrus asked.

'Charmides,' said the boy.

'How old are you, lad?' Satyrus asked, feeling a thousand years old.

'Eighteen – in a few weeks.'

'Months,' Phillip said. 'He won't be an ephebe until the Feast of Herakles. That's my feast of Herakles – in Pella.'

'I knew which one you meant,' Satyrus said tolerantly. 'What do you think of this, sir? Do you want him to go to sea as a marine?'

The old Macedonian smiled tenderly at the boy. 'I hope he never sees a spear flash in a foe's red hand,' he said. 'But for all that, he's eager for it, as we all are, eh?' Phillip made a face. 'You've seen a fair amount of action – for a Greek.'

Satyrus shrugged.

'I could send him to Antigonus, but he has the reputation of eating men,' Phillip said. 'Cassander may be regent of Macedon, but I can't love him. Ptolemy – he was always my favourite. But Aegypt is a long way away.'

'Are you asking me to take this boy?' Satyrus asked.

'Let me think on it,' Phillip allowed.

In the morning, the handsome lad was on the black sand beach of Mythymna with a heavy wool sea bag and wearing a fine suit of armour. Phillip stood by him in a cloak, half purple, half tan. It made Satyrus smile – the mark of the Companions of King Alexander. A magnificent brag. And a true one.

'I guess that he must go sometime, eh?' Phillip asked. 'I had hoped to send him with Draco—'

'He's holding Timaea for me,' Satyrus said. 'What's your name again, boy?'

The young man looked shyly at the ground – really, too well bred to be believed. 'I'm called Charmides,' he said.

The boy reminded Satyrus of someone, but he couldn't put his finger on just who that was.

Satyrus turned to Apollodorus. 'We have a new marine,' he said.

Apollodorus smiled. 'Likely lad, I must say. Can you throw a javelin, lad?'

Charmides dimpled when he smiled. 'Well enough,' he said, cautiously.

'Well enough to throw in the boys' events at the Olympics!' Phillip said. 'You take good care of my boy. I've been his father, in everything but blood.'

Satyrus clasped hands with the old man. 'I'll do my best,' he said. 'The sea is not always kind.'

'Let's see if I can make it kinder,' Phillip said. 'Walk with me on the beach.'

In a few minutes of walking, Phillip laid out the naval dispositions of Antigonus, Demetrios and the pirate Dekas. 'Dekas has sixty ships,' Phillip added, 'including four of mine.'

Satyrus made a face. 'I can't face sixty ships. I'd like to. I think

I could take him – but the risk is too high, and my merchantmen would suffer.'

'Wait a few weeks, then. Dekas can't wait for ever – Antigonus needs him to fight Ptolemy down off Cyprus. Or blockading Rhodes—' Phillip shook his head. 'You can wait here. I won't charge you much,' he added.

Satyrus nodded. 'Thanks,' he said. 'But no.'

'You mean to fight?' Phillip asked, and his glance at Charmides, already stowing his gear under a rowing bench, spoke volumes.

'No,' Satyrus said.

Satyrus went west out of Mythymna, rather than east through the Straits of Lesvos as he had planned. It was a risky course in late spring, and his next move was still riskier, leaving the safety of the Lesvian coast at Eressos on a clear morning, crossing the deep blue to the lonely island of Psyra, south by west, and raising her as evening fell. His men ate crab and lobster on the beach, and danced with the local men and women who came down to them when it became clear they were not raiders.

They sailed before Eos, the lust-filled goddess of the new morning, had touched the sky with her rosy fingers, and they sailed due south all day, more than a hundred stades of the deep blue and never a single sight of an island or even a gull after they left the rocky slopes of Psyra astern. And into the night – the greatest risk of all, forty ships sailing the deep blue in darkness, and every stern lit like a temple on a festival.

In the morning, Satyrus' squadron was spread over fifty stades of sea but he sailed on, the wind fresh and dead astern, carrying him south by south until, at the rising of the stars, Mykonos rose between the bow post and the foremast.

Neiron nodded. 'Good landfall,' he said. Then he grinned like an Aegyptian jackal. 'Excellent landfall.' Few things made sour old Neiron smile, but good seamanship was always worth a laugh. 'What's on your mind, young man?'

Satyrus bridled as he always did to be called 'young man', but then he shrugged. 'The price of grain,' he said. 'It is never far from my thoughts, these days.' He looked out over the sea towards Mykonos. 'I have ten thousand *mythemnoi* of grain – more, I suspect. All the grain from my farms, all the grain from most of the Maeotae farms on the Tanais and all the surplus from Pantecapaeaum. At four drachma per *mythemna*, Athenian price, we break even. Not a good year for the small farmer. At five and a half drachma, we make a small profit.'

'I'm no farmer,' Neiron said. 'What's a small profit?'

Leosthenes, the priest of Poseidon, made a snorting noise. He'd been sitting on the helmsman's bench, reading from a scroll. He got up. 'Didn't you even grow up on a farm, old man?' he asked.

Neiron smiled and shook his head. 'Fishing boats and merchant ships.'

Leosthenes nodded. 'My *pater* was hard put to make his *zygote* quota of two hundred *mythemnoi* every year. Two hundred measures or more, and you are a full citizen. Fewer, and if the assessor wants to, he can take away your right to serve – lots of rights. If you don't make quota, your son can't train in the gymnasium.' Leosthenes looked out to sea, clearly remembering something painful.

Satyrus hadn't thought of it like that. Of course, except for being a terrified exile for a few weeks, Satyrus had never wanted for money. He looked at the priest. 'Did it ever happen?'

Leosthenes laughed grimly. 'Never. Once in a while we'd have a year where the crops were good and the olives were good and we'd make quota and then some – and pay our taxes and lay aside money for dowries. One year in five. The rest, we'd work in the fields with the slaves, gleaning every grain before the crows took them. In Athens, they have a special name for oat grains with dirt on them.' He shrugged.

Satyrus looked back at Neiron. 'So – at five drachma, we make a small profit. One of my Maeotae farmers is lucky to have two hundred *mythemnoi* – like Leosthenes' father. Let's say he has four slaves and a horse and oxen and a plough, six children – well, do the maths. Two hundred *mythemnoi* of grain at five drachma gets him a thousand drachma. Ten mina of silver. A sixth of a talent. Seems like riches, until you feed the children, the slaves and the oxen. Not to mention the horse.'

Neiron nodded. 'Every merchant ship knows the score, lord.'

Satyrus made a face. 'When I look back there,' he waved at the merchant ships in their trailing arrowhead, 'all I see are the hopes and fears of a thousand small farmers. If I lose it all in a storm – what then?

Pirate attack, bad choice of port, low prices when we get there—'

Leosthenes looked interested. Neiron frowned. 'That's life in the merchant trade, Satyrus. Every cargo bears its weight in worry, or so my *pater* used to say.'

Satyrus jutted his chin at Mykonos, now well up on the horizon. 'So it's not just a landfall. It's a risk passed. We should be around Dekas now. I could fight him. Hades, I'd *like* to fight him, outnumbered or not. But this isn't my grain. Or half of it isn't.'

Leosthenes nodded. 'Lord, you should cross the strait and visit the god at Delos.'

The idea appealed to Satyrus, and he was surprised he hadn't thought of Delos at all, separated from Mykonos by a narrow strip of water. 'My mind has been too much at sea,' he said. 'I will find the time to visit the god.'

They lay the night on the north beaches of Mykonos, with ships coming in all night. Satyrus declared the next day a day of rest, and the sailors mended ropes and sails while the oarsmen slept and the marines drilled, did the war dances and threw javelins until their arms hurt. Young Charmides threw so well that Apollodorus refused to be responsible for the boy.

'The men will either throw him over the side or get lovesick over him,' Apollodorus said. He shook his head. 'He's so *likeable*.'

Satyrus laughed. 'I'm just trying to decide who he reminds me of,' he said.

He took Helios and young Charmides with him, walked down the sand to Diokles and the *Black Falcon* and arranged to be rowed across the narrow channel to Delos and the Temple of Apollo – the holiest shrine in the Hellenic world. Satyrus had never seen it – never had a chance to visit. And while he led his ships in a long end-round of Antigonus' naval dispositions, he'd felt – perhaps as a result of his encounter with Amastris and its results – a sense of pollution, of having made himself unclean.

What did he owe Amastris?

Why had he *not* made sure to part on better terms with his sister?

Diokles' men rowed with a will, every one of them as eager for the market at Delos – one of the best markets on the sea – as Satyrus was for the temple.

'They must be pissing in their chitons,' Diokles said with a laugh, looking at the beach.

Satyrus came out of his thoughts to see the landing beach for the great Temple of Apollo – the *hieron* of Apollo's birth, and of his sister, Artemis. There were at least a hundred priests and acolytes on the beach.

Satyrus looked at them and shook his head. 'Is that for me?' he asked.

Diokles laughed again. 'You have twenty warships just a few stades away. This temple has backed Antigonus since the dawn of the war – and here you are.'

Glaucon, Diokles' master, was a man with one of the pleasantest voices that Satyrus had ever heard. He pointed past the headland to where the great temple stood by the sacred lake. Very little of it was visible from this close in.

'Worth a few drachmas to sack yon,' he said.

Satyrus gasped at the blasphemy. 'Are we pirates?' Satyrus asked.

Diokles shook his head. 'No, lord. We ain't pirates. They are.'

Satyrus smiled. 'My family has a legend about one of our ancestors being badly treated here – but he got a good prophecy, nonetheless, or so it is told.'

'Getting cheated by the priests is part of the pilgrimage,' Diokles said.

'Worth a few drachmas to sack this place,' Glaucon said again, his voice dreamy.

'Snap out of it!' Satyrus said, but now he was laughing. 'I forget that I am a king, and a sea wolf. I expect that, with a little effort, I can take a sociable revenge for my ancestor.'

'Bet it's worth a thousand talents of silver,' Philaeus said – but then he put his hand over his mouth.

Satyrus took Helios and Charmides up the beach, where they dutifully kissed the sand and were greeted enthusiastically by the priests.

Satyrus endured several hours of obsequious service in exchange for his sacred moments in the cleft of rock and his opportunity to worship the Lord of the Silver Bow, which he did, sacrificing a ram with his own sword, and another for Melitta on the altar of Artemis, to the high priestess's delight. He left them some of the loot from the pirates at Timaea, which seemed to please them more than his piety.

He stood by the sacred lake and looked into the black waters, but the god did not speak to him. And in the sacred cleft, he heard muttering and a shriek – a very dramatic shriek – but the voice of the god was still for him.

The place itself was dramatic and beautiful, ancient with the touch of a thousand years of worship, and perhaps a thousand years before that. And when he turned to leave the sacred lake, where he felt that he had stood too long, the hierophant was waiting for him.

'My lord,' he said quietly. 'Did the god speak to you?'

Satyrus shook his head. 'No. The cleft and the lake were equally silent. I confess that my thoughts are most often turned to my ancestor, Herakles, and perhaps I have neglected the Lord of the Lyre.' Satyrus shrugged. He regretted the impulse that had brought him here.

The hierophant shook his head. 'You have not offended the Lord Apollo.' He paused. 'Not in particular.'

'What, then?' Satyrus asked. The gods he worshipped, but priests sometimes annoyed him.

The hierophant gave him a hard look. Oddly, that made Satyrus like him better – it was the obsequious priests that Satyrus disliked.

'I had a dream about you, my lord. You bear the impurity of enormous blood guilt. You have killed many men – many men, my lord, and without apology. Your line are killers, back to the generation of Herakles, may his name be blessed.' The hierophant's eyes bored in on him, unblinking. 'You must consider expiation.'

'Sacrifice?' Satyrus asked. Even as a pious man, he was tempted to ask if a large enough donation would cover this supposed blood guilt.

The priest narrowed his eyes. 'You have a reputation as a man who loves and fears the gods,' he said. 'You act like a sophist from Athens.'

Satyrus squirmed. 'Both men may inhabit the same body,' he said.

The priest nodded. 'Even the body of a priest. Listen to my dream, and the word of the Lord Apollo, and act on it or not, because the gods grant men their will, to do or not to do, and expect men to take the consequences, I think. Apollo asks that you make a sacrifice of your *time*, and learn to play the lyre. My dream tells me that you skimped on music as a boy. Apollo commands that you learn his instrument, and through it, perhaps, you will see things that you have not seen.'

Satyrus fell back a step, stunned by the simplicity of the god's demand and its subtlety. 'I thank you, lord priest. I will … I will consider the god's demand. Will act on it.' Indeed, the faintest whiff of damp cat's fur came to his nostrils, the first sign from his ancestor god in many passages of the moon, and he was moved. He embraced the priest, who nodded graciously.

'Teachers will come to you,' the priest said suddenly.

'A music teacher?' Satyrus asked.

The priest shrugged. 'I – some daemon gave voice. I spoke without thought.'

Satyrus was satisfied. The gods had spoken, and his visit was not wasted. Blood guilt – aye, Satyrus admitted that the deaths of many of his victims sat just below the surface of his mind, waiting for his every dive into deeper waters. The Sakje girl he'd killed in his first fight. The sailors he had once executed on a beach to maintain discipline. The dead of his battles. The women massacred when his marines stormed the town. A king quickly piled up corpses.

Back on the beach, Charmides thanked him prettily for allowing him to come along.

'Are you pious, Charmides?' Satyrus asked. He was deep under, seeing all his dead.

The young man blushed – a remarkable talent in a man who could throw a javelin half a stade. 'I – I believe in the gods, lord.'

Satyrus nodded. 'Helios?'

'I believe in the gods more strongly as a free man than I did as a slave,' he said. 'The gods have very little to offer a slave.'

Satyrus stared out over the stern. 'Helios, do you play the lyre?'

Helios looked uncomfortable. 'No, lord.'

Satyrus glanced at Charmides. He blushed, and stammered something.

'I'll bet he plays very well indeed,' Satyrus said to Helios. 'All the people of Sappho's island should be musicians.'

Charmides shook his head. 'No, lord. I never – I never put in the time. Music is difficult.' He shrugged. 'I spent my time running and learning to fight.'

Satyrus pursed his lips. 'I seem to have surrounded myself with non-musicians. And yet Theron and Philokles both loved to play and sing. Apollo commands me to learn the lyre, gentlemen. When I have engaged a teacher, I will invite both of you to learn with me.'

The two younger men beamed with pleasure, and that made Satyrus happy as well.

Satyrus thought about music all the way back to Mykonos.

South and east, down the 'gullet' between the Cyclades and the Sporades. A night on a beach with no name on an islet off the coast of Astypalaia, eating stores and keeping the fires small, and in the morning they were off again, due west of Cos. That morning, they saw two ships away north on the horizon – sixty stades or more.

'Miletus is off our port quarter,' Neiron said.

'With most of Antigonus' smaller warships, if Phillip of Mythymna was right,' Satyrus said. 'We should be south of Dekas, though.'

'Unless those were his scouts,' Neiron said.

'We won't beach until dark,' Satyrus said, and went back to watching the sea. Twilight found them coasting along a headland that should have been Telos but looked strangely different.

'Stay at sea,' Satyrus said. 'Light the stern lamps and press on.'

In the dark, the stars began to vanish overhead in the second watch, and Neiron woke Satyrus to take a turn at the steering oars. There was an oil lamp flickering fitfully in the sheltered space under the stern strakes, and otherwise it was as black as the cleft of Apollo.

'Poseidon, stand by us,' Satyrus whispered to the wind.

The wind stayed steady through his watch and the ship moved fast – perhaps too fast. But it had to be time to turn east and run between Syme and Chalke – *hadn't it?*

Satyrus waited as long as he felt he could, and he worried – about the ships behind him, watching for his lights, and about the silence of the god at Delos, and his sister's anger – and most of all, about Amastris. The middle of a night watch is a dark place, and all of his responsibilities came to him, the weight of every relationship, the numbers of his dead.

Then he leaned on his steering oars and his *Arête* turned east into a night as black as new-melted pitch. Behind him, he could see Diokles' *Black Falcon* make the turn – or rather, he knew the *Falcon* well enough to know that that was the ship astern. After that, he counted lights – six, seven, eight – and then the gloom was too much. Some of his ships were astern. He wished that he had gone ashore at Cos. He wished he had beached at least for dinner and to remind his captains—

Most of whom were his elders, and had sailed these waters longer than he had been alive.

Then he leaned forward, looking for breakers, listening for a change in the sound of the sea. Twice he gave the steering oars to Helios, who huddled awake because his lord was awake, and went forward to check on his lookouts, but they were awake, as sharp-eyed and anxious as only men at sea on a dark night can be.

'I'll never keep a squadron at sea in the dark again,' Satyrus said to Helios. The younger man sat with his back against Satyrus' back, sharing warmth. The cool, damp wind sucked the heat right out of them, worse than a winter wind on the Sea of Grass.

Helios laughed. 'So you say, lord,' he said. 'Don't swear to it, or the gods will hear you!'

Satyrus nodded at the dark. Was that the first grey light of day? 'I mean it,' he said.

'Oh, yes, lord. Until the next time it seems the best way,' Helios said.

Dawn, and rain – first a light shower, and then heavier, with some wind behind it, so that Satyrus ordered the sails down. Visibility was the length of the ship and perhaps a little more

'I don't hear breakers,' Neiron said, coming awake. 'I gather we lived?'

Satyrus squatted by the helmsman. 'Don't count your drachma yet,' he said. 'The morning fog's so thick I can't see my nose.'

There was a loud crash astern and shouting, swearing – all of which sounded as if it was coming from their own ship.

Satyrus could hear Diokles shouting insults at someone.

'Someone fouled the *Falcon*,' Neiron said. 'Not good.'

'Men are hungry,' Stesagoras said at his elbow. 'We need to get 'em ashore soon.'

'I know,' Satyrus said. He reflected on the causes of fear – in daylight, if they were where he expected, his men would be quiet, respectful, eager for port. But in the fog of dawn, they were hag-ridden with worry.

'Don't pace,' he said to Neiron.

Neiron stopped walking up and down the command deck. 'Yes, lord.'

Satyrus lay down in the protected stern area behind the helmsman's bench. 'Wake me when the fog burns off and Rhodes is in sight,' he said. He pulled his chlamys over his head and lay alone with his fears and apparently asleep, listening for the first presage of disaster.

But it had been a long night, and he fell asleep.

In his sleep, Herakles came to him and put a hand over his face. 'If you had everything you desired,' the god said, 'you wouldn't be much of a hero, would you?'

Then he was in the agora – the agora of the Tanais of his childhood. Men pressed around, and women too, Sakje and Greek and Maeotae.

And there was Ataelus, and there was Philokles. They stood together.

'Not for having everything,' Ataelus said with a shrug. 'You must be for choosing.'

Philokles nodded. 'When the time comes,' he said slowly, 'I suspect that the choice will be obvious.' He smiled ruefully, a smile that Satyrus remembered so well that even in his dream his heart flooded. 'Trust the musician, boy.'

Then, suddenly, there were two horses in a paddock. Both were fine – a black and a pale cream horse with a pale mane.

Stratokles came up, wearing the red felt hat of a Sakje horse-trader. 'Whichever you keep, I'll take the other one,' he said, with a leer.

'She bites,' Ataelus said, pointing at the pale mare.

'Touch that head and you'll land in—' Stratokles began, but the words 'head' and 'land' did something in the dream, and Satyrus was awake. Men were cheering.

'The headland of Rhodes!' Neiron called from the bow.

Satyrus smiled and waved, and lay at the edge of tears, so moved was he by the memory of Philokles and Ataelus. He wished himself back to sleep, but if he dreamed, he didn't remember it.

The sun was at its apogee when they passed the headland for the harbour of Rhodes.

Neiron pointed at the walls. 'Will you look at that?' he asked.

'By the spear of Ares,' Stesagoras said. His sailors were all over the main deck, preparing to lower the mainsail and then the mainmast. He stood with his feet planed well apart, amazed. 'They're building a *sea wall*.'

Work crews were labouring so hard that the walls of Rhodes

seemed to be rising before their very eyes. At the north end of the harbour, men were raising a tower of heavy stone blocks with a giant crane powered by men in a treadmill – slaves, no doubt. Even as they watched, the crane raised a block the size of Satyrus' chest, held in a sling of heavy hide, and deposited it where a foreman straddled the growing tower wall. Under his shouted directions, the block settled, meshing neatly with the rest of its brothers and sisters in the course.

At the south end of the great bend of the harbour, a second mighty tower was rising, and at its feet, a mole – or perhaps a long wharf – was already built in timber, and rubble-fill was being dumped between the standing uprights. Enough of the wharf was complete that ships were already tied up by the finished side.

For as long as Satyrus had known the harbour of Rhodes, it had been undefended, the unstated claim being that Rhodes' great navy was the bulwark against invasion from the sea. The last time Satyrus had sailed into this port, he'd been able to see the great Temple of Apollo at the centre of the curve of the bay, the Temple of Poseidon next to it and the gilded bronze rose that was the city's device sparkling in the distance towards the agora. Now there was a wall rising all along the waterfront, pierced with gates and crenellated with towers.

The landward side was getting its share of new fortifications, as well. To the south, Satyrus could see that an enormous tower had just reached its third storey. It appeared to be a quarter of a stade on one side – the length of twenty horses tied nose to tail.

The part of his head that could calculate the value of any new construction in Tanais was running like a colt on a spring day, and Satyrus couldn't believe the amount of money he was seeing being spent.

'By the Silver Bow of Lord Apollo,' he said. 'There's the value of our city in that wall alone.'

Neiron shook his head. 'They must be scared shitless,' he said. He pointed towards the new mole. 'There's some good news.'

Satyrus hadn't noticed Leon's ships gathered around the new wharf – they were built almost exactly on the pattern of the Rhodian cruisers, and they were berthed alongside the Rhodian navy, so that they vanished among the long rows of carefully anchored warships.

'I count one hundred and sixteen hulls, with Leon's ships included,' Neiron added.

'We have heavier metal,' Satyrus said.

'We won't be as fast or as handy,' Neiron noted. 'But if we can get the time to try these new-fangled engines, we might show my cousins a thing or two.' He looked back over the stern at the long line of warships and merchantmen coming in behind.

'Best close in the arrowhead,' Satyrus said, and waved to Helios, who raised his master's gold-faced aspis and flashed it several times. They were still missing six ships, but a long night at sea and a foggy morning were bound to cause some vessels to wander off course. The rest of them had gathered back to the arrowhead formation while Satyrus napped, and now he put them in a column astern to pass the arms of the Rhodes harbour.

Ashore, men stopped working to watch. Many raised their arms and cheered.

'Good to be popular,' Satyrus said, to no one in particular. Heads came up all along the deck – the perfect rhythm of the oars faltered as men gazed at the shore. Sailors swung up on to the rails to get a better look, and the ship heeled a strake as the sailors all gathered on the landward side.

Helios smiled and looked at Charmides, who blushed.

Neiron frowned at everyone on the command deck. 'This is a working ship,' he barked.

Everyone went back to work.

The landing was smooth enough, especially as the pilot vessel that met them cheered and waved them away from the stony beach and alongside the new wharf. As if to make amends for their moment of inattention, the rowers were as sharp as a blade approaching the stone and wood, and the starboard-side oars shot in as if pushed by a god's hand, and the ship settled against the leather-padded pilings like a seabird onto water.

The first man to meet them ashore was Panther, Lord Admiral of the Navy of Rhodes, and the second was Leon. Satyrus hadn't seen the Numidian in more than a year, and his dark skin contrasted sharply with his white hair.

There were crowds – anxious crowds, Satyrus guessed – and they poured out of the side streets onto the main wharf and cheered. Panther had forty Rhodian marines – mercenaries, mostly, and a hard-looking crew – all around him. Leon had eight of his own men, four black men from Africa and four blond barbarians from the far north, yet all were matched like brothers, wearing identical muscled bronze cuirasses and fitted Attic helmets with red and white plumes. They were eight of the largest men Satyrus had ever seen. He opened his mouth to say something complimentary, but Leon spoke first. Then Panther shouted.

Whatever both of them said was drowned out by the sound of the crowd.

Satyrus pushed forward and tried to hear.

'I don't want to hear about how white my hair is,' Leon shouted, and grinned. He took Satyrus' hand and they embraced.

'It's a little scary,' Satyrus said. 'Do we need all these guards?'

'Wait until it's on your head,' Leon said. Then he laughed. 'I thought you meant the white hair. Guards? Yes. The people here are *not* happy.'

'White hair isn't so bad,' Satyrus said.

'Better than none at all,' Panther added. The top of his head glistened in the sun like a well-polished helmet.

Satyrus waved at all the activity on the walls.

'Is Rhodes in such imminent peril?' he asked. People were pressing close, calling out to him.

Behind him, Helios called for Apollodorus. Satyrus was forced to notice that Helios had grown powerful lungs.

Panther shook his head. 'This is not the place,' he said. 'When you have settled yourself, I'll come.' He looked at Satyrus' squadron – the last ships were just clearing the northern headland, and in the distance, the masts of another pair could be seen. Or at least, Satyrus hoped they were his. The rest were being guided to moorings by Rhodian harbour officials.

'You didn't have any trouble?' Leon asked.

Satyrus spoke just loudly enough to be heard. 'I took Timaea from the pirates,' he said. 'I took fifteen warships and destroyed as many again.'

Panther smiled. 'I knew you were a good ally,' he said. He looked around, located his phylarch and spoke to the man.

'Make a lane, there!' shouted the phylarch. 'Admiral Panther will speak! Step back, there!'

Panther stepped up onto a bale of cloth. 'Listen, citizens! Satyrus, King of the Bosporus, has landed with twenty warships and forty more ships laden with grain from the north. There will be no bread shortages! Further, he has defeated the pirates and taken one of their bases! I will see to it that all this news is posted in detail in the agora! Now *please* go back to your tasks!'

'And Dekas?' Leon asked, while Panther was speaking to the crowd.

'No idea. Last intelligence – courtesy of the Tyrant of Mythymna – is that he's waiting for me off Chios.' Satyrus shrugged. 'I went round. I had all my grain ships to think of.' He looked at the people. There seemed to be more slaves and women than citizens.

'You did well,' Leon said. Panther stepped down off his bale of cloth and Leon nodded to him. 'That should help, for a while, at least.' Leon waved at *Arete*. 'If Dekas is still at Chios,' he said quietly, 'we could have a go at him.'

'With the whole fleet?' Panther shook his head. 'I can't chance it.' He shook his head. 'The *boule* – the little assembly – is meeting. I have to be there.'

'Lord Ptolemy—'

'Tell me tomorrow,' Panther said. 'Lord Satyrus, you have done well – very well – to bring your grain fleet here. We will reward you and your captains as heroes. Until tomorrow?'

Satyrus embraced him, and the Rhodian admiral gathered his friends, his marines and his courtiers and set off up the street, through a gate so new that the plaster over the bricks wasn't dry, and men were sketching on it with charcoal anyway.

'They are too cautious,' Leon said. 'And Ptolemy is too rash. I fear—' He looked around. 'Well, not all the news is bad. I have your friend here – young Abraham.'

'His father let him come?' Satyrus asked.

'His father *made* him come,' Leon said. 'Ben Zion moved much of his business to Rhodes in the last two years. Abraham is here to – well, to run it. I leased part of his house for you.'

Satyrus laughed. 'I feel more like a mercenary than a king,' he said. 'No palace?' He looked around at the wall of Leon's marines – and his own. Helios had led the whole contingent off the *Arete*. Apollodorus frowned at him from the rear files, still tying his cheekpieces. Beyond the soldiers, the crowd was calm and orderly, but hands kept reaching out to touch him. Satyrus found this disconcerting. 'Do we take an escort wherever we go?'

Leon smiled. 'You have been away from civilisation a long time, my boy,' he said. 'Even in Alexandria, I go nowhere without a dozen swords. May I say without offence that you are ... so grown-up now.'

Satyrus laughed, the mood of foreignness broken. 'Why, thank you, uncle of my youth.' He stopped and put an arm around Leon. 'I had a dream about Philokles,' he said, 'and Ataelus. It made me cry.'

'Were they trying to tell you something?' Leon asked.

'I think so,' Satyrus said. But he couldn't remember what it was. 'Is Nihmu here?' he asked.

'Alexandria,' Leon said. Something unpleasant passed over his face. *If I am grown-up now, you are feeling old*, Satyrus thought.

8

Leon's encroaching old age wasn't visible as he sprang up the streets of the city. He walked fast, talking all the time – scribes followed him, copying letters as they walked on tablets of wood and wax suspended from their necks.

No, Satyrus noted – not as they walked, but whenever they stopped. And talking to Leon was quite frustrating, because whenever a scribe finished a document, Leon took it and read it.

'Your big penteres is magnificent. And you have six of the new engines aboard!' Leon nodded approvingly, then went back to a bill of lading. 'Have you decided on a price for your grain?' he asked.

'We haven't practised with them—' Satyrus began.

But Leon's attention was on a letter quickly thrust into his hands – the scribe flashed Satyrus an apologetic smile, as if to say *you may be a king, but if I don't do this he'll have my head*. The letter was on a wax tablet, which Leon held close to his eyes to read. '*Paideuo* is a bad verb to use when we speak of instructing a peer, Epiktetos. *Paideuo* means, 'I will teach you as if you were a child'. Leon winked at Satyrus. 'Which in fact is the case, but let's not say so out loud. Perhaps *didasko.*' Leon paused, watched his scribe until he saw the stylus scratch away the old word and replace it with the new in the wax, and then looked back at Satyrus. 'You haven't trained with the new weapons?'

'We've been a little busy,' Satyrus said. Leon made him feel like a child, sometimes, without meaning to.

'You stung Dekas, and that's something.' Leon's dark eyes caught his. 'Have you set a price for your grain?' he repeated.

Satyrus nodded. 'I know what my farmers need,' he said, a little more sharply than he had intended.

Leon nodded, eyes on another tablet. 'They'll take your grain if you aren't careful. That's what I came down to warn you of. They're desperate – far more desperate than the situation requires.'

Satyrus found the press of people threatening. 'This is worse than being a popular kithara player in Alexandria,' he said.

Leon nodded. 'You are a famous man. I am a famous man. You just brought this city ninety days of grain. Maybe twice that. All in all, you are cause for celebration, and the two of us together are enough for a riot of celebrity. Ah – here we are.' He paused. 'Send a runner to your ships and tell your captains to moor and keep their crews aboard,' he said.

His escort began to pass into a walled courtyard through a high gate. To the right was a synagogue – Satyrus knew the signs over the door in Aramaic and Greek.

Abraham was just inside the gate. Satyrus' eyes passed over him for a moment because he expected a tall, athletic navarch, and what he saw was a heavily bearded Jew dressed in long robes.

But it registered – quickly enough that Satyrus doubted anyone had seen him hesitate. He opened his arms, and Abraham wrapped him in his own long arms.

'King of the Bosporus!' Abraham said. 'Be welcome in my house.'

'The Jew of Rhodes!' Satyrus said in an equally dramatic voice. 'Come and visit my kingdom!'

Abraham laughed and swatted him – a not-so-gentle backhand straight from adolescence and the gymnasium of Alexandria. 'I'm impressing my neighbours, you useless aristocrat!'

Satyrus hugged him again, and then the gates closed behind the last files of Satyrus' marines, and Apollodorus pulled his helmet off. He and Helios exchanged glances – Satyrus couldn't help himself.

'Trouble?' he asked.

Helios shrugged. 'I apologise, Captain.'

Apollodorus shrugged. 'He ordered me and the marines off the ship. He's your hypaspist – not my officer.'

Satyrus forced a smile. 'This is not the place or time for this.'

Both men had the good grace to look abashed.

Satyrus turned to his former slave. 'Helios, for your sins, you can run an errand for me. Leon – a tablet, if your scribes can spare one?'

Leon laughed, took a dark panel of wood from one of his people and handed it over with a bone pencil, and Satyrus wrote quickly in the hard wax. 'Straight to Neiron, and not a word to any other man,' he said, keeping a smile on his face.

Helios saluted, Macedonian fashion, and trotted off, head high, with his aspis still on his shoulder.

Satyrus turned to his host. 'Abraham, you remember Apollodorus?'

Abraham laughed and embraced the marine officer. 'Too well.'

Apollodorus laughed, too. 'Not many men I've played "feed the flute girl" with, in public,' he said.

Satyrus passed over that remark to introduce Helios. 'My hypaspist, Helios, is the man I just sent away.'

'I remember him well,' Abraham said.

'I don't,' Leon said. 'I saw him several times lurking at your shoulder. He looks like a Greek.'

Satyrus nodded. 'Yes, sir, he is.'

'Former slave?' Leon asked.

'Citizen of Tanais!' Satyrus proclaimed.

'How does one "feed a flute girl"?' asked a sweet voice.

Satyrus turned his head. Behind Abraham was his sister, Miriam. Satyrus had met her once, in her father's house in Alexandria. Their eyes met.

She didn't drop her eyes this time, any more than she had four years before. She had the boldest glance Satyrus had ever seen – well, with the exception of his sister, Leon's wife Nihmu, and most of the Sakje women he knew. Her eyes were brown – deep brown, with flecks of gold in the iris. Her hair was a glorious profusion of browns with the same gold highlights as her eyes.

All of the men were staring at their sandals.

Satyrus laughed. 'You have not changed,' he said.

Abraham cleared his throat. 'My sister Miriam,' he said. 'We should go inside.'

'I apologise for the soldiers,' Satyrus said. 'I had little choice. The crowds were ... enormous.'

'And you'll need them the whole time you are here.' Abraham raised his arm and pointed. 'I have towers on my courtyard, here. Archers in the towers. Barracks for fifty men, and I employ thirty full-time. I can feed your men. Besides,' he said with something of his old humour, 'you're paying.'

'How splendid of me!' Satyrus allowed. The courtyard was not very decorative, it was true – heavily cobbled, but with no statues and no garden. Archways led away into warehouses – archways big enough for a wagon to clear – and into the house. Satyrus took a moment to realise that this was bigger than his palace in Tanais. Then he laughed, and followed his host through an arch.

On the other side of the arch, he might have been in another world. They went into a rose garden with paths laid out in white marble, and small trees – apples, it appeared. The whole garden smelled like jasmine, although Satyrus couldn't see a jasmine flower anywhere.

The house was typically Greek, with a colonnade that ran around the rose garden. But the walls, although brightly coloured, decorated with patterns, or painted with flowers, were devoid of gods, goddesses or dancing girls.

All very thought-provoking. Leon bowed to Abraham. 'I have a lot of business, Abraham. Will you excuse me?' and he was gone in a cloud of scribes, flashing Satyrus a look he couldn't interpret.

Satyrus was ushered into the main room of the ground floor – like an old *andron* with a new mosaic floor. Satyrus laughed at the conceit; it was covered with bits of food, ends of bread, discarded bones and a sheep's skull, all rendered lovingly in mosaic as if a feast had just been completed.

'Beautiful!' he said.

'We're Jews,' Miriam said behind him. 'We don't use representations of people in our religion. But this seemed innocent ... and charming.'

Satyrus nodded. A slave came and took his chlamys and his sword.

Abraham brought him a cup of wine. 'Welcome again to my house, brother.'

Satyrus raised his cup to both of them. 'It is a pleasure to be your guest.' He wondered why Abraham was suddenly so *very* Jewish, but he decided not to mention it. He put it down to the presence of the sister. She certainly had an effect on *him.*

'Feed the flute girl?' she asked.

'Please drop the subject, Miriam,' Abraham said.

She must be nineteen now, or perhaps twenty. Quite old to be unmarried. Or was that just among Greeks? Satyrus was suddenly struck with a desire to enquire, and he doubted Helios would know of whom to ask.

Satyrus smiled wickedly at his host. 'I could tell her,' he said.

'Only if you want to find somewhere else to stay,' Abraham shot back.

'Shall I guess, then?' Miriam asked. 'I think it is unfair that my brother had such a liberal education and I'm always to be left at home, wondering what Plato said and how flute girls are fed.'

Satyrus realised that this was a game – that Miriam knew exactly how 'feed the flute girl' worked, that she was embarrassing her brother in public and that an astrologer might have marked this day with red ink against the possibility of social humiliations in all directions.

'I have a great deal of grain to sell,' Satyrus said. 'I need to get down to it.'

Abraham nodded. 'I was going to let you get your sandals off.' He made a motion to his sister to leave. Instead, Satyrus felt a weight settle on his *kline*.

'Miriam!' Abraham said.

Satyrus turned his head. She was quite close – actually, she was at a perfectly respectable distance, one that would cause no comment among Greeks. But she was close enough for him to see the way the light played on the brown mass of her hair. He couldn't help but smile.

'I'm a widow,' she said, and shrugged. 'I can't be expected to remain in hiding. Besides, Abraham, I am your hostess. Satyrus – the king – is as much my responsibility as yours. We are not in Father's house.'

Satyrus thought that Abraham looked ready to explode. He put out a hand and touched his friend. 'Grain,' he said. 'If my ships are unloading, now is not the time to bicker.'

Satyrus turned to Miriam. 'I am delighted to renew acquaintance with you, Despoina. But your brother and I have business to discuss, and your teasing him will not help him dwell on the business at hand. Can the two of you suspend hostilities while I'm in the house?'

Miriam blushed. 'My life with my brother is none of your business,' she said.

Abraham looked stung. 'Miriam!'

Satyrus made himself smile. 'If you are my hostess, surely I can beg you to get me a cup of wine and a little privacy for some business?'

Miriam paused on her way to a display of temper. She looked at him for a moment, and a smile almost came to the area around her eyes. She rose to her feet and stalked away. She was very slim, Satyrus noted. Her legs must be very long indeed. He dismissed the thought as born of long abstinence and insufficient devotion to the Foam Borne.

It was a hard thought to dismiss as the transparent wool of her chiton outlined her hips and waist as she turned, the silken cloth hiding very little. And she smiled – not provocatively, but the smile of a person who likes another person. 'I will see to your wine and comfort, then. And since we are speaking frankly, may I then bargain for time with both of you? I might play for you, for instance.' She arched an eyebrow at her brother.

He relented immediately. 'Of course! As soon as we have settled the fate of the world, love. And please join us for dinner. You are the hostess, and this is Rhodes, not Athens.'

After the sound of her sandals slapping the floors retreated into the peristyle, Abraham slapped his thigh. 'If you ever retire from kingship, come and live with me and keep my sister in line. By Jehovah, Satyrus, that was well done.' He frowned. 'Since her husband died, there is no controlling her.' He caught himself, with the air of a man who has said too much.

Satyrus suspected that there was more going on than an uncontrollable girl – and he knew his own sister would not let the word 'controlling' go by without comment. But he had grain to sell.

He shrugged. 'I've always liked her, and my sister valued her company,' he said. 'And given my sister's views on sequestered women, you will have to allow me to take her side.'

Abraham grinned his old, open grin. 'She's a widow, now. And rich enough. And to be honest, I've been tempted to ship her off to your sister to learn to ride and shoot. She's far too intelligent to waste – she could run my warehouses without me, and no mistake.' He shrugged. 'If we weren't Jews I'd buy her a temple post, and she could be high priestess of Artemis or Athena. Then she'd have some sort of life.' He shrugged. 'But she is a Jew – more a Jew, I think, than I. Shall we talk grain? How much do you have?'

'I don't know the exact count of my grain,' Satyrus said. 'More than ten thousand *mythemnoi*, anyway. What's a *mythemna* of grain worth on the dock?'

Abraham raised an eyebrow. 'Six drachma and some change.'

Satyrus grinned and his spirits soared, almost as if he'd won a victory. Perhaps he had. 'I'm going to make a lot of farmers happy!'

Abraham nodded. 'I'd like to buy the lot.' He raised an eyebrow. 'If my credit is good. I don't keep that kind of cash here. This city may fall – or may be called on to provide exceptional fines to buy off Antigonus.' He shrugged. 'This is poor bargaining. I'll take your entire cargo at six drachma and three obols per *mythemna*, Athenian weights.'

'Is Alexandria safer?' Satyrus asked. He shrugged. 'I'd be happy to sell to you, anyway.'

Abraham shook his head. 'Nowhere is safe, so we divide our silver and gold among all our houses.'

Satyrus nodded. 'Pay Leon in Alexandria, then. But take your fee for my ships and my men; and I have a list of things I'd like to buy here.'

Abraham looked interested. 'What can I find for you?'

Satyrus made a face. 'It's a long list, brother – I live at the edge of civilisation. Spices, metal and skilled labour. Mostly smiths and tanners. I'd like to buy a whole industry's worth of both. I can promise freedom and employment to every slave I buy – they have to be free in Tanais.'

Abraham whistled. 'Skilled labour is cheap these days – Antigonus takes so many cities and sells so many into slavery. I'll see what I can find you.'

'Helios has the whole list,' Satyrus said. He remembered his promise to the god. 'I'd like a musician – a music teacher. For myself.'

'Kithara or lyre? Very well – get me the list. I'll get him to pass it to my factor. Anything else?' Abraham smiled. 'You are doing me a powerful favour. I'll see to it you get the best music teacher ever taken in war.'

Satyrus nodded. 'Good.' He laughed aloud. 'I've dreaded this moment for a month, and now it's over. Oh – my farmers are saved.'

Abraham shook his head. 'We're not finished. First, I should only take about half. That way, I keep all my competitors as friends. Besides, if all your ships come in, we're talking ... what did you say? Ten thousand *mythemnoi*?'

Satyrus nodded.

Abraham nodded back. 'In any other year, you'd merely make money. This year, you can make a killing. You and me both, of course.'

A slave entered silently, spoke into Abraham's ear and slipped out.

'We have a visitor,' Abraham said. 'Nicanor is the Archon Basileus of Rhodes. Have you met him?'

'Briefly. He was on the council of fifty when Rhodes approved the loan of a squadron to me in the last Olympic year.' Satyrus stood up.

Nicanor son of Euripides was a small man with a slightly damp hand clasp. He tossed his chlamys to the slave. 'You came with *all* your grain!' he said as soon as he'd been given a cup of wine. 'You don't know what that means to us!'

Satyrus smiled. 'You loaned me a squadron when I was an almost penniless adventurer,' he said.

Nicanor frowned. 'Yes, yes. It really is too bad – but I must tell you that the *boule* has just voted to take all of your grain at four drachma per *mythemna*. We passed a law.'

Abraham sat still for a moment, and then he took a deep breath. 'I'm sorry, you passed a law to forbid Satyrus of the Bosporus to sell his own grain?'

Nicanor nodded. 'Yes. We – that is, the city – are buying all of it. At a perfectly fair price: four drachma per *mythemna*. Nothing to fear there.'

Abraham stood silent – stunned.

Satyrus saw the ground crumbling under his feet. 'Except that the grain is worth far more, and you know it. And if you do this, Nicanor, no man will ship grain here during the siege – if it comes to a siege. No one. You cannot do this.'

'We have to prevent a panic and a run on bread prices,' Nicanor said. 'The safety of the city is at stake. Antiochus and his worthless son have agents operating in the city – among the slaves, among the lower classes. Agitators. There was almost a riot on the docks when you arrived.'

Abraham let out another sigh. 'You forced every lower-class man in the city to work on the walls for a fixed price, but didn't fix the price of bread,' he said. 'No one needs outside agitators to make trouble when you do that.'

'If they don't like working for us, they can leave,' Nicanor said.

Satyrus shrugged. 'I'll sell you half my grain at seven drachma,' he said. 'The other half I'll sell at a price that seems best to me, and to whomever I choose to sell it, including Leon's factor in Alexandria.

And if you mess me around, sir, I'll take my warships and my as yet unloaded grain and sail away.'

The silent slave slipped in again and whispered to his master.

Nicanor rose to his feet to protest. 'We *need* that grain. We have benefited you in the past, young man. You are, I believe, an honorary citizen of this city. You have obligations—'

Panther appeared at the door. 'Nicanor, are you an idiot?' he bellowed as soon as he entered.

'We are stabilising the grain price!' Nicanor said.

'You are destabilising the city!' Panther said.

Satyrus looked back and forth as they sparred – an argument of long duration and ancient antecedents, as far as he could tell. Interesting; Rhodes had always seemed like the most unified and powerful of cities. But now, with the threat of siege imminent and the enemy at the gates, the lines of fragmentation weren't just obvious – they were dangerous.

As the two politicians argued, Abraham commented quietly. 'They're really all oligarchs, here. No democratic party to speak of, although with every generation, students import some democracy from Athens. But Nicanor's people want direct control – really, *polis*-wide ownership of everything. Very Platonic. Mind you, they also want to limit the franchise to about two thousand men – the richest two thousand.' Abraham sipped wine and gave a nasty laugh. 'They're foolish enough to believe that they can use the threat of siege to deprive the lower-class citizens of their rights. Everyone knows exactly what they have in mind. It's ugly.' He lay back. Nicanor paused to take a breath and Panther shouted him down. Abraham smiled. 'If lungs are the weapons of oratory, Panther's storm voice will win every time. Panther isn't really in a party. He's a sailor and a military man. But he understands trade. And the navy doesn't want the oligarchs to do anything that will jeopardise trade. The navy needs free rowers with an interest in rowing well – in other words, an enfranchised lower class.'

Satyrus swirled the wine in his cup. 'I think I should go back to my ship,' he said. He felt the anger of a man who'd been at the point of an important victory and had it taken from him.

Abraham nodded. 'I'm sorry. Very sorry; I had so looked forward to seeing you – but yes. You'll strengthen your own hand by being on board.' He shrugged. 'Sorry for your farmers, too.' He smiled a bitter smile. 'And my sister, who, quite frankly, looked forward to your visit to relieve the tedium of her life. She has created errands for herself for a week.'

Satyrus nodded back. 'If you'd summon my marines? And I'd like to see Leon.'

Abraham growled. 'Leon was kind enough to leave us together so that we could renew old friendship. And I'm just a foreign metic here – I can't even intervene in this argument. But I guarantee you that if Nicanor has his way, you'll lose your grain – and his friends will sell it at a profit.'

'I could always go and join Antigonus,' Satyrus said.

Abraham swatted him. 'Don't even say that,' he said.

Nicanor turned away from Panther. 'You cannot bargain with the council, king or no king.'

'On the contrary,' Satyrus said. 'I'm about to return to my ship and leave. I won't bargain at all – you are quite correct.'

'There will be a riot! I forbid it.' Nicanor pulled his chiton up on his shoulder. 'If the little people see all that grain leave us—'

Leon came in from the garden. This time, he didn't have any scribes with him. 'Nicanor, have you lost your wits?' he asked.

'I'll sell you half, as I said,' Satyrus put in. 'Half, at seven drachma per *mythemna*, Athenian weights. The rest, to anyone I choose. You can have the cheap grain to keep bread prices low, and the merchants can make a profit off the rest.'

'You call seven drachma *cheap*? Grain should cost less than three drachma!' Nicanor was red, and his hand shot out. 'Merchants like this *Jew* make a profit off of gentlemen!'

Panther laughed. 'Nicanor is unaware, apparently, that we are a city full of merchants. Down, Nicanor. Heel, boy!' He pushed himself into Nicanor's face. 'Grain was three drachma a *mythemna* when all of the Asian shore competed to sell us their grain. Well, Antigonus owns Asia now. If Satyrus didn't bring us grain from the Euxine, we'd have none at all.'

'Regardless, that is *not* what the council voted, young man. You may be a king up in the Euxine, but here on Rhodes you are just a foreigner.' Nicanor smiled. 'Four drachma is a fair price.'

Satyrus held out an arm, and one of Abraham's slaves put his sword belt over his head while another slipped his chlamys over his shoulders. 'Not to me. I'm sorry, Nicanor – I have people to whom I have a responsibility – small farmers, landowners, merchants. And I am not, as you have said, a *xenos*, a foreigner. If you seek to constrain me, a citizen, I suspect you'll be lynched.' Satyrus gave him a calculated grin. 'I'll tell you straight – if a man lays hands on me or my marines, blood will flow.'

Nicanor frowned. 'This is your gratitude?' He all but spat. 'We gave you your kingdom, boy!'

'Take my generous suggestion to the council and put it to them,' Satyrus said gently.

'We need your grain!' Panther said. 'However foolish Nicanor and the council are being, we need that grain.'

'I am a dutiful son,' Satyrus said. 'I understand why Rhodes might want to have a supply of grain at a low price. I know that you helped me to my throne – help that resulted in a sea clearer of pirates and better grain prices. Help for which I paid in silver. But forget that. Take the council my counter-offer. Half – five thousand *mythemnoi* – at seven drachma. And even at that price, I would, of course, be mortified to find later that the same grain was being used to undercut other prices or to make private profit.'

Nicanor shook his head. 'You mistake me entirely, Lord Satyrus.' He drew himself up. 'No *king* is going to dictate to the council.'

'Very well. But please – take the *boule* my counter-offer. Half, at seven.' Satyrus crossed his arms. 'Or none at any price.'

Nicanor was angry, and unsure of himself – and aware that Satyrus was willing to call his bluff. 'I will summon the speaker,' he said, and swept from the room.

'Pompous arse,' Panther growled. He turned to Satyrus. 'You understand that I cannot allow you to leave the port.'

Satyrus was chilled. 'Panther, you cannot mean that.'

'I do.' Panther shook his head. 'Sorry, sir. But your grain is the measure of our survival.'

'Then let us hope the council sees sense,' Satyrus said. 'Because otherwise we'll have a fight inside the harbour. And only Antigonus and the pirates will benefit.' He cast a look at Leon. 'I'm going to my ship.' He offered his hand to Panther, and Panther took it.

'I must put duty before friendship,' Panther said.

'Put good sense before both,' Leon said.

'I think your people are panicking,' Satyrus said. 'I think that if everyone takes a deep breath, all will be well.'

Panther nodded, took his cloak and all but ran from the room.

Leon raised a hand. 'I'm with you. Let me send to have things brought to me.' Leon spoke to a slave and nodded. 'Nicanor is no more of a fool than an Athenian democrat – and better in a fight.' He looked at Satyrus. 'You handled that pretty well.'

Satyrus laughed. 'I think I did. But will they agree?'

Leon shrugged. 'You might have been a little less aggressive. Abraham here will tell you that the point is the deal, not who has the bigger cock. Right, Abraham?'

Abraham blushed. But then he raised an eyebrow. 'I'd have been less antagonistic, yes. But you need to get to the harbour before some-one – even Panther, and he's a friend – decides to keep you from your ships. This could get ugly – uglier if the street mob becomes involved. 'By the way, do I get the other half?'

Leon raised an eyebrow. 'I thought *I* got the other half?'

Satyrus nodded. 'You two can split half at seven drachma, and we'll make up parcels for the other merchants at eight.'

'Six and change – you accepted!' Abraham protested.

Satyrus said, 'Circumstances were a little different an hour ago.' He shrugged. 'Very well – you two at today's market price. Everyone else at eight.'

Abraham seemed to relax. 'Sorry. Life in Rhodes has been a little too exciting lately.' He shook his head. 'You stood in there – for me and for my price. I won't forget.'

'This from a man who used to make a hobby of being the first sword onto an enemy deck?' Satyrus asked. 'You are the brother of my heart, Abraham. I don't have enough friends that I can afford to screw any of them on a deal.' He embraced the man.

'Risking my life is easier than risking my father's money.' Abraham rubbed his beard after they had embraced. 'Six and change?'

'Yes,' Satyrus said.

'Run for your ships, now,' Abraham said. 'If Nicanor relents, come back. We have quite a dinner for you.'

Leon shook his head. 'Panther was about to tell us that Smyrna and

Miletus are empty,' he said. 'Antigonus' fleet is gone. Where has it gone, probably Cyprus?'

'So there's no risk of siege,' Satyrus asked, 'and the grain price will fall?'

Leon made a clucking noise with his tongue. 'Rhodes is going to be besieged, my friend. This summer, next summer – the walls and the grain will not be wasted. But if Plistias – that's Antigonus' admiral, Plistias of Cos – is not here, then he's off for Cyprus to get Menelaeus.'

'Ptolemy's half-brother?' Satyrus asked. 'Ptolemy trusted his useless half-brother with a fleet?'

'That's just what it is,' Leon said. 'Trust. Ptolemy can't give one of his Macedonians the fleet – they might just hand it over to Antiochus. Or Demetrios. Golden Boy has spies everywhere, and he pays good money for a little betrayal. It's one of the reasons we all have body-guards.'

Satyrus nodded. 'I thank the gods every day for the men my father and mother left me,' he said.

'Never trust a Macedonian,' Leon said. 'At any rate, if Plistias is at sea, heading for Cyprus, we have a free hand with Dekas. If we put to sea immediately, we can catch him off Chios – or hit him as he sails south to join Antigonus.'

Satyrus grinned. 'I have twenty-two ships.'

Leon nodded. 'I only have eight. But if Panther will bring us a dozen, we'll have enough.'

Abraham shook his head. 'I can tell you what Panther will say. He has to get cruisers to sea. To cover *our* grain ships. And to be frank, my friends – and I shouldn't be telling you this – the *boule* is negotiat-ing with ... with Antigonus One-Eye. Rhodes cannot spare a ship that might appear to be making war on One-Eye.'

Leon's dark skin paled and then flushed. 'Rhodes is selling Ptolemy out?' he said. '*That's* why Nicanor feels he can take such a high hand with Satyrus!'

Abraham raised an eyebrow. 'Rhodes is not part of Lord Ptolemy's kingdom,' he said. 'They offer no betrayal. In fact, they warned us, last winter, that this would have to be tried.'

Leon sat down suddenly on a couch. 'What in Tartarus ...?' he asked. 'Titans below! Witness the confusion of an old man. Ptolemy agreed to this?'

'Ptolemy had no choice,' Abraham said. 'He cannot compel Rhodes, any more than Antigonus can, short of a siege. The death of Demostrate was the last straw. Rhodes needs peace.'

Leon put his head in his hands for a moment. Satyrus had seldom seen the man he called his uncle so defeated.

'Leon?' he asked. 'What can we do?'

'We can catch Dekas,' Leon said, raising his head. 'If we can defeat him, we put Rhodes back on the board, back where they were before Demostrate died.' To the gods, he said, 'They had a choice – to strike at the pirates themselves, and tell One-Eye's ambassadors that piracy was none of their business.'

Abraham shrugged. 'Two years ago, perhaps. But Antigonus waxes and Ptolemy wanes. Even I think that that Farm Boy is almost finished.'

Leon frowned. 'Very well. The king and I have much to discuss.'

Abraham nodded. 'I'm sorry.'

Leon got up and embraced Abraham. 'As am I. You know that I love Rhodes second only to Alexandria.'

Leon turned to Satyrus. 'I have landed you in this. If you choose to take your warships and sail away, I'll understand.'

Satyrus shook his head. 'No. I like a good risk. And the Rhodians are behaving … irrationally. Antigonus wants their city. Not their alliance. Or so I hear it.'

Leon poured himself some wine. 'Agreed. So we strike. Can you put straight to sea?'

'All depends if my trierarchs let my rowers go ashore.' Satyrus saw Helios in the doorway. 'Message delivered?' he asked.

'Yes, lord,' Helios said, and saluted. He nodded and vanished.

Leon got to his feet slowly. 'Old age is a curse. If we put to sea today, we can camp on Telos tonight and be at his throat in the morning.'

'I'll follow you out of the harbour,' Satyrus said, swinging his sword scabbard under his arm.

'Like old times,' Leon said.

'Better, I hope,' Satyrus said. The last time they'd fought a battle together, they'd lost. Badly.

Apollodorus had all the marines on their feet in the courtyard. Satyrus smiled at Charmides, trying to remember who it was he looked like.

'Abraham?' Satyrus called.

As if summoned by magic, Abraham appeared at his elbow. 'I wish you could stay.'

'I'll come again.' Satyrus said. 'I have a half-arsed navarch in a big trireme – sure you wouldn't like to come and fight a ship?'

Abraham hesitated for as long as a musician might play three notes. 'No,' he said at last. 'My place is here.'

Satyrus was disappointed, but he tried not to show it. 'Fair enough. Please give my regards to your sister.'

'You must teach me how to talk to her.' Abraham embraced him.

'Talk to her as if she were a young man,' Satyrus said. 'And get her a tutor. A good one.'

'Other Jews would be scandalised,' Abraham said. But he laughed. 'I should have thought of that myself.' He looked around. 'How big a ship?'

Satyrus tried to hide a smile. 'If I gave you my own penteres, would you come?'

Abraham hesitated.

'You know the offer is open,' Satyrus said. Despite the rush of the last hour, and the deep disappointment over the grain, he felt a huge surge of affection for Abraham; his heart pounded as if he was in action. 'Come with me!'

Abraham evaded the closest part of the embrace and stepped clumsily backwards. 'No,' he said. 'No, my place is here.'.

And then Satyrus was out of the gate, surrounded by his own marines and moving fast, almost at a trot.

What has happened to my Abraham? he thought, and then buried that with all the other disappointments – a habit that was getting too easy, the rapid compartmentalising of anger, social failure, anything that got in the way of the next task. He wondered if the Rhodians would use force, or do something foolish to prevent them from leaving. That was the immediate peril. Abraham would have to wait.

There were people in the streets – lots of lower-class men, a few women. But they offered only a few cheers, and did nothing to slow Satyrus' passage, and he was in sight of the pier in the time it would take a man to run two stades. A fast man.

On the big wharf, he found that Abraham had sent supplies – a warehouse full of wine, oil and cheese. Diokles was standing under a pole crane, watching hampers of oil jars being swung aboard the Bosporan ships.

'We'll be ready for sea in an hour,' he said. 'Got your message. Helios ran his lungs out.' Diokles grinned. 'I've ordered the ships to go over to the headland and shoot practice bolts as soon as they are loaded.'

'You're a prince,' Satyrus said. He was back aboard his ship, and the last few hours seemed like a dream. 'But they'll have to stay at their moorings unless we all leave together.'

'We'll need water,' Neiron said as soon as he'd stowed his armour again.

'On the beach tonight – some place Leon knows.' Satyrus was lost in thought. 'If we leave.'

'We going to fight?' Neiron asked.

'Yes,' Satyrus said. 'Maybe right here in the harbour.'

'Heavy odds?' Neiron asked.

'Two to one. Pirates.' Satyrus answered. 'Or six to one against the Rhodian navy.'

'I won't fight Rhodes, and neither will Diokles,' Neiron said.

'Not even if they plan to steal our grain?' Satyrus asked.

Neiron sat heavily on the helmsman's bench. 'That bad?'

'That bad. It's as if all the spine's gone out of these men,' Satyrus said. He slammed his hand down on the rail. '*Shit!* I was *so close* to selling our grain and being done with this.'

Neiron stared at him.

'What?' Satyrus said. 'I'm tired of fools and ambushes and greed!' He shrugged at Neiron. 'I'm tired of—' he began, and clamped down on the words. He had been about to say that he was tired of being king, and being alone, with no peers and no friends, merely subordinates, followers and critics.

Neiron looked away, discomfited. 'Someone coming,' he said, sounding relieved. 'Someone important.'

Satyrus looked past his trierarch and saw Nicanor coming down the wharf, a purple cloak flashing behind him, and in his train a dozen more cloaks each worth the price of a small ship. The *boule*.

'Time to get off my high horse,' Satyrus said. 'No attendants. Helios – give me your plain cloak from under the bench. Hold mine. Look friendly.' Satyrus put a plain dun-coloured military cloak over his finest chiton and leaped straight onto the wharf and strode towards the councillors, obviously alone and unarmed.

Panther was there, and Herion, and another couple of men that Satyrus could remember from former visits to Rhodes.

Before Nicanor could speak, Satyrus raised his right hand like an orator, and forced a smile. 'Youth often causes hot words,' he said, 'and I beg you gentlemen to forgive my desire to be a good king to my people and a smart merchant on these docks. I will offer you one half of my grain for six drachma, not seven. Five thousand *mythemnoi* at six drachma will make it the cheapest grain in Rhodes. And perhaps will settle any ill feeling.'

Nicanor raised an eyebrow. 'You are less truculent than I expected.'

Satyrus nodded. 'I do not seek conflict here. Like you, I am not in open war with Antigonus – but I *am* at war with your pirates. And any fracture between us will only cause our enemies to celebrate.'

Nicanor nodded at the rest of the councillors as if to say, *See, is it not as I have foretold?* He crossed his arms. 'As you seem willing to negotiate, perhaps you will meet our price. Which remains four drachma for the entirety of your cargo.'

Satyrus did not lose his smile. He felt like he did when he took on a new opponent at *pankration*. 'At that price, I sail away. Or fight your navy in your harbour, and do you every damage I can do. This is not boyishness. It would be the result of your treating my offer with contempt – with hubris. My grain does not come from ten stades away across the straits. My grain comes from thousands of stades away, and requires a fleet to defend it, and at four drachma my farmers are *losing money*. Losing money after four years of war.' Satyrus tried to catch the eyes of the other men – tried to move them with his sincerity.

Nicanor tucked his thumbs in his girdle and smiled. 'You won't fight,' he said.

Satyrus looked past him at the other merchants, the admirals of the fleet, the countryside aristocrats. 'This man is risking your future and mine on an amount of money that is essential to my small kingdom and, quite frankly, nothing much to your city. I put it to you that he does so for his own purposes—'

Nicanor spat. 'Put the fleet to sea and take these barbarians,' he said to Panther.

Satyrus felt a whirl of rage – frustration and rage together – that this *one man* should baulk him, for no other reason apart from his own greed and power. The temptation to take the man and break his neck was so powerful that he shook, and Nicanor stepped back suddenly.

Panther shook his head. 'Nicanor, I beg you,' he began, and Leon appeared, running along the wharf like a much younger man.

'Nicanor,' Leon said.

Nicanor was too angry to respond. 'I demand,' he began.

'Nicanor, Demetrios is *at sea*. He may be after you, or after Menelaeus and Ptolemy. But the war is on, Nicanor. And if you do this to Satyrus – by all the gods, I promise you that no independent merchant will ever sail here again. You've already lost Athens. Would you lose Alexandria and the Euxine, too? And the rest of you – I am only another rich *metic*, but by Poseidon's mighty horses, has Zeus stolen your wits? Do you think that you can dictate your will like this? I am no boy, Nicanor – I have years on you – and I tell you that you are threatening the foundations of your city more thoroughly than Demetrios and his three hundred ships!'

The men of the *boule* shifted uncomfortably, and Nicanor's face grew so red as to be almost purple. He spat. 'You, too! You betray us, too, in our hour of need!'

'What betrayal?' Leon shook his head. 'Nicanor, you act like Agamemnon on the beach, trying to seize Achilles' bride. Consider the result, Agamemnon. And relent.'

Nicanor stood, breathing heavily.

Satyrus extended his hand to Nicanor. 'Five drachma six obols, and half my grain. I *cannot* make a better offer. Please, sir – as the younger man, I make apologies for my intemperance. Let us not make this personal, but do what is best for our city.'

That was the last arrow on his bow, and he shot it well. Instantly, he could tell that the *boule* was with him now. And Nicanor would look not just ungracious, but foolish to refuse. And he would still make a profit that would bring a smile to Gardan's face. He locked eyes with Nicanor and made himself smile, and blink, and act the lesser man.

Nicanor took his hand. 'You have good manners, for a king,' he said. But he didn't smile, and Satyrus did not think that they were friends. 'Order your grain unloaded.'

Leon stepped up beside Satyrus. 'It is customary to sign the contract first,' he said with a gentle smile. 'And I happen to have a scribe right here.'

Nicanor shrugged. 'What a lot of fishwives you foreigners are,' he said. 'Panther can sign for Rhodes. I have friends to entertain.' The man nodded – the least civility that was not a direct offence – and left with a flash of his magnificent cloak. Satyrus noted that half a dozen of the *boule* left with him.

The richer half-dozen.

Panther glanced after him with a look not far from pure hate. 'And now it is *my* name on this contract. For the next time he wishes to cut down the budget of the navy, that protects him. What a worthless cur he is.'

'Sadly,' Leon said, a frown on his face, 'my scribe has already written *The lord Nicanor and the* boule *have agreed* at the top of the document and we don't have any more papyrus. So if you could simply sign "for the *boule* of Rhodes", I think we might all' – and here Leon smiled like the lion he really was – 'rejoice quietly. And let our boys stand down and find themselves a wine shop.'

Satyrus nodded. 'What about Dekas?' he asked.

'Too late now. Too much time spent haggling. First light.' Leon smiled at Panther. 'Ten ships, and we are certain of victory.'

Panther shook his head. 'I can't spare one.' Then he grinned. 'Well – I can spare one. Mine.'

'Long odds,' Satyrus said.

Leon nodded. 'We must. Or Rhodes is off the board.'

Satyrus did not soon forget his dinner that night at Abraham's house. He was welcomed again, as if he had been gone for another pair of years – and he sat to a dinner of Numidian chicken and Athenian tuna, lobsters, subtle spice, subtle changes of texture and temperature, bowls of ice exchanged for soup that burned the tongue, and wines each more exquisite than the last. And dancers – not the usual erotic dancers, but fine young men and women dancing like temple dancers, and tumblers who performed prodigies of leaping and landing, and a pair of men in armour who started to fight as if to the death and then began to turn coward, the broadest and funniest mimes that Satyrus had seen since he left Alexandria. He laughed so much that tears started in his eyes and he had to wipe his nose, taken utterly by surprise.

His eyes met Miriam's, and she, too, was wiping her nose, and she laughed all over again. 'You are a good guest,' she said from her own couch. 'Every hostess dreams of pleasing guests as much as you are so obviously pleased.' She pointed at her steward. 'This is Jacob, a cousin; he found many of these men and women.'

Jacob bowed from where he was running the entertainment. 'Delighted you are pleased,' he murmured.

Abraham came and lay next to Satyrus. 'She chose them all herself,' he said. 'She has a wonderful head for it, and she did it without offending any of our laws. Jacob helps, of course. No lewdness, no Hellenistic religion. I could never have found the time, and already my dinners are renowned for being dull.'

'Not after tonight,' Satyrus said, and he raised a golden cup to Miriam. His eyes swung back to Abraham. He was a little the worse for wine, and needed a clear head to command his ships in the morning, but he couldn't hold his tongue for ever. 'You didn't used to care a whit for such things, brother. You used to attend parties that could never, ever be called dull, for all that they might have ended in chaos.'

Abraham nodded. 'I must seem a hypocrite to you, Satyrus. But blood is thicker than water, and I have made my father a promise: to live according to the law for three years. It is not so bad, except when the man I love above all others offers me a fighting ship and a sword.' Abraham lay back. 'By God, I miss the sea.'

Satyrus was drunk enough to think of pressing the argument. But respect for parents was a core belief for Satyrus – the more so as he had never known his own father, who was worshipped as a hero, and sometimes as a god, by many men.

'A promise to your father is a sacred thing,' Satyrus said, after the temptation to seize the moment had passed.

Abraham hugged him. 'Thanks,' he said.

When Abraham slipped off the *kline* to see to Panther and Leon, locked in discussion of a sea fight, Satyrus looked around for Miriam – eager to praise her arrangements, he told himself. Perhaps just too eager to see her brown eyes, and the pleasure she seemed to take in his pleasure.

But her couch was empty. Nor did she reappear.

He had one more cup of wine, from which he poured a libation carefully couched to offend no one. He passed the cup among his captains, and Leon's, and Abraham drank too, for a few moments one of them again.

9

South of Chios, a strong south wind lifting the sterns under full sail and no wine fumes in his head, Satyrus was as content as the rich blue sea, speckled with white wave tops spreading away from the sides of his ship like the most fabulous cloak ever imported from distant Qu'in.

Twenty-two ships in three columns. Satyrus led the centre column in *Arete*, because she was the heaviest ship, and the slowest. To starboard, Leon led his own column and to port, Panther's *Amphytrite*, the longest ship on the seas, a quadreme built with extra oars on length rather than breadth in a manner that only Rhodes, so far, had used to build a ship. Satyrus admired *Amphytrite* every time his eyes fell that way, rather in the way that even the politest of men may admire the breasts of a beautiful woman without meaning to stare.

Ahead, Leon's scout-pentekonter had warned them, lay Dekas with forty-four triremes and a pair of heavy penteres as big as *Arete*. Satyrus rubbed his beard and looked at Neiron, who was fiddling with the stern starboard war engine.

Twice, they'd practised while under way – both times sending the faster hemiolas forward with floating targets, which they engaged – well, tried to engage – as they floated by. Satyrus didn't think that they'd scored a single hit, but the value of a small farm had been shot away in iron-tipped bolts. Neiron continued to pronounce the weapons useless, but likewise he continued to tinker with them.

'Hull up!' came a call from forward.

Satyrus gave up trying to attract Neiron's attention. He walked forward from the helm – gone were the days when he needed to take the helm himself – to the midships command deck.

Apollodorus saluted. 'Bow reports enemy in sight,' he said. With both the mainsail and foresail fully drawn and the wind astern, no one could see anything over the bow except the men in the forward marine towers. Satyrus had noted that the Rhodians – innovators, every one of them – now had little baskets like nests attached to their standing masts, and men in them – lookouts raised a little farther above the surface of the sea, giving their masters a little more warning of peril.

Satyrus walked forward on the broad deck, ducked under the foresail and climbed the ladder to the forward fighting tower. It was very different from a trireme. *Arete* had never been in action, and Satyrus wondered if all this money was boyish folly. Big ships were no guarantee of victory, and could just be a slower, larger target.

Up the ladder and into the forward tower – and there, already hull up along the horizon, Satyrus could see the enemy. He shaded his eyes with his hand and watched them for as long as his eyes could stand the sun dazzle, and then turned away.

'They're all there,' he said to Apollodorus. Behind him Helios came up into the tower. Satyrus let him look for a moment.

'Put on your armour,' he said softly. 'And get me mine.'

They'd made their plans on the beach at Tenedos, when the scouts brought them word of the enemy. They were outnumbered two to one, and they were going to attack in a most unorthodox manner. A manner that would put *Arete* at great risk.

It was all a matter of timing, luck and the will of the gods, and Satyrus climbed down from the tower with a tension in his arms and legs that was not quite physical fear but perhaps fear of miscalculation, excitement, even joy, all communicated through his muscles.

Helios and Charmides helped him into his armour. Today he wore it all: heavy bronze breastplate and back, a pair of heavily worked greaves, thigh guards and arm guards and shoulder pauldrons of heavily tooled bronze, and Demetrios' silver-worked helmet on his head with a mixed crest of red, black and white. Before he took up his gold-plated aspis, he went to the rail with a heavy gold cup full of the best Chian wine, and he raised it high.

'Poseidon, Lord of Horses and of all the deeps, lend us your strength, protect our frail bodies from filling our lungs with your salt water, protect our poor thin hulls from the dangers of sea and ram, and allow us to fly on the face of the sea with the speed of your own horses.' Satyrus poured the good red wine into the sea and then flung the cup, the value of a small ship, into the water. 'For you, Sea God.'

His sailors murmured in appreciation. A rich sacrifice like that – a sacrifice that even a king would have to notice – was the best way to propitiate the touchy god of the waves. He heard Polycrates, the notoriously carping sea lawyer on number three oar, mutter 'That's right' in his dreadful accent, and he knew he'd done the right thing – although the cup had been a gift from his sister, and was his favourite.

Satyrus felt calmer in his gut and in his muscles after the libation, and he stood amidships, blind to the movements of the enemy and content to look unworried. Apollodorus would tell him if they manoeuvred, and messengers came aft from time to time, nodding or saluting and passing the word.

'Enemy is forming line, lord,' said the first messenger.

'Enemy line is formed – two lines,' said the second, a thousand heartbeats later.

'Enemy lines formed and now a crescent, tips forward like a new moon,' said the third messenger. His demeanour suggested to Satyrus that they were close.

Satyrus had his own rules of conduct, and one was that he must not show his nerves to his men. So now that combat was close enough to make the messengers nervous, he walked forward with the dignity of a priest, climbed the ladder and looked out over the sea.

In the time a man might run a six-stade race, everything had changed. As reported, the enemy was formed in a broad, deep crescent with the horns well forward, and their intent to envelop was as clear as the beautiful day.

Satyrus looked across at Leon, still in the stern of his beautiful *Golden Lotus*, and he looked to port and saw Panther watching him from *Amphytrite*. He waited several long minutes there, standing on the forward tower, looking back and forth and willing the ships around him to keep their places and not show their hands.

When the lead three ships were all but even with the far-flung horns of the enveloping crescent – and how prescient Leon seemed now, as the older Numidian had predicted that Dekas would use just this formation – Satyrus raised his aspis and waved it back and forth, so that the high sun caught the golden face and it shone like fire.

The effect was almost instantaneous, and very like the result of a boy kicking a hornet's nest that has fallen in the road. The rearwards ships of all three columns – every ship after the leaders, in fact, nineteen ships in all – turned like dancers, or greyhounds, and, crossing the wind, headed *out* to the flanks. It might have been chaos – in fact, Satyrus watched with his pulse blundering against his throat.

Leon's second ship shaved the stern of *Black Falcon* close enough to splinter an oar – but there were no other accidents, and the knuckle-bones of war were flung in the face of the gods.

Satyrus realised that he was wearing a grin so ferocious that it split his face. 'By the gods,' he said to the air around him.

He leaped over the rail from the fighting tower to the main deck, landed like an athlete in the pure joy of the moment and ran amidships, all pretence at dignity lost. He stood under the mainmast, caught his breath and made himself count to ten.

'Sails down!' He bellowed. His deck crew had been ready for ten minutes, and the sails shot down to the deck as if their ropes had been cut. He whirled, looking left and right – now he had a clear view of the enemy, already turning inward to close in on him, hunters who had set a trap and knew only one way to trip it. Leon's plan depended on the pirates having no battle drills that would allow them to switch formation. It was all risk. But informed risk.

As the last of the heavy linen canvas flopped to the deck and the way came noticeably off the ship, Satyrus nodded to his oar master.

'Ramming speed, if you please,' he said. He turned to Apollodorus. 'Commence fire. Concentrate all your bolts on the ships to our flanks.'

'Waste of money,' Neiron carped. 'No – god send I'm wrong.'

'I need you at the helm,' Satyrus said. 'Pick a ship in the middle of their line and take him – bow to bow.'

Neiron nodded grimly. 'They're going to be on us like pigs on shit,' he said.

'Let's try to be a greased pig, then,' Satyrus said.

Forward the first heavy engine fired, the thud of the machine's loosing communicating itself throughout the whole vessel, so violent was the vibration.

The result, caught in Satyrus' peripheral vision, was so spectacular that the starboard-side rowers lost the stroke for a moment and the ship shuddered.

Directly to starboard, a stade distant and more, the leading enemy trireme was bow on to *Arete* and the bolt, guided by Apollo's hand or Tyche's, passed over the trireme's bow and tipped over slightly to vanish into her unprotected oar decks. The body of a man flew up and out of the hull and a spray of blood was visible even at that distance, and the enemy ship suddenly turned sharply – too sharply – to her own port as her starboard-side rowers died as the heavy iron bolt thrashed around their deck. The ship's unintended turn threw the wounded ship across the bow of a second oncoming pirate ship, and the crash as the one struck the other could be heard clearly over the screams of the trapped rowers.

'Poseidon's glory!' Satyrus said, awed. His gunners hadn't managed to hit a blessed thing in two days of practice.

The sudden death of a trireme – apparently by a bolt from the heavens – affected the entire pirate fleet, and their ships could be seen to slow all along the starboard wing. The port wing, of course, could see nothing.

All around him the other engines fired, the crash of their release now heartening the crew as the tale of the success of the first shot spread to the rowers who hadn't seen it. The speed of the ship increased dramatically.

Satyrus glanced around. None of the other bolts had hit a target, but the eddy caused by the first shot had all but paralysed the enemy's left wing on his starboard side. Dead ahead, an enemy penteres *declined* to face his ship bow to bow and inclined away, leaving a smaller trireme to face his charge. A flight of arrows from the forward tower of the penteres fell on the deck of the *Arete* and not on unprotected rowers, and Satyrus held his aspis over Neiron and felt the heavy impacts of two Cretan shafts.

Arete's bow machine fired into the enemy penteres at a range of less than a stade and didn't miss – Satyrus thought that the enemy ship must have filled their sights – and the iron bolt raised a shower of splinters where it shattered the rail of the enemy ship and then carried on into the command platform, wheeling through the air, and Satyrus watched as two men in splendid armour were *cut in half* by the shaft.

Satyrus punched the sky.

The enemy ship carried on, her command deck suddenly silent.

Over the bow, the enemy trireme left to face *Arete* tried to manoeuvre. Her trierarch had either never fought in line before or he simply lost his head, knowing that he couldn't go bow to bow with a titan, but his last manoeuvre confused his oarsmen and placed him at an angle to the racing bronze bow of a comparative leviathan. His rowers were good – they followed orders and then ripped their long oars in through the oar ports, used to fighting smaller ships where the danger was the long rip of the beak down the side, snapping loose shafts, killing oarsmen as their oars were crushed.

But his rowers were as wrong as their trierarch. *Arete* was never a fast ship, and she had her faults, but she was both nimble and heavy, and Neiron, backed by Helios, put all his weight on the steering oars just a horse length from the enemy's side and their bow moved, perhaps the length of a man's arm, but the inexorable mathematics of Pythagoras and Poseidon put their massive bronze beak squarely in under the enemy cathead. In a lighter ship, it would have been the perfect oar rake.

Satyrus, with a clear view, was more appalled then elated. Their ram crushed the cathead as if it were made of thin clay and the way on *Arete* seemed undiminished as she crushed the slim pirate under her forefoot – the top of the ram caught the enemy rail, just as it was designed to do, but instead of *tipping* the enemy ship, the ram smashed through her, cutting the bow of the enemy craft off like a farmer's wife snaps the neck of a chicken before a family feast.

The enemy trireme filled with water in ten heartbeats, so fast that Satyrus' sailors were almost as horrified as their drowning enemies. And then they were gone, sucked beneath the waves so that in later years, Satyrus' sailors would say that they'd seen Poseidon come and suck the ship under, snatching with a massive hand.

And *Arete* carried on, still moving faster than she would cruising under oars, as if the death of two hundred men was no great matter for Her Majesty.

'Poseidon!' roared Satyrus.

The engines spoke again – doing no further harm, but sowing fear. To port, Panther's long *Amphytrite* had rammed the leaderless penteres amidships while to starboard, Leon had chosen to race through the huge gap in the enemy line untouched – and now he would be first into the enemy second line.

Except that the enemy second line had hung back, and rather than launching counter-rams they were breaking and running.

It didn't seem possible, and Satyrus was too pious to curse success – but the enemy was broken by the daring rush of three heavy ships and didn't abide the flying trap of the swift Rhodians, Bosporans and

Alexandrians racing at their flanks. The sudden destruction of four of their ships shattered any courage they'd brought, and they fled.

'Cowards!' Neiron shouted. 'Damn them! We had them!'

Every man aboard, from the lowest thranite to the navarch, felt the same, but Satyrus restrained them. 'Give only thanks for victory,' Satyrus called, and he ran below to repeat his orders on the subject.

To port and starboard, the fastest Rhodians and Alexandrians caught the slowest pirates. Their execution was swift – but so were the rest of the pirates, happy to buy life at the expense of their comrades.

Satyrus' ship was the slowest in the fleet, and the transition from sudden killer to helpless observer was painful. But there was one more thing he could do, and he did it. He climbed the forward tower and signalled a long-practised set of shield flashes.

'General pursuit', he sent.

And then he ordered the *Arete* turned and the sails raised, in the hope that they could at least keep the fleeing enemy in sight.

10

Night, on a beach – an islet south of Cos. Satyrus had left his beloved *Arete* for the speed of the *Black Falcon*, and the fleet had scattered – Satyrus suspected that there were ships from Miletus to Rhodes now, as the pirates had run in every direction. But *Black Falcon* and Diokles' *Oinoe* had stayed together.

The taste of too much wine in his mouth, and the tension in his shoulders from three days and two nights in armour and no sleep, no rest – two sharp fights, against desperate men who knew they would have no mercy. And now, wrapped in his cloak under the stern of *Black Falcon* at the edge of sleep, something tingled in his head – some stray thought, some sound from the surf. He sat up in the cool night breeze.

Running feet. Not a horde – just one man, or perhaps two. He leaped up, kicked Helios who lay to his left and slapped his left side to be sure that his sword was there.

'The king! Take me to the king!' said a man. There were torches.

The sentries were awake and alert and the alarm was being called, and a squad of marines pounded down the sand at his back. Satyrus relaxed.

Helios uncurled at his feet. 'Lord?' he asked.

'A cup of water, if you would be so kind,' Satyrus said.

Apollodorus appeared at his shoulder, still – or already – in armour. 'Fisherman came into the outer picket post down the bay. Says there's three triremes laying across the channel on the Asian shore.' Apollodorus shrugged. 'Could be Panther or Leon, lord. But it could be the fucking pirates. And they'll be gone with the sun.'

Satyrus stood there, his shoulder aching, the promise of the fatigues of middle age already very real in his young body. His hands hurt. He rubbed his jaw and felt the stickiness of three days without washing, without oil, without—

'Let's do the thing,' he said. One of his father's expressions. It made Apollodorus smile in the fitful torchlight.

Helios rose as gracefully as a temple dancer, fresh and handsome the moment he awoke. You lay down in your armour, lord!' he said.

'It seemed the quickest way to get some sleep,' Satyrus said with a rueful smile.

Someone put a hot cup of wine into his hands and he drank it down, followed by a full canteen of water, and then he put his shoulder against the sternpost and helped get *Black Falcon* off the beach and into the hissing surf. His feet were wet, and then his legs, and then the hull was afloat and alive. He wondered if he could find the strength to drag himself aboard.

But he found the power to turn and sprint down the beach to where Diokles had his ship ready to launch. Satyrus stood under the stern in the blood-warm water.

'Diokles!'

'Here, lord.' The navarch was at his own steering oar.

'Let me decide if they are friend or foe. If I go in to the beach we all go, fast as thought. Land *everyone*. The Tanais way,' he finished, with a smile.

'I hear you. War cry?' Diokles asked.

'*Tanais*,' Satyrus said. 'If I've got it wrong and they're friendly, *Tanais* ought to clear the whole thing up. Otherwise, I want prisoners.'

Diokles was invisible even an arm's length away – just a bearded shadow – but Satyrus had the impression of a frown. 'We'll try,' Diokles said.

'Stay under my stern until I make my move,' Satyrus said. He slapped the hull of *Oinoe*, Diokles' ship, and ran off down the beach to his own vessel.

'King's aboard,' Neiron called as soon as Satyrus had his feet on the deck, and the sailors pushed the ship's stern off the beach and the oar master sang the first words of the paean to start the men all together, and they were away.

Fires were scattered across the beach like fallen embers from a fire pot. Too many fires – there were five hulls, not three, and the camp was too chaotic to be Leon's.

Easy to make the decision, but once he'd ordered the marines forward and the rowers armed, he had lots of time to worry that he'd been wrong and was launching a desperate attack against over-heavy odds, or attacking his uncle, and friends would be killed in the dark.

He walked back to the helmsman's bench, where Neiron had the oars himself.

'Five ships,' Satyrus said.

Neiron spat. 'Scum,' he said. 'They ran when they had us at long odds. They'll panic now.'

Satyrus was oddly reassured. 'You think I am doing the right thing?'

Neiron made an odd sound in the dark, which it took Satyrus a long and disorientating moment to discover was laughter, not choking. 'How would I know?' Neiron coughed out, and he laughed again. 'You're the king.'

So much for reassurance. Satyrus went forward. *Black Falcon* had neither tower nor was she fully decked, and Satyrus crouched against the familiar bulk of the marine box over the bow. His left pauldron was badly padded and the bronze was cutting his skin where his aspis sat too heavily on it – and his left arm was too damned tired to hold the shield so that it wouldn't cut his shoulder. And he could just have left the bastards to get away into the dawn.

He pulled his cloak tighter and smelled the whiff of wet cat – and his heart raced, his eyes opened, his arms filled with *power*.

The bow cut into the sand – softly. Neiron had put them ashore at a walking pace.

Satyrus stood up. 'Follow me,' he said to the marines, and went over the side into the water – water only to his ankles, and he ran up the shingle in the dark. There were shouts from the fires. Satyrus was a quarter-stade from one of the enemy triremes, a beautiful shape silhouetted against the enemy campfires, long and low like a lethal snake: a Phoenician design, or perhaps Sicilian – but nothing from his own scratch fleet.

'Praise to you, Lord Herakles,' he said aloud. And ran up the sand.

There were still men asleep. Satyrus disdained to kill them, but he left Charmides and Helios to watch a dozen, and led Apollodorus and Diokles' marines across the beach. Twice they fell into knots of men in the dark – and Satyrus' arm was warm from the spilled blood – but cutting down running men is no battle, and after the second group begged for mercy – for slavery, no pirate could expect aught else – the fight was over. Fear, surprise and daring had done all the fighting for them.

The oarsmen and marines cheered him on the beach like a god.

Diokles embraced him, and Neiron helped him drop his shield to the sand.

'Don't forget it,' Neiron said. 'It won't always be the same, but when you win like this, men don't forget. It's the feeling of invincibility that they remember until they are old.'

Satyrus had to hug him again, and then he ran into the sea to wash as the sun came up. Bathed in salt, he made sacrifice in the new dawn of three lambs, and Helios brought him his best chiton and sandals as if he were going to the temple to pray.

'It's a special day,' Helios insisted.

He could feel the exhaustion just at the edge of his awareness but he held it off, and he walked among his men, handing out portions of meat from the sacrifice and awarding anything he could think of to award. There was good plunder: twenty gold cups, themselves almost a sign from Poseidon for the one he'd thrown overboard off Chios. There was some silver in bars, and more in scrap, and a little gold. Satyrus distributed it all, on the spot – two months' wages for the oarsmen and double that for the marines. The ship and marine officers – sixteen men, all told – received a gold cup each, and most of them were men who'd never so much as drunk from a gold cup. Apollodorus laughed, richer by a farm. Thrasos, the red-haired Kelt who had become Diokles' helmsman, made so bold as to hug his king, and Stesagoras, Satyrus' sailing master, filled his cup with wine from a captured skin, and then walked about filling all the cups.

'We must all give a thanks-libation together,' he said.

Philaeus, the oar master from *Arete*, just kept smiling at everyone in the rosy light.

They poured libations in captured wine to all the gods of Olympia and a few more – Asian gods of the sea and coast, a nymph or two and Nike, over and over. Finally, Satyrus insisted that they drink to Kineas, his father.

Apollodorus shocked him by displaying an amulet. 'I worship your father every day,' the marine said. 'Kineas, Protector of Soldiers.'

So Apollodorus led the libation.

When the frenetic quality of victory was calming, and they were drinking wine rather than pouring it on the sand, Diokles put his arm around Satyrus and pointed with his nose and jaw at four long lines of men kneeling on the beach.

'Now what?' Diokles asked, slurring his words. 'All those shit-eating prisoners.'

Helios, a patient shadow at his shoulder, pushed in. 'Lord, there are things that you should hear. Charmides and I—'

Diokles laughed. 'We have the prettiest marines on the ocean sea, lord. Perhaps that's why the gods love you so much. Look at the fine down on his jaw. And yet his hand is red – no light hand, your boy. A killer.' Diokles laughed again.

Helios tried to ignore Diokles. 'Lord, you need to hear what these men have to say.'

Satyrus nodded. 'Bring them.'

Charmides prodded two pirates up to the officers. 'Tell the king what you told us,' he said.

One of the pirates had pissed himself, and he stank. The other simply sank to the sand in the kind of abject exhaustion that Satyrus could understand all too well.

Satyrus stood straight and walked over to the two of them. 'I swear before the gods that both of you shall live and go free. Speak and know no fear.'

The exhausted man nodded. 'Poseidon's blessing on you. You'd be King Satyrus, then.'

Satyrus nodded.

'Your marines want us to tell you that Dekas is dead, lord. Our captain, Spartes, killed him last night for being a fuckwit. No one made any protest, lord.' The man shrugged. 'And now it appears that Spartes was no better, eh?'

'Tell the king the other thing,' Charmides prompted.

'Spartes told us all last night to make for Cyprus,' the man said. He shrugged. 'I am – was – a helmsman. Thus he told us.'

Satyrus looked at Diokles. 'Cyprus – to join Antigonus One-Eye.'

The man shrugged. 'Name I heard was Plistias of Cos.'

Neiron spoke up. 'Demetrios' admiral.'

Charmides prodded the man with his spear point, hard enough to start a trickle of blood on the man's naked hip. 'And the rest.'

The man looked at his filthy companion. 'Poke him. I've said everything.'

The other man wept. 'They'll kill us,' he said.

Satyrus shrugged. 'I could kill you right now.'

The man sobbed. 'There's six more ships in the harbour at Duria, and more down the coast – a fisherman told us last night.'

Neiron groaned. 'You can't. We can't.'

Satyrus forced his shoulders back, feeling the weight of every scale on his breastplate. 'We must. Ten more ships – even scum like this – could be the end of Menelaeus. We have to make for Cyprus.'

Diokles looked up the beach at the prisoners. 'And them?' he asked. 'Not the slaves – we can free them, or even use them to make up for our dead. I mean, the wide-arsed pirates.'

The words *kill them* actually formed in Satyrus' gullet. He could taste them on his lips like sour wine. Half a thousand pirates – two days' work to row across to Rhodes. Useless offal of humanity – men hardened to evil; rapists, murderers.

He could taste the words, the ease of disposing of them – twenty minutes' bloody work, like a big temple sacrifice, and it would be done. His men would do it – they were *his* this morning the way his other victories, hard fought and bloody, had not always made them his. Today he was like a god. He could order the pirates killed. And then he'd be free to sail to Cyprus. *Every minute might count.*

At his side, as clear as the sun in the sky, stood Philokles. 'Be true,' he said, and was gone.

Satyrus found that his hands were shaking. He spat the taste out of his mouth.

'Take *Oinoe* to Rhodos and get some of our grain ships, empty, and any soldiers that Abraham can spare. Leave your marines as guards. And then get them back to Rhodes.' Satyrus spat again.

Diokles raised an eyebrow. 'Killing them would be faster, and then we could stay together.' He shrugged. 'Look, I know it's *wrong*. But these aren't men. These are animals.'

Satyrus found the energy to smile. 'I agree. But sometimes *arete* makes its own demands, Diokles. If we know we're right and our enemies are wrong—' Suddenly he was confident in the *rightness* of his decision. 'Being right means being *right*. We are the better men. We must behave accordingly.'

Diokles snorted. 'You can be a pious prick, lord.' Then he stepped back. 'I could get it done if you walked down the beach.'

Satyrus shook his head. 'You have your orders,' he said, and his own doubts made his voice colder than he wanted it to be.

Diokles did a sort of skip to keep his balance and threw an arm around Helios. He was drunk, even by his forgiving standards of the sea. 'You'll go off in one ship and *die*. And we love you! Kill the fucking pirates and let us stay with you.' He looked around. 'Go up the beach and see the captives. See the girl who's been raped so many times she can't talk. See the farmer who watched his whole family killed for sport. Talk to them. They'll convince you.'

Satyrus refused to be offended. 'Diokles – get moving. I'll be fine. And *you have your orders*.'

But some perverse sense of duty made him walk down the sand, past the long lines of captive pirates. Charmides came with him, and Helios. He knew what he would find – he'd seen war, he'd seen cities sacked and he'd lived with pirates, when he needed them. He didn't much like where that thought led.

Charmides said, 'Lord, I didn't know there really were men like you.'

Satyrus said, 'Charmides, shut up.' He wondered if Diokles were, at some level, right. But Philokles – he'd been *right there*.

Still he walked towards the former captives – two hundred men and some women who had been taken as rowers or sex slaves or cooks – or all three. Satyrus stopped in the midst of them and motioned to them for silence.

'I'm King Satyrus of Tanais. All of you are free. Would you rather be freed right here, or on Rhodes?' He looked around. Many of these people were broken – but not all. He saw hope and care and despair and rage in as many faces.

No one answered him – or rather, everyone did.

'Silence!' he roared in his storm voice. 'I must sail away before the sun is a handspan higher. There will be Rhodians here in a few hours. My marines will see that every one of you has' – Satyrus looked at Helios and mouthed *twenty drachma*, and Helios shook his head slightly – 'ten drachma to travel home. You must decide for yourselves whether you plan to go to Rhodes, or you will travel from this beach.'

One young woman with a baby at her breast fell to her knees weeping. Other people had other reactions – joy, terror.

Some simply stared at him blankly. One haggard woman patted his cloak in a way that scared him more than the angry men would ever have scared him. Her wits were gone, taken by the gods. Apollo, she wasn't even old. Just broken.

Diokles had followed him across the beach and stood at his shoulder. He pointed at the weeping girl on her knees. 'Pirates did this. And this *thing* used to be a gentlewoman of Lesbos. And this man was a farmer. *Just kill the fucking pirates.*'

Satyrus met his eyes. 'By that logic I'd be best to kill her, too,' he said. 'And the baby – no man's brat. What choice of life has he? *But I am not a god.* Neither are you. I am, however, your king. You are making this something that is between you and me. Obey me.'

Diokles smiled, not as drunk as he had been. 'Had to try, lord. I *really* think you are doing the wrong thing. But I *will* obey. If, on the other hand, you go and get killed away from me, I will personally come to the underworld and pour dung on your shade.' He reached out his arms, and Satyrus embraced him.

And then he turned back to the people on the beach. 'Can anyone speak for the others?' he asked.

A man, a man with a spark in his eye and the accent of education and command, spoke up.

'I was a captive, not a slave,' he said carefully, 'but I did what I could for some of them, and they all know me. I think – if you mean what you say – that they would like to stay together.'

Satyrus looked around. 'Together?' he asked.

One of the men nodded.

The girl with the baby spat in the sand. Through her tears, she said, 'Lord, you think I should go back to my *village*?'

At his shoulder, Helios said, 'Tanais could take them, lord, and they'd be no worse. Maybe better.'

'Apollo,' Satyrus said. 'A ship to Tanais? That'd cost.'

Helios held out his new gold cup. 'I'll pay, lord. *I was one of them, once.* Lord – you have no idea. The shame … the terror.' Helios' eyes filled with tears. 'None of us could ever go home, lord. That world is gone. Who will wed her? Who will take this man in his forge, or on his farm? What of the ones who saw their families killed? Who will understand them?' Helios stood straight.

'Surely people know that the gods love us when we take care—' Satyrus paused. That was what Pythagoreans believed.

Helios cut in – perhaps the first time he had *ever* cut off his master. 'Lord, you may live like that, and the men who are your companions. But peasants would say that she is unlucky. That he is cursed. He lived with pirates – he's a pirate. She's a whore.'

Satyrus looked at the educated man who had made himself their orator. 'Is this ... true?' he asked.

The man nodded. 'Your hypaspist speaks for them better than I could, lord. If you find it in your heart to send them somewhere together, it would be best. Some will die anyway, but some might make new lives. And any who disagree can simply walk away.'

Satyrus felt as if his brain was filled with glue, but he managed to make the wheels turn over a few times.

'Helios, you will see to it that all these people go to Rhodes – in a different ship from the captives. Yes?' He smiled at his hypaspist.

Helios nodded.

'See to it that they are lodged by Abraham at my expense, and add them to my freedmen who will be going as colonists to Tanais. See to all that, and then rejoin Amyntas as a marine aboard *Oinoe* and await my return.' Satyrus smiled. 'Think of this as a way to reintroduce them to life.'

Helios grinned. 'But who will see to you, lord?'

Satyrus raised an eyebrow. 'I lived before I had you, boy. Besides, Charmides never does any work—'

He straightened his shoulders, heartened. Feeling morally good. A rare feeling for a soldier.

'You go to pursue the rest of the pirates?' asked the man who'd been a captive.

Satyrus nodded.

'May I come aboard as a volunteer?' the man asked. 'I'm a capable spearman. And I would dearly love to put iron in a few bellies. And I play the lyre – I'm a musician. I could play for your oarsmen—'

'Do you believe in the gods?' Satyrus asked suddenly.

'Only a fool does not,' the man said.

'Welcome, then. Have you ever taught the lyre?' Satyrus asked. He could see that both *Black Falcon* and *Oinoe* were almost loaded, the loot crowding the gunwales, the prisoners herded together under the watchful eye of Amyntas the Macedonian, who had a spear in one hand and a golden cup full of wine in the other.

'Alexander never gave me a gold cup,' he shouted. 'I drink to you, lord king!'

This must be what it is like to be a god, Satyrus thought.

'Lyre and kithara, too. Some dancing, and some sword work, yes. I teach rich men's sons. Anaxagoras of Athens. Friends call me Ax.'

Satyrus held out his arm, and they clasped. 'Most of my friends are dead,' Satyrus said. 'Most men call me "lord".' He hadn't meant to sound so bitter.

Anaxagoras nodded. 'That's natural, and I'm an obsequious bastard myself. Shall I call you "godlike Achilles"? or perhaps "Alexander come again"?'

Satyrus laughed. 'And the pirates didn't gut you?' he said. 'I mean, you talked like this and lived?'

Anaxagoras shrugged. 'Some people find me entertaining.'

Antigonus One-Eye was seventy-eight years old, a shambling monster of a man, still strong, still quick, possessed of so much energy that men spoke of it in a hush and made signs against the supernatural. His hair was the colour of old steel – the steel of a good sword, carefully maintained. His shoulders were still broad, the sinews that knit his arms to his neck still thick like rope. Men gathered to watch him exercise in the gymnasium.

His son Demetrios had all the godlike grace and beauty that his bestial father lacked: golden curls, a perfect, slim physique. Not for nothing did men call him 'the Golden'. But when his temper flared and his annoyance rose, men died.

The procession had just reached the steps up to the Acropolis of the city. The Temple of Poseidon rose above the steep hill, the largest temple in Miletus and, some said, in all the world. Twelve thousand men and women crowded the steps, restrained in their enthusiasm by another four thousand of Antigonus' soldiers, elite silver shields who had served Alexander. They were old men now themselves, those veterans of Arabella and Issus, Jaxartes and India; the youngest of them was nearly half a century old, and the oldest well beyond that – their shields and hair were silver, but their bodies were iron hard.

The priests – Antigonus had demanded the attendance of every priest in the city – were late. At the top of the steps, Demetrios could see the priestess of Artemis – coldly beautiful, a distant and arrogant figure. Demetrios fancied her instantly and began to wonder what he'd have to do to win her – even for an hour. It was a pleasant enough fantasy, and it passed the time.

'You think this is foolish, don't you, boy?' growled the old man.

Demetrios smiled beatifically. '*Pater*, you are rarely foolish. And you have been right so many times when I was wrong—' the golden god shrugged. 'If you wish us to be kings, let us be kings.'

'Symbols matter, boy. Ptolemy stole a march on us when he had himself crowned. Helped solidify the very loyalties we've worked so hard to break.' The old man coughed into his hand. 'Let us be kings.' He looked back at the procession and the crowds. 'From soldiers to kings. A long climb. Like these endless fucking steps.'

Below them, at the base of the long stoa of columns that ran away down the hill, the place where the richer townsmen congregated, all built and paid for by Antigonus, Demetrios could see a man in a military chiton, running.

'When we finish all this, you take the fleet to Cyprus and I'll get the main army in transports.' Antigonus smiled at his golden son. Subtle as a snake, vengeful, mean, bestial, monstrous – Antigonus was called all of these things, but the one thing the world knew of him was that he loved his son.

The smile that broke across Demetrios' sun-like face suggested that Antigonus' affection was not wasted. 'At last! I hoped we were just waiting for this – that is to say, that's fine, *Pater*. Cyprus?'

Antigonus paused for a moment, savouring his words. Above them, the beautiful priestess of Artemis made a small motion with her hand, infinitely elegant, and a long line of trumpeters stepped up onto a temporary platform. The sound of their trumpets was the sound of elephants and the neighing of horses, and for a moment, Demetrios was in battle inside his head – battle, for which he lived, better than the sighs of women under him and the roar of acclamation from fifty thousand throats.

The trumpets died away, and the echoes returned slowly from the cliffs east of the city, where the Persian siege engines had been placed two centuries before.

Antigonus put a hand on his son's shoulder. 'Cyprus matters. I need you to win there. Scatter Ptolemy's fleet. Because the target is Aegypt.'

Demetrios, used to his father's deep strategy and sudden changes of direction, was nevertheless taken aback. Heads turned – it looked as if the old monster and the young god were having a quarrel: big news at court.

'But ... we've already lost a quarter of the season. And we're no better supplied than when I—' Demetrios was seldom at a loss for words, but he was surprised.

'I have the stores laid in. We supply ourselves from the sea – after you defeat Ptolemy. We use the sea to outflank his defences in Gaza. We move so fast that we're in Alexandria before winter.'

The procession began to move.

'You are brilliant – or mad.' Demetrios smiled, waved at the crowd. 'So that's why we aren't being crowned at Athens.'

The old man nodded to an equally old Silver-Shield – the nod of one veteran to another. 'That's right, boy. I needed the spring to gather grain. When Dekas brings me the Euxine grain, I'm ready.'

'Effeminate idiot,' Demetrios said. He had no time for Dekas.

Antigonus paused, his foot on the top step of the triumphal steps that rose ten times the height of a man from the streets below, a conscious effort to best the steps up Athens' Acropolis. 'Lad,' he said, and turned his head so that the full weight of his mighty stare rested on his son. 'Lad, you must rise above these "likes" and "dislikes". Dekas is not, perhaps, an epic hero. You would not, perhaps, invite him to a select symposium hosted to reward your best men, your loyal friends. But he is *our tool*. His hatred of the Euxine upstart and Ptolemy is the break for which we have waited four summers. Loathe him if you want – but remember that he was sent us by the gods, and he is an instrument of the gods.'

Demetrios hated it when his father spoke of the gods. Demetrios was a modern man – a rationalist. His father's superstition annoyed him. And Dekas was loathsome. Whereas Satyrus of Tanais, the 'Euxine upstart', was a worthy adversary – the sort of man whose measure made you bigger. *Hektor to my Achilles.*

Demetrios managed a small smile, because if he could believe that Satyrus was his Hektor, he was as superstitious as his *pater*. And *Pater* was no fool. 'I will pay Dekas the respect he is due,' Demetrios agreed. 'The priests are waving to us, *Pater*. We should square our shoulders and move.'

The runner in the plain military tunic had almost reached them, though. He was obviously a messenger, and this close it could be seen that he bore one of Antigonus' personal messenger tubes – an iron scroll plated in solid gold, the only badge the runner needed.

'This won't be good,' Antigonus said with a grin for the crowd. 'No officer of mine would send a runner through the crowd with good news. Brace yourself, and don't show it, whatever it is.'

Pater thought of everything.

Demetrios schooled his face and stood with his father. The runner didn't slow for the steps, moving with a lithe grace that equalled that of the priestess of Artemis. He sprang up the steps, his pace unabated, until he arrived at the old *strategos* and extended the tube, his eyes cast down.

'Just tell me, lad,' One-Eye said gruffly.

'The Rhodians and the Euxine prince have routed Dekas, lord.' The runner bowed. It was never good to deliver bad news. On the other hand, the Antigonids were professionals, not petty tyrants.

Demetrios smiled, touched the runner's face with his right hand. 'What regiment?' he asked.

'Spears of Isis,' the young man replied.

'You run well,' Demetrios said, to put the young man at ease.

Antigonus shrugged very slightly, giving nothing away to the crowd. 'Come, my son,' he said. 'Let us become kings together.'

He took his golden son's hand in his and raised it over his head like a man winning an athletic contest, and the crowd roared its approval. Flower petals fell thickly, sweet poppies and roses.

'Fuck Rhodes, and fuck Satyrus of Tanais,' Antigonus said under his breath. 'I'll see them destroyed.'

Pater didn't like to have his plans thwarted. But for Demetrios, it would be all the sweeter that he, and not the useless Dekas, would go to defeat Satyrus.

BOOK TWO

AEGYPT

11

The moment they were aboard, Satyrus and Neiron got the wind under their stern and the bow pointed south, and virtually the entire crew of the *Falcon*, with the exception of the deck crew, went to sleep as quickly as if Circe herself had ensorcelled them. Satyrus slept so long that when he awakened the ship was dark and still – and empty – and he was utterly disorientated for a long moment until he realised that the keel must be fast in the sand.

Charmides was asleep by his back, and the new man – did he really call himself Ax, or was that just his sense of humour? – sat on the helmsman's bench, strumming empty air with his fingers as if he had an instrument in them.

'You are awake,' Ax said quietly.

'I am,' Satyrus said. He felt like going back to sleep.

Ax grinned. 'Your Neiron conned the ship ashore at the edge of day, and they left you to sleep.'

Satyrus managed to climb over the stern, drop to the beach and find his tent. Then he fell on a pile of skins and went straight back to sleep.

Dawn, and Charmides was forcing him awake, and they were away over the wine-dark sea again, sailing south and a little east into the deep blue, as sailors called it. There were no islands now between them and Cyprus, home of foam-born Aphrodite. No islands and no refuge.

But the weather was spectacular; high golden clouds in the morning, and by mid-afternoon a sky of such dazzling, brilliant blue that it might have seemed as if they had sailed across the very top of the world. Satyrus sacrificed the only animal aboard (except for the cat), a rooster, to Poseidon and to Aphrodite for the day and the sailing, and they cooked the rooster over the fire pot, a big clay pot that ships used to carry fire from one beach to another.

Down the wind they flew, and no hand touched an oar from dawn to dark.

They raised Cyprus well before darkness fell, and sailed into a harbour on the west coast – a harbour that had seen its share of pirates, for the only lights were on the mountain, six stades and more away in the clear evening air. But fishermen – a brave lot in any land – came in an hour to sell them lobsters and snapper and mullet, and they made big fires from driftwood and cooked, and Satyrus was asleep again.

But in the morning, the oarsmen had to earn their keep. Now the wind was from the east and east along the coast was where they had to go, and rowing into the eye of the wind was miserable work, the more so as no man aboard was fully recovered from three days of fighting without sleep.

Satyrus passed the day learning the convolutions of Anaxagoras' mind. He was strangely humoured – a man who seemed utterly unafraid of causing offence, for whom a jest was more important than meat or drink. His great-grandfather had been the famous philosopher and opponent of Socrates, and he had many anecdotes about the philosophers of Athens that Satyrus had never heard.

He had been born to an old family, and he'd held one of the priesthoods of Nemesis as a boy and fallen in love with singing and music. And dance. 'I danced in armour at two Panathenaic Games,' he said with pride. 'And I was a chariot runner at a third.'

Satyrus smiled. It all seemed a little fantastical to him. 'Chariot runner?'

'In Athens – you have been to Athens?'

'I'm a citizen. My father was Kineas of Athens.' Satyrus sat back against the shrine of the sea god, which in between sacrifices made a fine backrest for the helmsman.

'Of course. Have you seen the games?' Anaxagoras asked.

Satyrus shook his head. 'I was too young to attend, and then—' He smiled. 'And then I was an exile, a soldier and then a king.'

Anaxagoras' face darkened. 'Kings are all the rage, at Athens.' Then his face cleared. 'At any rate, I was a chariot runner. That means that, dressed in full armour, you leap on and off a chariot moving at speed.'

Satyrus smiled. 'Sounds dangerous.' He paused. 'Have you ever … fought? Hand to hand?'

Anaxagoras shook his head, deflated. 'No. When the wide-arsed pirates took us, I was asleep, and then I was a captive. I've never faced a man across the spear points.'

Satyrus raised an eyebrow. Charmides smiled at the Athenian. 'I have – twice! Terrifying ... beautiful, sir. You will enjoy it.'

Satyrus held out his horn cup to Charmides for a refill. 'No one – and I mean no one I know – has ever called combat *beautiful*.'

Satyrus accepted that Anaxagoras was god-sent. He bore the mark of Apollo, the golden hair of the god, and he was a musician. What more could Satyrus want? And Satyrus had rescued him from pirates, as his father had rescued Philokles from the sea.

'Sometimes things are simple,' Satyrus said, after he had drunk some more wine.

'Almost never,' Anaxagoras replied.

'My father rescued Philokles from the sea, and they were friends for life,' Satyrus said, as the rowers under his feet cursed his need for speed.

'I would wager that there was much more to it than that,' Anaxagoras said. 'Some basic similarity, some appreciation and some shared experience – perhaps shared immediately after the rescue. Let's face it, rescued men rarely love their rescuers.' He winked at Charmides.

Charmides had been listening with rapt attention. 'Why? How ungracious!'

'Perhaps, but human.' Ax laughed. 'Listen, lad, nothing spoils a man's image of himself than being in debt for his life. The myths are full of such stuff.'

'But Philokles was a great man,' Charmides said.

Satyrus looked at the Lesvian boy. 'How do you know that?' Satyrus asked. 'I mean, you have heard the older men speak of him?'

Charmides shook his head. He looked away, and then looked back, and he was blushing. 'He fought for some time on Lesvos.'

Satyrus nodded. 'Yes, of course. That's where he was before *Pater* met him. Mythymna.'

'If this Philokles overcame self-love to love his rescuer, he was a noble man indeed. Are we talking of Philokles the philosopher? Of Alexandria?' Ax looked interested.

'My tutor. And one of the noblest men who ever lived. But you, sir – are you ungracious? I rescued you, and you seem to take it in good part.' Satyrus smiled. It was a pleasure to have someone to tease.

'I think it only shows how very noble I am,' Anaxagoras said with a slow smile.

'I think you spent half an hour setting me up for that line,' Satyrus said.

'Yes,' Ax said, and grinned.

A day of rain, and they rowed east along the coast, still into a head-wind, and made less than two hundred stades. Satyrus was tempted to go ashore and take a horse, he was so impatient to get to Menelaeus of Alexandria.

But off Lampasdis, where the shrine of Aphrodite towers over the sea, he found two ships moored for the night – his own *Marathon*, and *Troy*. And there was better to come; Sandakes, the Ionian mercenary who had *Marathon*, twirled his oiled moustache and pointed east.

'*Arete* is in the next bay with *Plataea*,' he said.

Satyrus went to bed easier at heart, and awoke to command a squadron of powerful ships. He moved all his officers back to *Arete* in the morning, and dark-visaged Aekes, the current navarch of *Black Falcon*, pretended to be angered by the exchange.

'All those tall decks!' said the short man. 'I could walk in the oar lofts without bending over!'

But the way his eye passed over the *Falcon*, he was clearly happy to return to his own ship, and to be free of the responsibility for his very expensive temporary command.

Laertes, Apollodorus' second, had exercised the heavy engines every day they'd been apart, firing wooden billets to save the iron bolts.

'How'd they beat us here?' Satyrus asked Neiron.

'Aekes guessed we'd go for Cyprus,' Neiron said. 'He's a good man.'

The next day he pushed them as hard as he could, still into the wind, but he was nearing the seat of war, and the requirement to keep his rowers in shape to fight prevented an all-out effort to reach the anchorage at Cyprian Salamis, where all the fishermen and the rumours agreed the two enemy fleets were anchored – that of Ptolemy, to help his brother who was laying siege to the city, and that of Antigonus One-Eye, who was trying to save the city or at least trap a portion of Ptolemy's ships.

That afternoon they spotted a merchantman – which proved to be the last of three vessels, a trireme and two big grain ships. Satyrus thought for a moment and decided that his need of information outweighed his need to arrive, and he gave chase.

The trireme fled as soon as she saw them, making no attempt to protect her consorts, and Aekes vanished over the horizon in pursuit. *Marathon* and *Troy* picked up the grain ships – they couldn't sail against the wind, and the Bosporans were downwind and they never had a chance. They were Asian ships from Tyre, laden for Antigonus' fleet, and Satyrus took them with private glee – big grain ships were worth a fortune in the Euxine, if he could get them home.

The next dawn brought *Black Falcon* with her foe under her stern, a small trireme, pretty with new paint and decoration and a shrine to Ba'al in the stern galley. Satyrus put a skeleton crew of rowers aboard out of the mighty *Arete,* and led the way around the long point of Cyprus and south again to Salamis.

They raised the headland, with the largest temple of Aphrodite on the island, just a little after the sun crossed the top of the sky, and Satyrus breathed a deep chestful of air in relief to see the black hulls drawn up in three places – sixty ships of Menelaeus under the walls of the town; further west at the camp of Antigonus at least a hundred hulls, and some great ships, and still further west in the fortified camp of Ptolemy Sator, the King of Aegypt.

Three fleets. Hundreds of ships. He was not too late.

He was not too late, but as soon as he saw the might of the armament against them, he felt as if a piece of cold bronze had been pressed against his back.

'I count—' Satyrus said. He paused. They were well out from the shore, and Plistias of Cos seemed not to feel they were worth his trouble. Not a single ship left his anchorage. 'I count two hundred and sixteen hulls. Nineteen penteres. And something that looks bigger yet.'

Neiron had Thrasos at the steering oars while he counted. 'Two hundred and eleven, by my count. But aye, lad – yon's a monster, and no mistake.'

They stood in shared and silent contemplation of the vastness of Antigonus' preparations, and then they were racing along the beaches held by Ptolemy. Ptolemy had fewer ships, even with his brother's force in the town, and smaller ships, too.

'I wish now we had *Oinoe*,' Satyrus allowed himself to say. The big fourer was almost as powerful as *Arete*, and Ptolemy was clearly short on capital vessels.

'Where is the rest of the Aegyptian fleet?' Satyrus asked.

'Where in all the seas did Antigonus get so many ships?' Neiron asked.

'Rhodes should be here,' Satyrus said. 'Fifty ships of Rhodes would break Antigonus for ever.'

'Hmm,' Neiron said. 'If we win. Not a risk Rhodes would want to take, I think.'

'If Ptolemy wins, there will never be a siege of Rhodes,' Satyrus said. 'By the gods, Neiron, we've shattered the pirate fleet and now, with the favour of the gods and a little luck, and some sea room, we'll see Ptolemy do the same. And then we can go home!'

'Aye, perhaps,' Neiron said.

Ptolemy looked older. He had just a fringe of hair on an otherwise polished head, almost like Panther of Rhodes. His lips still curled automatically in a sneer (which belied his pleasant disposition) and he had liver spots on his hands – and wore a diadem.

'I suppose we're all kings, now,' he said in greeting. 'It seems just a few summers ago that I sat in Alexander's tomb and told you the story of his life. And now you are a king.'

'Well,' Satyrus said, kneeling, 'I'm king over some horses and sheep. I can bow to you without shame, mighty lord of Aegypt.'

Ptolemy rose and embraced him. 'I never really thought you'd take the bloody place, boy. But you did. The only victory for my side in this gods-cursed war, in four years. I hear a rumour that you have fought the pirates this summer.'

Satyrus provided a précis of his squadron's activity.

Amyntas, Ptolemy's admiral, nodded along. 'You beat them – but how many did you destroy?'

Satyrus counted aloud. 'Sank four. I took five more myself, and sank another pair over the next few days. I can only hope that Leon and Panther took more.'

Amyntas nodded. 'I hope so, too. But you must admit that it is possible that another thirty ships could join Plistias over the next few days.'

Satyrus shrugged. 'It could be so. But equally, the rest of my squadron could come in. Diokles will rally any ships he found at Rhodes. He should only be a day behind me – two at most – and he may not have met the cursed headwind that pushed against us all the way along the coast of Cyprus.'

'My lord, with all due respect, I must deal with the war as it is set before me. With your four ships – your beautiful penteres – we are closer to even than we have been yet. One hundred and ninety-four to two-hundred and seven ships that will stand in the line of battle.'

Amyntas raised his arms to Ptolemy of Aegypt. 'I do not feel that we can risk waiting for more of Lord Satyrus' ships. We could just as easily see thirty pirate ships sail in to join Plistias tomorrow noon.'

Satyrus couldn't argue the odds. 'My crews are tired,' he said.

Ptolemy grinned ruefully. 'Offer them hard cash,' he said. 'Tomorrow, we throw the knucklebones.'

12

'Hulls are wet,' Neiron complained as they got aboard *Arete,* the new-minted sun a red disc on the horizon.

'Pardon?' asked Satyrus.

'All of Ptolemy's hulls are dry. Light. We've been in the water four weeks straight – heavy. We should have a day or two to dry the hulls.' Neiron shrugged.

Satyrus watched his oarsmen pushing the heavy hull into the water, one step at a time, as the oar master tapped out their pushes on a small drum, very like the tambours that temple priestesses used.

'I don't much like the look of the weather to the west,' Neiron said. He scratched his beard. 'Lord, I have a very bad foreboding about today.'

'How about *not* sharing that with the rest of the crew?' Satyrus said. 'We're outnumbered, but not badly. Ptolemy got a messenger to his brother in the night, so all we have to do is rendezvous off the breakwater and our numbers are nearly even – holy Demeter Mother of Grain, what's that?' he said aloud, running to the leeward side.

There were new ships on the beach, over where Plistias of Cos had his camp. Fifteen or more new ships, all beached together, hulls glistening in the new sun, black with tar, and among them a giant hull like a vast wooden tortoise.

'Thetis' shining tits, that thing is enormous.' Neiron whistled. 'Quarter of a stade. More. Zeus Sator, stand by us.'

Satyrus watched them launch it. Men crawled over the hull like ants, and long lines of men pushed with poles.

'Herakles,' he said.

'I've never seen a ship so large,' Neiron said.

Underfoot, their own ship was suddenly free of the land and took on a life of its own, and men began to pile aboard up the rope ladders trailing the hull on either side, climbing in disciplined rows and racing for their oars. Launching and landing were the hardest manoeuvres for big ships, and the custom was increasingly for such ships to moor off the beach and not to land.

Anaxagoras came up the ladder and sprang down into the helmsman's station. 'Good morning, lord king. And Neiron, great councillor, tamer of horses.'

Neiron, whose love for the *Iliad* Anaxagoras had discovered, swatted him with his free hand, but Satyrus smiled. 'Are you the old horseman, Nestor?' he asked.

'Wait until you are my age and younger men mock *you*,' Neiron said.

'Zeus *Saviour*!' Anaxagoras said, as Charmides came up the side. 'Please tell me that leviathan over there is on our side!'

Satyrus shook his head. 'I'm afraid not. My guess is she's Demetrios' flagship. I assume the golden boy sailed in during the night, meaning that we are now outnumbered,' he paused to calculate, 'somewhere around two hundred and twenty against one hundred and ninety-five.'

Anaxagoras looked at the enemy beach from under his hands. 'Is that bad?' he asked.

'Be still for a bit, sir,' Charmides said. Neiron and Satyrus were rattling orders at the deck crew. Almost alone of all the ships launching, the *Arete* had her foremast up and rigged, and Satyrus called to Stesagoras to hoist the foresail.

Under the stern, a runner was shouting.

'Lord,' Charmides tugged at Satyrus' chiton. 'Lord – a messenger.'

'Summons to a command meeting,' Satyrus noted. 'Send a boat ashore for me, Neiron. Charmides – on me, no arms. We may have to swim.' Satyrus leaped up onto the handrail and caught the ropes of a trailing ladder, swung out and dropped to the beach. 'Why couldn't we have our meeting before I had my ship afloat?' he asked the gods, and ran off down the beach, Charmides at his heels.

Amyntas – one of hundreds of Amyntases who served in the various Macedonian armies of the world, and known as Amyntas of Alexandria to his subordinates – stood at a table in Ptolemy's tent with a chart of the bay of Cyprian Salamis. He had a pair of dividers in his hand – a tool Satyrus had seen only in the hands of architects.

'Three bodies – three commands. All of our heavy ships in the centre, to match their heaviest – Demetrios apparently came in the night and he has an eighter. An octareme. May Poseidon roll the cursed thing in the surf – it's larger than any ship we have, and twice as heavy as our heaviest sixer. One of our lord's spies says it mounts *twenty* engines of war.'

Ptolemy spoke up from his golden chair. 'Amyntas, you're here to command us, not to demoralise us.'

Amyntas shrugged. 'This isn't the time for horse shit, either, lord. Very well. All our heavy ships in the centre – you too, Lord Satyrus. Sorry to split you from the rest of your ships, but I can't afford to put a single heavy ship on the flanks. Very well, the fastest ships with the best crews – Meleager's, and young Satyrus' triremes, and all the old fleet ships with professional crews – in the right wing. And when we link up with your brother, lord – with Menelaeus, then he'll form our left wing, closest to the beach. Our tactics must be simple, and antique. Ship for ship, our enemies have heavier ships, more marines, more towers and more engines. So we must fight the Rhodian way – the Athenian way. With rams and oar rakes and rapid flight. No closing. Once we start locking up with grapples, we're lost.'

Satyrus was not happy – was, in fact, deeply unhappy – with being split away from the rest of his ships. In effect, his beautiful *Arete* was being sent to live or die at the whim of strangers. But he had to admit that in every other way, Amyntas, a man he had never liked, was giving a sound plan based on a rational appraisal of the enemy.

Satyrus raised his hand.

Amyntas ignored him for a moment, but when no one else had a question, he nodded.

'How do we stay away?' Satyrus asked. 'We have to go at them, if only to pick up Menelaeus.'

Amyntas tapped his dividers on the table. 'That part will be touch and go – especially if Plistias tries to keep us apart.' He shrugged. 'Watch the king's ship for signals. We'll back water when we get close to them – perhaps draw them off the land.'

Satyrus wanted to ask if all of them were well enough trained to back water for an hour. Only a few years before he'd watched Eumenes, his enemy, lose all cohesion – and his crown – because his ships could not back water together. But it wouldn't do to speak out.

Ptolemy leaned forward. He looked older, all of a sudden. 'How do we form? In columns?'

Amyntas shook his head. 'Too unwieldy; too big a fleet. I wager that Plistias does the same – forms lines off the beach. I'll have Phillip Croseus form our right with the fast ships, and command it, while I arrange the centre. I've written out the order of ships, from beach to open sea. Check the list and take your places, gentlemen.'

Satyrus found that his warships – *Marathon*, *Troy* and *Black Falcon*, had been given positions at the very rightmost, or seaward, edge of the line. It was flattering – Amyntas was no fan of Leon, nor of Satyrus, but he was admitting that their crews were the best.

Satyrus himself was right in the centre, four hulls to beachward of Ptolemy himself, in a fine, enormous sixer. He had a great red cloth flapping from a pole on the stern, marking the flagship – another recent innovation.

Satyrus found Neiron holding *Arete* just off the beach. Satyrus stripped his chiton over his head and swam out, grabbed the ladder and climbed aboard. Charmides went below and returned with towels.

Satyrus grinned at Neiron. 'That felt good.'

Neiron shook his head. 'Pray it's the only swim we have today. What's our station?'

Satyrus spat over the side. 'We're with the king,' he said. 'A place of honour, no doubt, but Akes and the rest are four stades off at the top of the line.'

Neiron nodded. 'Lucky them. We're with the king?' he asked. His face grew very still. 'In the centre – where the fighting will be hardest.'

Satyrus looked around. He had no wish to dishearten his men. 'Amyntas is backing water after we're close to the enemy,' he said.

'With this lot?' Neiron asked quietly.

Satyrus shrugged. 'Let's not wish ourselves ill. Our fleet is made up mostly of Alexandrian professionals and a handful of mercenaries. We all speak the same language, and many of them – many of us – have sailed together before.'

Neiron nodded. 'Aye, lord, and Plistias has a horde of Asiatics and Cilicians and Phoenicians. But he has some big ships. And if he keeps it simple, it'll be hard for us to win.'

Satyrus shrugged again. 'Plistias is not an innovator. He'll form up in two lines and come for us, and try the contest with the gods. *If* we can back water and *if* Menelaeus comes out on time, we'll do well. Remember, Neiron – for all our griping. We don't have to win. We don't even have to stay even. Plistias has to score a *sweeping* victory.' Satyrus grinned.

Anaxagoras, who had remained silent throughout, spoke up. 'Why? Pardon me – I'm a novice at war. But a victory is a victory, surely.'

Satyrus shook his head, and so did Neiron – so exactly simultaneously that other men on deck laughed aloud.

'No. Look at the bigger picture. Antigonus is on the attack. He has risked a great deal to build this enormous fleet. Now he must destroy our fleet – and our ability to resist him at sea. Unless we're wrecked, he can't proceed against either of his two main objects – Alexandria or Rhodes.'

Neiron smiled – a rare enough expression for the man. 'And since we defeated the pirates, it is worse for them.'

Anaxagoras said, 'But this is as complex as a dance! Why worse?'

Satyrus turned aside and issued a string of orders as *Arete* passed along the rear of the first line and behind the royal flagship with her great red banner, and he began to count hulls. The line was forming well – there was none of the chaos he had feared. In fact, the Alexandrian fleet, for all of Ptolemy's legendary parsimony, was well trained, and his rowers appeared well fed, fully paid and in good spirits. Satyrus felt his own spirits rise. His experience – not as wide as Neiron's or Diokles', but he had a few years behind him, now – was that a fleet that formed well would fight well.

Behind his shoulder, Neiron explained.

'Worse for them because the pirate fleet effectively functioned to keep Rhodes out of the war,' the older man said. 'Antigonus is a subtle bastard. He uses the pirates to isolate Rhodes, and he uses diplomacy and the Rhodians' own conservatism to threaten them into staying clear of joining Ptolemy's alliance outright. But with the pirates scattered, or better, the Rhodians may decide to come in, with sixty ships – ships better, frankly, than anything either side here has to offer.'

Anaxagoras grinned. 'It's like the plot of one of Meleager's comedies,' he said.

'It's only a comedy if we win,' Satyrus said.

*

The Alexandrian fleet formed first. Satyrus had the *Arete* in line early – and with lots of time to wait. He walked up and down the decks, looking at the stacks of bolts for the machines, the spare oars in racks, the full water jars. He walked down onto the oar decks, chatting with his rowers – he'd drunk wine, by this point, with many of them, and they were no longer a sea of alien faces in the murk of the thranite hold but men he knew – funny, sad, outrageous, lewd, or plain. His number two thranite, hard against the bow, was called Kronos, as he was old enough to remember the birth of the gods and still hale enough to row.

'Good morning, Grandfather,' he said, and got a laugh from all the men.

Rowers had to be nervous, going into action, especially down here on the bottom benches, where the first they'd know of defeat was the water running in to cover their faces. They rowed right at the water line – *down in the farts*, as the old-timers liked to say. They received the lowest pay, on most ships – although like the Rhodians, Leon and Satyrus paid their thranites the same as the other oarsmen. A ram that penetrated the hull would kill the thranites instantly, and more would drown, whether the ship survived or not. The other rowing decks were not so dangerous. Many captains used slaves in the lowest rowing deck.

'We're in the middle of the line, near the King of Aegypt,' Satyrus shouted into the gloom. 'We'll go forward for a while, and then we'll back water. That's the most important manoeuvre in the whole battle – and not a reason for any man down here to worry. We're fighting the Athenian way. For those of you younger than Kronos, here, that means we try to hit and run.' He nodded at the silence. He always found it better to tell his men – on land or sea – what to expect. 'Remember that all of our lives are bound together. I won't abandon you. You, in turn – *keep rowing*. If your hearts are good, we'll drink together on the beach and count more silver in our caps. Understood?'

He gave the same speech on the second deck and the top rowing deck, too. It was just as spontaneous each time – he'd had good tutors – and every time he got a growl of approval from his rowers.

On the main deck, he found Anaxagoras playing an odd lyre for the top-deck rowers. It was a heavy instrument, the base made of wood but covered like a drum or tambour in sheepskin, so that the notes resounded. It had a harsh, military sound, and the Athenian was playing the hymn to Nike over and over, and men were singing.

'Hail, Orpheus!' Satyrus said.

Anaxagoras smiled and kept playing.

As Satyrus stopped to listen, Stesagoras came aft from the bow. 'Lord?' He seemed unusually hesitant.

'Speak your mind,' Satyrus said.

Stesagoras fingered his beard. 'Neither Neiron nor I think much of the weather, lord. And ... I do not seek to anger you, but we're in the *centre*. If all does not go well – We're lost.'

Satyrus managed a smile. 'Tell me news, Sailing Master.'

Stesagoras sighed. 'I'd like to run heavy ropes to the foremast head. Big ropes – like anchor cables.'

Satyrus stepped away from the lyre player and looked up. 'Why?' he asked.

Stesagoras looked around for support. 'I think – that is, Neiron and I both think – it'll keep the mast stable if we have to ram. Or if we are rammed. Even if we have the sail up.'

'Aha!' Satyrus could see it. 'Especially if two of the ropes run right aft along the sides. You'll have to be careful to keep clear of the engines. But yes – and another stay made fast forward to the ram. Make it so, Stesagoras.' He was still looking up. 'And while you are at it – sling a basket from the masthead, like the Rhodians do. With the new cables, the mast will surely support the weight. And put an archer or two in the basket.'

Stesagoras smiled. 'There's a thought.'

'Who knows?' Satyrus asked the gods. 'A lookout might tell us something good.'

Another hour, and still the Antigonids' second line was struggling to form. Stesagoras had had the foremast down on deck, laid down the middle of the top deck, and the whole of the deck crew had been employed pounding iron staples into the crown of the mast and then running cables round and round. The fire pot was brought out – carefully – and a pair of bronze loggerheads heated red hot, to put hot pitch over the newly roped masthead.

Anaxagoras played for them – songs of horse races and symposia, until they were ready to raise the mast, and then he played an old

Spartan marching song with a heavy beat and the mast went up as if Apollo himself had lifted the new cap between his great fingers.

'That'd be why Orpheus was so popular with the Argonauts,' Neiron growled.

Satyrus had seldom seen any unit – on land or sea – with so little in the way of jitters before a fight. He himself got nerves that came in waves – he'd be deep in the process of pulling a rope, or helping lace heavy leather to the basket so that the two archers there had some protection from their rivals – and then he'd look over the side and his heart would beat faster and his mouth would go dry.

But the music would carry him out of it, either because of the natural tendency to sing along, or because the man's playing was *so good*.

'He's god-sent,' Satyrus said.

Neiron nodded. 'I agree,' he said. 'And how often do I say that?'

They shared a laugh while the mast went up, and then the new ropes were pulled taut by forty sailors and all the marines, taut as bowstrings, and lashed to the heavy posts that held the fighting rail. It looked ugly as dung on a dancer, but the mast appeared as solid as if it had been planted like a seed, and the leather and tar-coated basket rose on pulleys into the masthead without the heavy oak pole giving so much as a creak.

'Your lyre is the best new weapon on this ship,' Satyrus was just saying to Anaxagoras, and the man was beaming in response, when the masthead called.

'Lord Satyrus!' called the men in the basket. Even thirty feet above the deck, you could see that they were excited.

'You're safe enough, lads,' Satyrus called. In fact, their basket swayed with every movement of the ship, but they were volunteers and had each been promised a ten-drachma reward.

'Enemy's all formed up!' the lead archer called down. 'And – there's a big squadron rowing *away*.'

'You should get into your armour,' Charmides said at his shoulder. 'Lord – the king is signalling the advance.'

Satyrus stood for a second, paralysed – but surely the advance would be slow, and followed by backing water and retreat. Lots of time to get into his armour. 'Put young Orpheus in armour, lad,' he said, pointing to Anaxagoras. 'I don't want him going to this dance naked – he may find that his partner's not as cooperative.' Then Satyrus leaped for the stays that held the mast and started to climb, hand over hand, praising Poseidon that there'd been insufficient pitch to coat the new standing rigging and he wasn't smearing himself black.

He climbed to where he could hold the lashings of the mast and brace a foot on the archer's basket, which made it rock a little.

'Leto Mother of the Archer,' Satyrus muttered.

The apparent confusion of the Antigonid front line was a sham. Now he could see over the first line. In the second line, the gigantic turtle-ship held the very centre – his impression was that it was larger than an eighter – perhaps even a tenner, though he'd never heard of such a thing. But it was not the giant war machine that drew his attention, but a squadron – fifteen ships – rowing *away* from Plistias' second line, headed north and west toward Menelaeus. They were all big ships. He counted fifteen – fifteen quadremes and penteres, all in a crisp line abreast.

Menelaeus had sixty ships, but they were all smaller ships, in the old Athenian style, undecked triremes and such. He was just forming – late to the dance, as Neiron would say.

'Good eyes, gentlemen,' Satyrus said. 'Listen – when we close, you two shoot down into the enemy command deck. Nowhere else. Don't waste a shaft on sailors. Marines and officers.'

'Wasn't born yesterday, lord,' the senior archer replied. 'You could send up some more arrows, if you'd a mind, sir.'

Satyrus wrapped his legs around the stay and slid – carefully – down the heavy rope, sparing a hand to keep his chiton off the rope where the fine stuff would be ripped to shreds. As soon as his feet hit the rail, he ran aft.

'Another two hundred arrows to the top,' he ordered Apollodorus. 'Then attend me on the command deck.'

'Yes, lord,' Apollodorus saluted.

'He's thinned his centre and sent his best, heaviest ships against Menelaeus,' Satyrus said to Neiron, who had Thrasos at the oars. 'What does that mean, old councillor?'

Neiron rubbed his beard.

'Enemy is advancing!' came the call from the masthead.

'That basket is the best new idea I've seen in ten years,' Neiron said. 'Rhodians think of everything.'

Satyrus turned to Charmides. 'Find the sailor with the biggest lungs and have him pass the word from our masthead to the ships of the centre – so the king gets the word. Enemy is advancing.'

'Foam under their bows!' from the masthead.

'What's that mean?' Anaxagoras asked.

'It means they've already gone to ramming speed.' Neiron clapped his hands. 'I'll take the conn. Give me the oars.'

Thrasos nodded, braced and Neiron put his hands on the oars. 'You have the oars.'

'I have the oars.' Neiron ducked under the big Kelt's arms and was in the helmsman's place.

Close by Satyrus' ear, a mighty voice roared, 'Enemy at ramming speed,' at Hermeaus' *Poseidon*, the next ship beachward from the *Arete*.

Satyrus suddenly realised that the two fleets were closing at the combined speed of a pair of galloping horses and that he was unarmed and unarmoured.

'Charmides!' he called.

The young man was at his elbow, arms full of bronze and iron.

'Arm me!' he said, his eyes still on the enemy line – what he could see of it. His own foresail blocked his view forward.

'Foresail down,' Neiron called, reading his thoughts. 'But brailed up, ready for raising.'

Sailors ran barefoot along the deck – the greatest advantage of the new full decking was the speed with which sailors could react to any part of the deck without climbing over rowers.

Satyrus got his corselet around his waist, and Charmides tied the waist laces, then the chest ties.

'We're going to ram,' Satyrus said to Neiron. 'Too late to back water.'

Neiron watched as the foresail came down in a rush, and suddenly they could see the centre of Plistias' line, a stade away, coming on like a cavalry charge.

Ptolemy and Amyntas must have thought the same, because the king's ship sped up to full ramming speed.

Charmides got the top laces done up under Satyrus' armpit, and Satyrus reached back for the yoke of the cuirass. 'Get my greaves on!' he said. He began to fumble with the ties of the breastplate. 'Herakles, Lord and Ancestor, stand by me.'

Close – very close. He felt the surge as *Arete* went to full speed.

The ship might be heavy, but his men were in top form: well fed, well trained and confident.

Apollodorus was tying the pauldrons to his waist ties. 'You keep commanding,' he said quietly. 'We'll keep you alive.'

'Are the machines loaded?' Satyrus asked.

'How stupid do I look, lord?' Apollodorus asked. 'Heh – don't answer that.'

Satyrus felt the greaves snapping onto his legs. Someone was buckling the silver buckles behind his knees and his ankles.

'Arm plates?' Apollodorus asked.

'Yes.' Satyrus didn't turn his head. 'Neiron – take the nearside one, the vessel closest to *Poseidon*.'

'Aye, lord.' Neiron flicked the oars. 'Thrasos, here – I need your arms. You with the lungs – tell *Poseidon* I'm taking the wide-arse with the green awning.'

The big sailor put his hands to cup his mouth. '*Arete intends to ram the green awning!*' he roared.

'Acknowledged,' the man said to Neiron. 'The helmsman waved.'

'We won't fuck that up, then.' Neiron looked over at Satyrus. 'I think we're in trouble,' he said quietly.

'Punch through their centre and see where we are,' Satyrus said. 'I mean it, Neiron – *diekplous* and through into the second line.'

Neiron nodded, all business.

Satyrus felt the familiar weight of his harness, bent his arms, crouched.

Behind him, Neiron and Thrasos together leaned against the steering oars.

The men in the masthead shot their arrows.

Apollodorus looked at Satyrus. Satyrus nodded.

'Engines! Fire at will!' he called.

Only the bow engines had clear shots, and they went off together. The deep, ringing *thrump* of a bolt striking their fore hull showed that their opponents had heavy engines, too.

Half a stade.

Satyrus turned to Charmides. 'No second chance now. Every armoured man to go with the marines. Apollodorus – if we board, do it like lightning, get the thing done and back aboard.'

'Aye, lord.'

Satyrus ran forward, the straps on his greaves a little too tight and cutting at his ankles. Too late now.

Too late for a lot of things.

'Marines! Brace!' shouted Apollodorus, and the forward engines fired again, together, racing to be first.

To port, the king's ship was a ram's length ahead, aimed at the largest ship in the enemy first line – an octeres that was, timber for timber, virtually identical to the king's. They struck, bow to bow, in an explosion of timber, a storm of splinters and a hail of arrows. Then Satyrus put his own head down, caught his cheekpieces and pulled them together and fastened the toggle at his throat.

The impact wasn't the greatest he'd ever felt – in fact, while it pitched him into the back wall of the tower, it didn't throw him off his feet. Above his head, the archer captain chanted orders as his men nocked and loosed and nocked and loosed again. *Arete* carried a much heavier contingent of archers than most ships: twenty men, most of them Sakje, with fluid recurved bows of horn and sinew and barbed arrows tipped with bronze. The Greeks were Alexandrians or Cretans, with heavy bows that shot long arrows capable of punching right through bronze.

The return volley from the enemy tower was late, and weak.

'His bow's crushed!' came the call from the tower.

Satyrus, his blood up, ready to repel boarders, felt a sag.

Neiron made the hand signal for the rowers to reverse benches, and the oar master gave a great cry.

'She's going to sink!' called a marine, and then the enemy came at them in a rush – fifty marines, crossing in three places where the bow towers were locked together.

Satyrus got to the starboard rail before the first enemy marine. Luck – good or ill – left him alone except for Charmides, as the enemy were trying to jump down into the waist behind the tower, where he was, instead of going to meet their peers; a tactic born of desperation.

Satyrus speared the first man in the helmet – a clean thrust into the very front of the man's horsehair crest – and his head snapped back, he lost his grip and he was gone over the side.

'Cut the grapples!' Satyrus roared at Charmides. Charmides ignored him, roared a war cry and threw his spear. It hit the second enemy marine just above the nose and the broad blade collapsed his face – and he took Charmides' spear over the side with him.

'The grapples!' Satyrus bellowed, and now he was facing three men – he took a big risk and attacked the middle one, counting on the tendency of all men to want to be sure of their footing before making a lunge. His thrust went in over the man's shield and just ticked the side of his unarmoured throat, and he went down. Satyrus was too close, now – no choice but to be wild. He roared, dropped his spear, grabbed the right-hand man's shield in his right hand at the base, and shoved it up under the man's helmet plates, breaking his jaw.

The third man rammed his spear into Satyrus' unprotected back and knocked him flat. The scales held the point, but the pain was intense – like a *pankration* opponent's punch to the kidneys. The world went white, then red and Satyrus was dead.

But in the time it took him to think that he was down and dead, he realised that he was still in control of his limbs and he rolled, got his back against the marine tower and pushed against the deck with his legs. A sword rang off his greave. Charmides threw himself across Satyrus and took the spear thrust from overhead meant for his king, and Satyrus sat heavily, his back against the marine tower, with Charmides' weight on top of him.

Apollodorus roared, and the *Arete*'s marines charged out of their tower. Charmides squirmed.

An Antigonid marine stood over them, raised his spear and grinned from sheer lust of killing.

Anaxagoras stabbed him from behind, a brutal, short spear jab, and then spun like a dancer, putting the butt of his spear into the next marine, using the power of his rotating body, and though his shaft snapped the enemy marine went down like a tree before a woodsman. Charmides screamed – there was blood flowing out of him – but Satyrus had no time for that, and he threw the boy off his legs and stumbled to his feet.

Hand up under arm – sword hilt – draw – lunge!

Satyrus put his point through an enemy marine's eye. The man fell back over another marine, also dead.

'Cut the grapples!' Satyrus croaked.

Anaxagoras was at the rail, watching his third victim fall away into the sea. He looked up. 'The boy is right. This is wonderful.'

Satyrus vomited over the side, and there was blood. 'See to the boy,' he said.

Swords and axes were slashing at the grapples, and the enemy ship was sinking, his bow ripped away in the first contact – bad timbers, shipworm, bad design – it should never have happened, but the *Arete*'s ram was caught in the sinking ship and Satyrus could hear his own timbers popping.

'Row!' Philaeus called. 'For your lives!'

The last grapple rope parted with a crack like lightning and thunder on a stormy day, and the enemy ship slid – grudgingly – off their ram, and suddenly they were floating free, the oars moving them away.

Satyrus was unengaged, still retching, and he could see an enemy trireme, low in the water from his vantage, coming around the wreckage to ram them broadside or break their oars.

He spat and raised his head. 'Oars in!' he called. 'Starboard side!'

Philaeus heard him, with the help of the gods – and repeated the order. 'Starboard-side oars *in*!' he roared, and Anaxagoras sang it, and the oars came in as if the ship were a machine built by mighty Hephaestos – and the trireme's bronze beak struck low into their unprotected side and the timbers held.

Idomeneus raced his archers to the engaged side. 'All together, now – *loose*!' he called, and twenty arrows fell into the trireme's unprotected rowers. Then all the starboard-side engines fired together – one, two, three, their bolts going downwards at point-blank range, down through men and benches and probably right through the bottom of the enemy ship.

The enemy trireme tried desperately to back water, but he had twenty dead rowers or more, and his oar loom was in chaos, his oar master nearly cut in half by an iron bolt thicker than a man's arm. The trireme wallowed in the swell, and Idomeneus ordered another volley right at Satyrus' ear.

'The king is finishing off his adversary,' Apollodorus said.

Satyrus felt his head clearing. 'Get me water.'

'Wine?' Apollodorus asked, and thrust a canteen under his nose.

Satyrus drank, spat and drank again. 'Good wine,' he said.

'Why die with the taste of cheap wine on your lips?' Apollodorus asked.

Anaxagoras was bent over the Lesvian boy. Satyrus tottered over.

'Alive?' he asked.

'He'll dance again, if the gods will it,' Anaxagoras said. 'I've seen this done – never done it myself. I need help.'

Satyrus crouched by him, and Apollodorus, with two marines, took the boy's shoulders and held him while Anaxagoras searched with slippery fingers. 'Got it!' he said. He had a loop of sinew in his fingers – a piece of bowstring. 'Apollo, brace my fingers. Pull!' he said to a marine, and the other man pulled on the sinew like a poacher pulling a snare – and shook his head.

Blood spurted across the deck.

Satyrus looked up. Neiron was calling – pointing.

'Sailors, here!' Satyrus called, and gave Charmides' feet to two men. He loved the boy, but he had four hundred men to save.

'It's too slippery!' grunted the marine.

Two more low triremes were coming out of the enemy line. They were warier than the first, but they had the marines to board, at least between them.

'Leave him!' Satyrus called up to Idomeneus. He waved at the stricken trireme under his feet – a ship he could take if he could get ten marines into the hull, but for what?

He glanced up, and saw both of the archers in the masthead shoot – they were methodical, and fast, for men shooting from a swaying basket. The one tapped the other and pointed at something out over the bow.

Satyrus couldn't watch any longer. 'All engines, all archers – that one!' he cried, and his voice broke from fatigue, already. He pointed a spear – whose spear? Where was it from? – at the nearest of the two new attackers, and almost as quickly as thought an iron bolt flashed out and struck the trireme's bow a glancing blow and then it wheeled down the rowing deck. The enemy rowers lost the stroke and fell off to their starboard, and the other ship was coming on alone.

He had time to note that the engines killed comparatively few men. But they killed them in a spectacular, horrifying fashion, so that they sapped an entire ship's morale.

Satyrus stumbled back to the helmsman's position. Thrasos was screaming, down on his stomach, an arrow in his back low and deadly. Satyrus looked to port for the first time in what seemed like hours and saw a big penteres – a ship as big as his own – approaching broadside on. Their archers were shooting across at him. Even as he watched, an arrow screeched off the bronze facing of his aspis and vanished behind his shoulder.

'You have to get Idomeneus to fire at their archers!' Neiron screamed, while ducking under his aspis.

Satyrus shook his head. Neiron couldn't see, but the broadside-on penteres was *not* the greatest threat. The two triremes were. Amidships, the huddle of men over the body of Charmides gave a cry, and men pumped their fists. There was a heavy *crash* as the enemy trireme hit their starboard side, and then all of Idomeneus' men leaned out over the side and shot straight down into the bow of the enemy ship.

'We have to get clear!' Neiron shouted. 'They're concentrating on us! Gods only know why!'

At some level of his tactical thought, the notion that they were matched against five enemy ships pleased Satyrus extremely. But it couldn't last, and the timbers of his strong new ship would not stand for many more ramming attempts, despite all the manoeuvring Neiron could manage and the puny size of the enemy rams. But he blessed the shipwrights, and every obol he'd paid them.

Another volley of arrows came in, hitting his shield like wind hitting a man's cloak in a storm at sea, and two hit his leg on the greave and a third his helmet, so that he staggered.

Two marines appeared from amidships, bearing big shields. 'Apollodorus says to let us protect the helm,' Phillip of Tarsus said. He was an old friend, a veteran of all Satyrus' battles, and allowed the king to feel that he was leaving Neiron in good hands.

Overhead, his masthead archers had switched targets. They began to shoot into the penteres to port – and every other arrow seemed to mark a man down. Even as Satyrus ducked and moved aft, stepping over a shocking number of bodies – Polycrates, dead with a pair of javelins in him – and what was he even doing above decks? Satyrus saw, in his peripheral vision, as the enemy oar master went down, rose to his feet and took a second arrow in the top of his shoulder and fell like a sacrificial victim – and the enemy helm was empty.

The port-side engines fired, point blank – everything was suddenly point blank. They were clearing their opposite numbers, firing into the enemy engines, an excellent strategy and one Satyrus wished he had thought of himself.

He looked down and realised that he was losing blood – in a bad way, flowing out of his groin.

'Shit,' he said, and stumbled.

'Hold hard there, Achilles!' Anaxagoras said, getting a shoulder under his sword arm. 'If you fall, we'll all be too busy weeping to fight.'

'I'm hurt – shit. Look at the blood.' Satyrus couldn't even work out where it was coming from, but his back hurt enough for five wounds. The sight of his own blood made him feel weak.

Arrows hit his shield. Anaxagoras winced and looked down to where an arrow had passed right through his thigh. He opened his mouth and fell silently to the deck.

Idomeneus had switched targets – high in the forward tower, his men had swept all three of the trireme's command decks, and now he was firing volleys into the penteres to port.

Satyrus shot a look over the starboard side. One of the triremes had fallen foul of the other's oars, and they were no threat – at least, not for some long minutes.

Satyrus made his way across his own ship to the port side, but the penteres had had enough. His rowers were untouched, but his top deck ran with blood – an easy thing for poets to sing about, but in this case, the archers and engines had massacred the sailors and enemy archers, and there was no armour to be seen. Someone was telling the rowers to row – but there was no command.

Satyrus looked up at his masthead. 'Where is the king?' he called.

'Moving south. Prize in tow.' Came the reply.

'Where's that big ship? The huge wide-arse?' Satyrus shouted.

'Half a stade north!' they called.

Satyrus turned – and his back hurt. But he wasn't dead yet, and it was time to do more than survive, noble as that seemed against the odds.

Apollodorus. He had his marines formed under the loom of the tower – safe, for the moment.

'Apollodorus – see the penteres? No crew on deck. Fine ship.' Satyrus knew when a little acting was called for. 'I rather fancy her. Let's take her.'

The men whooped.

Satyrus ran aft. 'I'm taking the penteres and turning her around. You go through the hole and head *south*.'

'South?' Neiron asked.

Satyrus nodded. 'If we're winning, you and I will break their line. If we're losing, we're running downwind to our own ships. Either way, we go south. If you lose me, and we're losing, go for Alexandria. Understand?'

'Yes, lord!' Neiron said. 'Go with the gods!'

'Stesagoras!' Satyrus managed to attract his attention. Apollodorus had a dozen men throwing grapples, and Neiron already had the oars out. 'Stesagoras – you and every sailor not required to manage the foresail. And a spare foresail and a yard. And *right now*.'

Stesagoras nodded and ran down a ladder.

Satyrus looked over at the penteres. Even as he watched, Neiron and Philaeus got the oars out – just the aft oars, a miracle of command and control – and laid the *Arete*'s ram gently alongside the enemy's stern, making a path for Apollodorus' marines. They rushed the handful of enemy marines left – one was shot down even as he rose from cover. Satyrus had meant to lead the rush aboard, and instead he was the last armoured man to cross, and there was *nothing* alive on the enemy deck, a deck remarkably like his own, but with only one engine a side, fixed forward, and now wrecked. All this he took in in a glance, and then he had the steering oars in his arms.

Stesagoras crossed after him, and twenty sailors with a great bundle of canvas and a long yard.

'Get the foremast up,' Satyrus said. 'And the sail and yard on it. I need you at the helm, here.' He turned to Apollodorus. 'Storm the oar galleys,' he said. 'Accept no resistance, and tell them that if they row, we'll free them, and if they fight, we'll sink them here.'

Apollodorus grinned – the man was untouched amid the maelstrom, not a mark on him. 'Aye, lord,' he said. 'Give me a moment to *persuade* them, and I wager they'll row as well as any in Piraeus.'

The man charged down the central ladder with all his marines.

The *Arete* had blood running from her scuppers, and one of her port-side machines was a wreck – and from here he could see the damage to deck and rail, and shattered strakes in the hull that had to be leaking water – but Neiron had her under way and moving well, already half a boat length off, scattering the little triremes the way a shark scatters bream.

'I need an oar master,' Satyrus said. 'Stesagoras – who do I take?'

Stesagoras shook his head. 'Laertes is my best, and he's putting up that mast. Patrocles was the big voice when we were coming up to fight.'

Satyrus nodded. 'Well, he's loud. Get him amidships.' He stooped at the stern and spat blood into the water and his eyes caught the ship's name, done in Asiatic Greek letters of gold under the stern planks – *Atlantae*; the huntress, beloved of Artemis, his sister's heroine. Satyrus decided to take this as a good omen, although when he raised his head he saw stars, and he had to spit blood again to clear his mouth of the bitter copper taste.

He decided to let himself believe that there was less blood flowing out of his back – in reality, if it was as bad as he'd feared, he should have passed out. As he was still standing, the odds were he'd live, unless the god of Contagion and Infection struck him with a poisoned arrow. He offered a prayer to Apollo, and another to Poseidon, and yet a third to Hephaestos for the fine construction of his ship – and then Apollodorus was up, breathing like a bellows but grinning.

'Slaves!' he said. 'It's a miracle from Ares, lord!' He embraced his king – under the circumstances, it was an embrace that Satyrus was happy to return.

Slave rowers meant men who would be free if their *new* side won the battle; men with no loyalty whatsoever to their dead masters.

'Listen,' he said. 'Go below – get this right. We're going to back oars for two ship lengths – and then we're going to turn hard to port, port oars reversed. Forty strokes back, port side reverse benches, fifteen strokes all ahead.'

'Forty back, port reverse, fifteen, port reverse, all ahead,' Apollodorus said. 'Ares – I'm a marine, not a sailor.' And he was gone.

The new oar master had a spear. He broke it between his hands to be rid of the saurauter, and thumped time on the deck.

'Row!' Satyrus called. 'All benches back!'

Fear, or passion, or courage – it scarcely mattered, but the rowers were motivated and the ship moved – heavily for five strokes, and then like a bolt from an engine, so that Satyrus realised that his estimate of forty strokes was far too high. But he also knew what changing orders on a raw crew would mean. The stern shot 'ahead', and the ship began to turn to port – simply because his steering oars couldn't correct from the temporary 'bow'. But he was turning in the direction he'd wanted. He was just plunging much deeper into the enemy second line than he'd intended.

It was empty here. To the south, he could see the giant tenner crushing one of Ptolemy's penteres, and turning to engage a pair of quadremes – ships that were otherwise considered heavy, but in this case, hopelessly outmatched. And to the north – ruin. Ptolemy was *not* winning.

But Satyrus had time: the enemy's centre was all but empty, stripped by the ships detached to face Menelaeus and by the failure of the smaller ships to engage *Arete* successfully.

Arete was close – twenty horse lengths to port, just turning to go south. But the gap between them was widening because of the speed of Satyrus' retreat.

Thirty-eight, thirty-nine, 'Reverse your benches!' Satyrus called. 'Still have your wine?' he asked Apollodorus.

Wordlessly, the man put his canteen into Satyrus' hands.

The bow began to swing – too fast.

'All benched for rowing ahead!' Satyrus called. Trying to fight the overswing with his steering oars made his back hurt like ice and fire on bare skin. He'd miscalculated by many degrees of turn – their current course took them right into the side of the distant leviathan, the enemy flagship, which towered above the battle like an elephant over infantry.

The new oar master was on top of it. 'Starboard side – trail your oars!' he roared – no missing that voice. 'Now *row*, you bastards!'

And now they were moving. He was clear of the enemy line and he was moving – right along the sterns of the enemy ships, far too close for comfort. He could do devastating damage – once – with his own ship, but it looked to Satyrus as if the battle had been lost. Upwind, Ptolemy was backing out of the action, covered by the heavy ships of his bodyguard – *Poseidon* was backing water slowly, her engines still firing away into the triremes that *Arete* had crippled. But elsewhere, there was little cheer for the Ptolemy side. Menelaeus had either never come out or been bested, and so the Aegyptian centre had collapsed from shoreward – always the weakest part of Amyntas' plan. To the south, the enemy flag was trying to close the gap to take Ptolemy's flagship, itself desperately backing oars to get clear of the trap.

But as he watched, the foremast in the bow of his new capture began to rise, stayed by four lines running aft. The marines were pulling like sailors – not the time, apparently, for old grudges – and the foremast came up and was belayed as smoothly as if it had been done in a yard.

Neiron was lagging, holding the *Arete* at a walking pace. He was waiting for his king – when Satyrus ranged alongside, his hands white-knuckling on his oars, afraid he'd slip and send his oar loom into *Arete*'s oar loom – Neiron called out across the water.

'Fight, lord? Or run?' he called.

Satyrus leaned on his oars again. 'Give me space!' he called. 'I want to get clear of their sterns!' The enemy was far too close. 'Run!' he called.

Neiron waved.

The *Arete* turned to port and Satyrus tried to do the same, getting his vulnerable starboard side clear of the enemy, but the port-side steering oar snapped under his hand – probably victim to the original collision and the boarding action. Then chaos ensued, his marines trying to find a spare oar in a strange ship, and their new oarsmen afraid – afraid of massacre, of defeat. Neiron fell in to port, keeping station just a quarter-stade distant. Both had their foresails up now, and with the wind in them they began to move well, even for heavy ships.

Satyrus spared time for a glance around. He could see trouble to the south – either there were new ships there, or someone had worked out that he was not on their side. But the rear of Demetrios' fleet was all confusion – the confusion of victory, but no ship challenged them as they began to pull away. Laertes was trying to compensate for the lack of steering oars by trailing the ship's oars, first one side and then the other, but the result slowed the ship and sent them in a lazy curve back under the sterns of the enemy. No ship responded – no ship seemed to notice them.

No ship except the great tenner, the mighty deceres that had started the battle behind the centre. Satyrus assumed that the ship was Plistias' command ship, and he had no intention of engaging. Through no choice of his own, he had to pass close under the stern of the leviathan, and just as he began his pass, wincing to be so close to so much danger, the enemy flagship began to back away from the pair of quadremes that she had engaged – grappling both and boarding them simultaneously, so large was his marine contingent compared to theirs – a hundred men massacring perhaps fifteen on each quadreme, leaving them adrift, with blood running in trickles from the deck edges like a child's attempt to write on parchment where the rowers had been murdered to save time. And the vast weight of the enemy ship backed under control, her oars sweeping like the legs of some ungainly millipede.

Neiron saw the enemy flagship begin to move at the same moment that Satyrus saw it begin to back, and both of them shouted orders at their oar masters. The same orders.

'Ramming speed! All oars!' Satyrus shouted, and Neiron gave the same command.

Satyrus felt the surge of power through the soles of his feet, but the huge enemy vessel was already moving and her stern towered over their side, and the enemy crew was now aware of them – shouting at them, assuming they were friendly – and then realising their error.

Satyrus stood tall at the starboard oar, testing his weight against them. 'I intend to sheer off!' he shouted at his temporary oar master across the length of the deck.

Laertes nodded and shouted down through the amidships hatch at the rowers. Satyrus shook his head. His hands were clenched on the red-painted steering oars like a *pankration* fighter in the last grappling of the bout, and his brow was covered in sweat. There was blood down his right side and back, and he was cold.

Apollodorus stood by him, covering him with his aspis. The enormous enemy ship had archers, and they were firing down at him.

'Thanks,' Satyrus said.

'Why not turn?' Apollodorus asked, grasping the rail.

'Too close,' Satyrus said. 'If I turn to port, our stern is no farther from them. If I turn to starboard, I'm running right down their side – look at those war engines!'

The tenner loomed over them like an adult over a child. Her sides rose like cliffs, and she had the same advantage over *Atlantae* that *Arete* had had over the light triremes. Neiron, a quarter-stade astern, had one advantage, however: all of his starboard engines could bear, and none of the enemy's engines could – yet.

Satyrus caught at the shoulder of Apollodorus' chiton. 'Get the forward engine firing,' he said.

Apollodorus nodded. 'I'll have a go,' he said.

So close.

Satyrus jerked the remaining oar as another marine came up the main ladder dragging an oar. Satyrus managed to nudge the bow off to port and then straighten again – port, and back straight – trying to cheat away from the enemy stern and yet maintain all his speed. And the marine – not anyone Satyrus really knew – had a head on his shoulders. Now he was lashing the new steering oar home against the side with quick, professional knots.

But the new oar was just too late.

'Oars in! Now!' Satyrus roared, and Laertes repeated it instantly. They were too close – there was no way to avoid the collision, and Satyrus could already see – as if it were a maths lesson – that if the enemy ship hit his stern, the two ships would come to rest broadside to broadside, each pivoting on the collision at the stern, crushing their oars between them.

Grapples were flying, now. The deceres wanted them. One thumped home into the stern rail just an arm's length from Satyrus' shoulder, and another into the deck just forward, and then the enemy stern tapped into their stern – the angle was too acute for the enemy ship to damage them, but momentum and the grapples spun them to starboard, so that as the mammoth ship coasted, her rowers desperately trying to get their oars in, the smaller *Atlantae* crashed alongside like a tethered foal against a fence, splintering oars and making a mess of the magnificent enemy ship's paintwork.

Atlantae's oarsmen got their port-side oars in and home before they were rubbing alongside.

A flight of arrows struck all around Satyrus, but by luck or the will of the gods none of them struck him.

Satyrus wanted to curse. He felt a tide of despair, the spiritual kin to the feeling in his back and the cold in his spine, but he shook his head. *We were that close to escape*, he thought. Even as he watched, his newly raised foremast collapsed, splintering, and the sail obscured the whole foredeck. There was a pause.

Surrender?

But there was no surrender in a sea fight. If he'd considered it, the gouts of blood painting the sides of the pair of derelict quadremes just to the east told of what lay in store for him.

Forward, Apollodorus got the one heavy engine on the port side to fire. The whole ship moved when the great bow released, and the bolt went right in through an oar port and appeared to vanish into the hide of a great beast, like a barbed arrow into an elephant.

Just aft, the *Arete* fired all three of her engines together, and the bolts slammed into the deceres. But they had no more effect than a child's sling does against a mad bull.

Satyrus let go of the oars and slipped his aspis onto his shoulder. He felt perversely annoyed to have to die here, in a lost battle for a monarch who didn't deserve his sacrifice. Nothing about the situation was remotely heroic – he was only in this position because he'd mistimed his turn as he backed away from the battle, and it was his own hubris in seizing the stricken *Atlantae* that had brought him to his death.

He got his helmet strap in his right hand and pulled it tight. 'No one's fault but my own,' he said. 'Herakles, stand with me.'

The smell of wet fur was sharp, heady, pungent. The smell heartened him – meant he was still in touch with the other world, the world of the heroes. But it touched him in another way; he'd never smelled the cat so clearly, and he suspected that the veils between his world and the world of the heroes were stretched thin.

I'm going to die, he thought. It was not a new thought, but it had never been so immediate, and he had a frisson of hesitation as he thought of fifty inconsequential things he would like to have done. He thought, among a hundred other foolish thoughts, of Miriam's hips under her chiton. It made him smile.

'Not dead yet,' he said aloud – so loud that the marine at his elbow grinned back.

'No, we ain't, lord.' The man stood taller for a moment, and then settled his apsis on his shoulder and raised his spear.

'Here they come,' he said.

Satyrus wished he could remember the man's name. He'd got a new oar from below, lashed it in place and then got his aspis between Satyrus and the enemy arrows. None of it was the stuff of the *Iliad*, but it was all done fast, and well – the sort of things that could tip a battle one way or another, as completely as a commander's decisions.

There were fifty enemy marines in the first rush – fifty professional soldiers. Apollodorus had his twenty all formed up, and Satyrus and his companion – *he's called Necho*. Satyrus suddenly found the man's name against a welter of recollections. Together they raced forward, abandoning the helmsman's station and apparently fleeing. Enemy marines, clambering over the stern, mocked them.

As they came up to Apollodorus amidships, the marine captain was stating his orders – calmly and quietly so as not to be heard by the enemy.

'Look scared. Hang back. Look unwilling – and when I give the word, charge. Any man who shirks is a dead man.' He paused. 'Look like the crap you aren't!' he said. He pointed aft, past the enemy. '*Arete* is on the way. Show some yourselves.'

This speech seemed to put heart into the marines, who were, of course, used to Apollodorus and his acerbic commentary. No man who followed him would expect a salutation to the gods or a flowery speech.

The enemy marines came over the stern, and Apollodorus let them get aboard – most of them. He played that he was terrified – that his men were hanging back.

He flicked a look at Satyrus, who nodded. Apollodorus was a marine for a living, and Satyrus was merely a king. The nod permitted Apollodorus to keep the command.

'Cowards!' Apollodorus shouted. An arrow from the enemy stern hit his helmet and danced away. 'Stand your ground, stay with me – NOW!' he bellowed, all play-acting gone, and he raced down the deck for the mass of enemy marines.

Satyrus would have said that it was impossible to surprise men in open warfare, on an open deck in the midst of a battle – but the enemy marines were plainly shocked when the whole of his marine contingent rushed them as one man. Perhaps they had been counting on negotiation, surrender, massacre—

Satyrus slammed his aspis into his first man, an officer in an ornate blue and gilt Attic helmet with a pair of feather crests, and the man went down hard, flying back into his file partner and he, too, went down, and Satyrus put his butt-spike into the second man's eye slot, ripped it free and plunged the fighting point, the sharp steel, into the neck of a third man. Then blows rained on his shield like storm-driven waves on a ship's bow – three, four, five and he was rocked back as one blow almost cost him his balance. He thrust his spear out, stabbing blind, his eyes under his shield rim in a storm of pain, and he felt his needle-sharp point cut – slide – plunge like a knife into roast meat, and then the shaft was snapped by a blow from the right, and he had nothing but a bronze butt-spike and a few feet of ash. He blocked an overarm blow from an axe with his shattered shaft – the axe cut away part of his own crest in a shower of blue and white horsehair – and he threw the butt-spike at an unarmoured giant to his front and made the man flinch back, and then Apollodorus was *into* the man, under his guard, stabbing as quickly as thought, once, twice, and the big enemy marine folded and vanished from Satyrus' limited line of sight. What felt like an armoured fist struck Satyrus' helmeted head and he rocked, tottered but did not fall because he was hemmed in so close by other fighters – he stumbled, recovered his balance, blessing long days on the sand of the palaestra. Without conscious thought he got his right hand under his armpit and pulled out his sword, stepped forward and cut overarm at the first man to come under his hand, and hit the man on top of his helmet crest so that he fell, unconscious.

The enemy was roaring, shouting, and marines were *pouring* onto the deck, but Satyrus and Apollodorus has cleared the deck around them, and the first batch of enemy marines were penned into the stern, terrified and yet shouting for aid – for something – *Save the king!* they called to each other and came in again.

Satyrus looked down between his legs and realised that he was straddling the enemy commander, who he had felled with his shield rush in the first seconds of the melee. He only had to look at the man for a second to know him.

'Demetrios!' he said.

'Satyrus the Euxine,' said the man lying under him. Demetrios the Golden grabbed his ankle and threw him in one practised move, and then Satyrus was on the deck, his left arm encumbered by his shield – a wonderful implement in a sea fight, but an impediment in grappling – and Demetrios reached out for his windpipe but Satyrus drove his sword hilt into the golden man's faceplate and the silvered bronze buckled under the blow and Demetrios grunted. Blood fountained. Still, Demetrios landed a heavy blow to Satyrus' throat just as Satyrus got his feet under him and he was rocked back, blackness encroaching on his vision and his breathing ruined, just as the second group of enemy marines charged.

Apollodorus' men met them like gods with a charge of their own

– heavily outnumbered, but desperate and charged with Apollodorus'
quiet courage – and the sight of *Arete*'s foremast looming up close.
Demetrios was back-pedalling like a crab on his hands and knees,
trying to get to his feet. Satyrus managed to cling to consciousness
– Demetrios was leaking blood from under his helmet, but Satyrus
had to assume that was just a broken nose. *That's why they're dumping
every marine they have into my ship*, he thought. *Save the king, indeed.*
He got to his feet, as did Demetrios, just a spear length or two apart.

'You are the man I wanted to fight,' Demetrios said. He drew his
sword with a deadly flourish. Under his helmet, the bastard was grinning. 'The Hektor to my Achilles. A worthy hero for me to conquer
– not poor old Ptolemy.'

Satyrus could see that Demetrios was fresher, and unwounded,
and thought, as if from a distance, that if the man had simply struck
without the Hektor speech, he might have finished the fight there and
then. Satyrus was unarmed – in bashing Demetrios' helmet, he had
shattered the pommel of his sword and the bone hilt was in shards.
Satyrus dropped it, stepped back once and his now empty hand found
a spear stuck in the railing by his shoulder. He pulled the weapon
free, skipped his return speech, set his feet, took a choking breath and
threw.

The spear was not light. It was a full-weight *longche*, the weapon
most marines carried, and Satyrus took a big step forward as he
released, the whole weight of his hips behind the missile, and it struck
the Antigonid king right in the centre of his torso, knocking him flat
to the deck. But kings wear good armour, and Satyrus' best throw
didn't lodge – no mortal blow – but skittered away down the deck.

Satyrus stumbled two paces. The enemy marines from the first rush
were rallied – and then stopped in their tracks to see their gallant king
laid low, again. Instead of a making charge that would have finished
Satyrus, they were gathering around the fallen Demetrios. They were
poised to rush into the rear of Apollodorus' men—

Oarsmen erupted out of the rowing decks, led by Stesagoras swinging a great twin-bladed bronze axe. The axe head glowed like fire
– like fire …

Like fire.

Satyrus gulped another breath while he considered his ludicrous
plan, which appeared fully formed in his head like Athena from Zeus,

and another while Stesagoras cut a swathe through the enemy front rank with the axe, before the inevitable – a spear in his guts and death, for him.

It was one of the hardest decisions of Satyrus' life, because the natural decision – the Heraklean decision – was to throw himself swinging into that fight and die with his newly freed oarsmen, with Stesagoras, a gallant man who had just died like a hero.

But in the flash of Stesagoras' axe, Satyrus saw a way to save them all – a poor chance, but some chance.

He leaped down the central ladder of the ship in a single jump of faith, and fell flat when some outside blow moved the ship. He got to his feet, tried to ignore his own blood all around him on the deck and staggered forward along the central gangway. There were oarsmen here – only the bravest, most desperate, least sane had joined Stesagoras – and he pushed past them, headed forward, past the midships stations, past the forward rowers, past the elite lead oarsmen who sat in the bow, to the tabernacle, the small space under the forward tower and over the ram where the sailors kept the fire pot that allowed them to heat iron or to start fires on the beach. A heavy, carefully protected clay pot the size of a man's head that was full of coals set in leaf mould and bark to smoulder slowly. Satyrus picked it up by the heavy linen wrap which surrounded it – sailors fear fire the way Ares fears Athena – and pushed himself erect, got to the forward ladder and climbed, now two horse lengths *behind* the fighting. He climbed up the ladder on willpower and staggered to the side of the ship, and looked up at the immense height of the enemy's sides – and his heart seemed to stop, to die within his breast. At his most fit, unwounded, he would never have been able to throw the heavy pot over the enemy rail.

He took a shuddering breath and stood straight. An arrow struck his helmet and ricocheted away, and a second hit his chest so hard that he staggered, but the point didn't puncture his armour and he got his feet under him and lifted the pot off the deck by the linen bag, and in a moment of inspiration he whirled it above his head – the pain in his back flared as if the coals had burst into flame there – and he ignored the pain for the movement, the purity of the great circle over his head, and he twirled, his feet moving nimbly, and then, when it seemed right, when the god spoke to him, he let the fire pot go.

It was never going over the enemy rail. For an instant, in the perfect physical moment as he spun, he had thought that perhaps, by the glory of Herakles ... but his throw was too flat.

Too flat, and too hard. No arc at all, and it shot like one of the bolts of the war engines, straight as an arrow across the deck and over the water – into the staved-in oar port where Apollodorus' first missile had hit, so that where the iron bolt struck, all the oarsmen were dead; the pot went through the hole and shattered, spilling coals onto the summer-dried wood of the rowing benches, and there was no one by to pour a canteen of water or wine on them.

And then Satyrus had to turn away, because it had been an act of desperation, and the gods had, at least, seen his throw go aboard the enemy, but there was no result – no smoke, no tongue of flame.

His sword was broken, lost somewhere. His aspis was leaning against the podium where the fire pot usually rested in the tabernacle, close under his feet but as far as Hyperborea.

But there were plenty of them on the deck, and Satyrus scooped up a short, heavy weapon almost like an iron mace, and an aspis, stripped from one of his own dead marines.

Now for death.

He was behind the enemy marines, and he would kill a few of them before they, in desperation, turned on him. He took a great shuddering breath, and his back hurt, and he wondered why it would matter how many enemy marines he killed – he was going to die, and were they not men, as he was? Perhaps better men. Perhaps men with loves, with lives ashore. He was saddened, as he cleared the breastplate from his neck and freed his right arm for one more fight, to discover how little he had to live for. *My sister,* he thought. *And her son. They will miss me, and I them.* Pater, *I have failed, and I am sorry.*

Then, by an act of will, he banished doubt, banished self-pity, shook his head to get the sweat out of his eyes and charged into the rear of the Antigonid marines.

He pulled up short – no need to commit suicide – and slammed his heavy sword into the back of a helmeted head, and the man fell. Satyrus took his time; his shoulder hurt. He put a second man down, and a third, and *now* they were aware of him.

But instead of closing on him in a pack, Satyrus saw, as if down a tunnel, as one of those things men talk about over wine – the real veterans, the men who've stood in the closest fights and who find humour in the horror, or at least room to live with it – the Antigonid marines slide to the right and Apollodorus' men, exhausted, just let them go, as if, by agreement, the vicious fight was over. Each side watched the other like dogs in a dogfight, but no weapon moved, and Satyrus joined the unspoken truce, although he was in a position to reap another man or two. It was, in fact, the oddest moment he had known in combat.

Satyrus stepped up to Apollodorus, who stood, unwounded and magnificent, in the midst of a dozen of his men, the survivors of the fight.

The truce was broken when enemy marines began falling as if cut down with a scythe – arrows, appearing out of the air, took two of them even as Satyrus slumped over, the pain in his back conquering his training so that he could no longer stand erect. *Arete*, game to the end, had ranged alongside, and her archers were reaping the enemy. Even as he watched, Idomeneus leaned far over his own rail and shot an officer who was trying to force another charge.

In the stern of *Atlantae*, a knot of enemy marines, shields over their heads in desperation, were lifting Demetrios the Golden off the deck where he lay as if dead, and passing him up the side of his great ship. Sailors and oarsmen cut at each other – Satyrus could no longer determine which side was winning, but the enemy marines were dying and they had clearly had enough, and even as he watched, the balance was changing. He was sure of it.

'One more charge!' He managed. He raised his borrowed sword, and Apollodorus lapped his shield onto Satyrus'.

As a charge, it wasn't much – they stumbled down the deck in a line, but Satyrus had read his opponents right. Their king was down and the archers were killing them and they had no way to reply. For some reason, all the archery from their own mighty ship had ceased. Satyrus' short shield wall shoved the enemy into the helmsman's station at the stern. One brave man stood his ground to cover the retreat of his comrades – and for a few long seconds he held Apollodorus and Satyrus both, his shield everywhere. He managed to slice Satyrus along the calf, and he got his spear point into Apollodorus' shoulder and then Necho, in the second rank, knocked him flat with his butt-spike and the melee surged over him, but Demetrios was gone, and most of the rest of the enemy marines had escaped due to the superb bravery of one man.

'Cut the grapples!' Satyrus bellowed – or perhaps inside his head he bellowed, because what came out was between a groan and a squeak. But Apollodorus, untouched, heard him, and leaped for the side. Satyrus stayed with him, bludgeoning a wounded enemy sailor to the deck when he tried to resist the marine captain, and Satyrus got his shield up to cover Apollodorus against archery fire.

Twice they moved to cut another hawser, each time sawing at the rope like children cutting string with dull knives, until the motion of the stricken *Atlantae* changed and they were free. Satyrus could not believe that they were alive – that they were afloat – that they weren't taking the hideous damage of the immense line of war engines that hovered over their heads, a horse length away – ten engines on this side alone.

But even as he raised his head from cutting the last grapple, he smelled the smoke. The enemy leviathan was pouring smoke like a wounded beast drips blood – smoke from the entry point forward and more smoke amidships, coming out of oar ports so that the whole incredible beast seemed to leak blood.

'Pole her off!' Satyrus croaked, and Apollodorus repeated the order. Satyrus stumbled from the ship's side, pain forgotten in a surge of hope – real hope. He crossed the deck to the port side and got his hands on the rail. 'Pass us a line and tow us clear!' he called.

'Get off that wreck!' Neiron shouted back. 'Abandon ship!'

Satyrus felt the god in him, and he stood taller, towering over the pain in his back. 'No! Get us a line and tow our stern clear!'

The fire on the enemy ship was burning now, flames visible all along his side, and Satyrus saw a curious change in his own men, exhausted heroes from the fight – they panicked, as if fire was an enemy too dreadful to be faced – or perhaps, after such prolonged stress, they simply couldn't endure another crisis. Men – brave men – broke away from the side, ran across the deck and cowered against the port-side bulkhead. A sailor dared the jump to the *Arete* and leaped, only to miss his grip, fall between the hulls and be crushed like an insect as the waves threw the two hulls together.

If the flames get aboard— Satyrus caught the line that a sailor threw him and moved forward with it, belaying it on the stump of the foremast.

'Come on, lads,' he croaked. 'Almost there. Don't burn to death – no point. We're going to *live*. Come on!' he waved, and the two men closest to him trusted him – came away from the illusory safety of the bulkhead and joined him in fastening the tow rope.

'Get the deck crew moving and get the foresail back up,' Satyrus said. They both looked too wild-eyed to respond. Satyrus stumbled away; everything was a matter of heartbeats now.

The tow rope began to straighten.

Satyrus saw the marine, Necho, by the rail.

'Necho! Stand up, man! Come and get these sailors to do their duty. Come *on*!' Satyrus called. He slapped the man on the back, as one comrade to another – and Necho's face cleared and his courage returned.

'My lord?' he said, as a man awakening from sleep.

'Foremast up! And the sail cleared away so that it doesn't catch fire!' Satyrus called, as loud as his throat could manage, and Necho looked as if he understood. Then Satyrus went aft. He could feel the *Atlantae* leaning to port with the tow, and he knew she was moving – not fast, but her bow was coming off the enemy vessel.

Apollodorus had never panicked. He and Laertes were in the stern, pushing at the enemy stern with spears, trying to pole off. The fire was so hot here that Satyrus knew another moment of terror – sparks were coming aboard, hissing into the pools of blood that lay like puddles after a rain shower where the fighting had been thickest.

Other men had followed Satyrus, and they threw themselves against the spears and long poles, pushing with what strength they had left, and as one more sailor leaped to help them the stern moved, and suddenly they were sliding through the water, the bow curving off to port to follow *Arete*, and Satyrus felt life in his steering oars. The brave man – the one who had held them there at the very end – was lying across the steering oars, fouling them, and Satyrus got his feet and Apollodorus his head and they moved him a few feet, setting him down as gently as they could in unspoken respect for his heroism.

Then Satyrus settled into the oars. 'Laertes!' he said, in what voice he had left. 'Get the rowers to their stations – oars out.'

'Aye, lord,' Laertes answered. He had a cut on his brow and blood was running down his face.

To Apollodorus, Satyrus said, 'As soon as the rowers have way on us, cut the tow.'

Apollodorus nodded. 'You going to pass out?' he asked.

Satyrus managed a grim smile. 'Not if I can help it. Now get to it. We'd look like idiots if some cruiser snapped us up now.'

13

The promised storm held off, the clouds towering from the horizon to the very peak of the heavens away to the south and west, so that a superstitious sailor might imagine that Zeus in his wrath was present, hovering over the sea. The sun reflected on the clouds and down on the darkening sea, a sheet of bronze over a sea of blood.

Arete and *Atlantae* were not the only ships crewed by heroes – this was evidenced by the fact that the titanic enemy tenner had got her fires out, off to windward, and the column of smoke was carried away by the rising wind. Satyrus could imagine what it must have been like – the rowing decks an inferno, and a handful of brave men forcing themselves into the fire to pour helmets full of water on the flames. But the burning ship had covered their retreat, and the desperation of every Antigonid ship to come the aid of their stricken king had saved Ptolemy's centre.

Satyrus, leaning exhausted between the oars of his helm, had no need to count the Ptolemy fleet to see who had won. The result was obvious. Ptolemy's fleet was badly gored – thirty or more ships lost in the action and the rest moving sluggishly, running downwind towards Aegypt, abandoning their camp.

The worst of it was that Demetrios and Plistias were so relatively unhurt that their lighter ships were mounting a pursuit. As the storm clouds piled up to the west and the sun set in wrath and thunder, the squadron of penteres – every ship the size and weight of *Arete* – that had spent the day inactive, facing down Menelaeus and his *sixty* inactive ships, now came on, rowing powerfully in the fading light, determined to capture a dozen more of Ptolemy's limping triremes. And from Plistias' centre emerged another two dozen triremes, equally eager to continue the contest.

Most of Ptolemy's ships had left all their masts and sails ashore, and now they ran downwind under the power of their exhausted oarsmen. They were slow. Only darkness would save them.

Arete and *Atlantae* had their foresails up, and were ten stades south and east of the rest of the retreating Ptolemy fleet, already safe by the inexorable mathematics of the sea. But in late afternoon, when the last sight of Cyprus was gone, the promontory now below the horizon, and when the storm clouds were beginning to look like something supernatural to the west, *Arete*'s lookout saw sails to the east and his shouts alerted Laertes, amidships on *Atlantae*, and he ran aft to Satyrus, who was dozing at his oars.

'Sails to the east,' he said.

Satyrus had trouble focusing. Every part of him hurt – and from where he was slouched between the oars, he could see the marines, or at least the dozen survivors, crouched in attitudes that expressed the same weariness and pain.

'I can take the helm,' Laertes said.

'Have you ever done so?' Satyrus asked.

Laertes shook his head. 'No, lord.'

Satyrus nodded. 'Sail's drawing well. Rowers are resting. All you have to do is go straight. I'm willing to give you a try, if you'll take the responsibility.'

Laertes managed a smile. 'I would be proud to try, lord.'

Satyrus nodded. 'Put your hands on the oars. Now you say, "I have the helm".'

'I have the helm,' Laertes said.

'You have the helm,' Satyrus said, and slipped under the man's arms from between the shafts and Laertes passed him, clumsy in his eagerness to do it right. The ship seemed to skip, the stern moving the length of a man's arm to port as Laertes tried to balance the two shafts, and then he got the pressure right – right enough – and the ship steadied on his course.

Satyrus walked to the port-side rail and watched the basket suspended from the *Arete*'s foremast. Neiron was standing at the foot of the mast, and the men in the basket were gesturing and speaking.

'They don't looked panicked,' Satyrus said.

'I don't have the strength to panic,' Apollodorus said. 'Lord – it's a pity that we lost, because that was our best fight.'

Satyrus sketched a smile. 'Your men were like gods.'

Apollodorus nodded, and Satyrus saw that tears were flowing down his face, although he didn't sob – his expression didn't even change. 'Eight dead already, and three who probably won't make it.'

'And Stesagoras,' Satyrus said.

'Yes.' Apollodorus hung his head. Satyrus realised that the smaller man with his arrogant posturing and his endless energy – his annoying superiority, his fighting skills, his near *perfection* and his apparent contempt for his men and all those about him – was weeping inconsolably.

Satyrus put his arms around the marine captain. 'Sometimes it's worthwhile to remember that *we're alive*,' Satyrus said. 'I was sure I was dead there – twice, I think.' He found that he was crying, too. 'I think that – that – that I may work a little harder on being alive. And the men that died – Zeus Sator, Apollodorus, a least we can look to see that they died *for* something.'

'For the King of Aegypt?' Apollodorus asked, his voice raw. 'For *glory*?'

'No idea,' Satyrus said. He took a deep breath. Men were cheering on the other deck, and pointing east. 'No idea. But we should find something, before we're dead ourselves.' He was rambling. Apollodorus didn't seem to mind. The smaller man stood straighter.

'I'm all right. Sorry, lord. Sorry. Poseidon, I didn't know I had such weakness in me.' Apollodorus stumbled away, caught himself on the rail and threw up into the sea.

Satyrus walked back to the helmsman's station, found his own canteen under the bench and poured a horn cup of wine. He looked at Laertes, who was focused on his task with heroic intensity, his whole being urging the ship to stay on course. Laertes flicked a glance at him and tried to smile. 'Doing my best,' he said.

'Notch in your wake,' Satyrus said. It made him smile, despite everything. 'When you looked at me, you let up on your port oar.'

He turned and walked back to Apollodorus. 'Wine?' he asked.

Apollodorus raised his head, and his eyes were clearer. 'Thanks.' He drank the whole cup off. His head came up; something had caught his eye. 'You there!' he shouted past Satyrus' head. 'What in Hades do you think you're doing, Stilicho?'

Neiron was waving from the other deck, and Satyrus leaned out over the rail to hear. All he caught was *Diokles*. But when he looked again, he understood.

Marathon was coming on from the east, under foresail and mainsail and oars, with *Troy* and *Oinoe* and half a dozen other ships in line astern. Even Satyrus could see that the third ship in line was their capture from the beach on the Asian shore, the beautiful long, low trireme of Phoenician design.

'Well,' Satyrus said. There was no one near him except the marine, Necho. Necho was younger than he had expected, and with his helmet off he didn't look like a veteran at all. In fact, he looked pathetically young. He had two black eyes from some blow that had rocked his helmet into his forehead, and he looked terrible. Terrible, but alive, and his eyes glittered as they met Satyrus'.

'Lord?' he asked.

'Well,' Satyrus said. 'I think we're going to live.'

Night, and the swell was rising, and Satyrus feared for the remnants of Ptolemy's fleet, last seen strung out over thirty stades of water and with the enemy in sight to the north. Ptolemy's bodyguard had hung together, managed somehow to rig foresails to rest their oarsmen and the big ships, who could better endure the coming weather, began to pull away to the south.

In the last light, Satyrus went below on *Atlantae*, passing along the oar benches, talking to a rower here and another there. 'We lived,' was the burden of what he had to say, and they were glad to hear it.

'You men don't know me,' he said. 'I'm Satyrus of the Euxine, and at least for the moment, you're my men. I'll see you paid and fed, and no man on this ship will be a slave as long as you keep slavery away by pulling your oars. Any of you who want to leave this ship may do so – once we reach Alexandria. Until then, I need you to row!'

He didn't get much of a cheer, but it hadn't been much of a speech, and he felt that, on balance, they were content enough – *alive* and *free* were powerful feelings – but he also felt that Stesagoras might have taken all the real leaders with him in his mad rush to glory. The rowers seemed remarkably unspirited. They needed reinforcements, officers, lead rowers, and his handful of utterly spent marines and sailors were not up to the job – and neither was he.

He went aboard *Oinoe*, all but falling to the deck from the rail, his legs no longer interested in supporting him, and Diokles and Helios caught him.

But in return, dozens of deckhands, junior officers and oarsmen went aboard *Atlantae*. They winched across a spare foremast from *Oinoe* that was to be raised as a temporary mainmast, come the dawn.

As darkness fell, all the Euxine ships lit oil lamps and placed them in bronze storm lanterns on their sterns. All the captains preferred communications to stealth. Under close-brailed foresails in the bows, with the oar ports closed and the thranites cleared off their benches because the lowest oar deck *always* leaked, with men already queued on the decks to straddle the side-pumps, the squadron stood south. *Oinoe* fell back at dark to the centre position.

Satyrus tried to listen to Diokles, but he couldn't. He fell asleep.

He awoke to a red, red dawn. The sun was rising in the east, his bronze-bright light reflected oddly all around them.

'You're awake,' Diokles said.

Satyrus was no longer in his armour – he was wearing a frowzy wool chiton over a heavy linen bandage that was wrapped around his middle, over and over so that he couldn't bend at the waist, and even as he thought about his back, pain bloomed there.

'So,' Satyrus grunted. His mouth felt as if someone had painted it with rust.

'You smell like blood. We let you out of our sight for a few days, and you go and try to get killed. Just as I said!' Diokles shook his head.

Helios was washing his feet and legs. They were covered in dried blood. 'I was afraid to wake you,' he said. 'Lord.'

Satyrus shook him off – kicked him off, more precisely – rose to his feet with heavy effort and went to the downwind rail. He hiked his chiton and pissed downwind – and felt his heart stop as he pissed red, red blood.

'Oh, Apollo,' Satyrus said weakly. His kidneys hurt like fire by the time he was finished, and the stream was as red at the end as at the start, and Satyrus felt weak.

'I had a master who beat me with a stick,' Helios said quietly. 'I always pissed blood after he beat me.'

Satyrus lay down on the sheepskins they'd piled up for him. He was cold, and Helios put a cloak over him. He felt better for Helios' words. 'I didn't know. I've never pissed blood before – well, once after a fight in the palaestra, but not – not so much.' He grunted.

'You'll heal,' Helios said gently.

Satyrus went back to sleep, even as the wind's note in the stays rose an octave.

'We need to beach,' Diokles said, somewhere off in a dream of riding on a winged monster. Satyrus struggled to the surface of the dream like a man pulled under by a breaking wave on a beach, and he managed to get his head above the nightmare to get his eyes open. The light was the same as it had been before.

'I guess I didn't sleep,' he said to Helios, before he realised that the boy was asleep himself.

Diokles smiled. 'You slept all day, lord. Now the sun – such as it is – is setting. And the wind is rising, and we're in the middle of nowhere.' He shook his head. 'Wind is veering right round – into our faces, and the sails all have to come down, and there's sand in the wind off of Africa. Bad night ahead.'

'Where's Aegypt?' Satyrus asked.

'A hundred stades or less off the bow,' Diokles said, and he didn't bother to hide his bitterness. 'Might as well be ten thousand stades, Satyrus. It'll be in the eye of the wind in ten minutes, and we can't row into this. And we haven't had a hot meal in three days. The rowers aren't fresh, we're short on food and very short on drinking water, and there's no haven short of Alexandria into the wind or back to Cyprus. Into the teeth of the enemy.'

Somewhere in Diokles' recitation, Satyrus came awake. He had to piss, and he was afraid to do it. Afraid of the stream of dark red urine. Somewhere in the fight off Cyprian Salamis, he had discovered that he loved life and had a great many things that he wanted to do. And now he wondered how badly he was hurt. It scared him more than all the fighting had scared him, more than the threat of a storm.

Facing his fears, he rose to his feet, stumbled to the rail and relieved himself. The stream was as red as Tyrian dye.

'Where are the enemy?' he asked. He felt faint, but he wasn't going to surrender to it.

'Due north. If you can get up on the stern rail, you ought to be able to see them,' Diokles said.

'How much left in the day?' Satyrus asked.

'An hour, at most. Hard to guess with this odd light.' Diokles shook his head. 'I'm sorry I was late. Men are saying ... it was close. We might have made the difference.'

Satyrus managed a bitter laugh. 'Five ships? Diokles, don't be so self-important. We lost by *sixty ships*. Menelaeus stayed in port and let us die. We were never in that fight, my friend, and all you would have done was die.'

'And yet you took a ship – a beautiful ship,' Diokles said.

'I'm a clever bastard and my father is halfway to a god,' Satyrus said, intending humour. He climbed the rail, balancing on the slippery wood and clinging to the arching wood of the ship's stern that rose over the helmsman's station.

He could see them, just helm up in the failing light. He counted fifteen before he grew confused. He slipped back to the deck, feeling clumsy and light-headed.

'Get us alongside *Arete*,' he said. 'Have you ever seen weather like this?'

Diokles shrugged. 'No. But one of the Aegyptian marines says he's seen it upriver, and it means a sandstorm.'

Their eyes met. Satyrus had seen small sandstorms to the east, in the Sinai. 'That's where I've seen the copper sky,' he said.

Diokles shrugged. 'Sure, if you have. Any ideas?'

'Yes,' Satyrus said. 'My idea is that we should ask Neiron.'

Draco, who had been one of Satyrus' companions from childhood – who had once mistaken the King of the Bosporus for a child prostitute in the Macedonian barracks at Heraklea – came up and embraced him. 'I hear that was one fine fight,' he said. 'Young Necho seems to think that you and Apollodorus are gods.'

'Gods don't get wounded as often as I do,' Satyrus complained.

'That's pretty much what I said. Here, have some warm wine. Always good for you when you take a wound. Boys say you're pissing blood.' Draco, as always, was the very king of straight talk.

'I am,' Satyrus mumbled.

'Yeah, well, stop acting as if *this is the end*.' Draco laughed. 'How has a big bastard like you got through as many fights as you have and never pissed blood?' He laughed again, a little cruel in his attitude. 'I – I thought I was going to die, the first time. And it went on for days. Days!' He laughed a third time.

Diokles pointed at the *Arete*, now under their lee. 'Lord?' he said.

'Thanks,' Satyrus replied. He leaned out, cupped his hands and called, 'Neiron!' so loud that his back and kidneys hurt all over again.

Neiron appeared and waved.

'Sandstorm?' Satyrus called. He pantomimed puzzlement like a tragic actor.

Neiron nodded agreement and waved. 'Yes!' he roared back, his deep-sea voice carrying like the voice of Poseidon.

The problem was that Satyrus had to have this conversation out loud, where every man on the deck and most of the rowers could hear him. Their confidence in their king was not going to be increased by the process.

'What do you suggest?' Satyrus called.

Neiron looked blank.

'What do we *do*?' Satyrus asked.

Neiron put his hands to his mouth. 'Pray!' he called.

'Oh, that's fucking helpful,' Diokles muttered at Satyrus' side.

'Should we run *north*?' Satyrus called. He hoped – he prayed – that Neiron could read into his suggestion: north, so that their sails would keep them moving, keep the seas astern, keep the deadly sand at their backs. But right into the enemy squadron.

Neiron looked surprised – even stunned.

The wind howled, and the first gustful of sand stung them, and everyone scrambled for spare cloaks and light wool chitons to wrap round their heads.

Satyrus stayed at the rail, watching his senior navarch, a man with ten times his own sea-keeping experience. Neiron talked to someone at the helm – the man between the oars.

'YES!' he roared back.

Suddenly Satyrus felt his pulse quicken and his gorge rise. All very well when it was just a bold idea. Now it was real, taking six ships and their exhausted crews into the teeth of a larger enemy force. But dark was close.

'Head of the line, if you please, Diokles,' Satyrus said. No point in waiting. 'Get the foresail laid to by the mast and have every sailor you've got hold it down. Ready to raise, on the yard. Understood?'

Diokles laughed. 'I taught you this trick.'

Satyrus grinned back. 'So you did. I want the other ships to *see you doing it* and get the message.'

Diokles nodded. He gave orders – a series of rapid orders that sent men running in every direction.

'Helios – gold aspis into the stern. Fast as you can.' Satyrus went to the helmsman's station. Helios, awake for a few minutes, managed to get the great gold-finished shield out of its cover and stood by him.

'Raise it so they know there's a signal coming,' Satyrus said.

'Foresail laid to. Ready to come about – oars are warned.' Diokles nodded. 'You'd best do it – it's going to be hard to get the heavier ships around already with the wind. We've barely headway with the rowers going full on.'

Satyrus turned to Helios. 'Signal – READY.'

Four of the five ships sent a return flash. The fifth, *Atlantae*, probably didn't even have a signalling shield.

'Signal "SHIPS TO COME ABOUT IN SUCCESSION".' Satyrus raised an eyebrow at Diokles, who shrugged.

'We've practised it fifty times,' he said.

Helios had brought Satyrus his best cloak when the sandstorm started – a glorious Tyrian purple with embroidered eagles, ravens and stars. It was warm and thick at his throat, pinned with the family raven done in gold by Temerix the smith, a gift for his mother. He held it around himself for a long moment. He could remember his mother wearing the raven pin at her throat when she gave justice at Tanais when he was a boy. The memory pierced him like the pain in his kidneys. Then he ripped the cloak off over his head, stood on the stern rail and offered the cloak to the sea.

'Poseidon, Lord of Horses, take this as a token of the hecatomb I will send thee, and spare my ships!' he called into the wind, and let the cloak go. It caught the wind and swirled – up, then down, spreading flat on the sea as if a sea nymph intended to spread a picnic on it – and then it was gone, as if plucked down by some invisible hand.

'Signal COME ABOUT,' Satyrus said.

Oinoe, temporarily the lead ship, was ready, and port-side rowers dragged their oars while the starboard men continued to row forward, and the ship turned so fast that Satyrus barely had time to fear for his stability as the full force of the south wind out of Africa caught her broadside, but the rowers were pulling for their lives, and the bow came round – round fast, and before Satyrus could even frame the words, Diokles ordered that the foresail be set, and the whole deck crew and all the marines raised the yard, sail and all, and the wind caught it, even brailed tight, and suddenly the ship's motion was altogether different, smoother, less choppy.

Arete was next in line, and she followed *Oinoe* around in fine style, although her port side leaned so close to the surface in the turn that all decks must have taken water. Aboard *Oinoe*, the bulkhead pumps were manned already, and water flew high into the wind from all three pumps as men raised and lowered the handles – brave men, men who had to stand on the rail to work the wooden pumps.

'Rowers stand down and close the oar ports,' Satyrus said to Diokles, without taking his eyes from the ships following him.

'We're going to fight *under sail*,' Diokles asked.

'I don't have a lot of fighting in mind, my friend,' Satyrus answered. 'I intend to run right down between their squadrons, and if you want to fire your engines, be my guest. But look, Diokles – what choice have they? Turn broadside to this wind to try and move to stop us?'

They were passing *Atlantae*. Her inexperienced officers had made a mistake, and were turning on the spot rather than playing 'follow the leader' and turning in succession. The rowers were tired, and the volley of strange and unexpected orders had caught them out, and oars were flailing out of time. The ship crept around, took a big wave square on the flank and the whole ship shuddered.

Someone up forward had climbed the foresail mast and cut the lashings on the sail – it spread with a crack that carried like lightning, and the ropes attached held. One blew out, but the rest merely strained and suddenly the head of the stricken ship came round like a restless horse turning under her rider.

For whatever reason, *Troy* duplicated *Atlantae*'s movements and further confused the manoeuvre by turning to starboard rather than to port, so that she just missed falling foul of *Atlantae*, her bow shaving past *Atlantae*'s stern and her oars, by the luck of the gods, pulling in just at the point of closest approach.

Diokles walked to the rail and threw his sword over the side, gold hilt, scabbard and all, the fruit of a whole season of fighting in the year that Satyrus and his sister had won their kingdoms. 'Poseidon be with us!' he called to the restless, red-hued sea.

But they were around, all six of them. By the will of the gods, they were in two sloppy columns, with *Oinoe* and *Arete* following

Plataea, while *Troy* was well to the west and slightly behind *Atlantae* and *Marathon* far astern, her confused navarch having tried to compromise between the two styles of turn. Now he was six stades behind.

But *they were around*. They had their sails up and the storm was under their sterns, the rising sea rolling in against the part of the ship designed to meet a Mediterranean storm.

And dead ahead were the Antigonid ships. The badly executed turn meant that Satyrus' ships were not a cohesive whole, but spread over several stades of sea. There was no possibility of communication or further manoeuvre, with the wind howling and screaming, the foresails blown into rock-hard bubbles of canvas in the bows, the steering oars thrumming like live things.

'If we did ram ...' Satyrus said, and paused.

Diokles' eye grew wide. 'We'd die. The bow would blow in. Lord, we've never moved a ship this size at this speed. We're moving faster than a galloping horse.'

Satyrus nodded. Perhaps. Perhaps not. At this speed, the ram might cut the enemy ship in half, breaking every strake – and they would sail on—

Lunacy.

Satyrus was grinning. 'Smile, Diokles! This is going to work.'

Diokles had to shout to be heard. 'It is the best plan, given where we are,' he said. 'But it is not dark yet.'

Satyrus got up on the rail and was soaked to the skin by the flying sea – even this far aft, spume rose off the crashing bow and soaked everyone. He missed his cloak. He couldn't find the Antigonid ships for a moment, and then there they were – so close aboard he'd mistaken them for his own.

Even as he looked, Neiron's marines opened fire with their machines. Satyrus could see the bolts fly, black against the red-bronze sky, but they were far too small to see after the moment of launch.

But the Antigonids – at least some of them – had decided to turn. Satyrus watched one of the lead penteres start its turn, oars coming out and moving, port side forward, starboard side reversed. It was well done, and the ship came about like an automaton, reversing its course with a professionalism that called for admiration.

The second ship chose to drag oars and turn to port, and someone misunderstood the order and the port-side loom crashed in missed strokes, the whole rhythm lost as the ship lost way and wallowed in the trough of the last wave.

The next wave, sweeping down from Africa, caught the oars first and threw them up, and men must have died as the oars were forced into the ship and off their thole pins, but it scarcely mattered because a heartbeat later the wave reached the hull and rolled it back, and someone forward let go of a corner of their brailed-up foresail – the whole sail was ripped from the hands of its crew and before Satyrus could blink, the ship was gone, turned turtle and sunk under the great wave that even now was under *Oinoe*'s counter. But the wreckage was still there, just under the surface, as was always true in a battle, and the first ship that had turned so bravely struck it with the whole weight of the storm behind her.

And the Euxine squadron sailed on north, moving as fast as a herd of panicked horses on the Sea of Grass. They passed between the outstretched arms of the two Antigonid squadrons and sailed on for Cyprus.

When Draco went to load the engine on the port side, Satyrus sent Helios to stop him. 'Tell him that tonight we're all sailors,' he said.

Draco came aft. 'You're too soft,' he said. 'One split foresail and they're dead,' he allowed, pointing at the nearest Antigonid trireme just a stade to port.

'A thousand men just died,' Satyrus said. 'So far, Poseidon has preserved ours. Let's let them go, and see if the god might let us go as well.'

Draco nodded. 'You're soft,' he said. 'They'll be *wild* to kill us in the morning.'

Satyrus felt a gust full of sand sting his back.

'Helios!' he cried. 'Another chlamys!'

It was the longest night of Satyrus' life. Or perhaps the second or third longest. Nights like that are incomparable – while you live them, they are eternal, and when they are over, there is little enough to remember but fear, blown sand, fear and wind, fear and water, fear and the sandy taste of hastily snatched wine.

When the sun rose, it was never more than a white disc lost in flying sand. Satyrus had the presence of mind to order all the ropes on the foresail checked and replaced – the sand was wearing the lines.

'Cheat west, if you feel you can steer to port at all,' Satyrus said to the helmsman when there was light. The sand was everywhere. There were little drifts of sand in the bilges, and in his mouth. So much to worry about, and now he could add the worry that they might run right on Cyprus and he'd never know.

Midday – he guessed – and the rain hit. It hit them like a fist, and a squall tore overhead, ripping the foresail clear off the pole and out into the sea, heeling them over so far that men fell off their benches.

But Poseidon accepted their sacrifices and let them go, and they got the ship righted and wrestled another scrap of canvas onto the foremast and sailed on at the same nightmare pace into a second night. They were so short on water now that Diokles was sending wine around instead. That wouldn't last long, and the sand made it worse. They got some water from the rain and drank it all, men laying their chitons out on deck, standing naked in the rain and dark, wringing the clothes nearly dry into their mouths, drinking three-day-old sweat, blood, urine and salt as well as water.

The second dawn: for most of them, their fourth at sea without a rest, and this for rowers who were used to beaching every night to cook their food. The oarsmen were so hungry they could barely speak, and so dry that when they did open their mouths very little came out.

Noon on the second day, and the wind began to develop fits and flaws and Satyrus thought it might be blowing itself out. The sand was gone from the air – blessed relief – and men emerged from their head wrappings to stare at the sun on a windblown sea. But the sea wasn't finished with them yet, and in late afternoon the wind changed direction, turning back from south to north, grew colder and Satyrus put the oarsmen to their oars and turned the ship about again, guessing that he was three hundred stades south-south-west of Rhodes – which was now in the eye of the wind. It might have been funny if he hadn't been so tired.

He was so tired he didn't even notice when he pissed over the side and it was yellow-brown rather than red. Helios did, however, and they laughed together like boys. Of such things are triumph made, when you are in your third day of a storm after a day of battle.

But they made it through the night alive, although there were oarsmen who were beginning to feel the hunger in ugly ways, and Diokles put marines at the ladders just in case.

Satyrus had the steering oars – *Oinoe* was tragically lacking in officers, having sent her best into *Atlantae*. At present, that looked like a poor decision, as they hadn't seen another ship in three days.

But an hour later, Satyrus saw *Arete* running south with mainsail and foresail set, ten stades off their starboard side, and he yelled and men cheered. *Arete* steered close and fell in under their stern.

Just at full dark, they found *Atlantae* and *Plataea* rowing patiently into the wind. As soon as they saw who they'd found, the other two ships abandoned rowing, turned and raised their sails. The wind was dwindling to a comfortable roar, and Satyrus guessed his location, put his helm down and ordered the mainmast raised and the mainsail set.

Dawn found all four running fast, the wind dead astern. Noon revealed *Troy* dismasted, wallowing in the waves but still afloat, and Satyrus put marines into her – there had been trouble – and *Plataea* emptied her stores for yards to rig a makeshift foresail mast.

Twelve hours later, a marine killed an oarsman who attacked him to get his empty canteen.

And an hour after that, the coast of Africa rose above the bow.

14

They landed on a beach a few stades west of Cyrene, a Greek city hundreds, if not thousands of stades west of Alexandria. Satyrus, usually a fine navigator, had lost his way utterly.

Neiron was no better, and after a feast of slaughtered cattle and wine and fresh-flowing water, no man on any of the four ships seemed to feel that any error had been made at all. They stood by their fires, watching the sea, looking for *Marathon*, and told each other how close they'd come to death, how narrowly they'd avoided capsizing, catastrophe – and then they hurried to expiate this sin by telling how very good a sailor Sarpax was, how unlikely he was to make a mistake.

By a curious twist of time, the battle seemed to have happened long before, so long before that it felt odd to hold funeral pyres for the dead who hadn't been bundled over the side in the hellish moments of the storm.

Satyrus walked along the line of dead – mostly his own marines from *Arete*. Here was a man who had been at Gaza when they fought elephants. Here was a man who'd taken a wound at the Battle of Tanais. Dead, now. Dead for him.

He had gold aboard his ships and he spent it like water, for a grave stele the size of an Aegyptian monument for his sailors and marines.

There were three happy surprises – men he had counted as dead, and who lived. Charmides, the beautiful boy from Lesvos, would never be quite as beautiful, as he would always limp. But he was alive, and his smile raised Satyrus' heart. And Anaxagoras, the musician, had taken four wounds and lived, and none had taken infection. He grinned at Satyrus.

'It's a miracle,' Satyrus said, seeing the way a sword had stripped the flesh from the musician's leg and side.

Anaxagoras managed a smile. 'I enjoyed it too much, I fear. You always pay in the morning for a good night.'

'I suspect it will be a while before you teach me the lyre,' Satyrus said.

'As we're both alive, at least it remains possible,' Anaxagoras answered.

And the brave young man who had covered Demetrios' retreat was alive. Nechos had struck him with the butt of his spear, knocking him unconscious – he had recovered his wits in mid-storm, risen from the deck and helped to sheet home the foresail. Laertes, who had circles under his eyes like a debauched rich boy, came up with the man on his arm.

'Clearchus of Crete,' he said. 'I promised we wouldn't enslave him, lord. He's been like an officer for me.'

The man bowed. 'Lord.'

Satyrus felt no enmity for this grave man. He was past middle age, grey at his temples and in his beard. 'Are you a mercenary?' Satyrus asked.

'No, lord.' Clearchus shrugged. 'I was a volunteer. I have served One-Eye since I was young – since just after the Great King died.'

'You'll want to go back to them, then,' Satyrus said.

'I doubt,' the man said, and hesitated. 'I doubt that I'm worth ransom. Lord.'

Satyrus nodded. 'Well, sometimes excellence must be its own reward – yours and ours. We'll be going straight back to war, Clearchus – against your Demetrios, who even now must be recovering from the storm. So; walk up the beach and turn left. In a few stades you'll come to Cyrene. You can find a merchant to take you to your people.'

Clearchus bowed and stammered his thanks. Common soldiers were seldom rescued or released. They were usually sold as slaves – or slaughtered.

Satyrus shook his head. 'Wait.' With Helios' help, he sat and wrote a long note to Demetrios, who he addressed as 'My Noble Adversary'. He praised the Cretan and said that he thought that, but for the man's reckless bravery and loyalty, he, Demetrios, would have ended the action as a prisoner, or dead. *That will anger him*, Satyrus thought, but he didn't see Demetrios the Golden as the kind of man who punished messengers.

'Here's a letter for Demetrios, and here's a gold daric to see to it that you get there,' Satyrus said. 'Keep your arms.'

Clearchus surprised him by bowing like a Persian and kissing his hand. 'You are the deserving son of a godlike father,' Clearchus said. At his throat, a blue bead gleamed – the same bead that Apollodorus wore.

Satyrus was no longer sure that he loved the increasing deification of his father. But he smiled at the man until he turned with a salute and walked off up the beach.

'That was a good act,' Diokles said.

'You're too soft to live,' Draco said.

'You're both right, more than likely,' Satyrus said. 'Now, before we make this a debate, let me issue some orders. I've paid the merchants here for six days' provisions and we're almost full on water. Are we ready for sea?'

'When?' Diokles asked.

'At the rising of the sun,' Satyrus said. 'Even now, Demetrios and his admiral are just where we are – watching the sea for survivors, trying to get to sea. The first one to sea—'

Diokles shook his head. 'You're mad!' he said.

Neiron appeared, back from a swim. A slave brought him a towel, and he dried himself at the fire while he drank wine. 'He *is* mad, but he's right, too.'

Satyrus ran his fingers through his beard. 'If Demetrios gets uncontested to the coast of Aegypt, Ptolemy is done.'

Diokles shook his head. 'Who gives a shit?'

Satyrus wasn't angry. It was odd how the last few days had focused him, but he wasn't mad at Diokles' usual intemperate disobedience, nor anything else. He could *see* what needed to be done, and he was going to do it.

Satyrus finished the wine in his cup. 'Diokles, I value your opinion, and when you find yourself king, you may do as you wish. Right now I intend to risk all of your lives to keep Aegypt independent of Antigonus One-Eye. Why? Is it for some magnificent end reason? Some moral that old Aristotle might admire? No, gentlemen. We are going to fight – and perhaps die – so that grain prices in the Euxine remain stable. So that foreign soldiers don't come to *our* shores. Because we have an ally, and if he falls, we're next.' Satyrus gazed around at them in satisfaction. 'I wouldn't do it with any other team. You, gentlemen, are my team – even Gelon the fop and Apollodorus the martinet.' The last named pair had just walked out of the approaching darkness. 'I can well understand why a man might hesitate to give his life for the stability of Euxine grain prices, but friends – that's what we're fighting for. And if you don't want to – well, Cyrene is right over there. In the morning, I'll take this squadron and any other ships I can rally, and I'll have a go at harrying Demetrios while he tries to support his father's attack on Aegypt.'

Diokles laughed. 'Damn. That was well said, lord.' He raised his cup. 'For Euxine grain prices!'

Gelon, the Syracusan, laughed. 'To the grain!' he said, and drank.

The sun rose over a light chop and a brisk wind, and the orb itself was a red ball on the eastern horizon, but Satyrus already had all his ships on the water sailing downwind, due east, in line and abreast spread wide apart, sweeping for friends, for enemies, for news.

The first ship they found was a friend, *Ephesian Artemis*, the Phoenician-built capture that *Black Falcon* had made north of Cyprus. Satyrus barely knew the man who had the command – Nikeas son of Draco of Pantecapaeaum, who had started the campaign as the assistant sailing master of the *Black Falcon* and now had his own command. According to him, neither *Black Falcon* nor *Marathon* nor *Troy* had been damaged in the fight at Cyprian Salamis, which was welcome news. The four ships had attempted to stay together in the rout, but Ptolemy's fleeing navy had made any formation impossible.

Ephesian Artemis had lost the others as soon as the sand began to blow. Her crew had rowed and rowed – rowed to total exhaustion, and then on for a few strokes more. They had spent a day almost in sight of Cyrene, but without enough strength left to row ashore. However, when they landed they'd eaten and drunk, and they'd just put to sea to look for friends. Such a coincidence was clearly heaven sent, and by nightfall every man was ready to make sacrifice.

Of *Black Falcon*, *Marathon*, or *Troy*, on the other hand, there was no sign.

In the second dawn they picked up a Ptolemy trireme. All marines and officers were dead, killed by the rowers, and some evil acts had been done aboard. Apollodorus crossed over with all of his marines, hanged a pair of men from the yard of the foremast, and Satyrus took all the rowers out of the ship and distributed them among his own ships and had *Arete* take the ship in tow.

To the south, over Africa, there was another storm simmering. Satyrus beached for the night, exhorted all the rowers to redouble their efforts and the next day they reached Alexandria.

As he expected and feared, the Royal Harbour was empty. He sent a boat ashore at Diodorus' house, to tell Sappho that he would use the yard and to ask for news of Leon. Then he led his squadron into the moorings between the warehouses that he knew so well – the home of his adolescence, of his first love, of his first war. Just the smell of Alexandria was the smell of home.

Leon's harbour facilities were the finest on the ocean, because he was a rich man with a fine merchant fleet and he could afford the best. His factor was Nicodemus, and Satyrus embraced the man as an old friend.

'Two fights and a storm,' he said, by way of greeting. 'I need a refit from stem to masthead, every ship – scraped clean, dried a day at least – the hulls are so heavy that the rowers would be hard put to make ramming speed if they were fresh.'

Nicodemus bowed. 'We are at your service,' he said. 'The more so as you are a paying customer.'

Satyrus took the opportunity to unload the chests of gold and silver from Rhodes into the guarded basements below the Temple of Poseidon. He embraced the half-Aegyptian high priest, who had served with him in the first Antigonid war at Gaza.

'Brother, I need men,' he said. 'I need everything – rowers, soldiers, officers. Ships, if your people have any hidden away.'

'Alas,' said the high priest of Poseidon. 'Alas, we have no ships, or we might throw you Greeks into the sea and be a free people,' he grimaced. 'But in the meantime, you and Ptolemy are a far cry better than Antigonus. Rowers and marines I'll find you; men who served with us at Gaza.'

Satyrus nodded. 'We are, if anything, more desperate,' he said. 'Ptolemy lost the battle badly – so badly that I fear for the king himself.'

'Fear not,' said the priest. 'Ptolemy lives, and he and his bodyguard ships are on the way – a rather circuitous way. They beached at Gaza four days ago, and the wind has been against them, and they've already had a skirmish with Demetrios.'

'It must be nice to serve an all-knowing god,' Satyrus said.

'I wouldn't know. I have a good intelligence service. And Old Gales and I exchange information. You should see him – he may have more recent news. Of course the public word is that the king won the battle.'

Sappho he embraced like a lost mother, and for a moment, wrapped in her arms, he didn't think about cordage, iron darts for his bolt throwers, leather helmets for new marines, or dried bread. Or amphorae for his water supply. He just *was*.

'My poor boy,' Sappho said. She was older – he was startled to see how much four years had aged her.

And then he borrowed her enormous and well-oiled household to be the machine of his staff, and he used them to fill his ships with goods while the priests replaced his dead rowers and marines, and while he fully crewed his captured ships and the Aegyptian trireme that had mutinied.

In the royal yard were two triremes so heavily rotted that they'd been left behind. After two days and nights of work by daylight and torchlight by Aegyptian shipwrights promised eternal redemption by their priests, the two were barely seaworthy, with scratch crews officered by retired merchants from the town. Satyrus worked like a dog, but he sent messengers everywhere, and men came to him and he issued orders as if he were king – and was obeyed. Timber from the Levant, worth its weight in spices, donated by the Jews. Clay fire pots like the one he'd used on Demetrios' flagship – every ship carried a dozen now, and sacks of charcoal to fill them, donated by the charcoal burners. Alexandria was a city that loved itself, and while many – most – affected to despise old Ptolemy, they fought for him – the best of many evils.

One of the first men to come to him in the yard was Dionysus – still beautiful, still given to wearing transparent wool chitons and expensive perfume. Despite which, Satyrus, covered in pitch soot from recaulking the *Amon-Ra*, embraced him.

'I need a captain,' he said.

Dionysus wrinkled his nose – whether at Satyrus' rank sweat or the condition of the *Amon-Ra* was difficult to determine.

'Not this,' Satyrus said. 'One of Ptolemy's, out at the moorings – to the right of *Arete*. See her?'

'Smaller than *Wasp*.' Dionysus allowed his lisp to slip away when talking of ships.

'Same as *Wasp* exactly. I think they must have come out of the same yard – Ephesus or Miletus, I suspect.' Satyrus squeezed the young fop's hand. 'Come on, brother. Dump your social calendar and come to sea.'

'But of course!' Dionysus said. He pulled his India-made chiton – the value of four strong slaves – over his head and tossed it to his boy. 'Get me a working chiton,' he said to the boy. And set to work pitching seams.

Eight days after the defeat at Cyprian Salamis, despite the best efforts of storm and Antigonid, Satyrus got to sea with ten ships under his stern, as well crewed as could be managed. His crews were rested and his own precious hulls had enjoyed almost three full days out of the water.

He wished for the squadron he'd led from Tanais. In his wake were only four of his own ships – *Oinoe*, *Plataea*, *Tanais* and *Wasp*. Every other ship was a capture or a replacement. He was missing some of his best ships: *Thetis*, *Nike* and *Ariadne*, all quadremes, with engines mounted and fully trained rowers and heavy marine crews. Poseidon only knew where they were.

Diokles, of course, had *Oinoe*; *Plataea* and *Tanais* were commanded by the brothers from Syracuse, Anaxilaus and Gelon, and *Wasp*, the smallest trireme in his force and perhaps on the surface of the ocean, continued under her veteran commander, the oldest of the trierarchs, Sarpax. The Aegyptian ship that had murdered its navarch and marines he'd stripped and renamed *Ramses* to please her Aegyptian crewmen, and Dionysus had that ship and a crew of enthusiastic volunteers with very little seagoing experience. *Amon-Ra* and *Asp* he'd found rotting in the yard, and they had scratch crews of Aegyptians under untried trierarchs – *Amon-Ra* had her own captain of marines, with Apollodorus in command, and *Asp* had his oar master, Philaeus. *Ephesian Artemis* had survived the storm under Nikeas of Pantecapaeaum, and there could be few higher recommendations of a man's competence. And Laertes had the mighty *Atlantae* by the same logic, although he now had a dozen junior officers chosen from among the best sailors on the *Wasp* and *Oinoe*.

He himself was back on the deck of *Arete*. With the exception of Neiron at his elbow, the officers were all new men; *Arete* had lost heavily in two actions and then given up still more officers to other ships. Neiron seemed untouched by the storms and battles, and the new men weren't actually new – Satyrus had had all summer to learn their worth – or rather, eight days of constant action, which now seemed to stretch away like a full season of war.

Laertes, the bronze-lunged sailor who had replaced Stesagoras, who was himself now a trierarch, was replaced as sailing master by Jubal the African. Apollodorus chose Necho to command the marines. Andromachus of Athens was the number one oar, way forward under the bows on the starboard side, replacing Polycrates. Satyrus wasn't sure that he knew the names of every sailor on the deck, but he knew most of them because he had stood with them by torchlight, splicing rope and hammering pegs into new decking in Leon's yard, or he'd kept watches with them. Xherses, a Nemean, was as thick as a rock and had to be told to do everything with elaborate sign language, but he was strong and willing and the other men liked him. And Jubal – once Stesagoras' nearly invisible third deck officer – was some form of North African or other – he had lost all of his teeth in a fight and had the habit of looking at Satyrus from under his eyes when talking, like a flirtatious flute girl. The combination of the averted glance, the missing teeth and the deep ritual scarring on his dark brown face left an indelible impression that was often mocked by the other sailors – but he had a quick wit, and he could navigate by the stars. Xiron – a big-bellied Corinthian – was the new oar master, promoted from the number one port-side position. He laughed a great deal, and made men sing, and yet was widely feared for his temper, a far cry from gentle Philaeus.

But for all the new officers, the crews themselves were no longer a collection of professionals who shared the cramped space of the black hulls. They were crews, for better and for worse. If they survived the summer, these men would sit in wine shops and brothels from Alexandria to Pantecapaeaum and nod, and say *that there's Jubal – he's a mean son of a bitch, don't cross him, mate. We shipped together under Satyrus, who was King of the North back then, see? And we got fucked in the arse by Demetrios – oh, but he shattered our line – but we served him out, didn't we, mates? Aye, and burned his precious ten tiers of oars, set her afire, almost captured the sod. Our oar master – Stesagoras, and wasn't he your uncle, young Leon? He died in that fight, roaring like a lion.*

In every ship there had been the same process, so that Diokles had a better crew in *Oinoe*, and Sarpax in *Wasp*, than either had started the summer with. Every ship was different – every ship had her own personality, and some were better; *Oinoe* and *Arete* were as good or better than Rhodians, while Dionysus and his *Ramses* were doing well to row in a straight line. *Amon Ra* leaked like the proverbial sieve of Sisyphus.

And out over the horizon, north and east, was the enemy – two hundred or more ships, most of them heavier than his heaviest.

And perhaps a few of his own. Perhaps the king. Perhaps Leon.

Forward, by the mainmast, Jubal barked something and his few teeth glinted, and the men around him laughed.

'Gaza,' he said to Neiron.

'Gaza,' Neiron repeated.

And behind his right shoulder, the pillars of cloud were still simmering and brewing over the African desert like something brewed up by the God of the Jews.

15

Last light off Gaza, and the beach was crawling with men – Antigonids – and there were almost a hundred ships beached there. Satyrus approached from the setting sun, all masts down, his ships in a close column behind him, under oars.

'Must be Antigonus himself,' Neiron said. He spat over the side, perhaps indicating what he thought of his king's plan.

'Seventy-five, seventy-six, seventy-seven,' Satyrus counted.

'Look at the grain ships,' Jubal said.

'Shut up and let me count,' Satyrus said. He was standing on the forward marine tower. 'Eighty-three, eighty-four. I make it eighty-four. And no ship larger than a trireme.'

Neiron shrugged. 'Just odds of eight to one, then. Easy as eating fish. Let's get 'em.'

Satyrus nodded. 'Exactly.'

The Alexandrian squadron manoeuvred from line ahead to line abreast with the elegance of a Nile hippo walking out of the river mud. *Ramses* responded late and turned the wrong way, and Satyrus could hear Dionysus' rampage across the water; *Amon Ra* was so slow that he didn't appear to be in line at all.

It didn't matter, because no one was watching. Plistias' fleet thought that they had the seas off Gaza and Palestine to themselves, and they were still recovering from the worst sea storm in nautical memory. So when Satyrus' ragged line swept in and began to grapple the empty hulls, the crews took long, long minutes to believe what they were seeing, and to react, and by the time armed men were at the shingle and archers were fitting arrows to their bows – mostly dry – the Alexandrians were away to sea, towing behind them a capture apiece, except *Amon Ra*, who'd come so late to the beach that he'd had to reverse oars and row away empty-handed.

Satyrus' squadron rowed into the darkness, laughing.

'We have to burn them,' Satyrus concluded after he'd examined every one of the captured hulls the following dawn.

Neiron agreed. 'It kills me,' he admitted. 'But if we have to crew them, we'll be making men who were thranites on *Arete* in the spring into trierarchs. And we'll all be equal – equally bad.' He shrugged. 'Even as it is, I think the quality's spread too thin, lord.'

Apollodorus nodded. 'We're like a slaves' breakfast, lord – too little olive oil, too much dry bread.'

Satyrus scratched his beard. 'These two are particularly fine – these two long ships. Let's call them *Amon Ra* and *Wasp* and burn the worn-out hulks you've rowed the last week.'

Dionysus shook his head. 'All that wasted work makes me want to cry.'

'What waste?' Satyrus said, relentlessly cheerful. 'They got us here. Now we have better hulls. Get it done, gentlemen.'

Followed by as much confusion as if they were under attack, hundreds of oarsmen moving their cushions and gear along the beach: fire pots, food, amphorae of wine, all the flotsam and jetsam of life at sea. But *Wasp* launched with the dawn and patrolled off the beach, and they made the transfer unmolested and got their sterns off, the shore party left behind to burn the ships that couldn't be crewed swimming out, leaving nine columns of smoke rising to the heavens like funeral pyres for the heroes in the *Iliad*.

Neiron was looking at Africa under his hand while Satyrus watched the last swimmers come up the side.

'Poseidon's throbbing member, I think we're for it again,' Neiron said.

Jubal spat between his teeth. 'Sand,' he said. 'I hate sand.' Without his front teeth, his S's sounded like th's, and he said *thand*.

Satyrus looked at Africa and then at Asia. 'Are you *sure*?' he asked.

Neiron shrugged. 'Nope,' he said.

'Very helpful,' Satyrus murmured, and Jubal laughed.

They sailed due west, towards Alexandria, until they'd sunk the land and were safely out in the day's haze, a red-hot African breeze against their port sides, and then Satyrus ordered the sails up and turned to line abreast, the ships six stades apart so that his line covered an enormous distance. The sea was a muddy, shiny blue under a deadly white sky, and the sun beat down like a merciless foe, the heat like a living enemy – but the African wind filled their mainsails and kept them dead astern, sweeping the sea north along the coast so that *Arete*, the ship closest to Asia, could see land at the top of the swell, and *Oinoe*, seventy stades to the west, could see the towering pillars of cloud over the Nile Delta.

They sailed north for an hour over a sea empty even of fishing boats. Alexandria's fishing fleet was keel up on the beaches of Pharos, her fishermen pulling oars for Satyrus.

It was almost noon when the lookouts shouted.

'*Amon Ra* just made the signal – something to the east. She's turning that way,' came the shout. They had very simple signals – four manoeuvres and two sightings.

Satyrus had just formed the words *Let's go and see what they've found* in his mind when the lookout reported again.

'Sail to landward.'

The opposite direction, of course, and all his ships were now running down to look at the something to the east. If he went west – towards the enemy – he'd be alone.

He clambered up onto the rail – the wound on his back had scarred over, but it still shouted its presence whenever he went to climb anything – and then he began to pull himself up the main brace, hand over hand, feet braced against the rope – slow, by sailor standards, but steady. At home, he'd have been on the sand of the palaestra three hours a day. Here, he climbed the rigging.

Aloft, at the top of the foremast, he locked his legs around the trunk of the mast, rested his arms over the edge of the archer's basket and looked across the sparkling sea, west, out of the eye of the sun.

Two sails – big, square sails. Grain ships.

'Keep an eye out for more. Tell me when you see sails – tell me whether they're triangles or squares. Understood?' Satyrus was pleased to find that he wasn't even breathing hard.

'Yes, lord,' said the man in the basket.

Satyrus got down the rope without burning his hands. The pitch and resin on the standing rigging was sticky in the blazing sun, and he had a line of sticky black like bad honey on his legs.

Helios laughed aloud. 'King of the Zebras!' he proclaimed. He and Charmides laughed, and Satyrus decided that he could afford to be the butt of some humour. But to Neiron he said, 'Grain ships for Antigonus. Take north by east – we'll have them in an hour.'

Like the men on the beach the day before, the crews of the two tall grain ships – round-hulled, high-sided cargo ships with eyes painted under their bows, both Athenians – were mortified to find that they had enemies in these waters.

'We had an escort,' said one captain bitterly. 'He lost us last night.'

Satyrus took the captains as hostages and sent the ships – with a dozen trusted marines in each, led by Draco and Amyntas, because he was out of other trusted men – sailing north by west for Rhodes. By this time he was all but in the surf of Antigonus' beach at Gaza – and again, the men on the beach ignored him as if he weren't there.

Arete had to row into the wind to get back to the coast of Africa, and since the heat was so vicious, Satyrus ordered that they row soft and slow, creeping upwind with steerage way and no more.

Late afternoon, and the lookout sighted something in the water ahead, and an hour's rowing took them to a capsized trireme, floating upside down just at the surface of the water. Gulls were picking at corpses.

'Not one of ours,' Charmides said from the bow with the ruthlessness of a veteran. He limped back to the sternward edge of the marine tower. 'Just happened – there's sharks still feeding.'

On and on, into the blazing sun and dead into the wind. Satyrus had sweated through his lightest chiton during his turn at the steering oars. He couldn't imagine what the thranites were going through, so he descended into the choking depths of his ship.

The air was so close and hot in the bottom range that it was like coriander soup – except that it smelled much worse. Sweat and urine and faeces and old cheese.

'Everyone here still alive?' Satyrus asked.

'Neh, we's all dead men!' called one old sweat.

'Wish we's dead,' said another.

'Is we there yet, *Pater*?' called a third.

Satyrus had to smile despite the stench. If the thranites were in such spirits, then he was in good shape.

An hour later, and the clouds over Africa were unmistakable. Neiron pointed them out to Satyrus, who was standing with Idomeneus, the archer-captain. The Cretan didn't know it, but he was slated as the next prize master. Satyrus was testing him on his navigation.

'And Cyprus to Rhodes?' Satyrus asked.

'I'm from Gortyn!' Idomeneus said with a rich chuckle. 'I was at sea when I was born. Cyprus to Asia and due west along the coast – west by south to weather the cape at Cos, and then across the strait to Rhodes. A child could do it.'

'If we take any more ships, Charmides will have a command,' Satyrus said. 'And that's as close to a child as this ship holds.'

Neiron pointed at the bronze sky to the south. 'Wind's growing stronger,' he said. 'Just like before.'

'We should get on the beach,' Jubal said.

The edge of darkness, and they saw fires to the west along the coast, and Satyrus breathed a sigh of relief when he recognised *Wasp* and *Ramses* beached stern first. And Diokles was waiting – the whole squadron had already fed, and he lined them up on the beach, got ropes aboard the *Arete* in the rising surf and pulled the big ship right up the beach until the heavy bronze bow was on dry sand. Every ship in the squadron rested on the sand.

'I count twelve,' Satyrus said, when he had his back against a chest and a golden cup of wine in his fist.

'Sank two, took one,' Diokles said. 'Ugliest action you ever saw – if you like to see a plan. But our ships kept coming up, and finally we swamped them. Your young Dionysus did very well – his men backed water almost like real oarsmen.'

'Shut your gob, wide-arse,' said Dionysus in mock sailor talk. 'We's as good as any man – better than some, aye.' He growled low in his throat.

Satyrus laughed with the others. 'He's not my Dionysus. It's my sister's breasts he wrote the poems to, after all.'

Apollodorus laughed. 'I'd wager he's never touched a breast in his life.'

Dionysus narrowed his eyes. 'Better than raping corpses for a sex life, Corinthian.'

Satyrus stepped in. 'Are we pirates now, friends? This is pirate talk.'

Diokles nodded. 'Lads are excited. It was a good day. Let me tell it – and let's not hear any more asides.'

Apollodorus raised an eyebrow. 'I apologise, Dionysus. I meant my comments as raillery – nothing more.'

Dionysus grinned and lisped. 'Apologies accepted, O Gift of Apollo. And returned. I'm sure some of your rape victims are alive.'

Apollodorus didn't explode. He smiled. 'I might find the time to convince you otherwise, Child of the Wine God.'

Satyrus put a kingly elbow into Dionysus' ribs with all the energy of the gymnasium, and Dionysus spewed wine across the fire. 'Apollodorus, you must forgive him. He's always been like this – I think the technical term is *insufferable prick*. And you two will not fight. Save it for Demetrios.'

Dionysus was laughing uncontrollably. 'I miss this,' he admitted, rubbing his ribs.

Apollodorus gave the fop a hand to his feet. 'Let the man tell his story.'

Diokles spread his hands. 'So Dionysus found two of them, and he went right at them. Then he backed away – took a light ram, got his oars in. And *Amon Ra* and *Wasp* came up and they all chased each other in circles—'

Apollodorus laughed. 'It was pitiful. My rowers made mistakes, I gave the wrong order—'

Dionysus laughed. 'I ordered my men to reverse benches, and only about a third of them did it, so that we turned broadside on to one of the enemy ships—'

Satyrus winced.

Diokles shook his head. 'So I came up in *Oinoe* and it looks like a seaborne circus, with ships in what appears to be a circle, chasing their tails like kittens. And then the biggest enemy ship turns out of its circle to ram *Ramses*—'

'And my lads all pull their arses out of the air and suddenly we're like a ship – I put my ram into their ram,' Dionysus said. 'We aren't moving as fast as an old man walks—'

'And this big trireme *impales* himself on *Ramses*,' Diokles said. 'His bow must have either been rotten, or wormed, or the gods blessed Dionysus. But that ship just *sank*.'

'And just like that, the other two lost all their spirit and we had them as fast as I can say it,' Apollodorus said.

'And my lads, who've been rowing in that infernal heat like heroes

209

to save these fools, are left as the cheering section. By which time we could see the storm clouds over Africa and we ran for the beach.' Diokles looked over his shoulder at the grey wall – almost black – shot through with lightning. 'I pity any man at sea tonight. Friend or foe.'

'You must have taken prisoners,' Satyrus said.

Apollodorus nodded. 'Plenty. It's not all wine and cheese for Demetrios. Half his fleet is here, and half is strung out between Cyprus and Alexandria. He set one rendezvous and Plistias, his admiral, set another. Antigonus needs food, right now – his men crossed the Sinai at midsummer and they need *everything*. That's what they were saying five days ago at Tyre, anyway. That's where these two rode out the last storm.'

Neiron came and stood by his king. 'You're plotting in there,' he said.

A gust of wind scattered cinders and coals across the beach, and several stung Satyrus. 'I'm always plotting. I'll turn into Stratokles, eventually.'

'Perish the thought,' Diokles said.

'Last storm blew three days,' Satyrus said.

Neiron nodded.

'If we put to sea the moment the sand dies away—' Satyrus said, and Neiron interrupted him.

'You'll be launching into the biggest seas of the summer.' Neiron shook his head. 'Day three was better, but only by comparison.'

Satyrus shook his head. 'It all depends,' he said. He shrugged. 'Ask me in a day or two.'

Two days of sandstorm, lightning and rain.

Mid-morning on the first day of the storm, and Satyrus was lying on his pile of skins, watching the sail over his head move and flap and wondering if it would tear its pegs out of the sand when Anaxagoras ducked under the heavy rugs blocking the open end of the tent and stepped in, streaming sand from his red chlamys.

'Time for a music lesson,' he said.

Satyrus sat up with a laugh, boredom vanquished, and spent a difficult hour trying to make his calloused hands match the gestures of his master on the strings of the kithara – ten strings, all running from a fine ebony rod at the tips of the instrument's hollow wooden horns, down across the belly of the instrument to lie across the sound box. Anaxagoras' kithara was a beauty, as befitted a professional musician, all lemonwood and ebony inlaid with ivory.

'Pluck the strings with the *right*,' Anaxagoras said for the eighth or ninth time. 'Calm them with the left hand.'

Satyrus had no trouble using the plectrum to strum the strings with his right hand – it felt quite natural – but his teacher's constant demand that he dampen the sound of some strings while allowing others to ring true puzzled him.

'But you say you have studied the mathematics of Pythagoras,' Anaxagoras said, clearly flustered and perhaps growing angry with a very stubborn student.

Satyrus sighed. 'When I see a ship running diagonally across my course, I *see* the mathematics of Pythagoras,' he said. 'You can tell me about the lengths of a chord until you are blue in the face, and it does nothing for me.'

Anaxagoras took a deep breath and forced a smile – a very false smile. 'I believe that you were ordered by the god to learn to play?' Anaxagoras said.

Satyrus was about to tell Anaxagoras exactly what he and the god could do with a kithara when there were shouts from outside.

One of the captured triremes *had blown over* and the sides splintered as the ship rolled on her beam ends. The sea rose until Satyrus feared that *Wasp* would be pulled out into the water, and they got the men out in lashing, sandy rain to pull the little ship higher on the beach – and then they endured two more hours of it to pull *Oinoe* and *Arete* higher up as well.

'You bastards *sailed* through this?' Dionysus asked on the evening of the second day. 'It scares me on the beach.'

Apollodorus and the Alexandrian had reached some sort of understanding.

Apollodorus shot the younger man a smile. 'I won't say this storm isn't worse, m'dear. But yes – we sailed in this for three days and three nights.'

Dawn of the third day, and Satyrus rallied all his men – over two thousand, rowers and oarsmen and marines all told – on the beach. But the wind off Africa hadn't blown out, and the sun didn't come out from the clouds until noon.

'Too late in the day,' Satyrus said, as the wind began to fall away and the mosquitoes from the swamps to the east rose from their enforced rest to find a rich source of blood waiting on the beach. They made it the worst night of the three, their high-pitched whine eventually forming a terrible sound, like the distant breathing of a malignant insect god. They didn't relent with full dark, and it was hot and airless.

Satyrus launched his ships in the dawn on a sea that seemed to have been blown absolutely flat; but a stiff shore breeze sprang up, banished the evil insects and sent the squadron winging north over a sea so calm it looked like wet faience in the new sun.

'Three days' full rations,' Jubal reported, and spat through his teeth. 'That's after dividing everything we took out of the captures.'

Satyrus nodded. 'Mainsail up. Head for Cyprus.' He shook his head. 'Let's see if we can make some trouble.'

Their first capture was two hours later – a swift message boat that had been dismasted in the last of the storm and lay helpless under their bow, snapped up almost in passing and then sunk to prevent recapture. The captive oarsmen reported that the storm had damaged Antigonus' resupply badly, but that he'd sent to Cyprus for his son and all the ships of the victorious squadrons there.

Satyrus spent the day in the lookout basket forward, shielding his eyes from the sparkling sun, watching the north and then a long line of dark clouds piling up on the western horizon. Storms from the west were all but unknown in the Cyprian Sea, but so were sandstorms out of Africa.

'I may have made a poor throw,' Satyrus said back on the deck, talking to his officers and miming a cast of the knucklebones. 'We've got no beach under our lee, and that storm ... is coming.'

'So we sail until the wind rises,' Neiron said. 'And then we row. You're too nice to the rowers, lord. They can do it.'

Satyrus went to sleep worried, and awoke with the first of the thunder and then it was morning, a grey-white morning, hot and airless. The rowers groaned and set to, a cruising stroke, and Satyrus put his little fleet into two columns of six ships, headed due north.

The sun was high in the sky and past noon when the first gusts of wind from the west hit them. By the third gust they could see a squall line coming, and Neiron ordered all the sails struck down, the masts lowered and stowed and the ship rigged for heavy weather.

'Where do you place us, Old Man of the Sea?' Satyrus asked Neiron.

Neiron made a sign to avert evil. 'A hundred stades south of Cyprus, give or take a hundred. Hard to tell how much northing we made in the dark last night. Eh?'

Jubal spat between his teeth. 'More *thouth* than that,' he said confidently. 'Not enough wind for a fart latht night, lord.'

Satyrus walked forward with Anaxagoras.

'Teach me,' he said.

'Only if you will learn,' Anaxagoras said.

Satyrus sighed. He called for stools, and sat down in the shade of the forward tower. So that he was the closest officer when the lookout shouted.

16

'Sails! Sails to the east! Ten square ... fifty triangles!' The man sounded as if panic had taken the lower registers of his voice.

Satyrus sprang up the steps into the marine tower without feeling a twinge in his back. Away to the north and east was a great fleet – all their sails up, running east and south on the wild west wind.

Running for the coast of Asia.

Satyrus kept himself still for several long breaths, counting sails. The closest squadron was hull up – big ships, and in a crisp formation, and he guessed that these were the squadron of penteres that had faced down Menelaeus. Beyond were two more squadrons of triangles, hull down, and perhaps another further. And at least twenty merchant ships – and more away to the north.

Satyrus looked away to the west, away from the enemy. A line of squalls all the way to the horizon.

Helios climbed up the ladder. 'Neiron asks, how many and what are we doing?'

Satyrus managed a smile. 'I'm sure he put it in a more direct way than that.'

Anaxagoras came up the tower, the kithara still in his hand. 'Sex acts were mentioned,' the musician laughed.

Helios handed his master an apple. 'You haven't eaten, lord.'

Satyrus took the apple and ripped at it with his teeth. He looked at the enemy fleet, which now filled the horizon. Then he looked back at the squalls.

'Let's take this aft,' he said, and by the time he reached Neiron at the helm, he'd made up his mind.

'We're going to fight in the storm,' Satyrus said.

Everyone nodded – even Neiron.

Despite the fact that no one demurred, Satyrus felt he had to explain. 'We're going to get caught in the wind, anyway,' he said.

'The crews are as good as they'll ever be. And if we can hit them this afternoon, any ship we even damage is dead in the night.'

Neiron nodded. 'But no ramming, and no boarding,' he said.

'That's it,' Satyrus said. 'Oar rakes, archers, the engines if we can get them to work. And fear. Don't forget fear.' He looked around, and they seemed confident. He was proposing to fight a galley action in a storm and they looked like they agreed.

He nodded, chewed the last bite of his apple and threw the core over the side. 'Line ahead. We'll row another half an hour, get the foresails up and run free – oar ports closed. *Arete* in the lead. If we do it well, we should come in *behind* the penteres and right into the grain ships.' He smiled at them; he felt few of his usual pre-battle fears. He grinned. 'Because, my friends, this is about grain. Burn the grain, and Antigonus can't invade Aegypt.'

'For grain!' Anaxagoras shouted. Despite his obvious irony, the other men answered.

An hour later, under foresail alone, and still it took two men to keep *Arete* to her course, one on each steering oar, so great was the pressure of the speed. *Oinoe* was just astern, and now the rest were lost in the spray, and the storm line was so near astern that it would be a close race whether Satyrus came up with the grain ships ahead before the storm, with all the rain it seemed to hold, came crashing up behind.

All the ships were running the same way – east, towards the coast of Asia. But the enemy's supply ships were slower, even under sail and with the wind dead astern, than the slim warships, most of which had raised their mainsails and raced ahead. To the south, a pair of penteres loomed like sea monsters in the grey light. Beyond them were other ships, south and west.

Satyrus' hulls were smooth from the yards and dry, and for once it was he who had the speed advantage – an advantage that was as clear as the waning day as *Arete* caught up with the trailing grain ship like an Olympic runner overtaking a fat man.

'Light the fire pots,' Satyrus ordered. He was literally playing with fire. 'Poseidon, forgive me the use of this foreign flame on your sea – my need is desperate.' He had nothing to hand to offer as a personal sacrifice.

The grain ship was a merchant – probably Tyrian – with rounded sides like a wooden soap bubble, virtually storm-proof. She had two tall masts, with only a scrap of linen set on the foremast. The captain gave Satyrus a wave as he drew alongside assuming, as so many others had, that Satyrus was from his escort.

Neiron barked an order, and the *Arete*'s bow swung a few degrees. The oars were in, and the big penteres' marine tower matched the grain ship's side for height. The best athletes – Anaxagoras, Charmides, Necho – threw fire pots across the few feet of water, and then they were past, their port-side engines and all their archers firing into the helpless ship. The wicked west wind whipped the coals to flames that seemed to explode from the wounded ship's bow as her captain sank to the deck with one of Idomeneus' barbed shafts in his throat.

Every ship in the squadron fired into the hapless grain ship, but the damage was done – she broached, cutting across the wind, her helm empty.

Two more ships fell in quick succession, and then the enemy began to respond the way fish respond to a pod of dolphins – the grain ships began to scatter, throwing their helms wildly to port or starboard, choosing the perils of crossing the wind against the immediate and definite threat of the ships coming up so fast from astern, but the wind had risen to a gale behind them and the edge of the storm was a palpable thing, somewhere just aft of *Wasp*.

Satyrus watched a grain ship roll – too much canvas, too wild a turn. She rolled to port, her rail went under the water and Poseidon took her – just like that. Gone.

He turned to Neiron. 'Done. And worth it: if we all go to the bottom now, Aegypt is safe.'

Neiron made a face. 'That makes it worth it?'

And then the storm hit.

As men told the story in later years, it wasn't much of a battle, as battles went. None of Satyrus' ships received as much as a single arrow. It was more like the storming of a city – ugly work, a massacre of the almost innocent.

But war is an ugly tyrant, and the tactics of terror and death were the only tactics that Satyrus had left. His ships pounced out of the storm like sharks on whitefish, like furies avenging an insult to the gods, and every ship they forced to turn out of the wind died.

As battles went, it was more like a massacre.

But as a storm, it was quite a storm. Men talked about the storm for the rest of their lives, those that lived.

No one on *Wasp* lived. A freak cross wave caught *Wasp* before night fell, rolled her too far and the ruthless wind served her and her two hundred rowers as the Athenian grain ships had been served – with death, no reprieve, for Sarpax and all his crew. Satyrus saw them go, and something harsher than rage – something like *fault* choked him. Losing men he liked to Ares was the stuff of war, but the sea was cleaner and worse – two hundred men in between breaths.

No one on *Ramses* lived. Ramses was just astern of *Oinoe* when the light failed, riding west under a scrap of sail, and they died so close astern that the men at *Arete*'s helm heard them scream as a wave filled them, or as some plank failed, or the bow split against wreckage or a floating log. Poseidon had a thousand ways to take a man down, and Dionysus went to the bottom with his men.

And when the sun rose somewhere over Asia, too close under their bows, so that they could see the surf in the first light, the others were gone. *Arete* ran west until there was no more water, and the sea behind her wake was empty of life. Neiron conned the ship close to the beach, stripped the last scrap of canvas at the edge of the surf and ran the great vessel ashore ram first, taking his chances with the sea god to keep his men alive, ignoring the king's protests in his ear. And under the lash of Neiron's anger, Satyrus leaped into the water with his deck crew and his marines and oarsmen and hauled and hauled again until the penteres was clear.

Not every ship had been so lucky. There were wrecks on the beach, ships which had run ashore in the dark and died there. Satyrus counted four wrecks on this beach alone. He had to visit them. He walked, alone, from wreck to wreck. None was his.

Men started fires.

Men cooked food.

The sea was empty. By noon the sun emerged and the wind, the killer west wind that had sent a thousand men and more to crawl the sea bottom with Amphitrite, lungs full of water, finally died away, and the sea was the deep blue of innocence: it was as empty as a drunkard's purse.

Satyrus walked off by himself, sat on a rock and wept.

Neiron came up.

Satyrus looked up, uncertain.

'Well?' Neiron asked. 'Was it worth it? Because you *lost them all*.'

The older man turned on his heel and walked away.

Antigonus One-Eye didn't need an ivory stool to look important. He was sitting on an iron stool with a pair of fleeces on it, and his shoulders were as square as those of a man of fifty. Or thirty. He was eighty.

His son came in. He did not look himself: his hair was pale and dry, not the flame of gold it usually seemed. He had circles under his eyes like bruises, and his skin looked more like a waxen image than the skin of an active man.

'A chair for the King of Aegypt,' Antigonus said to a slave.

Demetrios laughed. 'Ptolemy is the King of Aegypt, *Pater*.' A slave put a cup of wine in his hand and he drank the whole cup.

'May the gods curse him!' Antigonus shouted. 'What have I done to be treated so by Tyche?' He looked like an outraged falcon, and Demetrios rose and embraced his father.

'*Pater* – it's the will of the gods.' He wrapped his arms around the old man.

'I spit on the gods!' Antigonus shouted. 'Whores and bastards! Two years of work lost in a storm! A *storm*! Aegypt was lying naked, waiting for me to plough her!'

Demetrios wondered if his *pater* was losing his wits. He hugged the old man harder. '*Pater* – *Pater*. No hubris.'

'This, from you? Who claims to be a god incarnate?' The old man hadn't lost his wits. He managed a laugh. He stroked his son's hair, then pushed him away. 'A curse on the lot of them, then. We must start again. If I don't order the retreat tonight, I'll lose good men – Macedonians – in a few days. The swamp here is putrid – the miasma is from Tartarus, and men are sickening already. Wait until you've spent a night here – the mosquitoes are worse than Parthians. Worse than the cursed Sakje.'

Demetrios drank a second cup of wine. 'No reproof? It was me, *Pater*, who said I could supply you from the sea.'

'Bah,' Antigonus said. 'You gathered the ships you promised. Even that harlot, Athens, did her part. And you beat Ptolemy at Cyprus – I gather Menelaeus surrendered, that arse-cunt.'

'As soon as his brother's ships were over the horizon,' Demetrios said. 'My only success of the summer, I fear.'

'How many ships have we left?' Antigonus asked.

'At least one hundred. All the big ones – they weathered the storms best. Perhaps more – in truth, the biggest mistake I made was to give a different rendezvous from Plistias. I don't really know what I have left. Neither does he. They will be spread from Syracuse to Tyre now.'

'And Ptolemy?' Antigonus asked.

'Fewer.' Demetrios lay back on the bed. 'You know who actually worked to defeat us, *Pater*?'

'Poseidon?' Antigonus asked.

'Satyrus of Tanais. He almost had me at Cyprus.' Demetrios grinned. 'I like him. I want to kill him in single combat.'

'Son, sometimes when men tell me that you are mad, I'm tempted to believe them. We do not fight in single combat. We win empires.' Antigonus snapped his fingers for more wine. 'I'd wish I could trade Satyrus for one of our useless allies, though. Why do we get Heraklea when Ptolemy gets Tanais? Eh? I can't trust Dionysus of Heraklea as far as I can throw him. And as he's fatter than Milos, that's not far.' The old man spat.

'We'll have the winter to rally the fleet,' Demetrios said. He was staring at the silk tapestry hanging from the ceiling of the tent.

'If you can keep the *fucking* Rhodians from putting more troops into Alexandria, we can be right back here in spring,' the old man said. 'A curse on all the gods. Fuck their mothers. I was right up into the forts on the river, you know that? And he's all but lined the bank with artillery. One of his engines *killed an elephant*. If the storm hadn't come up, you could have turned his flank at sea—'

'If wishes were bread, beggars would never go hungry. *Pater* – let me take the fleet and go for Rhodes.' Demetrios shot off the bed, suddenly filled with energy. 'Rhodes is the key. Aegypt will stand or fall with Rhodes – and Rhodes is the easier nut to crack.'

'Rhodes is a boil on our behind. Aegypt is the key to the world.'

Antigonus stared into his son's blue eyes and wondered how he had *ever* fathered such a handsome boy.

'Lance the boil,' Demetrios said. 'Lance the boil, and you'll have the key.'

Antigonus puffed up his cheeks and then blew out suddenly. 'My gut aches and my insides turn to water,' he said. 'My legs hurt all the *fucking* time. Half my nights, my little Persian girl can't get my rod stiff with a barrel of olive oil and the best breasts in the Eastern Ocean. I *hate* being old, and the only good thing about my age is that it is better than death.' Antigonus looked at his golden, marvellous son. 'You know what keeps me alive?'

'Love for the gods?' Demetrios asked.

'You, and dominion. And gods-cursed Ptolemy. I hated him when he was Alexander's butt-boy and I want him under my heel now. Before I'm *dead. I want Aegypt.*'

'The road to Aegypt is through Rhodes,' Demetrios said.

Antigonus wrapped his son in his still strong arms. 'Do it, then. Lance the boil. Get me the key, whatever image appeals to you, boy, but *get it soon.*'

Demetrios smiled over his father's shoulder, and in his head, the cogs and wheels that drove his planning began to whirl.

'It will be *incredible,*' he said.

BOOK THREE

THE SIEGE OF RHODES

17

Kineas of Athens, rendered in bronze, the whites of his eyes pure gold, the pupils lapis, stood in the dressing room of the gymnasium, a slim staff of vine in his hand. When he spoke, his teeth shone in shining silver inside his mouth against his bronze tongue.

Satyrus was mesmerised by the effect. But the words his father spoke were clear and businesslike, heavy with import. Satyrus leaned forward, trying to listen, but the play of light on his father's metal face distracted him again, and filled his eyes so that he soared away like a child avoiding his lessons, daydreaming of flight, of the sky, of clouds—

Satyrus! Pay attention! Philokles' voice: the sharp 'I mean it' voice of a sober, angry tutor. Satyrus cringed in expectation of the teacher's rod across his shoulders and he sat straighter.

He turned his head, and Philokles was standing behind him, also rendered in precious metals – the very statue that had just been delivered in Tanais, now animated. And sitting behind him, where Xenophon had always sat for lessons in Alexandria, was Stratokles the Informer, who looked every bit as terrified of Philokles as Xenophon had.

There were other boys: he saw Demetrios the Golden off to his left, and could the round-headed boy be Panther of Rhodes? But now the stick struck him with all of Philokles' accustomed force; pain leaped through his body, not from the back but from the lungs, and he had blood on his chest.

Satyrus! Pay attention!

Is he going to die? Srayanka asked. His mother was beautiful – her hair was carved from a black stone and it hung free, beautifully combed, as it did when he was a boy, on the rare occasions when she dressed as a Greek woman.

I guarantee it! Philokles said with a snort. *He's mortal, is he not? And death is the required condition of all mortals, is it not?* The tutor's rod struck his back again, and more blood fountained from his mouth across his chest.

Do you spend so much time with your father that you can ignore him when he speaks? Philokles asked.

Satyrus looked at his father, and was fascinated by the play of light on his father's golden eyes. He forced himself to listen to the lecture, ignoring the host of questions that beat at the doors to his mind—

How can my dead father be speaking in the gymnasium of Alexandria?

How can a statue speak?

Who has allowed my mother, a woman, into the gymnasium?

Is she, too, not dead?

Why is Stratokles here? Where is Xenophon? He is dead. He should be here. But I am here – am I dead?

Is this death?

The rod struck him again, forcing him forward, coughing and coughing, and with every cough more blood flowed out of his mouth – gouts of it. Finally, exhausted, he fell backwards.

Xenophon caught him, as he had so often done at lessons.

You should listen, Satyrus!

Satyrus lay back with his head on his friend's legs and watched his father, the statue.

His father looked down at him and smiled.

So glad I finally have your attention, lad.

It was as if he could see himself. Zeus Sator, he looked bad – blood all over his bedclothes, eyes rolling – Apollo! His eyes were as yellow as the golden eyes of the statues!

He was in a room that looked familiar, and the room was full of people who looked familiar, but just at that moment, Satyrus couldn't put names to the actors or to the place, and he just floated, watching as the dark-haired woman washed the blood off his chest, as the old woman forced something down his throat, as two young men stood by, watching with the helpless eagerness of men who don't know how to do anything useful.

The old woman completed her task and shook her head.

'He's going,' she said. The woman paused and rolled her head, flexed the muscles in her shoulders. 'I said he's going, child. Let him go. Leave the washing of the body for the corpse-cleaners.'

The dark-haired woman kept washing, her hands moving with a fierce determination. Satyrus, even from so far away, could read that this woman intended to wash him clean – clean of death, if only she could.

Satyrus winced to see his body, which was so thin – where was his muscle? Where was his strength? His arms were like sticks, his legs like a woman's legs. He wished his eyes would close and hide the hideous yellow.

'He is not dead yet,' said the younger woman.

The old woman looked at the men. 'Get us some water – as cold and fresh as may be.' They hurried from the room, and the young woman's eyes widened.

'You have thought of something?' she asked. To say that her eyes glimmered with hope would be to suggest too much. Perhaps, thought Satyrus, this is what the hope of a hope looked like.

He wished that he could remember this woman's name, as she was very devoted to him, and he wished that he could reward that devotion. For himself, he wouldn't have touched that body with a sword.

I am a ruin, he thought. *Let me die – I would never wish to live like that.*

The old woman shrugged. 'No, dear. I just wanted them out of the room. I am going to give him poppy juice.'

'But—' The younger woman shook her head. 'You said—'

And the older woman managed a smile. 'You are a good girl. Two months ago, when we were fighting the disease with a strong body, I feared to take him back to – to his addiction. Now, I seek only to let him die easy. There will be no addiction for him where he is going.'

The girl turned on the old woman, and Satyrus could see that she was not a girl, but a grown woman. And not his sister. He had rather hoped that she was his sister. He loved his sister – and that feeling, that love, the loss of Melitta, wherever she was, rolled over him like a wave and snuffed him out like a lamp.

The siege is the deadliest form of war for both the soldier and the citizen. The siege is the only battle where women and slaves are soldiers; the only battlefield where men, not the gods, create the terrain; only in the siege can a man be forced to fight all day, sleep, rise and fight again. Armies that undertake long sieges are often ruined and never useful as an army again. Cities that survive a siege may die of exhaustion; cities that are taken in a siege are sacked – the laws of war that protect the captive and the ransomed are as nothing because an army that lays siege to a city must take risks, gambles and hideous casualties to accomplish their goal, and as a consequence, when that army is victorious, they take their revenge. Every man is killed – free or slave, noble or thetis. Temples are looted and burned, and it is reckoned no impiety. Women are raped – not once, but again until their minds are broken, and then they are sold as slaves, to work another's loom and another's bed until they die.

And yet, by the same remorseless laws that dictate that the victorious besiegers will act like animals and sack the town, the town itself will use any device, any stratagem, any tactic no matter how reckless to avoid the sack. They will bribe, coerce, seduce; squander their citizens in sorties to burn the enemy camp, turn the slaves from the town and watch them starve beneath the walls, old family retainers and all. They will sacrifice citizens like the priests sacrifice goats, and count the cost light. Because defeat means extinction, degradation, horror and death.

And this contest is conducted with every science that men have ever developed, with all the passion that the gods gave to men for better things, with the ruthlessness that men ought to save to fight beasts. Well might old Plato say that to see the worst that men might make of themselves, you need only watch the siege of a city.

But today we will discuss how it is best to take a city, and how it is best to defend a city. I have done both. And to aid you in this consideration, I will use what Philokles has taught you of the body, and I will ask you to use the body as a model of the city – I am hardly original in this, as Plato and Aristotle are both there before me.

How does illness attack the body? I will argue that it can attack in two ways, just like a besieger. It can come forward by stealth. After carefully scouting the body, it can attempt to seize the body by a sudden assault on the gates – taking a side gate of a postern, perhaps, in a brilliant rush at the break of dawn while the body's sentries are asleep. And in rushes the contagion, and the body's defences never have a chance to respond before the healer can pray to the gods or administer the least medicine; before a bath can be prepared to wash, the citadel has fallen to the deadly swift disease and the man is a cooling corpse. Have we not seen this?

But the swift onset of the secret force will seldom triumph in the taking of a city. As a besieger, it must be tried – even at the cost of losing the picked men of your army, the savings in blood and gold of such an attempt is almost incalculable. Never, when you are commanders, allow yourself to count the loss of such a picked group against the possibility of success. If a city must fall – if that is the objective of your campaign – there is no personal price you should not be willing to pay short of impiety or immorality in the taking of the city.

I lost my hyperetes – my oldest friend, as well – in the taking of a citadel. I mourned him but I counted the cost as light.

Likewise, if you find yourself defending a city, you must be prepared from the outset for a swift assault on your gates by secret forces. You must assume that every suggestion of parley cloaks an attack. From the first suggestion that a siege may be undertaken, you must change the guards on the gates regularly, and also change the officers who hold towers, assuming, always, that every man can be bribed. This is a caustic way to deal with your fellow citizens, but everything about a siege is caustic. Many will die, and many things and ideas will die that we hold dear – love dies of hunger as much as of disease, and honour is all too frequently sacrificed or lost, because the siege is not a one-day battle that shows the best in the best men, but an endless contest that gives every mind the opportunity to show its darkest excess.

But let us consider what happens when the secret force has failed. In an attack on the body, the disease now settles down to a siege of the citadel. Already, the disease has a lodgement – has hold of some part of the body. A wound, perhaps, that becomes enflamed, or the fever that sprouts from bad air or miasma. This sort of disease cannot win the citadel in a single attack – the human is much too strong, unless already eroded by bad food, little sleep, no exercise, age, infirmity, or other diseases – just like a city that survives the initial assault will last a long time, unless already weakened by internal strife, military defeat, weak governance, starvation and the like. So the disease must work carefully. It must undermine the walls of health by wrecking the body's sleep; by fatiguing the muscles while stifling exercise; by raising and lowering the temperature of the body to simulate an adverse climate, stimulating dreams that wreck the moral fibre and destroy the will of the body to resist, exactly as the besieger will seek to send spies and spread false reports.

And when the body is sufficiently weak, it will fall. Or it should fall.

Sometimes the body comes with an exceptional defender – the will. And the will can command the defences like a tyrant commands his bodyguard. Tyrants are poor rulers, in many cases, but they are often the toughest nut to crack in a siege because they have the will to resist to the very end. If the mind has this singleness of purpose, it may resist the disease to the point where the disease itself dies. Likewise, a city that does not lose its wits, that remembers the cost of failure, that has the will of a tyrant even if the city is a democracy, may endure, and break the besieger.

Another day I will speak more on tactics – on how to reinforce a gate, on how to construct a tower, on how to use hot sand or molten lead, on how to construct a secret tunnel. But I have spoken enough for today – there are some among you who are ready to sleep.

Satyrus, I say this to you. If you wish to live, then live.

With those words ringing in his ears, Satyrus awoke.

Perhaps it was wrong to say that Satyrus awoke. He emerged from the dream of his father – a dream built with colours more vivid than the waking world, with statues that talked and the souls of dead men – to a world much more like the world he inhabited every day, with the exception that he saw it from a distance, as if for the first time. There, in the bed, lay his emaciated body.

Helios – he knew the boy immediately – dozed in a chair. The bossy woman with the iron-grey hair was asleep on a *kline* under a grand window. Outside, the sun shone brilliantly over the harbour of the town, and the work on the walls continued unabated. Across the harbour, tied to the new wharf, *Arete* rode at her moorings, the tallest ship in the harbour of Rhodes.

So I am at Rhodes, Satyrus said to himself.

The long-legged woman of his earlier dream came into the room with a small *lekythos*, from which she poured white milk into a cup. Satyrus could smell the poppy juice as soon as she poured it, and he longed for it as soon as he smelled it.

She took a small bone spoon and put some in his mouth. He wondered that she could bear even to touch him – he looked like a corpse. His head seemed to have grown out of all proportion to his body, and his shoulders – once heavy with muscle – were all bones.

'What shall I tell you today?' she began, and something in her voice told him that this was a habit – an old habit. *How long has she been talking to me? A week? A month? Two months?*

'Demetrios has two hundred and twenty ships gathered at Miletus, or so Panther says. He comes here often, he and Memnon. No one here has forgotten what you did for us, Satyrus.' Her voice was gentle, and she took his hand and ran one of her fingers up the middle of his palm. 'They say he is bound here, on the first good wind of spring – with forty thousand men in transport ships. So the whole city makes preparations for the siege, and oh, how my brother wishes for your recovery!'

She bent down and kissed his brow. 'Everyone asks after you, King Satyrus.' Then she rose, and walked quietly across the tiled room, edging carefully around Helios. At the door she spoke, and her tone was different – Satyrus saw that she was speaking to a scroll hanging on the wall.

'Would it be so much, O high and lonely god, to let this man live?' she said, addressing the scroll.

Never take that tone with the gods, Satyrus wanted to admonish her, for she sounded bitter, angry and reproachful, like a young child who has discovered the fallibility of her parents.

Helios awoke with a start. 'Mistress Miriam?' he asked.

Miriam.

She stepped back into the room. 'I'm sorry, Helios.'

'Gods, Despoina, it is I who should be sorry. I should be awake.' Helios rubbed his eyes. 'He was calling out last night – calling to his father and to Philokles, and coughing blood again.' Helios looked over at the old woman lying on the *kline*. 'Aspasia no longer believes that he will live. Am I ... right?'

Miriam made a face. She was not old enough to act the matron, but she tried, controlling her emotions as best she could. 'You are right. She may also ... be right.' Miriam sagged against the door jamb and rubbed her eyes. 'No man should be able to live so long without food. But I am giving him poppy, and so is Aspasia. It will ease his end ... or allow him to eat.'

'He has a strong will,' Helios said with the careful deliberation of the young who have come to great knowledge. 'He will not die easily. And yet ... Oh, Despoina. He blamed himself for all the ones lost in the storm. Anaxagoras says that, not the miasma, brought this on.'

'Anaxagoras believes that he can be healed with music,' Miriam replied. She sighed. 'And yet Anaxagoras is full of wisdom, too. Why are we all so wise, and none of us can save him?'

Lost in the storm echoed in his mind. Yes. Diokles, Sarpax, Akes, Dionysus. How many ships lost? Seven? And all their crews? Fifteen *hundred* men lost because he felt that he had to—

It had to be done. Am I just defending myself from the charge of rashness? Or do I actually believe it had to be done?

I lost my hyperetes – my oldest friend, as well – in the taking of a citadel. I mourned him but I counted the cost as light. His father had said that. *In a dream.*

The body on the bed twitched and started, and Satyrus fell from above into the corpse's eyes – down long tunnels—

Philokles sat between two men that Satyrus knew only from statues – Socrates and Arminestos, the family hero. The Plataean who had saved Greece. All three were immortal in bronze and gold, wearing chitons of marble. Behind them stood the chryselephantine statue of Athena Nike.

Philokles leaned over the table in front of him. Satyrus didn't dare turn his head, but he thought that they must be in Athens, of a sudden – in the Temple of Athena Nike on the Acropolis. No idea why.

'You charge yourself with the loss of fifteen hundred men,' Philokles said. 'Do you really wish a full examination? Or will you merely wallow in guilt for a time, and then wall that guilt away?'

'An unexamined life is not worth living,' Socrates said. 'Let the trial be a fair one.'

'Any commander who wastes his time counting the corpses of his friends isn't worth a shit,' Arimnestos said. 'All this sentimentality will only make you weak.' He, in turn, leaned over the table. 'Unless you just squandered them, eh? That's shameful. Men have lives – even slaves. Even oarsmen. Perhaps not as worthy as ours, but they aren't there to be squandered.'

'Let the boy speak,' Socrates said gently. 'Listen, boy. Once we start down this path, you will try yourself, and if you find yourself wanting, it will be far worse than the fools who ordered me to drink hemlock.' He snorted. 'No man can run from himself. Nor does any man need to account himself wise for knowing that the worst furies are one's own.'

Philokles had a pair of dividers in his hand. 'Come,' he said, just as *he had when he had summoned a much younger Satyrus to give him an answer in geometry. 'Come – will you try the case?'*

Satyrus sat up. 'I will.'

Arimnestos laughed. 'Then I am ready with my verdict.'

Socrates nodded. 'Yes, boy. I, too, am ready.'

Satyrus felt as if he'd been struck by a storm. 'But – the evidence!'

Philokles nodded. 'Is complete. Listen, boy – it's all in your head.' He gave one of his rare grins to Arimnestos. 'I would hate to have to tell his father that he was found guilty.'

Arimnestos nodded respectfully to Philokles and then turned to Satyrus. 'You, lad, are rash.'

Socrates nodded. 'Over-bold. Foolish. Given to taking risks because you believe that you can overcome them with luck and planning.'

Philokles nodded. 'In fact, it is this very talent – the ability to take an enemy at a rush, to make a plan on the fly, calculate the risk and overcome it in your head – that is at risk in this tribunal. Having lost fifteen hundred men, will you ever trust yourself again?'

Socrates nodded. 'Exactly.' He glanced at Philokles. 'You say you are from Sparta?'

Philokles shrugged. 'It's true.'

'Hmm,' Socrates said. 'An educated Spartan. Still, the world is wide and no man in it has the knowledge of the gods, or even of other men.' He ran his fingers through his beard. 'Listen, boy. When I made my stand at Delium – when young Alcibiades rescued me – I lost my two closest friends, because when I stood, they stood. And later, men all but worshipped me as a living hero – and I believed the men. And yet, I knew that I killed my Nikeas and my Cassander as surely as if I'd taken my kopis to their necks. And yet I was sure – with all the surety of the young – that I was doing the right thing. The moral thing. The thing that Achilles would have done.' Socrates shrugged. 'They haunted me all my days, of course. Even while I remained sure. In fact, I could say that their ghosts made me Socrates the Sophist. I had to search for answers.'

Arimnestos looked at Socrates and smiled – not a very nice smile. 'I'm sure that all that sophistry does you honour,' the warrior said. 'I lost friends the way children lose toys. What of it? Always for me the place to fight was wherever the fight was thickest – gods, how I loved it. And if my friends would follow me there – follow me to where Ares danced – then they would die, many of them. Was it my fault? I'm no madman, Satyrus. I

233

worried about it like any commander worth two farts. But I didn't worry too much. When the bronze rings and the iron shines, you kill or you are killed. And afterwards, you make what peace with yourself you can, or you go' – the warrior looked at the sophist – 'goat-fucking mad.' He shrugged. 'Or you lose your touch of the divine and become an animal.'

Philokles made a face. 'Satyrus, I sit between these two for a reason, as you, who were always a bright boy, can easily guess. Now – please. What is your verdict?'

Satyrus looked out of the temple – and he saw the shades of thousands of men. There was Ataelus and there was Samahe, and Philokles himself, and the Sarmatian girl he'd shot, the first person he'd knowingly killed, and there was a Macedonian he'd put in the dust at Gaza – Ares, there were thousands. Was that Diokles, at the back? Shades – wisps, and yet they seemed to stretch away down the Panathenaic Way. They murmured. He couldn't hear them, and yet they made him profoundly afraid.

The three statues were immovable in front of him, and behind the three was Nike, slim and beautiful and remarkably like Miriam, holding a sword. She was made of marble, gilded and painted, and she smiled at him.

'Who are they?' Satyrus asked, annoyed by the fear in his voice. He jerked a thumb at the shades.

'The jury,' Nike answered. 'Don't even try to bribe them. They're dead!' and she laughed, a fluid sound like a brook in spring, easy and light.

Back to hovering above the room, and watching Aspasia – that was her name. She'd healed him before, discovered his addiction to the poppy juice and set him on the road to recovery.

She moved around the room with purpose, like a trierarch on the deck of warship under oars. She stepped quietly and confidently, preparing a tisane of herbs and drugs, adding warm water, feeding it to him with a spoon.

Satyrus, watching himself, wondered why they bothered. His skin was transparent like the most expensive parchment, and the tone of the parchment was yellow – a hideous colour. Even as he flinched at the colour, the stick figure on the bed rolled and cried out.

Aspasia murmured endearments, tenderly wiping the hair from his face. At some point while pushing the straggling curls away, she stopped, muttered something inaudible and laid the back of her hand against his forehead, and then against his cheek. And then she peeled back the bedclothes and thrust her hand into his groin.

'Alas,' she said. And folded the bedclothes over his face.

Troy – the siege of Troy – endless. Satyrus fought and fought, day after day – he was Menelaeus, he was Achilles, he was Hektor, and Aeneas. Diomedes ...

She returned with Abraham, already weeping, and Miriam, Helios, Anaxagoras and Neiron – Neiron was dressed in a full chiton, a man of property going to the assembly.

She had a silver mirror in her hand, and she buffed it against her chest until it shone.

'Any news of his sister?' she asked.

'None,' Neiron replied. 'And now – her son is king, I assume. A raven's feast if the Herakleans—'

'Are you gentiles so heartless?' Miriam asked. 'Was this not a man? Not your friend? And all you want to talk about is his inheritance?'

Neiron shrugged. 'Despoina, he was a king. If he had lived, he would want his kingdom to live, and not be cut up like a pig is cut by a butcher.'

Zeus Sator! Too right, old man.

Miriam sat on the edge of the bed and put the silver mirror in front of his lips. 'It never hurts to be sure,' she said, matter-of-factly.

'He's cold,' Miriam said, and took a shuddering breath. 'Neiron, I'm sorry.'

'Nothing to be sorry about, Despoina. I liked him. More, I fear, than I let him know, but I'm old enough not to want the world to see everything that crosses the bridge of my thoughts.'

Abraham shook his head. He raised his fists towards the ceiling. Then he composed himself. Miriam took his arm, and he embraced her.

Helios wept.

Anaxagoras sat in the chair, lifted a small lyre and began to play.

Aspasia shot him a look.

'Worked for Orpheus,' he said with a smile.

'To Hades with your blasphemy,' the doctor-priestess said.

But the simple tune he played was like a dirge, like a march, like a hymn – his hands seemed to flow over the strings of the lyre and it rang, louder than might have been expected, the notes slowing until they fell one by one like drops of water falling on a desert, and then Anaxagoras moved his right hand across all the strings like a man wiping a slate clean, and he began to tap his sandal on the floor, a rhythm so compelling that Miriam, clutched in her brother's arms, found herself patting her brother's back in time, and Helios through his tears was slapping the chair arm in time and Neiron's chin moved fractionally up and down.

'Come and take your stand, Satyrus,' Anaxagoras said. 'Achilles said,' and here his rhythm beat harder, 'Achilles said that it was better to be the slave of the worst master among the living than to be a king among the dead.'

And then his right hand moved and the notes began to fall and then flow, faster and more insistent—

Anaxagoras began to sing, and Neiron's harsh croak joined in instantly, and Aspasia, her eyes shining, and Helios, hesitant—

Daughters of the muses, who walk the slopes of well-wooded Olympus! rang the paean to Apollo, the song that maidens sang to the newborn god and that men roared in defiance when preparing to sell their lives dearly.

Notes fell like a waterfall of sound and glory, and Satyrus found that he might make the choice, if he willed it, and he chose to fall down the waterfall of music back into the deep pool of his body—

And the music rolled on, man's most potent magic against the dark, the oarsman's salvation, the aid of the warrior, the light of the dancing maiden until his head was more full of the notes than of the fever.

And when the music ended, there was silence, and dark.

Far, far away, he heard the healer say, 'Look, there. I'm wrong, and all that fuss for nothing, dear. See where his breath mists the silver? Always best to be sure.' But her breath caught and there was the hint of a sob, and behind her, Helios and Anaxagoras finished the hymn.

18

Satyrus awoke to the sound of music, and he slept to the sound of music. The *Iliad* and the *Odyssey*, the war poems of Tiresias, sea shanties, drinking songs, hymns to the gods. And another voice, lighter but pure, singing women's songs – Sappho's songs about the purity of love:

Some say that a body of cavalry is the most beautiful,
And some say the phalanx is the most beautiful,
And some say a squadron of ships is the most beautiful,
But I say that the most beautiful one
Is the one that is loved

And his eyes opened, fluttered and stayed open. At the foot of his bed Aspasia sat in a chair of ebony, her wrinkled face composed in sleep. And closer, sitting so that her hip rested in a pool of warmth against the sticks of his own hip bones, Miriam played the lyre and sang through the whole of Sappho's greatest love song, singing of how Helen chose love over war, and how great was the beauty of that gift.

Satyrus lay for a long time with his eyes open. He couldn't bear to look at his shoulders against the coverlet, but he could watch Miriam's face in repose and song for a long time.

A long time.

She sang another song in a very different voice – a strange, almost discordant song that was almost more like a chant than Greek music.

In his head, he smiled to realise that he was actually awake – these were real people, not phantasms; that his brain still worked. The word *Hebrew* floated to the surface of his thoughts – the language of the Jews in their home. She was singing in Hebrew.

And then he was asleep again.

Days – days of gorging on soup, retching at simple beans, swallowing clear broth and then accepting more complex meals until he ate bread, and kept it down, and his friends gathered at his bedside as if it was a feast day at the temple, or as if his sickroom was a symposium.

'You lived,' Neiron said.

Satyrus managed a smile. 'If you call this living,' he said in a whisper. If he had gained any weight, he couldn't see it. 'How long?'

'Almost three months, lord,' Helios said.

A jolt – a daemon of energy coursed through his body.

'Any ... more?' he asked.

'More what, lord?' Helios asked.

Satyrus tried to raise an arm to gesture – tried to speak more precisely, and all that emerged was a moan.

'You tax him too much,' Aspasia said. 'He is still close to the edge. Let him be.'

Neiron shook his head. 'Nay, Despoina. He asks if any ships have come – if any survived the storm. Lord, it is winter here, and the worst sailing weather in fifty years. No ships have come into the harbour. There is almost no news from the world.'

'And Demetrios has the shore opposite, and when the weather clears his ships sortie to close the blockade,' Helios said, all in a rush. 'He intends to lay siege to the town as soon as the weather clears ...'

Satyrus could no longer make sense of what he heard, so he went back to sleep.

Sleep, and dreams he didn't remember, except that he fought against opponents appointed by Herakles, and in his dream his physique was the same poor wasted thing he was in life, and Herakles mocked him.

How will you save this city with the body of a dead man? he asked.

Awake, and Aspasia fed him, and he forced himself to eat, the taunts of his patron ringing aloud in his ears. He ate and ate, and Anaxagoras came and played music for him, and the notes seemed to enter his *psyche* like bronze nails hammered into a shield rim.

Asleep, and awake to Miriam singing, and he tried to smile at her and she played on, oblivious to his presence, alight with her own singing. And awake, he could read the depth of her unhappiness as if it was written on her face in stonemason's letters. Tending to him wasn't just the duty of the woman of the house – it was release.

She sang on, and he slept.

And woke, and ate.

And slept.

And eventually, became aware of the rhythm of the house, the passage of the sun across his window, the wheel of time and life. The sun was warmer. Winter was fading. There were fewer smiles from any of his visitors.

Rhodes was pleading with Demetrios to let her surrender.

Abraham and Neiron came to him to tell him of it, and it saddened him and set his feeding back a week, because he wasn't sure he wanted to live in a world where Rhodes cravenly surrendered. Worse – humiliating – Rhodes had to send ambassadors to the Golden Man, the conqueror, and *beg* him to be allowed to surrender.

Across the straits, Demetrios had invited the pirates – all of them – to join him for the rape of Rhodes. Over three hundred ships had joined him: some said it was every pirate left on the face of the seas, and Demetrios, instead of destroying them, promised them the unimaginably rich plunder of the richest city on the ocean.

Abraham sat in the ebony chair, his hands clasped as if he were the one pleading to be allowed to surrender.

'Antigonus turned our envoys away and said that he would prefer to see us as slaves,' Abraham said. He frowned. 'But Demetrios is made differently. He sees himself as being greater than men – as a god come to earth. He will relent, if only for his reputation.'

Neiron did not look so sure.

Satyrus could see it. All too well. 'He will not relent,' he said. 'Because he thinks he is a god, and that he has no need for the morality of a man.'

Neiron narrowed his eyes as if seeing something new.

Satyrus fell asleep. And dreamed dark dreams of defeat and enslavement, and spurned his food.

He awoke to music. Anaxagoras played him awake, and then stopped – stopped in the middle of a rousing war tune. 'Wake up, you sluggard!' Anaxagoras said. 'You think we saved your hide so that you could die? There are men here who need a king, a leader. A fighter. Wake up and strive, or lie back and die. My fingers grow tired of playing for you.' And he laughed, his big laugh rolling out through the windows into the spring air like a hymn to Dionysus.

Satyrus took his medicine, and then he ate.

He lay back and listened to the tales men told him.

He tried to raise his legs in the bed, and he lay, humiliated, while Aspasia and Miriam and a host of slaves rolled him over, cleaned his body of excrement and laughed at him.

'The baby I never had,' Miriam chided him.

'If I had let you die, I'd have saved us all a lot of work,' Aspasia quipped.

After another few days – perhaps a week, although his grasp of time was not yet strong, and there was poppy juice in his water, he suspected – he dreamed again of his father, Kineas, the statue, speaking of the ways of the siege. When he woke, the dream was far away and unclear, very unlike the immediacy of the first. Except in one regard.

He asked Miriam to summon Neiron, and he came soon enough, again dressed in the long sweeping chiton of a citizen in formal attire.

'You were at the assembly?' Satyrus asked.

'We went to hear the ambassadors,' Neiron said. His face told Satyrus everything.

'Demetrios refused you,' Satyrus said flatly.

'Demetrios intends to raze this city to the ground, kill every man, sell all the women as slaves and salt our fields. He intends to leave nothing, so that men will see what defiance of the Antigonids receives as a reward.' Neiron looked away. He choked a little. 'He escorted the ambassadors from town to town to show the completeness of his armaments. He has five hundred ships of war with the pirates. He has four hundred merchant ships to carry fifty thousand soldiers.'

'Troy,' Satyrus whispered.

Neiron strained to hear him. 'What's that you say?' Neiron asked.

'Troy!' Satyrus said aloud. 'He's playing at being Achilles, or perhaps Agamemnon.' He laughed a little. 'Or perhaps he merely plays at being Alexander.'

'If he's playing, he's playing in earnest. He has a thousand ships, or near enough.' Neiron sighed.

'If we are to be the Trojans, we had best prepare to resist,' Satyrus whispered.

'Resist?' Neiron barked a bitter laugh. 'Men are more interested in discussing who bears the fault of this disaster than in discussing defence. The harbour wall is not finished because the oligarch party will not spend the money to complete it. The only reason they haven't run to exile is that they fear being captured by the pirates.'

'If Demetrios has refused the offer of surrender,' Satyrus said, as loudly as he could manage, 'it is time to resist.'

Neiron shrugged.

'Our men, Neiron?' Satyrus asked.

'Many were sick, lord – the same sickness that you had. Indeed, it is rumoured that Ptolemy had it, and died. It is one of the reasons that the town despairs. There is no hope.' Neiron put his face in his hands.

Abraham took a deep breath. 'Your captain of marines – Apollodorus – had the worst fever, except you; his eyes turned yellow as yours did, but he lived, and that gave us hope, lord. But he has been up for two months, and exercising in the gymnasium for a month. Four men died, and fifty were sick. The marines were sicker than any oarsmen.'

Satyrus nodded. 'But they are recovered?' he asked.

Neiron nodded. 'And Abraham has cared for them and paid them, so that they remain a crew.'

'Good,' Satyrus said. He squinted. 'Get me Apollodorus.'

It seemed that he had only to blink, and things were done. The next time he opened his eyes, Apollodorus was there, sitting in the ivory chair. As soon as he saw Satyrus' eyes on him, he sank to one knee and kissed Satyrus' hand. 'Lord – I feared for you. I will send a hecatomb to heaven, to Asclepius.'

'Better send another to the deadly archer, for it was his bow which shot me, and you. Anaxagoras changed the balance with a hymn to Apollo. I saw it – and many other sacred things. This is what I want to say to you, Apollodorus.' Satyrus beckoned with his stronger hand, and Apollodorus came closer.

'Listen to the words of my father, spoken in dream,' Satyrus said, and was satisfied to see the marine captain touch the blue amulet at his throat. '*The swift onset of the secret force will seldom triumph in the taking of a city. As a besieger, it must be tried – even at the cost of losing the picked men of your army, the savings in blood and gold of such an attempt is almost incalculable. Never, when you are commanders, allow yourself to count the loss of such a picked group against the possibility of success. If a city must fall – if that is the objective of your campaign – there is no personal price you should not be willing to pay short of impiety or immorality in the taking of the city.'*

'Your father is warning you that Demetrios will try to take one of the gates by stealth – before his fleet lands.' Apollodorus rubbed his hands. 'I will see to that.'

'You must be secret,' Satyrus croaked. 'The simplest way to take this city would be by treason, and there are plenty here to play the traitor. I charge you to look for him … or them.'

Apollodorus nodded.

Satyrus sagged back against his pillow. 'There is another thing,' he said. 'It does not come from a dream – or rather, something was said in dream and I have thought and thought on it, sometimes in fever and sometimes as clear as the sea. I need you to accomplish it without demur. It will take all our sailors, and keep them employed. Will you see it done?'

Apollodorus grinned. 'Anything you ask, lord – so long as you will obey me in physical things, and allow me to begin training you. It took me a month to restore my flesh – and you are far worse than I have been.'

Satyrus nodded. He was burning to transmit his idea.

'Buy a house,' he said. 'Buy a house in the western part of the city, close to the wall. And dig a tunnel.'

'An escape tunnel? Under the wall?' Apollodorus asked. He sounded surprised, and not particularly pleased.

'The tunnel must run all the way to the low rise beyond the great tower – there is a barn. Your tunnel must run to the barn.' Satyrus nodded.

Apollodorus shrugged. 'I doubt that anyone on the face of the earth can tunnel so far.'

Satyrus forced himself up. 'Dig, damn it,' he said. 'You have months.'

And then he was asleep, again.

Sleeping, waking and eating. Now he tried to walk, and fell into the arms of Helios and Anaxagoras. But he would not lie still, and he walked – his stick-figure arms over their shoulders until his muscles burned like those of a man who had fought a long bout against a heavier man on the sands of the palaestra. When they left him, laughing, joyful at the pace of his recovery, he wept to be so weak.

But walking brought its own rewards, and exercise created appetite, and appetite fed exercise. He walked on other men's legs, and then with a stick, his arm around Miriam as he crossed his chamber, back and forth, five times and then ten and then fifty, the circle of her waist a delight.

But as fast as his body healed, the world outside seemed to rot. The sun shone, and then a burst of spring storms wrecked a pair of grain ships that had almost run the blockade, and the spirit of the town fell again. Demetrios caught another grain ship and crucified the captain, and that was the end of blockade-running. His ships began to be visible in the straits all the time, and even Miriam was touched by fear and Abraham seemed to age before Satyrus' eyes.

'We have food for five months,' Abraham said. 'Oh, Satyrus! I should have sent my sister away. May God keep me from having to open her neck.'

'Brother,' Satyrus said, and put his hand on Abraham's shoulder. 'We will stand side by side again, and we will not lose this city.'

'Almost I believe you,' Abraham said.

'We worship different gods,' Satyrus said. 'But perhaps you will understand if I say that I was sent back to save Rhodes, if I may. Or so I believe.'

'May these words be true,' Abraham said. 'For a heathen, you are pious. I have never known you to blaspheme. Is this the truth?'

'By Zeus Sator,' Satyrus said. 'I swear to you – my father spoke to me of saving the city, and Philokles, too.'

Abraham stood up. 'I think that I want to believe you too much,' he said.

Later, Helios came in with his hands dirty, dirt under his nails.

'You are filthy!' Miriam said.

Helios looked guilty, and he slunk away to wash. He returned when Miriam had gone to manage the household affairs. 'We are digging, lord,' he said.

Fifteen days he walked, enjoying the feel of Miriam under his arm – some appetites return very easily, he mocked himself. Miriam was a widow, the sister of his closest companion, and a woman who was deeply unhappy. She did not need to be the king's mistress to add to her evils. Satyrus knew this, but the sickness had drawn a bond between them like a fetter of iron, and he felt it keenly. And her hand would linger on him when she washed him, or touched his face, a fraction of a heartbeat longer than it needed to – or was that his imagination?

Fifteen days, and then Apollodorus brought him an old slave from the gymnasium, a professional trainer of the new sort, a grizzled man with scars on his arms and a missing finger.

Apollodorus introduced him. 'This is Korus,' he said. 'I have promised him his freedom when you can wear armour and swing a sword.'

And with Korus' introduction to the household, torment began that was worse, in many ways, than the illness that had preceded it. Korus ruled like a tyrant, ordaining food and exercise, and the exercises were brutal – lifting jumping weights, at first, until Satyrus couldn't use his arms. And his legs – he was forced to run on the spot, his feet on towels of linen on the smooth tile floors, half crouched with his legs behind him, until he would fall forward and crack his head.

And then food: he heard Miriam's voice raised in anger – rage, really – at the demand that the kitchens produce roast pork in quantities suitable for a feast, and this in a household that forbade pork. Pork became the cause of a war: Miriam would allow none in her kitchen, and Korus acquired it elsewhere and forced Satyrus to eat it until he loathed the smell. Miriam fed him fish and chicken, and Korus fed him pork – five or six meals a day – and sometimes he vomited from surfeit.

Korus had no conversation at all. He was not an educated man, like Theron, and he didn't debate philosophy or discuss religion. He did not speak of war threatening the city. He had no interest beyond Satyrus' body, and he was remorseless in the pursuit of his goal.

Some days into this regimen, when Satyrus had just laid his head open smashing it against the tile floor in sheer fatigue, when Korus stood over him requiring him to rise and carry on, Satyrus lost his temper.

'I wish to rest,' he said in the voice of command.

'Fuck that, boy,' Korus said. Everyone was a boy, a *pais*, to the trainer. 'Get your arse off the floor. You can do better.'

Satyrus rolled to his feet, proud that he could control parts of his body again after five months of illness – and then fell on the bed as he lost control of his legs and the room spun.

'Get up, you useless turd. Get on your wide-arsed feet and move.' Korus didn't even raise his voice.

'Can't you see he's exhausted?' Miriam asked sharply. 'How dare you speak to him like that!'

Korus looked hurt. 'Like what, Despoina? Now you – get on your fucking feet.' He ignored Miriam and stood over Satyrus. 'On your feet.'

'He's finished!' Miriam yelled. 'How stupid are you?'

Korus looked at her. 'Not stupid at all, Despoina. Smart enough to know that he has some power left in them arms and legs, and I want to milk every *fucking* drop of his strength so that I can put it back into him twice over in food. In *pork*.'

'Get out of my house!' she said with murderous intensity.

He nodded. 'No, Despoina. I have your brother's permission. It ain't pretty, what I'm doing. But I do it well.'

'You are hurting him.' Miriam said. 'Do you like it?'

Korus shrugged. 'Not me getting hurt, is it? But the sooner I do him, the sooner he's strong. And can fight. That's what the contract says. And if it's all the same to you, Despoina, I'm fighting for my *freedom*. Been a slave too fucking long. Let me get him ready, and you can do anything you like with him.'

His meaning was so clear that Satyrus rose from his bed in anger, and Miriam flushed right from the roots of her red-brown hair to the middle of her back, where it showed among the folds of her long chiton.

'Knew you had some power left, laddie,' Korus said as Satyrus rose.

Rumours came, of Demetrios. More rumours that Ptolemy was dead, and Satyrus told Abraham that this was just the sort of deadly rumour that Demetrios would send into the city to cause panic.

More sleep. Another day of endless agony – lifting, carrying and falling – more failure than success. Satyrus hated Korus' voice, his rudeness, his lack of conversation.

And then, in the night—

He awoke to the sound of fighting – fighting close by, at the sea gate, and when he had his eyes open he could see the golden-red reflection of fire against the ceiling of his room, and he got to his feet.

He had no sword, no armour. But an attempt was obviously being made – he could hear voices, the unmistakable sound of mortal combat. The voice of the sword blade, the song of the axe, the ring of the hollow shield under the spear and the keening chorus of the wounded and the dying. From his window, which opened on the harbour, he could see it as clear as day – the new sea gate on the mole was flooded with men, and there were ships against the mole that hadn't been there before. Satyrus found a chlamys – probably one of Helios', left by chance – and wrapped himself in it and walked to the head of the stairs that led down from his room to the courtyard garden.

He hadn't put a foot on a step in five months, and by the base of the steps he had a two-handed grip on the stair rail like a dying man at sea grips a floating spar. Down the steps to the courtyard gate – it was shut. And a heavy bar laid across.

A bar he could have lifted when he was thirteen; a bar of heavy wood that would have made Theron laugh. He couldn't budge it – couldn't move it in its well-worn channel of stone. As if he were an infant.

He gritted his teeth and put both hands on the bar. Once, he could have cut through a backstay with a single blow of his sword. Once, he could have severed the head of an ox with a single axe blow. Now, all he desired was to move the bar on a house gate. He strained, and prayed to Herakles, and the thing slid – a hand's breath and more, and the gates opened wide enough to admit a man and he slipped out, even as the shouting began behind him.

He tried to run towards the sea gate, and he fell – caught a foot on the cobbles. Ahead, a troop of men ran at him, armed and armoured. He was helpless – now that he was down, he didn't think that he could get to his feet. Weak and unable to resist, he watched them come. They ran right over him. A single foot found his ribs – the massive pain of a hobnailed boot in his belly, and then the squad of men was gone, running on, ignoring him lying in the filth of the street.

It was almost enough to make him laugh. They were Antigonid marines, and they had unknowingly ignored the King of the Bosporus, lying in the muck of a Rhodian street. But he hurt too much to laugh, and he tried to roll onto his side to protect his guts.

A clash of iron and bronze erupted at the head of the street. The sounds came clear, and his head was working even if his sinews were not. The men who had passed over him were under attack.

'You are surrounded,' he heard Apollodorus say over the sound of men dying. 'Throw down your arms, or die.'

Even in a haze of frustration, rage, pain and fear, Satyrus was glad.

The joy of the defenders at saving their town from the attempted escalade was tempered by finding the King of the Bosporus lying in the street outside the house of Abraham the Jew, cursing his own weakness. Many men carried him back to his bed, and Aspasia, looking like a fury with her iron hair flying in all ways around her head castigated him like a boy and humiliated him far more thoroughly than Korus ever had.

'You thought perhaps to take a sword and shield? To help the city in its defence? You are a fool, King Satyrus. Did we save you so that you could risk your life like an idiot?'

And Neiron stared at him. 'It is like a sickness, this rashness. Listen, *King*. You killed half a thousand men in your hubris in the storm – and you almost killed yourself last night. This city needs you – who was it who made the preparations to repulse the surprise attack? And you are still such a lackwit as to *go yourself?*'

Satyrus lay on the bed while Aspasia and Miriam cleaned him and put him on clean bedclothes. Both of them were clearly so angry they couldn't speak. Miriam handled him roughly – again he had the feeling of being a small boy, this time one who had displeased his mother and aunt.

But in himself, he felt unaccountably *better*.

With dawn, any residual anger at Satyrus was burned away by the new sun. Spring was fully on the ocean and the water was as blue as new-cut lapis, and the sun was a red-gold dish in a shining bronze sky. The day was as beautiful as all of the memories of youth of all the people watching from their windows, from the walls, from the hills above the town and from the smoke-blackened harbour where Apollodorus had sprung his trap, destroyed the assault and burned their boats.

The beauty of the day was lost on all of them, as was the fleeting triumph of the night before. For the sea to the north, which stretched away in unshadowed blue, was crowded almost black with ships. A thousand ships. An invincible horde of ships.

19

DAY ONE

Satyrus was almost instantly asleep, despite the obvious disapproval of his caretakers. He was awakened by Miriam, with a cup of hot soup. The sun was high in the sky. Miriam's dignity seemed, at first, a further reproach for his rashness of the night before, but Satyrus had spent enough time with her, asleep and awake, over the last month and a half of recovery to know her.

'What's the matter?' he asked. Very unGreek. Greeks never admitted weakness.

'You behaved like a boy last night,' she said bitterly. 'A rash boy. A foolish boy who must always try himself against every obstacle.'

Satyrus managed a smile. 'I was just such a boy,' he said.

'Why? Why waste all the effort of so many people? Did you think your puny arm would save us all?' She looked at him, but her eyes kept straying to the window.

Satyrus drank his soup. 'I do not like being an invalid,' he said. 'Do you think it is pleasant, lying here while the town is threatened? Sending my friends to fight while I lie in bed?' He shrugged. 'May I tell you something, Miriam?'

Her eyes were out on the sea. 'I have washed your body and listened to you rave. I don't think there are any secrets that you have from me.' She meant it to sting, and it did.

'I might have a secret or two, yet,' he said, trying not to rise to her. She was angry. He thought that he knew why, and he wanted to help her, but her armour was thick.

She tore her eyes away from the window, turned herself with visible effort to face him on the bed. 'Surprise me, then.'

'I'm a coward,' he said.

She laughed. But that was an automatic reaction, the woman's response to the man. It was false laughter.

'No – it's true. I think it is true of many men, and I'm just bitten worse than others by the snake of fear. I am afraid of so many things: death, betrayal, the loss of those close to me. But most of all, I am afraid of showing fear. Even to myself. I throw myself at things that scare me, and sometimes,' he said with a smile, 'they hit back.'

She narrowed her eyes. 'Nicely put. But somehow, you have succeeded in sounding *more noble* rather than more like a small boy.'

He started to rise from the bed.

'Satyrus, put those feet back in that bed this instant.' She spoke at him, like an officer giving orders. Like a nurse giving directions to small children. 'You must stop it, Satyrus. Neiron despairs of you. Abraham is sure you'll die. And Satyrus, you don't know it, but this town is already hanging by a thread. For myself, I would like to live – free, unraped, in my own house until I grow old, and you, sir, are my chief hope of surviving this – the famous soldier-king of the North. If you die in the streets fighting, your name may well be remembered for a generation, but *my* chances of ending my life in a brothel are greatly enhanced.'

Satyrus nodded. 'You are afraid, Miriam.'

She narrowed her eyes. 'Of *course* I'm afraid. Have you looked out there? Fine – get out of the bed. Be my guest. *Look!*'

While every armed man in the town stood to the walls and watched, Demetrios' vast armada sailed unopposed past the harbour and down the coast, to land at the next curve of beach beyond the next headland – a handful of elite ships full of Argyraspides first, and then a full *taxeis* of pikemen who formed on the dry ground above the shingle. *Psiloi* splashed ashore to cover them, and then a full squadron of cavalry, the horses pushed over the sides of the horse transports to swim ashore where their equally wet riders waited, rode off into the low hills and spread out in a long line of vedettes to cover the initial landings. It was all very professional.

'Some say a squadron of cavalry, and some a phalanx of infantry, and some a squadron of ships is the most beautiful,' Satyrus said. He leaned against the sill of the window, warm in the Mediterranean sun.

She turned to look at him. She was suddenly very close – there was jasmine in her hair.

Both of them knew the next line of the poem perfectly well.

Satyrus made himself turn back to the window. 'I can't say that I'm happy to be in this town, or happy that any of my friends are here,' he said. 'We are Troy. Young Achilles there is determined to take us, and all of his father's ambitions require our fall.' He glanced at her. Her eyes were lowered – her cheeks had the faintest touch of pink, the way a new dawn brushes the grey sky at the break of day. He could feel the heat in his own face – and in other places, as well.

Miriam had none of Amastris' sensual marvels; no one would write poems to Miriam stating that she was Aphrodite fallen to earth. Her nose had too much shape; her hair rose from her head in a cloud of red-brown curls that could never be ruled by the hand of man or woman, and she seldom dressed herself to best advantage, a thing Amastris did every day. But in the erectness of her carriage she ceded Amastris nothing, and in her chin and in her eyes was *character* – strength of purpose, depth of spirit. She could be stern.

All of this came at Satyrus rather like the band of Antigonid marines had the night before. He was helpless before a rush of observations, as he *saw* her all at once. And he felt the heat on his cheeks increase.

'But,' he managed, trying to keep his tone light, 'for all that, with the gods, we'll stand.'

She turned to him, and suddenly she was very close indeed, and he was unsure which of them had bridged the last handspan but now, without touching, he was close enough to feel the heat of her hip and her breasts and her face—

'Good morning, lord,' Korus said from the doorway. 'Despoina, good morning.'

'I have work to do,' Miriam said. She didn't whirl away, which Satyrus rather admired – he had flinched when Korus spoke. Instead, she looked up into his face and smiled. 'Heal fast,' she said. And then she smiled at Korus, who was as surprised as anyone, and left the room at her usual dignified pace.

'I hear you went out last night and tried to fight,' Korus said.

Satyrus nodded.

'You fucked in the head? Die like that, I'm still a fucking slave. You fight when *I* say.' Korus shook his head. 'Apollodorus says you were an athlete. That true?'

Satyrus shook his head. 'I never competed anywhere. But I had a trainer, and I fought *pankration*.'

Korus grunted.

'Something wrong with *pankration*, trainer?' Satyrus asked. He was lifting the jumping weights already – Korus didn't say anything unless he executed a movement incorrectly.

'Fought in the game myself.' Korus nodded. 'Time to give you heavier weights.' He pulled open a bag and took out two iron bars. 'Let's go down to the garden, lord. Time you let the sun kiss your skin.'

An hour later, Satyrus was all sweat.

'You know you'll never be the same, lord,' Korus said. He had the grace to sound sad.

'I wondered, yes,' Satyrus admitted, and what he felt in his heart was something like grief. Like the loss of a good horse, or a friend. His body – his physique – kept him alive in battle. And caused men to follow him, to look at him as something special.

'You spent your whole life building that body,' Korus said, handing him a rock as effortlessly as he handed over leather straps. 'It's gone, and now I have a few weeks to rebuild it. It won't be the same, lord. And when we start fighting – and that's soon – you need to learn to fight differently. I'm going to wager you was one of the strong ones – kicked the shit out of weaker men by hammering the sword home until it kills. Now you need to fight smart.'

Satyrus nodded. 'I think you may be surprised,' he said. 'But I take your point.' The rock – about four *mythemnoi* in weight – fell to the ground by his hip, crunching the gravel.

'Herakles,' Satyrus said. The muscles in his left arm had simply stopped working.

'Don't let that happen again, lord. When you reach the point of failure you must *stop*. Understand? Tell me, and I'll take the fucking rock.'

Satyrus nodded, extended a hand and Korus pulled him to his feet. 'Get a rub-down and a nap, lord. I'll send you up a meal. This afternoon, we go again.'

Satyrus could barely stand his muscles were so tired, but he was as hungry as a horse – the first time he could remember in months that he'd been burning to eat.

'I could eat a lion,' he said.

Korus gave a fraction of a smile. 'About time.'

Afternoon, and he ran – up and down the street. Every citizen he saw was in armour, and while many laughed to see his emaciated figure running, more called out greetings. When he stopped to lean on his thighs and pant, a dozen men with Memnon, Aspasia's husband, came up, shook his hand and thanked him.

'Your man, Apollodorus, he saved the town. We all know who to thank – he told us you warned him. Zeus, lord, we have few enough soldiers in this town.' The speaker was an older man, with grey in his hair but big and well proportioned, like an athlete.

'Damophilus,' Memnon said. 'I don't think you two have met. One of our best trierarchs.'

'A pleasure, sir,' Satyrus said, shaking the man's hand again. 'As far as I can say, every man in this town and most of the metics are well-armed, well-trained soldiers. I know that my friend Abraham the Jew has served – quite gallantly – at Gaza, and elsewhere. With me.'

Damophilus nodded. 'Abraham we know. And yes – we've all seen service, Satyrus. But few of us have commanded in battle on land, or even seen a siege. I suspect that every man in this city has now read Aeneas Tacticus – but what's written down—'

'What's written down is better than no advice at all. And it will be some time before I can stand in a breach and fight.' Satyrus shook his head. 'But I am a citizen here, even if only an honorary one – and I will serve. I'll help in any way I can.'

'Good man,' Damophilus said. 'So, what's next?'

Satyrus was as confused as if Damophilus had struck him. 'Next?' he panted. Korus was leaning in a doorway, watching – his disapproval obvious.

'You guessed that they would try an escalade,' Damophilus said.

Satyrus stood up straight. 'Anyone could have guessed that. But you have to ask yourself – what's the weakest point in the circuit of the walls?'

Memnon nodded – the whole group nodded. 'The curtain by the great tower on the landward side,' they all chorused, although in different ways.

Satyrus scratched his chin. 'I don't agree,' he said.

They all looked at him as if he was mad. Memnon raised an eyebrow. 'Flat ground, almost no ditch—'

'And a great tower full of artillery and Cretan archers within bowshot – a tower that renders the curtain almost superfluous.' Satyrus shrugged. 'I've been sick, gentlemen, but I do look out from my bedroom and see things. My window's right there,' he raised his hand. 'I can see out over the harbour. From the second floor. Because,' he said dramatically, 'the sea wall is unfinished. A man can climb it in a dozen places that I can see from my window.'

'Nicanor is an *idiote*,' Memnon said. 'He's blocking the inner council from spending any money on the sea wall. He says we need the money for grain.'

Satyrus laughed. 'You have to be alive to eat,' he said. 'Look to the sea wall.'

The men all shook his hand again. It raised Satyrus' spirits, to be accepted as one of them. To see that they were ready to resist; to be able to contribute.

'Some people will do anything to avoid their workout,' Korus said.

'You live here too,' Satyrus said.

'I'm a slave,' Korus said. 'When I'm free, it may seem different. Right now, it's all the same to me whether the town falls or not.'

Satyrus looked at the man. 'Korus, I understand, and better than you can imagine, coming from a king to a slave. But you are wrong. If this city falls, you'll die. No man escapes the sack of a city like this. Slave or free.'

'Maybe I'll just slip over the wall,' Korus said.

Satyrus knew immediately that anger was not the right response. He ran another sprint, came back and spat. 'Trading one kind of slavery for another,' he said.

'What's that?' Korus asked.

'Slipping over the wall. And you'll be building siege machines and digging trenches for Demetrios until you die, or until he takes the city. And then you'll be sold.'

Korus smiled. It was the first smile Satyrus had seen on the man, and it wasn't a pleasant smile. 'You think I'm stupid,' the man said.

'No—' Satyrus began, but the trainer interrupted him.

'You think I'm stupid. You think I don't know that Demetrios is no better – maybe worse? Fuck you, *lord*. I know. But when you're a man like me, and they've made you a slave, you get to the point where any change is better – and when maybe seeing all the fucks who made you a slave die, in a sack, seems like a reward in itself. Lord.' Korus stopped, and had the grace to look frightened for a moment – frightened that he had said so much.

Satyrus was too tired to argue. 'They made you a slave? Here? What were you before – a pirate?'

Korus spat. 'Maybe,' he grunted.

Satyrus looked at the man. 'You were a pirate, Korus? Oarsman? Marine?'

Korus glowered at him from under his heavy brows. 'I'm a trainer. I was took off Sicily. I thought it was better to pull a fucking oar than to die.' He shrugged. 'It wasn't a bad life.' He shrugged again. 'But the high-and-mighty Rhodians took us, and we was all sold as slaves.'

Satyrus felt as if his thighs and shoulders were about to refuse to support his bones. 'And in a few weeks, you'll be free. I need a trainer. Why not take what the gods offer? I can make you free – and comfortable. I'm a good friend to those who stand by me.'

Korus laughed. 'Is that what they tell you?' he said. 'What I hear is that everyone who stands close to you dies.'

DAY TWO

When Satyrus awoke, every muscle in his body hurt. But for the first time in months, he awoke to the sun on his own time, without interruption, and he felt like rising. He threw off his blankets and rose, stretched, rubbed his shoulders and walked across to the windows that gave on to the harbour.

He could see right down the coast to the south. He could see fires flickering in the distance, towards Afandhi, and there were columns of smoke across the horizon. Satyrus walked out onto his balcony to have a better view, and then, thinking better of it, he climbed the ladder – not without pain – to the roof of his room, from which he had a panoramic view of the city.

Demetrios had already begun to fortify his camp. He was a very active commander – Satyrus already knew that, but if he'd needed more evidence, it was provided by the fact that in the first light of dawn, Demetrios' whole cavalry force was in the field, well forward, almost within bowshot of the city, and behind them, covered by the armoured cavalry. Bands of men were cutting down every olive grove on the north end of the island, piling the trees and sending them by sledge to the camp, where other work parties were sharpening the branches and making them into a giant abatises, a sort of bramble entanglement that would surround the camp as a first line of defence. Within the abatises, as tiny as ants, more men dug into the loose soil and the rock under it with picks, and still more men wove giant baskets to hold the sand and soil, and yet more men filled those baskets with shovels, so that a line of earthworks reinforced by baskets made of olive rose over the ditch inside the felled trees.

The pace of the work, man for man, was agonisingly slow, as the soil was virtually non-existent over the rock. But taken as a whole, the pace was staggering – Demetrios must have enslaved the entire farm population of the island overnight, and his work parties would have his ships enclosed in a wall in two or three days.

But despite the activity of the men around the camp – the thousands of men around the camp – what drew Satyrus' professional eye was the activity on the distant beach. He looked and looked, and couldn't decide what he was seeing.

It dawned on him that he'd been on the roof for some time, and that he'd heard something—

'Satyrus!' came a call from below. It struck him that someone had been calling his name for a while.

'Up here,' he said.

Aspasia came out onto the balcony beneath him, a long Persian robe over her shoulders and her grey hair unbound on her back. 'You frightened me, idiot boy. I thought you'd run off again.' She motioned. 'Come and have your medicine. Gracious gods, boy, you are naked.'

With some chagrin, Satyrus realised that he was, indeed, naked.

'I've seen it all before,' Aspasia said. 'Come along.'

Satyrus climbed down, now painfully aware that he was climbing a ladder in the nude. Among Greeks, showing your body was allowed – welcomed, even – but only if that body was beautiful. Satyrus still felt like a bag of sticks.

'How are you today?' Aspasia asked. There was something in her tone that alerted him.

'Tired. But ... solid, somehow. And I'm hungry.' He smiled at her.

'I've lowered your poppy to almost nothing,' Aspasia said. 'You haven't craved it?'

Satyrus shrugged. 'Is that why I hurt so much?' He made a face. 'I had thought it just fatigue – but now I remember it from before.'

'You *are* doing well. You're almost clear. I will resign you to Korus and go to my other patients: my husband, for one, will welcome my cold feet back into his bed. You are one of the greatest triumphs of my life as a doctor – and I will never understand just how you survived when I was certain that you had died. Do you remember it?'

'No,' he lied.

'Well, it is a gift from the gods. Don't squander it. I like to think you were sent back to deliver this city.' She smiled. 'At my age, I don't have the fears other women do – if the city is falling, I can be gone from this body before the least indignity can be visited on me. But for the others – for my children, for girls like Miriam – they deserve to be saved.'

Satyrus took his medicines, emptying the clay vials one after another.

'What are the odds, Satyrus?' she asked.

'Pretty bad,' Satyrus said. He drank off the bitterest – a taste so strong he'd almost come to like it. 'Demetrios is no fool. He's very professional, and he can hire the best engineers and soldiers. He won't make many mistakes.' He made a face at the taste. 'And I can't save you. You can only save yourselves.'

'Ourselves?' Aspasia asked. 'Does this look to you like a world women have made? Men made this – war and slavery and death as far as the eye can see.'

'Women are no different,' Satyrus said.

'Women nurture. Men destroy,' Aspasia said.

Satyrus laughed. 'You really must meet my sister. Who I miss, and whose ungentle hand of destruction would stand this city in good stead. I don't know if you are right or not, doctor. But I have seldom taken war to those who hadn't already visited it on me. You want me – and men like me – to stand between you and the destruction of this town.'

'Oh, you think I'm attacking you. And I am not, young king. It is my own husband – and many other men here – who I blame. We only reap the results of our own policies. Why make war on pirates who do not prey on us? Why support Ptolemy against Antigonus, instead of merely trading with both? So many decisions … and now, here we are.' She shrugged.

'It is always thus, Despoina.' Satyrus heard Korus' heavy tread – he had to wonder if the man thought him a lewd satyr and now made a noise every time he approached. 'War comes when men have made mistakes – or when men are so foolish as to want it, like inviting the Tyrant to rule your city.'

Aspasia nodded. 'Do your best for us. That's all I can ask. And … Satyrus. I have eyes. Miriam—'

Satyrus made the same face he had made with the bitter medicine. 'Miriam is not for me,' he said.

'Praise to the Cyprian that you know that. I thought that you did. How can you be so wise and so foolish?' She asked.

Satyrus laughed. He kissed her hand. 'Human, I think.'

Korus cleared his throat and came in. 'Time to eat, then train,' he said.

Noon, and a rest. Satyrus sent Helios to assemble all of his officers, and Abraham agreed to be present.

'Starting tomorrow, we exercise at the gymnasium,' Korus announced after he had run.

Satyrus raised an eyebrow. 'For as long as there *is* a gymnasium,' he said.

Korus pulled out a coarse linen towel and started to rub him down. 'What the fuck you mean by that? Lord?'

Satyrus was face down on a *kline* by then. 'I mean that the gymnasium will be one of the first buildings pulled down,' he said. 'This town will need building materials – ready-made. Dressed stone. Garden walls will only go so far.'

'Ares,' grunted Korus. 'My livelihood.'

'Come and work for me,' Satyrus said.

'Hunh,' Korus grunted. 'Getting some meat on your bones. Good for you. I'm that much closer to freedom.'

Exhausted, dressed like a gentleman for the first time in five months, Satyrus sat on a woman's chair while Neiron, Abraham, Anaxagoras and Helios as well as Draco and Amyntas, last seen boarding the captured grain ships so long ago it seemed like a different lifetime, and Charmides, came in, led by Abraham's slaves, embraced him and settled onto couches. There were other men, as well – men it lifted his heart to see. Sandakes, the handsome Ionian, all but glistened with oil. He commanded *Marathon*, last seen vanishing into the storm wrack off Cyprian Salamis, the night of the lost battle. And Daedelus of Halicanarssus was there. He was not, strictly speaking, one of Satyrus' men, but a mercenary captain with his own ship, the big penteres *Glory of Demeter*. Satyrus embraced them both. With them were three of his other captains – men he knew well enough; Sator, son of Nestor of Olbia who had *Thetis*, one of his best quadremes; Xiphos the Younger, also of Olbia, a former slave who had fought his way up to the position of trierarch – a crude man and hard to like, tall, stooped and scarred, but a dependable captain, commanding *Nike*; and Aristos the Lame, another Athenian gentleman fallen on hard times. His wooden foot and leg gave him his name, and the constant pain they brought him fuelled his infamously bad temper. He had *Ariadne*.

'I can't tell you how heartened I am to see all of you,' Satyrus said.

Neiron gave him a hard smile. 'Good to know we have a few ships left,' he said.

Satyrus refused to be bowed. 'Yes, it is. Daedelus – what in Tartarus are you doing here?'

'Heard you were hiring. I picked up some prizes, brought them here to sell – I was cruising the pirates – independently, you might say.' He smiled. It wasn't a pleasant smile. 'The storms caught me here in autumn, and the blockade sealed me in.'

Satyrus smiled at Sandakes. 'I missed you. We had a few fights off Aegypt.'

Sandakes returned his smile. 'I heard that it might have been best for me and my crew that we missed the second storm – the first blew us west of Sicily, lord. It took us a month to beat back – I went all the way down to Africa because the rumour is that Athens is actively supporting Demetrios, and her fleet is on the sea.' He shrugged. 'We came in here after you – you were already flat on your back, and Neiron ordered me to stay.'

Satyrus looked at his other captains, all three of whom had been missing since the fight with the pirates off Cos. They all shrugged. 'Lord, we went to the rendezvous and then the storms caught us.' Xiphos was more belligerent. 'You suggesting we've done something wrong? Eh?'

Satyrus wasn't offended – far from it; the sight of them made him feel better than he had in days. The sound of Xiphos' hard voice made him feel better than he had in weeks.

'Not at all. I'm delighted that you have preserved your commands – it raises my hopes that some other ships might have been saved.' He glared at Neiron, who glared back. Then he swept them all with his eyes.

'Korus!' Charmides called out into the silence, and then blushed. He clearly hadn't meant to be heard.

'How's the leg?' The trainer asked.

'The better for your work. I'd like to do more. Do you have time?' he asked.

Satyrus smiled. 'I seem to own all of his time, Charmides. But if you'll share, I will.'

'He's wonderful,' Charmides proclaimed with the enthusiasm of youth. 'Saved the muscle of my leg after the wound.'

'He's certainly effective,' Satyrus said. 'Gentlemen, allow me to call you to order. Ship states – Neiron?'

Neiron had a wax slate in his hands. 'I could have given you all this,' he said.

'I'm sure you could – I'm sure you are an excellent navarch. I want to do it this way. Humour me.'

Neiron exhaled strongly. '*Arete* is in most respects ready for sea. We're twenty-four oarsmen short. Full load of water in the jars, full load of oil. Can't say the Rhodians haven't been gracious. Bolts for the artillery. I'd like to make up the oarsmen and the deck crew, and you know as well as I that we're very short on officers.'

Satyrus nodded. He went around the room. 'Daedelus? You with us?'

The mercenary smiled. 'You paying?' he asked.

Satyrus grimaced. 'Yes.'

Daedelus nodded. 'Then I'm yours.'

In general, their reports were the same – they'd had the winter to refit, at least before the blockade tightened, and aside from manning, all of them were fully supplied, fully armed – in most cases, in better shape than when they'd left the Euxine almost a year before.

'Apollodorus, how many marines do we have?' Satyrus asked.

Apollodorus indicated Draco, who stood. 'One hundred and fifty-eight of our own, lord. Lord Daedelus had been kind enough to train his men with ours this winter – another thirty-eight. Given the rumours of the coming siege, and the town offering, we've acquired a great deal of new armour, and have practised fighting in it – leg armour, bronze-plate cuirasses. And lots of practice on the engines.' He nodded. 'With the officers in armour, I can put two hundred armoured men on the walls.'

'What's the garrison?' Satyrus asked. 'How many hoplites can the citizens provide?'

Apollodorus winced and looked at Abraham.

Abraham shrugged expansively. 'Fewer than six thousand, with every metic and every *thetes* in the town armoured and standing on the wall. The town is offering many of us citizenship – I've accepted. Memnon and Panther are asking the *boule* to free the able-bodied slaves, arm them and make them hoplites.'

Satyrus nodded. Other cities did the same. The casualties would open huge holes in the male population. 'And?' he asked.

Abraham made a face. 'Things aren't bad enough yet. The oligarchs believe we'll negotiate a settlement – they don't want to make *unnecessary changes*.' Abraham all but spat as he said the words.

Apollodorus shook his head. 'We're fucking doomed,' he said.

Daedelus smiled. 'Can I withdraw from our contract, lord? We haven't been paid yet.'

Xiphos rose to his feet. 'Fuck that. Lord – I'm your man, hilt and blade. But we have five ... six good ships. Give us a dark night and a fair wind and we're gone, and none of Demetrios' lubberly captains can stop us. Why die here, like a fox trapped in her earth? Let's get back to Tanais – to Olbia.'

Satyrus looked around. Sandakes kept his council – he was an aristocrat born and bred, and he had the training to keep his thoughts hidden – but it was plain that he agreed. Neiron looked away. Draco grinned and looked at his lover, Amyntas. Amyntas shrugged.

'Famous fight,' Amyntas said. 'Men say it's the biggest siege since Troy.' He grinned at Draco – an impudent, boyish grin that looked odd on a fifty-year-old man. 'I'd like the glory – one more time.'

'You're mad,' Draco said. 'Sieges aren't glorious – it's all dirt and dust and choking smoke and disease.'

Satyrus nodded. 'Let's put the discussion on cutting and running on hold,' he said. 'I'm not against discussing it, but I want all the news first. I've missed five months of my life – I didn't even realise that half of you were here. Abraham – you're the merchant prince. You collect news. How strong is Demetrios? And what of the rest of the world – Athens? Tanais? Alexandria?'

Abraham gestured and Miriam entered, dressed beautifully in the Greek fashion, her long legs barely covered by transparent wool. Behind her were twenty slaves, paired males and females, with platters of barley bread, spiced chicken in the African manner and wine

– quite a bit of wine. She stood among them, moving from couch to couch, making every man feel at home. Satyrus noticed how Amyntas, who disliked women as a matter of manliness, smiled at a joke she was telling him. Draco had a rough chivalry that she employed to shift a table. Xiphos she disarmed – Satyrus couldn't see what she said, but the brutal fighter grinned like a boy and blushed. Anaxagoras rose to help her, stood by her elbow as she gave the slaves orders like a general, and then went to a corner of the room to sit in a chair and take up his kithara. Then she went and sat by him, almost at his feet, and Satyrus suddenly saw that they were close – quite close. The way they sat showed a long intimacy – of course, they were both musicians, and they had been together five months.

He was overcome with unaccustomed jealousy – a feeling he scarcely recognised and immediately loathed. Anaxagoras was a gentleman of means, an honourable man, unwed, a legitimate match for the sister of a citizen of Alexandria and Rhodes, a rich man with twenty ships.

They began to play, and the sound of music changed the gathering. Xiphos might have made a comment – he spurned what he called the 'fake graces' of the gentlemen captains – but Miriam had disarmed him already, and instead he listened, caught in the web the two instruments spun, and he was not alone. Daedelus played – Satyrus remembered it from beaches across the Ionian sea – and his fingers moved in sympathy, as if he desired to play himself, and certainly Sandakes felt the same.

They drank wine, ate their spiced chicken and their barley rolls, and the music died away to laughter and applause.

'Soon enough we'll have neither barley nor chicken,' Neiron said.

'You are the very life of the party, aren't you, Neiron,' Satyrus said.

'I think—' Neiron began.

'Shut up,' Satyrus said. He was human enough to allow the bile created by his jealousy to flow out over Neiron, and he regretted it, but on another level, the man had it coming. 'Either you are one of my captains, or you are *not*. I am absolutely sure you did a fine job commanding in my absence. You think me ungrateful? You do me *another* disservice. I am not. But by the gods, Neiron, I made the decision I had to make – as I have in the past. I am *deeply* sorry men died. Men I *loved*. Dionysus!' For a moment, Satyrus choked on his emotion and he was ashamed of the outburst, but hardly anyone was listening except Neiron, who looked as if he'd been struck by lightning, white-faced on his couch, and Miriam, who happened to be pouring him wine. 'Zeus Sator! Herakles, my ancestor – you think I am *careless*? *I am not.* But now I am in command. These men – and this town – need heart. Soul. Passion. Belief. Not carping and short answers.'

Neiron stirred – and Miriam vanished, fully aware she should not have heard any of this.

'I think that you were wrong to take us to sea in the second storm,' he said. But then he shook his head. 'But you are king, not I. I apologise for my attitude, lord.'

Satyrus took a deep breath. 'Thank the gods, Neiron. I couldn't win here without you. But I need you willing, and not doubting my every thought because I'm *rash*.'

Satyrus smiled at the other men – they'd mostly noticed that something was happening, but Anaxagoras had intercepted their stares with a bawdy story that made Miriam blush as she arranged her slaves, and caused Aristos to roar and shake with laughter.

'Finish up,' Satyrus said. 'We need to hear from Abraham.'

The men settled down. The double file of slaves swept in again, collected everything – down to the last crumb – with an efficiency that bespoke good training and some elan, rare in slaves, and swept out again.

Abraham cleared his throat. 'You play beautifully, Anaxagoras. I have seldom heard the like.'

Other men joined him in praise.

The musician bowed. 'All praise is sweet. Your sister has a unique talent – few women are so accomplished.'

'Few receive the training. My father said it was the best way to shut her up. She has quite a mind.' Abraham smiled, and Anaxagoras smiled back.

It is all arranged, Satyrus thought. *I should be pleased. Why am I not pleased?*

'At any rate,' Abraham went on, 'let us look at the world.' He went to stand alone in the centre of the circle of couches. 'Of Tanais, Pantecapaeaum and Olbia I know little – but the little I hear is not bad. Your sister is not returned to Tanais – not yet returned from her journey east. So much I heard from Leon's factor in Alexandria.' He glanced around and shrugged. 'This news is no better. Dionysus of Heraklea is dead – he died just four weeks ago.' That got everyone's attention: small news in the big world, but mighty news for the men from the Euxine. 'Amastris is now queen.'

Satyrus felt a qualm. 'And I am here.'

'So you are,' Abraham said. 'Amastris has sent five ships to support Demetrios.'

Satyrus nodded. 'She has to. Her father had a treaty.'

Abraham raised an eyebrow and moved on. 'Ptolemy is alive. He retains control of Aegypt. I had a bird today from the mainland – and may the messenger still be alive who sent it. Ptolemy is preparing an armament, to come here. And Leon is alive, and at Alexandria.'

'Praise the gods,' Satyrus said, and many of the officers echoed him.

'I only received as much news as would fit on a piece of papyrus as small as Miriam's hand,' Abraham said. 'But it is less bad than it might have been. If we can hold – even for a few months – Ptolemy will come.'

'Ptolemy has never won a naval battle with Demetrios,' Neiron said.

'Ptolemy has never fought supported by Rhodes,' Sandakes added.

Satyrus ran his fingers through his beard. 'Well. Since you are so well informed, how stands Demetrios?'

Abraham laughed. 'Forty thousand soldiers, twenty thousand slaves, two hundred thousand oarsmen.' He made a wry face and provided them with an elaborate shrug like a Greek mime in the theatre.

'Can he feed them?' Xiphos asked.

'Has to be his weakest point,' Satyrus said.

Aristos winced – everything hurt the man – and put his wooden foot down on the floor with a thump. 'We're better at sea,' he said.

Satyrus nodded at Abraham, who sat, and Satyrus stood up.

'I've had some months to do little but think,' he said. That got a chuckle. 'I want the option to cut and run – I won't fool you gentlemen. I'm King of the Bosporus, not the King of Rhodes, and behind closed doors, I don't intend to die here. I agree with what I see on all of your faces – we can vanish on any moonless night. I'll be cocky – we don't even need a moonless night to vanish, do we? I suspect we could beat anything they could chase us with.' He looked around. 'But if we can help save this town, we will. First, because I'm a rash bastard and I promised.' He grinned at Neiron, who winced. 'Second, because all of us – even me – serve the people of the Euxine. All our grain comes through this city, and much of it is sold through the very merchants we're trying to defend. The loss of Rhodes would make us much poorer, gentlemen. And when Aegypt falls, Antigonus will turn his piggy eyes north.'

They were nodding. He had a headache – his fatigue had reached the state where his stomach felt like a vat of acid – but he had them.

'With Panther's permission, I want to send you to sea – tomorrow night, if we can do it. Commence raiding. Don't bother to fight Demetrios' warships. Just take the grain ships – and, of course, bring them here.' He looked around. 'Let me predict the future for you, friends. In a week, maybe more, Demetrios will make a grab at the harbour wall. I don't want my ships to be here because, win or lose, that harbour is going up in flames.'

He looked around. 'And finally, Apollodorus, I'll be keeping half the marines. The best. You choose them and stay with them.' He looked at the small man. 'How's the digging?' he asked.

Apollodorus nodded. 'Nowhere near complete.'

'Well, it was just a thought. We'll rotate oarsmen through it when ships are in port. I'll send to Panther and tell him what we intend. Any comments?'

Daedelus raised a hand. 'Easy to get out – once. I agree. Getting in? Not as easy.'

Satyrus nodded. 'Point taken. That's why you get paid so much.'

'And the second time will be harder, and the third time harder still. Surely Demetrios will try to build a close blockade.' Daedelus gave a sweep of his hand to indicate the harbour.

Satyrus smiled. 'It's one of the biggest problems facing him,' Satyrus said after a pause. 'The harbour is huge – a double harbour, two different entrances, the mole, the wharf and the northern sea gate on the open beach – he has to cover three wind directions and twenty stades of sea wall, and I don't think he can do it – not if Leon and Ptolemy start threatening him so that he has to put a squadron to sea to cover them. There's no obvious way to stopper up Rhodes. He can't just sink ships across the entrance. There's no really good upwind port like Alexander had at Tyre. At any rate, gentlemen, let's show the Rhodians how to run the blockade. And every ship you take is grain out of their mouths, and into ours. He has a lot more mouths to feed than we have. And Apollo's deadly shafts fall on besiegers and besieged alike. Dysentery, plague, the fever I got in Aegypt – one epidemic and Demetrios is finished. Pray for luck. Pray to Apollo. And get us some food.'

'It's about the grain,' Charmides laughed. 'That line should be in Homer.'

DAY THREE

Exercise. Eat. Plan. Sleep. Eat. Plan. Exercise.

Another day.

Night on the great wharf – and no torches.

'We need to build the harbour walls so tall that no one can see in,' Panther muttered. 'For moments like this one.'

Five Rhodian warships were going to sea with Satyrus' ships. One by one his captains – men he'd been so happy to have back – shook his hand and boarded their ships. Neiron was last, and Satyrus embraced him, hugging him close. Tried to tell him with an embrace how much he valued the old mariner.

Neiron had the most difficult mission of all, because he was viewed as having the best ship. At dawn, he would sweep down the beach past Demetrios, risking interception and capture to have a look at what was going on behind the enemy's new camp walls. *Arete* was the mightiest of the ships in the port, and fast – the most likely to survive a dawn patrol along the enemy beach. Charmides was going with the ship – his mission, just as difficult and dangerous – was to re-enter the city from the south, disguised as a slave, with the report.

And then, when the moon set, they slipped away, only a handful of oarsmen rowing until they were near the harbour mouth, and then the oars would go, all together, unfolding like the wings of swift swallows, shining against the night, and they were away.

All ten ships slipped away into the darkness, and there were no answering shouts from the enemy sentries.

The harbour seemed empty in the not-so-dark darkness.

And then Satyrus went to sleep.

*

He was awakened by Helios. Dawn was pale outside – Helios looked like a ghost.

'Time, lord. Neiron will be making his run at the beach.' Helios had an oil lamp in his hand, and hot oil spilled on Satyrus' shoulder. He yelped.

'Watch yourself, youngster!' he said. 'Do I *look* like Eros?'

Helios laughed and helped his lord into a simple chiton, and then they climbed the tower together.

Satyrus could see the line of dawn, but not much else, and not a sail nicked the horizon that he could see.

Noise below – first in the courtyard, then on his balcony, and then Abraham appeared, followed by Anaxagoras and Miriam. She looked very beautiful in the first flush of dawn.

'You all right?' Anaxagoras asked him. He was a social man, and he could tell that something was amiss.

'I'd rather be *doing* it than watching,' Satyrus said. He was quite proud of his answer, because it was a perfect dissimulation. He was telling the truth – just not the truth about why, suddenly, he was cold to the music teacher.

Abraham put a hand on his shoulder.

Miriam smiled. 'May I stay?' she asked.

Satyrus couldn't muster even a shred of coldness. 'Of course,' he said. She sat close to him – between him and Anaxagoras, in fact. It was chilly.

You are in a bad way, Satyrus thought to himself. *You need to go and offer sacrifice to Aphrodite – and perhaps find a nice pliable slave-girl, too. Neiron is about to risk your ship, your crew and your friends – and you are angered by where this girl sits.*

The worst of it was that he knew – knew very well, in his heart – that he wasn't training like a madman for the noble purpose of saving Rhodes, but for a much simpler reason.

When Miriam and Anaxagoras were comfortably distant – say, downstairs – he could see how much they suited one another. And he was going to marry Amastris – any day. Amastris was her own mistress now, Queen of Heraklea, and together, they would rule the Euxine. He could remember the swell of her breasts; the line of hair that ran up her thigh into her groin, the smell of the nape of her neck—

So different from the woman next to him.

'There he is!' Helios said.

They all stood up together, like spectators at a horse race.

Satyrus hadn't even been looking in the right place. Neiron had used the night brilliantly. He was approaching from the *south*, sails down, masts down, moving quite fast, right along the beach.

Even on the rooftop overlooking the harbour of Rhodes, the enemy camp was less than six stades away – close enough to hear the sudden hum of activity, hear the screams – and see the tongue of fire that shot out of the dead ground invisible to them.

And then nothing: except that they could see Demetrios' army stand to. Men poured from tents, not even ants at this distance, more of an impression of men than palpable men, and they mounted the new walls and poured into the fields.

Ships were launching, all along the beach.

In the enemy camp, something went up with a *whoosh*, as if a god had taken a deep breath and coughed. A column of flame reached to the clouds.

Nothing. Just waiting.

More waiting, except that men were shouting all along the enemy camp. The enemy cavalry emerged, and cantered out into the scrub to the south.

'Gods send that they are not already tracking Charmides,' Satyrus said.

Now the camp seemed to descend into chaos, and more ships were launching – indeed, it seemed as if the entire enemy line of ships was moving, and then *Arete* emerged from the smoke, the flames and the dead ground, still moving at a racing pace right along the beach, and she was suddenly *close*, less than two stades distant, and even as they watched, all her port-side machines fired together and a hail of lethal iron flew into a half-formed infantry unit standing by the beach, and their screams carried the most clearly of all as they were flayed off the beach the way fat is flayed off a stretched hide when the tanner starts his work.

Now there were Rhodians on every wall and tower, and they were cheering the way people cheer for a great runner as he nears the finish, and *Arete* passed the sea tower at speed, already dragging his oars on the port side, and suddenly the great ship turned like a dancer turns as the music doubles the tempo – turned and darted into the harbour.

'That wasn't the plan,' Helios said, with the inexperience of youth.

Anaxagoras caught Satyrus' eye – no longer a rival, just a staff officer. 'Shall I go, lord?' he asked.

Satyrus shook his head.

'I can only expect he saw something too important to leave to Charmides,' he said. 'Let's run – he'll want to be away.'

They ran to the port – even Miriam, running on her long legs like a maiden runs in the Artemisian Games – but it was too late. By the time they reached the port, there were fifty triremes just outside, and two floating upside down where they had dared to test the range of the sea tower's artillery and been destroyed.

Arete entered the harbour at racing speed and slowed on his oars, the men putting their backs into holding the water, and the great ship slowed, Neiron piloting him brilliantly – he made the turn under the Temple of Poseidon and brought the great ship close in to the beach, almost at Satyrus' feet.

He jumped straight from the helm to the wharf. 'Too important to leave to Charmides,' he said.

Panther came running up, with Memnon, Damophilus and thirty other leading Rhodians. Nicanor was there, already proclaiming that they were *provoking Demetrios*.

'Wait – tell us all at once,' Satyrus said. Miriam was leaning against him – very slightly, but the pressure was real. Anaxagoras was already aboard *Arete*.

Satyrus smiled.

When most of the *boule* was assembled, Neiron looked out of the harbour. 'He's built a dozen double ships,' he said. 'Two big hulls – they look like penteres to me, lord, as big as our *Arete*. Decked between the hulls, with massive engines – Zeus, I've never seen *any-thing* like this.'

'How big are the bolts, do you think?' Memnon asked.

'No bolts,' Charmides said. 'Baskets. They aren't bolt-throwers like ours. Different design entirely. Here, I drew it.' He handed round a sketch, and the waiting men shook their heads.

Anaxagoras was back. He looked over Charmides' shoulder. 'Counter-weight.'

Sandakes agreed. 'Lord, you've never been to Sicily. The old tyrant there loved the things. They can throw a stone – a thirty-mina stone. Even a talent. Even five talents, although not very far.'

'By Hephaestos!' Panther declared. 'Ten double hulls, each the size of a penteres, carrying one of these great engines?'

Charmides shook his head, curls flying in all directions. '*Five* engines on every platform.' He grinned. 'But only nine platforms.'

Neiron allowed himself a satisfied smile. 'We put fire into one. And there was something on their wharf – they have built a wharf.' His smile widened. 'They won't store oil there any more.' He grinned. 'And the wharf itself is *gone*.'

Panther raised his arms. 'That was a great deed – under the eyes of every man in the city.'

'A deed which will only provoke King Demetrios further,' Nicanor said.

Ignoring him, Panther went on, 'But despite your best efforts, you tell us that he has *forty-five* engines that can throw a talent each – on ships.'

That silenced everyone.

'They're coming for the sea wall,' Satyrus said. 'Short and sweet – bombardment, and then a rush. Demetrios means to take the city in one attack. As befits a god.'

20

DAY EIGHT

Arete floated, as empty as the day she was launched, below Satyrus' window. Every ship in the harbour was empty. Forewarned, the Rhodians knew that the attack and the great engine-ships were coming at the harbour defences, and they had stripped every ship remaining in port of all engines, all oars, oil, drinking water, amphorae – anything that might give comfort to the enemy. And the ships were moored together with heavy ropes, all across the front of the beach wall, so that there was a wooden wall in front of the unfinished land wall.

The sea wall was not so much as a span higher – Satyrus hadn't bothered to argue with the oligarchs, who still attempted, every day, to negotiate with Demetrios. He had spent his own money, and that of Abraham, and a legion of slaves had laboured *behind* the wall.

Four days they had worked like slaves, and the fifth dawned clear and pink, and as soon as the light was strong, Demetrios put his great fleet to sea. Not the pirates. Not the riff-raff. Only his own magnificent fleet, escorting the ten great platforms, each as big as a herd of elephants.

Satyrus, still pained in every joint from yesterday's exercise, stood on the roof of Abraham's house. The roof had changed – flying buttresses now reinforced the front walls and the corners of the main towers, and the reinforced roof now held a pair of *Arete*'s ballistae behind stone curtains. Four days can be a long time, if you have enough men to work.

The Theatre of Dionysus was no more. The Temple of Poseidon had lost its east face and its retaining wall. A decree stood in the agora that promised every god so affected a ten-fold return should the city survive. The decree – and the permission to tear down public monuments – had been passed by the *boule* by a single vote.

'Ready to try, lord?' Helios said by his side. His hypaspist had his armour laid out on the roof. Satyrus had not worn armour since before his sickness. He had muscles, now – he could see them on his arms – but they were *nothing* like the muscles he had carried a year ago. Abraham's armourer had taken his breastplate in, and made him plain greaves for his legs. His old greaves were merely a painful reminder of the body he once had.

But when the breastplate was buckled securely onto his thorax, he bore it only as long as it took the enemy fleet to silence the battery of engines on top of the harbour tower with their dozens of ballistae, sweeping the crews right off the tower – minutes – before he was breathing hard, and stooped under its weight.

Humiliated, he allowed Helios to take it off him. Satyrus felt better immediately, and he watched the unfolding action as his sweat cooled.

Demetrios was in no hurry. In fact, he was making a demonstration. The great engines worked – but the crews were untrained, and it took them *hours* to get the range. Stones the size of a man's head fell harmlessly into the harbour a stade or more from the target. Rhodians jested that Demetrios meant to fill the harbour with stone.

By afternoon, the jests had fallen away. All at once, all of the great machines, which fired about four times an hour, found their range. Three great stones in a row reached the top of the tower, and then, with a rumble, the fourth drove in the top of the tower the way a big man can be driven to his knees by a strong man – and then six or seven more stones hit, all low, and the tower vanished in a cloud of dust and a roar of shattered timber and cracked stone, as if the fist of a god had smashed it flat.

A hundred Rhodian citizens perished in five heartbeats.

'Lord?' Helios asked. Miriam was behind him. She had something in her arms.

'I had this made for you,' she said. 'Because you are stubborn and rash. And weak.' Her smile belied the harsh words.

She looked like Thetis on the old vase paintings, holding a man's breastplate – of leather. Beautiful, Athenian leather, tanned and then coloured with alum, the edges bound in bronze, with an iron belt over the kidneys.

It weighed very little. It was plain – as plain as something a marine might wear, but it fitted, and he could bear the weight. She closed it around his waist with her own hands, and Satyrus kissed her – a decorous kiss, in thanks, but their lips touched for too long, and when Satyrus turned back to his men, her brother looked at him, his brow furrowed.

The loss of the harbour tower signalled the end of the day. Demetrios' fleet withdrew, jeering at the defenders.

Rhodians wept.

Satyrus went down to his room, ate and exercised. In the agora, the assembly met and voted to offer complete submission to Demetrios, and ambassadors were dispatched immediately.

Satyrus went to sleep.

DAY NINE

In the first grey of dawn, Helios woke him and together they ate dry bread soaked in wine. Korus came and made him exercise – before dawn's rosy fingers extended over the harbour, Satyrus had run half the circuit of the walls, and he walked back to the house, greeting the other men of the city. Rhodes was a true democracy – it did not appoint a single commander, even in war. The *boule* commanded. The oligarchs feared a unified command – feared, with some reason, to create a tyrant worse than Demetrios who could never be ejected. Satyrus was wise enough to know that he, as a king, was dangerous to the oligarchs, more even than to the commons, and he went running through the town naked on purpose, as much to show his essential vulnerability as anything.

The loss of the harbour tower had crushed any spirit the Rhodians had. The officers of the paid troops – the professionals – had expected nothing else, but the *boule* were panicked. Even Panther shook his head. 'Surrender is the best we can expect – and a garrison of his soldiers,' the older man said. 'Will you take me, at Tanais?'

Satyrus nodded. 'I'll be happy to,' he said. 'But Demetrios will not accept your surrender. He doesn't need to. Try to surrender just after you sting him with a victory. When he's won one, what needs he to treat with you contemptible mortals?'

Panther winced. 'Avert,' he said, making a peasant sign.

Nicanor shot back. 'Is that how *you* think, O great king?'

Satyrus was a small, thin naked man among a dozen rich men in armour. He laughed. 'Do I threaten you?' he asked. And ran back to Abraham's house, where his trainer made him lift weights until Helios called him to the roof.

Korus handed him a basket. 'Pork. Eat it. You need bulk.' The slave frowned. 'You are doing well,' he said grudgingly.

Satyrus sat on the roof, chewing pork and watching the sun walk across the ground between the camps. When it reached the enemy walls, he heard the murmur before he saw for himself.

The ambassadors had been crucified.

Satyrus scratched his beard and finished his pork, then licked his fingers. Sometimes, he had to wonder if he was, indeed, like other men. He'd known two of the ambassadors. Good men, with children. But seeing their corpses, he smiled. He thought of his father, and of Philokles, and even, a little, of Socrates.

The enemy fleet came in fast. There was no counter-fire from the harbour batteries, so they burst into the entrance, forty big ships, quadremes and penteres mixed. They cleared the harbour entrance, and behind them came the great engine-ships, their double hulls gigantic in the morning light.

They got into the harbour, and fired their first salvo at the sea wall. A single stone flew right over the wall, over Abraham's house, to strike the roof of the next house and crush it flat, so that the two machines on the roof were masked in a thick cloud of powdered mud and concrete that rose from the collapsed building. Men who had survived major earthquakes said how much like one this was.

But before they could reload, the town unleashed its first surprise. Engines, stripped from ships or purchased before the sailing season closed, had been placed on the roofs of the highest houses – and *not* on the unfinished towers of the sea wall. Now they fired, all together, when a red flag was raised by Helios.

Most of the bolts used by the defenders were wood, with iron tips – nowhere near heavy enough to penetrate the thick hulls of the heavier ships, although they might have been deadly enough to a trireme.

But Satyrus and his men were not the only innovative men in Rhodes, nor did Demetrios the Golden have the only engineers. His engines were carried in ships. That imposed limitations.

The defender's engines were higher. And every one was on a rooftop – the roof of stone buildings with kitchens and giant hearths. Their bolt-tips had been heated red hot.

Some missed. They were wasted, sinking hissing into the blue water of the harbour.

Others struck metal and screeched away. A few hit unlucky flesh, destroying a man – and every man around him – in a grim shock of heavy metal and wood.

And the best of them struck the ships.

The results were not immediately apparent. Red-hot metal will not straight away ignite wood – even carefully dried wood exposed to the Mediterranean sun and coated in black pitch.

But just about the time the fastest of the great engines aboard the nine double-hulls were being readied to fire, ships began to burst into flame – as if Apollo had rained fire on them. The result was so sudden and so spectacular that it surprised the defenders as much as it surprised the attackers.

The Golden King was no fool, and he had no intention of running risks or losing.

He withdrew. In minutes, the harbour was clear, except for the burning wrecks – infernos now – of fifteen of the Golden King's ships. The trapped oarsmen screamed, and the citizens of the town carried the smell of roast pork with them for a day. They burned to the waterline, and then sank.

DAY TEN

Satyrus never did his exercise on the tenth day. Before he was fully awake, Demetrios had his fleet on the water and the Rhodians, warned by their sentries, manned their machines and heated their missiles.

Demetrios' ships had wet hides across their bows and decks, and they came on boldly into a withering fire. Their boldness was misplaced. Three handspans of red-hot iron with a barbed tip cares nothing for a sodden bull's hide. Sailors wrestled with the red-hot shafts, trying to prise them loose, and the town's mercenary archers and all the archers from sixty Rhodian triremes – hundreds of men – shot shaft after shaft across the harbour into the sailors and the harbour began to fill with corpses, the way dead flies can litter the surface of a bucket of wine in the sun.

After an hour, the engine-ships had fired three times, and found the range. A hail of stones fell on the sea wall, just two streets to the south from Abraham's house, hammering the half-built wall down on its underpinnings. Dried mud bricks vanished in puffs of mud-smoke, and stones cracked under the onslaught, and the facing broke and broke again.

At the centre of the maelstrom a breach was opened, fifty paces wide.

But Demetrios' ships could not stand the counter-battery of heated missiles, fire arrows, javelins – anything that could be thrown or shot across the harbour. Two thousand of his sailors died in that one hour, and ten more ships caught fire, and the other trierarchs, threatened with ruin, backed water against orders and fled. Because they fled without orders, they jammed the harbour entrance, and then the slaughter commenced.

It was the most terrifying kind of war Satyrus had ever experienced, and he had stood his ground against a charge of elephants. But here, great rocks fell from the sky without warning and without mercy. A single stone might kill an entire family – might wipe out a bloodline two hundred years old, or a huddle of terrified slaves, or a family cat or dog – the stones were merciless and like some dark embodiment of Tyche, and veterans began to flinch every time the telltale hissing of the passage of one of the big stones was heard.

A marine – a good man – screamed and threw himself face down on the roof.

Apollodorus was there – not a terrifying disciplinarian, but a hero, who took the man by the shoulder and raised him, speaking into this ear until, red-faced, the man returned to his engine.

'Imagine ten days of this,' Neiron said, at Satyrus' side.

'Imagine a hundred days of this,' Satyrus said.

Miriam came up the ladder with a basket, followed by a dozen of her maids. She was smiling. If she was afraid, she was above it. Satyrus and Anaxagoras caught each other watching her. But with death falling like granite fists from the gods, Satyrus could only smile. And Anaxagoras could only smile back. When she reached the top of the ladder and lifted a long leg around to clamber onto the roof, every man at the machine smiled.

Then Satyrus saw the enemy ships retreating – hard to see, with the smoke of burning ships, collapsed buildings.

'Neiron!' Satyrus said.

Neiron was munching bread from Miriam's basket. 'Lord?'

'Is that an engine-ship?' Satyrus asked. He was looking clear across the harbour through the battle haze.

'By Hephaestos!' Neiron said. He ran to one of the engines, and Satyrus to the other.

Down in the courtyard, the slave-women had heated a pair of bolts – too much heat, in one case, so that the barbed point was deformed.

'No matter,' Satyrus said. 'Load!'

Men got the thing into the firing channel – already charred in places where hurried men had made mistakes – and winched the heavy cord back. Men were standing straighter, taking their time, making fewer mistakes – there were no stones falling. And, of course, Miriam and her women were on the roof, passing out bread – no marine wanted to be seen by a woman to flinch.

'Ready!' Necho said. Satyrus waved – the marines had practised all winter while he had lain helpless, and he wasn't taking charge of a weapon now when there were men better fitted to shoot, but it galled him. He wanted to *participate*.

He leaned over the roof, caught the eyes of the head woman and waved. 'More missiles – four more, red hot, as fast as you can!'

The woman all but saluted. She was enormously fat, and as strong as an ox, and she had mastered the heating of the heads without crisping the heavy shafts better and faster than any other person.

'Hit!' roared Neiron, and he turned but couldn't see a thing. Neiron wore an unaccustomed grin, and he waved his absurd Boeotian hat at the enemy.

Necho's machine fired, and then they were raising the next pair of red-hot shafts, hurrying to avoid the moment when the shaft caught fire from the head. Satyrus could no longer see the principal target. But Helios could, and he leaned over to help Necho.

After a pause, both machines let fly together with a crash that shook the roof.

Far off, across the harbour, a tongue of flame leaped to the sky like a sacrifice to the gods.

Satyrus joined the cheer, and even as they whooped the vast double-hulled leviathan caught – a single sheet of fire, and then two.

But that was not the end, because now the burning ships were acting as a barrier to the escape of their other ships. Satyrus' crews could no longer see anything for the smoke, but other machines on the other side of the harbour could, and they shot and shot again into the helpless enemy ships. It was over an hour before a handful escaped.

Nineteen enemy ships burned in the harbour mouth, and the engine-ship's double hulls were visible just above the surface of the water at low tide. Eight engine-ships slunk away, and Satyrus doubted that there was celebration in Demetrios' tent that night.

He sank onto his own bed, exhausted. He slept the afternoon away, dreamed of his father again, rose and dressed without help – little things were becoming easy again, and he was to begin *pankration* and swordsmanship again the next day. The thought cheered him.

He awoke clear-headed – and with the memory of a dream of

Herakles and a firm notion of his next step. He leaped from his bed, put on yesterday's chiton without repinning it, buckled on a belt and was pleased to see that it was tight. He was so excited, he almost forgot sandals.

He found Miriam outside his door – each as surprised as the other – and she froze like a deer caught by a stealthy hunter who does not use dogs.

'I was—' she said.

'I'm awake,' he said. 'I have to talk to the *boule*.'

She flushed. 'Of course,' she breathed.

She smiled, and walked away down the hall. 'Don't be late,' she called over her shoulder.

Satyrus shook his head and walked down the steps without feeling light-headed – a matter of some pride – and then into Abraham's receiving room, now one of the command stations of the defence.

There were a dozen messengers waiting, and Panther, in full armour, seemed to be in charge.

Satyrus shook his hand. 'I wanted a word,' he said. 'With the whole *boule*, if I can manage it. Even as he said the words, it struck him. *What was she doing outside my room? Was she about to come in? And then?*

His heart beat as if he was in combat.

Panther put a hand on his shoulder. 'You doing all right, lad?'

Satyrus smiled. 'The *boule*?' he managed.

Panther nodded. He wrapped his salt-stained military cloak around his shoulders, summoned a pair of ephebes as bodyguards and messengers and led Satyrus out of Abraham's house. Together they walked up the street to the row of statues outside the Temple of Poseidon, and then left up the steepest of the hills to the agora. Everywhere they walked, there were dead and wounded people – men, women and children – the dead laid out on the street, many already wrapped in linen according to the Ionian custom, the wounded screaming or silent. A small boy lay with both of his feet crushed and amputated, his eyes huge, his mouth open and flies everywhere about him. A woman lay on a bier, the side of her head crushed so that her hair and the shards of her skull were a single grotesque shape – but she was alive. Alive, and lying on her funeral bier.

'If your people want to surrender,' Satyrus said, 'tonight is the night.'

'What?' Panther asked. 'This, from you?'

Satyrus followed the Rhodian navarch into the agora – already, slaves were stripping the facade from the gymnasium to get at the big stones underneath the marble. But the round *tholos* of the *boule* was untouched, and they walked into the cool, shaded interior, which cut off the sounds from outside – the sounds of people dying.

Panther led him into the main chamber, where thirty men – most in armour – sat on benches or lay on *kline*. There were charts, chalk drawings of parts of the walls and baskets of scrolls – every book in the city on the art of war was being devoured at speed by the government.

'Satyrus of the Euxine would speak to us on matters that affect the city.' Panther looked around. 'I move that we allow him to speak.'

Nicanor rose, red-eyed, from his couch. 'He is a king and a tyrant. I stand against your motion.'

But when the men present were summoned to vote, Panther's motion carried easily.

Panther spoke quietly to Satyrus. 'I should have told you on the way, but your thoughts put my head in a whirl. Nicanor's sons – two of them – died in the collapse of the tower.'

Satyrus nodded. Then he stood in the centre of the floor.

'Demetrios will be as mad as Ares tonight, but he's had his first taste of defeat. Look – this is my opinion, nothing more – but in some ways, Nicanor has a point. We do think much the same, Demetrios and I – we are kings, we are used to getting our way. And surrender – a surrender that keeps the city intact and your families alive – gentlemen, I'll fight as long as it takes, but let's not kid ourselves. You've seen what just half an hour of bombardment does. Just imagine – imagine that we survive the harbour attack. And I think that we will. Then – then he builds *more* of those engines, and goes after the land wall – and there's nothing to sink. My mathematics says he can concentrate a hundred engines on fifty paces of wall. We won't even be able to hit back. *Every day* he'll clear another fifty paces of wall. A breach a day.' Satyrus shrugged.

'You are in favour of surrender?' Nicanor asked. 'Surely this is a sudden reversal?'

Satyrus bit his lip. 'No. First, I doubt he'll accept. Second, he's as likely to butcher us after we surrender as anything. He respects *nothing* but his father's will. *But* if the *boule* is still set on this course, the time will never be better.'

Panther nodded. 'I am still against it,' he said.

Nicanor made a face. 'I have only one son left to me. People died today. We lost *almost a twelfth* of the total citizenship of military age in *one day*. I am surprised that Satyrus the Tyrant has come around to my way of thinking – but I move that we take his advice and send a deputation.'

Satyrus gave the man a wry smile. 'Who will lead this deputation? He has the bodies of your last ambassadors crucified on his camp walls.'

Damophilus rose. 'I think that Satyrus seeks only to show us all the possible paths. And I, for one, would not trust Demetrios to count the coins in a warehouse. I say we fight. I will go farther, gentlemen. I say we need a centralised command. I move that we appoint Panther as polemarch – as war archon. And three *strategoi*, as in former times, to command the city.'

Nicanor rose. 'This is the first breath of tyranny. Let this city be governed as she has always been governed – worthily governed by men of worth.' Nicanor looked around. 'And who are these *strategoi*? Yourself, Damophilus?'

Panther rose and thumped the floor with a spear. 'We are not barbarians. Vote the items as moved, one at a time. For the creation of an embassy of surrender?'

Almost five hundred citizen soldiers had already perished. Many had been in the tower when it collapsed – the Rhodians had thought it impregnable. More were in their homes, or on the sea wall, or simply unlucky. And citizen women, children, slaves – the casualties from the initial bombardment were staggering.

A twelfth of the citizen population was already dead. By the twists of bright Tyche, six of the dead were oligarchs – and members of the *boule*. And not one of the Demos party or the Navarch party had died yet.

So, by luck, the domination of the *boule* by the oligarchs had been broken in the first hail of the besieger's engines.

The vote to surrender failed by three votes.

Only then did Panther and his allies realise that they had the *boule*. Nicanor was a proud man – and a mournful one. He rose, pulled his himation about him and stared at them all.

'Now you will order everything your own way – and you will fail. Democrats can never govern – the so-called people lack the *arete* to succeed. When the conquerors are riding your daughters like whores, do not look to me.' He turned to go.

Panther raised his arm. 'Nicanor – you are grieving, and any mortal man would do the same. Stay, and help us choose our *strategoi*. It is in my mind that you should be one of them. Why not? You are a worthy man, a good spear-fighter and you lead a party that is of account. Let us not count every vote. Let us act together for the good of the city.'

Nicanor paused in the doorway. 'You seek only to catch me in the toils of your own failure.'

Panther made a dismissive noise. 'Nicanor, I am a *sailor*. When the storm blows, I do not ask the oarsmen for advice. Nor do drowning men criticise me if I'm wrong. If we fail, *there will be no politics in this city, because we'll all be dead*.'

Nicanor had more dignity in defeat and anger than he did in victory. 'No. I will serve on the walls, but I will not lead. I resign my seat. Good day to you.' He turned and walked through the door. Two of the younger oligarchs rose to follow him – Hellenos and Socrates – but they paused.

Damophilus intercepted them at the door and spoke to them, and they returned to their couches.

The *boule* chose Panther to command the defence. And then the *boule* elected Satyrus of the Euxine to be a member. No one present was more surprised than Satyrus.

He was led to a couch, and Menedemos, the young aristocrat, but a democrat, came and lay by him. 'You are an aristocrat like us,' he said fiercely. 'We play kithara with your friend Anaxagoras and we know you are one of us – Nicanor is blind with grief.'

Satyrus shrugged. 'I'm a king,' he said. 'And my people were aristocrats in Athens and Plataea since the time of the gods.'

Menedemos nodded. 'Exactly. And you are friends with Panther – and with Damophilus. The three of you will unite the parties.'

'I am a foreigner,' Satyrus whispered.

Menedemos laughed aloud. 'You are a king, and all the foreigners know you. There are a thousand metics in this city. Many are worthy men: Abraham the Jew—'

'Is a citizen now, but I agree he's a worthy man.' Satyrus looked at the other man – who was his own age, or even a little older. 'Where is this going?'

Menedemos pointed at Panther. The navarch rose.

'I move that the *boule* appoint me three *strategoi* for the conduct of the siege,' he said. 'I request Damophilus son of Menander, Menedemos son of Menedemos and Satyrus son of Kineas.'

Satyrus lay back and laughed. 'Now I see,' he said.

DAYS ELEVEN TO EIGHTEEN

Satyrus stood on the sand of the gymnasium's palaestra – still smooth under his feet, but a breeze blew across the sand where the whole front wall had been removed, quarried for stone.

He was naked, holding a wooden sword, his left arm wrapped in his chlamys. Anaxagoras faced him. The musician had never been trained as a swordsman, and wished for lessons. Korus stood by them with a heavy staff. Satyrus was covered in sweat, and Anaxagoras gleamed only with oil, having just arrived.

'Again,' Korus growled.

Satyrus moved forward in the guard position, left leg advanced and left arm steady and high, the trailing folds of the cloak covering his side and leg, the cloak weights in the embroidered border holding the edge down. His sword arm was well back, so that his opponent could not easily get control of the sword – his right elbow was cocked back, almost like a boxer ready to throw a punch – the tip of the blade was high, pointing at his opponent's neck.

Anaxagoras smiled. 'I'm not convinced that a man can learn anything from a "sword master",' he said. 'Does Xenophon not say that holding a blade is natural to every boy?'

Satyrus nodded across the wooden blades. 'I'm not sure I'm strong enough to demonstrate the superiority of art over ignorance. But ask yourself, music teacher: how well does that same boy do at playing the kithara – with his *natural* skill?

Anaxagoras stood square on to Satyrus, sword well out, cloak held close to his body.

He grinned. 'I certainly cede the point intellectually. Well hit.'

Satyrus found it hard to dislike the musician, even when he had seen him standing at the entry to the women's quarters, exchanging witticisms with Miriam in the early-morning light while she coached her women on their weaving.

He smiled, and his cloak arm moved a fraction – he slid forward half a step, and his cloak arm shot out, pinned Anaxagoras' sword and his own sword tapped his opponent on the throat – hard enough to make the musician stumble back in pain.

Very satisfying, really.

When Anaxagoras came back on guard, his face was flushed. 'Trick,' he growled, and sprang forward, his sword swinging in vicious arcs. Satyrus ducked, parried with his sword and rolled his wrist, clipping Anaxagoras on the side of the head – a blow which he carefully pulled.

The big musician didn't pause, but cut back.

Satyrus blocked that blow, using the heaviest part of his wooden sword closest to his hand, and the two swords locked for a moment and Anaxagoras, even at a mechanical disadvantage, easily pushed Satyrus down and away – but Satyrus sprang back, substituting training for strength, and extended his sword, which Anaxagoras ran on – too late: he swung his sword, failing the parry and smacking Satyrus' right arm so hard that he dropped his weapon.

'I killed you twice, you ignorant *fuck*,' Satyrus said angrily.

'You never touched me!' Anaxagoras laughed. 'Just as I thought – you dance around and I hit you anyway.'

'I hit you on the head and I just poked you in the gut,' Satyrus said.

'Not hard enough to do any damage,' Anaxagoras said. 'Don't be a poor loser. Is this something about being a king? If I knew I had to lose, I'd have been better prepared.'

Satyrus felt the blood rush to his face. For a moment, he actually *saw red*. Then he counted – ten, nine, eight – slowly down to one. At the end, he took three deep breaths and set himself to guard. He was covered in sweat and his arms hurt, and he was naked. In armour – even light armour – he would already be exhausted.

'Ready,' he said.

This time, Anaxagoras put his cloak well out in front and ran at him, sword swinging.

Satyrus didn't move. Choosing his moment precisely, he punched with his cloak and swung his sword the same way. Even through his wrapped cloak, Anaxagoras' blow stung his arm. But Satyrus' blade caught the musician's out-thrust shin and the man went down like a sacrificial ram.

'Gods curse you, arse-cunt!' Anaxagoras said angrily. He rolled to his feet and thrust at Satyrus, who stepped back. Anaxagoras lunged forward, off balance, his sword held clumsily across his body, and Satyrus stepped forward, shoved the sword into the out-thrust cloak and put his wooden blade into his opponent's armpit. 'Don't be ruled by anger, musician,' he said.

Anaxagoras didn't pause: he cut overarm, a wild Harmodius blow, one, two, three, as fast as he could, heavy blows that jarred Satyrus' arm and made his jaw ache.

Satyrus punched his opponent in the gut with his cloak hand. Once, it would have been a stout blow, even for a left-handed jab. Now it was merely a poke. But Anaxagoras flinched away from it, and Satyrus rolled his blade off the other man's clumsy attempt to stop-cut and jabbed the blade where the punch had gone.

Anaxagoras didn't stop coming. But Satyrus was used to his rage now – he spun back, ducked, and caught the blow on his cloak and it stung.

There was a crack, and Anaxagoras stopped, stunned.

Korus had hit him with his staff. 'Stop, now,' he said.

Anaxagoras stopped. He was bleeding in three places: one was his head, where Satyrus' second blow had caught him. He was breathing hard. The fire died away from his eyes, and he dropped his oak sword.

'Oh, lord, I'm sorry,' he said. 'The fire comes on me ... fuck. You hurt me. I'm an arsehole.'

Satyrus hadn't seen the musician like this – angry, or remorseful. 'You scared me, Anaxagoras,' he said.

'Me too,' Korus said. 'You kill him, I lose my freedom.' The trainer grinned.

Anaxagoras hung his head. 'Sorry,' he said.

Satyrus dropped his cloak. The welt on his cloak arm was red and livid and already raised in a long ridge. 'You hit hard.'

Anaxagoras nodded. 'I find that it works, in combat.'

Satyrus had to smile.

Korus nodded. 'You hit like a girl,' he said to the king of the Euxine.

'You should see my sister fight,' Satyrus said. 'And I was *pulling* my attacks, you idiots.'

Korus spat on the sand. 'The music-maker doesn't want to admit how easily you hit him. You don't want to admit that you have no strength in your hand. You're a pair of liars.' He shrugged. 'Tomorrow, in armour.'

Three days of respite – Demetrios never left his camp.

Three days of fighting on the sand of the palaestra, while the gymnasium itself vanished around them.

The fourth day, Demetrios' fleet moved forward. The Rhodians stood to. Satyrus ran from the sands of the palaestra, already armoured, when the alarm sounded from the Temple of Poseidon, Anaxagoras at his side. They went up the ladders together, onto the roof of Abraham's house.

'Get the marines formed – four streets back, and well spread out, so no one rock can kill them all,' Satyrus barked at Apollodorus. 'You are the reserve for this sector. Any questions?'

Apollodorus got his chinstrap tied and nodded. 'I hate this,' he said. 'I want to hit something.'

Out in the harbour, a pair of light boats were manned. They were fire boats, directed by Menedemos. He intended to burn another engine-ship if he could.

But Demetrios was on to a different tactic. His fleet came up to the seaward edge of the main harbour, but they stayed outside the mole, beyond the headlands that marked the small harbour. Five engine-ships crept slowly across the mouth of the small harbour, and four dropped anchor just off the large harbour's southern headland.

In minutes, their lever arms were swinging and their stones began to fly – over the moles, over the harbour. They only had range to hit the northern and southern ends of town by the port, and about one hundred and fifty paces of wall at either end of the harbour.

Just as quickly, refugees were pouring out of the threatened parts of the town. They fled to the temples, which were out of range of the current bombardment.

At dark, the ships withdrew. The sea wall didn't exist anywhere that the engine-ships could reach: from the harbour entrance, north and south, almost three hundred paces of wall had been reduced to pulverised clay, broken concrete and smashed stone. Dozens more were dead, and fires had started where panicked householders had abandoned homes while lamps were lit in household shrines.

The northern quarter burned for two days. Panther ordered that the town's reserve simply destroy two rows of houses to isolate the fire, and return to their duty.

At the height of the fire, Demetrios sent ships into the harbour – thirty ships crammed with soldiers. But they had trouble navigating the wrecks, and there were dozens of Rhodian ships anchored, empty, in the shallow water by the beach under the sea wall, and despite damage, most of them had survived to impede navigation.

Not a single enemy soldier got ashore, and Panther's ruthlessness in abandoning the northern quarter to fire was proven sound.

Four enemy triremes were caught and destroyed.

On the seventeenth night of the siege, Panther, Damophilus and Menedemos each manned light guard ships in the dark, rowed silently out of the small harbour entrance and attacked the engine-ships with fire. Satyrus stood on the roof, unable to settle to sleep. The engine up there hadn't fired in days – the enemy didn't come within range – but the roof was the highest in the neighbourhood of the temples and Satyrus could see a long way.

Anaxagoras came up the ladder while Satyrus sat. The attack was secret – so secret that Satyrus hadn't even told Abraham – but everyone knew something was up.

'Am I welcome here?' Anaxagoras asked.

Satyrus grunted. He was standing on top of the left-hand ballista for the added eight, watching the sea.

'I brought wine,' he said.

Satyrus grinned in the dark. 'Well, in that case …'

Anaxagoras handed up a metal cup and then clambered onto the other machine. 'Night attack?' he asked.

Satyrus drank the wine in a single gulp. He was nervous, and angry – angry at his body for not being ready.

'All of the commanders,' he said. 'All except me are out there on the water.'

Anaxagoras nodded. 'They're amateurs,' he said.

Satyrus looked at him, but the musician was impossible to read in the moonless gloom.

'I'm no soldier, but I'm a professional singer,' Anaxagoras said. 'I know how to plan and execute a big commission. A huge party, a temple entertainment – fifty musicians, ten pieces of music, a chorus, a sex act and a fighting act and a pair of famous lyre players – how to keep them all happy and together so that the client is happy.'

Satyrus tried to get wine out of an empty cup. 'Do you have more wine?'

'Yes. Catch,' Anaxagoras said, and threw something.

Satyrus caught it – a wineskin – balanced on the main slide of the ballista, and was proud of the body he was rebuilding. He poured more wine. 'You have the right of it,' he said. 'They don't see the whole siege, just pieces of it. Demetrios will assault the harbour, perhaps tomorrow. But he's been moving men around the city for days, and he'll have a go at the land walls – another attempt at surprise, I expect. And the men of the city are as brave as lions, but they aren't looking ahead and they won't listen to me. They're thinking in days. This siege will last a year. That is, if we are lucky enough to survive tomorrow.'

Anaxagoras shuffled around in the dark. 'A year?'

Satyrus shrugged, not that the motion communicated anything. So he spoke. 'At least. All Demetrios needs to do is realise that if he kills one of us for every fifteen of his men, he'll win – and then we'll be finished. So far, he has disdained such tactics.'

Suddenly, there was fire on the water. One fire sprang up, and then another, and suddenly, as fast as Satyrus could take a breath, the fires leaped into pillars, the roar like the distant hum of bees.

'Poseidon,' Satyrus said. 'Herakles, stand with us.'

The flames grew until the whole area outside of the harbour was illuminated as if by daylight. The three Rhodian ships could be seen clearly, and a dozen enemy ships launching from the beach and a pair of guard ships already moving at ramming speed.

One of the Rhodian ships got fire into a third target at the price of being rammed – hard.

Satyrus writhed, his body moving to and fro as he tried to fight the battle himself.

'You drinking all the wine?' Anaxagoras asked.

Satyrus threw the wineskin back, and the musician caught it. 'Your arms are getting stronger,' he said.

Satyrus smiled to himself. 'Yes,' he said.

'We're not so different,' Anaxagoras said.

'No?' Satyrus asked, his eyes glued to the fight beyond the harbour. There were four enemy ships around one Rhodian. The other two Rhodian ships had made their escape.

'No. You'd rather be fighting – even at the risk of your life: you, a king, a rich man – than watching.' Anaxagoras snorted.

Satyrus saw that the third Rhodian ship had set herself on fire. That was courage. 'Yes,' he said.

'I hate to watch, too. I have to play – whatever everyone else plays. Music. Games. Sword work.' Anaxagoras snorted.

Satyrus joined him. 'It's true,' he laughed, although his heart was in his throat. Who had just died?

'And we're in love with the same woman,' Anaxagoras went on. 'I'm sorry about that.'

Satyrus all but fell from the ballista. 'What?' he asked.

'You want Miriam. So do I. I see how you look at her – Hades, I look at her the same way. I'd like to eat her raw, too.' Anaxagoras laughed. It was not a happy laugh. 'The thing is – you, the king – what can you offer her? I can give her music, and a good name. I would marry her, if Abraham would have me.'

Now more ships were burning – the three enemies grappled to the Rhodian ships, dying in the fatal embrace. Someone had made a noble sacrifice. Who was it?

'I'm doing this badly, lord. You have other things on your mind.' Anaxagoras made a noise like a man choking.

Satyrus jumped down from his ballista without another word, and then climbed down the ladder closest to him, ignoring Anaxagoras. He wasn't ready to consider the validity of Anaxagoras' claim – and he thought that he'd seen men going over the side of the distant burning ships.

'Apollodorus!' he called. 'Marines!'

He gathered the first dozen, with Idomeneus and some archers, and ran for the harbour mouth – slow going when they came to the edge of the southern quarter, where the buildings had been crushed as if by the hand of a god. They climbed across the rubble that covered the streets – whole houses collapsed, or walls that had fallen straight outward, dreadful footing – but the distance was short, and then they were on the breakwater of the small harbour. Satyrus led the marines and archers along.

'Look for men swimming!' he called.

One of the enemy ships was looking for swimmers as well – a trireme. She came on strongly, her archers shooting down into the water, and Idomeneus began shooting at the archers. His men supported him, and the glare of the burning ships backlit the enemy, while Idomeneus and his archers were invisible in the darkness. In heartbeats, the enemy archers were shot silent.

'I see men!' Apollodorus called. 'Spearmen, to me!'

Idomeneus glanced at Satyrus. The enemy trireme was coming right in – it was possible she intended to land her marines on the breakwater to cut off the swimmers.

'See if you can clear her command station,' Satyrus said.

'Aim amidships,' Idomeneus sang out. 'All together. *Loose!*'

A dozen arrows flew, and then another dozen before the first had struck, and suddenly the enemy ship turned – not to port, away from the breakwater, but to starboard, and in two breaths she struck, at cruising speed, her ram hitting the piled stone of the ancient harbour mole from the time of Agamemnon and Achilles.

Then the night was full of fighting. The enemy crew, desperate, poured over the side into the deep water and came up the side of the breakwater. Satyrus had only a half-dozen marines, and they had to move up and down the stone road on top of the harbour works, killing the men climbing.

And they had to be careful, because from the first, some of the climbing men were friends – swimmers from the burning Rhodian ship.

Satyrus stood at the head of an iron ladder built into the breakwater, and his shield felt as if it was made of iron on his shoulder – he could not remember feeling so tired *before* a fight. Some enemy had made it up this ladder or another, and most were unarmed or poorly armed, but Tyche sent a rush at him – three men in armour, who had clambered straight from the dying trireme onto the wharf, and a dozen unarmed sailors behind them – and he was alone.

He kicked another man on the ladder and the poor wretch retreated, and then Satyrus set his shoulder and the rush came in.

There was nothing he could do but retreat – he could not have held the head of the ladder even in top shape. He managed two good blows, both of which struck home, but not with enough strength, and neither of his first opponents fell.

Back and back and back again, cursing his weakness. A shape beside him in the dark, swinging wildly, and men fell back before them – and now a flicker of light, a burst of flame and Satyrus lunged, changing feet, and his point sank into a man's eye-slit and he died.

And then – suddenly – the breakwater was covered in men. Menedemos brought his ship in close on the *inside* of the breakwater and landed his marines and his deck crew, and they stemmed the rush. As soon as they pushed past Satyrus, he fell to his knees – a few seconds of wrestling with his helmet and he vomited from fatigue.

Anaxagoras held his hair out of the vomit, and then passed him a rag, silent in the fitful light of the dying ships.

Satyrus got to his feet. 'Thanks,' he said. 'I think you saved my life,' he continued.

Anaxagoras grinned. 'I think you saved mine, back in the fight at Salamis.' He shrugged. 'Even?'

Satyrus couldn't raise his arms above his shoulders. 'I can't help myself,' he said.

Anaxagoras nodded. 'Me neither.'

The Rhodians cleared the mole, killing every enemy on it and offering no mercy. All of the Rhodian swimmers were rescued, including the three men supporting Panther, who was still in armour and had nonetheless made it across the harbour.

'There's a man more tired than I am myself,' Satyrus said. He went and embraced the old navarch.

'Now he'll go away,' Panther gasped.

Satyrus shook his head. 'Now he'll get serious,' he said.

21

The next morning, Demetrios stayed in his camp and the defenders slept. There were now two thousand people, free, slave, citizen and foreigner mixed, sleeping in the agora and on the open ground in front of the Temple of Poseidon, and families were building shacks from blankets, old sails, baskets – anything they could find. Wood was at a premium: Satyrus' sailors had taken every bit of wood that could be spared, and men were cutting down the olive trees that grew in gardens.

The sortie had destroyed three more engine-ships, leaving Demetrios with six. His engineers and slaves spent the nineteenth day of the siege hard at work, and thirty triremes escorted a dozen merchant ships away to the north.

'What do you think he's up to?' Anaxagoras asked between bouts. Korus was leaning on his stick. They were in Abraham's garden – there was no longer a gymnasium to visit.

'Getting wood to build more engines,' Satyrus said.

Fighting in Abraham's garden meant fighting where all the marines and sailors could watch. And Miriam, of course, who smiled at both men. And raised the intensity of the mock fighting enormously.

Both of them were limping when they finished. Miriam had watched all of their bouts, and now, as Charmides went forward to fight Helios, she watched them, as well. Other marines were pairing up.

'Have time for me?' Abraham asked.

He was wearing armour.

Satyrus grinned. He took the practice sword from Anaxagoras' hand.

'Brother!' he said, and they set to.

Abraham was in good condition, but his technique was rusty and Satyrus drove him down the garden and then got a thrust to the abdomen.

'I deserved that!' Satyrus laughed.

'I enjoyed it,' Abraham said.

He managed two more good bouts before fatigue crushed him, and he saw that Abraham was pulling his attacks, and raised his hand. 'That's it for me,' he said, and the two embraced. 'Good to see you in armour,' he said. He went to stand with Apollodorus, watching the marines. He didn't mean to stand where he could overhear Anaxagoras talk to Miriam. It just happened.

'How odd men are,' Miriam said to Anaxagoras. 'My brother is here every day – but when he dons armour to be a killer, Satyrus loves him more.'

Anaxagoras shook his head. 'Nay, Despoina,' he said. 'It is far more complicated than that – as I think you know. War made them brothers. When Abraham is dressed as a Jew – I mean no offence – Satyrus doesn't know what to make of him. But the king is courteous, and he loves your brother. But when your brother puts his armour on and shows his legs – why, that's the man he knows; knows to the centre of his heart.'

Miriam wasn't visible to Satyrus. He wished he could see her face – she made an odd sound, almost like a moan. And he thought, *Anaxagoras, you bastard – you're right. And Abraham deserves better, however he's dressed.*

And then they ate, and slept, and Demetrios launched his largest attack yet.

Satyrus was caught by surprise – he'd expected Demetrios to be patient, get more wood from the mainland and continue his careful bombardment. It was, after all, a crushing strategy.

Instead, at dawn on the twenty-first day, all six engine-ships came on, covered by a hundred triremes and two dozen penteres.

The Rhodians scrambled for their defences. They got to their stations, and Satyrus had time, no matter how fast the enemy rowed, to alter his local dispositions. His was the responsibility for the centre of the sea wall. His work crews had laboured in secret for fifteen days. His sailors and marines manned some of the walls. His beloved *Arete* lay moored in front of the weakest wall section.

'Apollodorus?'

'Lord?'

'All the marines into the reserve. The sailors have been training on the engines – let them take over. I want every armoured man ready to stem a breach – well back, all the way to the agora. I won't lose one of you to bombardment – and my reading is that he's going to bring the engines in close.' Satyrus slapped him on his armoured shoulder. 'Go.'

'Yes, lord!' Apollodorus saluted.

Demetrios' fleet formed off the small harbour and the large – and at a trumpet blast, a dozen triremes dashed into each harbour to be met by a hail of ballista bolts, fire arrows and spears.

But it is difficult to sink a determined ship with bolts. The trireme's oarsmen were brave, and they had been promised rich rewards for success. They drove their ships beak first into the moored defensive line – the wooden wall of ships defending the sea wall – and it burst into flame.

'Shit,' Satyrus said. One of the first ships to catch was *Arete*. And all he could do from his rooftop perch was to watch his beloved burn. It was like looking on at the death of a friend – a lover. A best-beloved. For three years of peace he had poured his desire for action, for a life outside the Euxine, into *Arete*. And she burned so fast – his dreams of freedom, his secret desire to sail away and leave Tanais to rot, never to attend a council of farmers, or count drachma when ordering statues – she burned, and he couldn't tear his eyes from her, as she seemed to achieve some final perfection, as if the ship itself was summoned to Olympus and went through an apotheosis of fire.

Demetrios had chosen his men well and planned carefully, and the whole line of the wooden wall caught fire and the sea wind pushed the smoke ashore, into the faces of the defenders. And while their eyes streamed and they choked on the smoke, the heavier ships entered the harbours, and the engine-ships behind them.

Then their engines began to range the sea wall. They were shooting blind, into the smoke – but they had engineers who had been trained by philosophers and mathematicians, and they had the range from other forays into the harbour. The deadly hail crushed the sea wall in three places, opening breaches as wide as a small ship was long. Two hours into the action, as the waves lapped over the waterline of the blackened *Arete* and she sank in the shallow water, extinguishing the last fire in the harbour, and the air cleared, the whole force moved in, undeterred by the defender's desperate counter-barrage. The harbour was *filled* with enemy ships. The two rooftop ballistae shot as fast as bolts could be provided – a few red hot from the kitchens, most cold and straight.

In the harbour, enemy ships caught fire, enemy captains fell, enemy oarsmen died, but still the fleet pressed forward – and now the great engine-ships raised their aim points. Their big stones ceased to fall on the sea wall. They shot a hundred paces further inland, creating a line of destruction far behind the wall.

'He's cutting the beach off from the town,' Satyrus said. He shook his head. 'He's good. I hadn't thought of using the big engines to keep men away.'

Anaxagoras ducked as a stone whistled past close by and crushed the rubble of the house behind Abraham's – again.

'Here they come,' Satyrus said. 'Now we see.' He turned to Helios. 'Get Abraham.'

In moments, his friend was beside him in the street. Satyrus took him aside, into the courtyard. He motioned to Anaxagoras to join them.

'Abraham,' he said. 'The town may fall in the next hour.'

'I know,' Abraham said.

'If you agree, I will leave Helios here to kill … your sister.' Satyrus shrugged. 'Anaxagoras, am I wrong?'

The musician shook his head. 'No.'

But Abraham shook his head. 'It is taken care of,' he said. 'I thank you for your … thought. But she has her own way.'

Satyrus nodded. 'Good, then. Let's be to work.'

He saw Miriam at the window of her weaving room. He waved.

She didn't wave back.

The streets were grim. The air was full of smoke and dust, and splinters and shards of rock had hurt many people, so that slaves and injured children drifted listlessly, or ran screaming.

Satyrus moved forward through the rubble. The closer he got to the sea wall, the worse the destruction was. Many of the stones had missed, and fallen on the town. The worse for his plan.

By the time he reached the sea wall – or the rubble of the sea wall; a continuous breach for four hundred paces, now – the enemy was beaching thirty light ships, all packed with soldiers. Two were already on fire – one had taken a ballista bolt right into the packed phalangites – but the others came on, and the men leaped into the shallow water and came up the beach screaming.

Picked men, all volunteers. Veterans of fifty actions, hard Macedonians, Greeks and Asians who had faced cavalry and elephants and fire and sword for twenty years, they came up the beach into arrows so thick they seemed the embodiment of wind. Men fell, and more pressed behind them. Dozens died. Dozens fell wounded, and more than a few cowered in the bilges of their light assault boats and refused to press ashore – but two thousand men set foot on the beach and most of them crossed the shingle to the foot of the breach.

It was darkly comic, like Menander's best work, that Demetrios had forty thousand soldiers and yet his assaults were limited by the number of men he could fit into ships and cram through the small harbour entrance. If he'd been able to fill the beach with men – even four thousand men – the town would have fallen in minutes.

Satyrus waited in his defences. Two weeks of work by his sailors and the town slaves. *Was he right? Did Demetrios suspect?*

The town's half-finished, badly mauled sea wall didn't even *slow* the Macedonian professionals, and they were into the streets.

'Stay together!' an officer called. 'No looting until the garrison's dead!'

They cheered like madmen. They were in the town, their ships dominating the harbour—

Satyrus watched them come.

The lead men were dying under renewed archery volleys – stronger, if anything, than before. And now the Macedonian officers began to raise their heads and see.

A city block behind the sea wall was another wall, disguised among the houses. It was built of rubble and the stones of the Temple of Apollo and the gymnasium. It was only twice the height of a man, and instead of towers, the biggest houses had been crudely reinforced and loop-holed. Every archer in the town was in the houses, and they shot into the packed Macedonians like hunters killing a herd of netted deer.

The Macedonians screamed in fear and in rage, and they didn't break. They went up the narrow streets between the loop-holed houses. They were veterans. They took the casualties to get them to the wall, because they knew to a man that the only way out was forward.

Satyrus had seen second-rate Macedonians at Gaza. But he had never seen the ferocity of the best of them: the old farmers of Pella, the men whose courage had made Alexander master of Asia. They roared like the lion roars when trapped in the barnyard by the herdsmen, trying to attack the cattle in the barn on a cold winter's night and now, cornered, too angry to run. They bellowed, and they climbed their own dead to get over the walls.

They gained the top of the wall in three places. In two, local counter-attacks cleared them – later, Satyrus learned that Idomeneus, the finest archer he knew aside from his sister, had led his unarmoured Cretans out of their houses into the flanks of a breakthrough.

But that was later. Right in the centre, where they received some supporting fire from the engines on their ships, the Macedonians went up the wall three times, and on the third attempt, climbing a hundred corpses to reach with heavy hands for the lives of the defenders, they crossed the wall, gave a great cheer and roared into the town.

Satyrus turned to Charmides. 'Get Apollodorus,' he said. 'Don't die on the way.'

He had Anaxagoras and Helios, Abraham and a dozen half-armoured sailors.

Neiron's hand closed like a vice on his shoulder. 'Not you, lord.'

Satyrus shook his head. 'Every man. I have armour.'

Neiron shook his head. 'You are *rash*.'

Satyrus caught their eyes, tied his cheek-plates down and hefted his spear. His shield threatened to drag him down. He ignored his fatigue. 'Ready?'

The men around him growled. Sailors were pouring off the roof of Abraham's house. The street was full: from side to side it wasn't much wider than a chariot, and thirty men filled it six deep.

Anaxagoras looked at him, huge and ferocious in a leering bronze helmet – a Thracian with a wicked faceplate. 'At least stand in the second rank,' he said.

'Never,' Satyrus said. He could see Miriam on the roof, watching. At some remove, he knew that he was a fool, a rash boy, but Miriam was standing right there and he was the King of the Bosporus, not some shirking second-ranker.

The Macedonians paused at the edge of the street, cheered and charged.

'*Charge!*' Satyrus roared.

They pounded down the street at the enemy, sandals slapping. A Macedonian caught his foot on rubble and fell – the enemy charge faltered, but the men were trained and they flowed around the fallen man and came on.

Satyrus wished that he was stronger, and then the daemon came to him, and he ran—

Both sides slowed as shields came together. Neither side had sarissas – the huge long pikes that Macedonians carried in open warfare. They were too long for siege work, and the enemy phalangites had javelins and *longche*, the sort of spear that Greek cavalrymen and hunters carried. They had the smaller round shields as well, and Satyrus and his companions had the advantage at contact. Satyrus put his shoulder down, and his shield face slammed into an enemy—

And he was knocked flat, the man stepped on him and died, his blood all over Satyrus' face as he tried to rise, and a blow rang off his helmet and he was down again, something heavy on his legs. Another man stepped on his shield and his shoulder shrieked with pain. For a moment he was twelve years old, fighting in the dark beneath Philokles' feet when assassins attacked their house in Heraklea. He let go of his spear, got the sword out of his scabbard under his armpit and hurt *himself* as someone kicked his out-thrust right elbow – lost the sword, took a blow to his helmet.

It was tempting to give up and lie flat, but his city was dying. He got his shield arm out of the porpax of his shield, fought the wave of pain and put his left hand under himself, pulled at his legs and began to drag them free – there were dead men on his legs and hips – a shield slammed into his head and he went down again, and he was on his chest now, eyes full of stars and a forest of legs and hips above him, the star of Macedon on the shields. Satyrus found his sword hilt under his hand and he cut up with his *xiphos* and the blow had little strength, but the edge and point went into a man's groin and the man screamed and folded, falling right onto Satyrus' outstretched sword arm; he lost his grip on the sword. Another blow to his back and he was down, and the weight on his back was so great that he wondered if he was to be crushed alive. Men died above him, and now he was imprisoned, someone was screaming curses inside his helmet—

Darkness.

HERAKLEA, SPRING, 305 BC

'Satyrus of the Bosporus is dead.'

It was said in the agora and in the barracks, in the private houses where merchants lived, in bedchambers and in *andron*. Some said it with conviction, and some said it with hesitation.

In the citadel of the city, high above all the other whispers, Stratokles of Athens sat on an ebony chair in his mistress's presence, a bag of scrolls by his side. He lifted another scroll – his third of this stormy meeting – cracked the seal and read the long, florid salutation aloud.

'To the Divine Amastris, light-bringer, herald of beauty, beloved of Aphrodite and Athena, this humble supplicant sends greetings, beseeching your Divine Majesty for your continued protection and favour.' Stratokles looked up and raised an eyebrow. 'I'm *so* glad we don't pay by the word. However, Phiale is an old and trusted agent – ha, although the mere use of the word *old* will probably cause her pain from here. And there it is, Despoina – Satyrus is dead. Died of some sort of poisoned wound, or perhaps a fever, oh, a month ago or more.'

Amastris picked up a fine *pnyx* of Aegyptian alabaster, looked at it for three full heartbeats and slammed it into the wall by her head. It shattered into a thousand shards, which a pair of slaves leaped to clear away before she stepped on them and had the pair beaten for their failure.

Stratokles watched her, and he winced – his persistent fondness for the woman was often jarred by the blinding selfishness of her rages. The way she weighed an item before destroying it … In other rages he'd watched her pick up an item she actually liked, weigh it, and then place it back on her side table. She never seemed to destroy anything that she truly valued.

'He is not dead,' she shrieked. 'I will not believe it!'

Stratokles was careful to keep any expression off his face. 'There is always some small chance, my dear. But he was on Rhodes, facing Demetrios. He chose to support the doomed city – against our interests, may I remind you. And now he's paid the price. You may be as angry as you please with the fates – rage against the *Moirai* if you will – but it is time we faced facts. You weren't going to marry him anyway ... were you?'

He hadn't meant to say it; it was a nasty truth, the sort of thing that a careful politician like Stratokles kept between his teeth, the sort of knowledge that could constitute power if used carefully. But sometimes her selfish, pretended devotion annoyed him, and this time it got the better of him.

'I – love – Satyrus,' she spat at him. Her favourite maid – the Keltoi girl – was on her hands and knees, picking up bits of the destroyed *pnyx* as fast as she could. Amastris emphasised her love by kicking at the girl viciously to clear her path across the floor. 'How dare you, you Athenian scum, pretend you have no finer feelings. Get out of my sight!'

Stratokles leaned back in his chair. 'No,' he said. He was having one of those moments when he rebelled – he often deplored the results, but he couldn't resist the opportunity to show her to herself. 'Stop abusing your slaves and pay attention to me, young lady. Antigonus and his golden son have risked everything – *everything* – to take Rhodes. By all accounts, they are winning. Your father had a close alliance with them – we must have a closer. And Satyrus is dead. His sister has vanished into the east and if we're lucky, she's dead, too. *This is our moment.* Get a hold of yourself, get some warships together and send your father's bodyguard in those ships to aid Demetrios – a public avowal. He's going to need ships and men – a siege like this one will eat men like a pig eats cabbage. Get his alliance – his approval – and then move on Tanais. It can be ours by the end of the summer. There's no one to stop us – their fleet is all away. Probably destroyed.'

Amastris threw herself on the curtained bed. She sobbed inconsolably, for several minutes and then, like a child, she sat up. 'Who do *you* see me marrying?' she asked.

Stratokles nodded. This was the princess he loved. It often took time to reach her, but the trip was always worthwhile in the end. 'I see several possibilities,' he said. 'If you are willing to be queen to the Emperor of the World, I think you could do worse than Demetrios. He's beautiful, he's going to own the whole of the ocean sea—'

Amastris shook her head. 'I never want to be second,' she said. 'Although he *is* beautiful, and I remember that he has this delicious belief that he is more than mortal – it's the most gorgeous thing about him. Perhaps I can ... befriend him, before I wed.'

Stratokles laughed. 'Or after, dear.' Amastris had seldom gone a month without a lover, and he didn't expect that the future would be any different.

'So, if not the great man himself, you might take any number of local men and make them your consort. Melitta's mercenary commander – he'll need to be bought anyway – he's handsome and he's nobody.' Stratokles laughed. 'Once we have Tanais, we can always make him go away.'

'Anyone else?' she asked, dangling her feet over her head as she lay on her stomach. She danced constantly, with a dedication that belied her apparent sloth – she had the body of a temple dancer, and in fact she often led the religious dances in person. She was remarkably flexible, and Stratokles had to look away. She did it on purpose: he knew it, she knew it. And yet she could tie him in knots.

She smiled, her eyes already losing their red rims. 'What about young Herakles?' she asked. Banugul's son – the last surviving child of Alexander's body. Not born within wedlock, of course. But Stratokles had him, and his mother ... hidden away, he wouldn't tell anyone where.

'He's a little younger than you,' Stratokles said, rubbing his beard. 'And to be honest, his time is *not yet*. My instincts tell me that Antigonus will make a mistake – and then it will be time for my boy.' Stratokles looked at her. 'You're both young. Time to wed the mercenary, ride him for a year or two and then see what's on the horizon.'

'Queen of the Euxine. Queen of the Bosporus.' Amastris smiled. 'Girl, what *are* you doing on the floor?'

The slave flinched, but Amastris merely smiled. To Stratokles she said, 'And what of Lysimachos?'

'Lysimachos and Cassander must be at their wits' end,' Stratokles said. 'Lysimachos can only prosper if Asia and Europe are at war and he controls the middle ground. Cassander will lose Greece as soon as

Antigonus had dealt with Rhodes and Aegypt. The handwriting is on the wall, dear. But – let us not jump too fast. You have a great deal to offer, and the time is at hand to increase your flocks. Make Demetrios your ally and then take Tanais, Olbia and Pantecapaeaum. We'll need more troops – perhaps Demetrios will rent them to us when Rhodes falls.'

She made a moue, then smiled. 'You have it all thought out, as usual.'

Stratokles raised an eyebrow. 'If you agree, you must send ships for Demetrios. And we need to deal with your father's captain, Nestor. He doesn't approve of you.'

Amastris smiled in a way that showed her teeth, like a predator, without reaching her eyes. 'I think that mostly he disapproves of *you*, dear advisor.'

Stratokles returned the smile, tooth for tooth. 'I think that in this situation our interests run in harness like a chariot team.'

Amastris watched her maids on the floor for a hundred heartbeats. 'What do you have in mind? I could send him with Uncle's men to Rhodes.'

Stratokles shrugged. 'That's a short-term solution.'

'And you can go in command,' she said.

BOOK FOUR

DEMETRIOS' CAMP, ISLE OF RHODES, LATE SPRING, 305 BC

Stratokles watched his mistress flirt with Demetrios with all the unease of a father watching his daughter flirt with a pimp.

He was forced to admit that at some level, they belonged together. He had seldom seen two such perfect bodies, each with the same blaze of golden hair, and they seemed to recognise something in each other – something that allowed self-love to be interpreted as *love*.

And she was coy with the golden man, in a way she was seldom coy. Five days in his camp, and his hands had yet to touch her body. Stratokles had to give her full marks for discipline, in this instance. She was *not* Banugul. She had other strings to her bow, other arrows in her quiver.

'I take it that you have brought me here to see me die?' Nestor asked him. The black giant was standing at his shoulder.

Stratokles had many faults, but cowardice was not among them. So he didn't flinch, even in his heart. 'We're not exactly friends, are we, Nestor?'

Nestor shook his head. 'No.'

'I expect you could organise my death as easily as I could organise yours,' Stratokles said. He nodded to his lieutenant, Lucius, who had arranged to stand very close to Nestor. The Italian was the deadliest man Stratokles had ever known, and Stratokles was a veteran fighter himself.

Nestor was as unperturbed as Stratokles had been. 'Perhaps,' Nestor said. 'Although not all men are vipers.'

'Shall we have a truce, Nestor? I have to lead these men – our mistress will expect nothing less. I will not work your demise if you will not work mine.' He looked into Nestor's eyes. The warrior was absolutely honest: if he meant to deceive, Stratokles would know instantly.

Nestor smiled. 'Will you swear an oath, Athenian?'

Stratokles nodded. 'Of course.'

Nestor smiled. 'What oath would I accept?' he asked.

Stratokles stood up to the other man. 'I keep my word,' he said angrily.

'Really?' Nestor asked. 'I ask all the gods to witness, then. By the River Styx, on which the gods themselves swear. By Zeus, who hears all oaths. By the furies, who haunt the oath-breaker. I swear that, as long as I serve my mistress Amastris, I will take no action by thought or word or deed to harm you, Stratokles.' He laughed. 'Will you swear the same?'

'What need, since you are already bound?' Stratokles laughed.

Nestor returned his laugh. 'What need to ask of me an oath, Athenian?' he said. He grinned at Lucius. 'Since we both know that I would only kill you face to face. You seek me to demand an oath that you would need from a man like you. But I am not a man like you – and if I were, my oath would not bind me. Isn't it droll?' he asked.

He walked off. Stratokles looked at Lucius, who shrugged his massive shoulders. 'Don't look at me, boss,' Lucius said.

'I may need him dead one of these days,' Stratokles said.

'Kill him yourself, boss,' Lucius said. 'My sense is that that one will take a lot of killing.'

Stratokles had to laugh. 'I don't need you to tell me that. And can I tell you a secret, Lucius? I rather like him.'

'Me too,' said Lucius. He shrugged in his Italianate way. 'I've had to kill men I liked and I've never fancied it. So I won't do Nestor. OK?'

Stratokles nodded. 'Fair enough. We'll die like autumn flies in this siege, anyway. You've been a soldier more often than me.' Stratokles nodded at the camp walls. 'How is our golden hero doing?'

Lucius gathered his cloak around himself. It was late spring, and the water temperature was still cold, and the breath of wind off the ocean was not warm. 'He was badly beaten the other night, before we came in. He lost two thousand men – that's two thousand men *dead* – trying to storm the harbour defences. I talked to a handful of survivors who swam out – the Rhodians built a hidden wall a stone's throw behind the harbour wall. Fucking clever, if you ask me. Never seen it done in Italy. Heard it talked about, but these bastards went and did it – a stade of it.'

'Two thousand men,' Stratokles was dismayed. He'd expected to find Rhodes on the verge of falling.

Lucius shrugged. 'He's got men to burn – not many as good as ours, but he has a fair number – he has some of his father's men, and some good Macedonians, and some Argyraspides that his father probably *wants* him to kill off, if only to save their pay.' He shrugged again. 'He'll win – never fear. But I think this siege has a month left in it. Especially since he seems to be getting ready to have another go at the harbour.'

Hours later, walking on the sand, trailing after his mistress as she walked arm in arm with the Golden King, he heard Demetrios.

'Is it not like Troy?' Demetrios asked. He waved a bronze-clad arm at the line of ships. 'A thousand ships have their sterns in the sand, my dear. A thousand ships. And we are the noble Achaeans, come to take lofty Ilion – not so lofty, but damned strong.'

Amastris laughed at him. 'It is a little like posturing, Great King. Windy Ilion took ten years and more to fall. And none of your attacks has taken any ground yet.'

Demetrios paused and looked at her – a long look, a look that went on to the point where everyone stopped, all the courtiers and guards, all the attendants, all the slaves.

'A lesser man would explode in rage that you should doubt him,' Demetrios said. 'But lesser men are ... lesser. They lack confidence, and they choose rage when what they truly express is fear. I am not like them. I will take Rhodes because I am the best man – indeed, because I am like a god. I have a great army, a great fleet, superb engineers – and over all of it, my own commanding will. They have none of these things – but they have a strong wall, and they are brave. In a way, I love them for it. This is the contest of my life, Amastris. If they were unworthy, I would lose as much as they lose. If this siege takes ten years, let them be years of greatness.'

Amastris looked into his remarkable eyes with her own. Stratokles was close enough to hear her. She made him proud. 'You speak like a god, my lord. Next you will compare me to Helen.'

Demetrios grinned, not like a god but like a boy. 'That would be foolish, lady. If you were Helen, you would be in the city, wretched at your betrayal of your husband and your infidelity.'

He didn't see how his words, meant to flatter, narrowed her eyes instead.

He went on, oblivious. 'You are outside the city,' he said.

'Oh,' she shot at him. 'Am I Briseis, then, or another spear-won trull?'

Demetrios laughed his golden laugh. 'Do not mistake me for a fool, lady, and I will not mistake you for a mortal woman. You are no Helen. You are Aphrodite incarnate, come to see the siege. And I am Ares. Tonight I will assault the city again. Will you come and watch?'

'Nothing would give me more pleasure,' she said. 'And perhaps you would like to use some of my men in this assault?'

Stratokles winced.

'Ah,' Demetrios nodded. 'The sport is always sweeter when you have a team on the field, is it not?'

22

Melitta sat on her riding horse, watching the smooth steppe roll away to the east broken only by tall clumps of thistle and lappa. She was munching an apple so dry it was almost inedible. Her horse's breath rose in clouds of steam.

'Well?' she said to Coenus.

'Wait for the scouts,' Coenus advised her.

'We've waited three days,' Melitta said. She finished the apple and tossed the wrinkled core on the snow.

'Thyrsis and Scopasis are not likely to fail,' Coenus said.

Melitta didn't want to admit that it was failure she feared – failure, and her own roil of emotions when it came to that pair. Scopasis, the former outlaw and her long-standing bedmate. Thyrsis, the Achilles of the Sakje.

'They could be dead, now, or captives,' she said pettishly. 'Why on earth did we do this?'

This constituted a twelve-hundred-parasang journey into the east. The Tanais high ground lay far behind – they had ridden north around the bird-filled marshes at the north end of the Kaspian Sea where their horses shied at storks and geese, and then south again along the eastern shore, where they'd hunted the abundant game; they ate saiga every night for three weeks and left the entrails for the birds and dried the extra meat under their saddles; killed endless numbers of bustards, and ate them every conceivable way. Despite good hunting, they took the time to purchase supplies in Hyrkania. Twice they'd fought bandits, and twice they'd spent a fortnight with other Sakje or Sauromatae tribesmen, trading for fresh horses and food, and once they'd lain two days under hides, horses pulled tight against them, while a tide of locusts rolled over the plains – and then they'd eaten all they could catch, in fresh honey.

Everyone east of Hyrkania had been raided by the Parni – the new tribe, fresh from the deserts beneath the high walls of the Qu'in. Distant cousins of the Parsi and the Parthi, or so men said. But no one seemed to know where they were.

Until, after thirty weeks of riding, they had crossed the salt lake and camped on the outskirts of Marakanda, where Alexander had camped and where her father had fought. And there they'd met rumours of the Parni, and how they were moving into the lands of Bactria, lands emptied by a generation of war by Alexander and his satraps. Alexander had not conquered Bactria cleanly – but none of the Bactrians who had resisted him had lived to tell the tale, and their forts were as empty as the beds of their wives.

And the Parni had ridden south from the steppe to occupy some of the richest grazing land in all the known world.

Sitting in the agora – the souq – of Marakanda, Coenus had tried to convince his charge to turn back.

'If the Parni have moved into Bactria,' he said, 'they're no business of ours. They'll never trouble us again. They came west, all the way to Hyrkania. Now they've turned south. You've shown your power – you've ridden across the steppe the way your mother did, and shown that the Assagetae still have a long arm. Let us ride home. There are other predators besides the Parni.'

Melitta shook her head. 'I will show the length of my arm with my arm,' she said.

And so, fifteen days later, east along the Polytimeros, and then south with the first break in the weather, losing horses to climb the high passes of eastern Sogdiana – the same passes that Leon and Ataelus and Temerix had crossed twenty years before. Now their knowledge, transferred through their sons and daughters and friends, was more precious than gold, and the Assagetae and their Tanais cavalry allies descended into northern Bactria through the back door of the Dushanbe Valley, where they bought musty grain and warm food. And information.

The people of Bactria had no great love for their new overlords.

Melitta had sent her best to find the right target. And then she had tried to sit back and relax and stay warm. In Bactria, it was still winter – high, howling winter, and the passage of the Sogdian Mountains seemed impossibly rash in retrospect.

'Why did we do this?' she asked again. But she could tell that

Coenus was avoiding telling her the truth – that she'd made every choice that had brought them here.

An hour later a snow squall hit from the south, the snow blowing in their faces, and Melitta retreated to her warm felt tent, where the other leaders might look at her and where she had to wear the armoured mask of impassive command.

But when the snow squall cleared, Scopasis pushed into the lodge, brushing snow from his long leather coat, grinning like a boy with his first horse. Behind him was Thyrsis. They didn't look like rivals for her love – they looked like brothers.

'Lady,' Scopasis said, and when she waved, he sat. Coenus brought him a cup of wine, and another for Thyrsis. Nikephorus made room at the brazier for the two men, and Listra grinned at Thyrsis.

Melitta writhed at that grin. Jealousy was not an acceptable trait among the Sakje – and showing jealousy to a peer over a man you don't bed yourself was not just unacceptable but beyond the imagining of the Sakje. So Melitta had watched her beautiful Thyrsis grow closer and closer to the Grass Cats leader all summer. Now they openly shared their furs – Melitta had lain awake, listening to them quietly make love.

There is no privacy in a winter yurt. And Melitta was alone.

I will not go back to Scopasis, she thought. So she slept next to Coenus, curled in his arms, or alone in extra furs as her mood took her.

And Listra was ... observant. And not insensitive.

Except now. Her eyes devoured him, and he all but caressed her openly.

Melitta cleared her throat.

Scopasis drank his warm wine. 'That was brutal,' he said. His grin didn't belie his words. It just made him look like the tough bastard he was.

'And?' she asked.

'The Parni are a big concern,' Scopasis said. 'Twelve thousand warriors, give or take a thousand. They'd have more, but they don't let their women fight.' He grinned. 'They've moved in here like an avalanche falling.'

Coenus muttered, 'Tell us something we don't know.'

'They have Diodorus as a prisoner,' Scopasis said, flat as the crack of a big tree in heavy ice.

Coenus sat up. 'That's it!' he said. 'Oh, the fading mind of the old. Diodorus is here on an embassy!'

'And now the Parni are keeping him against Seleucus' good behaviour.' Seleucus was another of the rivals of Antigonus One-Eye and Demetrios – a strong ally of Ptolemy of Aegypt, and he held the mercenary contracts of Kineas' father's friends, the Exiles. 'And something about tribute.' Thyrsis smiled at Listra, and then back at his queen. 'Lady, we talked to Diodorus. He's well. He said he could run any time he wanted.'

'Where was all this?' Coenus asked.

'Down in Alexandria of Bactria,' Scopasis said. 'Three days' ride. In the summer.' He smiled a hard smile. 'Listen: the new Khan of Bactria has his horse lines there – ten thousand horses, all his wives, a palace of yurts and buildings, too. Alexander's old camp – Ganax of the Parni has taken it for himself.'

'Guards? Warriors?' Coenus asked.

Scopasis grinned, and this time it was genuine mirth.

'The Parni are desert people,' he pronounced.

'So?' Tuarn of the Hungry Crows was soft-spoken.

'So they don't ride in winter,' Scopasis said. 'And they can't imagine anyone else doing it, either.'

Melitta's people scouted Alexandria of Bactria four times. She herself rode through the horse herds, wearing a plain fleece coat. She saw a sentry, and heard the man complain of the misery of standing winter guard. She rode across the souq unchallenged. She counted the guards around the palace of yurts.

Listra went with Philokles of Olbia and Thyrsis. Tuarn went with Scopasis and Nikephorus and Coenus.

Then they built a model of the town in the snow outside Melitta's yurt.

Then they slept, sharpened their arrows and their swords, and two nights later, in a snow squall, they attacked.

Melitta chose to ride with the Greeks. They had heavy armour and good discipline, and she put all the Olbians together with the men of Tanais and the mounted mercenaries under Coenus and Nikephorus. The snow squall was fortuitous, but not entirely so, and they lost their way twice in the darkness before a lucky glimpse of a watch-fire put them back on course.

In fact, getting to the main gate of the complex of yurts, wagons and outbuildings was the hardest part, and the part that made her stomach turn. She prayed to her gods that no bow would shatter in the cold, the sinew or the horn giving way. Most of them rode the last hour with their bows under their legs. But when they came into the clearing before the gate, her fears fell away and her numb fingers clamped an arrow to her string.

And then there was no more time for worry, and they were riding easily over the tramped snow in front of the gate, and the sentries died without a cry.

The gate was a joke – in Alexander's time there had been a ditch and palisade, but it hadn't been maintained and five feet of snow made a mockery of it. Nor was the gate closed. Melitta rode over the corpse of the first sentry, his blood impossibly red on the snow, and passed under the gate into the heart of the tent palace. Philokles of Olbia took a squadron north inside the gate, and Nikephorus took another squadron south. They paused only to kindle fire in their cold hands, and then they were away – screaming. And men began to emerge from the tents, yurts, wagons and lodges – angry men – and Melitta and her warriors killed them in the streets, riding them down, shooting them with arrows at point-blank range.

The night was full of screams and fire, and her only fear now was accident – to her men or to Diodorus, who might rush into the street unwarned and perish. But such things were in the hands of the gods, and even while she chewed on the ends of her worry, she shot a beautifully dressed man in the back as he ran from her pony's hooves, and when he attempted to rise she shot him again.

Besides, Scopasis had sworn to rescue old Diodorus. And she trusted Scopasis to do anything he said.

She gave a long whoop, and then she was in the central market, where the ring of wagons marked the Khan's own family. And even as she rode out into the fire-lit night, her men emerged from the flanks – young Philokles, his hood down and his hair streaming behind him, and Nikephorus, considerably less dramatic but just as successful, rode out of the street to the north. They immediately began to fire the wagons.

Coenus was taking very little part. He rode behind her, watching, looking for an ambush that never appeared, keeping his own men in reserve against a crisis that she didn't expect. In fact, his disgust was written plainly on his features. This was steppe war, not Greek war. He didn't like it.

Too bad for him.

She rode her pony forward across the hard crust of snow to the edge of the fire circle.

'Come out, King Ganax!' she shouted.

'Don't be a fool, girl!' Coenus called, and the knights of her body-guard, led by Scopasis, surged forward to surround her, but no arrows flew out of the dark.

'Stay and burn, or come out, King Ganax!' Melitta called.

And Ganax came. He had little choice – as the leader of a tribe, he knew his duty. He came in his armour, gleaming in the red light.

'Who the fuck are you?' he demanded. 'Dogs will eat the corpses of your people.'

Melitta laughed. 'I am Melitta, Queen of the Assagetae.'

Ganax had an axe – a big axe with a four-foot handle. He put the head of the axe in the snow and rested his weight on it. 'Assagetae? The Royal Clan of the West? What do I have to do with you, bitch?'

Melitta grinned. She *had* done the right thing. She could feel it.

'Your warriors killed some of my people, and took two women as slaves. For fifteen dead, I take a hundred of yours dead. For two women enslaved, I take you, Ganax. Let your people feel my hand. My reach goes where the grass grows and the snow falls.'

Men watched her from the wagons.

Ganax raised his axe.

'All I hear is talk,' he said.

Melitta rode in close. She reined in her horse just two horse lengths from him.

'What do you offer me for your life?' she asked.

'Fuck you!' he roared.

She shot him contemptuously, so that her arrow tore into his groin and he fell to the ground screaming.

'Goodbye, Parni,' she yelled. 'Don't come across my river again.'

She and the bodyguard and all the Greeks galloped away, out of the bloodstained snow and the fire-stained camp and into the darkness.

On the high ridge above the camp of the Parni, she met the other bands – Tuarn with his Crows, bundled like children in the cold air, and Listra with her warriors, and behind her, the snow was black with horses.

'How will we ever get them all home?' Tuarn laughed.

'Let's find out,' Melitta said. 'The Parni will not lie down and take this. In the morning, they will count their dead and find our tracks and they will be on us.'

Scopasis shook his head. 'They will count the horse herd gone, and they will despair. And the horses will cover our tracks so that they will never know how few we are.'

A deep male voice spoke in the dark. 'Why not take the short road home, lady?'

Diodorus rode out of the darkness, and Melitta embraced him.

Scopasis made a face behind him.

'He'd already rescued himself,' Scopasis said, and spat. 'All I did was escort him.'

Diodorus shook his head. 'No – I count this as rescue,' he said. 'Seleucus will love you for this, Melitta. The Parni have been a threat to him for two years – invincible. Now they won't seem like such a tough nut.' Diodorus shivered. 'May I suggest you ride south? We can be out of Bactria in two days.'

'South will put no horses on my grass,' Melitta said.

'Sell them to Seleucus and sail home,' Diodorus said. 'You've come five hundred parasangs. Why go home that way?'

'He has a point,' Coenus said.

Her tribal leaders looked troubled, but no sooner was the press of combat off her breast than she wanted to be home. Months in the saddle for a night of fire – it was time to leave.

'How long to Persopolis?' she asked.

'Thirty days?' Diodorus suggested. 'I took fifty getting here.'

She nodded, and they rode south and west.

South and west was like riding into spring, so that after just four days of riding down the passes out of Bactria, they had grass for the horse herd and no snow. The ground was soft and muddy, and they lost the smaller horses.

The third night out of Ganax's camp, Scopasis caught a pair of

Parni scouts and killed them and left their bodies in the muddy tide left by the passage of so many horses. Every man had many horses now, and the Assagetae and the Greeks moved like the wind, riding and changing horses every hour; the likelihood of traps or pursuit began to look remote.

Tuarn rode up beside her on the fourth day.

'This will live for ever in the memory of the people,' he said. 'But I do not want to ride to Persopolis. Many visits make long delays. We should come on the Kaspian Sea from the south – just ten days' ride. We can be in the high ground of Colchis by the first moon of summer.' He grinned. 'And keep this horse herd. And lady – I speak not as a Ghan but as a man – when you bring these horses home, no clan will *ever* question you again. Do not sell them to the Seleucids. They have more value on the hoof – they show the length of your reach.'

An hour later, Scopasis rode up beside her and said nearly the very same.

So on the fiftieth day, she embraced Diodorus and sent him on his way south with a hundred horses and all the goods he had rescued and most of Nikephorus' men – all perfectly happy to accept extra land grants to get back to civilisation all the faster. Alexander of Phokis led them, and he saluted his captain and the Lady of the Assagetae, and then they rode away into a light rain.

And Melitta turned her column north and west, towards Hyrkania, Colchis and home.

23

Herakles, massive muscles rolling at the strain, locked in a straight pull – with Apollo, Lord of the Golden Bow. Apollo's physique is slimmer: he is the eternal naioi, the eternal ephebe, the image of strong youth, while Herakles is the warrior's epitome. They are well matched.

Between them, a tripod, wrought in bronze – the sacred tripod that supports the priestess at Delphi, the very symbol of potent and accurate prophecy. Both strain to hold the tripod, to wrest it from the other.

Even as he watches, the tripod goes through a transfiguration – it lengthens and changes and becomes richer, fuller, the gleam of the bronze becomes a different highlight, and suddenly it is a woman caught between two men, one holding each arm, pulling, and she—

The mathematics of Pythagoras, made incarnate in colour and shape, perfect circles falling from the sky, one at a time, first slowly and then faster, and now Apollo's hands are on his lyre and Herakles dances the Pyrriche with heavy feet, the rhythm of his right foot like the beating of his heart, and the circles of white burst as they touch the lyre in a riot of colour – colour that leaps away in waves that are themselves the embodiment of another mathematics. More and more – the circles, the waves, the lyre of Apollo and the great god dancing—

The notes leaped from the strings to fall through the air – no, Satyrus thought, the notes rolled through the air like wind rolls through tall barley.

'You're awake,' Anaxagoras said. He put his kithara down on the table next to him, laying the instrument reverentially on a cloth. 'How's your head?'

Satyrus took a deep breath. He hurt *everywhere*. His lungs seemed to hurt, and his arms had bruises and lacerations – deep cuts up on the biceps.

'Herakles, stand by me,' he said. He raised his head, and a smith's hammer of pain hit him right between the eyes, and he fell back onto his pillow.

'I – what happened?' Satyrus asked.

'You tried to fight in the front rank while you were forty pounds underweight,' Anaxagoras said. 'Or that's what Apollodorus muttered.'

'Herakles!' Satyrus murmured.

'You went down fast – and then we all fought over your body. It was Homeric, I promise you.' Anaxagoras laughed. 'But we held. Apollodorus came with the marines. By then there was a pile of corpses filling the street – you were under most of them. We charged over the pile, and then were pushed back onto it. I went down somewhere there, but Apollodorus and Neiron cleared them out – all the way to the beach.' Anaxagoras shrugged. 'I need to learn more about fighting.'

Satyrus rolled on his side, spat blood into a pot and drank some water. 'I need forty pounds,' he said.

He ate as soon as his head had cleared – a whole day wasted – and watched from the roof as a dozen heavy triremes sailed in to reinforce Demetrios.

'So many things I'd like to know,' he said to Abraham and Neiron, standing at his shoulders as if to hold him up if he fell. He was tired of being an invalid. He wanted his body back.

'Try me,' Abraham said.

'Are those ships part of the squadron he sent away last week, or are they new ships?' Satyrus asked.

Something passed between Neiron and Abraham, and Satyrus noted it. Something was being kept from him, something he guessed was personal: Leon's death? They'd be idiots to keep that from him. Someone else? Sappho might be dead – or Amastris.

Odd, that he thought so little of Amastris these days. Of course, there was little to think of beyond fighting and preparing to fight. He sent a thought of love like a prayer to distant Amastris, and went back to watching Demetrios' camp in the distance.

'We should review the whole circuit of the walls,' he said.

They had to walk. Every horse in the town was already meat. Satyrus took his professionals – Apollodorus, Draco, Amyntas and Neiron, and he added the priest, Leosthenes, and Charmides, because the boy had to learn. His own head still hurt, a tiny twinge at every step, a vague pain when his eyes went too close to the sun.

'You will *not* lead from in front again,' Apollodorus said, out of nowhere. 'Not until you have the body of a man. Ares, lord, I'm small – my *pater* said I was too small to stand the shock of war. You are too thin. And men died, lord – Gorgias fell over you, and young Necho.'

'Ah,' Satyrus said. He said it the way a man exclaims when he bangs his shin on his bed – an unaccustomed pain. 'Necho?' He could barely remember Gorgias. But Necho—

'He and Helios and Anaxagoras stemmed the rush when you fell, or so I hear it.' Apollodorus turned along the Street of Temples, which now ran close to the once secret wall.

Satyrus noted that behind him, Neiron was busy extolling the virtues of the hidden wall to the others – a loud dissertation clearly planned to cover the dressing-down of the king by his subordinate.

Satyrus felt his spirits plummet. It was like a black cloud settling on his head – like the hand of chance pressing him into the earth. 'Herakles,' he moaned.

'Bah – he was a good lad, and he died a hero. Tonight we'll burn his corpse the old way, and that's that. If you hadn't been there, we'd have lost the town and that's no mistake. Them Macedonian fucks were hard as bronze nails.'

'I make a great many mistakes,' Satyrus said bitterly.

'Aye, Neiron said you'd go off on one about your failings – so spare me. We're doing well enough, and you know it. But if you die – lord, if you die, we're fucked. You do good work as a commander, and men love you, and you have a name. Apollodorus the Marine is not going to get this town through three more months of siege, eh? So stay alive, lord, and more of us'll stay alive. And let's not have a lot of crap about your failings. You have lots of failings. Petty, arrogant, tyrannical—' Apollodorus laughed aloud, because he'd got Satyrus to smile.

'We have a lot in common, then,' Satyrus said.

'Takes one to know one,' Apollodorus laughed aloud again.

'This is supposed to make me feel *better*?' Satyrus asked.

'Pep talk over. Back to work,' Apollodorus said, and slapped his commander on the back.

*

The circuit of the walls was more than a dozen stades, and took them from the harbour, where they were intimate with every foot of the defences, both old and new, south to where the great tower was complete, rising a hundred feet above the stone-based, mud-brick wall of the main battlements – the most modern defensive structure in the world, with three levels of war machines and a new killer on the roof: a counterweight engine that Neiron and Jubal had built from the washed-ashore wreckage of the engine-ship destroyed in the harbour. With the iron fittings in hand, Jubal had rigged the engine in just four days.

Satyrus hadn't seen the black man in weeks – Jubal had reinvented himself as an engineer, where his skills as a sailor were most helpful to the city. Today, he led a dozen carpenters in building a second counterweight engine.

'We was out of wood,' he said after he clasped hands with his king. 'But since Golden Boy keeps knocking people's houses down, we took to lifting the roof timbers. I want to put four of these things up here, but all the smiths in the city are making armour and spears and arrowheads – and I need fittings.'

Satyrus looked at the carefully built wooden models of elbow joints, a pivot bearing, a dozen binding plates. 'I'll take it up with the war council,' he said. 'We could certainly do with these at the harbour.'

Jubal nodded. 'Nah, you're wrong.' He smiled.

Apollodorus grew purple-red. Neiron laughed aloud. 'Jubal, we try not to tell the king straight out like that when he's wrong.'

Jubal nodded. 'Aye – but he's in a hurry. Lord, look here. Golden Boy has forty of these engines, and he's building more today. See?'

Sure enough, Jubal's sharp eyes had seen what the dozen incoming triremes had brought – heavy timber. Demetrios' engineers were making up their losses in engines. Satyrus watched them work for a minute, his eyes watering and his head pounding.

'I see that,' Satyrus said, his heart falling flat again.

'If we put five engines at the harbour, Demetrios knows we have them and his engines pound them to splinters.' Jubal shrugged. 'Put 'em here first – I can hit his camp, I think. Not that I want to let him know. But this is one tall-arsed tower.'

Neiron was leaning out of the east rather than the south face of the tower. 'Storm coming,' he said. 'Hadn't noticed it. Look at the sky.'

Long lines of dark clouds raced along the eastern horizon.

Satyrus nodded, but his thoughts were elsewhere. 'Strong enough to bear the weapons firing?'

Jubal grinned. 'Neiron asked the same. I don't know, and that's a fact.'

Satyrus made a face. 'All right. But we shouldn't be building these a few at a time. We should have forty of them that we can shift wherever we need them.'

Jubal smiled. 'Have to knock down every house in the city,' he said. He looked rueful. 'And you understand – I haven't even loaded one yet. We've fired them empty, but I can't afford to have Golden Boy see what we're up to. I don't intend to shoot until he's come close.'

Satyrus rubbed the back of his head and then the spot between his eyes where the pain came from. 'That may happen,' he said.

Neiron took him on a tour of their excavations under the wall. The city was built on rock – most houses had cellars cut out of the rock – and the progress of the tunnel was slow until they got free of the rise of rock that the first city had used for foundations. After the rock there was clay, and Satyrus stood with a reeking tallow torch in his hand, looking at a tunnel the height of a man and a little wider than his own shoulders that stretched away into the darkness. He felt as if the weight of the earth above was pressing on his shoulders, but he had to admit that his headache was less down here.

'It stinks,' he said.

'Most men don't go above to relieve themselves,' Neiron said. 'They're sailors, after all.'

'Getting a lot of complaints?' Satyrus asked while he walked forward.

'Did I mention they were sailors?' Neiron quipped. 'The bickering is constant.'

The gallery was surprisingly long, shored up at intervals with timbers that looked remarkably like the stem of a heavy ship.

'We salvaged *Arete*'s keel,' Neiron said.

'Where are we?' Satyrus said. He was at the forward face of the shaft, and there were a half-dozen of his oarsmen, some cutting at the rock face with picks, some collecting the resulting rock and dirt and clay in baskets.

'Just under the wall. If you go back – see here? We think that's the lowest underpinning of the south wall, about a dozen horse lengths east of the great tower.' Neiron shrugged.

Satyrus shrugged back. 'Keep digging. If we hold the sea wall, then I guess he'll come here next. The north wall is impregnable and the west wall is like adamantine, all new construction and *all stone*.'

'Jubal thinks he'll go there anyway, to avoid Jubal's precious tower. Boy loves that tower.' Neiron smiled as they turned and started back out of the shaft.

Satyrus got to the foot of the ladder. 'Jubal's as smart as a whip, but Demetrios won't want to have the siege happen so far from his camp – and he'll want to bring that tower *down*. And the way I see it, if he *does* go for the west wall, we'll have plenty of time to prepare.'

'You have a point there,' Neiron admitted.

'But let's go and have a look at it anyway,' Satyrus said.

The west wall looked like what people imagined a city wall to look like. It was three times as tall as a man, stone sheathed on both sides with no mud-brick at all. In between the stone sheathing – whole cells of stone, in fact – there was heavy earth and gravel fill that would simply eat the shock of the largest engine's strike. And the wall was crowned with heavy towers – squat, low towers just twice the height of the wall, and the whole length was crenellated. There were four sally ports that passed under the wall, and behind the wall was a ditch and a low rampart, and in front of it was a wide, deep dry ditch.

'If they'd done this to the whole city, we could whistle at Demetrios,' Apollodorus said, and all the other officers made noises of agreement.

'He'd be a fool to come at this,' Neiron agreed. 'Jubal's putting lotus in his wine.'

Satyrus looked at the west wall with a jaundiced eye. 'But here, his engines are at much the same height as our own,' he said. 'Forty of those big killers out there – he could turn a few feet of wall into rubble in a day. The collapse of the wall would fill in the ditch. Jubal may have a point. If he's patient—'

'Messenger coming,' Charmides called.

Satyrus straightened. He'd been leaning out over the wall. He was already tired, and it was time for his workout. His head hurt and his every limb hurt – of course they did, men had walked on his arms, fought on them, died on them. He was lucky that they weren't broken—

'Demetrios is moving his fleet, lord. Panther sends to say it is in the harbour. Again.' The messenger stood and panted – he'd run hard.

'You are *not* fighting in the front rank,' Apollodorus said.

They ran across the city. Satyrus was already tired when he put his light armour on. Today he took a long spear from the rack Abraham had installed in the courtyard.

Miriam was in the courtyard, too, arming Anaxagoras. Her hair was in a scarf, and her long chiton was kirtled up, showing her legs like a dancing girl.

Abraham shouted something at her – something that sounded like mockery – and she snorted as she tied the laces under Anaxagoras' arm, and Satyrus felt another stab of jealousy: it should have been him in the heavy armour. But he answered her smile and waved. She called something else in Hebrew, and Abraham looked serious as he hefted a spear.

'What did she say?' Satyrus asked his friend.

'It is a feast day for us,' Abraham said. 'And I am going to fight. It is allowed – but I didn't make any observance this morning, nor did I pray. It is as my father says: I can be a warrior, or I can be a Jew.'

Satyrus nodded. 'Perhaps. But for the moment, I suggest that we save the city and hope that our gods stand by us.'

'There is but one God,' Abraham said stubbornly.

Satyrus gave his friend a steady look meant to convey a number of things – that this was not the time, that he did not happen to agree, that he loved Abraham and would take all kinds of crap from him – and Abraham smiled.

'Come on,' Satyrus said.

The marines and many of the sailors and oarsmen – most of whom now had some armour, helmets and good weapons – gathered in the streets behind Abraham's compound. The marines were in front, already formed in their ranks, and Neiron and Satyrus set to organising the sailors into a phalanx.

Panther appeared with a dozen armoured men. 'The engine-ships are just dropping their anchor stones,' he said. 'Ten minutes until they open fire.'

Satyrus clapped his hands for silence. 'Listen to me!' he called.

The sailors fell silent, then the marines, and then other men – Rhodians on the hidden wall, engine crews on the rooftops.

'I want every man off the hidden walls and every man off the rooftops and down here in the centre,' Satyrus shouted. 'Into the agora, formed in your companies. *Now*.'

Neiron faced the sailors about and led them through the now familiar web of alleys to the agora. He led them to the western edge, and formed them and set them to rest in the shade of the trees that fronted the ruins of the gymnasium. The marines formed in front of them and used the portico of the Merchants' Stoa for shade.

'Enjoy it,' Satyrus said to Apollodorus. 'It's next on my list to quarry for stone.'

Panther's eyes widened. 'You will leave us nothing to defend.'

Satyrus shook his head. 'Lots to defend,' he said, thinking of Miriam. 'Stone can be replaced. The west wall is beautiful, by the way.'

The Rhodian ephebe company – two hundred young men, the sons of the wealthiest citizens – manned the northern end of the hidden wall, and now they formed across the northern edge of the agora. Satyrus went over to their captain, a mercenary professional from Thebes called Gorgus.

'This isn't a complex plan,' he said.

'Good,' Gorgus said. He managed a smile.

'I intend to leave them nothing to shoot at. I want to let them get their men ashore. Then I'll feed our archers back into the buildings, and then we'll attack. We'll be up-slope and organised. And we'll have the numbers.'

Gorgus looked around. He looked at Panther. 'It's a risk,' he said. 'Letting them into the city.'

Panther looked at Satyrus. 'I've never heard of anyone doing this, Satyrus.'

Satyrus nodded. 'The Plataeans did it against the Spartans,' he said. 'Over and over. And the Spartans have done it once or twice.' His eyes were locked to the east, where he expected to see the first volley of stones appear.

Panther mopped his brow. 'I'll tell the citizen company in the south,' he said.

Menedemos came up, and Nicanor, who looked different in armour.

'You are insane!' Nicanor said – he said it with emphasis, but he did not shout it, so as not to dishearten the men.

Satyrus had not had a day of light, but a day of darkness, and his spirit had been heavy with foreboding. But once he'd made a decision, it was not in him to change it.

'Right or wrong, sane or insane, the knucklebones are cast,' he said as a hail of heavy stones fell into the town with the sound of the thunder of Zeus from a clear blue sky, and a cloud of mud-brick dust rose from their impact.

The second hail shower fell, and the third.

Satyrus watched the stones fall. 'Everyone out?' he asked Abraham. In his heart, he meant Miriam.

Abraham had his aspis against his legs, his helmet cocked back on his head, the cheekpieces open, and he had never looked more Greek. He pointed at his sister with his chin. 'She's appointed herself the polemarch of women,' he said.

Miriam was shepherding women and children into shelters on the western edge of the agora.

Satyrus turned to Neiron. 'You think Jubal is high enough to see what's happening in the harbour?' he asked.

'I could see the harbour this morning,' Neiron said.

Satyrus nodded. 'Charmides – go to the tower, get an eyeful of the action in the harbour and come back with a report. And tell Jubal to send me a runner when the landing ships stand in.' To Apollodorus and the other officers he smiled, hoping that he looked confident. 'We ought to know anyway – the engines will stop firing.'

He was proud of them. His head was pounding, and he was not sure he hadn't made a terrible mistake in pulling all of his forces out of the beaten zone of the enemy artillery – it seemed so obvious, to him, that they should *not* be under the bombardment, but the engines were so new that the tactics to use against them were equally new, and everything had to be tried. There were fewer than five thousand armed men in the town, and he had two thousand of them in the agora.

Under his eye, a couple of his marines were playing knucklebones in a helmet. One of them was Phillip, he thought, one of Draco's men.

'Winning or losing, Phillip?' Satyrus asked.

'Who the fuck cares?' the man grunted. 'And what's it to you? Oh – lord. I'm sorry. Didn't see you there.'

Satyrus laughed. 'I thought that you old sweats could smell an officer.'

'Fucking stones from the sky must have covered the sound of your sandals,' Phillip said.

'Smell of all this shit covers your scented oil,' said the other man. But he was grinning.

'Caryx the Gaul,' Satyrus said.

'Got me in one, lord. Didn't even think you knew my name.' The man smiled.

'Herakles guard you, gentlemen.' Satyrus bowed to them and moved on, to where a dozen marines were watching a pair of sailors sewing with heavy bronze needles. They were repairing sandals – sandal straps took a beating, and men were wearing their footwear long after they would have expected to replace it in a city not so thoroughly blockaded.

Men were pushing forward to get their sandals repaired, paying a couple of obols for the service. Satyrus pushed in behind two big marines, craning to see who the sailors were.

'Think the king knows what he's doing?' one man asked.

'Nary a fucking clue, mate,' said the other. 'He looks calm, and Soldier Boy looks eager, and all that's a gods-cursed act to keep thee happy and ready to fight.' The man laughed.

'We just gave up the wall, like.' The first marine sounded puzzled.

'Well – we ain't being crushed to death by rocks falling out of the sky, is we? We is not, mate. That we is not. So worry thee not about the king. He's as shit-scared as thee.'

I am lucky to have these men, Satyrus thought.

The bombardment continued all afternoon. By the time the sun was well down in the sky, it was plain that no assault would come that day, and Satyrus dispersed the garrison troops to cook.

The promised storm brought no more than cool winds and an hour of light rain at dusk, and the bombardment stopped as Demetrios' ships drew back out of the harbour for the night.

As the light began to fail, Satyrus climbed the tower again. This time he had Panther with him. They spent the whole of the end of the evening watching Demetrios' fleet at its moorings off the town.

'We could do it,' Panther said. 'I have nine ships left. Turn half into fire-ships and go after them.'

'They have something in the water, there,' Satyrus said, pointing. 'Jubal? Can you see it?'

Jubal watched for a while and shook his head. 'I see something – it flattens the waves. Can't make it out, though.'

They watched a while longer, but the light was failing fast.

'Tonight, do you think?' Panther asked.

Menedemos shook his head. 'That storm means business. I think tomorrow. We want to go at them just before the storm.'

'Pray we survive tomorrow, then,' Satyrus said.

Abraham's warehouse was gone. His slave barracks were just a mound of fired brick and mud-brick dust. But by the irony of the gods, his beautiful house, with the vulnerable war engines on the roof, was untouched.

'Symposium, gentlemen?' Abraham asked while they were all wriggling out of their armour in what remained of his garden. 'I don't expect the house to last another day, and I have a great deal of wine to be rid of. And I owe my God a feast.'

Apollodorus laughed, but he looked at Satyrus.

Satyrus shrugged. 'Demetrios keeps city hours in this siege. I think we can drink.'

It was a rough-and-ready symposium, with every cup of wine scented with mud brick and sewer water. But Abraham was as good as his word – when the slaves had finished clearing the courtyard and the main rooms sufficiently for the men to recline, he invited them – and all the sailors and marines – to partake of his wine.

'It's in *pithoi* in the basement,' he said. 'It'll be gone tomorrow, anyway.'

Dozens of huge *pithoi* – cheap wine for slaves, sharp wine for sailors, Cretan wine and Lesvian wine and the deep red of Chios. Satyrus moved from couch to couch – this was not just relaxation, it was command responsibility, too. He lay beside Abraham, thanking him for the largesse.

'I missed you, brother,' he said. 'It is almost worth being trapped in a doomed city to see you.'

'The problem with you, brother,' Abraham said, 'is that having lost your parents, you seek constantly to create a family.' He leered, as if he'd said something profound. Perhaps he had. He was already more drunk than Satyrus had seen him in some time.

Satyrus rolled to the edge of the *kline* and poured a libation. 'To the one God of the Jews,' he said. 'May he stand with us here.'

Abraham's eyes grew wide. 'We do *not* pour libations to our God,' he said.

'And look how well you're doing,' Satyrus said.

Abraham managed a smile. 'You are incorrigible,' he said. 'Do you mean to marry my sister?'

Satyrus froze. 'I will marry Amastris of Heraklea,' he said carefully.

'No, you won't,' Abraham said. 'She's a fucking whore from hell, your Amastris. Time somebody told you so. You look at my sister ... I could be angry. Sometimes I *am* angry. She's a widow, not a flute girl.'

Satyrus couldn't believe what he was hearing. 'Talk to me when you're sober,' he said curtly, and rolled off the *kline*.

'Shit on that, *brother*. You can trust me to back you up in war – is that it? That's what makes us *brothers*. Listen – I have brothers, brothers born of my mother. When they do things to piss me off, I tell them. When they blaspheme against our God, for instance. And I have a sister, and I am responsible for her. You look at her in a way that is *fucking inappropriate*. How's that, *brother*?' Abraham had come to his feet, and he was breathing hard.

'Please withdraw your comments about Amastris,' Satyrus said.

'Her cunt's as wide as the harbour entrance. She deceives you, *brother*. No one wants to tell you this, but she just sent Demetrios five more ships bursting with marines. Marines commanded by fucking Stratokles the Athenian. With *Nestor*. And she's sitting in that camp over there, watching us die.' Abraham shrugged, suddenly appearing both smaller and more sober. 'I'm sorry, brother. Someone had to tell you.'

Apollodorus appeared at Abraham's elbow and hissed, 'We talked about this.'

Abraham looked at the floor, glanced up and then shrugged. The party was falling silent.

Satyrus looked at his marine captain. 'These are not drunken ramblings, are they?'

Apollodorus shook his head. 'No,' he said. 'Prisoner report.'

Satyrus nodded. 'There's probably a reason. She's a queen, gentlemen. She has things that she has to do – for her people, for herself, to ensure her rule. And she has Stratokles – that wide-arse wouldn't hesitate to put a sword in me.'

Apollodorus looked him in the eye. Satyrus realised that the smaller man seldom did – hadn't noticed how eagle-sharp the man's brown eyes were. 'I think he already has,' Apollodorus said. 'Put a sword in you. Our prisoners say the word is that you're dead.'

Satyrus shrugged. 'It was close,' he said.

'You're not going to run off to the enemy camp to reassure her? Win her back?' Apollodorus asked.

Satyrus shook his head, pursed his lips. Now they were all standing around him – Neiron, Charmides, Anaxagoras, Abraham. 'You all think I'm a fool,' he said.

Neiron shook his head. 'You think – differently,' he said.

'I need more wine,' Satyrus said.

Outside, the moon rose. Satyrus had matched Abraham's wine intake for two hours, and the man just kept apologising. Satyrus hugged him close and went to lie beside Anaxagoras, who raised a cup in welcome.

'Charmides and I are talking of Eros,' Anaxagoras said.

'Do you two want to be alone?' Satyrus asked with a smile.

'Might ask the same of you,' Anaxagoras asked. 'Sorry about the queen. Never met her. Don't know what to think.'

'Are we talking about Eros?' Satyrus asked.

'Charmides says that men and women can never be friends. That the tension is too much, that they can only be lovers, competitors, or enemies.' Anaxagoras raised the cup to the beautiful Lesvian man. 'While I think he has a point, I find that women make good friends.'

Satyrus honoured their attempt to have a real symposium with good talk by participating. 'You are a musician, Anaxagoras. And Charmides is, if you'll pardon me, young. So as a musician, Anaxagoras, you have something to *share* with women. You can perform together. You can honour the god together. It is like standing in the battle line – yes? I get that much from my lessons – if we play and play well, together, we have shared something *real*. Yes?'

'Ahh!' said Anaxagoras, delighted. 'You are not just a pretty face.'

'While Charmides – pardon me, lad – is beautiful, rich and young. Women want him in their beds, especially in the marriage bed. Am I right? And you hold them in contempt when they fawn – and when they behave ill to each other, in competition. And seeing this, you think, *they cannot even be friends with each other*.' Satyrus lay back, satisfied that he had contributed to the conversation like a proper guest.

Charmides waited while the *kylix* was refilled. 'My lord, you speak well, and I am chagrined to admit that you have a point.'

'Women are quite worthy, when men allow them to be,' Satyrus said. 'And when they behave like children, you will usually find that men have forced them to act like that.'

'Who made you so wise?' Anaxagoras asked.

'His sister,' Miriam said. She sat so that her back pressed against Satyrus' back – her sudden warmth against him caused an instant physical reaction that he had to hide. If she noticed, she didn't hesitate. 'His sister is a magnificent woman – the sort of woman other women either admire or despise. She is brave and strong, and she lives almost entirely the way a Greek man thinks men live.'

Charmides had eyes as big as wine bowls. 'I meant no disrespect,' he said.

'I took none. Women are like men in this – that every one is a kingdom to herself, and no one should ever be judged by another.' She rose to her feet, and now Satyrus could see her. 'But I do appreciate when one of you rises to defend us,' she said, and her mocking smile was briefly serious as she looked at Satyrus.

He watched her as she moved away. Then he looked at Anaxagoras, who shot him a wry smile.

'That's one to you,' he said.

'This isn't a competition,' Satyrus said hurriedly.

'No?' Anaxagoras asked. 'Could have fooled me.'

24

DAY TWENTY-SIX

There were some hard heads in the morning, and Abraham made men stand at his well and drink water until they vomited it. Satyrus felt better – much better – than he had in days, and he took exercise with Anaxagoras, Apollodorus and Helios in the agora while the men sat in the shade. He wrestled briefly with Helios – a boy who would not, a year ago, have offered him anything like a match – and he lifted jumping weights and rocks under Korus' harsh eye until he'd sweated out the last of the wine.

The stones fell and fell. The men of the town had to watch the methodical destruction of their waterfront temples, which had been the city's pride for a hundred years. They were dismembered stone by stone, and when the roof of the Temple of Poseidon crashed to the ground, the answering cheer from the Antigonids sounded just as loud.

Satyrus was chewing a dried apple. 'That was our counter-attack route,' he said to Neiron.

'Best do something, then,' Neiron said. And the day ended, and Abraham's house still stood, by a miracle. Satyrus arranged through Panther for the town slaves to clear him six routes through the temple rubble.

The naval sortie wasn't ready. So they all went to bed, and woke in the morning to a red sunrise and another promise of a storm on the eastern horizon. Satyrus woke and found Korus asleep in the courtyard.

'Exercise me now,' he said. 'They will attack today.'

When Panther appeared, Satyrus briefed him on the use of the town slaves even as he exercised, and he asked Apollodorus to get the men into position and drill them at passing through the gaps built by the slaves and reforming the phalanx in the clear ground east of the destroyed temples. He wanted it done before the engines were in position, and quickly, while it was still barely light, unobserved by the enemy.

Another hour, and a breakfast the size of a dinner, and Satyrus donned his light armour with more ease than he had in weeks.

'I might consider wearing bronze,' he said.

Korus nodded. 'You have some muscles, but I'm not finished yet,' he said.

Then out to the agora, to their now accustomed places, and the fall of the shot, the rising columns of clay dust, and fires – the enemy was throwing fire into the rubble. Or into the ships in the harbour – what remained of the ships. A pang hit Satyrus again – that his beloved *Arete* was dead, her charred keel supporting the tunnel under the walls.

Messengers ran back and forth from Jubal's tower, explaining the movement of the engine-ships. Sometimes Jubal lost sight of them for an hour at a time – a column of powdered masonry or woodsmoke could hide the whole harbour as effectively as a blanket over the eyes. But his reports were accurate and timely, and Satyrus depended on them.

By afternoon, the men were completely relaxed, and many were sound asleep when the stones ceased to fall.

'Stand to,' Satyrus ordered.

Before the last men had fallen into the ranks, a messenger from Jubal confirmed that lighter boats full of assault troops were coming into the harbour.

Satyrus sought out Idomeneus. 'Archers forward,' he said. 'All the *psiloi*. Get into the buildings – whatever is left – and kill what you can.'

Idomeneus nodded warily.

'I'm not asking you to fight them hand to hand,' Satyrus said. 'Just break them up and harass them.'

Idomeneus raised an eyebrow. 'We're *mercenaries*," he said.

Satyrus nodded. 'And you'll be well paid.'

'Man likes to live to collect,' Idomeneus said.

Satyrus realised that the Cretan was serious, not making pre-battle small talk. 'Idomeneus, I could talk to you about loyalty, about my

338

sister's esteem for you, or about how we've raised you from an archer to a captain.' Satyrus paused. 'But instead, I'll talk to you as one professional to another. I'm not Ptolemy – I haven't turned you out for the winter and rehired you in summer. I've paid a steady wage – a damned good steady wage – for three years of peace.'

Idomeneus bowed his head to the logic of the argument, but he made a face. 'This is like suicide, lord.'

Satyrus shook his head. 'Not at all. Brief your men, lead them into the rubble and stay alive. We're less than five minutes behind you.'

Idomeneus looked desperate. 'I'm doing this on behalf of my men. I can't—'

Satyrus wasn't angry. He liked Idomeneus – he was one of the best soldiers he'd ever known. And he knew the pressure that was on the man from his archers, who felt naked when not covered by armoured men. But time was being wasted – Satyrus could feel the water-clock of fate somewhere in his head, running fast. Drip, drip, drip.

'Go now. Promise them a bonus, if you must. But get them into the rubble.' Satyrus pitched his voice just *so*. The voice that meant the argument was at an end.

Idomeneus met his eye. 'On your head be it,' he said. In his glance was a straightforward accusation: his eyes accused Satyrus of sacrificing the archers.

But Idomeneus sprinted to his men, already spread wide along the cross-street where the gymnasium had stood, and he blew a long note on a bone whistle round his neck and they followed him into the rubble.

Satyrus went and walked along the front face of his formed phalanx. On the right, he set Apollodorus and the picked men of the marines and sailors in heavy armour – two hundred men of bronze. In the centre, with a thin front of marines, stood the bulk of his rowers and some Rhodian rowers and citizens as well, almost eight hundred. After the second rank, there was no armour. On the left were the Rhodian ephebes – all very young, but brilliantly armoured as the sons of the rich always are. The sailors were only six deep at the centre, whereas the flank units were deeper and heavier.

The received wisdom of this style of warfare was that more lightly armed troops would operate better in the rubble. If Satyrus had possessed peltasts – fighters with light shields and javelins and perhaps swords – he would have been expected to use them as shock troops.

Satyrus was not following the received wisdom. Instead, he'd posted his lightest troops in the densest phalanx formation he felt that they could maintain, and placed them where they could move over the flattest terrain with the least rubble, east of the temples. And his most heavily armed men – men virtually head-to-toe in bronze – he'd put out on the flanks in ridiculously open formations, almost as open as the ancient writers suggested men had fought before Marathon – six feet or more per man. His logic was simple: in the bad footing of the rubble, a man might easily face opponents from several directions, and only armour would keep him alive. Or so it seemed to him, and there was no one to tell him how bad an idea it might be.

Satyrus finished walking along the front of the phalanx. He nodded to men he knew, or smiled at them, and they returned it. He knew most of them now – even the Rhodians. He had old Memnon right there in the second rank, Aspasia's husband. And one of his sons, Polyphemus, stood a stade away in beautiful bronze, in the front rank of the ephebes. Satyrus found his eyes meeting those of Apollodorus and Neiron, of Anaxagoras, of Charmides and Jubal, hurrying to join in from his observation post with his team of upper-deck sailors.

But no one spoke to him. He was alone. He smiled at them and they smiled back, but never the other way round.

He turned to find Helios close behind him.

'Korus says I am not to let you fight in the front rank,' Helios said.

'I'll keep that in mind,' Satyrus said with a smile. He looked up and down the ranks one last time, and his ears told him something – he could not have defined it, quite, but there was a quality to the enemy war cry that suggested men were being hit by arrows. He'd seen enough war to know the sound.

Now he had to fear that he'd waited too long, that his centre phalanx would take too long to file through the ruins of the three great temples into the clear ground to seaward. He reached up and tipped his helmet forward on his head and pulled the leather loop on the left cheek-plate against the pressure of the spring to hook over the right cheek-plate. An Italian design, men said. Very well made – much plainer than his magnificent silver helmet, taken years before from Demetrios.

Funny thing to think about, at that moment.

'Forward,' Satyrus said.

The sailors filed through the carefully cleared gaps in the smashed temples just as they'd practised. It was well enough done, and when men made mistakes, forgetting who they followed or what file went first, other men pushed them roughly but firmly. They flowed more than marched, but they crossed the deep rubble to the open ground by the harbour and reformed even as Satyrus, first across the rubble of the Temple of Poseidon, in the centre, watched the enemy forming his phalanx under a light hail of archery.

It was just short of noon, and the midsummer sun beat down like a fall of scorching sand, a second enemy to both sides.

Satyrus formed his phalanx with both flanks apparently empty. And then, when his whole body was formed – and it seemed to take for ever – he stepped out of his place in the second rank.

'Friends!' he roared.

Not much movement. Behind him, Idomeneus' men shot a volley of arrows and ran – they had done their part, as they saw it, and now they made for the safety of the sailors' phalanx.

'You can defeat these men. You have beaten them before. When you lock your pikes with them, put your backs into the push and wait for my word. When I call, let's hear your war cry – and not until then. Ready?'

There was the growl – the same growl with which, as oarsmen, they answered the call to ramming speed.

Not for the first time, Satyrus wondered if there was an aggregate creature in the head of every oarsman – if, when together, they formed some sort of thousand-headed monster with but one set of thoughts.

He slipped in behind Helios.

'Forward!' he called, and the centre bowed out as the phalanx went forward, but it was too late to worry about such things.

The oarsmen were wearing sandals – siege sandals, men called them, because they'd learned how nasty the rubble was on their feet, even the rock-hard feet of an upper-deck man, and they'd made light leather boots to wear under heavy-soled sandals, and the marines had pulled every hobnail from their 'Isocrates' sandals, because the lifesaving purchase on a wet wooden deck was a ticket to slipping and lost footing on crumbled rock and broken marble.

Satyrus was betting that the enemy would be barefoot. Greek soldiers – even Macedonians – often fought barefoot, for a surer footing. And if the men coming up the beach had never fought in a siege – *and who had fought in a siege like this?* – then they would probably be barefoot.

The flanks of the sailors' phalanx hurried to keep up, and the front rippled.

The enemy was already close. They were deeper and formed loosely, and they had a curious mixture of weapons.

Pirates.

It took Satyrus precious seconds to see that Demetrios had not committed any of his precious Argyraspides or his Macedonian phalanxes this time. These were the pirates – the men who'd come only for plunder.

Good or bad?

There were heartbeats to impact. The pirates had the numbers by a factor of ten to one, but they were curiously hesitant. And barefoot.

Crash!

Satyrus' men smashed into the front of the pirates like a battering ram into a gate, and men were knocked flat at the impact – men were actually impaled on the incoming pikes, as the pirates were so inexperienced, they hadn't closed up or placed their shields to endure the storm of iron that was a pike phalanx oncoming, even with just six ranks of spearheads going home.

But there were blows in return – a torrent of blows, a staggering ocean wave of blows.

Satyrus had never been in the second rank before. It was terrifying. In the second rank, you could *see*. Men in the first rank crouched, tucked their eyes mostly under their shield rims and endured, parrying on instinct. In the second rank, a fighter could *see* the enemy. Could feel the press of his file behind him and translate it to the file leader – carefully, not allowing the file leader to be pushed to his death.

Like most of the second-rankers, Satyrus had a heavy spear, not a pike. He had all the time in the world – it was *odd*, but all the fighting was two critical feet away – to cock his arm back and strike, a simple strong blow just below the crest box of the pirate's helmet.

The man dropped, and the spear returned to his hands and Helios stepped into the gap and cut – cut back – into the back of the helmet of the enemy pirate on his right, crushing the man's skull instantly so that the man's blood shot out of the faceplate of his helmet.

Satyrus was ready. He practised every day with Helios – he knew these routines cold. He stepped up behind his hypaspist, in the process stepping on the man he'd put down with his first thrust, and shot his spear across Helios' back into an oncoming pirate, this time thrusting *down* onto the man's outstretched thigh or knee – no way to know what he hit, but the man screamed and Helios all but beheaded him on his own back cut, and now they were deep into the pirates' formation and Satyrus could see Anaxagoras' blue and white plume just a horse length to the left, equally deep.

Satyrus had intended the attack of the sailors' phalanx as a feint to lure the enemy into going for the flanks.

No plan ever survives contact with the enemy. The sailors' phalanx was crushing the pirates against their ships.

Satyrus stood straight and took a deep breath – the pirates were cringing back – and roared '*Arete!*' as loudly as he could.

He counted to three in his head.

'Blood in the water!' he yelled.

The answering roar was like surf on a windy day – like the thunder of Zeus, like the rumble of fate closing the scissors. The oarsmen had the measure of their opponents, and their war cry was so loud and so awful that the enemy froze like fawns before a raging lion, paralysed as the tide of bronze and iron swept them down the beach.

Satyrus set his feet, picked a pirate in a fine helmet and threw his spear as hard as he could. He didn't pause to see the effect. He slapped Helios.

'I'm out,' he said, and turned. 'Let me through!' he called back, and he pushed against the flowing tide of his own phalanx, slipping back rank by rank – glanced back, and was delighted to see that the colourful side plumes of the pirate officer were gone. He punched out through the back of his own phalanx, paused and took a few deep breaths.

He felt good.

Rear-rankers looked at him.

He undid his cheek-plates and raised his helmet. 'You!' he said, pointing at one of Jubal's deck men. 'Go to Apollodorus and tell him to charge.'

'Aye, lord!' said the sailor.

'And you,' to the ephebes. 'Tell them to forget the plan and get right down the beach on the widest possible front. Go now!' Satyrus was shouting when he didn't need to. He needed these men to understand – to carry his orders.

'Aye, lord!' the man cried, and dropping his spear, he ran off up the beach, headed north into the rubble.

Herakles, stand with me. Something is wrong. This is too easy.

Where are the Argyraspides?

One thing at a time.

'Jubal!'

'Aye, lord?'

'The whole rear rank – on me, right now. Form up tight.' Satyrus stood a few horse lengths behind the rear rank and more than a hundred men left the back rank and fell in. Satyrus picked up the spear dropped by the messenger and held it out so that they formed along it – they were sailors, not Spartiates.

'Three deep! Three deep!' he yelled.

Sailors and marines milled about, but in fifty heartbeats they were sorted – not pretty, by any means, but the advantage of sailors over phalangites was that sailors didn't expect any kind of order in a fight. Chaos was natural to them.

'As soon as the right man passes the end of our boys, we will wheel to the left!' Satyrus yelled to them. 'Look at me! Understood? We'll link on our own left file and charge.' He used the pike in his hands to illustrate.

Men nodded. Other men looked blank.

'Listen! Look at me!' A few feet away, the sailors gave a great cry and the phalanx of sailors pushed forward the length of a great ox – and stopped. 'We link up on *that file right there* and wheel *like this*,' and he waved the pike again. Now he saw more recognition than confusion.

He was out in front, with nowhere to go when the fighting started. So be it.

'Forward!' he called.

His loose, thin line rolled forward, bowing like the amateurs they were.

'To the right! Wheel!' he roared in his best storm-caller voice, and *most* of the sailors wheeled, although at different speeds, and the whole front fell apart. Satyrus wanted to weep – this was the sort of manoeuvre his marines or his mercenary Macedonians could perform in their sleep.

There were pirates teeming around the left face of his main phalanx, and the right-most files of his tiny counter-attack swept them away – and then he was in combat.

His feet were on sand – they were actually on the beach. A man appeared in front of him out of the confusion of the fight, a small, wiry man with an earring and a bloody axe. Satyrus had lost the pike – where? – and he found that he had drawn his sword, and the little man cut overarm at him with the axe and Satyrus punched with his heavy shield, caught the haft of the axe on the rim of his shield and thrust, pushing with his legs to keep that axe pinned high in the air. The pirate tried to stumble backward, and when that failed he put his helmeted head down and attempted to headbutt Satyrus under the chin, but he got Satyrus' sword through his neck and fell in a tangle. Satyrus pushed forward, feeling the daemon of combat for the first time in what seemed like months, caught a second man unawares with a clean cut to the neck that didn't quite sever his head. Then Satyrus swung low against a third man, cutting the backs of his thighs under the rim of his shield, and then two blows hit his shield face solidly, rocking him back so that he stumbled, and a pair of impacts on his helmet staggered him again. He lashed out with his sword, a sweeping blow without skill, a stop-cut to buy himself a few heartbeats.

He fell to one knee, and now he was one man, alone, and he had a pair of men focused on him, and another in his peripheral vision, an opportunist looking for an easy kill.

Satyrus shot to his feet with a powerful push of his right leg, slammed his big aspis face into the two men in front of him, bounced off them and lunged – the full length of his reach – against the man to his side, the opportunist, who got the point of a *xiphos* through his collarbone and neck for his efforts. But as he fell, Satyrus' sharp sword caught in bone, and the falling man tore the sword from Satyrus' grip.

As if Herakles stood and coached him, Satyrus rolled his hips back to the left, reached out as if he'd practised the move a hundred times and caught the wrist of another pirate to his front, smashed his shield into the man's unarmoured face and took his sword, stripping it from the man's fingers. He felt that it was a *kopis*, a heavy chopping blade, and he turned back to his original opponents, pushed forward again with his supporting leg, raised his shield, saw his opponent raise his own shield in answer to the feint – an inexperienced man who was not going to live to learn. Satyrus chopped under the raised shield into hip and groin, and the man toppled like a small, straight ash cut by a strong woodsman and Satyrus viciously pushed the corpse – the man was already dead – into his file partner with his shield arm and followed it with a straight overarm chop and pivot on his left foot – so that the right foot passed the left, the whole weight of his body behind the blow, and the crooked blade of the *kopis* blew through the pirate's light shield rim and the thin bronze of his helmet, too.

Now no one would face him, and the whole of the pirate front bowed back before him and he stood alone, breathing hard like a boar that has slain all the brave hunting dogs and now faces only the curs.

His own men were hanging back as well. Combat had those moments. Men could only stay locked breast to breast for so long – a hundred heartbeats, two hundred for the strongest and best, and then they had to step back and breathe.

'The king!' called a sailor at his back, and they took it up. 'King!' they called. 'King!'

Satyrus raised the *kopis*, and blood from the blade ran down his arm, the warm lick of death on his skin. He inhaled, and he could smell the lion skin of his lord on the wind, and he could see, as if imprinted on his eyes, how he could kill every man facing him.

But his moment of divinity was stolen when Apollodorus and his marines charged headlong into the pirates at the south end of the beach. Satyrus heard the moment of impact, and it penetrated his battle-fogged head.

'Let me through,' he barked at the sailors nearest to him, and Jubal swatted a man out of his way.

Satyrus dashed back through the thin line of sailors – men who had thought themselves safe in the rear rank and had still managed to find the hero in themselves when asked.

Thank them later.

He ran up the beach to the soft sand, which ate his remaining energy the way a dog eats fresh meat. He turned, and looked over the beach.

It was not the battle he'd wanted – it was all being fought on the open beach west of the temples, not in the choked streets of the ruined town, out on the flanks where his well-armoured men could eat these ill-armed pirates in alleys at no cost to themselves.

So be it. You made plans, and they evaporated. His men were winning – despite that the pirates were still landing fresh men, farther out so that they had to wade ashore hip-deep. And men out there – really, only a quarter-stade away – were hesitating. He could see them waiting at the side of the light rowing boats, unsure whether to clamber over the side or stay aboard.

But while this attack was serious, all of Golden Boy's real soldiers were somewhere else.

Satyrus took the time to watch carefully the scene at his feet.

Apollodorus was cutting through the loosely formed pirates like an iron chisel through hot bronze – slowly but inexorably, the drive of the marine's legs like a great hammer pushing his spear point home. A few light pirate ships made to land men behind him on the beach, but Idomeneus and the archers had reacted without orders and the nearly naked pirates were being punished hard for their temerity.

No crisis there.

At the north of the beach, the ephebes advanced slowly and cautiously, but on a wide front, only four deep. They had doubled their width, confident in their armour, their training and their youth. They were not mistaken, and the pirates flinched and flinched away.

The fight on the beach was minutes from becoming pure slaughter.

To the south, though, there were ships trying to force the defences of the main harbour for the first time. They were taking heavy punishment from Panther's carefully sighted engines. Satyrus watched for a long time – the time it took forty pirates to die – before he decided that he was watching a feint: Demetrios had sent ships to tie Panther down.

But why?

He had no idea what had gone wrong, but he could feel it as surely as if he'd taken a wound.

'What's happening?' Abraham asked. He'd emerged from the rear face of the phalanx, breathing like a blacksmith's bellows. He sank to his knees in the sand. 'I'm out of shape.'

Satyrus continued to watch. The pirates were at the point of breaking – too many dead, and water licking at their ankles. Rear-rank men were throwing their shields away and swimming.

Curiously, they weren't shattered by Apollodorus or by the ephebes or even by the sailors pounding away at their front. What broke them, even as Satyrus watched, was the desertion of their boats – as suddenly as a school of silver fish attacked by a dolphin, the pentekonters and rowing boats that had brought the assault force ashore turned and ran, abandoning their comrades on the beach. Instantly their morale collapsed – a visible movement in the front ranks, and suddenly pirates were throwing down their arms in all directions and trying to swim, and they received no quarter. Satyrus' oarsmen – many of whom had been slaves – reaped them like a farmer reaps the last crop of barley, hurrying against the winter wind and the rain, gaffing them with long pikes as they swam or punching daggers into men trying to surrender.

'I need Apollodorus,' Satyrus said.

'I'll go,' Abraham offered.

'Good – go fast. I need him, and as many men as he can extricate. I need them now.' Satyrus gave Abraham a slap on his backplate, and noticed that blood was running out of Abraham's helmet and over his back.

'You're wounded!' he said.

'Bah – it's nothing.' Abraham got his helmet off and dropped it on the beach. It had a hole in it, and his hair was a matted mass of blood.

Satyrus turned his attention back to the fight on the beach.

The ephebes had joined the slaughter with all the impetuosity of youth.

Satyrus kept backing up the beach, trying to get high enough to see what might be happening at the south end of the harbour – the inner harbour. Panther's area.

Helios emerged from the slaughter and came up the beach.

'Good lad,' Satyrus said. 'Breathe.'

Helios' right hand was all blood, and his arm to the elbow, and his entire right side was spattered by the blood dripping from his spear. 'I can't get it out of my hand,' he said in a strange voice.

The blood had dried, sticking the spear grip to his hand.

Satyrus poured his canteen over the younger man's hand, and gradually the glue-like blood loosened, and then they shared the rest of the canteen.

Abraham returned, running well, with long strides. 'Apollodorus is going to break off.'

Helios pulled his helmet off and dropped it to the sand.

'I need you to run to Panther,' Satyrus said to Helios, who nodded without speaking.

'Get me a report. Fast as you can. Go, now.' Satyrus knew he was using the boy up, but his options were limited and the feeling of doom was growing. And the only knucklebone he had was that the pirates had died fast, leaving him with a reserve and some options. Perhaps. Maybe.

Down in the slaughter, Anaxagoras was cutting a swathe through the pirates. His blue and white plume was unique, and Satyrus had no trouble watching him. His wrath was terrible, like something from the *Iliad*.

'I do hope we don't take any casualties wiping them out,' Satyrus said, and his voice was like Ares' voice – a thing of bronze, inhuman.

Abraham watched for a moment. 'A moral man would say that they are men, like us,' he said. He turned, and his eyes had no trouble meeting Satyrus' eyes. 'But they are not men like us, and their deaths give me nothing but pleasure.'

'Kill them all,' Satyrus said. By his estimate – he found it remarkable how clearly he was thinking – there were three or four *thousand* of the curs caught in the pocket, facing a quarter of their own number, and dying. He could never feed so many – he couldn't even dare to accept their surrender, as they were men of no worth whose word could never be trusted. They would rise against him and slaughter his men if they ever understood the superiority of their numbers. Only Tyche – luck – and good planning had delivered them into his hands. He felt no mercy.

All this in three rapid beats of his heart.

'Tell the phalanx to kill them all,' Satyrus repeated to Abraham, and turned away when he heard his name being screamed from the ruined temples.

'Satyrus!'

He looked right and left. Helmets made such searching difficult.

'Satyrus!' Closer.

It was Miriam. She had blood on her face and in her hair.

Satyrus caught her in his arms – not his intention – as if his body acted without him.

She went into his embrace, blood and sweat printed on her chiton, so that the outlines of his shoulder armour could be traced on her for the rest of the day.

But she murmured no endearments.

'The enemy is in the town,' she said, her voice controlled, her own panic carefully held back. 'They are behind the agora, and a soldier I met says they are coming in through the west gates.'

Satyrus turned his head.

Apollodorus was coming up the beach, his two hundred intact.

Thanks, Lord Herakles, for the warning. May I be in time.

'In the streets behind the agora?' he asked.

'That's what I believe,' she said. Her voice trembled. 'I don't *know*.'

He wanted to say something like, 'Welcome to war', but there wasn't time. 'Get every woman you can, get onto the rooftops and drop tiles on them,' he said. 'Every woman you can find in the agora – listen. I may be sending you to your death, Miriam, but if your women can't slow them in the alleys, we're dead.'

'I understand,' she said.

'I love you,' Satyrus said.

She shot him a look from under her eyebrows that suggested that, even in the grip of fear, she had the wits to question his choice of words. 'I'll try not to die, then,' she said lightly. She pulled up her skirts and ran, her long legs flashing in the afternoon light, a rare sight on a battlefield.

Satyrus turned to Apollodorus. 'Enemy in the town behind us,' he said.

'Zeus Sator! Apollo, Kineas, be with us,' Apollodorus said.

'Follow me.' Satyrus led them up the beach, and his fears almost robbed him of the ability to run – had the town already fallen? Usually, once the enemy penetrated the walls, the defence collapsed although Rhodes was so big and so deep that both Satyrus and Panther had been using its depths as a defence.

He ran back across the rubble, ignoring the growing pain in his right ankle, through one of the tunnels and the fallen Temple of Poseidon and into the agora.

It was *not* a mass of enemy soldiers. It *was* a mass of panicked civilians, with Miriam trying desperately to motivate some of them to join her.

Even as Satyrus ran up, Panther's wife Lydia, and Aspasia, and other town leaders – the priestesses and the healers – stepped out of the mob and began to harangue them, and the mob fell silent.

Through the silence, Satyrus could hear the screams from the west.

'Form three columns – one on each main street. There must be some defenders – put heart into them.' Satyrus barked his commands and Apollodorus picked his three commanders, and even as men emerged from the rubble tunnels they were numbered off into three groups.

'I'll take the right,' Satyrus said.

'I should stay with you,' Apollodorus said.

Satyrus shook his head. 'You're no worse off if I die here – if the town holds,' he said. 'Besides, I have Draco and Amyntas,' he said, catching their eyes. 'They won't let me die.'

Both men managed a grunt that might have been mistaken for a chuckle.

'Ares' golden balls, this sucks like a flute girl at an ephebe's symposium,' Amyntas said. 'I hate sieges.' He turned to his men. 'Have I ever told you lads how I saved Alexander?'

'Not above a thousand times,' Draco grumbled. 'Come on, or the young king will try and do all the fighting himself.'

Amyntas spat. 'He's just doing it to impress that girl,' he said.

'I can think of worse reasons,' Draco retorted.

Even in fear of imminent death and loss of the city, Satyrus found that his cheeks could burn.

Into the streets west of the agora, new terrain for Satyrus and all the marines, they went slowly, well closed up, checking side streets as they came to them.

They went half a stade before they found men looting. A dozen men, all enemy soldiers, who had decided that the town was fallen and they could start the promised sack.

Their paralysis, their total surprise at his force gave Satyrus some hope.

'Forget the side streets,' Satyrus said. 'Form close. At the double! Forward!'

Their feet pounding the stones, the marines moved fast, flowing along the gently curving street at the speed of a running boy or girl who hears the call of a distant parent – and they saw the enemy, a clump gathered around a small olive tree in a town square no more than two horse lengths on any side. The square was packed with Antigonids sacking a rich house, raping two women they had caught, drinking fine wine – all the delicious, evil spoils of war in one place – and Draco's marines slammed into them without slowing, and the slaughter was fast and their was blood in the spilled wine and the fountain at the centre of the square was choked with dead men.

But behind the initial assault of plain pikemen had been a corps of veterans, a reserve, and now they reacted like professionals, coming up from the west and punching straight into Satyrus' marines, and the pikes and spears were crossed, locked and the killing began in the square.

They were pushed out of the square, step by step. Amyntas died there, who had saved Alexander's life in far-off India, who had killed men from Thebes to the Hindu Kush and beyond. Draco saw him fall, and he planted his feet over his fallen lover and his spear rose and fell as if he were Ares incarnate, and the Antigonids feared to face him – indeed, as the enemy was reinforced, some of them shouted his name because they were facing the old veterans now, the best of Demetrios' force, and the men in the front ranks of the Argyraspides knew Draco by sight and they drew back in respect.

Another marine dragged Draco back, and Satyrus grabbed his ankles and pulled and they made it alive around a corner.

'Rally!' Satyrus said.

Draco was weeping, all rationality gone, like a beast that has lost its child. 'Give him to me!' he shouted at Satyrus, and would have struck him if Satyrus hadn't been watching. He let the body fall, backed away as a man would back away from a dangerous predator, and only when he saw Draco crouch over Amyntas did he turn his back on the man.

'On me!' Satyrus bellowed. His voice was failing, and he felt fatigue sapping his will to fight, and the fact that they could not hold the square suggested that the town had fallen indeed.

'Satyrus!' Miriam shouted. She was above him – it hurt him to look that far up, with the neck plate on his back armour biting into his neck under his helmet as he craned to see her. But there she was, a roof tile in her hand.

'On me!' he roared, his spirit soaring. And the change in his tone was more convincing than the words, and suddenly the marines hardened around him even as the Argyraspides charged around the corner—

The corner took them by surprise, and the marines held the rush and thirty-year veterans died there, men who had climbed the banks of the Ipsus and the Jaxartes and stood their ground at Arabela. And Satyrus had no time to think: all he knew was the rush of blades, the hollow sound of his shield taking impact after impact, the endless roar of the battle cries and the screams and curses as men were hit and went down. He stood his ground, a front-ranker now, and the men on either side stood their ground, and that was all that could be said. He thrust with his spear as often as he dared, and had no idea if he was hitting or not – over his shoulder, men thrust, and there were screams – it seemed almost impossible to Satyrus that he could still be unwounded, and the fighting in the street seemed to have gone on for hours.

Then, almost as if an order had been given, the marines backed away three steps – all across the street – and the Argyraspides *did not follow*. And now that the front-line fighting stopped, the silver shields had time to realise how many of their men were down – how hideously they had been thinned by falling roof tiles and mud bricks from the houses on either side, which were reaping them with more efficiency than the tired marines.

Just as a young child, her knee skinned in a fall, may take long heartbeats to scream for her mother, so the Antigonid veterans stood for long seconds before realising how many dead they had.

But they were the best soldiers in the world. And they had not lived so many years in the hands of brutal Ares without learning all the hard lessons of the battle haze. When they found how badly hurt they were, how deep they were in the noose of the women on the roofs and in the alleys – they did not fail. Calling to each other, because so many of their file leaders were dead, calling out from man to man, they lapped their shields and charged.

Satyrus took the rush on his shield in a state of despair, because *any other troops would have broken*. All he could do was stand his ground, and die.

The man on his left died almost immediately, and Satyrus and his rank-mate to the right – he saw that it was Jubal the sailor, a man who had no business being here – were pinned to the street wall by the rush of Macedonian veterans. But Jubal grunted, struck out with his spear and put a man down – a man with a shield rich in ivory and silver, and instead of flinching, the Nubian pushed forward and Satyrus got his shield up, lapped it on the Nubian's and *pushed* his legs against the house foundation at his back. Someone filled in from behind, pushing into Satyrus' left and lapping his shield, and suddenly they were filling the street. They held like a smaller wrestler holds a larger when his slipping feet find a small rock, buried in sand, wide enough to catch the flat of the foot and give the fighter that heartbeat to gather his wits—

And then Apollodorus stormed into the side of the Argyraspides from the flanks of the square. The enemy commander had never understood that Satyrus' counter-attack was in three columns. He'd committed everything in the centre. And in a street fight, ignorance is death.

Apollodorus' column burst into the square, fifty paces behind the Argyraspides' front rank, but their shock was translated instantly and *that* was too much for the veterans. And they *still* didn't break. They knew that to break was death. Instead, they retreated through the streets, leaving dead men at every step, dead at the hands of Satyrus, Apollodorus, Charmides – but more dead from the endless rain of mud brick and roof tile.

They never broke.

They moved fast, and they killed even as they retreated, and when their Macedonian comrades broke and deserted them, they covered the younger men's retreat at the gates and died there as well, and Satyrus thought that they were the most magnificent soldiers he'd ever seen.

And then they were outside the gates. And just beyond the gates, coming hard, was a fresh phalanx – a whole *taxeis* – two thousand men. Two thousand *fresh* men.

The gates were still there – a mystery to Satyrus. *How in Tartarus did they get in?* he thought.

'Gates!' he panted to Apollodorus.

A file of Argyraspides came to the same conclusion – and turned to stand in the gates. Half a dozen men – men in their forties and fifties, with silver beards over their silver shields.

The gates opened outwards. To close them, the Argyraspides had to go.

The enemy *taxeis* was close. Close enough that he could see the puffs of dust their sandals raised as they ran – *ran* at him.

Apollodorus didn't hesitate. He ran forward, all mad recklessness. The Argyraspides braced, but he stopped just short, raised himself on his toes and thrust *down* into the back of one man's helmet and nailed him to the ground. Satyrus was a half-step behind – he'd mistaken Apollodorus' intention and he went hurtling over the smaller man, into the midst of the Argyraspides in a sprawl. He should have died, but he hit them like a missile and three of them went down – and suddenly they were all locked together on the ground, grappling desperately.

Satyrus ripped his arm out of the porpax on his shield, got the dagger from its sheath beneath the porpax and stabbed – as fast as the strokes of Zeus when he sends the lightning – at anything his dagger hand could reach, while his free right hand – he'd lost his sword – caught a man's throat and he squeezed and stabbed with all the ferocity of a *pankration* fighter in his last hold. Someone was biting his bicep as hard as he could, and another blow landed between his legs, the shattering agony of a groin shot, but he rode it, stabbed again and felt his opponent's carotid collapse under his thumb, felt the crack of the cartilage of the man's neck. His hand moved – he felt the man's face, and buried his thumb in the soft not-flesh of the man's eye.

A blow caught him in the back and sent him rolling over, and the pain in his groin flooded over him like a wave. But he could see his marines cheering, all around him. He got to one knee and threw up, and then fell forward into his vomit.

And they were still cheering.

He rolled back and forth for an eternity, his knees locked tight, his back on fire. Gradually, it became merely pain. A sort of cold, evil ache that owned the whole lower half of his abdomen.

Apollodorus was leaning over him.

He was grinning.

'You'll live,' he said.

Lying on his back, Satyrus could see that what had hit him in the back was the gates as his men pulled them shut. And in the towers either side of the gates, Idomeneus' men were pouring arrows down into the *taxeis* that lay helpless at their feet.

Miriam came out of the fog of pain. She looked like a fury – blood and dust and a look to her face that was far from beautiful – far, at least, from the kind of beauty poets and potters praised.

She studied him for a minute.

'I think—' She steadied her voice. 'I think you've looked better, my lord.'

'You—' Satyrus said. And mercifully for everyone, he bit back what came to his tongue. 'Well done,' he said instead, like an officer to a well-disciplined spearman. 'Well done, Miriam,' he panted.

But their eyes were locked, and her eyes spoke louder than the shouts of pain in his guts and his groin.

25

DAY TWENTY-SEVEN

Satyrus had no more wounds than any man who has fought all day in armour – long scrapes, mysterious bruises, three deep punctures in his lower back where spear heads were held off by his leather armour – but the points had licked through. He had a bruise on his upper left arm that turned a horrendous colour so that other veterans winced to look at it, and he had another on his butt where the gates had struck him that made it almost impossible for him to sleep.

Altogether, he felt wonderful.

Part of the euphoria he felt was caused by the poppy juice that Aspasia had given him for the pain in his groin, and part due to his success – by any standard, he and his men had won a notable victory. Demetrios had launched his grand assault, with almost twelve thousand men involved at its height, and he had been repulsed – repulsed with hideous losses. The heaviest assault had fallen on the beaches, and been massacred.

But the greatest part of the euphoria came from the casualties – or rather, the *lack* of casualties. Luck, planning, divine aid – for whatever reason, the phalanx of oarsmen had lost just fourteen men; the city ephebes had lost just six, and the combined marines of all Satyrus' ships, engaged all day in the very heaviest fighting, had lost nineteen men – including Amyntas, the only one of Satyrus' *hetairoi*, his close companions, to die.

Panther and Menedemos had each held minor attacks – real attacks, but with fewer men – and each had lost fewer than twenty men.

It was a miracle – sent by Athena, men said.

Satyrus lay on his bed and ached, and thought that it was indeed a miracle, and it was sent largely by Demetrios' arrogance, and a great deal of luck. And some forewarning from Herakles.

The sun rose on a new day – the summer festival of Apollo – and Satyrus lay on a low couch, on a magnificent Persian rug in a tent crowded with furniture rescued from the wreck of Abraham's house. The house was gone, hit four times by rocks the size of sheep. But his slaves had remained loyal and protected his belongings from looters, and now Abraham, his family, retainers and slaves had a compound of tents in the agora, made from *Arete*'s sails, at least temporarily out of the range of Demetrios' machines.

Slowly, cursing from time to time, Satyrus swung his legs over the edge of the low bed, sat up slowly and managed to rise to his feet.

Helios appeared at his side. 'My lord!'

'You fought like a hero, yesterday, lad,' Satyrus said. The word *lad* escaped from his teeth unbidden. *I am growing old*, he thought, *if I can call men lads.* Twenty-four years old. And another year for every day of the siege.

Helios grinned at him. 'I did, at that, lord. Charmides says so, as well.'

'Well, that certainly makes it true,' Satyrus joked.

Helios grew more serious. 'As you're awake, there's business, lord. After the pirate slaughter last night, Demetrios managed to throw some assault troops onto the mole – the town mole. They've barricaded the townward end, and they have a pair of great machines there.'

Satyrus winced. 'How many men?' he asked.

'Six hundred, and some ships in support. And Demetrios has pulled his engine-ships well back, and rebuilt the spiked boom. You can see it on the water. Panther was here, almost an hour ago. He's asked for all the *boule* to meet. Abraham refused to have you waked.'

Satyrus rubbed his jaw. 'Gods, I stink. Abraham is a prince. Can you get me a bath and some sweet oil, Helios? And a cup of hot cider?'

Helios handed him a cup – warm pomegranate juice. 'I'm ahead of you, my prince.'

Satyrus sat back, sipping the juice. The euphoria was still there. 'We won a noble victory, didn't we?'

Helios laughed. 'Only – lord – why does he not give up and sail away?'

Satyrus finished the juice and stood up. 'He's barely started, Helios.'

*

'Shall I wake the others, lord?' Helios asked.

Satyrus shook his head. 'Let Neiron and Apollodorus sleep.' They were stretched under awnings near his tent.

Clean, in a *chitoniskos* short enough to cause comment in Athens, Satyrus walked out into the blaze of sun in the agora. He went to the *boule* by way of the square where Amyntas had died. He found the olive tree he remembered, and he cut a long frond and made a wreath and handed it to Helios.

'Wear this, hero,' he said.

Helios knelt and took the wreath, and burst into tears.

Satyrus cut three more and twisted them into wreaths as he walked. 'When we are finished with the men of the city, we will return, set up a trophy and bury Amyntas,' Satyrus said. Then he walked to the *tholos* where the *boule* met.

'Lord Satyrus,' Panther said, and came to meet him at the entrance. 'The hero of the day. We have just voted you a statue, should our town ever rise from the rubble to have such things.'

One by one, men rose and took his hand, or embraced him. These were good men – noble men, whatever their birth, and their thanks – their very heartfelt thanks – were better than a hundred golden wreaths.

Panther indicated the podium. 'I think we'd like to hear a few words from you, sir.'

Satyrus smiled curtly and went to the podium. He cast his chlamys back over his shoulder – he was very informally dressed, for an orator – and he looked around the dim room, picking up every eye.

'I'd like to bask in your admiration, gentlemen,' Satyrus said. 'Indeed, it is a great honour to have served you well. And yesterday was a victory. A very real victory.' He nodded at their smiles and plaudits, and then he raised his voice and chopped at them with it like a woodsman with a sharp iron axe.

'It will take a hundred such victories to preserve this city,' he said, and they were instantly silent. 'Every day, every assault, we must be as victorious as we were yesterday, and by such a margin. We lost *sixty men*, sixty good men. We killed two thousand pirates and perhaps five hundred of his Macedonian professionals. He has thirty-five thousand more soldiers and twice that many pirates. If we lose fifty men a day and he loses a thousand men a day, *we will run out of men first*.'

359

Silence.

'We have other enemies,' Satyrus went on. 'I live on the rubble of the agora now. I can smell the shit of three thousand people from here. We must do better than that. Soon enough, the whole population of the city will live on the agora. We must have sanitation, organisation, proper latrines, proper wells and districts measured off. No rich man should have more tent space than he actually needs.'

Men looked around.

'Further, we need to consider our slaves,' Satyrus said. 'Many have been loyal. But as the food fails – and mark my words, gentlemen, we face food shortages almost immediately – their loyalty to us will dwindle. We should consider inviting them to be citizens. And when this town survives, I promise you that we will need their numbers to make up our losses.'

Grumbling.

'And finally, gentlemen, for all that we managed to incur Nike's good pleasure yesterday, *someone opened the west gate to Demetrios.*' Satyrus glanced around. 'Let's not mince words. If not for Miriam, Abraham's sister, the town would have fallen. No amount of heroism by our converged marines, by our ephebes, by anyone could have saved us, except that Miriam came to the beach and told us that the west gates were open. The women of the town – your wives, gentlemen – bought us the minutes we needed, and then helped break the best men Macedon has to offer – and still, they would never have been in the town except that *someone let them in.*'

Consternation.

'The west wall garrison had been withdrawn. Who gave that order? Decimus, the lead phylarch, died in the fighting. No one seems to know who ordered his men to leave the walls. In a way, that traitor did us a favour – we saved the west-wall garrison instead of losing them. But friends, it was so close – so very close – that even now, as I speak to you, my knees feel weak. Who is the traitor?'

'Any slave might have done it,' Panther said. 'You made the point yourself.'

Satyrus nodded. 'Almost certainly. But let us not make it easy for the traitor. Appoint a committee to investigate. Find out what slaves, if any, deserted yesterday. Question the west-wall garrison – who was there? Town mercenaries?'

Panther nodded. 'Cretans and Greeks – two hundred hoplites and four hundred archers.'

Satyrus nodded. 'And let us face the horrible possibility that the mercenaries themselves sold the gate.'

Panther nodded, and other men looked sober.

Menedemos rose to his feet. 'Satyrus – you have been an accurate weathervane so far. Where will Demetrios strike next?'

Satyrus narrowed his eyes. 'I'm no seer, Menedemos. Answer me this, first – how stands the naval sortie? What happened in the southern harbour, and does the enemy possession of the mole cut you off from the sea?'

Menedemos glanced at Panther, and Panther scratched his chin.

'We're ready enough,' he said. 'We have the ships ready. We're a little short on oarsmen, to be honest – all our oarsmen are on the walls. But we can put to sea any night, now.'

Satyrus nodded. 'Look, friends, I cannot guess what Demetrios will do – or even if I can, I can't be right every time. We have to make him dance to *our* tune. Our best course of action remains to strike him – to break the boom and destroy his engine-ships.'

'His men hold the mole!' Carias the Lydian was a former metic who was one of the town's richest men. 'We can do little while they hold the mole.'

'The engines on the mole can hit any point in the town,' Menedemos said.

Satyrus nodded. 'Demetrios wants us to try to storm the mole, my friends. And I predict he'll have those engines drop rocks – perhaps even bundles of small rocks – on the agora, in an indiscriminate killing to goad us to assault the mole.'

Panther looked at him. 'I think we must.'

Satyrus shook his head. 'No! Listen to me! We cannot afford to be bled like that. Retaking the mole – it might cost us five hundred men. We might lose that many and *fail*. His engines, however evil, will not kill so many.'

Panther shook his head vigorously. 'Not today, perhaps,' he said.

They argued half the morning. At last they decided to prepare the naval sortie and ignore the mole, and they appointed committees to organise the displaced citizens, another to begin recruiting slaves – the best of them – as citizens, and another to search for the traitor, if he existed.

Menedemos moved that the west-wall garrison be relocated to the north wall, and that the citizen hoplites, held on the north wall to avoid casualties among the richest citizens, be put on the west wall, at least temporarily.

The motion was carried unanimously, which showed Satyrus how seriously the men in the room took the threat of treason. The richest four hundred men were unlikely to betray their own town.

Satyrus shook hands with the other councillors and walked through the broken rock and clay of the streets. In every street, there were houses that had survived – some were shells, where a rock had dropped through the roof without touching the walls. Some stood because they had been overbuilt to start with, using heavy timber against earthquakes. Some were protected by the *Moira*. But there were few enough houses on the seaward end of the city, so that they looked like the teeth of an elderly man – more missing than remaining, and pitiful piles of rubble in between.

And there were bodies in the rubble – men and women, children, pigs and dogs and cats and rats, all rotting together, so that the east side of the town stank like an abattoir, or a temple the week after a great sacrifice. And that miasma would breed disease.

Satyrus walked through the rubble and headed south, to the great tower that the Rhodians had built to dominate the plain south of the town and the most vulnerable stretch of wall. Legs aching, he climbed the tower.

Jubal was already there. He laughed to see his king.

'You're up early, no joke, lord.' Jubal smiled.

'You fought well yesterday, Jubal,' Satyrus said. He reached under his chlamys and produced a rather straggly wreath of olive, taken from the tree in the courtyard where Amyntas died. 'Yours to wear.'

Jubal smiled. 'Heh,' he grunted, then shook his head. 'Not for Jubal, lord. Di'n want to be a hero. Just stood my ground.'

'That's about all there is to being a hero, Jubal,' Satyrus said. 'How're the engines?' he asked, leaning out over the tower.

'Had a try las' night in the dark,' Jubal said. One of his petty officers grinned like a death's head. 'Wen' pretty well.'

'Yes?' Satyrus asked. Jubal and his men were a pleasure to be around.

No big issues here – just the cat-and-mouse of siege engineering.

Jubal's grin was that of the raven putting one over on the fox. 'Reinforced the walls and floor, eh? And then we made the throwing arm longer, uh? And then we put yon heavier weight on the end. And then we shot her.' Now his grin was triumphant. 'Dropped a rock right over the west wall – don't you worry, honey, no one was awake to see or hear.'

Satyrus had to grin. 'You tested your range over our *city*?'

Jubal shrugged, and his gold tooth shone. 'One rock more or less ain't gonna do much harm.' He looked around. 'Made the whole tower move, though.'

Satyrus looked out from the great vantage point of the tower. He could see the new works built across the mole – four times the height of a man. And he could see that there were no defences on the flanks of the mole, because Demetrios had ships – a dozen warships – lashed all along it, full of men. And another four hundred men on the mole itself.

South, he saw that more ships were anchored out from Demetrios' camp. Either he'd sent another force away, or another force had arrived. Satyrus wished he had spies – good spies. But only a fool deserted from a giant army of comfortable, well-fed besiegers to the desperate garrison of the city – and such fools were thin on the ground. There had been a few, but most knew so little, they had nothing to offer.

'If we can just burn his engine-ships,' Satyrus said, and scratched his chin.

'Then he *have* to come at me,' Jubal said. 'I walk all round this fewkin' city. An' the only way in be *right here*.'

Satyrus was glad to hear Jubal say it, because he'd come to the same conclusion months ago, before the siege had even begun, and he knew that the Italian who had built the great tower had had the same view.

'We should start work on a false wall here,' Satyrus said.

'Oh, aye,' Jubal agreed dismissively. 'But first, I wanna shoot the squirtin' *shit* out of his landward engines. An' then he'll build more, an' more, an' finally he'll knock down the whole fewkin' tower, an' *then* we'll need a false wall.' Jubal shrugged. 'I've made the measurements, with Neiron. We done the maths.' He grinned evilly. 'I even know where the new tower'll go, when this one falls.'

Satyrus shook his head. 'Where'd you learn all this maths, Jubal?'

Jubal made a face. 'Anaxagoras. An' Neiron. An' me dad. Great one for countin' stars, me dad. Always fancied numbers.'

Satyrus grinned. 'I think I'll start a book of sayings: *You never know a man until you stand a siege with him*, is my first.'

Jubal raised an eyebrow. 'Not bad, lord. An' how 'bout *Them what overbuilds the foundation course can always put engines on their towers.* Heh?'

Satyrus hid a smile. 'I'll put it in the book, Jubal.'

DAY TWENTY-EIGHT

Satyrus woke to more aches and pains than even the day before – the siege was teaching him the rule of the second day, at least with bruises. He *hurt*.

He rose anyway, and Charmides brought him a cup of sage tea, and another of warm juice, which he drank down and felt better. And then Korus insisted that he exercise, and then he ate – more food than he felt he needed.

'You still need weight, lord,' Korus said. 'You're better than you were – you may be the only man in this town gaining weight.'

Miriam came up with a bowl of barley meal and coriander. The smell attracted him as much as the person carrying it, and he scraped the bowl clean before smiling at her. Then he went into his tent and emerged with another scraggly olive wreath.

'From the marines,' he said, and Apollodorus, just awake, came over and saluted her the way he would a man, an athlete or a hero.

Miriam blushed – a remarkable blush that started somewhere near the top of her head and seemed to run down to her navel – but she never lost her composure. 'Some of us are delighted with the opportunities for weight loss, Korus. My hips will be the better for it. Indeed, every single woman needs a siege: men, good company, opportunities for heroism and exercise.' She took the bowls, smiled at Satyrus and walked back to her own tent and the pair of cooking fires burning behind it.

Anaxagoras emerged from the open ground nearest the former Temple of Poseidon and took Satyrus' oil bottle without asking, scooping it from Satyrus' towel. He came and stood with Satyrus, using his expensive cedar oil liberally.

'Is she not the very wonder of the world?' he asked quietly.

Satyrus grunted. 'That's my oil,' he said.

'Learn to share, is my advice, lord king,' Anaxagoras said. From another man, the words might have been a calculated insult. Anaxagoras was too open for such petty things. 'Have you kissed her?'

'And you have?' Satyrus asked, stung.

Anaxagoras laughed.

Men compete in many ways, and Satyrus was not so petty as to pass on this one. If Anaxagoras could be the cheerful athlete, why, so could he.

'If you use my oil, we'll smell the same,' Satyrus said.

'And?' Anaxagoras paused.

'Well, when she kisses you, she'll assume it's me. Starving poets don't use cedar oil.' Satyrus smiled with a confidence that was entirely artificial – like showing courage when the Argyraspides charged, sometimes a man has to *make* himself stand to the challenge.

Anaxagoras sighed. 'I haven't kissed her.'

'Nor I,' agreed Satyrus. 'Now give me my oil back. Before Abraham kills us both.'

DAY TWENTY-NINE

Another day of inaction – exercise, food, stinking corpses dug from the rubble and burned. Funeral games for Amyntas, and a dinner by the tents. Scattershot dropped by the engines on the walls killed a dozen citizen children playing with some goats, and killed all the goats.

Towards evening, the storm that had threatened for a week suddenly began to manifest, and Miriam and Aspasia bustled around with other women arranging every unbroken vessel to catch water. The town had a dozen wells, but the constant rain of heavy rocks was damaging cisterns and dropping dirt and sand into well shafts.

The sun sank, a bright red ball in dark grey clouds, and Leosthenes the priest claimed it was an omen. He demanded Satyrus' attention.

'Lord, it is a sign from the Golden Archer. I had a dream to accompany it, and I take it to mean that we should attack the mole.' Leosthenes began a complex discourse on his dream and on the interpretation of dreams, and the importance of the dreams of a priest.

Satyrus nodded and walked away, leaving the priest to tell his dream to an audience of marines and sailors. Leosthenes – and Apollo, for that matter – wasn't telling him anything he didn't already know, and he took Neiron with him to find Panther in the small square at the south end of the port, where they'd first landed, what seemed like ten years before.

'Navarch,' Satyrus said, to greet the older man.

'My lord,' Panther said, rising from a late supper of olives and bread. 'A cup of wine for the king.'

Satyrus shook his head. 'I need my head clear. Panther, you're the best sailor here – how long until that storm breaks?'

Panther raised an eyebrow. 'Three hours?' he guessed, looking at Neiron as a gust of wind shot through his tent.

Neiron nodded. 'That's what I said.'

'Two hours after dark,' Satyrus said. 'I've heard it said that Rhodians are the best sailors in the world, Panther. Care to put it to the test?'

Panther shot to his feet. 'Ares, Satyrus, you want to hit them *tonight*?'

Satyrus shrugged. 'Neiron usually calls me rash.'

Neiron shook his head. 'Not this time. Navarch, we think that if you give us one of the ships you've readied – well, we have the best armoured oarsmen in the town. Perhaps in the world,' he said, with a piratical gleam. 'We'll land on the mole – right out of the storm.'

Satyrus leaned over to explain as another gust hit the tent. 'Even now, all those ships lashed to the mole have to cut their grapples and row away, or be dashed to pieces.'

Neiron nodded. 'Jubal saw it two days ago, but we couldn't risk talking about it.' The town now had desertions every day – so many slaves and mercenaries that there was no point in investigating the treason of the west gate.

Panther nodded, and finished his wine in two gulps. 'Let's do it,' he said.

An unfamiliar ship, in total darkness.

But he had the best one hundred and sixty rowers of *Arete*'s complement, and the best twenty marines of the whole combined force, and all of his own officers.

In fact, the town was *again* risking everything in one throw. Menedemos commanded the largest trireme, and Panther the second largest: both intended to break the spiked boom protecting the engine-ships and throw fire pots into them. Satyrus saw to it that they had dozens of householders' fire pots aboard.

'The attack on the mole will, at least, even if we fail, provide a diversion,' Satyrus said when they gathered the commanders.

And the *boule* voted to take the risk. All the knucklebones in one helmet.

It took an hour to get the men to their oars. They were in armour, with helmets and swords and spears which were lashed in piles on the main gangway – the trireme wasn't a cataphract and lacked a main deck above the rowers.

Outside the ship, the wind howled like the living embodiment of wind, and the stern of the ship crashed into the stone wharf again and again, even in the inner harbour of Rhodes. A stade away, across the harbour, the waves broke on the mole and arched up to the height of two men, even three, in the cool night air, and the wind brought the spume across the harbour.

'Bastards on the mole ain't too comfortable,' Neiron said.

'They'll be awake,' Satyrus said. 'Take the helm, friend. I'll go in with the marines.' He had Draco with him. Apollodorus was ashore, at the sea gate opposite the mole, awaiting some signal that the attack was on the mole before he led a hundred picked men out into the dark and up the landward face – the piled rubble, old barrels and sacks of sand with which Demetrios' men had built their temporary wall.

'Cast off,' Satyrus said softly, and men sprang into action. Xiron, the new oar master – better known now as the right file in the phalanx, a hard drinker called the Centaur by his men – called the beat softly, beating time with a spear butt, and the oars dipped, held water and moved.

Aphrodite's Laughter sprang across the harbour. It took fewer than four strokes for the crew to remember their profession, and then the warship moved at ramming speed.

Neiron had practised this route over and over, the last few hours, rehearsing how he would turn. His intention was to keep the ship hidden by the anchored ships in the inner harbour until the last *possible* second, and he'd talked them through it, every oarsman standing in the agora in torchlight, so that no man could say later he hadn't known the route.

Under the stern of a big grain freighter, and then a sudden turn to starboard, and another to port, and they were flying up a line of anchored hulks – a dozen once beautiful triemiolas now stripped to their decks, a wooden wall protecting the town, a screen. Only the most observant man on the mole might glimpse *Aphrodite's Laughter* running up the line – almost as far as the harbour entrance.

'Ready, all decks!' Satyrus called. He risked a yell – everything depended on this one turn.

The handful of oblivious men were slapped by their oar-mates. Men rose a little on their haunches, ready to back their oars.

'Ready about!' Satyrus called from amidships. The full weight of the sea wind caught them, but they'd planned for it, and the bow was already slipping south, just as they wanted it to—

'Hard to starboard!' Satyrus called, in case some laggard had forgotten the drill. 'Port side reverse benches all aback starboard ahead full row – row – ROW!'

Simultaneously, Jubal dropped a pair of heavy stones from the stern – stones roped by hawsers to the mainmast stanchions, so that the ship became a horizontal pendulum at the end of a pair of anchor ropes belayed amidships.

The bow came around like a living thing. For a second, their whole port side was exposed to the gale, and the wall of wind took them and moved the ship the length of a house, *sideways* and rolled them so far that some starboard-side oarsmen got their hands wet in the ocean and their oars were almost straight up and down, or so it seemed. But they held their ground and pulled like they had held their ground in the phalanx and the port-side men pulled like heroes, and the ship shot about in her own length, her force keeping her out against the hawsers of the fulcrum – turned at racing speed.

Jubal, armed with a great axe, chopped at his hawsers and they parted with the sound of close-in thunder.

Like a great arrow from the god's bow, *Aphrodite's Laughter* shot out of the storm-lashed darkness at the mole. Satyrus ran forward from amidships to join the marines.

'Ares!' Satyrus could see forward now – over the marines, every man already soaked to the skin – and he saw now that Demetrios had *not* recalled the flanking ships. Half were sunk, their ruptured timbers showing above the water like spiky teeth, and the others were rolling into the mole with mighty crashes, pounding themselves to flinders. 'Poseidon!' Satyrus prayed, and ran aft.

'The mole's still full of ships!' Satyrus yelled.

'Then we don't need to back water!' Neiron roared in reply.

'Brace!' called the men in the bow. Satyrus threw himself flat and grabbed a stanchion.

The bow hit something with a gentle tap, and then something else – Satyrus kept his helmeted head down, well clear of the stanchion, and felt impact after impact – four, five, a great shudder and a ripping noise, as if the veils that hid the world of the immortals from men had parted asunder, and then a crash forward.

Satyrus was on his feet without actually thinking that the way was off the ship, and he ran forward – the foremast had snapped off cleanly and lay over the bow, right across the deck of a half-sunk trireme – and onto the mole.

Satyrus ran down the deck, already knowing what he had to do. Because only a god could have delivered the foremast like a boarding plank, cutting across the half-sunk wreck the way that Herakles cut across most of the problems posed to him.

At full charge, Satyrus leaped onto the butt of the fallen mast and ran – *ran* along the rounded, slippery bridge, eyes locked on the mole, blocking his fear – fear of heights, fear of slipping, fear that no man would follow him. He ran across the fallen mast and slipped – at the very end – and skidded on his knees at the edge of the mole to fall in a heap—

—on the mole.

Only his greaves kept him from ripping all the skin off his knees, and the salt-water spume hurt like a hundred avenging furies, but he was up on his feet in a heartbeat, his spear still in his hand, shield on his shoulder – he'd hurt that shoulder falling, hell to pay later – and he looked back to see Draco coming across the foremast, jumping effortlessly onto the surface of the mole.

'Let's kill every fucker here,' he said, and ran off down the mole into the dark.

The oarsmen were clambering off their benches, impeded by their armour, but the marines were coming across the mast. Satyrus didn't wait for them.

He turned, and ran down the mole after Draco.

The whole length of the mole seemed deserted.

And it seemed to stay that way until he heard a scream, and then a massive lightning flash lit up the scene.

Draco was killing men. And the mole was packed – *packed* with men. All the men from all the ships.

Zeus sent lightning from heaven to give them light, Poseidon blew wind and rain at the men on the mole, and Satyrus and his puny handful came out of the storm and started to kill.

Satyrus ran shield first into a clump of men illuminated by the levin-bolts. The thunder seemed to roll on now in one continuous peel, and the rapid flashes of the storm strobed together in an almost continuous light that nonetheless had a terrifying quality to it.

Most of the men closest to him were unarmed oarsmen. Satyrus killed them anyway, because a night assault in the heart of a storm is not a time when a man shows mercy. He was economical, fighting as only a veteran of dozens of hand-to-hand combats can fight – killing as only the veteran knows how to kill, shallow jabs to eye and throat and abdomen, no long thrusts – the needle-sharp point of his best short spear was a reaping scythe, into temples, through skull-fronts, into necks – any stroke that left the victim dead without risk to the attacker, risk of a wound or of his weapon binding in the wound.

The storm roared. It gave the fight an Olympian quality, as no sound of mortal man could be heard.

Men came up out of the storm, more marines and more and more again, and then Jubal and the deck crew – and the oarsmen, packed like herd animals died without response, their screams lost in the scream of the storm.

But behind the living wall of oarsmen were good soldiers, professionals, men who knew how to shelter themselves on a stormy night, and knew when they were under attack, knew that their lives were forfeit if they failed. The oarsmen died to buy them time, and they awoke, took up their weapons and formed.

Satyrus could see them forming, and he tried to cut his way through the last fringe of terrified oarsmen, who now pressed back into the forming ranks of the enemy soldiers – now the enemy soldiers were killing the oarsmen as ruthlessly as Satyrus' men, defending the integrity of their formation. All in the lightning-lit roar that filled the senses.

Satyrus broke through the last rank of oarsmen, face to face with an officer in a bedraggled double crest. He thrust – hard – and his spear point caught on the other man's breastplate and knocked the man down, but failed to go through the heavy bronze. Satyrus stepped in, kicked the man in the groin and went for the kill—

A spear caught his in the descent, parried him, swung up, inside his guard – Satyrus sprang back and the counter-thrust *just touched* the front of his helmet under the crest, a killing blow a finger's width from its target.

Satyrus planted his feet, caught the replacement blow on his shield and went *in* with the other man's spear safe on his shield, and now the other man sprang back.

Time to think *this man is a brilliant spear-fighter* and then a flurry of blows, blocking on instinct, and an overarm swing with his spear point to catch what he couldn't see – pure luck, his bronze saurauter caught the man in the side of the helmet – just a tap, but it staggered him and they fell apart, and five flashes of lightning showed Satyrus that he was facing Lucius, who he'd seen before.

Lucius must have recognised him. The Italian grinned, showing all his teeth. 'Let's dance,' he said. And rifled his spear overarm, a beautiful throw.

Perhaps Herakles or Athena lifted his shield. Perhaps it was just the wind. The spear, meant for his eye, sprang off the bronze of his aspis rim and leaped high in the air over his head.

Lucius was right behind it, having quick-drawn his sword, and his swing blew chips out of the aspis. He was inside Satyrus' spear.

Satyrus dropped his spear and punched his open hand at Lucius' face, a *pankration* blow – he only caught the man's armoured forehead but he rocked his head back, powered forward on his leg change and knocked the Italian off his feet and went for his own sword, but the Italian's legs came up and kicked him square in the chest and he was down, his aspis rolling away into the light-punctuated darkness.

Satyrus had no idea which way the fight was oriented now, and he'd lost Lucius when he fell. He ripped his sopping chlamys over his head and rolled it on his left arm, shoulder burning – and took a pair of blows on his back, but neither was hard and he got to his feet, head swinging like a hawk's, looking for the Italian, terror stealing his breath.

And then he saw the Italian – the man had the officer he'd knocked down in his first rush by the heels, was dragging him clear.

Satyrus pushed forward and found himself facing an enormous man with a spear that hit as hard as an axe, and Satyrus was forced to one knee to parry the spear with his cloak. He couldn't take another such blow, so he powered forward, like a man tackling a goat, and cut behind the man's knees as the man's spear-butt crashed on his helmet – he smelled blood, saw a bright light and continued forward and the man fell back, cursing, fell to the ground, his hamstring cut, and Satyrus pinned his shield to his chest and thrust his sword point through the man's eye—

As he realised that he had just killed Nestor, the captain of his lover's guard. His friend, from childhood. Guest friend, sworn friend—

Satyrus screamed into the god-filled night, a cry of pain and rage as loud as his lord Herakles had ever bellowed, a cry so loud that it carried over the roar of the storm.

Men flinched from that scream. Something died in Satyrus with that scream, which tore from him whatever shreds of youth still clung to him, so that the sound leaving his throat might have taken something of his soul with it out of the trap of his teeth and into the hateful night.

Draco's head snapped around – because a man who has just lost a friend of forty years knows exactly what is contained in that scream – and the Macedonian fought his way to Satyrus' side and pulled him to his feet, heedless of the enemy, who had mostly fallen back to cower against the wall.

Satyrus looked at the enemy, eyes blank with hate – not hate for the men who faced him, either.

'Amastris!' he roared at the night. *Aphrodite's Laughter*, he thought. *I hate the gods.*

Draco plunged back into the cold inferno of the fight. Satyrus stumbled back, watching his life burn before his eyes as surely as if a lightning bolt had hit him.

Amastris was helping Demetrios. With her best. And Satyrus had just faced Stratokles, and Lucius, and ... Nestor.

He wrenched his helmet off his head, wiped the streaming water from his eyes and pulled the helmet back on.

The storm was less severe, now, and men were pouring over the makeshift wall at the south end of the mole – Apollodorus and his marines.

Satyrus watched a boat pull away from the mole into the teeth of the storm – three times its pair of oarsmen tried to leave, only to be smashed alongside, but the boat didn't capsize and the oarsmen kept their nerve and then the boat was away, climbing a breaker into the storm.

Lucius and Stratokles, of course.

Satyrus' face worked like that of a horrified child, and he ran to the edge of the mole, roared 'Amastris' at the storm and hurled his sword at them. It arched up into the storm and vanished into the huge waters.

The boat slipped over the height of the wave and vanished into the darkness.

And Satyrus began, like an adult, to work on controlling his fear, his anguish and his horror.

Behind him, in between the flashes of lightning in the dwindling storm, columns of fire rose to the heavens. Even in driving rain, pitch-painted ships burn well.

26

DAYS THIRTY AND FOLLOWING

Panther was dead. He had died in the lightning, killed by an unlucky spear thrust from an enemy marine as he led his boarders
into the engine-ships. His ram had broken the boom, flashing out of
the storm like a bolt of black lightning to strike the boom with the full
force of the wind and sea, and it had smashed in the whole bow of his
own ship. His men had followed him over the bows into Demetrios'
ships, taking a penteres and a trireme in exchange and bringing them
safely through the shattered boom.

Satyrus' men cleared the mole, and before they had finished, they
were so satiated with killing that they had two hundred prisoners,
who included many of Amastris' guardsmen. Satyrus sent them back
to his former lover in exchange for Panther's body – two hundred
men for a corpse. No one in Rhodes questioned him.

He walked out of the town with the dawn, the second day after the
assault on the mole. His eyes were dry and his mind clear.

He walked a stade from the town, as agreed by heralds, accompanied
only by his *hetairoi*. He had Anaxagoras and Charmides, Neiron and
Jubal, Helios, Apollodorus, Draco, Leosthenes the priest, Abraham
and twenty others, all wearing their best armour. Ten marines carried
Nestor on a bier made of his men's shields.

Demetrios met them on horseback – a magnificent golden horse
with a saddlecloth of leopard skin, his own armour a yellow gold that
caught the rising sun and made him glow like a god.

Surely, thought Satyrus, the intended effect.

Satyrus wore his best – his bronze armour, his silvered helmet. And
when he approached the mounted man, he had the satisfaction of
seeing the golden man's blue eyes widen.

Demetrios raised a leg over the saddlecloth and slipped from his horse as elegantly as a Sakje maiden.

'Satyrus!' he said.

'Demetrios,' Satyrus said, and saluted, as one priest salutes another.

Demetrios, rarely brought up short, was breathless. 'You – we understood that you were dead.'

Satyrus looked away. 'I live,' he said.

Demetrios embraced him. It was one of the strangest moments of his life to have this man, this implacable enemy, embrace him. 'You give me life, brother!' Demetrios said in his ear. 'I am not held at bay by a council of old men, after all. I am in a contest with a worthy foe.'

Satyrus started as if an adder had appeared between Demetrios' lips. 'This is no contest,' he said.

Demetrios' grin might have split the heavens. 'This is the contest of my life!' he said. 'Who could ask for more? We are not men, Satyrus! We are gods! And we contest for worthy things – glory, and honour! Not puny things like cities and women. This is the siege of Troy born again, and you, my love, are my Hektor.'

Satyrus met his eyes. Sadly, they were not mad. Madness might have been some excuse. He spat, in contempt.

'I am not Hektor,' Satyrus said. 'I return the corpse of a great man – a hero, who died for his queen when lesser men fled. I offer it free – although if she was worth an obol, she'd have craved his body as we craved that of Panther.' Satyrus waved at the two hundred prisoners who were marching out of the city. 'And these – I return. Where is the body of my friend?'

'He's just an old man!' Demetrios said, as if something about the scene made no sense.

'God or not, Demetrios, when you lack the sense to honour your own heroes, your men will leave you,' Satyrus said. He knew it was foolish to offer advice to the enemy, but he couldn't resist.

'You return two *hundred* warriors for a dead man?' asked one of Demetrios' staff officers. 'He is a fool, Lord King.'

Demetrios turned and struck the man so hard that he fell on his back. 'You are a fool, Phillip.' He turned back to Satyrus. 'You are winning, aren't you?'

Satyrus permitted himself to smile. 'I am winning by so much that

I can give you two hundred living men – good spearmen – for the corpse of a friend.'

A movement passed through Demetrios' staff like a wind through a stand of trees on a still day.

'I will take this city,' Demetrios said.

'No,' Satyrus said. He turned, and put his hand to Panther's bier.

'I will have you in ten days!' Demetrios called.

Satyrus kept walking.

At his heels, Neiron grunted. 'Best thrust of the siege,' he said.

'I thought so,' Satyrus said.

'Why?' Helios asked.

Apollodorus grunted. 'Demetrios just felt a cold draught of doubt, lad.'

The loss of all his machines cost Demetrios a month. His ships had to search the Asian shore for timber, and they did not make those forays without cost.

But timber came, and Satyrus, who went every morning to the peak of Jubal's tower to watch, saw the big machines take shape. New metal had to be forged for their parts, and new wood beams cut, in far-off Lebanon and closer in on the wooded slopes of Ida. Thirty days of labour, and Demetrios had again a battery of machines.

The city was not idle during that time. The tent city in the agora was reorganised, and men set their hands to improving their tents against late summer rains. Latrines were dug in the rubble of the former northern-harbour neighbourhoods. Makeshift taverns opened, and men looted the wine cellars of smashed homes to open a tent for one night that sold a little comfort against the hopelessness of the siege.

The second month of the siege saw a collapse of normality in the city. It started with the emancipation of a third of the slaves, made citizens with citizen rights – three thousand men and women altogether. These *Neodamodeis* (newly enfranchised) were formed into their own regiment, given their own living areas, and older citizens adopted many of them – some in place of lost sons and daughters, and others simply because they had been favoured slaves, or as insurance. Menedemos took command of them and formed them into a phalanx.

In their ranks marched Korus. Satyrus armed him, from top to toe, and Apollodorus provided his weapons. They invited him to serve with them – with the oarsmen, or the marines. But the trainer shook his head.

'I'll go with my own,' he said. 'They need me.'

The emancipation had bitter enemies, and Panther's death had re-empowered the oligarchs. Nicanor had returned to power. He openly advocated surrender on the best terms possible, and lampooned Satyrus for claiming that the siege could be won. But most painful, he held Satyrus up as war-mad, like a young man with his first woman might be love-mad. He made this allusion in every speech, every meeting, so that the men of the town began to look at Satyrus as *not* being one of them, but as an alien with different interests, like glory.

'He has no daughters in this town,' Nicanor proclaimed. 'And when we fall, his friend Demetrios will take him to his tent and feed him wine – while we are crucified.'

Satyrus admitted that there was truth to what the man said. There always was. He wasn't evil – he was merely driven.

Nicanor railed against the emancipation of the slaves, but it was done. Carried by Menedemos' slim majority. And the same for Satyrus' status as a commander. By one vote, Satyrus held onto his command.

Other changes came, and they angered men so that the tensions inside the political class of the town escalated. Women – maiden daughters of citizens – were caught in the beds of young men. Indeed, Satyrus saw women going to the fountains who showed themselves quite deliberately to the ephebes. And other women flirted openly – with married men and unmarried. Nor were they the only ones to make advances.

In a city at the edge of extinction, the old rules don't hold long.

Nor did the Demos party have much patience with the law courts of the oligarchs. A jury of rich men found a poor man guilty of cowardice in a skirmish and the man was carried away on the arms of his compatriots, and the jurors were threatened with stoning.

A pair of foreigners – Persian merchants – were killed by a mob.

Men knifed each other over clean water.

Satyrus tried to wall himself off from it. He concerned himself with the siege, day after day, drilling the *Neodamodeis* and raiding with his marines. Four times his men, unarmoured, crossed the open ground between the city and the enemy camp to massacre the sentries, until Demetrios had to build a wall to protect his wall.

On the fiftieth day of the siege, the *boule* had to cut the ration. Men received two-thirds of the grain they'd received before, and women just half. The rich had other food, and they made no protest – they made the rules, after all. But the poorer classes and the newly enfranchised had no other food, and they were angry.

Satyrus was angry, too. He walked from the *boule* to Abraham's tent, sat heavily and accepted a cup of clean water from Miriam, who now did the table service. Abraham was proud that he had freed *all* of his slaves.

'We cut the grain ration,' Satyrus said. 'Nicanor wanted it, of course.'

'Why? Are we short of grain?' Miriam asked.

Satyrus smiled at her. He barely saw her any more – he all but lived in Jubal's tower, preparing the southern defences for the expected assault. Nicanor had the harbour now. He'd demanded it in an early vote and been surprised when Satyrus exchanged it for the south and west without demur.

'No. Not yet. It will come, of course. Mostly he wants the poor to be demoralised, so that they will desert – or better yet, open another gate to the enemy.' Satyrus drank his water. 'Nicanor is willing to risk a sack to get the siege over.'

'He's mad!' Abraham said.

'I think so, yes,' Satyrus agreed. 'I think that grief and pettiness have pretty much stolen his wits. Today I actually considered killing him.'

Abraham shook his head. 'They forget so soon!'

Satyrus made a face. 'Not really. It's just that after we win a fight, everyone's confidence goes up for what – three days? And then we crash again. I can't blame them. I can't see the end from here – I watched Demetrios land another five or six tonnes of grain today. I spent an hour trying to imagine how to get at it. We can't – there's no raid we could launch that would do any good.'

Miriam smiled. 'You need music, my lord. Come and play. Anaxagoras and I will teach you.'

Satyrus smiled curtly. 'I would only be the third wheel on your chariot, madam,' he said, so sharply that Miriam turned away, her face red.

Abraham shot to his feet. 'What, exactly, did you mean by that?'

Satyrus stood. 'I should not have come here.' He gathered his chlamys and walked out, leaving Abraham as angry as he'd ever seen him.

So be it, thought Satyrus. He loved Abraham, but he couldn't abide – couldn't *abide*—

There were some truths even brave men hide from.

Luckily, such men often have friends.

Later, in the courtyard of Jubal's tower, when Anaxagoras approached him, Satyrus stared at him coldly.

'You need to relax, have a glass of wine, listen to my song about Amyntas,' Anaxagoras said.

Draco smiled softly. 'It is really very good, lord.'

Satyrus nodded. 'I believe, Anaxagoras, that you are the captain of the west gate – this very moment. But here you are, with a lyre under your arm.'

'I exchanged with Apollodorus!' Anaxagoras said. 'I protest, Satyrus! I did not expect to be an officer. The poetry came upon me.'

Satyrus nodded. 'You wish to be relieved of your command?' he asked. Anaxagoras was now a captain of twenty crack marines.

'No!' Anaxagoras was stung.

'Then go to your post and stop making excuses.'

'You are jealous.' Anaxagoras's blood was up. 'My time is my own. I exchanged with Apollodorus.'

'I may be excused for not answering you, sir. I know my duty – do you know yours?' Satyrus drew himself up. 'I might wish that I had time to visit certain people, but I do not. You must make your own choices.'

'I say you are an insolent hypocrite!' Anaxagoras said. 'You're afraid of her, afraid of me and afraid of yourself since Amastris betrayed you, and you seek to hide from it with work. And now you shout at me in this cold public condemnation – fuck you, sir!'

Satyrus turned. 'Draco, please take Anaxagoras out of the courtyard. You are relieved—'

Draco seemed to trip over a beam for a new machine, careened into the King of the Bosporus and knocked him flat.

'Uh?' Satyrus managed.

'*Stop being an arsehole*,' Draco whispered as loudly as a storm wind. And then he helped the king to his feet.

'Come on, lad. Let's go and have that cup of wine the king doesn't want,' Draco said, as Anaxagoras gave him a hand up.

'I didn't mean—' Anaxagoras looked stricken.

'Forget it,' Satyrus managed. Now exposed to himself, he didn't seem controlled and professional at all. He seemed like ... a jealous arsehole.

It made his stomach roil to find them together, but Satyrus made himself go – an hour later, last light, when he'd have been launching a raid if he thought he could get away with it.

They were sitting on stools in the soft evening air, playing their lyres – Anaxagoras with a kithara, and Miriam with the brasher sound of a turtle shell. They looked up as he brushed under the bead curtain Miriam had hung to keep her tiny courtyard inviolate.

Satyrus had done many brave things. It was years since he had seen himself as a coward. He knew himself to be brave – brave in the hardest way, the way of a man of intelligence and imagination who nonetheless faces his fears and gets things done. But facing her contempt and his pity was as hard a thing as he'd ever faced.

'I've come to apologise,' he said.

They looked at him.

He almost lost the will to go on. It was so easy to give way to anger – to allow himself to be the victim and not the aggressor. He could shout his betrayal and take refuge in violence. He could attack Anaxagoras. He could revile Miriam.

But that would be cowardly.

Excellence often exacts a terrible penalty.

'I've come to apologise,' he said again.

Miriam shot off her stool and threw her arms around him, lyre and all. 'You are an *idiot*,' she said into his ear, and pressed herself against him.

And Anaxagoras came and embraced him, too.

Excellence often brings its own rewards.

Later, he sat with both of them in the chill of the evening – they were all pressed together, sitting with their backs against a sun-warmed stone with a skin of wine none of them would ever have drunk two months before empty at their feet.

'And I saw him die,' Miriam finished. She was making a throwing motion, and she was crying.

Anaxagoras shook his head. 'I feel like I bathe in blood every day.' He spat into the sand. 'But the worst of it is that as long as I'm fighting, it is more intoxicating than wine, or sex.'

'Oh, *sex*,' Miriam said wistfully.

Satyrus put his hands to his ears. 'La, la, la,' he sang, putting a brave face on his jealousy.

'I haven't had sex with either of you,' Miriam said. 'So you can both relax. I shan't.' She shrugged and lay back against them. 'Unless you'd like to share me on alternate days?'

Anaxagoras shot a mouthful of wine out through his nostrils and across the remnants of a street. His coughing went on for a long time, and did a fine job of covering Satyrus' feelings.

Miriam looked back and forth and laughed. 'Men are so *easy*,' she said.

Anaxagoras drank more wine.

Miriam laughed – a dark laugh, the laugh of a maenad. 'What woman wouldn't envy me?' she said to the darkness. 'Two great heroes who love me. But when I choose one, I betray the other. Don't bother with your denials, gentlemen – you are what you are. And who cares? Aphrodite? Who cares if I lie with you both – both at the same time, one each day, one each hour? I'm no virgin, and *we will all be dead soon*.'

Miriam didn't burst into tears. It might have been better if she had. She laughed again, her laughter like the surgeon's scalpel – the sharp bite of truth. 'Your Greek gods are so much more understanding of my predicament than my old patriarch,' she sighed. She rose to her feet and kissed each of them on the lips, and then picked up her chiton skirts and ran off into the dark.

Satyrus sat still for a moment, and then looked over at Anaxagoras. The musician shrugged. 'You going to marry her?' he asked.

Satyrus rubbed his chin. 'You?'

'She kissed me first,' Anaxagoras said.

'Fuck you, you ... wide-arsed musician.' Satyrus laughed, and picked up the skin of wine.

'Last one alive gets her?' Anaxagoras said. 'Don't hog the wine.'

'I'll share the wine,' Satyrus said. 'And don't think we get to decide the terms of the contest, either.'

Her kiss burned on his lips like a wound.

27

Daedelus came out of the late-summer dawn mist like Poseidon's chariot. His ships were at ramming speed, and Demetrios' guard ships died under their rams. The distant screams of the trapped rowers were like the sound of gulls, and Satyrus might have slept through the whole thing, but Jubal caught the fighting with his sharp eyes and woke everyone in the tower.

Satyrus knew the Labours of Herakles instantly. He whooped like a child watching a race, laughed aloud when the fire pots began to smash into Demetrios' beached ships. And his smile was just as broad when the man himself stepped down from the deck of his ship onto the wharf.

'You bastard!' Satyrus said, embracing the mercenary. 'Where have you been?'

But he couldn't maintain any kind of fiction of anger – less so, even, when the grain ships began to enter the harbour. Six of them.

'These are Phoenician ships?' Satyrus asked.

'Demetrios didn't seem to need them,' Daedelus laughed. 'Have you *no news*?'

Satyrus shook his head. 'None!'

Daedelus nodded. 'Leon is at Syme with six thousand men and forty ships. Demetrios has made two tries at him and failed both times – he can't spare the ships. And your sister and Nikephorus are raising the Euxine cities – we hear they have another twenty ships and all your mercenaries.'

Satyrus laughed. He felt ten years younger.

'Wait – you haven't heard the best. Diokles is in Alexandria, refitting.' Daedelus smiled.

Satyrus paused a long, long time – maybe twenty heartbeats. 'Diokles?' he asked softly.

'All those sailors you sent to Poseidon?' Daedelus shook his head. 'Diokles has seven heavy ships.'

'Dionysus?' Satyrus asked, hope bursting from his chest.

Daedelus shook his head. 'Sorry lord, no. He was lost. And every man aboard. But *Oinoe, Plataea, Atlantae, Ephesian Artemis, Tanais, Troy, Black Falcon* and *Marathon* are refitting at Leon's yard.'

Satyrus breathed a prayer to Poseidon.

'Let's celebrate,' Satyrus said.

'I brought wine,' Daedelus said, 'but Leon hits the beach with his diversion in about an hour, and I have to be ready to sail. But from now on, you'll know we're out there. Demetrios doesn't have it all his own way at sea. And we hear that the Greek cities are begging his father for aid – Cassander is hitting them hard, undoing five years of their work.'

'I never imagined I'd be on the same side as Cassander,' Satyrus said.

'I never thought I'd help save Rhodes,' Daedelus said.

Satyrus took the news straight to the *boule*. The council was bitterly divided – many of the town's leaders wanted to try to negotiate a surrender while they were still holding out, and it had become more and more obvious that the oligarchs intended to starve their own lower classes into forcing such a surrender – the most craven strategy Satyrus had ever seen. He wasn't sure they were even doing it consciously.

Nicanor seemed to fight Satyrus automatically, and he made no pretence of his contempt for the man he always referred to as 'our young royal'.

Despite which, news of six grain ships was received with universal acclaim. Nicanor rose and proposed that all the grain be placed in the central store immediately.

Menedemos rose and argued that one-half of it be served out immediately as a donative, and to raise morale.

Satyrus let them wrangle. The hardest part for him – aside from his desire simply to take command and issue orders for their own good – was that *each* side had excellent arguments which were perfectly sensible and yet, most of the *men* on each side made these arguments with a cynical lack of conviction and a devotion to their own faction that lowered them daily in his estimation. Even Menedemos – the best of them, to Satyrus' jaundiced eye – was so devoted to his democrats that he could lose track of what was best for the survival of the city. Damophilus was a great man with a spear in his hand, but in the council he spoke only for party interests. The only man who cared solely for his city was Panther. And he was dead.

Satyrus waited his turn to speak, and eventually he rose. 'I neglected a point which may affect your deliberations,' he said, and he did a poor job of hiding his contempt. 'Daedelus and Leon will be back in two days, just after dawn, with a second load of grain and two hundred more soldiers. And they have landed a hundred more marines already.'

'What time?' Nicanor asked.

'That will depend on wind and tide, I assume, Nicanor.' Satyrus tried to sound pleasant.

Celebrations were short-lived. Fresh grain put heart into the lower classes, and the presence of a friendly fleet – a fleet which had some of Rhodes' own ships in it – raised everyone's expectations.

But two days later, they watched Daedelus' squadron try and run a second convoy into the town, and get decisively beaten. Demetrios' ships were waiting, manned, on the beach, and when the first trireme sail nicked the horizon, they launched, all together.

To avoid be overwhelmed by the in-sweeping flanks, Leon had to back water, and he lost four triremes and did no damage – and all six grain ships were lost, within sight of the port.

Morale plummeted.

And Demetrios, as remorseless as death, or time, moved his heavy engines forward across the hard ground south of the south wall. They began to move on the sixty-fourth day, and by the sixty-seventh day, they were almost in range.

Satyrus climbed the tower. The last light of day was shining on the besiegers, and their horde of slaves were dragging the final pair of heavy machines across the hard sand, raising a long column of dust.

'Watch them,' Jubal said.

At the front edge of the enemy machines was a full *taxeis* of pikemen, fully armed, their weapons throwing long shadows. They were just three stades away, neatly formed, standing to protect the machines. Even as they stood there, Satyrus wondered how they would react if he emptied his garrison at them in one mad dash to take the engines. When they started to throw their great rocks, the town was doomed.

Or at least, the suffering would begin again.

Jubal had filled the top of the tower with engines, and raised canvas and wood screens to hide them. The two captured on the mole had been strengthened, lengthened and now allowed the nautical mathematician four shots in his battery. He refused to commit more engines to the tower, which he said wouldn't last the day.

'My job is to kill as many of his engines as I can,' Jubal said. 'You watch.' He pointed. 'You see they? They's his engineers. Look.'

Just beyond the engines themselves, the enemy engineers were examining something on the ground. It wasn't a complex machine. It was a large rock, deeply embedded in the sandy soil, painted bright red.

'They found your aiming rock,' Satyrus said sadly.

Jubal smiled, and he bore a striking resemblance to a wolf. 'They foun' it,' he said. 'But they don' know what she be.'

He did some calculations in the last light, based on the distance the enemy engines were parked from his rock.

Jubal opened fire when the Pleiades were high in the sky. His first cast was a rock coated in tar and set alight – using a major portion of the town's spare tar. But it landed with a crash in the darkness and flames roared from the tar, and based on its position, Jubal began to issue orders, glancing from time to time at his wax tablet.

The canvas and hide sides dropped away from the tower.

His engines began to fire. The first four rocks elicited screams and crashes, and then the night was full of pandemonium and fire, and Satyrus released his sortie – just twenty men. They ran out of the postern, crept as close as they dared and began to shoot arrows at any man who was silhouetted against the flames.

After that, the tower engines fired as fast as they could, but they didn't seem to add to the chaos in the dark.

Satyrus went down out of the tower to Anaxagoras and Apollodorus, waiting with blackened faces and armour on in the open ground behind the postern gate. All his elite marines were there, reinforced by the men brought by Daedelus – almost three hundred ready to rescue the archers if they got into trouble.

Idomeneus came back in through the postern, shouting the counter-sign.

'The king?' he asked.

'Here,' Satyrus answered.

Idomeneus was panting so hard he couldn't speak. 'They've run – abandoned the engines.'

Satyrus and the marines were out of the gate as soon as they had fire. He almost forgot to tell Jubal to cease fire.

Fifteen engines were destroyed by fire or by bombardment: two weeks' work by every slave in Demetrios' camp. The next day they saw the great man survey the carnage on horseback. He issued orders, and his men raised a deep cheer.

No hesitation in that camp.

Satyrus saw Amastris riding at his side. He spat.

Neiron raised an eyebrow. 'Sure she's not just doing what a monarch has to do?' he asked.

Satyrus shook his head.

When Demetrios' engines came out again, two weeks later, they rolled forward under cover of night. Jubal sprayed them with fire – he sent burning wads of straw and pitch, he sent rocks, he threw hails of stones. Men died.

But in the morning, sixteen engines stood where thirty had been. And as soon as they could see, their rocks began to hit the tower.

Jubal's men were already out. He'd loaded and aimed all four engines, and he waited, alone, adjusting aim – he wouldn't take a chance. Then, one by one, his four engines let loose, and each shot hit – one ploughed a red furrow through the slaves, one crushed a dozen veterans like a boy crushes ants, and two crushed engines.

And then he swung down on a rope and watched as the remaining enemy engines pounded his precious tower. It took them all day, and another day – and then with a rumble, the tower fell.

The people of Rhodes saw it as a defeat. Jubal just laughed.

For nine days the machines crushed the south wall under their rocks, and on the tenth day, when there wasn't a house standing around the wall, the *taxeis* came forward.

The archers emerged from cover and bled them for a while, and then withdrew. The pikemen pressed forward, unopposed, but by now they knew what to expect, and they went up the breaches with their heads bowed and into the rubble of the town, and when they found the hidden wall just beyond the range of the engines, they simply fled. Many dropped their pikes.

Satyrus watched them run from some archers, and smiled. His smile wasn't very different from Jubal's.

The next day, the enemy machines pressed forward until their missiles could fall on the new wall.

Well behind the new wall, free men were already excavating the next wall. And the enemy machines were just forward of an old barn, a huge stone building that served as a cover for men wounded in the endless archery sniping.

The marines needed a rest, and Satyrus took the ephebes. Nicanor tried to forbid him to use them, and Satyrus took him aside in the *boule*.

'I have a tunnel,' he said. 'It runs from just under the wall at the west gate out into the hardpan just past the gully. From there, the ephebes will be able to run straight into Demetrios' camp.'

Nicanor nodded. 'I see.'

Satyrus got his men. And he nodded to Helios as he emerged from the *boule*, where his hypaspist stood with Miriam. Both of them nodded back.

Then he went to the agora, found the ephebes and led them to the house he'd ordered to be purchased five months before.

Jubal was ready with fire and pitch – every support was coated. The moment the sortie returned – or was beaten – the tunnel was to be destroyed.

Then Satyrus briefed the ephebes on their mission, and briefed Idomeneus and three of his best scouts on their mission.

It took them too long to crawl down the tunnel, which was as narrow as a man's waist in too many places. Satyrus went in after Idomeneus and his scouts. The tunnels scared him – they were dark, cold, like the land of the dead, and when his cuirass scraped along the walls, he felt as if it would all fall on his head. But Anaxagoras was the man behind him.

They emerged in the dead ground by the walled enclosure near the old barn. Idomeneus and his three men vanished – first up the ladder – into the darkness.

Satyrus was next. He got up the short ladder and lay down.

Anaxagoras lay next to him, and then the ephebes began to emerge. Satyrus could feel his nerve fraying away – it was all taking too long.

About half his men were out of the tunnel when the slaves tripped over Anaxagoras.

'What the f—' one muttered.

Satyrus rose to his feet as quickly and silently as he could and beheaded the man who had spoken.

'Zeus S—' the second man started to shout, and he got Satyrus' backswing.

Silence.

But there was a third slave, and he screamed.

'Now,' Satyrus yelled. 'Go for the engines!'

The ephebes rose and ran out of the yard. They were fifty men against an army – but a sleeping army that had no idea the ephebes could be so close.

'Now what?' Anaxagoras asked. They were virtually alone, except for two boys who'd come up out of the tunnel after the ephebes rushed off to burn the engines.

'Gather the next fifty and go and rescue those boys.' Satyrus tried to sound calm.

They could hear men shouting for other men to rally.

Satyrus' patience held out to the tune of thirty-five more ephebes. He could hear fighting everywhere, and he needed to get moving. 'Follow me,' he said, and led the young men into the dark.

He paused at the gate to the enclosure. 'Anaxagoras – go back. Tell the rest of them to turn around and go back, and then tell Jubal to fire the supports.'

'No,' Anaxagoras said. 'Send one of these boys. Where you go, I go.'

Satyrus laughed. 'You are insubordinate, sir.'

'You're right. No way am I going back to Miriam and saying, "He nobly sent me back, and meek as a lamb, I went".' Satyrus saw the flash of his teeth.

'Right.' Satyrus turned to one of the many young men – all thinner and harder than they had been half a year before. He searched for a name, and found it. 'Plestias? You're my messenger. Turn 'em round, all back to the start, and fire the supports.' He touched his helmet to the young man's and saw the hesitation, the desire and the pleasure at being saved and the disappointment all at war in his eyes by the light of the first engine to burst into flames.

Then he led the rest of them into the darkness.

They didn't do as much damage as he hoped. The engines were hard to light – Demetrios' men fought hard. But Satyrus got most of his boys away cleanly, leaving five engines afire. The white chalk on their helmets showed up well enough, and when he blew Neiron's sea whistle, they turned and fled north, all the way to the new postern gate.

He lost six men.

Jubal pointed at the fire raging at the edge of the wall, and they all heard the rumble as the tunnels collapsed under their feet.

Idomeneus came up out of the darkness from the west gate, saluted and raised an eyebrow. 'Exactly as you said,' he grinned. 'You have some sort of spell that allows you to see into Demetrios' tent? There was a *taxeis* of pikemen waiting just where you said.'

Satyrus shook his head. 'The opposite. He's had a look into ours. When the gate opened. When Daedelus made his second try at the harbour.' He motioned to the archer. 'Come with me.'

And then he gathered fifty ephebes and fifty of his own marines and set off at the double.

Helios met him near the Temple of Poseidon. 'Lord?'

'I missed you, but I'm alive. We only got five engines.' Satyrus kissed his hypaspist on the cheek. It always pleased him to see how much the young man loved him.

'The lady and I had an adventure as well. And Mistress Aspasia – the lady invited her to join us.'

'Because she's not a nasty foreign Jew,' Miriam said, dropping down off the remnants of a wall. Like most citizen women under fifty, she'd taken to wearing a man's chitoniskos, Artemis-like. The moon glowed on her legs.

She is very like my sister, Satyrus thought, and found the thought uncomfortable.

'No one would doubt your word, Despoina,' Helios said.

'That's what you think,' Satyrus agreed. 'Aspasia?'

'You look better,' the priestess growled. 'Heavier. Meaner. Yes, we saw it all. He sent a pigeon.'

'Not a slave?' Satyrus asked.

'A bird. All the merchants have them.' Aspasia shrugged.

At his back, Neiron spat. 'What in Tartarus are we about, here?'

Abraham pushed forward, too. He'd spent the watch on alert with the citizen hoplites – the full-grown men – and he was angry. 'What is my sister doing out – Miriam, that manner of dress is shocking!'

Miriam kissed him. 'No, dear brother. A month ago it might have been. In another month we'll make love in the streets. Listen to Satyrus, now.'

Other men were coming up – there was Memnon, no more pleased to find his wife in the streets than Abraham had been – and Damophilus and Menedemos and Socrates.

Satyrus took Damophilus' arm. 'How many of the *boule* are here? Round them up.'

'I do not take orders from you,' Damophilus shot back. Then he relented. 'We were all on the walls – they should be here.'

Satyrus raised a hand for silence. Helios had a pair of torches now, and he stepped up behind his master.

'This is for us,' Satyrus said. 'Not for the *Neodamodeis* or the mercenaries.'

Memnon understood immediately. You could see it in his face. And Menedemos.

'Gentlemen, when the west gate was opened to Demetrios, I smelled a rat. So did Panther. We took some action – to be honest, we hid certain things from the *boule*. Some weeks ago, I was fool enough to give Daedelus timings out in open council – and Demetrios was waiting for him. Last night, I told a member of the *boule* in detail how I would make my attack with the ephebes.' He paused to let that sink in. 'I lied. By some stades. Idomeneus, tell them what you saw.'

The Cretan stood forth. 'I went to the west wall – to the gully where Lord Satyrus told me to wait. There was almost a full *taxeis* waiting there – waiting in blackened armour. If I hadn't been warned, I would never have seen them.'

Satyrus grinned mirthlessly. 'They call it the poisoned pill, gentlemen. My tutor, Philokles, taught me the technique. Tell different men different lies, and wait to see who acts on which.' He turned. 'Lady Aspasia?'

'We saw Nicanor send a pigeon, immediately after the *boule* met,' she said.

At Nicanor's name, the crowd of citizens shifted nervously.

Satyrus led them to Nicanor's house. The man himself was not at home, an old slave reported.

'Fetch him out,' Satyrus said to Apollodorus.

'This is illegal!' Memnon said.

Satyrus motioned to Apollodorus. To Memnon, he said, 'The laws of the city will mean nothing if the city is destroyed.'

There was a shout – the ring of a blade – another shout of anger, curses. And then Apollodorus emerged, a piece of his plume cut away. 'He'll be out shortly,' Apollodorus said cheerfully.

'Your *creatures* killed my slave!' Nicanor said. He was in a chiton and a Persian over-robe. His arms were pinned by two Cretan archers.

'I took the liberty of securing his garden first,' Idomeneus said. He and Apollodorus exchanged a look.

Satyrus nodded. 'Nicanor, I accuse you of treason to the town. You opened the west gate and murdered the captain there. You informed Demetrios of our fleet movements. You attempted to have the *taxeis* of ephebes destroyed tonight.'

Nicanor met Satyrus' eyes easily enough. 'Well, well. We shall have quite an exciting trial. People may learn a great deal.'

Satyrus rubbed his chin. 'There will be no trial,' he said.

Memnon pushed forward. 'We are Rhodians!' he said. 'There *will* be a trial. Nicanor – if you have done this, the curse of every man and woman in this town is on your head.'

'Really?' Nicanor asked. His words were mild. Satyrus heard in them the words of a man with nothing to live for. 'Really? Or do they curse you and the young tyrant here for keeping them in this cesspit? We could have surrendered months ago—'

Satyrus shook his head. 'No. We tried. You tried.'

Nicanor turned on him and spittle flew. 'You – you carrion crow! All you want is war and death! It is *sport* to your kind. Not to us. My sons are *dead*. My wife is *dead*. I alone try to save this town when every one of you labours to destroy her. What do you have? *You have nothing*. The temples? All destroyed. The gymnasium? You pulled it down with your own hands. The agora is choked with slaves and *shit*. You eat *shit*. Look at the Jew's sister, dressed like a whore! And Memnon's wife – *shit*. You are no longer Greeks, no longer men. You are not even Hellenes. You are animals, you have lost even the semblance of civilisation. Because this Tyrant has taken your minds. Years ago, I told them to abandon Ptolemy and go with Antigonus. Had anyone listened, we would have had *none of this*. Now, everything we have ever had is gone, and it no longer matters whether you hold Demetrios off or whether he comes and his pigs rape every one of you to death, for the city is *destroyed*.'

Satyrus waited, impassive except when the man called Miriam a whore. 'Was that your defence?' he asked. He flicked his eyes back and forth to the two archers holding Nicanor. They were veterans.

'I need no defence. And when the Demos hear what I have to say in court, they will surrender the town faster than you can stop them.' He looked around. 'As you, the so-called worthies, ought to have done. Put halters around your necks and go and face the Golden King.'

He looked at Satyrus. 'And you – perhaps you made all this up? You and the metic woman and the Jew?' He grinned with confidence. 'You will regret this.'

'Not for the reasons you think, Nicanor,' Satyrus said, and his right hand rose under his armpit, his sword leaped from his scabbard and Nicanor clutched at his throat as blood burst from his severed neck.

The archers held his arms and his knees buckled.

Satyrus turned. 'I wanted it done in public. I did it myself, so that no other man need soil his hands. We do not need a trial – Nicanor would have won, even as he lost, poisoning one man against another.'

Memnon's face was parchment-white in the moonlight. 'You've – killed – him.'

Satyrus nodded. 'Listen to me, now. I have the soldiers and the crowd, and I could, very easily, declare myself Tyrant. To be honest, I think you people need a single voice and a strong hand. And yet, Nicanor said many things that were true – and here's the worst. We are losing the city. We may endure, and endure, and still have the heart of your city perish. So I think that we should try to rule through the *boule*, and I will take the chance that you gentlemen will feel that I need to be arrested.

'But hear me.' Satyrus looked around. They were silent – in shock, he thought. Nicanor's blood was dripping onto his foot. 'I demand – I *beg* that this night and this callous murder mark the end of faction. There is only one good, friends – the survival of the city. No party is more important than this, and if the city falls, you must believe me, the besiegers will leave *nothing*. Nicanor was deranged by grief. I am not. Put your factions on the shelf, link hands and swear to the gods to carry this thing through to the end like brothers and sisters, or by Herakles, I will wash my hands of you and sail away.'

Roughly – deliberately – he turned and wiped his sword blade carefully on Nicanor's cloak until the blade was clean. Then he put it back in his scabbard.

'Goodnight,' he said.

His officers closed around him, and his *hetairoi* around them. It was some consolation that they trusted him. Killing a man in cold blood was always hard – probably a sign that he was not completely mad, but he felt cold, angry, hopeless. And Miriam looked at him as if he were a mad dog.

He might have dwelled on her disapproval, but Anaxagoras and Abraham walked with him step by step.

'Had to be done,' Abraham said.

Quite possibly the sweetest words of Satyrus' life.

He stopped against a mostly intact building and threw up.

'The ephebes are still with us,' Anaxagoras said.

'I think I just gave you Miriam,' Satyrus said, without thinking.

'What's that?' Abraham asked.

I am a fool, Satyrus thought. 'Nothing, for the moment, brother,' he forced out, because his head could only take on one crisis at a time. *Help me out, Demetrios. Launch a night assault.*

'Wake up!' Helios said, and rubbed his cheek.

Satyrus came awake easily, swung his feet off the bed and reached for his sword.

'What?' he managed.

Helios held a cup of warm juice. At this point, Satyrus had no idea where the man came up with juice. 'The *boule* is meeting immediately. You are requested.'

Satyrus rose. 'Dress me well,' he said. 'Not like a democrat. Like a king. Get me Neiron, Abraham, Anaxagoras – and Apollodorus. And Idomeneus.'

He finished the juice, swigged water, used a twig of liquorice on his teeth and Helios laid out his best chiton, a flame-coloured cloth with tablet-woven edges in white and gold thread, with hem borders

– woven scenes from the *Iliad*. A chiton with the value of a ship.

He waited while Helios tied his best sandals – the Spartan style, in leather dyed to match the cloak. When Helios kirtled up his chiton, he did it with a matching red leather belt that fitted – again. For the first time in a year. And over the chiton and belt he slipped his best sword belt, although the sword that hung from it was a plain enough weapon – he'd broken three swords in the siege.

Helios oiled his hair and braided it into two braids, and wrapped them on his head. He put over his shoulders the matching chlamys – long, the deep red of new-spilled blood, with black ravens and yellow stars, the signs of his house.

Satyrus examined himself in a hand mirror. 'Very satisfactory,' he said. He walked to the tent opening. 'You come too, Helios. I want you to hear this.'

He went out into the small courtyard formed by his tent, Neiron's and Apollodorus'. There was a fire, taking the autumn chill off the air, and a circle of his men – his best. His companions. His friends. It made his heart soar, that he finally had *friends*, not just followers. Neiron – Draco – Anaxagoras.

'Gentlemen,' he said, and they murmured their greetings.

'We're ready,' Abraham said.

Satyrus shook his head. 'I've called you together to prevent just such a misunderstanding,' Satyrus said. 'I expect no trouble from the *boule*. But they may act against me – indeed, they may arrest me. They may even feel that they *have* to arrest me, against their own desires.' Satyrus raised his arms and indicated his finery. 'I'm trying to dress to remind them who I am – but I may fail. If they take me, gentlemen, you are to submit absolutely to their instructions.'

That got a reaction. Idomeneus spat. 'Like fuck!' the Cretan said.

'Listen, friends,' Satyrus said. 'We're here to do a job. I've said this from the start – I'm *King of the Bosporus*, not King of Rhodes. If you quarrel with these men, *the town will fall*. We win – as a team – when Demetrios sails away from these walls, and our grain warehouses and all the merchants who deal with us are safe. We win if we beat Demetrios here, because by winning here, *we assure he will never come to our homes in the Euxine*. Arrest me, put me on trial – if you continue to fight on, if Jubal springs his lovely trap—'

'Jubal has a trap?' Neiron asked.

'I've avoided talking about it until Nicanor was ... put down.' Satyrus shrugged. 'Obey me, friends. Just this once – no heroics, no running amok.'

Idomeneus was the first to embrace him. 'I'll obey,' he said, 'but what you're really saying is that the stupid wide-arses intend to arrest you!'

Satyrus was mobbed by his friends, which he enjoyed thoroughly. It helped wipe some of the blood from his hands. 'Yes,' he said ruefully.

Neiron embraced him last. 'We've had our differences,' he said.

Satyrus had to smile. 'Better to say, "there have been times we've agreed".'

'But you were right to kill him. You're a tyrannicide, not a tyrant. And many here feel as I do.' There were tears in the man's eyes.

Beyond Neiron was Abraham. 'They're fools,' he said. He and Satyrus embraced.

And outside the courtyard was Miriam, hollow-eyed with fatigue.

Satyrus' heart rose when he saw her. She didn't shirk meeting his eye, and he felt that he had to say something.

'I had to do it,' he said. It sounded lame, put like that.

She stepped up to him and kissed him, causing her brother to go white with shock. 'Someone had to do it,' she said. 'As usual, you did it yourself.'

'You are the very mistress of ambiguity,' he said. Her chaste kiss felt like a new bruise. He wanted to lick his lips. Or hers.

She smiled from under her eyelashes, and then he was walking away, as if nothing had happened.

The *boule* did not arrest him, or order him to trial, or to be executed.

They appointed him polemarch, the war commander of the city.

28

DAY SIXTY AND FOLLOWING

The seventy-fifth day of the siege, Diokles slipped out of a long line of storm clouds with four captured Athenian grain ships – great ships, the height of four men – and ran them into the outer harbour before any of Demetrios' ships dared leave the beach. Diokles' former helmsmen had time to embrace him once, wave at the soldiers piling ashore and laugh.

'We're killing Demetrios at sea,' he said. 'And Leon snapped up a whole Athenian relief squadron. Do you need us to get you out of here?'

Satyrus shook his head. 'I'm the commander,' he said.

Diokles laughed. 'I should have known. If there's smoke, there you are, fanning it. Leon says to tell Panther to send all the rest of their fleet to sea – we have Syme and two other ports, and we're getting ready to challenge the bugger before winter sets in. We've got six thousand Aegyptians ready to land, and your impetuous sister is up at Timaea with Nikephorus and Coenus and all your mercenaries.'

Satyrus nodded. 'Superb – but only if you can keep us fed.'

'You must need more men!' Diokles said.

Satyrus nodded. 'I need men. I need archers – every archer is worth ten men. But food is the sticking point, and soon, very soon, Apollo will start to shoot his poisoned shafts into the town. There's people in the *Neodamodeis* camp who look ... well, like sick people.'

Diokles winced. 'I'll tell Leon. You tell Panther.'

'Panther's dead,' Satyrus said.

'Poseidon!' Diokles said. 'Hades. I loved that man.' He looked around. 'This place looks as if it has been crushed under Zeus' heel. Can you hold another month?'

Satyrus nodded. 'We hold this town one day at a time,' he said.

The disease started in the slave camps. Too many of them had *not* been freed – at least, in Satyrus' opinion. The ones left enslaved were prey to despair. And poor diet and despair were the breeding grounds of disease. Satyrus was a pious man, but he had no trouble noting that hungry men got sick faster than full men.

Women were next. And when they were sick, their men got sick.

Three weeks after his confident assertion that he had all the men he needed, Satyrus was guarding the walls with fewer than a thousand men. Apollo was stalking his own city, and his poisoned shafts were reaping a rich harvest.

Satyrus fought off a probing assault on the latest south curtain wall with his own marines and the ephebes. The rest of the garrison was sick. Or dead. Apollodorus' marines were curiously immune. Charmides, who was by then madly in love with Aspasia's daughter Nike, went from sick bed to sick bed, reckless of the disease, and it never touched him.

Miriam did the same, and Satyrus got a hint of the fear he might cause in those who loved him – she went from sick tent to sick tent, and he shuddered for her. Had Miriam not been a Jew, the town would have offered to make her Aspasia's deputy priestess – she went everywhere that the older woman went, to rich and poor, and neither of them had sickened.

So far.

On the eighty-eighth day of the siege, with the first breath of autumn weather off the harbour, heavy mist rising from the warm water on a brisk morning, Diokles appeared with a pair of ships – Tanais merchant ships, loaded to the gunwales with grain, wine, oil and archers.

Sakje archers.

Bundles of arrows – long, heavy cedar shafts for the Cretans. Cane arrows and stiff pine shafts for the Sakje.

The Sakje came off the ships in a mob, and the sound of their rough voices and the smell of their coats made him smile. He smiled even more when he saw men he knew – and women, too. Scopasis, and Thyrsis, both carrying heavy woolsacks.

'No horses here!' Satyrus quipped at Scopasis.

The former bandit with the scarred face squinted, and his scars made a smile that made most men blanch. 'Lady says come. We come.' He clasped hands with Satyrus.

'How is she?' Satyrus asked. 'Gods, I miss her!'

'Good!' Melitta said. She was wearing a pale caribou-hide coat worked in blue – their mother's, he thought. She was ... stronger-looking than ever. She looked like an intelligent hawk – small, fierce and ready to *eat* anything she didn't like. She had a line of white in her blue-black hair. 'I missed you too. And since you couldn't be bothered to come home and rule your own kingdom, I've come here to fetch you back.'

She hugged him, and he hugged her.

They walked up through the town, hand in hand.

'Smells like death,' she said.

'That's your war name, not mine,' he said.

'This town smells like death. Like shit.' She shook her head. 'Why are you here?'

Satyrus stopped. 'They need me. And this is our grain centre.'

Melitta grinned. 'Save it for people who don't know you.'

'I'm in love,' Satyrus said.

'That's more like it. So – can I kill Amastris?' Melitta waved at Demetrios' camp.

Satyrus hugged her. 'I've missed you.'

'I've missed you, too. Where is this paragon? Have you married her?' She asked.

Satyrus paused. 'She – she may love someone else.'

Melitta raised an eyebrow. 'Let me get this right. You are squandering our kingdom's riches for a town where there's a woman you love who you don't know, for *certain* sure, loves you?'

Satyrus found himself smiling.

'Sister, it's the siege of Troy.' He shrugged. 'Wait until you meet her!'

'Gods, you are doomed.' She laughed. 'Any handsome young princes?'

'Eh? What of Scopasis?' he asked.

Melitta saw Abraham in the distance, and waved. Abraham waved back. 'I can't go around sleeping with my officers. It's bad for discipline,' she said.

'Doesn't seem to hurt the Spartans,' Satyrus quipped.

'Are you joking?' she asked. 'Did you listen when Philokles described the inequities of the king's justice?'

'It *was* a joke, Melitta,' Satyrus managed. 'Abraham – you remember my sister?'

Abraham got a crushing embrace. 'How could I forget – the very Queen of the Amazons?'

He smiled, and she smiled, and then he turned. 'You remember my sister, Miriam?' he said.

Miriam stepped forward – Satyrus knew her well enough now to see that her motion was very tentative. She was unsure of herself with Melitta.

Melitta had, when Miriam last saw her, been a Greek woman with good clothes, beautiful hair and a philosophical education that Miriam envied deeply. Now she was a scarred woman with enormous, shockingly blank blue eyes and an armoured shirt over a barbarian coat and trousers.

Miriam saw a woman with a mob of brown hair and long, naked legs.

Satyrus could only marvel at how much similarity he saw between them.

'Well,' Melitta said. She kissed Miriam. 'I must say, that style suits you.'

Miriam laughed. 'We call it the "Great Siege of Rhodes" style.'

Melitta grinned. 'Ever do any archery, Miriam?'

That night, in honour of his sister's arrival, Satyrus gave a party. A symposium. The recent loss of the third line of the south wall had placed the southern fringe of the agora within the long range of Demetrios' engines, so Satyrus got his marines and sailors to clear the tiled floor of what had been Abraham's dining room – they needed the rubble anyway, for the fourth south wall – and then he moved *pithoi* of wine, fresh from the ships, and fresh-baked bread and some olive oil and cheese – riches in a town under siege – to the excavated floor.

The invitees brought cushions if they had them, and all lay on cloaks, and there was a fire in the hearth, as the evening held an autumnal chill. As polemarch, Satyrus had arranged to issue every man and woman in the town with some wine, some oil and some bread – the symposiasts weren't getting anything that any other citizen didn't have.

Six months of lessons had *not* made Satyrus a master lyricist, but he managed the first fifty lines of the *Iliad* and received the applause due a swordsman who has learned the harp – that is, there was some jeering and some good-natured mockery.

Anaxagoras played with Miriam, and they played Sappho's ode to Aphrodite.

Apollodorus was, at that moment, sharing Satyrus' cloak. 'That's a dangerous song to play at a symposium,' he said.

Satyrus shrugged. 'They play beautifully.'

Melitta took Apollodorus' place. She was warmer, but she wriggled and wriggled under the cloak like an eel in a trap. 'You are sharing Abraham's sister with that beautiful man?' she asked. 'Does he fight?'

'Like a young god,' Satyrus said happily. 'Yes.'

'Good, then,' Melitta said. 'I approve of her indecision, and I approve of your choice. Worth ten of Amastris.'

She lay still. The wine bowl came by and he rose out of his cloak, drank and noticed that she had shed her Sakje clothes under the cloak and emerged as a Greek woman in a very short chiton. He choked.

'If Miriam can play Artemis, I certainly can,' Melitta said. 'I have good legs, and the moon is full. Here, have some wine.' He took back the cup, and his sister slipped away.

Other men rose to play. Damophilus played the kithara. Memnon and Apollodorus sang together, and Charmides played a few halting tunes. Helios sang.

Melitta and Miriam were hardly the only women. Aspasia lay with her husband, Memnon, and her daughter Nike did not – quite – share Charmides' cloak, although she sat *very near*. As the drinking moved on to the third bowl, Satyrus noted that women – and some men – came out of the darkness to sit or lie by their partners – Plestias the ephebe and his sister, whose name Satyrus didn't know, but who he realised he had seen near his tent – *near Helios' tent*, now that he gave it a moment's thought. A slave-girl with brilliant red hair – he'd certainly seen *her* – looked utterly out of place until Jubal scooped her off her feet and carried her to his couch.

Satyrus made his way to his feet. Three bowls of wine, and he was light-headed – they were all out of practice.

He stood. 'I wanted everyone to have a lovely evening,' he said.

They fell silent a little at a time. He smiled around at them until they were still.

'I want to welcome my sister,' he said, raising the *kylix*, and there was a cheer.

'And I want to tell you that we're about to enter the very worst part of the siege,' Satyrus said.

Memnon said something to his wife – meant to be quiet, but quite loud, in the tension. 'Here it comes,' he said.

There were giggles.

Satyrus walked a few steps. 'Jubal?' he said, and handed the black man his *kylix*.

Jubal rose, patting his girl's haunch. 'Not much to say. Maybe two days, maybe three – then Demetrios – he rush the fourth wall. They fall faster an' faster,' he said, and he grinned. He swept an arm through the air in an arc. 'South wall used to be straight, like an arrow, eh?' He nodded. 'An' now it bends, like a bow. Little by little, Golden Boy punches deeper.' He looked around. 'Nex' punch, he go deep enough to hit th' agora with his engines. Lord, yes.' Jubal was grinning like a jackal.

'Course, 'less he's got lot smarter, he won't notice that his engines are inside the bow, when he moves them.' Jubal drank from the *kylix*.

'And then what happens?' Melitta asked.

'Jus' you wait an' see, lady.' Jubal's grin rivalled the moon. 'Got to be a surprise!' He nodded. 'But what Lor' Satyrus wan' me to say is this – this wall's the las' wall we lose. No more room to give groun' – no more. This wall gotta stan'.' He handed the *kylix* to Satyrus.

Satyrus looked around. 'You think we're goners, friends. We've been here more than four months. Some of us have already been here a year. We're getting regular supplies, and we've all heard there's thousands more men ready to come to us, fifty ships at Syme and twenty more across the straits. Abraham says that the Greek cities are begging Demetrios to give up the siege. Athens will be under siege from Cassander this winter.'

He nodded. 'If we were facing One-Eye; if we were facing Lysimachos, or Ptolemy, or Seleucus – this siege would be over. We're not. If we win here, the Antigonids will never be the same again. Demetrios' notions of his own deity will never be the same

404

again. Demetrios will very soon become desperate. Indeed, if Jubal's trick works, it will be the last straw. And then—' Satyrus took a deep breath, 'and then he'll stop fucking around and throw the whole of his fifty thousand men at the walls.'

They gasped all the way around the fire circle.

'And we have to hold. So drink. Relax. But remember – in three days, we start the last part. For good or ill.' Satyrus went to Abraham, and sat on his cloak.

'One way to help the party along,' Abraham said.

Anaxagoras played a marching song of Tyrtaeus, and then a drinking song of Alcaeus, and they sang. Indeed, more and more people came out of the dark, some with their own wine, and the singers sang. More and more voices were raised against the night.

Scopasis came and lay with his back against Satyrus' knees.

'You still love her,' Satyrus said.

Scopasis shrugged. 'How's the fighting?'

Satyrus looked out into the ring of faces. 'Terrifying. The hardest I've ever known. The worst of it is that it is all the time – every day. There's no rest, except this,' and Satyrus raised his wine cup.

Scopasis sneered. 'You never outlaw. Outlaw fight every day.' Scopasis paused. 'No – not fight. *Fear fight*. Every day.'

'Well,' Satyrus said. He drank wine and stared at the embers on the hearth. 'Yes. That's what it's like.'

Scopasis nodded. 'I brought plenty arrows,' he said with professional satisfaction. 'Love her till I die,' he suddenly added. 'Want to die old.'

He walked off into the singing.

Later, they danced. Satyrus was surprised – shocked, even – when Miriam started it. She rose to her feet, gathered an armful of brushwood – someone's dead garden – and threw it on the hearth.

'Let's dance!' she called with the gay abandon of a maenad or a bacchante. Other women gathered around her, slave and free, beautiful and plain, tall, thin and they pulled off their sandals – those fastidious enough to have them in the first place, and men hurried to sweep the tile floor clear with their cloaks. And Melitta was there, her hand in Miriam's hand, and Aspasia, her hand in Melitta's – the redhaired Keltoi slave, rich men's daughters and poor men's daughters, some with high heads and straight necks like the dancers on Athenian pottery, and some watching their feet, one young maiden with her tongue protruding between her teeth like a kitten, concentrating on the complexities of the dance, and around they went, with Anaxagoras playing the hymn to Demeter and then embellishing it.

Satyrus sat with Abraham again, back to back on their cloaks, watching the women dance, their legs flashing – the trend to the briefest possible chitoniskos was even more daring when Persephone's birth was celebrated and her trip to the underworld re-enacted in dance. Satyrus watched them all, and Melitta paused in front of him, raised her arms with the other dancers and grinned at him before her eyes went ... elsewhere.

And then Miriam paused in her turn. And her eyes went through him – she was looking nowhere else, and the quarter-smile on her face was for him, her hands on her hips were his hands, and she leaped—

'Are you in love with my sister?' Abraham asked.

'Yes,' Satyrus said, with a sigh.

'God!' Abraham said. 'Job did not have a trial like Miriam. You *too*?' He shook his head. 'I make a joke – I always make a joke. In truth, my friend, I am – angry.'

Satyrus watched her long legs and her smile a quarter of the way around the circle. 'Someone should free the Keltoi girl,' he said.

Abraham nodded. 'The Keltoi girl is *not* my problem. My sister is. You can't marry her. What do you mean to do – keep her as a mistress? Hide her away?'

Satyrus sighed again. 'Friend, I have no idea. None. But I'll offer this – why *shouldn't* I marry her?'

Abraham turned to look him in the eye. 'Oh – you will become a Jew?'

Satyrus frowned. 'Don't be foolish.'

Abraham glared at him. 'Foolish, is it?'

Satyrus raised a hand. 'Let's be sure of our arguments, shall we? I have nothing but respect for the God of the Jews. But my god is Herakles.'

Abraham shook his head. 'Herakles is a silly myth for children. Gods do not personify themselves – they do not come to earth and make love to mortals and all that foolishness. Or perhaps he's merely the memory of a great man – a warrior. You claim him as an ancestor, do you not?'

'And the God of the Jews has done so well for your people – the "chosen". You rule the world, do you not? You Jews?' Satyrus had never said such a thing out loud, and he was none too proud he'd done it. He put his hand out. 'Sorry – that was uncalled for.'

Abraham was red, but at Satyrus' touch he shook his head. 'Don't think I haven't thought it. Sometimes it *all* seems a sham. What god would allow this?' Abraham looked up.

'What, a party?' Satyrus quipped.

'War. This siege. Nicanor. Demetrios.' He shrugged.

Satyrus frowned. 'The world exists so that we may compete, and by competing, show the gods our worth.' He shrugged.

Abraham narrowed his eyes. 'Those slaves out there, puking their lives away with fever – what are they competing for?'

Satyrus shrugged. 'No idea.'

'You are no empty-head. Don't you care?' Abraham asked. 'When you killed Nicanor, what did you feel?'

'You sound like Philokles, brother. No, I don't care. I care for them – when I meet them – one at a time. As a mass – slaves – I can't care. I can care for my men, for my city, for myself. I can work to make a better city on the Euxine, to make my farmers richer, to make my soldiers triumphant. I can't feed the slaves, much less free them. When Nicanor betrays his city, he is less than worthless – I cut him down as I would kill a mad dog. And he won't haunt my dreams.'

The women had stopped dancing. They were looking expectantly at the men, who were mostly applauding like mad, except for Abraham and Satyrus. Abraham stared off as if he didn't even know women existed. After a pause, he said, 'My sister loathed her husband. He was a good man. A merchant. A quiet, honourable man.' He rolled his shoulders. 'And when he died, she *rejoiced*.' He spat the word. 'And now she shares her favours between Hellenes. You know that she makes cow eyes at Anaxagoras as well? Eh?'

Satyrus laughed. 'How could I not know?' he said, and looked at Anaxagoras.

The musician was wrapped up only in his lyre.

Abraham spat.

Satyrus laughed. 'You, my friend, are suffering from an excess of bile. And the women want us to dance. I *know* that you know the dance of Ares.'

Abraham rose to his feet. 'Of all your Greek gods, Ares is the one I understand.'

Satyrus took his hand to lead him out. 'You understand *Ares*?'

'Hateful Ares? The brash, boastful coward, fomenter of strife, god of slaughter, ruin and mindless combat?' Abraham spoke with so much vehemence that spittle flew. 'I see him made manifest every day. How could I pretend he doesn't exist? Perhaps his mean and spiteful mind rules the world. Perhaps *he is the only god*.'

Satyrus was struck dumb, and he put a hand to his mouth.

Abraham picked up a cup, drank some wine and spat.

'Jews are great ones for blasphemy,' he said, and managed a smile. 'Let's dance.'

The men chose to dance the Pyrriche. It was no hardship – every man present had a spear and a shield, and months of incessant warfare made them so confident that no one even proposed that they bate their spears.

Because many of them were men of Tanais, they danced it the Euxine way, and the first two verses were a vicious tangle – Satyrus had a cut on his right bicep where Menedemos forgot the new steps. But they were all dancers – almost every warrior present had competed in the Pyrriche – and they learned fast, and by the time the third verse of the hymn rose to the heavens, the Euxine men's knees and the Rhodian men's knees all rose together, kicked, spun, leaped—

The first roar of the crowd, already growing.

Anaxagoras played – first the hymn to Ares, and then, subtly, he changed the tune, and he whispered to Miriam as he played, and she picked up her kithara and Aspasia joined in with a small lyre. Note by note they moved the tune from the brash striving of Ares to the military wisdom of Athens, the hymn to Athena.

And the men, in four lines, stood forth, brandished spears, fell back through ranks, turned, thrust, leaped, and parried all together, and if steps were missed, they were lost in the flood of *eudaimonia*.

At some point, the women began to sing, and more men and women were drawn out of the darkness by the fire and the music, so rare in a city under siege. Men sat on the crumpled ruins of houses they had once owned and raised their voices together, and women pushed forward until they could see the men dance, faster and faster.

Satyrus could see them at the edge of the old foundations, hundreds of people singing the paean to Athena – possibly thousands – and he was lifted out of himself to leap the higher, snap faster from posture to posture, as if Theron and Philokles were there to watch his every move—

He spun to clash his spear against a shield and there was Charmides, his beauty like a blaze of light, and the younger man leaped so high that Satyrus was able to sweep his spear shaft *under* the man's feet. Charmides landed, his smile so broad that it threatened to swallow his face, and his counter-thrust went *over* Satyrus' head as the polemarch stretched along the ground, front leg out-thrust, rear leg nearly flat, head ducked. The people nearest to them cheered, roared and pointed and Satyrus dared to *roll* forward, tucking his shield, and stood *behind* Charmides – the other dancers exchanged less extreme postures, but Satyrus was, for this one figure, the lead, and Charmides answered by flipping *backward* over his shield, a feat Satyrus had never seen done. The crowd by them erupted and the hymn drove on inexorably to the end, two thousand voices now—

Come, Athena, now if ever!
Let us now thy Glory see!
Now, O Maid and Queen, we pray thee,
Give thy servants victory!

Satyrus found himself weeping, and Apollodorus was weeping, and Charmides and Abraham. And Melitta took his hand and kissed him, and smiled boldly at Charmides. 'Our father's war song,' she said.

Then she kissed the boy. 'You are a very handsome lad,' she said. And walked off to congratulate the musicians.

Two stades away, wrapped in a cloak on the edge of the abatis that protected the Antigonid sentry wall, Lucius listened with Stratokles. Even two stades away, the hymn to Athena was loud enough to hinder conversation.

Lucius sighed. 'Can I tell you something, boss?' he asked.

Stratokles found that he was so choked up he couldn't speak, so there was a long pause. 'When do you not say whatever you like?' he managed, with tear-filled eyes.

'We're on the wrong fucking side, boss.' Lucius took out a gold toothpick. 'I'm a pious man, boss. Demetrios is – ah, cunt, I don't know what he is. We don't invoke the gods. The priests in this camp are lickspittles. The Macedonians just go through the motions – Hades, Stratokles, they worship demons and spirits! Fucking barbarians, if you ask me. Worse than Etruscans.' Lucius picked his teeth. 'You heard that hymn, right? Fuckin' arse-cunts had what – a thousand singing?' He looked at Stratokles, who was struggling between a desire unburden to the closest thing he had to a friend and the desire to discipline the closest thing he had to a subordinate.

Friendship won. 'I know,' he said. Under the circumstances, he was proud of the laconic reply.

'When our boys roll up that breach, they're already afraid. How many have the arse-cunts killed? And they just got reinforcements, eh? Our boys are *already whipped*. And the Rhodians are *singing hymns*.' Lucius got what he was after, stared at his toothpick for a moment and put it away. 'If they win this thing, people will remember them for ever. Like the fucking Trojans.'

'The Trojans lost, Lucius,' Stratokles said.

'My point exactly.' Lucius spat. 'An' they didn't lose. Aeneas brought the survivors to Rome. Ask anyone.'

Stratokles decided to pass on this point of regional belligerence. 'The problem is – Athens.'

'Always is, with you. Boss.' Lucius laughed. 'Mind you, it's why I stick with you. You ain't one of these godless cunts. You are a proper city man. Athens first and always. Eh?'

Stratokles smiled. In the doomed city, there was cheering and laughter. 'Athens is about to be besieged by Cassander,' he said. 'Because Demetrios is here with all his father's best troops.'

'Well, make me *strategos*, then, 'cause I can solve that in two shakes of a lamb's tail.' Lucius was flat on his back, watching the stars. 'Demetrios has *overcommitted*.'

Stratokles laughed. 'Oh, thanks. I had no idea.' He laughed again.

Lucius rolled onto his elbow. 'You got a plan?'

Stratokles rubbed his eyes. 'Yes. But the question – no really, friend, I seek your advice – the question is this. Do I help Golden Boy take the city? Or do I help the Athenian delegation that's on its way to convince him to drop the siege? Either way, I'm helping my city. And I, too, am ... how did you say it? Pious. I heard the hymn.'

Lucius nodded. 'Like that.' He stared off into the night. He rubbed his beard, spat and turned back to Stratokles. 'Well, nice to be asked, boss. Yes. Here's how I see it. War's chancy, and nothing chancier than a siege, eh? No matter what you do for Golden Boy, he could lose here. My professional opinion? His odds is no better than one in two, now. But if he walks away – well, Zeus Saviour, then he has the largest army in Europe and he can be at Athens in five days.' Lucius paused. 'Didn't you tell me that if he failed here, he an' his *pater* were done for?'

Stratokles had picked up a straw and started to chew on it. 'Yes. It'll take a few years. But they *must* win here.'

Both men stared at the distant city.

'Well,' Lucius said after a time, 'I have a plan of my own to put into effect, tonight.' He got up and dusted his chiton with his hands.

Stratokles was startled. 'A raid?' he asked.

'Only on Aphrodite, boss. A deep-penetration raid,' he said with a lewd chuckle.

The party was on the eighth bowl. It was hard to keep count by Greek standards, because the darkness was full of people and wine now, and there was more wine circulating than could possibly have come off the ships with Diokles – rich men much have broached their stores, or poorer men looted it from ruined cellars. Anything was possible – but Satyrus couldn't help noticing that his people were drunk. Very, very drunk.

He hoped that the ephebes were in their places on the walls, because Apollodorus – just as an example – wasn't going to be able to fight off an assault of kittens. The marine captain was locked in a passionate embrace with his girl – whoever she was, she was so wrapped in his cloak that he looked as if he was being attacked by the garment.

Charmides sat among three girls, all beautiful, dishevelled and determined to be last in the field. By sheer persistence, if not by charm or beauty. But he had eyes only for Nike, who sat with her mother, trying to be demure and failing in a most charming way. Satyrus wondered if any woman had ever looked at him with the same longing.

Jubal didn't bother to cloak himself, lacking Apollodorus' careful gentleman's education. But he was engaged in the same activity, and the slave-girl's red hair was almost as good as a cloak.

Satyrus tried not to let this evening's good humour be poisoned by the fact that Anaxagoras was missing, as was Miriam. He had accomplished a miracle in improved morale – and Melitta was here. Somewhere. Satyrus could see Scopasis – who was not alone – and a pair of Sakje spear-maidens who had seized two young aristocrats.

Satyrus locked hard on his jealousy. It was unworthy. What was *unfair*, he felt, was that *he* should be alone while all of them had someone. Aphrodite was heavy on the air, and he—

Self-pity is among the ugliest of the emotions, Philokles seemed to say in his ear.

Abraham was standing in the middle, near the hearth, like Dionysus – a vaguely Aramaic Dionysus in a long robe, a garland of olive on his head, a wine cup in each hand.

'People keep handing them to me,' he said. 'Have one, brother.'

Satyrus took one and kissed his friend on the cheek. 'You should go to bed,' he said.

'Want to play feed the flute girl!' Abraham said with drunken assertiveness. 'Want to *live*.'

'Not the right party, brother,' Satyrus said.

'I love you, brother,' Abraham said.

Even through the wine, Abraham's good will beamed and Satyrus embraced him.

'You too, comrade.' He got an arm around his friend, lifted him, wine cup sloshing, and walked him along the street.

'Even when I dress like a Jew?' Abraham asked. 'I am a Jew, you know,' he said, 'even when I dress like a Greek.'

'Always,' Satyrus said.

'You love my sister always, I can see that much,' Abraham pronounced, as if giving the law. 'My *pater* is going to kill all of us, you know that? You, me, her, Anaxagoras – dead, brother. Please tell me you haven't … you know …' And Abraham stumbled, caught himself, put his hands on Satyrus' shoulders. 'Please?'

Satyrus could tell that the man was earnest – deadly earnest.

He took Abraham's shoulders. 'Never,' he said. 'My solemn oath – on my ancestors.'

'Ah!' Abraham said. He nodded happily. 'Knew it,' he said,

unconvincingly. 'Please don't. Listen – siege is wrecking everything – don't. Please? Promise?'

Satyrus, painfully aware that Miriam had been off in the dark with Anaxagoras for more than an hour, felt his face go hot. But he was too much of a gentleman to tell his friend that he had the wrong suitor.

'I swear,' he said.

'On that ancestor – the old one – the hero?' Abraham asked.

'Arimnestos?' Satyrus smiled. 'I will swear by him. I swear on my heroised ancestor I will not debauch your sister.'

Abraham nodded. 'That's good,' he said.

Satyrus managed to lead Abraham across the agora – not that far, usually, but quite far with a loud, drunk man on your shoulder – and to his tent, where Jacob, Abraham's steward, was sitting outside the tent on a stool.

Satyrus shuffled to a stop. 'Some help here, please?'

Jacob got up heavily, placed his own wine cup on the ground with exaggerated care and got a shoulder under his master's arm. 'At your service, lord king!' he said with careful enunciation. Together, they lowered Abraham onto a pile of furs and blankets, and Jacob threw a heavy wool cloak over him. 'Good for him,' he said. 'Looks like he's had a good night.' Jacob, who was usually an invisible shadow, was jocund with wine. 'Not everyone did,' he said.

Satyrus had no idea what the man was on about, so he slapped him on the back in a meaningless gesture – the affections of one drunk to another – and stumbled out through the tent flap, feeling drunker by the moment, as if the exertion of getting Abraham to bed had accelerated the fumes of wine to his head. He paused, aware that he should walk the circuit of the walls – and be sure. Sure that they were safe. Was that drunk thinking?

And aware that he should be a lot more sober, and have a guard. He took a deep breath, and smelled jasmine – just time to flinch away, to think—

'It is you,' Miriam said.

'Mostly, it's your brother,' Satyrus said. He was confused – delighted – to find her here. Delighted, unless that was Anaxagoras in the darkness behind her.

She laughed. 'Aphrodite fills this night. Oh, I'm a poor Jew,' she said, stepped in and put her arms around his neck, and kissed him.

Satyrus was not an inexperienced man, but a man may have sex many times without being kissed – kissed at length, kissed thoroughly, kissed as the release of many months of longing. Satyrus never thought that he was standing in the door of Abraham's tent, or that Jacob had to be *right there*. In fact, Satyrus didn't think of anything at all. It went on and on – was uncomfortable, was too long, was passionate, was perfect. Her mouth was the entire universe – a better universe.

Then she pushed him away – not ungently. 'Please, just walk away,' she said. 'I went to bed – in my tent – to stop this.' In the distant firelight, he could just see her half-smile; longing, self-derision, amusement, self-loathing all mixed. 'And you brought him to bed.'

Satyrus caught her up, pressed her body against his. Dived into her again. But when her hands left his neck and pressed his chest, he stepped back.

'Please walk away,' she said.

'I love you,' he said, hopelessly.

'*Walk away*,' she said.

He did. In his head he heard Abraham's plea. *Please don't.* He shook his head, suddenly sober, aroused, his body heavy with energy and suppressed lust. He pushed into his own tent.

Helios was still up. He was lying blissfully with his girl, their faces beaming, their hair plastered against their heads with sweat. Satyrus felt guilty about interrupting. But before he could withdraw, Helios saw him and leaped to his feet. 'Lord!' he said.

'I need you,' Satyrus said. 'I'm sorry, lad, but I need to make a circuit of the walls.'

Helios nodded. 'Immediately, lord. I'll send her away.'

Satyrus shook his head. 'Tell her you'll be back in an hour, and leave her to sleep.' He put his shield on his shoulder.

Together, they walked along the waterfront, challenged by each of the ephebes in the makeshift towers as they passed. 'Sounded like a great party,' one young man was bold enough to assert. Satyrus smiled.

'Your turn will come, young man,' he said. Pomposity comes easily, with command.

Up the inner harbour, past the new false wall – Satyrus never let the slaves stop building. It was always possible that Demetrios would try another assault on the harbour. A long detour around the new construction where the harbour wall met the north wall, the sea wall that faced the open sea. Always neglected, because there was no real beach – or so it seemed until Memnon had shown him where smugglers landed routinely.

Past the construction, and along the north wall – only a handful of sentries, and Satyrus was surprised to find that most of them were his sister's Sakje. Where the north wall met the west wall and the robust new fortifications with their modern ditches and towers began, he found Thyrsis, also making his rounds.

'Who put you on duty?' Satyrus asked.

'Melitta,' he answered.

Satyrus shrugged. 'You missed quite a party,' he said.

'That's why she sent me away,' Thyrsis said. He shrugged.

'Aphrodite, not you too!' Satyrus said.

Thyrsis was rueful. 'Oh, yes.' He spat in the Sakje way, over the wall. 'If she does not marry soon, we will follow her around in packs.'

'She is very beautiful,' Helios put in.

Satyrus got a glimpse of how Abraham no doubt felt. 'You find her attractive? And her war name is *Smells like Death.*'

'What could be more beautiful?' Thyrsis said.

Helios nodded.

'Oh, Abraham,' Satyrus said.

Across the west wall. Satyrus didn't expect Demetrios would *ever* try the west wall, but it was so strong that he spent extra time there, peering into the darkness, trying to shake the perception that he'd allowed a night of drunken riot and that Demetrios was going to use that against him. Scaling ladders, perhaps?

And down along the south wall, now a deep, deep bow, from the corner of the west wall where the original fortifications still stood, along the bow – the fourth wall that they had constructed, now really more of a mound of rubble in a long deep curve, with a hasty ditch in front and a shallow trench just behind, and deeper trenches and loop-holed ruined buildings behind that. The wall and ditch were the highest since the loss of the outer wall – after all, Jubal and Neiron had agreed that this one had to be held to the end.

Walking the south wall was hard – and sobering. Twice, Satyrus clambered over the 'wall' into what was now the debatable ground: once to listen to see if he could hear sounds of digging, and the second time—

'Go and wake Jubal and get me twenty men,' Satyrus said to Helios. 'No questions, lad. Run!'

Satyrus stood perfectly still, tensed and completely sober, and waited. There it was again.

Chink. Tink.

And then nothing, for a long time.

Just when he wondered if he had torn Jubal from red-hair's arms for nothing ...

Clink.

'Here I am,' Jubal said.

'Shhh!' Satyrus hushed him. He was on the ground in front of the wall – fifty feet in front of the rubble wall, out in no-man's land.

A line of men were picking their way down the rubble slope. They made a lot of noise.

Over in the enemy lines, there was a shout.

'Get back!' Satyrus said, as low as he could. 'Back!'

Charmides froze. He had heard his lord.

A slim figure barked a sharp command. The file turned and began to climb the slope. Melitta was leading his twenty men – probably all the soberest men – and they'd been spotted.

More shouting in the enemy lines.

'Listen!' Satyrus whispered.

Clink.

Jubal nodded sharply. 'Got him,' he said. He tore a strip off his cloak with his knife, walked a few paces, picked up a section of pike shaft and stuck the rag on the end. Then he lay flat. From his prone position, he said, 'They mus' be stopped, lord. If'n they get through—'

Satyrus understood immediately. He tore another strip off Jubal's cloak as the man lay flat, and he used his sword to cut a second length of spear shaft.

A rock whistled out of the darkness and struck the rubble wall, and gravel and shards of rock sprayed. Satyrus was hit in the back, but he wasn't knocked down.

Then another rock fell.

'They jus' get better an' better,' Jubal said. 'Got him.' He reached out, and Satyrus put the second flag in his hand, and Jubal crawled a few feet and stuck the shaft between two rocks. 'One more,' he said.

Satyrus had to go quite a way to find another spear shaft. A rock came out of the dark – two rocks, he could tell from the impact. Too damned close. Now he had a cut on his cheek.

It occurred to him, lying scared and alone in the dark, at the very edge of the enemy zone, that he was the polemarch and that someone else could have done this. And it burst on him like a rapid sunrise that Miriam had *kissed him*.

He chuckled, and a hand closed on his mouth.

'Got you,' the man hissed.

Melitta waited in the dead ground beyond the rubble wall, her hip pressed – not without careful planning – against that of the musician. 'What are they doing?' she hissed.

'No idea,' Anaxagoras answered her. 'He's like this.' Anaxagoras laughed silently, and Melitta felt it through their hips. 'And I thought he'd gone off with Miriam.'

A rock hit the other face of the rubble, and chips sprayed like deadly mud from a child's pebble, when children throw rocks into a pool after rain.

'Ah – damn,' Anaxagoras said.

'Let me see,' Melitta said. 'Keep your head down – you – what's your name?'

'Hellenos, Despoina.' The young aristocrat was relatively sober.

'Tell the other men to be quiet. And get me Scopasis.' She waved. 'The barbarian – one of the other barbarians. Dressed like me.'

'Yes, Despoina.' If taking orders from a woman was a rare thing for Hellenos, he had the grace to do it well. He went back along the file of men and women – both aristocrats and their Sakje maiden archers, some marines – to Scopasis.

Melitta looked at the gash left by the rock chip on Anaxagoras' neck, pulled off the scarf she wore to keep her cuirass from rubbing her own neck and wrapped it around his wound to staunch the blood. Another rock hit.

'I can't say I'm fond of this,' Melitta said.

'I think it's very brave of you to come out at all,' Anaxagoras said.

'I mean the rocks. I adore a night raid – the taste of an enemy's blood on my blade, the gleam of the moon—' *Laying it on a bit thick,* she thought, but his male dominance annoyed her as much as his music and good looks appealed.

An ugly scream in the darkness; almost at their feet.

'Raid,' Anaxagoras said, and rolled to his feet.

The moment the hand clamped on his mouth, Satyrus reacted. It was, after all, something for which Theron and Philokles had trained him repeatedly. Before the hand was over his mouth, his mouth was open and he bit savagely, all but severing a finger – his right elbow shot back, he rolled his right shoulder down, fell heavily on the man on his back—

His assailant was screaming. Satyrus caught movement, ducked—

… into the blow, so that the man's hand punched his head instead of the sword cutting into it, and he snapped back, tripped over his first attacker and fell flat on his back – but he still had sword and shield. The aspis he pulled up, over his head and chest. He cowered, fighting for consciousness, trying to get a foot under him, blind.

'Alarm! Alarm!' someone was yelling.

His shield gave a great *thud* as a weapon crashed into it, and a hollow boom as a second one hit the rim. But he had his feet under him, and his sword, and his right hand shot out in a stop-thrust, almost without his volition.

He raised his eyes.

At least three of them – maybe more, but trapped like him in the shallow trench that had been the third defensive line. The trench walls were loose scree on both sides, difficult to climb. One man – with a pick – was above him, trying to get in behind.

Satyrus backed like a crab, praying to Herakles that he wouldn't catch his foot on a stone.

Two men had spears, and they attacked, confident now that he was retreating.

Five men. Satyrus knew that no one man can take five, so he backed away, watching the man on the edge of the trench—

The man went down, and in falling he fell into the trench, fouling his mates – Satyrus lunged immediately, missed his footing, swung wildly, hit a shield and was toe to toe with an opponent. Both of them swung, their hilts locked a moment, and then the man's eyes glazed over, something warm sprayed across Satyrus' shins and the man slumped to the ground, all the fingers of his sword hand severed in a poor parry.

Satyrus stepped back, because the trench behind the wounded man was suddenly full of men in Thracian helmets – ten, fifteen—

'Herakles!' Satyrus roared, and charged.

'That's fighting,' Anaxagoras said uselessly.

'Follow me,' Melitta said, and ran down the wall of rubble. She didn't pick her way with risky sobriety – she *ran*, and left the men behind her with little choice but to follow. She could see men moving beyond the next rise, men like black ants on sand. She made the bottom of the rubble-rampart without falling, pulled her bow from her *gorytos*, got an arrow on the bow and narrowly stopped herself from shooting the black man with the sword – she knew him from the party, but they came face to face and she could tell he'd come as close as she.

'My brother!' she said.

Herakles! She heard – close. She ran.

The men in the Thracian helmets were surprised, their night raid caught in their own trench area, and they had the natural reaction of raiders – retreat. It took them long seconds to realise that they were under attack from one man.

Satyrus' head rang like his shield under the assault of their spears, but he downed the first man with a thrust over his shield into the man's eyes – thrusts are more deadly in the dark, as there is less lateral movement to betray the blow – and then he pushed forward over the dying man and got his shield against the next man's shield and struck him in the moment of impact. Philokles' trick, as most men brace, even unconsciously, against the pain of the moment where the shields meet. Satyrus' sword wrapped around unerringly and found the neck between the helmet's tail and the top of the cuirass, and the man went down without a groan.

But that was the end of luck and mastery, and three blows on, Satyrus was again on his back, head ringing again where a blow had shot his shield rim into his forehead, and he pulled under his shield – again. Got his back to a downed timber, pushed against it, got a knee under him—

He *knew* it was Anaxagoras as soon as he got to his feet. The man had his shield cocked to one side to let Satyrus rise, and then the two of them filled the trench. Anaxagoras had a spear, and he used it brutally, slamming it into the enemy shields as hard as his massive physique allowed, rocking the smaller men back and punching the needle point of his spear through their shield faces, stabbing arms and shoulders.

And behind the men fighting Anaxagoras and Satyrus, there were screams, and the familiar sound of Sakje arrows buzzing like wasps and hitting home in flesh like an axe hitting a gourd.

Above them, the round, full moon beamed down upon the earth.

Satyrus got his feet set, his head at least clear enough to support his friend. When Anaxagoras killed a man, they stepped forward together.

Satyrus knew Helios was behind him when the spear licked over his shoulder, riding on the smooth bronze scales of his shoulder armour, exactly as Helios did when he was tired, in practice. And the point, thrust expertly, one-handed, went into the enemy helmet and came out red.

They heard more buzzing wasps – the crash of armour hitting rock – screams.

'Let's get out of here!' Helios said, tugging his cloak; the remnants of his cloak.

But Jubal had other ideas. 'No!' he said. 'Lord! Into they trench – fin' the fucking mine!'

Anaxagoras whirled. 'What are you talking about? This is insanity!'

Satyrus got it. 'A mine – they're mining under our new wall before they even storm the old one – right?'

'They do!' Jubal said. 'Now – follow me!'

Satyrus whirled on his friend. 'This could be the entire siege – right now. Win or lose. Follow him!'

Sieges make for a strange order of things: a king, a dozen aristocrats, some Sakje – following a sailor. But the sailor seemed to know where he was going, or so Satyrus assumed.

Up the slope of the last wall – half a dozen enemy fled before them. Now they were deep in the enemy area, a part of the walls that hadn't been in Rhodian hands in a month. But Jubal moved fast, and Melitta was at his heels, and Satyrus swallowed bile and followed as fast as he could.

The enemy was sounding the alarm in all directions.

Satyrus hoped Jubal knew what he was doing. Demoted by Tyche from polemarch to hoplite, he ran heavily across the open ground in front of the old wall, across a tenth of a stade of rubble and up the inner face of the second wall – currently the leading edge of the Antigonid trenches.

At the top, well lit by moonlight, Melitta stopped and shot – once, twice. Scopasis joined her and the two maidens, and their arrows *poured* off their bows – Satyrus was breathing so hard he could scarcely run, but he made it up beside his sister. Jubal was down in the rubble gully of the enemy trench, and enemy blood was black in the moonlight.

Melitta leaped down beside the African, and her *akinakes* was in her hand. She finished a sentry with an arrow in his gut, looked at Anaxagoras and licked the point, smiling.

Anaxagoras stumbled on the rim of the trench, his head whipping around in a double take.

Satyrus wanted to laugh and cry. His sister was *flirting*, showing off like a young girl.

'Here!' Jubal called.

A trumpet sounded, near at hand, and was answered from far off – the enemy camp.

One of the men had a pick, and there were torches burning along the trench. Jubal took the pick and a torch and dived into the opening in the ground. Satyrus let him do it – Helios went with him.

'I'll go and cover him,' Melitta said, sheathing her *akinake*. She took her archers forward.

He saw them rise to shoot.

Time passed ... heavy, terrifying time, and a rock fell out of the dark, far over their heads, and then a wave of them, pounding the ground where they weren't, over by their own lines.

'Better hurry,' Melitta said.

Satyrus was listening to the enemy engines. They were close – close enough to rush.

He moved forward, listening to the grunts as the torsion drums were wound tight, the thud as the heavy arm impacted against the upright, the snap-*crack* as the sling on the end of the arm released its load and snapped against the frame.

Less than a stade away.

No.

Satyrus saw that men were looking expectantly at him. But this was not the time for further heroics, and taking a handful of men, even his best men, deep into enemy lines in search of their engines would be beyond reckless.

Smoke was pouring out of the entrance to the enemy mine, and within a dozen heartbeats Helios was scrambling out of the hole. Jubal was right behind him.

'Run for it!' Satyrus hissed.

Melitta loosed a shaft. 'We'll cover you,' she said.

Other men hesitated – leaving a half-dozen Sakje, most of them women, to cover the men's retreat sat ill with the Greeks.

Satyrus grinned and grabbed Anaxagoras by the chlamys. 'Come on, young hero. She's got a *bow*. We have swords. Let's *go*.'

Jubal shot him a fierce grin and headed off at top speed across the ruined, moonswept landscape, his leather-clad feet scarcely making a noise. The rest of them weren't so quiet, and when they began to climb their own rubble wall, someone on the far side saw them and suddenly the night was full of projectiles, arrows and rocks from the smaller engines. The rapid hail may have assuaged the enemy's need to strike back – but it had no other effect.

The men crouched in the cover of the reverse slope of their own rubble wall, listening to the enemy engines drop rocks.

'Them needs new rope,' Jubal said. 'Torsion slipping – rocks landing short.'

'*They need* new rope,' Satyrus said.

'What I say,' Jubal shot back.

'Where's Melitta?' Anaxagoras asked.

'Out in the dark, killing Antigonids,' Satyrus replied.

Before the enemy engines could reload, there was the soft sound of gravel sliding, a padding of moccasin-clad feet across stone and Melitta jumped down into the trench. She looked around until she found her brother.

'They're not much for night actions,' she said, pointing with her chin at the enemy lines. In the darkness and the moonlight, the scars on her face made her appear another creature entirely, and her attempt at a flirtatious glance at Anaxagoras appeared, at least to her brother, more demonic than enticing.

'They're afraid of us,' Satyrus said.

There was a soft *crump*, and then another, and then a roar that filled the night and the bitter smell of burning oak and something darker—

Jubal punched his fist in the air. 'Got him!' he said.

Melitta, so in command of herself in the night raid, was cowering flat against the rubble.

Satyrus put a hand on her shoulder. 'Jubal and Helios went down into the mine and set fire to the timber shoring,' he said.

Jubal nodded at the young man. 'Had to fight, down there,' he said.

He clasped hands with Helios, the younger man beaming.

Jubal smiled at Melitta. 'So when they timbers burn through, she go down – bang, crash. Whole tunnel *collapse*.'

Helios leaned close to Melitta. *They're like flies*, Satyrus thought. Once again, he appreciated Abraham's point of view.

Helios said, 'If they drive the mine under our wall, they light off the timbers and when it collapses, the wall comes down. If we get it first, it wastes their work.'

Miriam shook her head. 'This is a foolish way to make war,' she said.

Later, she curled up against him on his bed. 'It is nice to have my brother back,' she said. 'Someone to sleep with.'

Satyrus tried to wake up enough to listen to her. 'You have friends,' he said.

'I have *no* friends,' she said. 'The Lady of the Assagetae has lovers and followers. I never thought I'd say this, brother, but playing at being a Greek girl tonight was the most relaxing thing I've done in a year.'

Satyrus thought back and frowned. 'How's your son?' he asked.

'Amazingly big. Growing like a weed. Talking.' Melitta stretched. 'Where'd Anaxagoras come from?' she asked.

'Out of a pirate,' Satyrus said. 'He's in love with Miriam,' Satyrus added, trying for just the right tone – not wanting to sound jealous, offended, or angry. Aiming for a certain *man of the world* quality.

Sisters have always been poor targets for false maturity. 'He is, too. And you don't like it. But he sees me. Heh, brother. I like that one.

As pretty as a picture – long, gentle hands. But like Hektor of the nodding plume – I saw him in the trench tonight. Like a lion. I'll take his thoughts from Miriam.'

Satyrus shook his head. 'No – Melitta, you can't just throw yourself at a man because—'

She laughed. 'Go to sleep, brother.'

Day, and a hangover compounded by the two heavy blows he'd taken in the dark. Satyrus could barely raise his head off his rolled cloak, and there was blood in his hair and all down his side, and Melitta went to find Aspasia.

'You really shouldn't have been allowed to sleep last night,' Aspasia said with asperity. 'Sleeping after a heavy blow to the head – it's not good.'

Satyrus shrugged.

She handed him a herbal concoction, which he drank – it was sweet and quite pleasant, especially when compared to some things she'd given him. She poured him another cup.

Melitta stripped off her Sakje clothes and began to bathe behind a screen. The screen hadn't been there the night before. Satyrus lay back with his warm drink and considered that his whole tent had altered. It was larger—

'You brought a felt tent!' Satyrus said.

'So observant, dear brother.' Melitta laughed and emerged from the screen as a Greek girl – a Greek girl with two scarcely noticeable facial scars and a tangle of blue-black hair.

'Warrior braids aren't all that fashionable here in besieged Rhodes,' Satyrus quipped. He already felt better.

The felt tent made him feel *safe*. It was remarkably like *home*, a vision of childhood. And Melitta was remarkably like his mother – he'd seldom seen her look so much like her.

'Miriam's going to dress my hair,' Melitta said. 'I'm out of the habit. Neiron's waiting for you.' She ducked out.

'You need more pins!' he shouted at her. The side of her chiton was open to the hip.

His head hurt.

Neiron leaned in the new tent. 'If you're awake enough to shout at your sister,' he began.

Satyrus got to his feet, a little unsteady, and Helios came in with a water basin and a cup of warm juice.

'Well done, last night,' Satyrus said to Helios. 'He and Jubal collapsed a mine.'

'I've heard – it's the talk of the army.' Neiron smiled. 'And not a man lost – that's a raid.'

Satyrus didn't like the judgement in Neiron's tone. 'That's luck,' he said. 'Lots of wine.'

'And judgement.' Neiron nodded. 'Good judgement. Now Demetrios has asked for a truce.'

Satyrus shot around so fast he tipped over the bowl of hot water Helios was using to bathe the blood from his hair. 'What?'

Neiron nodded. 'About ten minutes ago, a herald came. Two days' truce to bury his dead.' He paused. 'Jubal says it is a ruse to change the torsion ropes on his engines and build more to replace the ones we're destroying.'

Satyrus raised his hand. 'Get me Jubal, and Menedemos, and any other officers you come across. I'll get the blood out of my hair.'

Helios wiped his hands on a towel. 'Yes, lord,' he said, and went out.

'Have a seat. Pomegranate juice?' he asked. When Neiron had a cup, Satyrus knelt down and lowered the whole of the top of his head into the deep bowl. The warm water burned at his scalp. He began to probe the wound with his fingers – the dried blood was thick and flaked away gradually.

'Quite a party,' Neiron continued.

'Have fun?' Satyrus asked. It was hard to sound lordly when you are bending over far enough to have your head upside down in a basin.

'Yes,' Neiron said. 'But this stunt last night,' he began.

The bowl was red. Satyrus caught his hair, wrung it out, wincing at the pain, and sat up. He could see Abraham's Jacob outside. 'Hey!' he called, and Jacob put his head in.

'Can you get a boy to fetch me some more hot water?' Satyrus asked, and Jacob vanished with the bowl. Turning back to Neiron, Satyrus shook water out of his hair.

'There was no stunt, Neiron. We found an active mine and we launched a raid to destroy it. It had to be done. If their mine found *our* mine?'

425

'Gods keep us!' Neiron paused. 'Were they close?'

'Too blasted close.' Satyrus winced. The wound felt as if fire had caught in his hair.

'You managed to be caught, alone, by an enemy patrol. I've heard it all already. Lord – you must *stop*.' He shook his head, stared at his pomegranate juice and frowned. 'You must stop running off like a hero from Homer.'

Satyrus shrugged impatiently. 'I was there.'

'Call for others and leave, next time,' he said.

'There were no others,' Satyrus shot back. 'Damn it, old man, I was *there*. I didn't make some drunk-arse decision to launch a trench raid.'

'Huh,' Neiron said, in obvious disagreement. 'If you need an officer to make a circuit of the walls, wake me. Wake Apollodorus.'

'Apollodorus was too drunk to move his feet.' Satyrus shook his head. 'What do you want, Neiron?'

'I want you to act like a king and a commander, not like some young pup out to bloody his sword. Lead from the back. No one – *no one* – could question your prowess or your courage. Give it a rest. If the girl doesn't want you, she won't want you any more with your sword all bloody.' Neiron glared, looking more like an outraged cat than was quite right.

'The girl has nothing to do with it,' Satyrus barked. And was mortified when Melitta came in, Miriam at her heels. Satyrus was naked, with his hair half washed out and a sheen of blood-red water over him.

Melitta laughed. 'Miriam, my brother is naked,' she called over her shoulder – far too late.

Satyrus had no towel and nowhere to go.

Jacob came in with another cauldron of water.

Neiron got to his feet. 'I'm sorry, lord. We just seem to have the same disagreement again and again. And I feel like a nagging uncle in Menander.' Quite casually, he tossed his chlamys to Satyrus.

Satyrus tried *not* to hurry as he cast the chlamys over his shoulder. The girls were paying no attention.

Satyrus smiled at Jacob. 'Thanks,' he said.

'Think nothing of it, lord,' he said.

Neiron stood. 'I should—'

Helios came in with Jubal and Anaxagoras and Apollodorus, the last-named walking as if he, not Satyrus, had been hit repeatedly in the head. Menedemos looked about the same.

'He only wants truce to build engines,' Jubal said without preamble.

Satyrus raised an eyebrow and let Helios sink his head into the water.

'I'm going to teach Miriam to shoot,' Melitta announced. 'Is this truce real?'

Satyrus, upside down, managed to laugh. 'It's good to have you around,' he said to his sister. 'Yes, we'll accept his truce – won't we, Neiron? Menedemos?'

The Rhodian commander sat heavily on a stool that Helios unfolded for him, cradled his head in his hands and shook it. 'I need a truce to recover from drinking,' he said.

Apollodorus groaned. 'Out of practice,' he said.

Satyrus was upright again. 'What practical advantage would we derive from refusing the truce?' he asked Jubal.

Jubal rubbed his chin and then the top of his head. 'None,' he admitted. 'Not much we can do. We *wan'* him to attack, eh?'

Satyrus nodded. 'He wants to rebuild his engines for the bombardment. We *want* him to assault the wall. And we don't want him to discover we've already effectively abandoned the third wall – is that right? So during the truce, we can man it heavily and show all kinds of troops up there.'

Neiron nodded.

'And we can man the rest of the ships in the harbour and get them to sea the moment the truce expires.' This to Menedemos, who also nodded.

'That could turn the balance at sea,' he said.

'And we get two days' rest,' Satyrus added. 'What have we got to lose?'

Anaxagoras shook his head. 'Nothing,' he said. 'Makes you wonder why he's asking for a truce.'

29

DAY NINETY AND FOLLOWING

The Rhodians spent the two truce days making and mending equipment, and keeping the enemy from seeing their preparations. Parties of enemy troops repeatedly attempted to climb the south walls under various pretences, and Satyrus quickly understood that this scouting function was the reason that the Antigonids had asked for a truce. When Satyrus set up a trophy in the blasted ground between the lines, Demetrios sent men to tear it down, and made a formal protest.

The herald, beautifully dressed in fine wool from India, a cloak of shimmering silk and a golden fillet on his brow, was brought before Satyrus where he sat with his *hetairoi* in the agora, mending sandals. Satyrus had his entire panoply laid out in the dusty grass, and while Helios buffed the bronze and silver, Satyrus was busy with a needle and heavy linen thread, sewing the long flaps that covered his lower belly and groin where sword cuts had all but severed two of them. Anaxagoras was watching Apollodorus work – the marine captain was an expert with leather, and he was refitting the musician's military sandals, putting a leather sock inside, a trick the marines had developed to keep the grit of the siege out of their feet. Charmides was working with the intense concentration of the neophyte while his girl, Nike, mocked his efforts. Melitta was chewing sinew and spitting while explaining to Miriam the superiorities of sinew over linen thread. Across the agora, marines, ephebes and citizen soldiers, hoplites, mercenaries and Cretan archers had their kit laid out in the sun while they made the repairs that could mean life or death – a scale replaced, a bronze plate adjusted, a helmet strap tightened or loosened.

The herald stared at the activity as if he'd never seen soldiers at work before. 'My king bids me say—' he began.

He was addressing Anaxagoras. Anaxagoras raised his head from watching Apollodorus and winked at the herald. 'I'm not the polemarch, boy,' he said.

The word *boy*, with its implications of immaturity – and slavery – made the man flush. He whirled. His eyes found Menedemos, where he sat having the straps on his greaves reset by a bronzesmith.

'Which one of you is the King of the Bosporus?' he asked belligerently.

Satyrus bit off his thread amid the general laughter. 'I am,' he said.

The young man walked over to him. 'My lord, the king demands that you remove the trophy that you have erected on the south wall.'

'Or what?' Satyrus asked. His men fell silent.

'It is an effrontery that you have erected a trophy over such a small thing,' the herald continued.

'Your master asked us for a truce,' Satyrus said. 'He requested two days to bury his dead,' he continued.

Apollodorus spoke up. 'The law of arms lets us raise a trophy,' he said. 'Your master ought to know that, boy.'

Abraham laughed. 'I'm a *Jew*, boy, and *I know* you get a trophy when your enemy asks for a truce.'

'I am not a boy, and my king is not my *master*.' The young man was obviously Macedonian.

Satyrus nodded. 'Listen, lad. You go back to Demetrios and tell him that if he wants the trophy taken down, he should come and do it himself. When the truce is over. Until then, the trophy stands.' He stood up. 'Your audience is at an end. Blindfold him and take him back – west gate. Who has my wax?'

Apollodorus looked sheepish. 'I thought it was my wax,' he said. And more quietly, 'Isn't it a bit of ... hubris to have a trophy for so small an action?'

'It's a goad,' Satyrus said. 'We need him to attack that wall.'

Miriam released another arrow into the straw bale. It flew well, if a little short, and once again the string caught her forearm, which was already red – angry red.

'Damn it,' she said, in Hebrew.

Melitta shook her head. 'Keep your wrist strong. Don't relax it. Here – your left – hold the bow like this.'

Miriam took a drink from the canteen next to them. 'So you keep saying. You must have wrists like a smith, Melitta – I can't hold the bow like that and release the arrow.'

Melitta frowned. 'A six-year-old Sakje child can do it, Miriam. *Concentrate*.'

Miriam, angered, lifted the bow, took a deep breath, relaxed, made herself move the bow a finger's breadth with her wrist and released. Her shot was weak, and flew short – but the string did not bite her arm.

Melitta smiled. 'There you go. You need to strengthen your arms and shoulders – I don't have a bow light enough for you, so you'll have to get stronger.' She nodded. 'Sakje maidens lift rocks and throw them. And shoot constantly.'

Miriam smiled. 'I'd be delighted to have shoulders like yours,' she said.

Melitta smiled back. 'No – I'm all muscle. You have the beautiful curves. I look like a boy.'

Miriam laughed. 'No. Not at all like a boy. But you do *walk* like a boy. Fierce – determined. And always ready to fight.'

Melitta nodded. 'I *am* always ready to fight.' She wiped her bow, retrieved her arrows.

'You like him? Anaxagoras?' Miriam asked.

'He's pretty and brave,' Miriam said. 'He looks at me the way I like to be looked at.'

Miriam nodded. The silence lengthened.

'You can't have both of them,' Melitta said.

Miriam fiddled with her hair. She was blushing. 'I can't have *either* of them,' she said.

Melitta frowned. 'Why not?' she asked.

Miriam met her eyes. 'It's fine for you – it always has been.' She looked away, bit her lip and said no more.

'What do you mean, Miriam? I'm no different to you. We grew up together!' Melitta felt as if she were suddenly talking to a stranger.

'You ... you don't play by the rules. How many lovers have you had, Melitta?' Miriam blushed when she asked.

Melitta laughed out loud. 'Far fewer than you might think. Three. Just three. And the cost is ... high.'

Miriam's hand went to her mouth. 'Oh – I'm so sorry! I assumed—' She blushed again.

Melitta laughed. 'Honey, if I weren't the Lady of the Assagetae, I'd no doubt run up the score you think I have.' She got to her feet. 'I'm not offended, Miriam. Everyone thinks it – I hear what men say. I have a baby. I live out in the field with men. But men are fools, and if I seek to lead them, I cannot go from bed to bed. The petty jealousies alone would destroy my people.' She stretched.

'Oh,' Miriam said.

'On the other hand,' Melitta went on, 'since everyone already thinks you're sleeping with both of them – why don't you? You'll never convince people you're an innocent widow. And,' she smiled, the same smile she made when she licked her knife, 'it'd be good for you. Your marriage was unhappy?'

Miriam looked away. 'Nothing that's worth a story.'

'I'm not in a hurry,' Melitta said. She sat back down on a sun-warmed stone.

Miriam stared out to sea. 'Do you think we'll win, Melitta? I mean, here. In the end.'

Melitta looked at the other woman. 'Yes, of course. Why do you ask?'

Miriam smiled – a surprisingly bitter smile, for her. 'If we were all going to die, I'd pick one. And love him every night and every day and to *hell* with what people say. Except that something tells me that if I choose one, the other will die, and I could not abide that. It must be easy to die out there – a moment's inattention. And when they compete for me, am I insane, or does it help keep them alive – give them an edge?'

Melitta nodded. 'I wondered if you were thinking that. And yes – oh, yes. I suppose someone might argue that they'll be reckless – but I use my lovely eyes on warriors all the time. The aspiring lover is the deadliest of men. And has something to live for.'

Miriam hugged her. 'I have never said that out loud – even to myself. I feel like such a trull. And then, at the symposium, I watched that red-haired girl and I thought – oh, I thought things. So I went to bed. Before—'

Melitta smiled, somewhere between a true smile and a sneer. 'I tried to get Anaxagoras between my legs after you went to bed, but he isn't there yet. Will you be angry when I win him?'

Miriam took a deep breath. 'Do girls really talk like this?' she asked.

Melitta shrugged. 'I don't usually have much time for women, aside from my spear-maidens,' she said. 'All the girls I know talk like this. Sakje girls wager on men.'

'I want to be a Sakje,' Miriam said.

Melitta nodded. 'Fine. When your shoulders are stronger. But only if I can have the musician.'

Satyrus could hear his sister laughing with Miriam, and he assumed that no good would come of it. And it made him uncomfortable, so he finished his repairs, gathered an escort and walked down to the harbour.

The Rhodians had worked night and day since the truce was declared, and they had eighteen triemiolas ready for sea, stores and water aboard down in the sand by the keel – minimum stores, as the city had little food to spare. The oars and running tackle were aboard, and the waterfront was full of oarsmen – men who had been serving as light-armed troops for months. Only Satyrus' oarsmen from the wrecked *Arete* had armour.

Menedemos meant to take the Rhodian ships to sea himself. The town was running short on leaders.

Satyrus walked among the Rhodian oarsmen, wishing them luck and Poseidon's speed. They wouldn't sail until the truce had expired. Satyrus kept glancing beyond the ruined harbour tower, looking for Demetrios to challenge the ships going to sea, but there wasn't a sign.

Menedemos saw him looking. 'I don't think he cares,' the Rhodian said. 'I think he wants us gone – fewer troops to man the walls.'

Satyrus sighed. 'And more cases of fever this morning – as if a moment's relaxation makes more people fall sick. I worry you will take the contagion to Leon's squadrons.'

Menedemos nodded. 'I'll go to Samos first and spend a day or two there,' he said. 'I'll know who's sick by then.' He looked around. 'I'm more worried that you won't have enough men to hold the walls.'

Satyrus raised an eyebrow. 'Diokles brought us more men than you are taking away – and none of the new troops is sick. Get out there and win, Menedemos. We can't win here – we can only survive. Just make damn sure that you tell Leon, and Ptolemy. We're out of space to give up. The new south wall – the "bow" – is the last. Now we have to fight every sortie, every assault.' He turned and met the Rhodian's eyes. 'They don't have to be skilful, just lucky. Or Demetrios can throw everything at us.'

Menedemos nodded. 'I know. How long? Two weeks?'

Satyrus shrugged. He raised his hands as if praying. 'By Herakles my ancestor, we might last months – or fall tomorrow. But my best guess? And you've heard this before: Demetrios will come at the third wall as soon as the truce lifts. We'll move back and he'll occupy the ground – four days. Then we unleash the trap and retake the third wall. For a day or a week. And he'll have to spend time rebuilding – call it another week.' Satyrus shrugged again. 'And then? We live from hour to hour.'

'We'd best get to sea, then,' Menedemos said.

'May Poseidon guard you,' Satyrus said.

'And Apollo withhold his contagion from you,' Menedemos said.

The truce expired with the sounding of trumpets in both camps, and the Rhodian squadrons put to sea unopposed. The sea was rough, ideal for the better sailors, and Plistias, Demetrios' admiral, seemed content to let them go.

But Demetrios' army didn't stir. There was no hail of stones, no grand assault into the third wall.

Satyrus stood with Jubal on the third wall, just at twilight.

'He smell the rat?' Satyrus asked.

Jubal's eyes widened and he scratched the top of his head. 'Who know?' he asked. 'God, maybe.' He paused. 'Duck,' he said, and dropped flat on the top of the wall.

Satyrus had the sense to emulate him.

With a wicked hiss, a par of shafts whistled over them to shatter below.

'Somethin' new,' Jubal said, hurrying down the inside of the wall. Small parties of Rhodians – the ephebes were on duty – were active in the trench behind the wall, and Cretan archers shot over the wall from time to time. It was vital to Satyrus that the enemy not know how eager he was to abandon the third wall.

Jubal picked up an arrow – the oddest arrow Satyrus had seen. It was solid, like the bolts thrown by ballistae, but short – much shorter than the engines on a ship threw, for instance.

Jubal walked back, poked his head up over the ramparts and fell back instantly, his face bleeding from a dozen cuts.

He lay on his back and screamed. Ephebes came running and got water on his face – he had two bad cuts where another bolt had hit a rock, inches from his face and split, the shattered shaft flaying his skin.

Satyrus helped other men carry him back to his tent, and Aspasia gave him poppy.

He found Melitta and gave her one of the bolts. 'Tell your archers to beware,' he said. 'They have an engine – a small one, I assume. Very powerful.'

By the next day, one of her maiden archers was dead, shot through the head as she rose to shoot, and another had her bow hand broken by a tumbling shaft that had hit a stone. Others were hit, as well – two ephebes shot dead; a citizen hoplite screaming his guts out in the makeshift hospital.

Satyrus ordered a makeshift tower raised just south of the agora, on the foundations of the *boule*'s *tholos*. Idomeneus and Melitta used the tower to watch the enemy lines as soon as it went up.

Idomeneus came down almost immediately. 'Troops massing behind their engines,' he said.

Satyrus sounded the alarm and the town's whole garrison stood to – manning every inch of wall, with the marines and town hoplites in reserve in the city's agora. They stood to all night, men sleeping on their feet in their armour.

And nothing happened.

The next day, Jubal was back, the wounds on his face livid, giving him an angry look that ill suited his open nature. He climbed the tower, came back down and shook his head.

'You know why I don' buil' no tower?' he asked Satyrus.

Satyrus shook his head. 'No – I guess I assumed that you hadn't thought of it.'

His makeshift siege engineer spat. 'Don' wan' them,' Jubal pointed at Demetrios' camp, 'to buil' no tower. Buil' they a tower, see over our wall, see my lil' surprise.'

*

Two stades away, Lucius looked under his hand at the distant city. 'Arse-cunts built a tower,' he said to Stratokles. 'Now they can see everything Golden Boy does – so much for the surprise assault.' He laughed. 'Now, why didn't *we* think of building a tower?'

Stratokles took a healthy swig of wine and spat it out after rinsing his mouth – just in case he had to fight.

'Because so many of our slaves are sick with the fever that we can't repair our engines *and* build a tower,' he said. 'Plistias wants a tower. So does King Demetrios. But we're a little short on manpower right now.'

Lucius barked a laugh. 'Make the useless phalangites do the work. They're not worth a crap in an assault – they ought to dig.'

Stratokles cuffed his man. 'Don't let anyone hear you say that,' he said.

Lucius was uncowed. 'If I had half this number of Latins, I'd show them how to dig. And fight.'

Two more days of inaction. Tense, desperate inaction.

And the fevers began to creep into the ranks of the ephebes. First one, then ten men went down, puking their guts out, skin sallow.

Satyrus ran into Miriam and Aspasia at the northern edge of the agora, where the slaves lived, arms full of blankets. Miriam looked as if she was forty. Or fifty. Her eyes were hollow, red as if from weeping.

Satyrus hadn't spent five minutes in her presence since he had kissed her. He went to salute her.

'Stay away, polemarch!' Aspasia commanded. She'd been a priestess and a physician all her life, and her voice carried commands as effectively as Satyrus' own. He stepped back. He smiled at Miriam, eager to establish some contact, and she looked at him the way a veteran looks as a green stripling.

'What do they need?' Satyrus asked the two women. 'More blankets? Greater food supplies?'

'Hope,' Miriam said.

'I think Demetrios has the fever in his camp,' Damophilus said. 'It's the only explanation Jubal and I can arrive at for his hesitation. His engines still aren't firing – at least, fewer than half of them.'

'I'm sure you can all see the irony,' Satyrus said. 'Demetrios is held

435

back by the sickness of his slaves – and so our trap is going to fail.' He shook his head. 'Zeus Sator, we need a little luck.'

Neiron nodded. All the men of the *boule* – now meeting in the open air, as the stones of their elegant meeting place now formed the centre of the hidden wall, Jubal's 'bow' – nodded. Their eyes were hollow, and their bellies, as well. The squadrons had sailed, and nothing had come back, and the granaries were reaching desperate levels.

'We have to cut the grain ration,' Hellenos said. He made a face and raised his hands. 'Don't kill the messenger!'

Memnon shook his head. 'If we cut the grain ration, someone will surrender the city,' he said. 'That's how I see it.'

Neiron grunted. 'There's more than one irony at work here. What you're saying is that *inaction* allows people to think of how desperate they are.'

Satyrus nodded. 'I saw that days ago, Old Neiron. Demetrios does us more damage waiting than striking.'

Damophilus raised an eyebrow. 'Then what – attack him? Before all our hoplites are sick?'

Satyrus shook his head. 'Suicide. His entrenchments are sound – in fact, in *yet another* irony, we've taught him to build better entrenchments by our constant raids.'

Jubal nodded. 'An' they heavy blows's killin' us.'

Two days of further observation showed that the enemy had a mechanical bow. Old soldiers like Draco knew them as soon as they saw them – Alexander had favoured the weapon for sieges – the *gastraphetes*. The crossbow.

'It's not that it outranges the Sakje, or even my lads,' Idomeneus said. 'It's that they can shoot it from cover. No need to pull it – no need to kneel or stand. And once they cock it, they can watch for a whole cycle of the sun for a man to show his head.'

Satyrus looked around at his officers. 'Anyone have a suggestion?' he asked, looking at Jubal.

Jubal nodded. 'Do. Do, do. Seen women making baskets – seen men fill 'em with earth, building walls.'

There was no news there. 'So?' Satyrus asked.

'Weave big-arse baskets, an' mount 'em on the walls at night,' Jubal said. 'Fill 'em with earth. Now archers can stan' to shoot – behin' the baskets.'

'Until they concentrate engine fire on the baskets' position,' Satyrus said.

'An' so we need fifty,' Jubal said. 'Make that twice fifty. Best do the new wall at the same time, eh?'

Satyrus scratched his beard. He was pretty sure that he had lice. Everyone did, all of a sudden. 'Let's try it,' he said.

'And how exactly are we going to get the slaves to dig for us?' Damophilus asked. 'Most of them are either sick or faking it.'

Satyrus didn't think many were shamming. It was a charge aristocrats had levelled since the first cases of fever. 'I think it is time to free all of the slaves,' he said.

Not a single voice was raised against him.

Satyrus found Korus with a line of women, all of them lifting rocks in the shade of the remaining olive trees at the western end of the agora. The women didn't look away in maidenly modesty, but glared at him for interrupting their exercise.

'I need you,' Satyrus said to Korus.

'You look strong enough to me,' Korus said. Some of the women laughed.

'I'm serious,' Satyrus said.

'So are we,' Miriam offered, coming forward. The lines in her face were even more pronounced, today – she looked stern, more like a teacher or a head cook than a gentlewoman of leisure. 'We're learning to be archers. You sister says we need stronger arms.'

Satyrus bit back a number of retorts. His sister was behind this – and she was right. And these women were participating, which was good for morale. He took a deep breath – lately he'd begun to think that the art of command was in *not* saying things – and smiled gravely.

'That's excellent,' he said. 'Korus, when you are finished, I need you to be my spokesman.'

Korus nodded. 'What do you want? The slaves, I assume?'

'I'm going to free them. All.' Satyrus looked at the former slave for a reaction.

Korus' smile was small, but it was there. 'Then what?' he asked.

'Then I'm going to ask every *citizen* to work. Tonight. On the south wall.' Satyrus smiled.

Korus smiled back. 'I think the new citizens might do that,' he allowed.

A new moon, and darkness. Like a wave of spectres, the chosen work parties went up the third wall – still, despite Satyrus' best efforts to give it up, the defensive position of the defenders – and planted enormous baskets all along the top. And then, like ants, the citizens of the town, with shovels and smaller baskets and metal buckets and every tool at their disposal, began to fill the giant baskets – fifty-two of them. With thirty or more citizens to every basket.

The enemy was taken by surprise. It took half a watch for them to get their engines manned, and the moon was down before the first rocks flew – and bolts from various ballistae, large and small.

Men died. Women died.

The defenders died. The survivors went on digging, carrying the fill up the wall and dumping it into the baskets. The lucky ones worked on the new wall – the 'bow'. They were covered. The unlucky worked on the third wall.

Like a squall at sea, the first shower of missiles died away.

'Shot away their reserve of arrows and stones,' Satyrus said to Abraham. 'Now they have to send to the rear for more.'

'Where are you going?' he asked. The King of the Bosporus was stripping out of his bronze cuirass.

'You command the reserve,' Satyrus said. 'You used to be my best captain. You're a citizen. I need you to take command.'

Abraham nodded. 'I accept.'

'Good,' Satyrus said. 'Because I'm going to dig.'

The sun was a smear on the horizon, and no one had the energy to comment on the rosy fingers of dawn. The diggers lay like the dead, except for Aspasia, Miriam, Nike and a dozen other women, who were carrying the wounded to the rear. Men rose to help them – but not many.

Anaxagoras stepped out of the ranks of the hoplites, and a dusty ex-slave put his hand on the musician's chest.

'Back in the ranks, brother,' Satyrus said.

'But—'

'If there's an attack right now, you and the ephebes are all we have,' Satyrus said. 'The citizen hoplites worked all night.'

Memnon, who looked as much like a slave as the king, stopped next to him and leaned on a heavy shovel. 'We lost a prime lot of weight, though,' he joked.

And the Sakje and the Cretans, who had been kept back from the digging, manned the new embrasures with the dawn. Satyrus took a wineskin and climbed the tower.

It took almost an hour for there to be enough light to see – or shoot. But Satyrus watched the crossbow teams move forward, saw them scratch their heads, literally – at the change in the Rhodian south wall.

Satyrus and Jubal mapped out the positions of the crossbow teams and sent the information to Idomeneus via Helios. A Sakje was caught moving and was shot through both hips, and he died screaming.

'I need to teach you to read and write,' Satyrus said to Jubal.

'Heh,' Jubal said. 'Why you think I can' read?'

'You may be the best siege engineer in the world, just now,' Satyrus said. 'And I need you to learn the maths. For all of us.'

'I know maths,' Jubal said. 'I read Pythagoras.'

A whistle sounded, and as one, the whole of Melitta's Sakje force rose to their feet. Further east, the entire Cretan force did the same, standing up behind the great baskets. All together, they drew. Master archers called ranges and lofted their own bows, and the bone whistle sounded again, and all of them loosed – six hundred arrows.

Seconds later, they loosed again, and then again and again, until the arrow squall filled the air between the walls with a continuous flurry.

In the enemy forward positions, men were hit. The crossbow snipers suffered heavily, and the survivors of the first volley, shocked, hugged their cover.

Small groups of Sakje archers ran forward down the rubble wall and sprinted across no-man's land, unopposed, as the fourth and fifth volleys ripped through the air.

The bone whistle sounded, and not a single arrow left a string. The last volley flew, whistling arrows shrieking to add to the terror, and the sprinters were across, clambering up through the stakes and sharpened tree branches of the enemy lines. The enemy snipers raised their heads too late: the Sakje were shooting point blank – and the enemy had no engines registered on their own lines.

Thyrsis returned in triumph, brandishing a captured *gastraphetes*.

Satyrus let out a breath he hadn't known he was holding.

Demetrios did not ponder long on the new development. Before the morning was old, the men on the tower could see his pikemen moving into assault positions.

'Finally!' Satyrus said.

There were thousands of them. They blackened the ground behind the enemy's entrenchments – four *taxeis* and then a fifth stretched four deep across the rear.

'Using his veterans to push the newer troops forward,' Satyrus said. Abraham had joined him, and Hellenos, and they kept the younger men busy, up and down the ladders.

Jubal grinned. 'Now – now he take the poison pill. Let he have it!'

Satyrus shook his head. 'I'd love to,' he said, 'but if those men get onto the new wall, we're done for. We have to make a fight of it, and then we have to withdraw in good order – without taking too many casualties.' He spat. 'Zeus Sator, stand by us. Herakles, guide my arm.'

He raced down the tower – now he feared the power of that assault – and Helios was waiting with his armour.

'Every man,' he said. 'Every man into the ditch behind the bow.'

When they came, they came fast and hard. They knew that the defeat of their snipers meant that they would face massed archery, and they'd been coached.

They didn't have their sarissas, either. They had javelins and light spears, or nothing but swords. They came forward at a dead run, screaming with fear, rage, battle spirit. Their officers came first, and the arrows reaped them first.

It was the first time that Demetrios had attacked a wall without massive bombardment. It was the first time he'd put ten thousand men in a single wave.

It was the toughest assault yet, and the Macedonians didn't flinch at the arrows though they died in heaps on the wall. The last horse length of the climb was brutal – Jubal had deliberately built the walls at a changing pitch to lure infantry into believing that they could be climbed easily. Only when a man was halfway to the top did he see clearly how steep the last few feet were, and few men stopped to reason why every section had a sloped zone with easy climbing.

Into the heart of the archery.

The archers reaped phalangites like a woman cutting weeds in her garden, but they began to tire – even the Sakje – and their arrow supply ran short. And then, at the call of a bone whistle, they broke. The Sakje were fast, running to reform being a part of their core tactics. The Cretans were slower to break, and lost men to the triumphant Macedonians as finally they got over the wall.

Satyrus had the ephebes, the citizen hoplites and the oarsmen formed along the trench.

'Stand up!' he called.

The town garrison had their spears in their hands and they all but filled the wall. The Macedonians came over the crest of the rubble – the wall was fifty feet wide in places – and crashed headlong into the formed Rhodians. Spearless, spread out in no particular order, their feet punished by the sharp gravel of the walls, the Macedonians hesitated, and the Rhodians rolled them down off the wall in a single charge.

Satyrus was never in action – he was too busy calling commands. And as soon as his men cleared the wall top, he ordered them to face about. Already the enemy had missiles flying, heedless of hitting their own recoiling troops.

The Rhodians went back down their own wall and into the reserve trench behind it.

The Sakje came forward, rearmed with arrows, and filled in the strong places on the rubble wall top. The Cretans were slower to return.

Idomeneus was dead.

The second attack was half-hearted. The archers cleared off the wall, but the Antigonids had lost too many officers and the men hung back. The whole attack bogged down into desultory javelin-throwing, the Antigonids occupying the wall top but not pressing their advantage.

Satyrus waited as long as he felt that he could and then attacked them, clearing the wall top. This time, as soon as his men crested the wall, the enemy barrage struck, and he took casualties. But many of the enemy rounds dropped short or long, and his men got away with only twenty down – twenty armoured men he could not afford to lose.

The third attack failed to dislodge the Sakje. They shot and shot,

441

some of them using their bows at arm's reach, others drawing their long knives, and the Cretans held their ground too, and the enemy soldiers paid heavily for their timorousness in not pressing their attack. Caught in the open ground, they took casualties they needn't have taken.

'Demetrios is pushing new troops forward,' came the message from the tower.

'My boys and girls are down to five shafts each,' Melitta said.

Two hours until sunset.

'Give they the wall,' Jubal said.

Abraham nodded. 'You said to make it look like we wanted to hold it. We held it all day. Give it to them.'

Satyrus looked into the golden afternoon. 'No,' he said. 'Sorry, friends. We have to go hand to hand.'

Neiron started to say something. Satyrus glared at him. 'This is my call, gentlemen. Archers out, Melitta, all the way back to the "bow". Save your last shafts for – well, if we get broken.' He held out his hand. 'Give me that whistle,' he said, and she handed it over.

'Don't get killed, stupid brother,' she said. She kissed him. They grinned at each other.

The archers slipped away unseen, heading for the rear. Satyrus climbed the wall, took cover behind one of the filled baskets, which topped his head – just. It had been hit repeatedly, and the soft earth and gravel fill was a pincushion of bolts.

Now he could see the enemy forming. Stones slammed into the earthwork, but it held. A trickle of sand ran down the basket and onto his back. Another bolt thudded home.

Satyrus ran down the slope to his troops. 'Officers!' he roared.

He waited until they were all there. 'Listen to me,' he said. 'When the whistle sounds, you charge. Got it?'

Neiron looked up at the wall. 'How will you know?'

'I'll be on the wall,' he said. 'Don't leave me there. We have to stop this one. No second place, gentlemen. No speeches. Get to the top and hold. Ready?'

They growled, and he sent them back to the phalanx. He turned and ran up the inner face of the third wall, Helios on his heels.

'I didn't tell you to come,' he said.

'You don't tell me to get you juice every morning, either,' Helios replied.

Bolts fell, and a shower of rocks, small rocks being launched in baskets. One pinged off his silver helmet, hard enough for him to smell blood. But he peered out.

The enemy was already in the middle ground – running silently. Men were falling – they were going too fast for safety. They were *fast*.

Satyrus blew the whistle. He had left it late. Just below him, his men had to get to their feet – had to get their shields on their arms. Had to start up the slope of rubble.

But the Antigonids were slowed – again – by Jubal's cunning rubble wall and its apparently shallow slope, and they bunched up on the ramps—

– Apollodorus roared for the oarsmen to dress their line as they came up the wall—

– Abraham laid his spear sideways across a line of his fellow citizens—

– A Macedonian officer, resplendent in gold and silver, raised his shield at the top of the wall. 'Come *on*!' he roared, and men poured onto the wall top—

Satyrus stood straight – no missiles now – and set his shield on his shoulder.

The oarsmen came over the wall top formed like veterans, and their spears slammed into the forming Macedonians. The Macedonians were higher: they'd won the race to the wall.

But they were too far apart, still trying to form.

And that's all Satyrus had time to see. He'd intended to fight the man in silver and gold, but just as the left files of the oarsmen closed around him, a crowd of Antigonid phalangites howled into his position. He took a shower of blows on his shield and he was pressed back against the men coming up behind him – and Helios went down next to him.

The whole fight seemed to crystallise, then, and time seemed to slow down. He sidestepped – right over Helios as the boy gave a great shudder – and put his spear through a man's eye-slit, whipped the head back and rifled it forward at the next man's helmet, the point scoring on the crown just under his horsehair crest and punching through

443

the bronze to spill his brains inside his helmet, and he slumped down across his file-mate.

A blow caught Satyrus in the neck. It hurt, but he kept his feet. Now his oarsmen were on either side. The enemy's rush was stemmed.

'Push!' Satyrus called, and the oarsmen leaned on their spears, put their shoulders into their shields and heaved. Now the tiny differences told – the leather socks inside their sandals allowed men a secure stance on gravel – scarves on necks stopped sweat, cloth pads in helmets allowed the men to see a little better.

But the Macedonians were better fed, and they had not lived in constant fear for six long months.

At the top of the wall, the fight balanced out. Men coming up behind couldn't join the push – the fighting lines were *higher* than their supporting ranks in most places. But they could press in tighter, and the press became so close that men began to die in the crush, stabbed under their shields, jaws broken when someone rammed their own shield up into their mouth in the melee, or men were simply crushed off their feet.

The citizen hoplites with the old-fashioned aspis were at an advantage, now – bigger shields kept men alive in the closest press. The marines, too: Apollodorus, howling like a lion loose in a pen of sheep, killed two men. He demanded that the marines *push*, and they responded. Draco killed a man an arm's length from Satyrus, and blood sprayed from his severed neck – the Antigonids around him flinched, and Draco was into them like a wolf into a flock of sheep, slaying to right and left, his spear ripping their shades from their mouths and sending them shrieking to Hades.

Draco died there, roaring into the ranks of the Antigonids alone, exposed, outpacing the rest of the marines, but he created a hole – a flaw like a tear in the fabric of the enemy formation right at the top of the wall, and it collapsed in. Satyrus knocked a man unconscious with the butt of his broken spear – no idea when it had broken – and stepped into the gap. Apollodorus downed his man and Abraham, armed only with a sword, roared at his citizen hoplites and jabbed so fast that Satyrus couldn't follow his actions – brilliant – and his men shoved forward. And there, in those heartbeats, the attack was broken.

Satyrus looked down and realised that the man he had just smashed to the ground was the man in the gold and silver armour. He grabbed the man's ankles and pulled. Other hands reached to help him.

He let go of the wounded officer, raised his head and saw the enemy rushing to their machines as the broken attack began to filter back. The enemy weren't smashed – officers and phylarchs were reforming down in the rubble – but Satyrus suspected that they were done for the day.

'Off the wall!' he called.

Two marines were lifting Draco. Satyrus had seen him fall – known who he had to be.

Other men had Helios, and other wounded and dead men. Satyrus saw blue and white plumes – the anchor.

Neiron: his white Athenian armour covered in blood.

'Back!' Satyrus roared. 'Off the wall!'

Slowly, stubbornly, the citizen hoplites and the ephebes and the oarsmen came down the back of the wall, and behind them, the enemy machines opened up.

'All the way back!' Satyrus called. He made himself look away – Neiron was looking at him. 'All the way back!' he yelled, and ran down the line. The ephebes were slow – too damned proud. He ran up to their leaders and demanded they run.

'We have no need to run, polemarch!' a phylarch called.

A stone from the enemy engines crushed him, showering his age-mates with blood and bone.

'Run, damn you!' Satyrus called.

He went up the face of the new wall – the last wall, the 'bow', and looked back.

The third wall was lost under a deluge of stone and shot. Some shots were going over – enough to kill more men in a few heartbeats than the whole desperate fight at the top of the wall had killed in minutes.

I had to, he told himself. Helios? Neiron? Draco? Idomeneus?

I had to. If I didn't hold it as long as I could, Demetrios would smell a rat.

If he's already smelled it, I have just lost those men for nothing.

The new wall had the revetments that they had spent the night building on the forward wall – heavy pylons like squat columns full of rubble and dirt, and the archers were already occupying them.

'Well done,' Melitta said. She had a graze across one cheek, but otherwise looked calm and clean. 'Looked real enough to me.'

'Helios is down,' Satyrus said.

Melitta raised an eyebrow. 'Helios is dead, brother. Neiron too. He asked for you. *And you did what you had to do.*' She put a hand on his shoulder. 'Everyone lost somebody today. Don't show it. You *won*. You must *appear* to have won. Philokles would say the same.'

Satyrus took a deep breath. *Helios!* he thought. But he schooled his face.

'Reform!' he called.

Demetrios didn't move forward until just after nightfall. The night assault rolled over the rubble, sprinting across ground thick with corpses, and took the unoccupied wall in one rush – and shouted their triumph, and relief, into the night.

Jubal smiled. 'Now he move his engines fo'wards.'

Satyrus awoke to pain. His body hurt, his legs hurt – one of his ankles was swollen, and he'd ripped his shield arm on the plates of his cuirass and *that* hurt. He sat up, cursed the darkness and managed to swing his legs over the edge of the bed and put his feet on the floor.

He made noise, deliberately, so that Helios would know he was up. *Helios was dead.*

He found a chiton and put it on, got to the door of the tent and found Jacob sitting on a chair.

'Lord?' he said, raising red eyes.

'Jacob?' Satyrus asked.

'Master has the fever,' Jacob said. 'We're all going to die here.'

Satyrus shot past the man into the adjoining tent.

'Is that you, Jacob?' Abraham said. Then he said something in another language – Hebrew or Aramaic. Satyrus shook his head.

'I hear you are sick,' he said.

'Stay back, Satyrus. Stay out. Damn you!' This last when Satyrus barged in. 'It's a fever, not some poisoned arrows of your strange god of light and disease.'

'I know what disease is, brother. You seem very much yourself.' Satyrus put a hand on Abraham's forehead. He was burning hot, and his eyes were as bright as newly minted coins. 'I take it all back. You are sick. Has Aspasia seen you?'

'And my sister – at the break of day. I was told to sleep as much as I can. I'm already bored, and this takes a week.' Abraham managed a smile.

'If you are lucky,' Satyrus said. 'It could be months,' he added.

'I could die,' Abraham said. He laughed. 'I might as well have gone down yesterday, covered in glory, like Neiron or Helios.'

Satyrus poured himself some juice and poured more for Abraham, and brought it to him. 'You are covered in glory. I saw you break their line. I will see to it that you receive a wreath of olive. And you're young and strong,' he said. 'We lost too many men yesterday.'

Abraham nodded. 'I assume you know what you are doing. I saw no reason for the third fight – but Jubal does.'

Satyrus managed a smile. 'Jubal is, in effect, commanding the siege.' He waved his hands. 'Who knew that I had a genius as my sailing master?'

'You'll miss Neiron,' Abraham said. 'He wasn't afraid to tell you what he thought.'

Satyrus swallowed heavily. 'I miss them all. Go to sleep.'

'If I die, I want to be burned,' Abraham said, 'in my armour. It's not against my religion.'

'Like a hero at Troy?' Satyrus said.

'Yes,' Abraham answered.

Outside, Satyrus found Apollodorus waiting patiently at the entrance to his tent.

'Looking for me?' Satyrus asked.

'Demeter, Lord.' Apollodorus shook his head. 'Helios is dead, and no one knows how to find you.'

'I'll need a new Helios.' Satyrus winced at the callousness of it. But there it was – if he died, they'd need a new polemarch, too.

'Hyperetes or hypaspist?' Apollodorus asked. He looked in Abraham's tent. 'He sick? That's not good. He's one of the best.'

'Both.' Satyrus led the smaller man into his tent, found the amphora of pomegranate juice and poured two cups.

'When this is gone, I have no idea where to find more.' Satyrus looked at the amphora – Attic black work, a hundred years old. Probably from Abraham's house.

'I haven't had juice in a month.' Apollodorus drank down his cup. 'You took a prisoner yesterday.'

'I did, too.' Satyrus nodded.

'He's one of Plistias' officers. One of the siege engineers. He wanted to see our rubble walls first hand.' Apollodorus scratched under his beard.

Satyrus made a face. 'How are the oarsmen?'

'I'm keeping them and the marines separate. The city hoplites have it bad – two out of three men are down. The ephebes are almost as bad. It's as if yesterday fuelled it – suddenly men are down everywhere. And this officer – Lysander – has seen some of it. I think we should kill him. We certainly don't want Demetrios to know how many sick we have.'

Satyrus drank his juice. 'I know why you asked, but we won't kill our prisoners, even if they storm us. We are *better*, Apollodorus – never forget that. To be better, one must *consistently* be better.'

Apollodorus managed a smile. 'I knew I'd get the "better" lecture. Very well – what do we do with him?'

'Give him an escort and let him wander about.' Satyrus nodded. 'Save your protests – I want to trick him, but first we must give a reasonably good facsimile of allowing him to go where he will. Is Demetrios moving his engines forward?'

'About a third of them. The rest are on rollers, ready to move. Jubal thinks from what he's seeing that the fever is as bad in the enemy camp as it is here, and that Demetrios has severe manpower problems.'

Satyrus nodded. 'Whatever happens, this Lysander *must not escape* tonight. Tomorrow night will be something else again.'

'You have a plan?' Apollodorus asked.

'It will depend on a few things. Let's meet under the olive trees at noon. All of the officers, and let's have some *Neodamodeis* and some women, as well.'

Exercise – alone, without Helios. Anaxagoras came up while he was shadow-fighting with a sword.

'Wrestle?' he asked.

They stripped and fought, and even with so many sick, people gathered to watch, cheered and wagered.

'You have recovered your muscle,' Anaxagoras said. 'I cannot pin you.'

'I have trained since I was a boy,' Satyrus laughed. 'It would be a strange thing if you could. Shall we play?'

In the shade of the olive trees, Anaxagoras was the master and Satyrus the merest pupil, but they played scales, up and down the lyre.

'It is exactly like swordsmanship, or spear-fighting,' Anaxagoras said. 'You must do everything until you can do it without any conscious thought. A good musician can play while talking, play while reciting poetry, play while drinking. Your sister is ... very different to Greek women.'

Satyrus laughed. 'She is very different.'

'I saw her in the trench – killing. Killing from the joy of battle, like a man. Is she really an Amazon?'

'Alexander called our mother the Queen of the Amazons,' Satyrus said. He tended to bite his tongue when he had to bridge his fingers in the scale.

'You see? That was your best scale. You must not think – only play. Your sister is taking your part with Miriam, I think.' Anaxagoras laughed. 'Although I flatter myself that she likes me.'

'I had a cat once in Alexandria. When she liked a visitor, she killed a dockside rat and brought it, all bloody, warm and damp, and dropped it on the person she fancied. Most people screamed.' Satyrus smiled.

'Point taken.' Anaxagoras reached out. 'No need for your elbows to stick out while you play. No need to force the strings. Relax.'

'She thinks you the handsomest man in Rhodes,' Satyrus said.

'The competition's not much, is it?' Anaxagoras laughed. 'She's a beauty, your sister. I didn't see it at first, mind you – I saw scars and barbarian clothes. It's in her ... daemon. When she smiles; when she moves.'

'Careful there,' Satyrus said. 'My sister. You know. Mind you, I'm not a protective brother. My sister does not require me to protect her.'

'She certainly has a way with opposition.' Anaxagoras shrugged. 'You are probably the wrong one for me to discuss this with. But no woman has ever pursued me like this before. I find it ... disconcerting. I'm used to the kind of pursuit that Charmides disdains – all smiles and blushes and smouldering looks. Your sister is – not like that.'

Satyrus laughed aloud.

'Nor am I ready to cede Miriam, although—' Anaxagoras showed actual confusion, and his hands fell away from the strings.

'As far as I'm concerned, to hesitate *is* to concede,' Satyrus said. 'I want to marry her. Make her queen.'

Anaxagoras smiled – a broad smile. 'Ah,' he said. 'Now we really are competitors. I've already offered.'

Satyrus was surprised. 'Offered? To Abraham?'

'Dowry stipulations, land, assets and everything.' He shrugged. 'I have not been answered. Nor does my ... curiosity about your sister end my suit. I think that the Lady of the Assagetae is a bit beyond me, to be honest.'

That's what you think, Satyrus thought.

Leosthenes poured a libation to Poseidon and made a small sacrifice to Apollo – a ram, and a ram that no temple would ever have accepted in better times. But the animal died well, with its head up, and Leosthenes proclaimed its liver clear of inflammation or disease – in itself a good omen.

Panther had been the Rhodian high priest of Apollo, but he was dead. Nicanor had been the second priest, and Menedemos was the third. It had taken them an hour to decide to allow Leosthenes to perform the rituals on behalf of the city, and they had confirmed his citizenship and taken him to the ruined altar of Poseidon for some secret ceremony that left his forehead decorated with ashes.

There was one altar among the olive trees – initially an altar to Apollo, and now to every god, because the temples were either destroyed or dismantled, and the open-air altar was the lone sacred space left to the survivors. Satyrus stood in front of the altar once the sacrifice was made.

All of the officers were gathered under the olive trees. Melitta stood with Miriam and Aspasia, the only women present. They stood well clear of the altar: despite his plethora of daughters and female servants and wives, the sea god was not one for feminine participation in mystery. Apollodorus stood at Satyrus' right hand, next to the altar, and Charmides, injured in the ankle by yesterday's fighting, sat on a stool. Damophilus, Socrates and Memnon stood together in front of the altar on Satyrus' left. Jubal stood farther back, with Philaeus, formerly Satyrus' oar master and now, with Apollodorus, an officer in the phalanx.

The *Neodamodeis* were represented by Korus and by Kleitos, the red-haired barbarian who was Abraham's helmsman: a freed slave himself, he was now commander of their *taxeis*.

Satyrus glanced at Jacob, who had brought with him a stack of wax tablets and a stylus. 'Get all this down, eh?' he asked.

Jacob nodded.

'First, the numbers. Casualties from yesterday?' Satyrus waited, apparently impassive.

Apollodorus indicated Anaxagoras, already acting as adjutant for the oarsmen.

Anaxagoras nodded. 'For the oarsmen – four hundred and sixty-two fit for duty, and two hundred and twelve marines, for a total of six hundred and seventy-four. Thirty-six wounded from yesterday, eleven dead or expected to die. All front-rank men.'

'Helios, Draco and Neiron,' Satyrus said.

Damophilus nodded. 'Three of the best. We will, of course, bury them as full citizens.'

Leosthenes sang the hymn to Ares.

Satyrus waited for him to finish, and turned to Kleitos.

'*Neodamodeis*,' Kleitos said. 'Eight hundred and thirty fit for duty. More with fever than I can count – let's say another six hundred. Only lost four dead yesterday and another nine wounded. All expected to recover. 'Less they get fever, of course.'

Men looked aside at the fever numbers. Freed slaves were now the bulk of the citizen manpower – and they were sick.

Melitta stepped forward into the circle of men, as was her right. 'I speak here for the town mercenaries,' she said. 'Idomeneus died on the wall. He served me five years, and I will put up a statue to him in Tanais, if we live.' She bowed her head. 'Cretan archers, two hundred and six fit for duty. Over ninety sick with fever. Twenty-one dead, no wounded, from yesterday. They tried to get his corpse back. And succeeded.'

Satyrus nodded.

'Idomeneus of Crete will receive full citizen honours,' Damophilus said.

Melitta nodded. 'Of other mercenaries, the city garrison can, this morning, muster three hundred and fourteen hoplites. Another hundred, at least, have the fever. Fifteen or more are already dead.'

Memnon nodded and stepped forward. 'City hoplites – around

six hundred. We lost seven dead and sixty wounded yesterday, but men have been falling like flies since sunrise, with fever. Maybe two hundred already sick.' He looked around. 'Abraham is sick. And my daughter, Nike.'

'So is your number with sick, or without?' Satyrus asked. He felt callous.

'Without.' Memnon nodded.

'Ephebes,' Satyrus said.

Socrates spoke up. 'One hundred and sixteen fit for service,' he said.

'Apollo's light!' Memnon said. 'What happened?'

'Fever,' Socrates said. 'We lost but two men yesterday, and four wounded. All four of whom have the fever now.'

Satyrus looked around. 'The oarsmen and my marines seem immune from this fever.'

Aspasia stepped into the circle of officers. 'Miriam and I have discussed that. But your oarsmen camp right next to the *Neodamodeis*, who have the highest disease rate.'

Apollodorus asked, 'Is it the same fever we had after Aegypt?'

Aspasia shook her head. 'I don't know. It seems to show an excess of bile – like your fever – but none of the men seems to turn yellow. And both of you did. As did many of the oarsmen.'

Satyrus nodded. 'I remember.'

'But the bile is much the same, and the sluggishness of the blood,' Aspasia said. 'I have cast horoscopes and I get no one answer. It is *not* the wrath of Apollo – that much I would feel bold to say.'

Apollodorus clearly questioned all this scientific talk. 'We should fill in the latrines,' he said, 'and make people use new ones in the ruins, down by the port. Dug deep. I've seen this fighting in Syria – same fever, same conditions.'

Aspasia surprised them all by nodding. 'I agree. I support the empirical approach to medicine. Hippocrates says many of the same things – simple observation has to augment our science. Let's face it – the people closest to the latrines have the worst fever except the oarsmen.'

Satyrus rubbed his chin. 'Fill the latrines? So people will have to walk to the port side to shit? That's not going to make me popular.'

Apollodorus nodded. 'And it won't – pardon my crude speech – be worth a shit unless you enforce it so that the wide-arse who tries to use the agora gets caught and punished.'

Satyrus looked around. 'Friends – this is the sort of thing that can destroy morale.'

Apollodorus was insistent. 'It works.'

Jubal leaned in. 'It do. Listen to he. Any sailor know it, too.'

Memnon shrugged. 'I don't, and I've been at sea all my life.'

Satyrus looked at Aspasia. 'I trust Apollodorus with my life, but you are the priestess of Asclepius and the best doctor in Rhodes.'

Damophilus nodded. 'And people will see that we are *doing* something about the fever.'

Satyrus glared at him. 'Until it fails, and then comes the backlash. People are not fools, gentlemen. It's a poor politician who makes bad laws merely to appear to take action.'

Memnon smiled. 'You don't know very many politicians,' he said.

That got a laugh.

Into the lightened atmosphere, Aspasia spoke up. 'I say do it,' she said. 'I will take some auguries and cast another horoscope – I will ask some friends for help. And I think we would do well to propitiate Apollo and Asclepius publicly. And then move the latrines.'

Satyrus nodded. 'Who is now Priest of Apollo?' he asked.

Young Socrates stepped forward. 'I am. And I would be delighted – devoted – to support Despoina Aspasia.'

Satyrus rubbed his chin. 'Make it so. We move the latrines tomorrow night – every citizen must participate. There will be no exceptions.'

'Lot of work,' Memnon said.

'We should have a few days off,' Satyrus said.

That got a buzz of excitement. Satyrus shook his head. 'No – I won't say anything. But I want to see Aspasia and Miriam after this, and Jubal. Kleitos – all the sailors tonight, yes?'

Kleitos grinned.

Jubal grinned.

Damophilus stepped forward. 'You *must* tell us, polemarch. People need to have hope. These men are grinning. Why?'

Satyrus kept his face impassive. 'Damophilus, I value you and I hope that we are friends. But yesterday, I sacrificed men – good men. My friends. They are dead so that I could keep a certain secret, and by all the gods, that secret will be kept.'

Damophilus was angry. 'We are the town council! What's left of the *boule*!'

Satyrus shook his head.

'Are you a tyrant?' Damophilus said in sudden heat.

Memnon grabbed his arm. 'Come, lad. Uncalled for.'

Satyrus crossed his arms. 'You may remove me from command,' he said. 'That's harder with a tyrant. But in this, I will not be moved.'

Damophilus submitted with an ill grace.

Satyrus looked around. 'I'm sorry for my tone. But I will not speak of this. However, I have other military matters to discuss. I need all the armour in the town gathered. I'd like every *taxeis* to collect its own, paint a number inside the harness and on every other item and lay them out here in the olive groves – the cleanest air, in case the miasma is in the armour. I need this to be done immediately.'

Damophilus' blood was up. 'Armour is a man's private property,' he said.

'So were the slaves. The rules are different, now.' Satyrus looked around. No one else demurred. 'I need that armour, as soon as can be.'

'We'll see,' Damophilus said, belligerently.

Satyrus stared him down, waited for him to walk away and collected the women and Jubal, and they walked with Korus and Kleitos to the far end of the sacred precinct.

'It is tonight?' Kleitos asked.

Jubal nodded. 'He is moving engines *right now*,' he said.

'Why are *we* here?' Miriam asked. 'Is it about the fever?'

'No,' Satyrus said. 'I need every woman – at least, the biggest five hundred – to put on armour. Late this afternoon. And to stand in it all night – and to ask no questions.'

Jubal grinned. 'I get it. You one sub-tile bastard.'

Satyrus punched the black man in the arm. 'This, from you?'

Jubal thrust out his chin and laughed. 'Take one to know one, eh?'

The shadows were long on the agora when the alarm sounded. Men moved with purpose – alarms were part of every day, and most citizens no longer even felt a rush of the daemon of war when they heard the trumpets.

Satyrus was in armour already. He'd had to lie down on the floor of the tent to get into his cuirass unaided, but he didn't have a new hypaspist yet, and wasn't sure where to find one in the middle of a siege.

He got to his feet, drank a cup of water which tasted fairly bad, and walked out with his shield on his shoulder and a spear in his hand.

Apollodorus was waiting, with the prisoner by his side. Lysander looked like a tough man, a veteran, in late middle age with grey at his temples and a major scar at the top of his left shoulder that ran in under his chiton.

'He bowed to Satyrus. 'My lord? I gather I have you to thank for my capture.'

Satyrus took his hand and clasped it. 'I took you, yes.'

The man met him, eye to eye. 'May I ask if I am to be ransomed? Or treated as a slave?'

Satyrus nodded to Apollodorus, who saluted and headed off towards the alarm.

'You had a pleasant day?' Satyrus asked.

Lysander made a face. 'I was allowed to wander about. This scares me, lord. I do not wish to be a spy – or to be killed.' He spread his hands. 'I see that you have the fever here – not as bad as our camp, but bad enough. I offer this as proof that I am no spy. I cannot hide what I saw.'

Satyrus nodded. 'Come with me, Lysander. You are a Spartan, I think?'

Lysander nodded. 'No true Spartan, sir. My father was a Spartiate and my mother a well-born Theban lady – but they were never married. I was refused entry to a mess, and I have served abroad ever since.'

Satyrus stopped at the base of the ladder to his tower. 'You may know a man I loved well – Philokles of Tanais?'

'If he was Philokles of Molyvos,' Lysander said with a smile, 'I knew him for a while. We fought together – Zeus Sator, back when Archippos was archon of Athens. I was a great deal younger then.' He laughed.

'He was my tutor,' Satyrus said.

'I know,' Lysander said. He shrugged. 'I know who you are, lord. But it ill suits a man who must beg for his life to claim acquaintance.'

'You really are a Spartan,' Satyrus said. 'Come.'

'Why?' Lysander said.

'Because I wish to show you why Demetrios has no hope of taking this city,' Satyrus said. 'Come. I will release you in the morning. Alive. To tell what you have seen.'

Satyrus led the way up the ladder.

The shadows were long – indeed, the sun had dropped to the rim of the world, and the handful of standing trees visible from the towers threw shadows many times their own height.

'Demetrios has almost completed moving his engines forward,' Satyrus said. 'Thirty-one engines, by my count.'

Lysander turned to him. 'You cannot expect me to confirm that, lord.'

Satyrus shrugged. 'Worth a try. How's your eyesight?'

Lysander raised an eyebrow. 'Not what it was when I was twenty.'

'Take a look, anyway.'

Lysander looked out into the edge of night. At his feet lay the fourth south wall – what the Rhodians called the 'bow'. It ran in a broad curve from the ruins of the great sea tower back almost to the edge of the agora, and then out like the arm of a bow to the original corner with the west wall, where a heavy, squat tower full of ballistae had never fallen to Demetrios. The new wall was the tallest of all of Jubal's rubble walls, and the most complicated, and most of the town had dug for a month and laid weirs made from every house timber in the town to build the cradles to hold the rubble to make the wall.

Beyond the 'bow' ran the shallower curve of the third wall, with a loose cordon of pickets on it – most of them archers and crossbow snipers in covered positions. Their posts were obvious to a child from the height of the tower.

'By the gods – that's how you killed our snipers!' Lysander said.

'Yes,' Satyrus said. 'I'm showing you all of our secrets.'

'Whatever for, lord?' the Spartan asked. His accent made Satyrus pine for Philokles.

'Because Demetrios needs to offer us terms we can accept, or we will defeat him and his empire will be at an end. You know this as well as I do, Lysander. You are a professional soldier. How long did you expect us to hold?'

Lysander nodded. 'Ten days.'

456

'So we are on the two-hundredth day – or so.' Satyrus pointed at Demetrios' camp. 'Will this army ever fight again?'

Lysander shrugged. 'I take your point.'

'Good.' Satyrus looked over the edge of his platform where he could see, half a stade away, a lone man standing at the south-east limit of the 'bow,' in the earthworks built from the rubble of the sea tower. He raised his shield and flashed it – once, twice, a third time.

Jubal flashed his shield back.

Satyrus turned back to the Spartan officer. 'Kiss your engines goodbye,' he said.

Stratokles stood on the rampart of the third wall at sunset, safe behind one of the basketwork embrasures that the Rhodians had constructed. Lucius was looking it over.

'Innovative bastards. Have to give them that. Of course a basket of rocks is a wall. Fuck me.' Lucius cut a twist of the heavy basket loose.

Stratokles was watching the enemy respond to an alarm. 'What's got them excited?' he asked. He watched carefully, sniffing the air.

Lucius shook his head.

'Do you smell smoke?' the Athenian asked.

'I do,' Lucius said.

Stratokles was looking *behind* the wall, at the ground that had been no-man's land the day before. Thin curls of smoke were rising in two places.

'Off the wall,' Stratokles said. He ran down the wall to where two hundred of Nestor's crack guards rested in open formation. 'Off the wall. Now! Back! Back off the wall!'

He turned and grabbed Lucius. 'They've mined the third wall. We were meant to take it – Ares, I can see it. Run, Lucius – all the way to Plistias. Get to Demetrios if you can. Tell him I'm getting the men out.'

'He'll spit you.' Lucius was dumping his armour as he spoke.

'Fuck him. These are good men – too good to die for nothing. Now *run!*'

Lucius dropped his breastplate with a crash of bronze, and ran.

Stratokles ran among the Heraklean marines. 'On me. Now! Don't bother forming by files – off the *fucking* wall, you wide-arses! Follow me!'

Crossbow-sniper teams could hear him, and they began to rise to their feet.

'Ares, it's their whole garrison,' said a man. Stratokles grabbed him, slammed a hand against the fool's helmeted head. 'Run!' he yelled.

Finally, the Herakleans were moving. So were the crossbowmen.

Stratokles ran across the former no-man's land, behind almost the last of his men. The ground felt hot under his feet. 'Athena protect,' he panted.

Men were slowing as they entered the battery where the king's machines had been parked by sweating slaves, many of whom were still heaving against the tackles or digging, or grading the ground smooth. Smoke rose here, too. The smell was in the air. And Stratokles suddenly noticed that right at the edge of the artillery park was an enormous stone, painted red.

'Athena save us!' he said. Then, to the phylarch nearest him, he said, 'Run! All the way – right through the engines!'

The man looked at him as though he were mad. Perhaps he was. He was urging the entire garrison of the new salient to abandon it to the enemy.

Just to the right, on recently cleared ground, stood the reserve *taxeis*, two thousand men with pikes, waiting to face any attack thrown at the newly taken third wall – meant to support the men *on* the wall. Stratokles' men.

'What in the name of Tartarus and all the Titans are you doing, you Athenian coward?' bellowed the Macedonian *strategos*.

'Mines. Pre-registered engines. Massive attack. Run or die.' Stratokles panted.

'Your wits have deserted you,' Cleitas said. He drew his sword.

'Stupid fool,' Stratokles panted. Now the man was between him and escape. 'Feel the ground. Look at the smoke. Look at the enemy. Are you a child?' he bellowed.

The Macedonian was more interested in his own sense of honour. 'Child?' he roared, and cut at Stratokles with his sword.

Stratokles took the blow on his shield rim and stepped past the man. 'Arse-cunt!' he said, and ran.

The mathematics of a siege is inexorable. There is mathematics in every form of war, but the limitations of a siege bring them to the fore.

Ranges, for instance, are immutable. An engine of war has a maximum range, no matter how it is built. On a battlefield, a new weapon might surprise an enemy – but give that enemy two hundred days, and they will know the range of the weapon to the hand's breadth.

And the mathematics of destruction are equally inexorable. It will take so many engines with so much of a throw-weight just so long to knock down a given length of wall. And if you have engines to employ, you will set them in certain very predictable positions – predictable because they have a certain range and a certain throw-weight, and because the enemy has a certain wall with a certain construction and height.

These things proceed as if divinely ordained. Perhaps they are. But because of them, when the third wall fell, there were only so many positions – at the right range, free of rubble and half-collapsed walls, covered – in which Demetrios, Plistias and their officers could crowd their thirty-one engines to batter the new wall. The new, tougher wall. In fact, by the new, inevitable physics of siege warfare, there were only two places. Large, red-painted stones marked both of them.

Satyrus drummed his fingers on the deck of the tower.

On the right and left arms of the 'bow', great swathes of painted linen were pulled down.

'Ares!' Lysander said. 'Oh, gods.'

In orderly rows, like the toys of a well-mannered child, sat twenty-four engines – new engines. Jubal had not used an engine against Demetrios and his forces since the fall of the great tower.

Every engine was fully loaded, the throwing arms cranked right back against the frames, the slings hanging limply to the ground.

When the cloths were ripped away, Jubal raised a torch. It showed clearly in the twilight air. He lit the payload of the engine closest to him. A dozen more were lit afire. And then they began to shoot.

Most of them volleyed together. A few were late – at least one failed to function altogether. But a dozen flaming missiles and another dozen heavy rocks flew, carving streaks on the clear evening air.

'Ares!' Lysander said again. It was a sob.

The shots were exactly on target. It was unlikely any would miss – a month ago, when the Rhodians had owned the ground, they had ranged them in. A few fell short – ropes can change torsion in a month, even when loosened off – but most struck their targets within a few arm's lengths of a bull's eye, and fire blossomed.

The alarms started, trumpets blaring in all directions.

The Rhodian garrison stood to in a sudden movement, two thousand spears coming erect as the hoplites stood up from concealment behind the 'bow'.

'I have no shortage of soldiers,' Satyrus said.

'Ares!' Lysander said. His face was as white as a suit of Athenian armour.

The second volley left the engines – no fire now, but just stones. Some engines threw baskets of loose stones, and some threw sacks that opened in the air, and some threw heavy rocks – one-mina and even ten-mina rocks, carefully hewn to shape by stone-cutters.

The storm of death fell all across the wall.

The whole corps of the town's archers – all the Sakje and the Cretans – stood to on the 'bow'. They lofted a volley onto the enemy wall – the third wall, captured just a day before – and then they lofted a second volley and a third and a fourth, a reckless display of a deep supply of arrows, and a fifth.

As the heavy arms of the engines cranked back for the third round, there was a low rumble from the earth near the second wall: the ruins of the second wall, well behind the enemy engines. Columns of dust and smoke rose into the air – some springing from the ground like a desert storm, and some rising lazily like smoke from a campfire when herdsmen kill a sheep and eat it on a feast night on the mountains.

'That was our mine,' Satyrus said.

'But they are ... far from—'

'Now your relief columns cannot reach the third wall. Not for a long time.' The flames from the burning mines rose like the sacrifices of a pious army, or the huts of a defeated one – columns of thick, black smoke: every drop of olive oil in every warehouse in the richest city in the world.

The engines shot again – two dozen heavy missiles visible at the top of their parabolas before falling like the fists of an angry god on the terrified phalangites of the duty *taxeis*.

The archers got off the wall, and the phalanx, two thousand strong, went over the top. Perhaps it was a shambles on the ground, but from a height it appeared that every hoplite was animated by the same godlike hand, and the Rhodians crested the 'bow' and filed from the centre of their *taxeis* like the professional soldiers that the siege had made them. They filed down the ramps of the 'bow' that Jubal had designed, formed on the glacis at the foot of the ramps, men flowing into the rear ranks, and then they stepped off across the rubble, and not a single missile flew at them from the Antigonids.

Lysander's knuckles were white on the tower railing.

A second line of hoplites appeared in the dead ground behind the 'bow.' They stood to, their spears wavering slightly in the last light, and the setting sun gilded their points and the iron and bronze points of the city hoplites and the oarsmen as they went up the third wall uncontested, over the top of the wall where Helios had died the day before, and down the ramps on the far side with perfect precision – they had, after all, practised for this moment fifty times. On the far side of the third wall they formed again – and gave a great cheer.

The arms of the engines were cranked all the way back. Satyrus felt his heart thudding against his chest. This was the part that he and Jubal had disagreed on – and Satyrus had conceded.

In the distance, two *taxeis* of Demetrios' veterans had formed at the run and were now rolling forward. They had to hurry – the remaining sunlight could be counted in heartbeats. And Demetrios' entire artillery train was about to be lost.

Stratokles ran to Plistias.

'Stop!' he called.

The Ionian looked at him curiously. The phalanx was formed – four thousand men.

'You were the watch on the wall, you and your Herakleans,' he said. Not accusingly – but very seriously.

'I ordered them to run,' Stratokles said. 'The wall was mined – the wall and the engines. It is a *trap*.'

Plistias looked at his files as they moved forward. 'What kind of trap can resist four thousand hoplites?'

Stratokles grabbed the Ionian commander. 'Must I beg you? Listen to me! I have set a few traps in my time, and I know one when I see one. And this is a subtle man, Plistias. Satyrus is not some ignorant chieftain in a hill fort. He knows that you will counter-attack with overwhelming force.'

Plistias had heard enough. 'Halt!' he screamed in his quarter-deck-in-a-storm voice.

The lead files were pressed against the burning trenches as Stratokles and Lucius and Plistias of Cos and their officers tried to push the pikemen back.

It became easier as the first stones began to fall. They fell in silence – the pikemen were loud, and the roar of the fire close at hand was loud, and the first stone crushed three men and killed others with flying bone splinters and gravel, so great was its force. Then the front of the pike block heaved back.

Stratokles was still calling for them to get *back* when something hit his head, and he went—

'You may return to your camp at any time,' Satyrus said, rising to his feet.

The Rhodians had retaken the third wall and stopped – and the engines were now shooting over their heads, volleys of heavy stones whipped so hard that the slings cracked like lightning when the engines released – a low angle, and a new type of shooting. Satyrus hated it – he expected to see red ruin in the Rhodian ranks at every discharge – but Jubal was as good as his word.

Selected parties of pioneers and scouts – Sakje, Cretan and some from his marines – went forward into the inferno, to make sure that the enemy machines were afire.

There were screams – hideous screams – and shouts where the survivors of the baskets of rocks now attacked the third wall – out-numbered and with nothing but fire behind them.

It was slaughter. An entire *taxeis* was trapped between the fire and the Rhodian phalanx above them. No quarter was offered.

It should have made Satyrus smile. Unless he missed his guess, the siege was about to end.

Instead, it made him tired.

He watched another volley of heavy stones, and turned.

Lysander was holding himself steady, but his face was wet. 'I hate sieges, my lord,' he said.

'Me too,' said Satyrus. 'And this is my first.' He took a deep breath. 'Take Demetrios my request that he find a way to end the siege. And my offer of a three-day truce. He'll need it just to find his dead. Your dead.'

'And you will erect another trophy,' Lysander said.

Satyrus shook his head. 'The trophy was a goad, sir. We're beyond trophies, now.'

Satyrus felt curiously lonely as he wandered the celebration, having taken no part in the fighting, but Apollodorus would have none of it.

'There was no fighting. Don't be thick. Drink!' He said, and pressed his horn cup into Satyrus' hands.

Memnon embraced Jubal, and then embraced Satyrus. 'Our agora will have statues to both of you,' he said. 'In the morning, we will see him slink away, his tail between his legs. By all the gods, Satyrus – that was a victory.'

Damophilus was cautious in his approach, wary that Satyrus would ridicule him, but Satyrus felt rancour towards none that night. He stepped into Damophilus' cautious approach and embraced the man. 'Forget it,' he said. 'We won.'

The democrat nodded. 'We did. I didn't trust you – should have trusted you.'

Satyrus shook his head. 'Power corrupts.'

But he couldn't shake the feeling that the cost had been too dear, and that the slaughter of a *taxeis* might not settle the matter. He missed Helios every time he turned around. It saddened him that he had become a man who missed his hypaspist more than he missed his helmsman, or a man who had followed him for ten years, or his boyhood friends: Xenophon had died near him, and Dionysus had gone down in a storm, and he scarcely thought of them at all.

He drank more wine and walked along the lines of fires, dissatisfied, uninterested in company. He walked the walls, alone, surprising delighted sentries in the towers of the west wall, greeting tired mercenaries along the 'bow' and along the near-deserted sea wall.

The walk made him feel better. He came up the street that had been Poseidon's Way, when there had been a Temple of Poseidon, and found a group of Sakje crouched on the tile floor of the temple platform, where the Rhodian admiralty had once met – a tile floor laid down in the likeness of the eastern Mediterranean, with the islands picked out in white against a dark blue sea, among which Rhodes was marked in gold with a rose. The Sakje had swept the floor and made a small camp there – twenty or so young warriors, men and women. He could smell the smoke from their leather smoke tent – a strong scent like burning pine needles, but more pungent.

'Kineas' son!' shouted one of the young men, and in a moment he was surrounded. And he laughed with them, and drank smoke in the tent because they dared him, and stumbled away while they roared with laughter. He laughed too.

'You are not done yet,' Philokles said. His Spartan tutor was seated comfortably on a ruined foundation, and he had the lion skin of Herakles draped over a shoulder.

'Master!' Satyrus said, and flung his arms around the man. 'You are dead!' Satyrus babbled.

I represent something that is very difficult to kill, Philokles said with a chuckle.

There was no one there.

Satyrus walked across the tiles to where the altar of Poseidon had stood. The heavy marble plinth was carefully buried now, protected from the wanton destruction of the siege – but the gods were close, and Satyrus could feel them. He threw his arms wide.

'Lord Poseidon, Lord Herakles, and all the gods – one hundred and eighty days we have stood this siege with this town and all my friends. Deliver us, now. What town since Troy has stood such a great test? Need we be humbled? We are not so proud.'

'More like a demand than a prayer,' Miriam said, behind him.

He remained in an attitude of prayer for many heartbeats, craving an answer with his whole soul. And his soaring delight at the sound of her voice was parried like a sword blow against a good shield by his promise to Abraham and the presence of the gods, and his own lack of control – the smoke had put him on another plane entirely.

If the gods had an answer to make, they didn't give it voice.

Satyrus lowered his arms. His neck hurt, and he rolled his head and turned to meet her eyes.

Miriam was still wearing armour – that of some slim ephebe who had given his life for his town, because the spear wound that had taken his life and stained the white leather and linen corselet dark brown was obvious. But it fitted her – the shoulder yoke sat firmly on her square shoulders and the base of the corselet sat on her hips as if it had been made for her. Her short military chiton showed her legs in the new moonlight – legs too long ever to have graced a man, no matter how athletic.

'I'm glad you were in the rear rank,' he said with a smile. 'Any Macedonian who saw your legs would have smoked our ruse immediately.'

'I loved it,' Miriam said. 'Oh – I could become Melitta. To be one with the phalanx—'

Satyrus laughed. 'I hadn't expected you to like it.'

She sat down. 'That's what Anaxagoras said. And he sounded just as disappointed in me. I thought that you would understand.'

Satyrus rolled his shoulders. 'Of course I understand. But I think I may be forgiven for being surprised. I'm surprised that *anyone* likes it. I am surprised that Anaxagoras likes it.'

'You like it,' Miriam said.

Satyrus shook his head. 'Not particularly.'

Miriam gave a sour giggle. 'You sound like a girl trying to win more compliments.'

Satyrus sat next to her. 'A subject on which I expect you have some experience.'

She shook her head. 'I want to know. Are you just posturing? Do you really not like it – the struggle? The fight?'

Satyrus shrugged. 'You want a real answer, and I'm not in the mood to give one, honey. I'm full of wine and old worries and smoke, and if your lips touch mine I'll have you right here, armour and all. Is that honest enough for you?'

She looked at him. A level stare; in no way a come-hither.

Satyrus sat back, getting the scales of his cuirass comfortably seated against the stones behind him. 'I love how good I am at fighting – in that, I am like your beautiful young girl, who loves to stare at her own reflection and basks in the admiration of every young man in the agora.'

Miriam chuckled. 'You've met some girls.'

'One or two. But honey, when the god-sent power falls away, I have a dead friend or two and I'm covered in other men's blood, or unconscious from a wound. And sometimes, when the wine goes down the wrong way, I have to remember that every man I've sent to Hades had a life like mine – love and hate, wine and olives. And Achilles says:

Better a slave to a bad master
Than king among the dead

'They're dead when I kill them. And the next fight, or the fight
after – I'll be dead. And when I look at you, when I play music with
Anaxagoras, I can't help but see that there are *better things*.' He took a
deep breath, and all he breathed in was her – jasmine and a woman's
sweat. 'It's not a competition in the palaestra. What I mean—'

He was so close to her that he could see the pores of her skin, the
smudge of dark oil under her right eye, the trace of cosmetics hastily
rubbed out of her eyes.

Her lips filled his head, the way an opponent's sword can fill your
head. He saw nothing else, and wanted nothing else.

It was easy to fall into her, and it was easy to break his oath to
Abraham—

Who was lying sick in a tent.

Satyrus stood up, his erection painful against his leg, ashamed of
his weakness and his *stupid* moral qualms. He wanted her as he had
never wanted a woman. The cold eye of light might tell him that she
was a dirty, dishevelled waif, skinny from not enough food, dirty from
battle, wearing a dead boy's chiton and armour – but all he could
see was the perfection of the lines of her lips, the spacing of her eyes,
the swell of her breast when she reached up to touch her hair, her
collarbones, her legs—

'I promised your brother,' he said miserably, backing away as if she
had a dagger at his throat.

'Me too,' she said. She giggled. It was an incongruous sound. She
covered her mouth, bent double with laughter. 'Menander couldn't
write a better comedy, Satyrus.'

'I imagine he'd make it funnier,' Satyrus said. He sat down on a
different stone.

She adjusted her hair, taking her time. 'I once heard that this is the
most aesthetic posture a woman can adopt,' she said.

'I wouldn't know,' Satyrus said. 'At the moment, they're all pretty
much the same to me.'

She chuckled, her voice low. 'You do pay the very best compliments.'

Satyrus smiled to himself. 'Do you have any wine?' he asked.

She shook her head.

'I'll get some,' he said.

'I'll wait,' she responded.

Satyrus walked back through the ruined temple to the Sakje youths. Two of them were copulating – some of the rest watched or called suggestions – but not loudly. Sakje were never loud in camp after dark.

'Could you spare me a skin of wine?' he asked, averting his eyes. The ecstatic face of the Sakje girl – on top at the moment – was not what he wanted to see.

'Hah!' Scopasis rose from the ground – he had been lying on an animal skin, and he rose with a chuckle. 'Satyrus, son of Kineas – I have wine to share.'

Satyrus pointed off into the dark. 'I have ... a girl.'

Scopasis smiled darkly. 'As do I. I will give you half what I possess.' He pulled out a skin – a skin that seemed to have a certain stench – and took a long drink, and then poured some into his cloak-mate's mouth, and more into a cup. Then he tossed the skin. 'Drink to me when I am dead, Satyrus son of Kineas.'

The Sakje girl was breathing hard, fast and rhythmically beyond the small fire. She raised her face and gazed unseeing on the autumn night, and shrieked softly.

Satyrus caught the skin. 'Gods bless you, Scopasis,' he said. He went back through the ruins, stumbling. The girl shrieked again and her man laughed, a low, happy sound.

Satyrus sat close to Miriam, who had loosened and removed her armour. She was as close to naked as a person might be, wearing a single layer of thin wool that covered her to the base of her thighs.

'I'm cold,' she said. 'Give me your cloak and sit close.'

He untied the laces of his shoulder yoke, lay down and rolled out of the harness, feeling lighter and younger. Then he sat next to her, shoulder to shoulder, and threw his chlamys over them both.

He handed her the wineskin and she wrinkled her nose.

'The hide is untanned. The Sakje think it keeps the taste in the wine. There's a sheep's stomach inside, and the mouthpiece is horn – you'll take nothing from it but wine. But the Sakje drink like this.' He flipped the skin up expertly and a line of wine fell from the neck of the skin into his lips.

She reached for the skin, and he shook his head. 'Let's not spill it. Raise your mouth.'

She did, and he carefully poured wine into it.

She spluttered. 'This is unwatered wine!' she said. 'Oh – and good wine, at that.'

'The Sakje do not drink bad wine. But drink sparingly – this has something in it. Poppy or lotus or ground hemp seed. Coriander. Something else.' He drank another mouthful. 'The Sakje do not believe in moderation.'

Now the man was moaning, a campfire away.

'I can tell,' Miriam said. She took the skin and drank, leaving a line of drops spattered along the edge of his chlamys. They both laughed.

'One of us should go,' Satyrus said some time later, when they'd fallen asleep briefly with her head against his shoulder.

'Why?' Miriam said. 'I will be true to my oath. But I would rather be true with you beside me.'

Satyrus smiled into her hair. 'Will you marry me?' he asked.

'Ask me when the siege is over,' she said. 'We are living in a world of heroes and horrors, not in the real, waking world. When you awake, I will be a scrawny Jew with a big mouth, and you will be a godless Hellene who needs a dynastic marriage. But I will tell my granddaughters that I might have been a queen—'

Satyrus got a hand under the chlamys, and with all the practice of years of brotherhood and martial training, rammed his thumb in under her arm so that she leaped in the air and squealed.

'You're ticklish!' he said, delighted.

'Uh-oh,' she said.

He fell asleep with her sprawled across him for warmth, held closer than any lover he'd ever slept with – oath unbroken. And woke to her eyes on his in the light of a new day. She rubbed the tip of her nose on his, and her fingers pressured his, and she touched her lips against his – and leaped to her feet.

'It's a new day,' she said.

PART V

THE DESTROYER OF CITIES

The Athenian delegation might have been chosen specifically to argue *against* their own best interests, or so it seemed to Stratokles.

'You must explain to the king how hard pressed Athens is,' Stratokles said. Again.

'We don't want to seem like beggars,' Democrates said. 'No, that would never do.'

'We represent one of the most powerful states within the girdle of the ocean,' said Miltiades the Younger. 'It would not do to appear as supplicants.'

'No, no,' said a chorus of elderly aristocrats.

Stratokles all but tore his beard. 'Do you think that King Demetrios the Golden will come to *you* to *ask* if he can send troops to relieve your city?'

Miltiades nodded. 'Well put. That is exactly what we should do.'

'That would preserve the dignity of our city,' Democrates said.

'There is no dignity in a city sacked by a conqueror!' Stratokles said. These men appalled him – they were the scrapings of the *areopagitika*, the worst sort of orators. They had told him themselves that Cassander's forces were at the gates. That the olive groves of Attica were on fire.

Democrates looked at Stratokles as if he were a piece of filth. 'You would not understand, young man. We have the city's best interests at heart. We represent the *best* families. We have not exchanged the tyrant Demetrios of Phaleron for a new master. Our city must have her own rulers – good men, from good families.'

'We know how to rule well,' said the chorus of aged sycophants.

From the doorway of the tent, Lucius the Latin chuckled and farted.

Stratokles was too angry for reason. 'You are a group of aged idiots,' he said.

That got him silence, at least. 'You must go before Demetrios the

Golden as suppliants – as very beggars, because that's what we are! And we needn't care if Holy Athens is under siege! May Athena blast me if I speak a lie – I have watched six months of siege here. You *gentlemen* have no idea what Rhodes has survived – but you do not want this war to come to Athens. You do not want your maidens ravished, your lands burned, the Acropolis pulled down around your ears or torched the way the Persians torched it. Save yourselves – let me help you. Go to Demetrios with halters around your necks and beg him to break the siege here and send troops to Athens before it is too late.'

Stunned silence greeted his tirade. For a moment – just a moment – he thought that he'd carried them.

'You are full of passion,' Democrates said. 'But you have little idea how great nations do business.'

For a moment, Stratokles considered killing the man. For ten years he had served Athens – served in secret, hidden in shadows, gathering information and money and mercenaries. He had served with Cassander and the Tyrant, Demetrios of Phaleron, with Dionysus of Heraklea, with Antigonus One-Eye, with Ptolemy and with Demetrios the Golden, shifting sides as a breeze turns on a cloudy day at sea, all for the best interests of Athens.

And these old fools were going to throw it all away.

He was blind with rage for a long moment – perhaps fifty heartbeats. The chorus babbled.

Democrates said something that was lost in his rage.

When he was able to see them, they were cowering away from him in the edges of the tent, and he had a sword in his hand. He took a deep breath. And said the words Athena whispered in his ears.

'No matter how beautiful a woman may be,' he said, 'she wins no suitors sitting at home. You, *gentlemen*, are fools. Sit in this tent, if you like. I will endeavour to save our city without you.'

Straight from the chorus of useless old men to the tent of his mistress, Stratokles entered without announcing himself and walking past her maids, who shrieked. He found her sitting on a stool, reading.

'Pack, Despoina,' he said. 'You must leave – soon.'

She sat up. Raised an eyebrow. 'I had not expected this level of impertinence from you—' she began.

Stratokles struck her. It was not a hard blow, open-handed, a mere tap – but across her face. The shock of it knocked her to the floor and she squealed.

'Wake up, Despoina.' Stratokles was ashamed of hitting her, but he'd done worse things. 'Demetrios is going *down*. Now – soon – a year from now – perhaps five years. He gambled here, and he has lost badly and you are *dallying*. We need to cut our losses, save your best soldiers and sail away – and put some new pieces on the board.'

She lay on the floor, staring at him with enormous, hurt-filled eyes. 'You hit me.'

'You needed the blow.' Stratokles' voice was hard, and his face closed. 'I have served you well, as well as I am able, and I have to leave you soon. I will see you clear of the wreck. I guessed wrong, Despoina. Demetrios will either lose here, or win with such losses that he will destroy his father's best army. You have options. It is time to employ them.'

'You would *leave me?*' she asked.

'My city is threatened, Despoina. I have never hidden my first loyalty from you. Indeed, I intend to use you to save my city, and use my city to save you, all in one roll of the dice. Now, please cease your struggles and *obey*.'

She got to her feet. 'I have never seen you like this. I might like it.'

Stratokles shook his head. 'I apologise for the blow. And I have no interest in being your master, Despoina – I am in haste. Pack. Now.'

'I will,' she said. There was wonder in her voice. 'Should I leave—'

'Yes,' he said. 'Leave everything that is not gold.'

He nodded curtly and turned to leave.

She met his smile with a brave smile of her own. 'I'll get on with it. Is it so bad? Can we save me? And your city?'

He nodded. 'If the gods will it.'

Stratokles met Lysander in the great red tent where men waited to be received by Demetrios the Golden. The Spartan took his arm as he entered.

'Satyrus son of Kineas told me to send you his greetings,' he said.

Every head in the tent turned, despite Lysander's attempt to speak quietly. The name carried its own force.

Stratokles nodded. 'You saw him,' he said.

'I was his prisoner for a day and a night,' Lysander responded.

Stratokles nodded again. 'He is well?' he asked.

'He has *six thousand hoplites*.' Lysander shook his head. 'He has less disease than we have. How could he have so many men? He *started* the siege with six thousand.' The Spartan stared at the ground. 'I asked that you be present when I tell the king, because you know this man.'

Stratokles nodded a third time. A courtier was approaching. 'Well, thanks for the warning,' he said.

Demetrios was sitting in an alcove of a Tyrian purple tent of linen and wool, with hangings on every wall – scenes from the siege of Troy, worked by the needle and by loom, shot with gold and silver threads. He sat on an ivory throne set on a floor of lion skins, and he was wearing his golden armour over a spotless white wool chiton. Plistias of Cos stood at his right shoulder. The Ionian bowed – sardonically, it seemed to Satyrus.

'Stratokles of Athens,' Demetrios said, with a nod.

'Lord King,' Stratokles returned with a bow.

'Tell me of this delegation from Athens, Stratokles.' Demetrios did not look like a man who had just lost two thousand elite soldiers. He looked like a temple statue in ivory and gold.

'Old fools, lord. Men that Pericles would have called *idiotes*, devotees of faction.' Stratokles spread his arms. 'Just my opinion,' he said, to draw the king's laughter.

He got it. 'Please, Athenian, tell me what you really think.' The king chuckled.

But Stratokles refused to play the clown. 'I will tell you, Lord King. I think that Cassander threatens Athens closely. I think that you stand to lose Greece – Attica and the Peloponnese – unless you or your father can act swiftly. Cassander is at the gates of Athens, lord.'

Demetrios nodded. 'So I hear, Stratokles. But sieges take time – who would know that better than me, eh?' he laughed. 'Athens will keep, and in my way, I am delighted to know where crooked-minded Cassander *is*. If he is penned in in Attica, laying siege to Athens, then he is not harming me elsewhere.' Demetrios smiled. 'Greece is the *past*, Athenian. The future is Asia and Aegypt.'

The focus of the king's regard lifted from the Athenian and settled like the *aegis* on the shoulders of Lysander. 'You were a prisoner with the Rhodians,' he said. His voice was mild, and it made Stratokles tremble.

He had been dismissed – both he and his city.

'Yes, lord,' Lysander said.

'And?' Demetrios asked.

'Satyrus son of Kineas sends his greetings,' Lysander said. 'He offers you a truce of three days to collect your dead. He says he will raise no trophy to goad you. And that he asks that you name terms, that this siege may be brought to an end.'

Demetrios had an ivory wand, tipped with gold – the kind of staff Hermes often carried, and that Hephaestos had made for Atreus. He toyed with it. 'He is gracious, my Hektor. What do *you* think, young Spartan?'

Lysander shook his head. 'May I tell you a tale, lord?'

'As you will,' Demetrios said.

'Lord, their council met yesterday, after their victory. And one of the councillors demanded that the town's statues of you and your father be pulled down – turned to rubble – and used to fill fortifications. But Satyrus,' the Spartan paused, 'said that they were being short-sighted. And the statues were cleaned and honoured.'

Demetrios smiled. 'You are too subtle for me, my Spartan friend.'

'They want peace,' Lysander said. 'They will fight to avoid extinction, but they will accept any honourable terms. They have the same disease in the town that we have in our camp. They are as thin as rails. Given any kind of terms, and they will surrender.'

Demetrios looked at them. He smiled – a young god.

'Terms,' he said pensively. 'Terms. An agreement. Negotiated. Men sitting around a table, bickering.' He shook his head. 'How many hoplites has my Hektor got left?'

'I saw six thousand,' Lysander said.

'Lord Ares, so many?' Demetrios smiled. 'I love him for his resilience – six months, and more!' He smiled again, and Stratokles, who had known Cassander and Antigonus, could not help but shudder.

'We have thirty thousand,' Plistias said. 'Arming our oarsmen would double that.'

Demetrios nodded, eyes glittering. 'Let us not brag. It offends the gods. But we have soldiers. And the rump of the pirates – they are still some thousands strong.'

'They are the hardest hit by the fever,' Plistias admitted. 'And they lack discipline.'

'But I suspect that they can each be used as an arrow shield at least once,' Demetrios said lightly.

'My lord,' Plistias protested.

'Surely it suits everyone if we exterminate the pirates?' Demetrios asked mildly. 'Surely that is a moral act?'

Plistias hesitated. 'They came as allies.'

'We can bury them as allies. How about supplies, navarch? Do we have supplies?' Demetrios was mocking.

'We do. Food for another six months, if required. Although we're losing ships.' Plistias spoke hesitantly. No one liked to give Demetrios bad news.

'We have a new shipment of timber from the mainland. We have the ships we can pull to pieces for timber. We have iron and bronze and gold and silver, for that matter, and most importantly, we have *my will*.' Demetrios rose to his feet. 'Your Rhodians want peace. Terms. They may have the same terms Troy had. They will know peace when the dogs are finished with their corpses.'

Lysander swallowed. 'Yes, lord.'

'Go and tell them, from me.' Demetrios flashed the man a smile.

'Yes, lord.' The mercenary bowed.

'Don't come back. If you are so fond of them, you may die with them.' Demetrios nodded, dismissing the man.

Lysander was a Spartan. He walked out with a straight back.

Demetrios' eyes went to Stratokles. 'And you?' he asked.

Stratokles sneered. 'Well, I certainly don't want to join the doomed,' he said with precise honesty. 'Nor am I any kind of friend to Satyrus son of Kineas.'

Demetrios nodded. 'Your honesty always refreshes me, Athenian. If you were less ugly, you might stand at my right hand.'

Stratokles had once winced at such remarks. But age brings reality. 'If I were prettier, lord, I might.'

'Shall I crave your advice?' Demetrios asked.

'You know my advice, lord. Get the best terms you can, load your army on your fleet, crush Ptolemy's fleet at Cos or Lesvos and fall on Cassander like a bolt from heaven.'

Demetrios locked eyes with Stratokles.

Few men could hold his gaze longer than it takes a man to draw a long breath.

Stratokles didn't so much as blink.

'You have a strong will, Athenian,' Demetrios said, but his eyes didn't move.

'I'm a stubborn man,' Stratokles said. He would have to avert his eyes, because to do otherwise would challenge the king, and the man was mad – at least, just now. But he didn't want to. He wanted – just once – to tell the powerful of the world to *fuck themselves*.

But his political sense rose above his rage – a rage that seemed to be simmering along, just under the surface. Perhaps it was just the waste of it all.

He blinked.

Demetrios chuckled in victory.

'I wish to crave a boon,' Stratokles said.

Demetrios pursed his lips and nodded. 'Within reason, anything.'

Stratokles scratched his beard. 'I want to arm a trireme and look into their harbour. I think they've shifted their engines – all of them – to the south wall. You need a good captain, and a crew he trusts.'

Plistias looked at Stratokles with a new respect. 'You would do this?'

Demetrios laughed. 'Plistias thinks you are a coward who abandoned the third wall. I am not such a fool. I ought to reward you for saving so many – old Cleitas was senile. Lost in the glories of the past. You seek to prove yourself to me?'

Stratokles smiled. 'Yes. You will see exactly who I am.'

Demetrios nodded. 'Choose any ship you like.'

Dawn, of the siege's one hundred and ninety-third day. Autumn, a cold, hard sky with high clouds that threatened a heavy wind, a red morning that might force sailors to take shelter.

A single black hull slipped off the beach and crept down the shore in the first light, oars muffled. Demetrios strode past the building area, where fifty new engines and a massive framework were under construction. Behind him, framing his head, a wooden wheel the size of an elephant towered, shot in iron. A hundred blacksmiths were already awake, pounding out plates. Demetrios smiled at the work.

'When they see you,' he said to the air, 'they will know my power.'

Plistias, and the two mathematicians who had done the calculations on the new machines, followed him across the sand. 'When they see it,' said Ctesibius, greatly daring, 'they will surrender.'

Demetrios was watching the black ship moving down the beach. 'I don't want them to surrender,' he said. 'Troy did not surrender. I want them to die.'

The ship began to gather speed.

'Send a boy for the lovely Amastris of Heraklea,' Demetrios said. 'She will want to watch her hideous champion in action.'

'He can certainly handle a ship,' Plistias said.

A slave went running across the sand.

'How tall will it be?' Demetrios asked, looking at the scantlings – great oak beams from Epiros.

'Taller than the pyramid of Chios,' Ctesibius said.

Demetrios beamed. 'I like that.' He listened to the sound of a hundred hammers falling on a hundred anvils. 'I like that.'

The slave returned and spoke to a staff officer, who spoke to Phillip the Macedonian, who looked around wildly.

'Well?' Demetrios asked. He had an eye for weakness.

'My lord, Amastris is not in her tent. Nor are her maids.' Phillip took a breath. 'And her soldiers are not in their tents.'

Stratokles' black-hulled ship raced along the mole and turned like the great drum of a war machine, as if guided by cogs and pulleys, into the harbour.

He ran down the mole – and the bolts began to fly. Not many, but enough to resound like huge hammers against a great drum when a brace of them hit his ship.

He turned again, his port-side rowers pulling their oars aboard just as his port side scraped along the hulks moored to cover the sea wall. Many of them had been burned, but the inner harbour had ships intact – and now they were covering his movement across the harbour.

The Rhodians hadn't had time to heat any bolts, and many of their engines must have been moved – but Stratokles' ship was hit, and hit hard. It shuddered, slowed and was hit again but the rowers kept their wits, and now Stratokles turned for the harbour opening.

'Well done,' Plistias said grudgingly.

The black ship shot out of the harbour entrance.

*

Stratokles was white-faced in the stern, his hands on the oars, a jagged splinter of white oak all the way through his left thigh so that his blood poured and pooled under him on the deck. There were men lying dead all along the deck, and more dead below in the oar decks, where the bolts had punched right through the fragile timbers.

But the ship was intact, and he was fifteen minutes' row upwind of Demetrios' fleet, and most of his deck crew were still alive. Amastris, brave as a lion, had refused to go below, and now she had a splinter right through her left hand, despite which she stood laconic, awaiting events, the blood running down her chiton while her maids screamed.

'Shut them up,' Stratokles said curtly.

'Pull it!' she said to her red-haired maid.

The Keltoi woman wasn't screaming. She pulled the splinter out in one smooth movement. Amastris shrieked once, fell to the deck and then put her back to the mainmast.

'Foresail,' Stratokles called down the deck, and Lucius passed the order to the acting sailing master. The sail was brailed on its yard – two men cut the brails and it swung free and the wind caught it immediately.

A maid screamed. Amastris cuffed her. 'Shut up, all of you. You,' she said to the Keltoi girl.

'Yes, Despoina,' she said.

'You are free,' Amastris said. 'You are too brave to be a slave. And you never heat my milk properly, anyway.'

One last shot came from the defences – a long shot, a light bolt that skipped on the wave tops and passed the ship as he heeled with the wind, pressing down the bow.

Rhodes was falling away under the stern.

'We are all free,' Stratokles said. 'Goodbye, Golden King.'

Amastris kissed him. Lucius slapped his back. 'Pretty smooth,' he said. 'Now lie down and let me save your leg.'

Stratokles was suddenly aware of great pain, and a rushing noise in his ears—

And he was gone.

30

DAY ONE HUNDRED AND NINETY AND FOLLOWING

The sag in morale when it became clear that Demetrios had no intention of abandoning the siege was so great that Satyrus thought the city might fall to any determined assault.

The weather grew colder, and it was too late to expect relief from the sea – and starvation began to stalk the garrison. There was no more oil to be found; wine was a drachma a sip, and the grain ration was cut – three-quarters of a measure, and then half, for all citizens.

Two weeks after the battle at the third wall, women cursed him in the street.

Miriam lost weight. He could see it in her neck and then, after a month on half-rations, he could see it in her face.

His sister lost weight. Anaxagoras lost weight. Men who survived the fever – like Abraham, gods be praised – had no meat to replace the muscle they lost, and they hobbled about like incarnations of Death.

The beautiful Nike died of fever, and Charmides was inconsolable.

And yet, unaccountably, after the lone ship tried to raid the harbour, the enemy didn't stir. Demetrios sat tight behind his earthworks. The ring of hammer on anvil carried clearly, though, and the sound was more ominous than any war hymn.

Lysander the Spartan was a useful and professional addition. He kept tablets, counted things, men, arrows – and stones. Satyrus took him at face value for the sake of Philokles. He couldn't imagine a dishonest Spartan.

Even the marines began to grow thin. Satyrus didn't see it happen – he just noticed, all of a sudden one morning, that Apollodorus' armour hung from him like a stripling wearing his father's corselet, and that Anaxagoras was thin: Charmides, practising with a bated spear against the Spartan, had thin legs.

'We're starving,' he said aloud.

Korus shook his head. 'Nah,' he said. 'We're a long way from starving.' He shrugged. 'But we'll be weaker, and then weaker still.'

Satyrus took to walking the streets constantly – from fire to fire, from guard post to guard post. Miriam was often with him, or Aspasia, Anaxagoras with a lyre, Lysander with a wax tablet, Jubal with papyrus and a plumb line or a tambourine. The first time he carried a tambourine, Satyrus teased him that he was trying to ape Anaxagoras. 'Or perhaps you will accompany him,' Satyrus said.

'Needs a pair of flute girls,' Lysander said, hesitantly. He wasn't one of them, yet. He wasn't sure if his humour would be accepted.

Jubal laughed. 'Funny, eh?' He shook the instrument, laid it carefully on the ground, pressed his ear against it and listened. 'Mines,' he said.

Anaxagoras got it. 'The drum skin passes the vibration, of course.'

Kleitos the helmsman was stripping the sails from the remaining ships in the harbour and rigging them as warmer tents for the poor. The Sakje, ever practical, had hollowed out cellars of collapsed houses and made warrens and tunnels there, where they lived in the warm – and where they could light a brazier and smoke out the whole warren.

Melitta almost always walked with him. The people of Rhodes saw her as a deliverer no matter how desperate they became, and many an angry word at her brother she deflected. And the weeks stretched on without relief.

The feast of Apollo came and went, and the fever came back to haunt former slaves and free alike – a quarter of them died in a single week, and the charnel smell of their burning corpses, like a vast burned offering of pig and goat, made every hungry stomach churn in desperation. More than once, Satyrus retched bile.

But after the second round of fever, the sickness seemed to abate. Leosthenes had nothing left to sacrifice but birds. He prayed unceasingly.

Gangs of children roamed the ruined city, poking into houses with sticks, finding half-rotted corpses of dogs which they cooked and ate, or miraculous treasures – buried *pithoi* of oats and barley. The luckiest treasure-finders brought their goods to the agora and sold them, but by the two hundred and thirtieth day, there was no coinage that could buy food – all anyone wanted was food, and a jewelled brooch worth a small ship wouldn't buy a cup of olive oil.

Twice, sentries sent out to catch people defecating in public areas actually caught people roasting a corpse. And Satyrus knew they weren't catching all the attempts. Among the Sakje, it was not even a taboo act.

And still, Demetrios did not attack.

At night, Satyrus sat with Abraham, whose intellect was unharmed but whose body was wrecked. 'He's determined to starve us to death,' Abraham said. Jubal poured some warm water, just tinged with wine – the greatest luxury they had – and some honey.

Melitta agreed. 'He's had it with being a god. He has the men to surround us, and the means. Look at the boom across the harbour – six stades of wood, all spiked and chained together. Look at the new trenches on the west wall – not even close enough for arrows to be exchanged. We are *contained*,' she said, as if the word were an insult.

Satyrus looked up at the sound of Miriam entering the tent – with Anaxagoras at her back. Hunger had given her the edgy coltishness of a very young woman, until you looked at her face. She had the stern lines of a forty-five-year-old grandmother engraved on her skin. Her nose had grown hawkish.

Satyrus thought her the most beautiful woman he'd ever seen.

She sank down next to him as if she were twice her age, and Anaxagoras groaned just the same way as he rested his back against Satyrus'.

'I feel as if I'm being punished for hubris,' Satyrus said. He smiled. 'I know how selfish that sounds. But I wanted to *beat him*. So I did. Look where it got us.'

Abraham laughed weakly. 'I wish I'd seen it, though. How long did it take to plan?'

Satyrus smiled at Jubal, and Jubal grinned his big, friendly, apparently not-so-smart grin. 'Long time,' he said. 'Eh? Long time.'

Satyrus nodded. 'Jubal had the idea the night we lost the great tower. We started our mines – by Hephaestos, we started them *before* we had the plan to go with them. I wanted a bolt hole. That proved foolish. I had a dream – sent by Apollo, I think – of the tunnels, and we dug them. But it was only when the great tower fell to his engines that we saw how to use our tunnels.'

Miriam waved her hands. 'And then – oh, my brother – just when you got sick, you remember that Demetrios *wouldn't* take the third wall. And his men started a mine,' she giggled.

'And we had to storm the mine before it broke through into one of ours.' Anaxagoras said, suddenly understanding. 'That's why you were alone in the dark.'

'Not alone,' Jubal said. 'He was there with me.' He roared with laughter.

Abraham shuddered when he laughed.

Apollodorus came in, drank some warm water with honey and wine, and sat heavily. Charmides came in with Lysander, and they sat back to back against the tent pole.

Anaxagoras chuckled. 'You know how I can tell that the gods are kind?' he asked.

Melitta raised an eyebrow. 'This will be good.'

'The hungrier and thinner I am, the easier I get drunk,' Anaxagoras proclaimed. 'I may write a song about it. Anacreon never had such a subject. As we run short of wine, why, the gods give me the power to be drunk on less!'

He raised the cup, drank a polite sip and smacked his lips like a connoisseur. 'Ahh ... looted from a cellar yesterday, I believe.'

Melitta laughed and smacked her leather-clad knee with her hand.

Satyrus couldn't help but notice how firm her flesh seemed to be.

He looked around. 'I have a suggestion,' he said. Anaxagoras was right – he was light-headed on half a cup of watered wine.

'Silence for the polemarch,' Abraham said.

Satyrus got unsteadily to his feet. 'Melitta, we have hundreds of Sakje warriors,' he began.

'I knew you'd notice, brother, given time,' she said teasingly.

'Demetrios has a horse herd,' Satyrus said. 'We have the best horse thieves in the girdle of the world here inside these walls. I propose that we sneak over there, lift his horses, ride them back – and eat them.'

Melitta laughed and slapped her knees again. 'He must expect us to attack,' she said.

'Arrogance is its own reward,' Lysander said. 'I would be happy to lead.'

Melitta put a hand on his knee. 'If you are anything like our Philokles, you can't ride and you make more noise than a lion in a sheepfold,' she said. 'But if you want to lay out for us how the horses are hobbled, we'll try it.'

'When?' Satyrus asked.

Melitta laughed. 'The moon's dark. Now's fine.'

The horse raid rolled along with an inevitability that seemed fated – the Sakje gathered in the dark of the west gate as if summoned, and the Greeks had no idea how it had been done. Melitta spoke to them in the liquid tongue of the Assagetae.

They laughed. She drew pictures in the dirt by torchlight, and they laughed again.

Satyrus and Apollodorus took the marines out of the sally ports and across the empty ground towards the new enemy entrenchments – the contravallation that enclosed the town in a cordon of earth, sand and rock.

There were sentries. They were alert. They sounded the alarm.

The marines stormed the wall anyway – the sentries were badly out-numbered, and Plistias had not stationed a quarter-guard to reinforce the most distant section, so that Satyrus was on top of the earthen rampart fifty heartbeats after his sword had cleared its scabbard.

'Prisoners,' he shouted.

The enemy phalangites had the same notion. Fifty of them sur-rendered. But only after they had sounded the alarm.

The trumpet notes rang out into the night, and trumpets responded from the camp.

Anaxagoras came up next to Satyrus. 'I wish that I was with your sister,' he blurted out.

'Me too,' Satyrus said.

It was pure joy to be out of the city. Melitta hated the damned city, the rubble, the perpetual smell of shit, the corpses and rotting crap, the brown stink of her hands. It was like a special hell for Sakje. Her brother had no idea how much it hurt the Sakje to be penned inside the foolish walls.

Out here in the open ground west of the city, she took deep breaths. To her right, Scopasis did the same, and Thyrsis laughed aloud.

'We could take the horses and ride away,' he said.

'We're on an island,' Melitta reminded them.

'Bah. We are Assagetae. Put a horse between my legs and these Dirt People will never smell me.' He laughed again.

'I don't know, Thyrsis. You smell pretty strong.' Melitta got up as she heard the fighting start. 'We have time now. Let's move.'

It was, as always, the waiting that was hardest. Demetrios' men responded well – a *taxeis* marched within half a watch, carrying torches to light their way, and the night was full of *psiloi* and oarsmen mounting the earthworks.

The *taxeis* marched out, moving fast, and were hit by a light shower of arrows. Men died.

The commander of the *taxeis* stopped and sent for new orders and help.

More arrows fell. Not many – a dozen at a time.

The *taxeis* put out their torches.

From the stricken entrenchments, the trumpets sounded again and again, urging the Antigonids on.

Demetrios sent his cavalry out through the main gate, two hundred *hippeis* of his own guard, hastily mounted in the dark. They rode around for too long looking for the *taxeis*, found it, and arrows began to fall among them. Horses screamed in the dark.

The trumpets from the doomed entrenchment pleaded for rescue.

The *taxeis* marched out across the open ground the long way, safe behind their own entrenchments, a sensible decision by their commander based on the erroneous information available to him. Erroneous, in that he assumed the entrenchment was still held by his side.

'I get better every time I blow the damned thing,' Anaxagoras said. 'No wonder I stuck with the lyre.'

'They're biting, though,' Satyrus said. 'It's time to go.'

Satyrus ran along the earthen wall, giving orders, and the marines scrambled down the outward face and dashed for their own gate. Anaxagoras sounded the trumpet once again, and jumped.

Melitta smiled. *Smells like death*, she thought. She wished Anaxagoras was here so that she could show him how the Assagetae really fought.

The *taxeis* crashing through the dark to the rescue of their doomed comrades was just a goat tethered for the lion. Bait. They passed along the broad road that Demetrios' siege engineers had built – such fastidious men. So predictable. Melitta had watched it being built – she had the map of the siege as clear in her head as her internal map of the woods, gullies and plains around Tanais.

The enemy cavalry would travel west and south of the road, riding across the open ground, sweeping to cover the flanks of the *taxeis*.

She waited for the marching infantry to pass her. *It is never so dark that a Sakje warrior cannot count his foes*. She watched them go and counted to a hundred, slowly, in Greek.

Then she rose to her feet, put an arrow to her bow and gave the shrill call of the owl.

The owl call carried across the west wall, and Satyrus nudged Anaxagoras. 'Here she goes,' he said.

'Poseidon protect her, and Apollo,' Anaxagoras said.

'Artemis is her god,' Satyrus said.

The Sakje rose from the grass and ran at the cavalry.

They made almost no sound, but the horses heard them. Most were ambling along, deeply unhappy at crossing such rough ground at night, heads down, interested in the tufts of untouched grass. But now one head came up, and then another. A stallion stopped and pricked his ears, and gave a great cry.

Even the riders could hear the sound of running feet.

Melitta was almost close enough to touch the rider she was after – she ran up behind him, her dead run much faster than his horse's rapid walk. When she shot him, her feet were still flying at a dead run. The man gulped, pawed the air and fell, and Melitta was in his place, her heels on the horse's flanks, forcing the animal to a gallop, riding far to the flank – the south-west flank.

As soon as her seat was secure, she began killing men. She would ride alongside and loose her arrow from an arm's length away.

The *hippeis* died so fast that their commander fell to the ground still unsure as to whether he was under attack. Scopasis cut his throat and took his gold-hilted sword and his scalp in three efficient motions.

Thyrsis whooped and turned his mount in a tight circle. 'Ay-*yee*!'

he screeched, and the rest of the warriors took up the keening cry, and the night was full of it.

'They got the horses,' Satyrus said.

'Now what?' Miriam asked.

Anaxagoras was more worried than Satyrus had ever seen him.

Satyrus wanted to tell the man how much his worry was misplaced. But he smiled instead. 'Now a lot of people die,' he said.

The truth was that the *taxeis* of Macedonians and Greeks was well led and had excellent discipline. Their officers never lost their nerve.

But not one of them ever forgot the terror of that hour at bay, waiting for the horse archers to come out of the dark. More than fifty of them died, despite their armour, the darkness and close-arrayed shields. The war cries seemed to last for ever, and when a man was hit, he fell among them and writhed and screamed, and they couldn't move aside to let him die alone. And from time to time one of the barbarians would ride in close and throw a severed head at them, bouncing hollowly off shields, or falling with a hard, damp thump against a helmet.

They stood like professionals, and their officers praised them every time the hoof beats died away. And when the sun rose, they found they had lost slightly fewer than a hundred men.

Melitta cantered easily over the low walls, down the front face between the pilings where the marines had cleared the stakes and pits, and along the open ground to the west gate. She waited for Scopasis and Thyrsis, who whooped and raised trophies in salute, and the marines cheered her.

She saw Anaxagoras on the wall above her, and she waved her bow. He hurried down the internal steps and hauled her off the horse by virtue of height and strength. She laughed.

'What a beautiful horse,' he said, after he'd kissed her.

She laughed. He was big, and she like big men, and his beard was pleasant. 'She's an ugly plug,' Melitta said. She wrapped her legs around his waist and kissed him, and her warriors whooped. Even Thyrsis, who had had hopes. Let him hope. She'd started this for her brother, but now she was finding the whole prospect remarkably attractive.

So was he; she could tell.

'Horse needs a name,' Anaxagoras said, when she'd removed her mouth from his. He put her down. He slapped the mare on the rump. 'I'm going to call this one "Sausage".'

Satyrus laughed. 'Well done, sister.'

'Sausage?' she asked.

'To go with "Horse meat", "Steak" and "Meat Pie".' Satyrus jumped down off the inner wall. 'We've been naming them as your folks brought them home.'

Inside the gate, she could see half the population of Rhodes. The horses were already dead – all but a dozen, which were under the close guard of the marines.

'Scopasis insisted we keep the best,' Satyrus said.

The roar of applause that greeted her appearance in the gate rose like an offering to the gods. She'd never been cheered by so many people. He face lit up, and one of her rare, full-face grins buried her scars.

31

The horse meat lasted two days. It raised morale, and filled bellies. It probably saved lives.

And then it was gone, and the winter wind blew from the north in cold gusts that mocked their hopes, every dawn, for a relief fleet.

They ate the good cuts, and then they ate the rest: entrails, ligaments, hairless hides boiled into broth. The Sakje were used to hard winters – they knew how to get food out of the hooves.

The ten horses saved against an emergency were eaten, one by one. Then they were gone.

Satyrus cut the grain ration to one-quarter of what it had been at the start.

No one had the energy to jeer, or to spit at him.

A crane appeared in the enemy camp – four ships' masts lashed together as the base, and two more as uprights. It towered over their camp.

Then they built another.

And then another.

They were on the two hundred and eighty-fifth day of the siege. Satyrus heard about the cranes, drank a cup of warm water and walked out into the agora with his heaviest cloak on his shoulders. He was still cold.

'What do you think it means?' he asked Jubal.

Jubal frowned. It was rare for the Nubian to frown. He watched as the fourth crane was erected, chewing on a piece of rawhide, on and on. Long after Satyrus expected an answer and then gave up on getting one, the black engineer shook his head and turned away.

'It means we fucked,' he said quietly, and spat.

The next morning dawned crisp and cold and windless. No sails marked the far horizon.

In Demetrios' camp, the four cranes were slowly linked with cross beams, so high in the air that men took a quarter of a watch to climb the ladders up to the cranes' tops.

Satyrus didn't let himself watch too long. It was demoralising. Instead, with Lysander at his heels, and Charmides, who had taken over as his hypaspist, he walked down to the olive grove, entered the steps under the sanctuary of Demeter and inspected the *pithoi* of grain there – the city's remaining stock.

A pair of very lean cats sat by the guard's brazier.

'Out of rats?' Satyrus asked, but the joke fell flat. The grain guards – his own marines – barely raised their heads. A quarter-ration of grain was enough to sustain life. Just. And no more.

He walked along the ranks of the *pithoi*, and he opened them, and he and Lysander inspected them with the priestess, Hirene, and her assistant Lysistrada. Satyrus smiled to himself, but the smile was grim.

Lysander marked his tablets carefully, and they bowed to the priestesses and went back above ground. Satyrus paused to pat the cats. And noted, with a cold surprise, that his hand was thin. Skeletal, in fact.

'Puss, puss,' he said. 'Didn't anyone give you some horse meat?'

Hepius, a marine phylarch from Athens, squinted out of the dark. 'Aye,' he said. 'Let's fatten 'em up a bit before we eat 'em.'

Hirene let out a squawk of outrage.

Satyrus managed a smile. 'Despoina, your cats are safe as long as the town stands.'

But to Charmides, he said, 'All officers. Right now.'

'We have two weeks' food at quarter-rations,' Satyrus said.

They just looked at him. All the surviving members of the *boule*; all the officers of his long-lost *Arete*. His sister's people, and the captains of the ephebes. The surviving Cretans. They didn't raise their voices, shout, or even murmur.

They just watched him with flat eyes, waiting.

Aspasia was as thin as a mainmast stripped of the yard. And Miriam – Miriam's eyes filled her face, and her long legs were a mockery. Her hip bones showed through her chiton.

Nor was Charmides much better. He was thin, and Nike's death had left him bitter.

Abraham looked like a living skull. But he was the one to speak. 'I will go to Demetrios,' he said. 'Someone must try.'

Satyrus shook his head. 'No. No, if anyone goes, it will be me. After all, he wanted this to be personal. Between us.'

'What do we do?' Apollodorus asked. 'Sit and wait?'

Satyrus shook his head. 'I wanted you to know. I *believe* in Diokles. He will come back. I think we should eat our sandals and hold on.'

Memnon sighed. He looked at his wife. 'I thought we'd won. Ten times, I thought we'd won. But,' he looked around, 'we've lost, haven't we?'

Satyrus nodded in agreement, but Miriam stepped forward.

'No,' she said. 'No, we have not lost. By God above, men are fools. We have struggled, and we have *not surrendered*.' She looked around. 'Three years ago, I sat at my loom in Alexandria and wished that, someday, I could have a real life where I could breathe free air and be a person, a human being, free of the Tyrant who ran my life. We have held – for almost a year. Spring is coming. We had a year.' She stammered off at the end, and then gave a self-conscious laugh and was silent. But when no one mocked her, she said, 'If I die tomorrow, I will not bow my head. My God will understand. We Jews are stiff-necked people. Let us talk no more of surrender.'

She was embarrassed at her own words, but Memnon clasped her hand, and Damophilus and Apollodorus clapped her on the back.

Melitta cleared her throat. 'For the Sakje, there will be no surrender. And brother – I came to rescue you, not to die here.'

Satyrus nodded. 'Well, then. Thanks. All of you. Let's quarter the ruins and search the cellars – especially the first houses to take hits – and see if we can dig up a few *mythemnoi* of grain.'

Charmides managed a real laugh. 'It's always about the grain,' he said.

Dawn, and chanting from the enemy camp.

The stick figures of Rhodian citizens lined the sea wall and the south wall closest to the enemy camp.

Ropes – great hawsers, thick enough to be visible even at that distance – were rigged to the massive crane structure. And by early morning, they were taught.

The monster that rose over the enemy camp was so tall that it reached above the towers, and in its last seconds as it was righted, it rocked twice – leaning so far that one of the crane arms was dashed to pieces, and a dozen men fell to their deaths. But righted it was.

The tower was the height of twenty men. The wheels along its base were twice the height of a man. It was as wide as two houses and as deep again, tapering slightly from bottom to top like an immense pyramid, and through the open sides the Rhodians could see six floors.

No sooner was it steady on its wheels than slaves and soldiers raised a great cry and began to roll it forward.

It rolled well. The wheels worked.

It was the largest moving thing made by the hand of man that Satyrus had ever seen.

Demetrios watched his toy with the joy of the creator. His hands had shaped both wood and iron. He had marked the drawings, and his hands had pulled the hawsers to raise the recumbent tower from its building site. Its sheer size awed *him*, and he had helped design it. Ctesibius, the chief designer, couldn't stop looking at it.

'Now I am a god,' Demetrios said.

Ctesibius agreed. 'A pyramid on wheels,' he said, his voice low. 'Full of engines. Fifty cubits on a side.' The engineer giggled.

'What shall we call it?' Plistias asked.

'Helepolis,' Demetrios intoned like a priest. 'The Destroyer of Cities.'

The giant *thing* which towered over their tallest wall and made a mockery of their defences might have been the last straw.

But the men and women of Rhodes had endured ten months of war, and their sense of awe was dulled. Had the great machine been brought against them in the first month –

But no: it was the tenth month. For three days they watched as the smiths carried iron plates to the waiting leviathan. On the fourth day, artisans and slaves began bolting the iron to the frame – all nine storeys of it. More building was still going on at the top of the frame, and the whole edifice had been rolled clear of the abatises that surrounded the enemy camp onto a swathe two stades wide that six thousand slaves, the survivors of the fever, began to clear like a pathway for the gods from the machine right up to the south wall. They filled the deep places and levelled the smallest heights, long lines of them working all together so that they crept across the plain, too slow to watch, too fast for hope.

A whole *taxeis* stood guard all night in front of the machine, with a hundred Cretan archers.

Satyrus watched them with Jubal from his own, much lower tower. Watched them for most of a day.

And watched the empty sea.

One by one, Satyrus talked to his friends. He talked, alone, to Miriam. To Abraham. To Anaxagoras and Melitta, to Charmides and Lysander and Apollodorus, to Korus and Memnon, to Damophilus and Socrates.

None of them was interested in taking the two surviving ships. None of them was interested in surrender.

So at noon that day, the three hundred and third day of the siege, the one hundred and twenty-fifth day of the archonship of Pherecles of Athens, the one hundred and nineteenth Olympiad, Satyrus ordered his marines into the vaults of Demeter with the permission of the priestesses and removed the last eighteen *pithoi*. And he gathered the entire population in the agora and distributed the grain. All the grain.

'Tomorrow is Anthesteria in Athens and Tanais,' he said. 'When men rope up the temples and let the spirits of the dead roam free. When Dionysus walks the earth. Feast. Eat it all.'

Silently, orderly and disciplined, they took the grain – just exactly a double ration of grain for every man and woman.

In Abraham's tent, his friends were quiet. Satyrus took his turn with the two bronze cauldrons full of barley meal and coriander, and the whole of an unlucky migrant bird that had passed too close to Melitta's bow. The smell alone was like lust and gluttony together.

'So,' Miriam said, approaching him cautiously, like a hunter. 'We're done for?'

Satyrus shook his head. 'I trust my gods,' he said. 'We Hellenes are also a stiff-necked people.'

Apollodorus stuck a horn spoon into the porridge and tasted it, burning his tongue. 'Ow!' he said.

'Serves you right,' Satyrus shot back, smacking him with his wooden spoon.

Apollodorus didn't bother to look contrite. 'You're feeding us up,' he said. 'So we're going to attack.'

Satyrus nodded. 'That's right.'

Apollodorus embraced him. 'Good,' he said. 'Let's die standing up.'

It turned out that people can get drunk on grain, if they've been hungry long enough.

Anthesteria was not always the loudest of holidays – kept in late winter, a cry to the coming spring, usually celebrated indoors. But with a double ration of food in their bellies, the six thousand surviving Rhodians sang hymns to the night and all the gods, roaring away – hymn after hymn to Demeter and Kore, and then to Apollo, to Herakles, to Ares and Athena. Thankful only for food and one more day, they sang to every god. Hymn after hymn rose to the heavens, an endless paean from nightfall to midnight. Shivering sentries on the Antigonid entrenchments wondered how, how in *all Tartarus* the Rhodians had the strength to sing, or even to walk. They huddled in their cloaks and smelled the smell of warm food floating on the wind, and when the hymn to Dionysus came across no-man's land, disgusted sentries spat in contempt for their own improvident commanders – or joined the song.

Satyrus looked around the fire. The stars had wheeled away past the middle watch, and every man who could walk was in armour – and some of the women as well. Every officer was here, in the middle of the agora, at the biggest bonfire they could build – not really all that big. Carrying wood was hard work, and starving men are easily tired. And the wood was mostly gone with the grain and the oil. The beached ships were already consumed.

Satyrus looked at them in the firelight. It was a kind, ruddy light, and it gave Charmides and Miriam back their beauty, three months gone; gave Melitta back her youth, lost in the valleys of the Tanais, and Anaxagoras looked like a god.

'Listen to me,' Lysander barked, long before Satyrus was ready to stop drinking them in. One last time.

They were instantly silent. It took a year's siege to turn Greeks into disciplined men and women – but they were. The only sound was the hymn-singing, led by Leosthenes, out along the south wall.

Satyrus nodded. 'So,' he said. He smiled. Looked from face to face. It was almost funny, the way they expected him to provide a magical spell of victory. 'So. Friends.' He hung his head, embarrassed by their trust in him. And then he raised his head. 'Listen. There is no trick to save us, now. I don't have a fancy plan. When we raise the paean to Athena, we go over the south wall and go for the monster.' He shrugged. 'First man there is King of Misrule.'

Anaxagoras sighed. 'That's it?' he asked.

Satyrus nodded. 'That's it,' he said. 'Kill everyone who gets in your way. It'll be dark. That can't hurt us.'

Abraham raised an eyebrow – for a moment, his old self. 'And when the sun rises?' he asked.

Satyrus locked eyes with Miriam. 'Die well,' he said. Then he walked from man to man and embraced them all. He hugged Aspasia. He hugged his sister, and she shook her head.

'This is not what I came for,' she said.

'Then escape!' he murmured into her hair.

'No. No – I couldn't face Mother in the spirit world, if I left you.' She hugged him closer. 'You kill a thousand, I kill a thousand – Abraham's good for five hundred, Charmides looks capable – and we wipe them out.'

And last, he embraced Miriam. 'I would have married you,' he said.

'I would have accepted,' she said. She kissed him.

And then he led them to the foot of the wall, and the morning star rose, and four thousand voices started on the hymn to Athena.

Once, visiting Athens, Satyrus had watched a desperate older man beat a much better younger man at *pankration*, on the palaestra of the Lyceum outside the walls of the city. Hundreds of men had watched as the older fellow – a plain-spoken country man, trained well enough but no champion, stubbornly refuse to raise a hand in surrender, for the simple reason that the young champion had been rude in his challenge. And when he was groggy from blows to the head, the younger man mocked him as a drunkard, a satyr, a shepherd.

Satyrus had watched the older man's face absorb the insult. Watched as the man stopped, readied himself and threw everything he had left into a stupid roundhouse blow, the sort of big, long, easy-to-dodge blow that untrained men use. The younger man saw it coming. But somehow – through indecision or poor training, or, as Satyrus saw it, the punishment of the gods – the champion stood as if rooted to the spot in amazement as the other man's twinned fists slammed into the side of his head, and he slumped to the ground, completely unconscious.

On that night, the remnants of the Rhodian garrison swept over the south wall like a black sea and rolled over the remnants of the second wall and the first wall, crushing the sentries and the reserve, and raced across the plain like a well-ordered tide across a salt flat when the moon is full.

Like the young champion, the Macedonian *taxeis* awaited the garrison with confidence.

Satyrus kept the oarsmen to an easy jog once they made the good ground. They were keeping up with the ephebes and the town mercenaries, but the city hoplites were lagging behind and there was nothing Satyrus could do about it. So he led them at a jog across the open ground, and saw the enemy phalanx form with plenty of time to achieve close order.

Satyrus slowed his oarsmen three hundred paces from the glittering enemy line. Dawn was already a pale line in the east, and there were trumpets everywhere.

He smiled. It was too late. For these men.

'Files!' he called, and the oarsmen doubled to the front, a Spartan manoeuvre that left every front-rank shield firmly overlapped – the *synaspis*.

His men hadn't stopped moving. A year of continuous action allows a unit to achieve a degree of drill that borders on beyond human. Half-files merely slowed a half a pace, waited while the new file leaders marched into the intervals at a jog, and then, as the shields locked, gave a low shout – just the file leaders.

'Spears!' Satyrus called. Two hundred paces. And the Macedonians weren't moving. It was getting late for them to start forward – he could see their spears moving – but it was hard to read them in the dark, and Satyrus didn't really care very much what they did.

Behind and alongside him, the front three ranks levelled their spears, and the back seven ranks pressed forward tighter, still at a fast walk.

'Paean!' Satyrus called.

Apollodorus raised his head.

A wall of sound leaped out from the oarsmen, and the Macedonians reacted as if they'd been hit by arrows – they recoiled, and into their confusion came the marines, and the moment of impact was like a thousand bronzesmiths beating on a thousand cauldrons across the sky, and the Macedonian phalanx burst asunder at the impact, and was destroyed.

It shouldn't have happened.

Because it did, the first relief *taxeis* on the road was caught in the disaster, with routers and tent-mates bursting through their ranks, and the ephebes and the slightly late city hoplites crashed into the disordered second phalanx and drove it back.

And then the fighting lost any kind of order. The attack of the city hoplites was the last moment in the action when Satyrus could see anything, or tell his friends from his foes – or claim to be in command.

The marines were cheering all around him, and the women in the rear ranks ran forward with fire pots and in heartbeats the timbers of the leviathan were aflame. Assembled war engines around the great wheels were shoved together, and the flames began to light the sky, and Satyrus tasted victory.

But he knew the taste was false. He had two thousand men, and Demetrios, however surprised, had thirty thousand.

Demetrios' counter-attack fell like a hammer on the victorious Rhodians.

The marines were still together – Charmides was close to his back and Apollodorus was on one side and Anaxagoras on his other, with Abraham's skeletal figure at his back, when the counter-attack smashed into them. Satyrus took a shield against his own shield, abandoned any thought of command and was a hoplite – shield to shield, his spear sliding off his enemy's shield as his enemy's spear probed for his eyes and rang against his helmet, pressed so close that he could smell the cardamom on the other man's breath. So close that he hooked the man's shield with his own and punched with his rim – larger shield, stronger arm – and the man went down, and Satyrus was in his place. 'On me, marines!' Satyrus called, as if it was a ship fight.

Charmides got his next opponent, through luck or precision; the man was down before he could set his hips, a spear point in his eye. The enemy phalangites were silhouetted against the burning machines, and they paid.

Apollodorus downed his man and stepped forward and fouled a spear – Anaxagoras pushed with his shoulder, and the man facing Satyrus flinched, fear rising in his eyes as he saw the whole rank in front of him die, and he backed away. Satyrus pushed into him, slamming shield to shield and stabbing under the shield rush – sword into something soft, and he pushed, and a blow rang off his helmet. He managed a guard with his sword, stepped forward – right in front of left, rotated his hips and swung his sword like a meat cleaver into the next aspis rim and split the badly made shield clear through, breaking the owner's arm with a shriek that Charmides ended. Not just luck, then – the boy was a master spearman.

The men in front of him started to blur, and Satyrus gave and received blows – a heavy blow to his right side under his arm when he pushed forward too fast, a cut to his left leg from a spearman who was fast and bold. Darkness favoured aggression and teamwork, and Charmides saved him ten times and Anaxagoras another ten – and he saved them, parrying high with his sword to keep blows off Anaxagoras, killing Apollodorus' opponent with a wrap blow to the back of the man's neck. Abraham's weak spear thrusts were precise.

The enemy died.

Satyrus lost track of opponents and blows. He was alive – and then another moment, and he was alive. Alive.

Still alive.

He lost his sword in a dying man, and as if gifted by Herakles his right fist closed on his next opponent's spear and tore it from his grasp as if he'd danced a move in the *Pyrriche*. Satyrus killed that man with the saurauter of his own weapon, reversed the blade and slammed it into the next man. And on.

Still alive.

Usually in combat, men fall back after a fight – a hundred heart-beats of chaos and horror is all most men, even the bravest, can stand. Men will flinch from combat if they can – stand at spear's length and shout insults.

But in the darkness, men slammed unheeding into each other, and died. The fire in the mammoth tower threw enough light to make survival possible.

Satyrus parried with his spear, a sweep across his body, and slammed the shaft back into the man's helmet, knocking him to the ground, where Charmides finished him.

Still alive.

New armour – more bronze, less dirt. Satyrus saw this when he got a lucky hit – his right hand was so tired he could barely grasp the spear, but he got the point into the other man's eye-slit on his next attack and the man went down.

Still alive.

The sun was rising. Men were backing away from them. Apollodorus spat in contempt and pushed his short spear through an opponent's armour and into his groin, right over the man's shield. Charmides caught a man turning away and slit him over the kidney where he had no armour. Anaxagoras was toe to toe with a man as big as he, and they swapped blows like dogs fighting, and their swords threw sparks and then Anaxagoras hammered his pommel into the other man's teeth and Abraham's timed thrust went into his helmet and his head seemed to explode and he went down—

Still alive.

The five of them had put so many men into the earth that the enemy flinched away and the marines were able to survive, wheeling from a defeated flank, secure while their king and his companions bought them room to breathe.

The enemy had recaptured the tower. Thousands of them were dousing the fires – the engines were black with men in the new sun, like ants covering food left outside.

Again the enemy flinched back, and Satyrus, in his turn, retired a step to link his shield with Anaxagoras. He coughed.

Still. Alive.

Satyrus breathed. He looked right and left, and saw that most of his marines were still alive, too.

He got his canteen to his mouth. Drank it, never taking his eyes off the enemy. They were a well-armoured mob, and a man in gold armour pushed through the front rank and gleamed like fire in the rising sun.

'Your men have done a fair job against my Aegema,' Demetrios said. 'You still wear that helmet.'

Satyrus spat water and blood. He smelled the wet cat fur, and he knew he was where he needed to be.

Demetrios was magnificent in gold and leopard skin, fresh and neat and strong, with the physique of a statue of Herakles. 'It is fitting that we finish this – Achilles and Hektor. Would you care to run a few times around the walls?'

'Let me have him,' Anaxagoras said.

Apollodorus snorted. 'Give me a drink and I'll fight him. Only if I can keep the armour.'

Charmides tapped Satyrus. 'If allowed, I would be delighted—'

Satyrus laughed. He stepped forward out of the ranks and saluted Demetrios. Demetrios' Aegema – his companions – had made a space by retreating. Satyrus pulled his canteen strap over his head and handed it to Apollodorus. Almost as an aside, he said, 'Demetrios, you must confess – your men flinch from me, and my men long to fight *you*. Ask yourself who is Achilles, and who is just another mortal man in golden armour.'

Demetrios raised his spear. 'I think we should fight, instead of talking.'

Satyrus grunted. 'You want this to be the *Iliad*, not me.'

Demetrios rushed at him, a simple shield rush, and then his spear licked out – once, twice, three times, as fast as a man could think – high, middle, low, a brilliant combination.

Satyrus blocked, blocked and blocked without shifting a finger's width, and as their shields rang together, he *pushed*.

Demetrios landed on his back.

'I am Satyrus, son of Kineas,' Satyrus said to the wind. 'My father was hipparch of Olbia and founder of a great city. Get up.'

Demetrios rose to his feet. 'Well struck,' he said.

Satyrus moved – a long, leaning feint Philokles had taught him – and struck high, and his spearhead cut Demetrios across the arm above his shield where his guard was weak.

'My grandfather was a hipparch of Athens. His father came to Athens from Plataea, where he held the wall alone for an hour against a hundred Spartans and killed ten. Athens made him a citizen, and raised him a statue as a hero,' Satyrus said.

Demetrios seemed puzzled by his roaring boasts and hung back, and Satyrus thrust with his spear, putting everything into this arm: love for Miriam, hate of waste, rage, terror, shame, pride. Sorrow. Pity. Hope. *Everything*.

The spearhead punched through the gold face of the shield and through the bronze and two layers of rawhide and the willow-wood strapping, and bit into Demetrios' shield arm and the king stepped back and swore, and there was blood on his golden cuirass.

'His father Arimnestos led the Plataeans to victory at Marathon against the Medes, and he stood his ground when the Hellenes won the day at Plataea and he was voted *best* of the Hellenes.' He feinted with his spear and *kicked*, a low trick that Theron fancied, catching Demetrios in the kneecap and sending him sprawling.

He stood over the golden king, spear raised.

'Arimnestos' father was the Smith of Plataea, and he held the charge of the Spartans alone at Oinoe!' Satyrus said. 'Get *up*!'

Demetrios stumbled back into the ranks of his bodyguard.

Satyrus waited. Demetrios straightened himself. He set his feet.

'His ancestor was Herakles, who is a god, and sits in high Olympus, watching men and judging them.' Satyrus planted the saurauter of his borrowed spear in the sand. 'Those are my ancestors, Demetrios the king. You came to fight heroes. These men were heroes.'

Demetrios came forward and lunged, deliberately driving his spear into Satyrus' shield – a powerful blow that rocked Satyrus back – and his point tore through the shield's cover and cut right through the leather and wood.

Satyrus left his spear standing in the sand, reached out his empty right hand and grasped the king's shield rim and turned it the way a wheelwright turns a wheel. The sound of the king's arm breaking echoed across the field like a ship's mast breaking in a storm.

And Demetrios screamed, rage and frustration coming together, and hacked with his spear at Satyrus.

Then the Aegema pressed forward to rescue their king. But they were not eager to fight. Satyrus reached out and pulled his spear out of the ground, seeing the blood trickle down his arm. Demetrios had hit him. He could feel an earlier wound on his hip – he looked down, and there was blood by his left foot. And on his left greave.

He stepped back into the ranks of his men and the shields locked, but the Antigonids were not as eager as their numbers should have made them. And Satyrus had lost the will to die. Step by step the marines backed away, until they were backing up the old south wall.

Trumpet after trumpet of alarm sounded in the enemy camp, and the enemy king's bodyguard hustled Demetrios the Golden off the field.

Satyrus looked at Abraham. But Abraham was looking past him, over his shoulder. Satyrus raised his eyes, and there, to the east, was a line of sails – fifty sails and more, coming down the north wind from Syme.

Marathon and *Oinoe. Nike* and *Troy* and *Ephesian Artemis*, and many more he knew at a glance. With a line of grain ships he knew from their towering masts and heavy sails.

'Herakles!' he called.

The sky rumbled.

EPILOGUE

The end, which should have been climactic, was merely terrifying. Ptolemy's fleet covered a dozen huge merchantmen all the way into the harbour, with fifty thousand *mythemnoi* of grain from Aegypt and a letter from Ptolemy promising relief in a week.

And did it again, two days later, while Satyrus writhed in pain from his wounds and watched Miriam's colour return. Food. Food was hope made concrete.

Off Asia, Ptolemy's fleet caught the remnants of the pirates and exterminated them.

The entire grain supply sent by Athens to reinforce Demetrios, was taken by Diokles.

Lysimachos of Thrace sent aid to the city, and forty thousand *mythemnoi* of wheat – Cassander, who had no reason to love Rhodes, sent ten thousand measures of barley and five hundred Cretan archers.

They heard that, in the absence of Amastris, her half-brothers Clearchus and Oxathras seized the city of Heraklea. They immediately allied with Cassander against Demetrios.

And finally, two weeks later, Ptolemy's fleet landed – led in by Leon, reinforced by every ship that could be spared by Ptolemy's allies. Three thousand fresh mercenary hoplites were landed on the mole in three hours. Thousands and thousands of *mythemnoi* of grain flowed into the city, along with herds of pigs and legions of cattle.

Ptolemy's reinforcements included the Macedonian, Antigonus of Pella. He had served with Alexander – indeed, like Phillip of Mythymna, he wore the old dun and purple cloak of the *hetairoi*. He swaggered when he walked. He looked at the sea wall; he paraded the city hoplites and the oarsmen.

He came and visited Satyrus in his tent.

'How'd you do it?' he asked. 'Don't get up.' The Macedonian extended his hand.

Satyrus, taken unawares, managed to swing his legs over the edge of his low bed and winced. He felt the cold wetness that meant the wound on his hip was open again. 'Do what?' he asked.

Antigonus shook his head. 'You held Demetrios.'

Satyrus shrugged. 'We all held Demetrios. Menedemos is polemarch now, I think. Go and talk to him.' But he laughed. 'But we did hold, didn't we? So why doesn't he sail away?'

Antigonus shook his head. 'He'll try one more attack. With everything.'

They chatted amicably enough for an hour – about the war, about the last year. 'I remember your father,' Antigonus said. 'Fine cavalry officer. As good as a Thessalian.'

Satyrus smiled. 'I'll be up in a few days,' he said. 'I'll show you the walls, and make sure you know all the tricks.' He grinned at the older man. 'Is it hard, being called Antigonus? When Demetrios' father One-Eye is the arch enemy?'

The Macedonian officer shrugged. 'Half my phalanx is called Antigonus,' he said. 'I suppose it was the "in" name that year.'

Two days later, while Satyrus lay on his bed and Miriam held his hand, Demetrios' grand assault took place. He did it in broad daylight. The magnificent Argyraspides penetrated to the theatre. Then they were driven out. Again. The rest of the assaults were half-hearted. The fresh hoplites sent by Ptolemy had never been ill fed and had never had the fever, and Demetrios' men were broken by a year of defeat. They ran.

That was the last attack, and Satyrus lay on his bed. And held Miriam's hand as if it were his hope of salvation.

And then there were weeks of negotiations. But for all those weeks, the food poured in, so that the *pithoi* under the old temple floor filled with grain again. And as soon as the negotiations started, something changed in every man and woman. Although there was wine to drink, no one was drunk.

Miriam wore the full robes of a woman, and put off the boy's tunic she had worn for months. When she did, so did the other women who had fought to the last.

The newly enfranchised citizens were assigned homes.

No one kissed in the streets. But the law courts returned to their function.

The stone of the third wall was retrieved to reface the theatre.

Before the ink was dry on the papyrus, the city had begun rebuilding.

And then, one morning more than a year after he had landed, Demetrios, the remnants of his army and his fleet, packed and sailed away for Greece. They left six thousand wretched slaves, who were immediately fed by the city and put to work.

That evening, Satyrus and Abraham, Miriam and Charmides, Anaxagoras and Melitta and Jubal, Thyrsis and Scopasis and a half-dozen others sat comfortably on stools in the cool autumn breeze with members of the *boule* and Antigonus, the new commander of mercenaries. Demetrios' fleet was still visible, their sails like knife cuts in the edge of a parchment.

'He'll be back,' said Abraham, raising a wine cup.

Satyrus shook his head. 'Never. He and Antigonus One-Eye are finished.'

Anaxagoras was gently strumming his lyre. He looked up. 'Were we finished? At any point?' he asked softly. 'They are, in their way, great men. They will find more warm bodies to carry their spears and pull their oars, and the world will have no peace until they are hacked to pieces.' He began to play the hymn to Ares very softly.

Miriam sat back and stretched like a cat. 'I hate them,' she said. 'I hate them all. None of them is *great*. They are all little men trying to be that great monster, Alexander. I spit on his shade. They posture and kill and torture and inflict catastrophe – why? To be more like a man who died drunk and alone at thirty-three!'

Antigonus of Pella looked at her for a moment, and bit his lips. 'Alexander was a god,' he said very carefully, through his teeth.

For a moment, she looked at him, her face impassive.

And then Miriam laughed. And her laughter – the ancient derision of women for the foolish games of men – rolled out over the sea, and followed Demetrios.

HISTORICAL NOTE

Writing a novel – several novels, I hope – about the wars of the Diadochi, or Successors, is a difficult game for an amateur historian to play. There are many, many players, and many sides, and frankly, none of them are 'good'. From the first, I had to make certain decisions, and most of them had to do with limiting the cast of characters to a size that the reader could assimilate without insulting anyone's intelligence. Antigonus One-Eye and his older son Demetrios deserve novels of their own – as do Cassander, and Eumenes and Ptolemy and Seleucus – and Olympia and the rest. Every one of them could be portrayed as the 'hero' and the others as villains.

If you feel that you need a scorecard, consider visiting my website at www.hippeis.com where you can at least review the biographies of some of the main players. Wikipedia has full biographies on most of the players in the period, as well.

From a standpoint of purely military history, I've made some decisions that knowledgeable readers may find odd. For example, I no longer believe that the Macedonian pike system – the sarissa armed phalanx – was really any 'better' than the old Greek hoplite system. In fact, I suspect it was worse – as the experience of early modern warfare suggests that the longer your pikes are, the less you trust your troops. Macedonian farm boys were not hoplites – they lacked the whole societal and cultural support system that created the hoplite. They were decisive in their day – but as to whether they were 'better' than the earlier system – well, as with much of military change, it was a cultural change, not really a technological one. Or so it seems to me.

Elephants were not tanks, nor were they a magical victory tool. They could be very effective, or utterly ineffective. The same applies to the invention of the ballista and the various torsion engines. I've tried to use the siege to describe some of the strengths and weaknesses of these weapons. And again, horse archery could be decisive or merely annoying. On open ground, with endless remounts and a limitless arrow supply, a horse-archer army must have been a nightmare. But a few hundred horse-archers on the vast expanse of a Successor battlefield might only have been a nuisance.

Ultimately, though, I don't believe in 'military' history. War is about economics, religion, art, society – war is inseparable from culture. You could not – in this period – train an Egyptian peasant to be a horse-archer without changing his way of life and his economy, his social status, perhaps his religion. Questions about military technology – 'Why didn't Alexander create an army of [insert technological wonder here]?' – ignore the constraints imposed by the realities of the day – the culture of Macedon, which carried, it seems to me, the seeds of its own destruction from the first.

And then there is the problem of sources. In as much as we know *anything* about the world of the Diadochi, we owe that knowledge to a few authors, none of whom is actually contemporary. I used Diodorus Siculus throughout the writing of the *Tyrant* books – in most cases I prefer him to Arrian or Polybius, and in many cases he's the sole source. I also admit to using (joyously!) any material that Plutarch could provide, even though I fully realize his moralizing ways.

In this book, I have a siege that is lovingly and confusingly described by Diodorus, and I have tried to use his account to frame my story. There are issues with his story that I can't resolve across the span of history, so I can only invent—a tunnel to explain the destruction of a war machine; the character of Demetrios. For the novelist, it is sufficient to tell *a* story, perhaps not *the* story, of how that might have come about.

For anyone who wants to get a quick lesson in the difficulties of the sources for the period, I recommend visiting the website www. livius.org. The articles on the sources will, I hope, go a long way to demonstrating how little we know about Alexander and his successors.

Of course, as I'm a novelist and not an historian, sometimes the loopholes in the evidence – or even the vast gaps – are the very space in which my characters operate. Sometimes, a lack of knowledge is what creates the appeal. Either way, I hope that I have created a believable version of the world after Alexander's death. I hope that you enjoy this book, and the two – or three – to follow.

And as usual, I'm always happy to hear your comments – and even your criticisms – at the Online Agora on www.hippeis.com. See you there, I hope!

Chris Cameron
Toronto 2012

AUTHOR'S NOTE

I am an author, not a linguist – a novelist, and not fully an historian. Despite this caveat, I do the best I can to research everything from clothing to phalanx formations as I go – and sometimes I disagree with the accepted wisdom of either academe or the armchair generals who write colorful coffee table books on these subjects.

Destroyer of Cities breaks away from the simplicity of earlier books because Satyrus, grown to manhood and power, is going to be at the siege of Rhodos. In fact, the King of the Bosporus wasn't there. But many other people including a large contingent of mercenaries were there, and had a profound impact on what was, arguably, the greatest siege of the ancient world. There were mercenary ships on the seas, and they, too, had an impact, and I suspect the line between mercenary and pirate must have been very slim. At any rate, I hope that readers will forgive the intrusion of Satyrus and Melitta. The discovery a few years back of some trilobite Scythian arrowheads can be taken as justification – I smiled as I typed that.

And ultimately, errors are my fault. If you find a historical error – please let me know! Aside from allowing my characters to have a major role in the siege – the role held in the actual siege by a succession of mercenary officers supplied to the beleaguered city by Ptolemy, according to Diodorus Siculus, who I used (as usual) as my main source – I have tried to avoid altering history as we know it to suit a timetable or plotline. The history of the Wars of the Successors is difficult enough without my playing with it. In addition, as I write about this period, I learn new things, from research and from reenacting, and my ideas about things undergo change – sometimes profound change. Once I learn more, words or ideas may change or change their usage. As an example, in *Tyrant* I used Xenophon's *Cavalry Commander* as my guide to almost everything. Xenophon calls the ideal weapon a *machaira*. Subsequent study has revealed that Greeks were pretty lax about their sword nomenclature (actually, everyone is, except martial arts enthusiasts) and so Kineas's Aegyptian *machaira* was probably called a *kopis*. So in the second book, I call it a *kopis* without apology. Other words may change – certainly, my notion of the internal mechanics of the *hoplite phalanx* have changed. Even as I write this note, I'm learning more about Hellenistic Judaism that will probably impact on Abraham and Miriam in the next book. The more I learn …

But I really want to say that was great fun to return to the Hellenistic world. I missed these characters and I'm delighted that they will return one more time in *Force of Kings*. Well, perhaps again after that. There are always the Celtic invasions.

Enjoy!

Toronto
2012

ACKNOWLEDGEMENTS

I'm always sorry to finish an historical novel, because writing them is the best job in the world and researching them is more fun than anything I can imagine. I approach every historical era with a basket full of questions – How did they eat? What did they wear? How does that weapon work? This time, my questions have driven me to start recreating the period. The world's Classical re-enactors have been an enormous resource to me while writing, both with details of costume and armour and food, and as a fountain of inspiration. In that regard I'd like to thank Craig Sitch and Cheryl Fuhlbohm of Manning Imperial, who make some of the finest recreations of material culture from Classical antiquity in the world (www.manningimperial.com), as well as Joe Piela of Lonely Mountain Forge for helping recreate equipment on tight schedules. I owe a long paean of praise to any number of professional scholars and academics who have patiently answered my questions on anything from helmet crests to ancient sexuality, and I'd especially like to thank Prof. Donald C. Haggis and Prof. James Davidson. I'd also like to thank Paul McDonnell-Staff, Paul Bardunias, and Giannis Kadoglou for their depth of knowledge and constant willingness to answer questions – as well as the members of various ancient Greek re-enactment societies all over the world, from Spain to Australia. I'd also like to thank my friends who I think of as my 'corps of archers,' including, but not limited to, Chris Verwijmeren, Zack Djurica, Matt Heppe (also a novelist!) and Dariusz Wielec, who provided some much needed flora and fauna to populate Melitta's steppe scenes, as well as illustrating *Tom Swan*.

Thanks most of all to the members of my own group, Hoplologia and the Taxeis Plataea, for being the guinea-pigs on a great deal of material culture and martial-arts experimentation, and to Guy Windsor (who wrote *The Swordsman's Companion* and *The Duelist's Companion* and is an actual master swordsman himself) for advice on martial arts.

Speaking of re-enactors, my friend Steven Sandford draws the maps for these books, and he deserves a special word of thanks; and my friend Rebecca Jordan works tirelessly at the website and the various web spin-offs like the Agora, and deserves a great deal more praise than she receives. And Dmitry Bondarenko who has seen service as both an 18th century British Solider and a Greek hoplite and who continues to do illustrations for the maps in these books.

Speaking of friends, I owe a debt of gratitude to Christine Szego, who provides daily criticisms and support from her store, Bakka Phoenix, in Toronto. Thanks, Christine!

Kineas and his world began with my desire to write a book that would allow me to discuss the serious issues of war and politics that are around all of us today. I was returning to school and returning to my first love – Classical history. I am also an unashamed fan of Patrick O'Brian, and I wanted to write a series with depth and length that would allow me to explore the whole period, with the relationships that define men, and women, in war – not just one snippet. The combination – Classical history, the philosophy of war, and the ethics of the world of arête – gave rise to the volume you hold in your hand.

Along the way, I met Prof. Wallace and Prof. Young, both very learned men with long association to the University of Toronto. Professor Wallace answered any question that I asked him, providing me with sources and sources and sources, introducing me to the labyrinthine wonders of Diodorus Siculus, and finally, to T. Cuyler Young. Cuyler was kind enough to start my education on the Persian Empire of Alexander's day, and to discuss the possibility that Alexander was not infallible, or even close to it. I wish to give my profoundest thanks and gratitude to these two men for their help in re-creating the world of fourth century BC Greece, and the theory of Alexander's campaigns that underpins this series of novels. Any brilliant scholarship is theirs, and any errors of scholarship are certainly mine. I will never forget the pleasure of sitting in Prof. Wallace's office, nor in Cuyler's living room, eating chocolate cake and debating the myth of Alexander's invincibility. Both men have passed on now, since this book was written – but none of the Tyrant books would have been the same without them. They were great men, and great academics – the kind of scholars who keep civilization alive.

I'd also like to thank the staff of the University of Toronto's Classics department for their support, and for reviving my dormant interest in Classical Greek, as well as the staffs of the University of Toronto and the Toronto Metro Reference Library for their dedication and interest. Libraries matter!

I'd like to thank my old friends Matt Heppe (again) and Robert Sulentic for their support in reading the novel, commenting on it, and helping me avoid anachronisms. Both men have encyclopedaeic knowledge of Classical and Hellenistic military history and, again, any errors are mine.

I couldn't have approached so many Greek texts without the Perseus Project. This online resource, sponsored by Tufts University, gives online access to almost all classical texts in Greek and in English. Without it I would still be working on the second line of *Medea*, never mind the *Iliad* or the *Hymn to Demeter*.

I owe a debt of thanks to my excellent editor, Bill Massey, at Orion, for giving these books constant attention and a great deal of much needed flattery, for his good humor in the face of authorial dicta, and for his support at every stage. I'd also like to thank Shelley Power, my agent, for her unflagging efforts on my behalf, and for many excellent dinners, the most recent of which, at the world's only Ancient Greek restaurant, Archeon Gefsis in Athens, resulted in some hasty culinary re-writing. Thanks, Shelley!

Finally, I would like to thank the muses of the Luna Café, who serve both coffee and good humor, and without whom there would certainly not have been a book. And all my thanks – a lifetime of them – for my wife Sarah.

If you have any questions or you wish to see more or participate (want to be a hoplite at Marathon?) please come and visit www.hippeis.com.

Christian Cameron
Toronto, 2012